EDWIN J. BRETT'S
LIST OF
ONE-SHILLING VOLUMES.

COMPLETE VOLUMES NOW PUBLISHING AT 1/- EACH. ILLUSTRATED.
Post Free, 1s. 2d.

CAPTAIN OF THE SCHOOL.
RIVAL SCHOOLS.
KING OF THE SCHOOL.
FRED. FROLIC, HIS LIFE AND ADVENTURES.
NIGHT GUARD; OR, THE SECRET OF THE FIVE MASKS.
GILES EVERGREEN; OR, FRESH FROM THE COUNTRY.
POOR RAY THE DRUMMER BOY.
ALONE IN THE PIRATES' LAIR.
TOM DARING; OR, FAR FROM HOME.
BY THE QUEEN'S COMMAND.
WALTER THE ARCHER.
WILDFOOT, THE WANDERER OF WICKLOW.
JACK STEADFAST; OR, WRECK AND RESCUE.

JACK-O'-THE-CUDGEL; OR, THE HERO OF A HUNDRED FIGHTS.
BICYCLE BOB; OR, WHO'LL WIN?
DICK AND HIS FRIEND DUKE.
ISABEL'S FORTUNE.
GALLANT JACK.
TOM FLOREMALL IN SEARCH OF HIS FATHER.
NOBODY'S DOG.
TRAVELLING SCHOOLBOYS.
PAT O'CONNOR.
OXFORD AND CAMBRIDGE EIGHTS.
UNLUCKY BOB.
EVERY INCH A SAILOR.
FATHERLESS WILL.
CHEVY CHASE.
STRONGBOW.

Complete in Two Volumes, 1s. each.

TRUE TO EACH OTHER.
SCAPEGRACE OF THE SCHOOL.
SCAPEGRACE AT SEA.
SCAPEGRACE IN LONDON.
TOM FLOREMALL'S SCHOOLDAYS.

PANTOMIME JOE.
ALICE; OR, THE ADVENTURES OF AN ENGLISH GIRL IN PERSIA.
WITHOUT REPROACH.
ENGLISH JACK AMONG THE AFGHANS.

POSTAGE, 2d. EACH VOLUME.

Harkaway Series, Price 1s. each Volume, postage 2d. extra.

JACK HARKAWAY'S SCHOOLDAYS. Complete in One Volume.
JACK HARKAWAY AFTERSCHOOLDAYS. Complete in Two Volumes.
JACK HARKAWAY'S ADVENTURES ROUND THE WORLD, AMERICA AND CUBA. Two Volumes.
JACK HARKAWAY AT OXFORD. Complete in Two Volumes.
JACK HARKAWAY AMONG THE BRIGANDS. Complete in Two Volumes.
JACK HARKAWAY'S ADVENTURES IN CHINA. Complete in One Volume.

JACK HARKAWAY IN GREECE. Two Volumes.
JACK HARKAWAY IN AUSTRALIA. One Volume.
YOUNG JACK HARKAWAY AND HIS BOY TINKER. Two Volumes.
YOUNG JACK HARKAWAY AT SCHOOL IN AMERICA. One Volume.
YOUNG JACK HARKAWAY AMONG THE PIRATES. One Volume.
YOUNG JACK HARKAWAY IN THE ISLE OF PALMS.

VOLUMES COMPLETE, PRICE 1/6. ILLUSTRATED. POST FREE, 1/9.

BLESS HER HEART.
JACK-O'-LANTERN.
RIGHTFUL HEIR.

WARD'S SECRET.
HARRY HALLIARD; OR, THE YOUNG BRITISH TAR.

COTTAGE GIRL. COMPLETE. STIFF PAPER COVERS, 2s.
VALENTINE VOX. COMPLETE. HANDSOME CLOTH COVERS, 3s. 6d.
YOUNG APPRENTICE; OR, THE WATCHWORDS OF OLD LONDON. Three Volumes. 1s. Each.
BOB BLUNT THE TRAVELLER. Three Volumes. 1s. Each.

LONDON, 173, FLEET STREET, E.C.

No. 1, New Series.　　　　Price One Penny.

Boys' Library

HARRY HALLIARD:
OR,
THE YOUNG BRITISH TAR.

"TWO MEN STOOD WATCHING THEM, WITH EVIL GLANCES."

PROLOGUE.

THE BIRTH AND PARENTAGE OF HARRY HALLIARD.

CHAPTER I.

THE CORNISH WRECKERS—HYLDA, THE STORM-RAISER—THE DOOMED SHIP—THE FALSE SIGNALS—THE WRECK—THE PLUNDER—A FATAL DISCOVERY.

"Avast there, Harleck, where's the skipper?"

"Off the Shark's Fin, with the rockets, Agger. The wind has veered a point, and we shall have an awful night; the scud flies over the stars."

"And what kind of drift will the sea send us, think ye?"

"Middling good, Agger. The barque is stuck in a fog-bank out in the bay; her toplight shows through the mist like a burnt hole in a blanket. They say she was five hours feeling her way round Deadman's Point, beyond Falmouth."

"What craft is she?"

"The 'Willhelmine,' of Amsterdam, freighted with lace and broadcloth."

"And where's our she-cap'en?"

"Hylda Penreal? Curse her, wherever she be! A while gone I saw her at Polruth's Kiddleawink—she and that other devil's doxy, Wild Thyra, were at their 'runeing' and 'charming,' talking language quite blasphemous. I was forced to scratch my head to keep my hair down—the two faggots were rhyming on the gale."

"And for whistling up the wind I never saw Hylda's match. She knows every black spell that ever was mouthed at a witches' sabbath."

"Pshaw! All bogey to scare infants. I grant ye she's a good 'un to get up a breeze with her fancy man, or play the bo'swain among the crew; but the wind is not under her orders, for all the old tales."

"Well, deliver me from her evil eye, and her infernal bedevilments—I'd rather be in my hammock than on the main-top when she's mumbling and humming her incantations, for if ever there was a witch——"

"Stopper over all, mate, there goes the skipper's blue light off the Lizard—that's the signal. Come along."

The speakers were two ill-looking ruffians in pea-jackets thrown loosely over their guernseys; they wore high boots, and caps of scarlet flannel.

The scene was wildly picturesque. Heavy piles of rock scattered a rough and shingly beach, a thick mist veiled the fatal coast of Mount's Bay, and the beacons round the cliffs, or on the bluffs at sea, shone through the bay with a dim red glare.

The wind blustered hoarse and fierce in the caverns and crevices of the dread shore, and the waves leaped and dashed about the slimy rocks, and strewed, heap upon heap, the heavy tangles of seaweed.

The growling wind raised higher its threatening voice, and the big waves grew heavier in their massiveness and swifter in their speed as they thundered and foamed far up on land.

Lantern in hand the two men clambered down the craggy side of the cliff and through the bustling squalls and hurtling rain, pressed on to a sort of mole, built of piles and stones, and running literally into the sea, which poured and danced over it in clouds of spray.

Before the rising wind the fog was beginning to clear away in weird wreathings.

Upon reaching the mole, a woman appeared standing on the edge of a water-break, the surf flying about her and the monster billows bursting at her feet. With one hand she shaded her eyes and peered through the dense vapours, as if in search of some object far out in the offing; in her other she held aloft a flaming torch.

Her heavy black hair fluttered in the wind, her white arms were bare, and she was dressed in a short blue kirtle and a handkerchief thrown about her moulded breast—even in the mist and gloom of the tempestuous night it was perceptible that she was a woman of exquisite form and probably of great beauty, for the torch threw down a bright glinting on her rich-hued cheek, and her eyes shone wild, black, and lustrous through the sweeping darkness. She was muttering some superstitious jargon, and seemed to be addressing the spirits of the ocean that might well be imagined floating and hovering in the murky haze that rolled along the crests of the surly breakers.

> "Breaker of spars and render of sails,
> Heaver of mountains, breather of gales,
> Sapper of cliff, and scourger of shore,
> Rev'ler that leaps to the tempest roar,
> I charm thee by dark words, mystic and dread,
> That move in their depths the bones of the dead,
> That stir the wind-spirits in far and lone caves,
> To rouse at my runes and to serve me as slaves;
> Old ocean, great mother, our cabins are scant,
> Thy sea-born are famished by winter and want,
> Then, with thy green arms from thy wild-heaving breast,
> Fling treasure and food to thy sea-born distressed,
> My runes shall be hushed, and the storm-fiend have rest!"

"Harken to the young hag," muttered Harleck, to his companion, "she'll finish her runes in Davy's locker, spite of all her conjuring—you'll see that."

"My jib! if she hears you, you'll be sea-lagged with cramps and twitchings, or blighted by the evil-glance," returned his more credulous mate, in a whisper.

The woman turned sharply.

"What are ye doing here?" she asked. "Are you awaiting the second signal from the Lizard Point?"

"Aye, mistress," Agger replied, in a humble tone.

"Very well, then; go to your post at the curve, where the boat is to land. Be off," said the woman, imperiously, "I am engaged in a work that requires none of your assistance."

"I would your black helper, the devil, you conjure, would run off with your fine figure-head, which I hate worse than his horns, pretty as it is," growled Harleck, as he moved away with his companion.

"Harleck, what makes you so bitter against Thorkil's wife?" asked the other fellow, simply.

"This is no time to overhaul my black books, mate, but her name is marked down pretty clearly in more places than one. Look ahead, there's a light to the windward."

"It's the doomed ship, Harleck," said the man.

"Hark!" cried the other, touching his lip.

A dull, subdued boom, piercing the heavy air struck their ears.

A pair of rocket-lights shot up and burst in the sky, and the fire-bubbles floated along, changing from steel blue to rich orange and pure red.

The steady stroke of oars was now heard, and a lantern was seen rising and falling on the rolling waters.

"It is my husband," said the woman. "Lend a hand, or the boat will be swamped."

The men rushed breast-deep among the breakers, uncoiling a rope which they had taken from the mole.

"A-hoy! what cheer! Ho, lads! the pass-words," cried a voice, loud and ringing, though deadened by the fog.

"Fate gives all the sea sends!" shouted Harleck.

To this ambiguous watch-word the same deep voice trolled out,

"All's well, catch the painter! haul a-head, she's a-strand."

A bowling head-wave crashed behind the boat and sent it shivering up the rough beach, and then burst and tossed about it.

Six men jumped out.

Hylda drew to the side of the taller of the party.

He was a very fine fellow, tall, and broad-chested, his elf locks raven black, and his eyes dark as the sky they gazed on. The expression of his face was that of ruthless determination, ungovernable passion, and strong will; yet, around his mouth, were softer traits, and, savage as he seemed, he showed the utmost deference to his wife, excepting when she greatly angered him, and then there was something in his rebellious churlishness that betrayed his weakness and could not gloss over his innate subservience to his fierce and beautiful spouse.

Thorkil Penreal was decidedly a handsome fellow; he resembled Hylda—in fact, was her cousin.

"And you left the Seals' Cover without consulting me, Thorkil," cried Hylda, in shrewish accents. "Of course, I am nobody; I am a woman, and, by consequence, a fool; this is Friday, too, the moon waning in her last quarter; and three nights I dreamed a water-sprite warned me that if you wrecked the barque which tried to save you, bad would come of it, and bad *will* come of it, Thorkil Penreal; but, of course, I am a woman, and know nothing; I have no right to a voice in the matter. That for your manly wisdom! Michael Guldenhoff, the Dutch smuggler, and our best customer, lies out in the offing, in the French cutter, the Loup Garou; he will be decoyed and run into danger; but, of course, that's nothing, you don't care for *me*—your own wife. Of course, *he* may go to the devil, or the shark's fin, for aught you care."

"Quiet, lass! Michael knows my signals; and the Dutchman that we mean to break up is worth overhauling—there's a cargo of lace and stuff, and, they say, a purser's bank of guilders," returned the captain of the wreckers. "And, if you'll be a good girl, I'll deck you out a reg'lar Duchess of Cornwall."

Hylda gave a little hiss of contempt.

"Don't ware ship, my little craft, from a storm of your own brewing. You and Thyra were runeing up at Polruth's for this very squall."

"Yes, to wreck the cursed Devonshire revenue cutter, with all Nat Redfern's barrels aboard her—not to strike the Wilhelmina. I've had omens."

"Curse your omens!" cried her husband. "Be a good lass; we don't want any of your jawing-tackle to help us out of this mess. There goes another gun: the poor devils are in great distress; it will be a mercy to put them out of their misery. Here's a pretty night, too. You may depend on't, Hylda, your mate, Thyra, has bamboozled you, because she's

envious. Now, I don't want to be balked, nor I won't be; so, if you don't like the business, go home."

"Go home! What could you do without me?" cried the girl, disdainfully.

"Sail a merry cruise, and be free of squalls!" growled the captain. "Look you, now, I mean to take salvage of yon barque, if I swing for it, so no more palaver."

"Well, you'll rue this night."

"No, for I shan't sleep in your hammock, and your tongue is worse than a sou'-wester. Get home! Harlech, go up aloft; you're the best cloud-brusher. Take old Triton and the mare from their stables in the cave, lead them along the lower rocks of the cliff, and tell Puffin to fire the long gun from the rock to the lee of the shoals. The look-out on the barque will take the lanterns for ship lights, and the gun for a minute signal; and as the lubber has a heart as soft as a ball of molten pitch, he'll send off a jolly-boat to pick up the ducks; and between that gull's chase and the blue lights we shall have the beach strewn with his ship-stores before the tide turns."

"And what is the skipper's name?" asked Hylda.

"How the devil should I know?" returned her husband, gruffly. "Do you think I want to give him a land-lubber's funeral, and ticket his coffin? Heave ahead, Harleck; there's no time to be lost."

"No; since you are resolved to brave the warnings of fate, I am your wife, and will share your peril," said Hylda, sternly. "I will lure the ship; do you keep the shore, or attend to the blue lights on the foreland? Come, Murdoch and Agger; let Harleck remain where he is."

"Aye, mistress," returned the sullen fellow, stepping away and murmuring between his clenched teeth, "I'd rather serve as powder-monkey on a man-o'-war, or pull the bow-oar of a galley, than command as warrant-officer under that rip!"

"Hulloa! you swab! what's that you say?" cried Thorkil, turning fiercely upon the other.

"I say it's a good plan; that there's no decoy flag so good as a petticoat," replied Harleck, readily.

"Now, lads," cried the captain of the wreckers, ordering the men, "you know your plan of operation. The vessel yonder, though the fog is clearing, is thoroughly bamboozled. Also her bearings; look how she edges away to the leeward; she will shoal in half an hour. Mark me! a score of you line the beech, others man the boats, the rest come with me."

The crowd divided.

With a strong party of the heartless villains Thorkil mounted the cliffs. The haze was clearing, but the night was pitch dark, and the wind and the waves were raving and bellowing tremendously.

The men were obliged to keep a convulsive hold upon the points and corners of the rocks, or the fitful gusts would have hurled them from their foothold.

Upon reaching a rugged, perilous ledge, that ran along the side of the cliff, they made their way to a cavernous hollow, opening upon the little path, and here they mustered.

Thorkil clasped his arm round a mass of the rock, and laying himself flat on the path, looked over the fearful brink, his long black elf locks, fluttering fiercely in the sweeping squalls, and torrents of wind and rain.

Below him lay another path, and upon this, Hylda, and the two men who had followed her, were leading a horse slowly along. On the forehead and at the side of the animal were attached a couple of huge lanterns, and whether, only through his decrepitude and the ruggedness of the path he was treading, or whether as the result of careful training, the steed alternately tossed and lowered his head and neck, in a measured sort of way, as if to imitate the rise and fall of the stern lights of a vessel, staggering in a heavy sea.

Thorkil leaned still further over the cliff and shouted.

"Ho, lass! give the word, and blaze away."

Hylda drew back the horse and stood grasping the rein, humming and chanting her wild rhymes, like some weird spirit of the storm.

Agger and Redfern dragged from a crevice in the rock a small iron mortar, charged to the full.

Hylda, with wonderful coolness, thrust the flame of the torch upon the touch-hole of the piece.

It flashed, and the report shook the rocks beneath their feet, and then mingled with the thundering bluster of the raging gale.

Thorkil scrambled down the rocks, and stood by her side.

"That's our signal of distress," he said, with a grin.

"Now, lads, screech like devils. We strike! we founder!"

The wreckers set up a wild shout, shrieking for help and for a boat.

There was a dull boom from afar over the dreadful waters.

Hylda flinched and shuddered, and clung to her husband's arms.

"She answers us; she sends off boats to our rescue, to their own destruction;" murmured Thorkil, in a voice that betrayed his intense excitement. "But, what ails ye, lass, you are not used to be squeamish when the sea is in a bounteous mood? You never before lacked the good old Cornish spirit; what ails ye?"

"This deed is unhallowed!"

"What the sea throws on our coast is ours!" growled her husband, impatiently. "How long since you have been scrupulous?"

"This deed is excepted; a special ban is set on it. Thyra and I have seen the water wraith; we have dreamed."

"If you were now at home, in bed and dreaming, you would be in your right place!" returned Thorkil, stamping his foot. "See, she looms through the fog! she luffs! she makes way! Ha, ha! she drifts; there goes the rocket from the shark's fin. She is doomed—her boats have gone down in the heavy seas—and now she runs before the head-wind crash on to the rock. See! the jib blown from the bolt-ropes! how it rackets in the squall."

"By God! she's our's!"

"Hark!" said Hylda, suddenly clutching his arm.

A faint yellow glare lighted the dark horizon, and shone palely in the awful crests of the innumerable billows. A hoarse, stern muttering, as of some reproving spirit, rolled far away in the distance.

"The voice of the storm itself is against us," said the superstitious Hylda.

"Well, and who brewed this tempest?"

Hylda did not answer, but lowered her glance.

"If you would save the ship, rechain the storm-furies your spells have set loose; but, a curse on your folly. Stay here, or go home—I am off to the beach."

Loud shouts were now heard along the strand, mingled with cries of "A wreck! a wreck!"

A man could scarcely look on the breakers as they billowed in like trembling avalanches and steamed in dense clouds of spray, without being smitten with blindness, while the simultaneous roar of the great guns of a whole fleet would not have out-blustered the din of the warring elements.

The shark's fin is a rock, so called because in shape it closely resembles the dorsal fin of one of those monsters just protruding from the surface of the water; but the sea rushed over it, and the mists hung about it in such a manner that it was impossible to distinguish the luckless barque which had been lured by these fiends of the coast to such a fearful doom.

Hylda looked over the sea in mute terror; she could not account for the sudden awe and anxiety that oppressed her. If she had not been accustomed to these terrible scenes the effect would have seemed only natural. But she had exulted in the ruthless betrayal and destruction of many a tall ship and the pitiless murder and robbery of many a crew.

As her gaze ranged across the waters, vainly striving to pierce the gloom, a vivid, quivering flash of lightning illumined sky and sea, and played brilliantly among the dense mass of clouds.

In the intense light she could distinguish every rugged excrescence of the sharp edge of the strange-shaped rock. She could see the pretty wreaths in the emerald billows that splashed over a dark object at the lower end of the rocks; an almost shapeless mass, it seemed, a mesh of broken spars, and tangled cordage, a dreary hull—the quarter smashed in and the forecastle crushed upon the rocks.

With a gloomy light in her wild eyes, Hylda, the storm-raiser, descended the rock.

Thorkil Penreal, Harleck, Agger, and the rest of the wreckers, ran along the shore, their woolfish eyes aglow with greed for plunder, their arms motioning with violent gesture.

A party of bold fellows were seen rowing a stout boat towards the shark's fin, lifting and sinking upon the waves, and down in the trough of the sea.

A number of bales, mess-chests, barrels, bottles, spars, bolts and tackling were washed far up the shore, and then snatched back again by the mighty waves, as if in the fierce sport of tantalizing the grasping villains, who were nearly drawn among the breakers; and floating hideously upon the heavy swell, lost among the foaming billows, and then rolled up on to the beach, were flung the limp, passive bodies of the drowned.

"Ho! there, cap'en, a light!" cried Harleck, from a little distance.

"What do you want, mate?" cried Thorkil, who was busily engaged in hauling something ashore with a long rope he had caught by rushing breast deep into the waves. "There's the lantern, fetch it yourself."

Harleck ran to the spot indicated, snatched up the light, and returned to the place whence he had hailed Thorkil.

The latter had managed to drag ashore a heavy chest with a sail and hammock nettings.

He turned his head to look for the lantern, in order to examine his prize: his eyes fell upon Harleck, who was leaning over the body of a drowned man.

Thorkil Penreal rose and walked towards him.

There was a bright flash of lightning, and the thunder crashed and died away in slow reverberations.

"It's the skipper; I think he's alive," said Harleck, in his harsh, guttural tones.

"Well, scuttle his hull; but give me the lantern."

Thorkil snatched up the light, intent on returning to his own booty.

Harleck moved his ravenous claw about the breast of the man, and passed it beneath his armpits in the lining of his jacket ; on one side he clutched a square substance, which he concluded was a pocket-book, and around the waist of his victim were heavy pieces, seeming of metal, sewed up in a belt.

Harleck seized hold upon the jacket, and drawing his knife, fumbled for the place where he had felt the substance, in order to cut it away.

He felt a light grip about his left wrist, as if the man were recovering consciousness, and had instinctively raised his hand to save his property.

It was so dark, and the action so sudden, that the wrecker could not resist a cry of horror.

Another vivid flash of lightning intensely illumined the wild and cruel scene ; quick as it was it glinted electrically on a gleaming knife, and showed a welling stream staining the sea-drenched guernsey of the hapless seaman bright red.

Solemn darkness, and the awe-striking roll of Heaven's artillery !

Harleck gasped as he felt his hand wet with a warm, clinging moisture, which he knew was blood.

There was a wild huzza in the distance. The boat had returned to the shore, laden with plunder from the wreck.

Harleck cursed and growled at the loss of the lantern, as his agile fingers bore away the pocket-book, and thrust it into his own breast ; and he ripped up the belt, and he heard the tinckle and tink of coins falling among the pebbles, and he grovelled in the darkness to recover them ; soon the rich gold pieces glittered on the stones and in his blood-stained hands.

He started, and looked up.

The lantern glared in his face, and the dark eyes of Thorkil Penreal scowled down upon him.

"Ha! Master Harleck, this is against our law. Money in the mass is delivered in the mass for fair sharings ; money in single coins, and stray findings is the finder's. Is not that the law ?"

"Pardon, cap'en," returned the wrecker, quailing beneath the piercing eye of his leader. "Isn't the night as black as a wolf's mouth ? I haven't taken a shiner."

"Nor shall you. Mate, fair sharings and a percentage ; its our rule ; and when any man can say that I myself don't abide by it, let who will take the lot."

"Cap'en, here's what I've taken. I leave the carcass to you, and all its accoutrements."

Thorkil Penreal looked on the placid face of the dead.

"I'm sorry you knifed him, Harleck. I like the look of him ; he wasn't such a bad sort that would leave his own barque in such a storm to succour us. There is such a thing as 'seething the kid in its mother's milk.'"

At this moment the flare of torches betokened the approach of the rest of the party.

Hylda, and a crowd of wreckers, surrounded the body.

The wife of the chief ruffian bent over the dead man ; the torch fell from her hand, and, with a pealing shriek, she flung herself upon his breast.

The wreckers looked into each other's faces in mute surprise.

Hylda raised herself from the breast of the murdered man.

Her glossy black hair mantled her fair shoulders in its massy folds ; her fine eyes were upturned to the wild and lightning-blazed sky ; she stretched out her pale arms, and shrieked and shrieked again, as she saw them dappled in blood.

She rose on one knee, and in her agony clutched her white brow.

She took away her hand, and the red stains of her fingers were left branded on her forehead.

The crowd of wreckers recoiled from the storm-raiser with a general cry of horror, so awful, so unearthly looked she, as she knelt with elevated hands, and the red glare of the torches fell on her tortured features and the crimson finger-stains upon her brow of snow.

Hylda rose, and turned like a pantheress upon her husband.

"Did I not warn you, Thorkil Penreal ?" she screamed, wildly wringing her hands. "Were not I and Thyra both warned by the water-wraiths, that know all, by dreams, that are shadows of spirit-land reflected on the brain-mirror of the soul ? Did I not know by runes and by the stars that the wrecking of yon fatal ship would be a deed of woe ? But you would not heed ; you urged me to use my strongest spells to raise this tempest. And, now, what have I done ? I have called down the lightning to sear my own brow, smeared with the blood of—MY FATHER !"

"Your father !" cried the crowd in one voice, and starting backwards.

Thorkil snatched a torch from one of the bystanders, threw himself beside the murdered man, and eagerly scanned the dead face.

"By the power of darkness ! she is right !" he groaned. "It is Hardred Trevellyn !"

"Did you strike this blow ?" asked Hylda.

"No," muttered Penreal, hoarsely ; "It was not I."

Hylda turned savagely upon Harleck.

The colour died from his cheek, but the blood-spots of his victim remained to condemn their murderer.

"The cap'en gave the word ; I followed orders," growled the man, sullenly.

In an instant Hylda had drawn her knife.

She rushed upon Harleck, who retreated before her.

Thorkil caught her by the arm, and forcibly restrained her.

"No, lass ; blood enough has been shed," he said, solemnly. "It was a fatal mistake for which he is not responsible. Let us bury your father and his memory together. Fate's workings are strange, and we are the puppets of destiny ; henceforth, poor lass, I will heed well thy warnings."

"Against what shall I warn ye ?" cried Hylda, in wild grief. "Against self-murder ?—you have killed my father. Against shipwreck ?—you have wrecked the barque that brought my parent home. Oh, we are parricides ; we are accursed ! There is no more hope, no hope, no hope—my father !"

With a piercing cry, the wretched girl dashed herself down to all appearance as lifeless as the corpse upon whose pulseless breast her pale cheek and dishevelled tresses were pillowed.

Thorkil Penreal lifted his wife gently, and bore her in his arms.

"Get a spar and place the body on it," said the captain, addressing his gang, "and follow me to the cave."

These orders were soon obeyed, and six sturdy fellows raised some bolted sheathing-boards to their shoulders, over which was thrown a piece of a sail. On this rude bier they had laid the corpse of the murdered man.

The sea still lashed and raved along the fatal shore ; the lightning still blazed and leaped in the dark chasm of night ; the thunder crashed and rumbled ; the wind still shrieked as if with horror at its own work of destruction, while up the winding paths of the cliffs moved that sad party.

Thorkil bearing his insensible wife, the six wreckers carrying the body, and all walking with down-cast eyes and awe-striken faces beneath the frown of the cliff, only rendered darker by the flare of their torches.

CHAPTER II.

THE KIDDLEAWINK — A BRUTAL SUITOR — A DAS- TARDLY ACT—BRITISH TARS—JOYFUL NEWS—A DEADLY PERIL — A LOVED ONE'S RETURN.

THE morning succeeding the night of the storm was one of translucent clearness and balmy freshness.

The swell on the ocean had not quite subsided, though the wind had lulled ; the briny waters seemed tumbling and leaping in rough good humour, for the giant ocean makes no more of the little lives he has swamped out of little bodies, or the tiny toys he has crushed on his rocky teeth, than a rude and sportive boy heeds the crushing of a sun beetle or a butterfly that crosses the path of his frolic.

The pure blue sky was mottled with fleecy white cloudlets, and the dazzling sunbeams fluttered into the changeful waters like gleaming arrows of burnished gold.

Upon a little road that wound round on the landward side of the jutting cliffs, and on a rough piece of a common, bright with yellow gorse, stood a small, lonely house—or, rather, hovel—in which were sold spirits and malt liquors of high quality at low charge, the profits not being reduced by governmental deductions : such a house, as our readers are, perhaps, aware, is called in Cornwall, a kiddle-awink, and the establishment in question displayed the sign of "The Three Jolly Mariners," and was conducted by an old smuggler whose name was Murdoch Polruth.

In the largest apartment of this little hostelry a large, ungainly, cabin-like, wood-beamed room, cumbered with furniture of antique fashion, strangely mixed with sea-chests and ship-tackle, and by the window that looked out upon the common, and commanded a prospect of the sea across the rounding of the cliff on either side, a young girl was sitting.

She was not more than seventeen years of age, extremely pretty and engaging, with health-tinted cheeks, sweet, budding lips, and gentle, yet animated, brown eyes, and soft, rich hair, neatly braided upon her clear, ingenuous brow.

Her glance was down bent, and her long lashes were wet with shining tears.

By the door stood a tall, dark, evil-looking fellow, dressed in a velveteen coat and leather gaiters, with his hat pulled over his shaggy brows, and a heavy whip in his hand.

The door was half opened, and without was this worthy's horse, a little grey nag, tethered to the sign post.

"I would give you a more favourable answer if I could, indeed, indeed, William," cried the girl, tearfully ; "I know you are above me in station, and I am sure, if you are only wise enough to court some one worthier of you than a poor friendless orphan girl, like myself, you will in the end be much more satisfied with your better choice. Oh, pray, do not fret me anymore ; I would love you if I could ; but, indeed, I can never forget my first lover, I can never wed any other than him."

"And who is he, Rose ?" cried the fellow, roughly.

"What is he but a scampish, sea-faring fellow without out a penny to keep the devil out of his pocket, or the wolf from his home-door. His home ! Where is his home ? He has no home, and never will have, and, for that matter, I think he has gone to his last home ; for I was told by Nat Redfern that his ship was wrecked on the Guinea coast, and that he and all his shipmates were lost ; anyhow, he's no mate for you, for, besides that, I hate him and love you. He would leave you from one year's end to another to grizzle away your young days in some wretched cottage, while he was cruising after other lasses in foreign parts. I tell you, Rose, I love you, and I am a willful sort of fellow, and never was ba'ked yet by man nor devil, much less by a puling woman that does not know her own good. I'm your uncle Polruth's landlord, and he is in arrears with his rent ; let him look to it ! If you don't consent to go to church with me, Rose, your uncle shall go to prison, and you may turn out on the road. I won't stand any more of this infernal thwarting. What I say I mean, so look to it."

"But he will find the money, Mr. Trelawny, and, even if he could not, I am sure you would not be so cruel."

"Cruel ! If I have any more of your mawkish folly and opposing, I'll peach on him to the revenue men as a smuggler and a wrecker."

"You dare not !" cried the girl.

"And why not, my pretty minx, what's to prevent me ?"

"The band would kill you."

"Kill me, would they ? Well, if you don't come round to reason, and listen to the suit of a man that loves you truly, and will make you a good husband, I'l bring the parliament men on the whole gang and hunt them out of their hold with pike points and cutlass blades."

The girl's soft eyes lightened with strange fire ; she rose, drew herself up to her full height, and said, indignantly,

"You talk rashly, William Trelawny—you are base enough to threaten me, and, if I loved you as much as I despise you, I would never be so untrue to my own dignity as a woman to wed a man rich enough to take advantage of my weakness to menace me. Go ! rather than be your wife I would be the victim of your fellest revenge. I spurn you, and will talk to you no more."

"Nor will I talk with you, scorner ; I will act," cried the young farmer, with a demoniac frown. " Look you, Rose Lavington, one day I give you to form your resolve ; if you do not receive me as I deserve to be received, loving you as I do, by this hour to-morrow, I will ruin your uncle, and you shall be turned adrift to find, if you may, in your boundless beggary, one who will make you as good an offer as mine. Remember, these are not idle threats ; to-morrow your hand, or your uncle's debt. Reflect on it ; so, good morn, and yours as you use me !"

With this, the ruffianly fellow slammed the door, and mounted his horse to ride away.

A short, thick-set fellow, with a bloated, sensual-looking face, emerged from a kind of shed, and halloed the young farmer to pause.

Will Trelawny reined his horse, and turned his dark face with a savage glare at the other, who came limping towards him.

"Well, Master William, what luck ?" said the innkeeper. "I s'pose the young baggage received ye more gracious like ?"

"No. And if I don't get a more gracious reception when I come to-morrow—which, let me tell you, will be my last visit on love business—I will play the devil with you, and her too. You are her uncle' and her only protector; your influence ought to be great with her, and you promised to use it to the utmost. But I see ye are both fooling me. Well, Mr. Polruth, to-morrow I eject you from the house you rent of me, and, moreover, denounce you as a smuggler; for, let me assure you, I am one of those men who never forget an injury!"

With this, he spurred his horse viciously, and rattled away.

Murdoch Polruth shambled into the house.

Rose still sat at the window, silently weeping.

"Look ye here, Miss Finick," cried the innkeeper, fiercely, "you pretend to call yourself something extraor'nary, proper vartuous, and all that sort—eh?"

"No, no," cried Rose, pleadingly. "Pray, dear uncle, do not be angry. I will try——"

"And you think yourself by many a knot further on your cruise to a better world than the rest of us poor sinners. P'r'aps you think all your kith and companions are on the wrong tack entirely, and are flying before a head-wind to the infarnal regions, Old Nick, and blazes. You think so—eh! Tell the truth, now?"

"No, uncle, you have been good to me; you have sheltered and sustained me since my parents died."

"I have so, to fine purpose. But, I was saying, you considered yourself the real Lady Nonpareil, and quite over-freighted with a cargo of cardinal vartues——"

"Oh, uncle!"

"Well, then, will you enlighten the blind as to what sort of quality is one you are over-laden with, my pretty craft—what's ingratitude?"

"Indeed, uncle, I am not ungrateful."

"What's ingratitude, I say?" roared Polruth. "Ain't it the most infarnal, skunking, unvartuous qualification as ever a saint was cussed with?"

"I'm not ungrateful," sobbed poor Rose.

"No, not a bit of it; in course. Didn't I take ye a fatherless, motherless, moneyless brat? Didn't I feed ye, and clothe ye, and bring ye up useful? And what's my reward? To be turned out in my age like a beggar to starve; to be bullied and browbeaten by a saucy land-shark; to be peached on, and p'r'aps 'prisoned or transported, eh! That isn't ingratitude with you; in course not. Give a dog a bad name, and hang him; give a dog a good one, and the more he bites ye the better."

"Uncle, I will do everything I can to save you from the consequences of the vindictive spite of William Trelawny—everything but marry him, and I will rather die than become the wife of one so ill-disposed, so mean and treacherous!"

"That's speaking plain. Well, now, hark ye, lass! I've tried all sorts of soft means with ye, but now I mean to play the skipper. You *shall* marry him! Do ye hear that?"

"I never will!"

"Look ye, lass, you're now nigh eighteen. Do you remember what happened to ye two years agone?"

"I fell into the sea, and was nearly drowned. Oh, Heaven, keep me from wickedly wishing that I had been lost!"

"And do you recollect that you were fond of playing on the reef and along the piles of the water-break? You were always a wilful minx from your cradle. And after you were brought home, half water-logged, I took the best means to bring you to your senses and to restore the circulation of the blood in your dainty skin, for I found a bit o' buntline that suited ye to a nicety, and I laid on like a bo'swain's mate, till you had cause to remember your sousing, and ye never fell into the sea afterwards."

"Uncle, you need not remind me of that which I am willing to forgive and forget."

"By the rolling thunder! I'll give ye a reminder ye shall *never* forget," shouted the ruffian, furiously seizing her arm, and roughly shaking her, "for, unless ye promise to make your own fortune and mine by wedding Black Will Trelawny, I'll flog ye like a drunken skulk at the gangway."

"You may kill me, uncle; but I will never be forced, by your utmost cruelty, to perjure myself before the altar!" returned the girl, with womanly heroism.

The ruffian growled a savage oath, forced the girl on her knees, and, snatching up a piece of rope, whirled it round, and brought it down with fearful force upon her fair and tender shoulders.

The poor girl screamed and writhed in torture.

He had not time to repeat the dastardly blow, for two men broke through the door. The first of them seized the brute by the collar and dashed him across the room.

Polruth struck his head against a beam in the wall, stumbled, and fell prone.

His assailant straddled across his prostrate body, and glared down upon him with his huge fists clenched, and seemed bursting with fury.

"Dam'me, you precious spawn of a fresh-water shark! you dastardly, dirty-faced skunk of a pirate swab, will you strike a woman?" roared the stranger. "Is that the way you honour your mother, by ill-treating a female sex? Shiver my top lights! if you wern't aground, I'd smash your hull into a heap of molasses. But, come aboard and clear for action, and see if I don't send a broadside into your figure-head that shall shake all your timbers, fore and aft. Come on, you woman-beating swab!"

With this the speaker retired a step and began to pull off his jacket.

Murdoch Polruth scrambled up, and, snatching a knife from his belt, rushed towards his opponent with upraised arm.

The seaman—for so his dress and bearing proclaimed him—lightly ducked under the uplifted knife, and, seizing the ruffian behind by the collar, planted his toe on the seat of honour, and projected him "about a bow shot" through the open door.

Upon getting on to his legs the furious kiddle-a-winker seemed inclined to show fight.

But when the sailor flung off his jacket, intent upon giving chase, Murdoch seemed to think better of it, and, after shaking his fist threateningly, took to his heels and ran off towards the cliff.

The man re-entered the house, panting and laughing.

When Rose had time to scrutinise her deliverer, she found that both he and his companion were fine, hearty-looking fellows, dressed in white-duck and blue jackets, and evidently King's men, from some man-of-war.

"Sarve him right, Joe; sorry I hadn't the over-hauling on him," said the champion's confederate; "for, curse me, if ever I saw such a mis-begotten, ragged-jibbed son of a sea-cook, with no more grit than lies in the blade of his dirty cat-stabber; and she such a pretty craft, too. I'm glad you turned him to the right-about."

"Avast heaving, ship-mate; don't you see young ma'am is all in the downs. Never mind, my little cherub, never say *die* while there's a shot in the locker. As for that martinet skunk, you're my convoy now, and if I get athwart hawse with him he'll not soon forget his brush with Joe Juniper."

"Oh, sir! you are very good, your intentions are generous and kind," said Rose. "But my uncle is a dangerous man, aud I fear he has gone to fetch some of his companions to revenge the just punishment you inflicted on him; you had better not stay here."

"What, strike my colours? No, as I'm a cruising in these waters, I mean to take my soundings," returned Joe Juniper, "and to overhaul ship's papers of every craft as comes within hail. And, as for that 'farnal Jonah, I'd have the skunk know that I'm a true blue, and that if he tries to cut out my prize, I'll dismast him and blow his hulk off the waters. Dam'me, miss—nothing offensive meant or designated—but its a disgrace to human humanity that you should be taken in tow by such a pirate. I'll defend ye, miss, while I've a fin; we'll blockade the port, and the second lieutenant and half the liberty-men are coming ashore, and you'll have a whole fleet to protect you."

"Aye, aye, mate," rejoined his more stolid companion, seating himself at the table; "but, I'm as dry as a castaway that's lived a whole cruise on brine and salt-junk. We must freshen hawse here; what have you got to drink, eh? Nothing illicit that arn't good stingo." The seaman gave a knowing wink.

"Bill Hawser, miss, a messmate of mine;" said Joe Juniper, looking at his comrade with a patronnising smile, "as good a seaman as ever reefed a tops'l. He's fingering his fob, for he's taken a young bank of prize money; and aboard, Bill Hawser rates higher than this indiwiddle, but it arn't merit, you know, miss, its pity. The cocked hats pities him 'cos he is sich a lubber; well, here's a guinea, my beauty, and now I'll take the change, being nothing meant as ain't ship-shape. Lord bless your pretty peepers!"

With this the gallant sailor passed his arm round the girl's waist, and imprinted a kiss on her lips.

Rose lighted a lantern; she went into a little shed at the back of the house, and soon returned with a couple of black bottles, which she set on the table, with glasses and pipes.

The tars seated themselves, after turning their chairs round and round and exchanging comical glances.

They lighted their long pipes, and "blew a cloud" that soon hazed their good-humoured, weather-beaten faces, which beamed through the genial mist aglow with enjoyment.

"Now, Joe, sing us a stave, hearty," said Bill Hawser.

"Aye, aye, shipmate; what shall it be?"

"Them werses as that schoolmaster chap compoged as was purmoted and made a warrant officer 'cos he saved the hold from catching fire all along of his book-larnin'—you know it, Bill."

"I does, and a very good song it be, so here's the 'Red, White, and Blue,' and now I blaze away.—

"Come, lads, wet hawse, for while on shore
   A seaman's helm is lashed a-lee;
Our anchor's cast, our cruise is o'er,
   We've nought to do but jolly be.
For, when on board—we did no more
   Than duty bids, you'll say—but then
The tempest's nor the cannon's roar
   Could never daunt us foremast-men.

"Great Alexander, I have heard,
   Blubbered when he had whopped the world;
Such conduct, mates, was quite absurd—
   There's lots of work, though flags be furled.
That sarcy Sue a sailor flouts,
   But blinks and blushes now and then,
or, though the little cherub pouts,
   We know she loves us foremast-men.

"So, lads, wet hawse, for while on shore
   A seaman's helm is lashed a-lee;
Our anchor's cast, our cruise is o'er,
   We've nought to do but merry be.
We'll taste sweet lips, we'll toss the glass;
   All hands for fun—a hornpipe, Ben!
Let's toast our cap'en, King, and lass,
   True British hearts, and foremast-men!"

Rose stood at a little distance, with hands folded together, looking on the simple tars with a dimply smile and a tear-brimming eye.

When the song was concluded she chanced to raise her glance to the window.

Rose shrieked.

"Breakers ahead! miss," cried Joe Juniper, starting up, "what's in the wind? Some more pirates in the offing? Dam'me! Bill, we'll weigh anchor and give chase to the ragamuffins."

The sailor blundered to the door, which he opened and he rushed out.

Bill Hawser hitched up his trousers and looked from the window.

He perceived a scowling, black-browed fellow sneaking away behind the hedge.

Joe Juniper appeared not to have seen this person, for he ran round the house and across to the shed, hallooing in his cheery voice, and seemingly intent upon finding the object which had occasioned such alarm to Rose.

He ran back into the house.

"Shiver his mizen!" cried Joe, "he's slipped anchor, the skunk. What sort o' craft is he, miss? Blow me if I don't think we're mooring in 'farnal strange waters. Howsomedever, don't be afeard, miss, for I'm your humble sarvant to command for ever and a long Sunday, for you're the trimmist little pinnace that ever blessed my eyes: hair, long and silky as a admiral's pennant; bows round and taut——"

"Avast heaving, you swab!" interrupted Bill Hawser; "don't ye see as young miss is blushing like daybreak? Behave."

"Well, miss, 'scuse sea manners; I means respectful. I'm no scholard, but I sail straight and carries true colours, and, dam'me! you're a sweet little cherub, if I dies for it."

Joe took of his hat and bowed reverentially.

"And now," said Bill, "another brimmer of rum to drink flabbergastration to old Blowhard, the landlord, and then, as we're not used to land cruising, and are rather stiff on our pins arter our long sail, p'r'aps you'll tell us where we can swing a hammock just to sleep out a few hours afore dog-watch?"

"Oh, sir, let me persuade you," said Rose, earnestly, "not to stay here. You are but two men, and, however brave, you will be robbed, perhaps murdered, by some of the evil people that infest this place."

"Much obliged, miss," returned Joe, "but we're not the men as will crowd sail to run away from sich land-crabs as your uncle, with all Lands' End to back him. Wait till he comes—in course, I means our second lieutenant, Mr. Halliard——"

"Halliard!" cried the girl, eagerly, starting and trembling violently.

"Aye, miss; did ye know him? Heard say as he hailed from these parts."

"Oh, God! if it be Walter."

"Lord love your eyes, miss, Walter it is!"

"He is fair, tall, with blue eyes, and a face handsome and bright with manly kindness?"

"That's his pictur'," cried Bill Hawser. Joe and I has sarved under him since he was the very devil of a sky-larking mid aboard the Thunderer."

"Yes, it is he—it is Walter!" cried Rose, falling

SAVED.

back in astonished surprise, "I know by your words and by the glad feeling in my heart that it is the one whom I love."

"Right glad am I, then, to be the one to give you the first intelligence," said Bill Hawser, taking her small, soft hand in his large and horny one; "it's given my heart a warmin' to see the bright color come into your cheeks, and the light spring up into your eyes."

At this moment there was a loud outcry without; the sound of men's voices—men, who had evidently been indulging in more liquor than was good for them.

The girl shuddered, and clung close to Bill Hawser.

And no wonder was it that she felt terrified.

The sound was such as is made by a number of angry voices, and presently there came such a terrific outcry, that Bill would have been forgiven if he had considered a bombardment a contingency by no means unlikely to happen.

A thumping was heard, and a sound uncomfortably like the tapping of pistol-butts.

Joe Juniper went to the window and sang out,

"Shipmates, ahoy! What cheer!"

"Open the door and to hell with you!" roared the savage Harleck.

"Starn all, messmates. Blow me if one on ye comes aboard till we overhaul your log. Who are ye?—what do you want?"

"What the devil should we want in the kiddle-a-wink, but to booze like other Christians. Let us in, hearty; we're square; you needn't be afeard. We like king's men, they're true-blue," said one of the ruffians, in a gruff tone of conciliation.

"The fox persuaded the silly crow as she were a sweet bird and had a fine voice," returned Joe Juniper, sarcastically. "I larnt that out of a child's primer at the dame's school where I was edicated—for ye see, mates, I were born ashore and am used to land-service, and I knows the signal-book too well to be deceived by false buntings. You may preach as fine as the ship's chaplain; but you're only some 'tarnal pirate or smuggler, for all that."

"Am I to be shut out of my own house by a swaggering sailor fellow, that has already assaulted me?" cried Polruth.

"Halloa! Are you there, old cat-o'-nine tails?" shouted Joe. "A credit you are to be skipper of this bunk—arn't you, now? A snivelling, woman-whacking, fob-filching, cargo-running, cod-mouthed smuggler and sneak! Dam'me, you purser swab, if you come within reach of my grapnels, I'll smash in your cabin-windows, and shiver your figure-head."

"Rose, open the door, you baggage," shouted Polruth, "or I'll lace your stays with a knot of rope. Do you hear, my princess?"

This threat so exasperated Joe that he snatched up the grog-bottle, quickly put it to his lips and drained it, and then flung it full at the landlord's head.

It struck him right across the face and knocked him heels over head.

A pistol flashed and crackled.

A bullet whizzed close to Joe's cheek, and flying across the room pierced a rum barrel; the liquor flew out and swamped the floor.

"Sarves ye right," said Bill Hawser. "That might 'a' been your own hulk. What do you shove your lubber's head out of the port for?"

"Open the door at once, or it will be worse for you," cried a deep, clear voice. "We don't want to damage the place; but we'll burn you out rather than be braved in this way."

"It is Thorkil Penreal!" exclaimed Rose, with a shudder. "Oh, you are lost!"

"Are there any fire-arms aboard?" asked Bill Hawser.

"Pistols? Yes; but no—no—no. You must not; blood will be shed," screamed Rose, for Joe had caught sight of a huge, bell-mouthed blunderbuss that hung over the fire place.

He took down the monstrous engine of mischief and swayed it in his hands.

"Dam'me, here's a stern-chaser, Bill, as 'll wing some of the ducks."

There was a loud knocking, and then a rush made at the door—the timbers creaked and quivered; but the bar and bolts sustained them, and they did not give way.

The wreckers gave a growl of rage and execration.

Joe ran to the window.

"Now, my boys, I puts it to you," he cried to the wreckers, "either to sheer off, or to receive the contents of this pretty piece of ordnance, and, to judge by the bore, I should think its charge is a bomb-shell. One—two—brush, ye lubbers—THREE!"

A loud report shook the house; the glass flew out of the windows; the bottles and glasses leaped from the table, and Joe Juniper sprawled on his back.

The blunderbuss had exploded.

Rose and Bill Hawser ran towards him; they lifted him up.

Joe opened his eyes with a bewildered look.

"My limbs, Bill!" he exclaimed, "where are we? It's a blow up, ain't it? My starn quarters has run astern of summut—is it the moon?"

They helped him to his feet.

"Humph!" said Joe, "busted! But it was jist as good as a raking broadside; for hark ye, Bill, them cut-throat chaps is skeared, and are weighing anchor, and standing off."

Whatever might be the cause of their suddenly raising the siege, the wreckers were certainly moving away.

Bill Hawser stooped on his hands and knees, and peered under the crack beneath the door.

"They're under way," he said. "But, shiver me, if I trusts 'em, Joe. They wants to entice us to clear out of port, that they may run us down, the whole fleet on 'em—the cowardly lubbers; but we'll keep up a reg'lar blockade; so just shut up that port, and look out for another long gun."

"Avast there," replied Joe, ruefully shaking his head, "I've had enough of that duty; I resigns my berth to you. I'm top-man; I shall go aloft, and reconnoitre the enemy. You'r master-gunner."

Joe Juniper hereupon strode across the room. He seemed to be destined to meet with catastrophes; once more he stumbled and fell, this time on his hands and knees.

Rose and Bill Hawser turned to ascertain the cause of this disaster, when, to their horror, they perceived that he had stumbled over the edge of a square trap in the floor, which was slowly rising, pushed up from below.

Joe was on his feet in an instant.

Knife in hand, his small, demoniac eyes flashing beneath their shaggy brows, like a fiend in a pantomime, the savage wrecker, Harleck, leaped up through the floor.

Joe collared him, and dashed him down the trap.

A furious shout rose from beneath.

Rose flung herself upon her knees, and clasped her hands in a mute agony of terror.

Bill Hawser flew to the stove. A large copper kettle was boiling on the fire; he snatched it up, and in an instant was beside the open trap, and with wondrous coolness, poured the hissing, steaming, scalding stream of boiling water down upon the besiegers in their mine.

Shrieks, yells, and fearful oaths mingled together, rose from the writhing enemy in their pit of torment.

Bill Hawser tilted back the kettle; it was still half-full of water.

He looked down through the trap.

A head appeared.

Another hissing stream of scalding fluid rattled down.

An awful scream.

Bill again tilted back the kettle.

"Blow me, Joe!" he said, with great unction, "they're turning lobsters; they're red as marines. Can't we rig another pump? Come, my beauty, boil us up another sarcepan. We must pipe all hands to the fire-buckets, for there's a smother in the hold."

Bang!—bang! Two bullets thudded into the ceiling, and pieces of plaster and splinters of wood fell down.

A broad, fierce fellow sprang up, in spite of the last shower of the hot water or the concussion of the kettle hurled down upon him by Bill Hawser's sinewy arm.

It was Thorkil Penreal.

It was well for the man-of-war's man that the dauntless chief of the wreckers had fired his pistol.

Rose screamed, as the two strong men grappled each other.

As for Joe Juniper, he threw himself against the wall, and struck out so lustily right and left that the rascals who assailed him were floored in all directions.

Polruth rushed upon his niece.

She fell on her knees, breathless with terror.

Her brutal relative shook and buffeted her, and poured forth a torrent of invectives.

All was pell-mell, havoc, and confusion.

When, to the uproarious discord of the noisy fray, a new element was added—the deep baying and savage, rough, rolling growls of a huge Newfoundland dog, which had leaped through the broken window.

The chivalrous animal's attention was first directed to the lady's case. The canine champion of beauty flew upon Polruth, and fixing his sharp teeth in the most eligible part of that ruffian's unmentionables, dragged him to the ground, shaking and worrying him as if he had been a cat or a rabbit.

The door had been open.

A loud cheer was heard without.

Brandishing their cutlasses, a dozen sturdy sailors, headed by two officers, a lieutenant and a middy, rushed into the kiddleawink.

The dog still fought like a dragon.

"'Royals or Revenues!'" shouted one of the wreckers. "Run, mates!"

With this, he leaped down the trap.

Thorkil Penreal flung the table and chairs at the dodging seamen, while one by one his fellows escaped to the trap, down which they darted like rats running into a hole.

Thorkil was the last to leap after them.

The trap fell over them with a heavy bang.

"Up with the hatches, and after the rogues!" cried the lieutenant.

"Aye, aye, sir," responded the men, setting to work with great alacrity.

Polruth had tried to scramble to the trap, but the dog restrained him; and, crushed with terror, he laid doubled up on the floor, while the dog growled over him, and admonished him by a lancet-like nip whenever he tried to escape.

All the sailors had now descended through the trap.

With a wild cry of ecstatic joy Rose Lavington flew towards the officer.

He started back, uttered her name, and caught her tightly to his heart.

"Oh Walter! dear Walter! your good fortune has not changed you—you have not risen so high as to leave me out of reach of you? Say that I am still your own Rose. Ah, I have suffered so much!" murmured the girl, nestling her head on his breast.

"Dear Rose—my proudest prize! do not be so cruel as to suspect me; but, here's a true friend come to greet you, my birdie—old Neptune—make much of him, you owe your lover's life to Nep's fidelity."

The dog had turned his huge shaggy head towards the speakers; he gave a deep, sharp, joyous bark, and heavily bounded towards them, panting with delight; he yelped, leaped, and fawned upon the pair with endless caresses.

At this moment the men returned up the trap.

"Well, Joe, where are the skunks?" asked the lieutenant.

"Why, Mr. Halliard, I've heard tell on the Flying Dutchman, and how his phantom craft will wanish away like a water-spout afore a gunshot, jest as you think you are about to overhaul him; but, shiver me, if these land-sharks arnt oozed through the rocks like water through a sponge, without leaving so much as a wake behind 'em."

"What!—you could not find the outlets of their rats' run? But, here's the landlord, we'll clap him into bilboes, and examine him—he looks like a pirate, and I know he's a smuggler. Sit down, Mr. Armitage," he added, addressing the midshipman, "the court is convened—Tom Truepenny, you're provost-marshal—there's your prisoner—silence in the court!"

"Walter, he is my uncle," murmured Rose, who yet could not help smiling as the rough and jolly tars arranged themselves about the room.

Tom Truepenny, a giant of a fellow, with a face as broad and as red as the sun in a brown fog, and a bush of fiery whiskers, collared the cowering rascal; while Neptune sat bobbing his tail, and watching the prisoner with lynx-eyed vigilance.

"Now, yer honour, I'm the fust evidence," said Joe Juniper. "It was about five-bells, yer honour, in the forenoon, me and my messmate, Bill Hawser, were cruising in these waters, when all at once we heard a woman piping a signal of distress; we clapped on all sail we could stagger under, and made for this hulk; when we had run the port mouth, what should we diskiver, but young miss down on her blessed knees a swabbing her lovely peepers, and that infarnal catamaran was laying on to her beautiful bows and figure-head with a hank of bunt line, like a bo'swain whacking a lazy powder monkey."

"Yah!" groaned the sailors, with deep indignation.

"How—how, cr-gr-ue-l!" responded the dog, with a terrific howl, as if he had fully understood what was said.

"Cruel indeed, Nep," said Halliard laughing, but his cheek hot with anger."

"Well, Joe, what did you do?"

"Why, your honour, I jest took the purser swab by the back of his turtle's neck, and setting my starboard toe to his boom-end, sent him flying like a shot from a forty-pounder, right out through the port into the offing."

"Sarve him right, Joe; shiver his mizen, we'll make a target buoy on him," cried the others.

Polruth tried to speak.

Tom Truepenny shook all the speech out of him.

The dog snapped and snarled.

"What followed?"

"A whole fleet of ragamuffins; they ran out like a gang of Chinese pirates, and bombarded our fort; but we held our own, till all at once, when we began to think the enemy had got their likings, and were sheering off, I was tripped over the combings of that hatchway, and the blackguards leaped on our deck; we swept off the boarders, and sent 'em rattling back into the hold, where we kept 'em at bay, yer honour, with a kettle-pump o' steaming hot water, till our ammunition were exhausted, and then we fought 'em hand to hand, till you came to the rescue."

"Have the villain up to the gratings, and give him a taste of the cat, Mr. Halliard," cried the middy.

"No, Mr. Armitage," returned the lieutenant, "first let us hear what he can say for himself."

"Aye, aye! speak, you lubber," cried Truepenny, shaking the prisoner till his teeth and knees chattered like castanets.

"G-Gentlemen, if you p-please. O-lor, I'm f-falling to peices; my b-bolts are giving way, I shall t-tumble into t-timbers," gasped the helpless Polruth, "t-the g-girl is my niece; I've be-been a f-father to her; I'm punished enough, burnt, bruised, bullied and bitten. Do speak for me, R-Rose, my d-dear, a-arnt I allers kind to ye?"

"My good friends and defenders, he is my uncle; it was cruel of him to treat me so harshly, but I was obliged to refuse to obey him in one particular," said Rose, colouring brightly; "and consider he has been sufficiently punished already."

"Let him go, Truepenny," said Halliard. "But mark me, sirrah, you may look upon yourself as under arrest, and must not leave this house till I give you permission. And, in the meanwhile, attend to the orders of my men, and open your stores to them, or, though I am no revenue man, and don't want to meddle with other peoples' duty, I'll take you prisoner, put a Government seal on the door, and seize the house. So, lads, don't spare the grog-kid; but, no drunkenness. And now I leave you to your sky-larking."

"Hurrah!" shouted the jolly tars.

Halliard led his pretty sweatheart from the house. And as, fondly pressing on his arm, and carressing the dog, which trotted proudly by her side, she walked as in a dream of thrilling joy, the merry scrape of the fiddle, and the patter of nimble feet, proclaimed that the merry mariners had abandoned themselves to mirth and jollity.

CHAPTER III.

THE LOVERS' INTERVIEW—A DEADLY RIVAL—THE TEMPTER—A DANGER THREATENS THE LIEUTENANT—BLACK WILL TRELAWNY INCLINES TO JOIN THE WRECKERS.

THE lovers sauntered slowly along the hedge, and reached the brow of the cliff.

All about them was halcyon bright; the sky intensely blue, the fresh sea glancing and leaping right away to the wide horizon, the murmuring waves washing the pebbles far below, and the white-winged sea-fowl screaming and skimming about the cliffs, and swerving and dipping on the breasts of the billowets.

Neptune stretched himself on the short, crisp sward, his eyes blinking in the sun, his long, red tongue lolling from his snowy-white fangs, and looked with luxurious indolence across the expanse of sea and sky, or turned up his good-natured and noble head at his master and mistress, who stood embracing each other.

"Oh! Walter, how many weary, weary hours have I worn away in summer sun and winter snow, watching from this cliff over yon wide and pitiless wilderness, yielding weakly to the aching hope that whispered my heart, that you might—only that you might—some day return," said Rose, tenderly. "Two years—years! every succeeding day of which has been a fresh link to a chain that was getting too heavy for me to drag. But you have come to break that chain, Walter. I see you once more; you are the same as ever, only that absence has made you seem more dear to your forsaken one. Oh! Walter,

it is not wrong and bold in me, is it, to tell you how very, very glad I am to see you again?—how much I love you? My affection has been hoarded up increasingly so long in my heart, that my heart would burst if I did not open it freely, now that I can. Oh! I am so, so glad you are come!"

Walter Halliard pressed her fervently to his heart.

"And, my darling Rose, I have watched long and patiently for this hour. I have seen many changes, suffered many sorrows, braved many dangers since our parting. When we have been becalmed, or were making steady way before fair winds, I have walked the deck in deep thought; while my companions were revelling, my heart has been far away with you. I have been rambling with you the sunny shores, or the green glades of dear, bright England; I have started to hear your voice so plainly, to see your sweet face so vividly—my imagination pictured your dear self with such truthful power; and when in the storm, the rain, the sleet, and snow have poured upon me, when the stinging blast has pierced every nerve, when the death-bearing billows have pounced upon our deck, and scattered all in confusion about me, I have thought of you then, and have felt armed against their power, for I knew you were lonely and wretched, and even ill-used, and I felt that the All-bounteous would preserve me, for your sake."

"Oh, Walter, I could die for joy."

"Silly girl, you must live for happiness; but whither shall we ramble? Yon brake is the spot where we parted; it is there we carved our names on the old tree. But, tell me, why has your uncle treated you so cruelly?"

"Because—because, dear Walter, though they told me you were dead," said Rose, blushing, "and I feared it was true, I would not marry that stern and terrible man, Black Will Trelawny; he is the owner of the kiddleawink. My uncle is in arrears for rent, and Black Will offered to cancel the debt if I would consent to marry him, and threatened, in case of my refusing to do so, to put a distress in the house, and to ruin my uncle."

"Well, dearest, I will settle that matter by paying the debt, and you would not think it a hard condition if I were to exact your hand as an equivalent—you may tell me that there is no equivalent to your kind, good heart; and I will reply that I cannot imagine by what merit I have deserved the great luck of securing such a treasure. See, Rose, the old village church; its grim, owl-haunted tower shall soon merrily ring the wedding-chimes."

Thus talking, the lovers wandered back into the fields.

Neptune gambolled by their side.

They were not unobserved. Two men stood watching them from behind a clump of trees with evil glances.

One was the stern, wild-looking chief of the wreckers, Thorkil Penreal; the other, the dark-faced savage, Black Will Trelawny.

"That's a pretty picture, Master Will; that's a sight to gladden a lover's eye. Bah! why do you stand it?" said the wrecker, gruffly. "Have you got no spirit?"

"Curse her! yes—yes; she shall rue it," muttered Black Will, in hoarse accents, the blood rushing to his forehead. "I loved that finiking, fickle wench, and for her sake would have tamed the devil in my heart and treated her gently. Well, I'll plague the pair of 'em. I am one whose ruling passion is revenge upon those that wrong me. She *has* wronged me, for I really liked her. Well, I hate her now a hundred-fold more than ever I loved her;

hate's the stronger feeling of the two. I am one who never forgets nor forgives an injury!"

"She's kissing him."

"Blast her!"

"Humph! Don't swear; don't excite yourself."

"I was a cursed fool to leave it behind me," muttered Black Will, abstractedly.

"Leave what behind you?" asked the smuggler.

"My gun, Thorkil," Black Will hissed out. "By the flames! if I had it in my hand I'd kill them both where they stand."

"And swing like a salting pilchard, for their ghosts to have the laugh of you. No; I hate the dandy quarter-deck strutter. It's enough that he's in the Royal service; but I hate him for other reasons, and I'll work out my grudge, but sensibly, patiently, completely, and, as for Rose Lavington, when we kill a wolf we don't spare his mate and cubs. I will strike at him through her, and the barb will be poisoned. Such state-cabin supercargo have no right on the Wreckers' Coast, unless they come washed ashore, water-logged, from some rich laden barque."

"You may spare yourself the trouble of seeking a chance of venting your hatred on the cussed sea-dog; he is *my* mark. I have more cause to hate him than you."

"Pah! kissing again," cried Penreal.

"Thorkil," whispered Trelawny, wildly, "you carry pistols under your guernsey; lend me one."

"What for? To let them die in bliss, when you may watch them linger in misery, and kill them as soon as you are tired of the sport. Besides, we are not a score of yards from the kiddleawink; the sound of a shot would bring the blue-jackets upon us, and they would make short work with us. *You* never forgive an injury—*you* know how to wreak a man's revenge. Why, you are but a fool in these things. Look here, Black Will, I want to speak to you on a subject. Phew! our doves are billing again. Come, let us get out of the way, or you will go mad, and I shall be choked. The brazen-faced harridan! You shall have vengeance on her if you listen to me."

"I will do anything so I can have some sweet taste of revenge to soothe my maddened senses. Jilted—scorned! and before my eyes to see the callet fondled by such a rival. I will go back and fetch a gun from the farm, and will send a bullet through the heart of both of them."

Penreal laughed.

"A crack, a puff of smoke, a scream, a lover's grave, where they will sleep for ever, twined in each other's arms, out of the reach of your fury. The hunt—the capture—the yelling mob—the gallows! the death struggle, darkness, and——"

Thorkil paused, and shrugged his shoulders.

"That's your notion of vengeance. No, no, Black Will, I will teach you a better way. Now, I want to ask you how you like your present way of life?"

"Well, Thorkil, not much. Why do you ask? The cursed faggot, I'll tear her to pieces!"

"Patience! You do not care to be a tiller of the earth. This farming is a dull and boorish employment, that does not suit a man of your pith and mettle."

"Why, no, not exactly. A cursed, capering, powder-monkey! Lieutenant, forsooth! I wish I were a black pirate, and had him under my flag; I'd rend his liver out with red-hot pincers!"

"Ha, ha! Black Will, you're more ambitious than I took you to be. Have you any intentions *that* way?" said Thorkil, with a leer, drawing his fingers across his throat significantly, and then

crossing them to indicate the "cross-bones." "A rover! Well, I confess that I think you would head the deck of a pirate schooner more becomingly than you crumble the clods of a dirty ploughed field; such a boy as you were for the sea, too: such an apprenticeship as you've served with the Channel-pilots and fishermen. But, look you, Trelawny, there's a fortune to be made at less risk, with greater ease, and to be finally enjoyed in full security. How many cargoes of contraband goods think you, have I run since I turned smuggler, without the least mishap?"

"You have been fortunate," said the farmer.

"Devil a bit! The existence of my gang has been known to the authorities for many a year. No, I have been *prudent*, Trelawny. Not only plucky, ingenious, active, and watchful — but cautious; caution is the chief thing required. Now, the winter is setting in, and if there's any trust to be placed in signs and seasons—to say nothing of the predictions of my wife, Hylda, and that eldreth creature, Wild Thyra—the clerk of the weather-office is in bad humour, and we shall have some awful storms. Our Cornish soil is barren, and will scarce yield us an ear of corn with all our toiling. The sea is profuse of her rich gifts, and flings us plenteous harvests without our labouring for them. I want money for a venture I am about to make with a Dutch agent, Michael Guldenhoff. Why don't you pluck up a spirit, like a true Cornish lad, and dare the world as a smuggler and wrecker?"

"A wrecker!" cried Trelawny, with a start. "If I could bring this cursed Ha'liard on to the shark's-fin while his wife stood on shore and saw him go down, I should consider that piece of work a recompense for all the mortification the minx has wrought me."

Then, join my band; show that you have grit, and act like a man who is not to be wronged and insulted with impunity. I will pass you through the ordeals; you shall swear our oaths, and Hylda shall set the mark upon you, and bring you luck by her runeing."

"Well, we will talk more of this, Thorkil. I confess the thought of alluring some mighty frigate on to the shoals or sunken rocks with Halliard on board her—of pointing in mocking exultation to the dreary wreck while the young wife wails in vain to Heaven for mercy—is a devil's thought, but thwarted love makes one a devil. Come, is there nowhere we can retire to drain a cup of cognac or scheidam; the kiddleawink is garrisoned with the cursed man-of-war's men."

"Come, lad, I am glad to see you have some of the old Cornish spirit yet; it is dying out amongst us, woe the while! Come on; I will take you to a little cell in the rocks where they brew nectar, and there we can arrange our plans and drink success to our plots for vengeance!"

CHAPTER IV.

THYRA'S PROPHECY—A FOUNDLING FROM THE SEA.

THE lovers reached the little church in the hamlet.

The scenery about them was wild and picturesque in the extreme.

The scenery of Cornwall, especially in the districts near Land's End, is very romantic, but its beauty is of the sterner, severer type.

No lovely green hedges skirt the fields and

meadows ; they are divided by low, crumbling walls of stone.

There are few trees, but the rocky coasts are grand, and there is something of wildness and rugged sublimity about the appearance of the country that in a great measure compensate for the lack of that softer and more sylvan beauty which adorns other counties of our pleasant island.

As Halliard and Rose Lavington paused by the churchyard gate they saw a strange, wild-looking creature wandering among the graves.

It was Wild Thyra.

She has been mentioned several times in the early course of our story, and as, throughout our eventful history, she will play an eventful part, perhaps it will be well to describe her at once.

Wild Thyra was a slight but exquisitely moulded girl, about seventeen years of age.

She was very fair ; her hair, faint yellow, was very fine in quality, and flowed around her dishevelled and mist-like.

Her eyes were intensely blue, yet vacant in their expression.

Her skin was extremely white, and there was a delicacy of frailty, a sensitiveness of helplessness in her passive, melancholy demeanour, that was very touching and interesting.

Moments there were when it seemed that some sybilline spirit inspired her ; then a strange and powerful enthusiasm shone through her outward weakness—toned every trait in her face with a dignity that was almost majesty ; gave a deep and impressive strength to her gentle, whispering accents—added height to her figure, firmness to her steps, and rendered her a weird and awe-inspiring prophetess.

It scarcely need be stated that Wild Thyra was mad ; but the simple and superstitious people of the sea-girt refuge of the ancient Britons looked upon the unfortunate girl as one who was inflated with the influences of spirits, trusted with blind faith to her warnings and predictions, and mistook the wanderings of her disordered mind for promptings of fore-knowledge and oracles of wisdom.

Wild Thyra was gathering herbs among the graves.

The lovers mutually felt the colour fade from their faces, and could not repress the horrid creep of involuntary and unreasoning awe and foreboding.

They mutually clutched each other's hands.

Wild Thyra rose from the little heaving mound of turf on which she had been kneeling. She walked towards them with a wild vacant smile.

"How is it with you, Thyra?" asked Lieutenant Halliard, "have you forgotten me?"

"No," returned the demented creature, with a light strange laugh. "But you forgot me long ago." She heaved a heavy sigh.

Rose started—her eyes flashed.

Halliard's cheek reddened.

"I knew you would come back—I knew it—I did not wish it. Why did you come?" said Wild Thyra.

"Are you not glad to see me, pretty Thyra?" said Halliard, his voice a little husky, as he took her hands. "Come, look at me—speak to me, and tell me all the news—you are looking but weakly— why do you toil about gathering herbs and muttering nonsense; it does you no good, it only excites you, and makes you ill?"

"I wish to learn runes and spells," returned the girl, pettishly.

"You know enough already," said Halliard.

"Too much," replied the girl, shaking her head. "I see what I do not wish to see ; I hear what I do not wish to hear—hark !"

"I hear nothing."

"How should you? Your ears are stuffed with mortal deafness; the spirits are not charmed into you, so that they may speak to your soul's organs. I would teach you the charms that would bring men within the fleshly circle; but you would not heed them, you are faithless. Hark ! do you really hear nothing?"

"The ripple of the lark's song, or the cry of a petrel. What do *you* hear, Thyra?"

"The voice of a spirit. I will tell you what he says."

"No, Thyra, I do not wish to hear ; you are a foolish girl to think that the spirits leave their abodes to talk to you about the worldly concerns of us poor earthy creatures ; they have done with earth, their thoughts are bent on Heaven."

"Oh, Walter, let her speak. What does your spirit tell you, Thyra ?" asked Rose, eagerly.

"He speaks of you ; I will tell you. You will be very happy. He is true—your lover. The wedding bells will ring a clear echo in your hearts—in both your hearts ; yet there will be roused in his one little chord of regret. It will be for one whom he never loved ; but who loved him. All will be happy as when the spring morning breaks on the calm sea and the air fills the sails of the speeding ships, as if to caress them, and a man's heart shakes off its burdens, and says, the world is fair, life is desirable !"

"Is this cunning or madness, Walter ?" whispered Rose.

"Something of both, my dearest ; there is much self-deception in these cases," returned her lover.

"Thyra, we are much obliged to you for your happy predictions," said Rose, kindly, "and I hope you will come and see us often in those good times you promise."

"You have not yet heard all," said the crazy girl, shaking her head, and deeply sighing. "A change will come ; dark clouds will gather on the morning's brightness ; the morning sunlight cannot last all day. Oh, terrible will be the storm that bursts at noon-day. I see it all—I feel the sudden darkness, and I see the wild red beacon lights ; I read their warning ; but the sea-bird is dazed—like a moth that dashes to the flame, he plunges through the darkness to the luring lights that burn to destroy him ; then comes the thundering of awful waves, the grinding of pitiless rocks, the prayers of the unpraying, the shrieks of the fearless, the laugh, the gloating of the beacon-fiend, who revels among the death-shoals and the reefs of shipwreck, and counts the bodies of his victims as they rise and sink in the surging swell. A wife is on the shore—a young, fond wife—a yearning mother. She sees all, as I see all ; she hears not all, as I hear, for the tempest-fiend has shown his hideous features, and as she looks on them she is petrified ; he lifts her cold as a stone, and bears her away ; then come many winter nights, when the drenching rain dashes her windows, and the howling wind roves round her cottage, and taunts that lorn one with the names of her loved ones, her husband, and her son, the BOY SAILOR, whom he holds in his power ; he shrieks out his threats, and wings on his way of destruction, and leaves her a widow and childless !"

Rose gave a cry of horror.

Halliard took the girl by her hands, and looked her gravely in the face.

"Thyra," he said, speaking in tones of deep seriousness, "I cannot think you a mere imposter, but are you not sure that you act very, very wickedly, when you pretend to know the secrets of the future ; and do you not think it is very unkind and cruel to try to make us wretched by prophesying such dreadful calamities? I am sure we love you, Thyra, and do not deserve such a show of malice. Why should you wish evil to fall on us? The seas are in the hollow of His hand, and if I must meet the fate that has befallen many a better man, the 'Father of the fatherless, and the God of the widow' will watch over mine and protect them. Oh, try to be more rational and less presumptuous."

"Why did you stay me?" cried the crazy girl, fiercely: "I would have told you more, but the spirit has fled. He who brought sunbeams from the tomb of night can bring joy out of the darkest woe. I might have told you that which would have given you comfort; but it is all gone from me—all gone! Well, will you come with me? I wish to show you something—come!"

"Shall we go with her, Walter?" asked Rose timidly.

"Yes, Rose, I think so; there can be no harm in humouring her fancy, and I am in no hurry to return to my men, who are enjoying themselves at the kiddleawink."

"But is there no danger?"

"How can there be, love?"

"Why, dear Walter, you know that Thyra associates with those desperate wretches who nearly murdered your gallant seamen this morning."

"The wreckers?"

"Yes; she lives almost always among them."

"Will you come?" said Thyra.

"I will go with you alone," said Halliard.

"No, no; I will go with you," cried Rose.

"You must both go," said the girl, imperatively.

"But whither do you mean to take us?" asked the lieutenant.

"To a cavern among the rocks, where I have something to show you."

"Well, lead on; we'll follow you."

"But you will swear not to tell Hylda," rejoined the girl; "to tell no one!"

"Yes."

"Then follow me,"

Wild Thyra led the way.

The lovers kept close behind her.

She led them from the churchyard, and took a winding path along the edge of the cliff.

They pursued their way for some time.

At length Thyra paused.

They stood on the brink of the precipitous cliff.

A narrow, zig-zag pathway, rudely carved in the rocks, wound down to the beach.

Thyra walked so near to the edge that Rose could scarcely restrain a scream.

The wild girl stood erect, and scanned the curving strand, and looked back upon the inland scenery.

The hamlet church, and the few hovels comprising the village, lay far behind them.

Thyra descended the rocks.

Halliard offered his arm to Rose, but she smiled and bounded lightly and fearlessly after their conductress.

They reached the shingly strand.

Thyra still lead the way; she conducted them round many a bend in the cliff.

It was a glorious day.

The tide was going down.

The sea was calm as an inland lake.

They saw a dark object thrown far upon the beach.

As they passed it, they saw that it was some broken spars from a wreck of the fatal night preceding.

Rose sighed, and Halliard looked grave; his thoughts were busy with the crazy-girl's prophecy;

he was ashamed of himself for attaching any importance to the aberrations of her insanity, and yet could not shake off the heaviness at his heart.

Rose gave a faint cry, and clung closer to her lover, burying her head on his shoulder.

A dreadful spectacle was before them.

A broken stuns'l boom, and lashed to it the dead bodies of two drowned sailors; their faces were bloated and livid, and they lay prone, their clothes saturated with brine and stiffening in the sun.

Thyra passed on unheedingly.

Halliard bent over the bodies.

Thyra turned.

She stamped her foot impatiently.

"Will you come?" she said. "What have the living to do with the dead? Come!"

Halliard drew the shuddering Rose to his heart, and led her away.

"I will send some of my men to bury the poor fellows; but, as you are a child of the sea, like myself, Rose, you must not think too much of these calamities."

Rose trembled and sobbed, but she did not speak.

Her heart, too, was heavy with the burden of Thyra's warnings.

"When we are married, dear Walter," she murmured, "you must go no more to sea."

They had now entered within the circle of a little bay.

It was a wild and desolate spot.

The sea was rougher here, despite the calmness of the weather.

Precipitous cliffs shot up around them on one hand; treacherous, dreadful, dinted rocks ran far out into the ocean.

Massive groins of green, sea-mossed piles had been erected on either extremity of the amphitheatre of cliffs.

Masses of stone of Cyclopean hugeness, and of grotesque form, were scattered along the shore.

The breakers did not plash very heavily among the rocklets, for the tide was going down, and, as before stated, the day was so bright and still.

Yet the receding tide raced far and fiercely on the shore, as if loth to quit the scene of its triumphs, which the mighty pile of a land-slip and the rough inequality of the cliffs betokened.

Thyra led them to the foot of the rocks.

Stooping low, she entered a concave hollow.

Along this they travelled.

More than once Rose stayed her lover to whisper her apprehensions.

He reassured her, and they continued to follow their strange guide.

Clambering up a sort of stair-case of stones and shingle, they entered a sort of cavern.

Here Thyra paused.

"You have sworn—you will swear not to reveal my secret to Thorkil Penreal or to his wife Hylda?"

"You have not told your secret."

"Will you swear?"

"We have no dealings with those you mentioned."

"It is well for you. Hylda knows many charms; she can raise the storm-spirits, but she cannot lay them," said Thyra, in a tone of contempt. "I can do both; but I will show you what I have found."

With this she retired to a dark corner of the cavern.

She stooped, and drew from a crevice in the rock a little bundle.

She placed this at the feet of Halliard and his sweetheart.

What was their surprise, upon throwing back the covering, to behold a little babe!

A sweet little girl, some few months old, deeply sleeping, its cheek pillowed on its arm, its lips apart, softly breathing, its lids closed, and its tiny, dimpled fingers spread on its light-heaving breast.

Rose gave a cry of sympathy, and snatched it up in her arms.

The little one opened its blue eyes, and gave a plaintive wail, and then nestling close to the girl, closed its eyes and sank once more into slumber.

"Where, Thyra, did you find this child?" asked Halliard.

The girl did not answer him. There was a vacant expression on her face, and she was low-muttering some of her garbage.

Halliard repeated the question.

"She is a child of the sea. The great ocean saves some; they are often spring-buds like this," said Thyra. "They live for a purpose—there is some great wrong they must right, some great destiny they must fulfil. Hylda has no children, her heart is as hard as the logan-stone; she might have killed the infant. Thyra is more kind; it is nothing to her to raise the mighty tempest, to shiver the vast floating town with their proud wings and bands of iron on the rocks and shoals; but the innocents the cruel water-wraiths have spared she will not injure. But what should she do with a nursling babe? Take the foundling—take her—she will bring you joy. I tell you so, and I have my knowledge from a dread source; but, give me the child."

The crazy girl snatched the baby from Rose's embrace.

Halliard, who was alarmed for the child's safety, sprang forward.

"Back!" cried the girl, holding out her right arm with an imperious gesture. "Now, you *must* swear—swear to keep this secret from all—from Hylda Penreal and her husband, of all others. Swear to protect and to nourish my foundling, or I will dash out its brains upon the rocks about us."

Rose extended her arms instinctively to protect the little one.

Halliard moved towards the mad girl.

Light as a mountain-nymph, Thyra sprang upon a rock.

She raised the unconscious babe in her hands.

"Swear!" she cried, "swear by Him to whom you look for succour in your hours of sorrow, sin, and weakness—swear to preserve Thyra's foundling, to maintain her, to take her for better or for worse, and to cherish her as your own child!"

"We swear it!" cried the pair, excitedly.

Thyra deliberately walked down from the rock, and bending her face over the child, veiling it with her long, hanging tresses, she kissed it with passionate demonstrations of affection.

She then put it into the arms of Rose, who pressed it to her heart with a soothing murmur.

"Her story is doubtless true," said Halliard, looking at the strange girl with a glance of pity and interest. "The poor creature is not dead to the instincts of natural affection. The little one is probably the child of one of those lost in the storm of last night. Perhaps, Rose, we may find its parents; but, if not, we will supply their place. Are there any marks on its clothes by which it may be recognised?"

"Its clothing is of the finest texture, Walter, and here, in the corner, are some initials; read them."

Halliard looked at the spot indicated.

At the hem of the robe, in red marks, appeared the letters,

H. de l'O.

"What can her name be, think you?"

"I cannot guess. Well, we will call her Helena, as her name seems French, and the name is pretty."

A gruff voice was heard without.

Thyra sprang before the pair. With a wild look she waved them back into the gloom, and then rushed out of the cavern.

CHAPTER V.

THE CAVERN—THE WRECKER AND HIS COMPANION RESORT TO THE SECRET HOLD—A FOUNDLING FROM SEA—THE ERMINE MANTLE—THYRA'S ESCAPE.

LIEUTENANT HALLIARD grasped his side-arms, and stood in the darkness, ready for action.

Rose Lavington pressed the little one to her bosom to still its wailings.

The voices without sounded louder, as growing nearer, and now the body of the sound was concentrated, as if the speakers had entered the passage that led to the cavern.

Thyra entered.

Lieutenant Halliard and Rose shrank behind the angle of a rocky projection.

The crazy girl stood before them.

Two men came into the cave.

"Here I have run many a cargo in former days," said one to the other, in a deep, rough tone. "I don't use the place much now, the land-slip has spoiled it. We have a 'look out' just a little westward from hence, and there are my most important spirit stores; but this is a little grot known only to myself."

"And Thyra——"

"Thyra knows everything, I believe; but the girl is no spy, she is quite harmless," returned the other; "and now I will show you the way into my little private chamber, where we will decide upon some course of action with respect to the subjects broached just now—ha! Thyra, what is this?"

Rose peeped round the edge of the projection, and saw the wrecker had picked up a little mantle from the ground.

"It is mine; the sea sent it!" said Thyra readily. "You will not rob me of it, Thorkil."

"But it is warm, the sea sent it! It has not been touched by water, how is that?" asked the wrecker, as he squeezed the mantle in his hard hands; "it is lined with ermine; where did you find it?"

"I will show you," said Thyra, moving towards the entrance of the cavern, and beckoning.

"Let the girl alone," said his companion, in a grumbling tone, "you say she is harmless; no doubt the mantle belonged to some infant drowned in the wreck; perhaps this thing was found in a sea-chest; that would account for its being so dry, and for its being warm; it is long and ample; perhaps Thyra has been wearing it."

The girl snatched it from Thorkil's hand, and flung it over her shoulder.

"It is my robe, my robe of innocence," she cried, "The evil spirits will not approach too near while I wear it."

"Give it to me," cried Thorkil, roughly.

"No; I have charmed up the tempest for you, I have raised the big waves, have unchained the winds. You are rich with the treasures my runes have brought you, Thorkil, and this little gift of

No. 2, New Series.   Price One Penny.

Boys' Library

HARRY HALLIARD:
OR,
THE YOUNG BRITISH TAR.

THE DOOMED SHIP.

the ocean is mine. If you take it from me I have power to resent the injury."

A low wail, instantly hushed and subdued, sent the echoes trembling round the cavern.

"Hark! it is a spirit! these stones have been stained with blood, and though it is long ago, the spirit still croons here at seasons."

"To hell with your cursed japs mes, you lying hag! its a *child!*" cried Thorkil, shaking her roughly. "What have you done with it?"

Thyra shrieked, tore herself from him, and, like a bird decoying the fowler from her nest, rushe through a narrow opening on the side of the caver opposite to that in which Rose and her lover wer hiding, and imploringly waving them back, disap peared among the rocks.

"Come, Will, we must follow her, the young bag gage has found some puling brat thrown up from the shipwreck, maybe cast from the boat on to the reef when the boat was sinking. We must find it we cannot make our mage— a nursery for sma fry."

" You would not kill the child ?"

" Why not?—it's a mercy—the little wretch would die."

" Thyra might preserve it."

" She ! She will find a new toy to-morrow."

" Go alone ; I do not like such work," said Black Will.

" Bah ! you are a fine fellow to be so squeamish ; you, who talk of a pirate-schooner, and the scissors and red-hot pincers."

" But a child !"

" Is spared consciousness and will die in less agony than a man ; and, as the world goes, is much indebted to the friend who shortens its existence, for life's a misery. Come, or the crafty witch will elude us."

The two ruffians disappeared in the narrow rock-way.

Halliard and Rose stole from their hiding-place.

" Rose," said the lieutenant, " the villains will kill, or ill-use the poor girl ; do you run home with the babe ; there is little danger of your being seen if you keep close beneath the cliffs ; you can carry the child to the kiddleawink and give it into the hands of Joe Juniper, my coxswain."

" Oh, Walter, you will be murdered !" cried Rose, faintly.

" Pshaw ! they are but two, and only one of them is armed. I have my pistols and sword, and they will not venture to attack me."

" Oh, do not go ; I am sorry for Thyra, but I do not think they will harm her, they look upon her with superstitious dread ; besides, they will believe her story, perhaps, and think the sound they heard really came from some invisible being. Don't go— oh, pray don't go !"

" Fear not, Rose ; I will not see the poor half-witted creature maltreated."

A laugh rang through the cavern.

Rose, who clung to her lover's arm, entreating him to stay, turned with a cry of astonishment.

Thyra stood behind them.

" Do you think that I have but one entry to my house in the rocks ?" she said, gaily. " I am always searching for new and curious crypts and cells ; in some of them I find huge bones turned into stone by the dripping of water, or by the lapse of sleeping ages. These are the skeletons of strange huge beasts and reptiles that lived in the age of giants. I would show you these wonders—some day I may, but now we must think of getting away from Thorkil. He chase me ! He might as well hunt the will-o-wisp, or the erl-king. Come on, you must get back to the village before he finds out that you have been here ; he will search this cavern for traces, and he will find them ; so make haste."

The pair needed no prompting ; they emerged upon the beach and hurried on towards the village.

Meanwhile Thorkil and Trelawny had examined every nook and crevice among the rocks.

The chief of the wreckers seemed to be in high dudgeon.

He cursed Thyra and breathed the direst threats against her.

At length they returned by a difficult and circuitous route through the tunnellings in the cliff to the cavern from which they had at first started.

Here Thorkil lighted a torch, which he carried in a case by his side, and proceeded to search the ground for foot-marks.

The floor of the cavern was chalky and the imprints of feet were apparent in several places.

" Humph ! do the spirits tread so heavily ?" growled Thorkil.

" Perhaps they were devils, and their hoofs would leave a deep print, you know," returned Trelawny, with a laugh.

" These are not cloven," returned the other. " But I will cleave the heads of the owners, if I catch them."

" I don't see why you need make so much ado about a lost brat that no one will ever lay claim to, that this girl Thyra has picked up as she might have taken a stray lamb or a wounded fledgling."

" Well, we must give up the pursuit for the present," said Thorkil, in a tone of reluctance.

" Yes, I am sick of it," said Trelawny, impatiently, " and as I cannot assist you much, I'll return to the farm."

" What, lad, without a taste of the schnapps, or a word of our enterprise. No, that must not be ; I have sworn to have the vengeance satisfied which I have sworn against Walter Halliard ; you may gratify your own wish by being my agent in accomplishing it. Black Will Trelawny, I mean to make a wrecker of you."

CHAPTER VI.

THE CORNISH VILLAGE—ROSE LAVINGTON'S BRIDES-MAIDS — A SAILOR'S WEDDING — THE SLIGHTED LOVER AND HIS TEMPTER—BLACK WILL JOINS THE WRECKERS.

SEAWARDINE—for such was the name of the Cornish village, ever memorable as the birth-place of our hero—was a straggling hamlet of long, low, stone-built cottages.

It was picturesquely situated in a vale, surrounded on one side by uplands, and from the other commanding an extensive and splendid sea-view.

It was a glorious day in August, and the bluff sea gales wafted brackishly from the main. The village was crowded by the inhabitants, who blocked up the wide and straggling street, and stood in laughing groups, displaying much excitement and curiosity with regard to the " coming event," which was heralded right merrily by the " bells, bells," that rang their sweet chords and cadences on the " bosom of the palpitating air."

It must not be supposed that all the inhabitants of Seawardine followed the desperate and lawless calling of those atrocious ruffians—the wreckers of the coast ; nor was the village, properly so called, connected with the few wretched hovels, the abodes of smugglers, that were clustered near the kiddleawink of Murdoch Penreal.

On the day succeeding that distinguished by the events narrated in our last chapter, Lieutenant Halliard had paid the rent of Rose's uncle, and had condoned his offences on condition that he should allow of her removal to the house of a worthy blacksmith in Seawardine, whose name was Joel Britton, and who had always treated Rose with fatherly kindness.

In the cheerful kitchen of the pleasant cottage— with its cuckoo-clock, oaken shelves, with their array of bright-burnished pewter platters, and its general air of rural naïveté and substantial comfort —Rose Lavington was seated, her eyes downcast, her cheek richly blushing.

She was dressed in snowy white ; her auburn hair neatly braided on her fair brow, and bound with a wreath of orange blossoms.

On one side was seated a venerable, genial-looking dame, who held the hand and, through her spectacles, scanned the pretty features of the sailor's bride.

On the other stood a young girl, fair-haired, with laughing blue eyes, and a sunny face, roguishly dimpled. She, too, was dressed in purest white, and about her beaming tresses was twined a coronal of lilies of the valley. This was Nelly Britton, the blacksmith's daughter.

The old blacksmith himself sat in the chimney corner. He was smoking his morning pipe, and was dressed in his best velveteen and Sunday gaiters.

"I tell ye, lass," said Master Joel, with a dry smile, and knocking the ashes out of his pipe in an emphatic kind of way, "that births, deaths, and marriages be the three grand mistakes of life."

"Then, I should think, that life must be a mistake altogether," said his daughter, pouting.

"In coorse Nell, in coorse ; and long afore you come to years of discretion, if so be as women ever *do* come to discretion (for I make a doubt on it), you'll be sartain of that fact ; but the worst of the three mistakes is marriage !"

"So I have found, discreet or not, Joel," said his wife, smiling good-humouredly.

"In coorse you have, dame, cos' why ? you never thought, for instance, as you'd get sich a good husband, and I, knowing my own disarvings, expected to find my spouse a reg'lar angel : so we're both mistaken. But, as for Rose here, going to be married to a sea-faring chap ! the thing is unheard on. Depend upon it, Rose, he has more wives now than he'd care to count up : from some little humpty-dumpty roll of superfine spermaceti at the North Pole—one of those beauties they call by such disgraceful imperant names—Here's-queer-makes !"

"La, father !—E-quimaux !"

"Well, darter, didn't I say so? to one of the other kind of Poles ; I'spose they're *South* Poles, that wear polka jackets and often get a jacketing, poor creeturs. You may depend upon it, Rose, he's been married in every mortal way, from high mass to jumping the broom-stick, and has got more wives than old Harry the Eighth ! Dutch fraws, French femmes, Indian squaws, Chinese chow-chows, and other darters of bow-wows : everywhere, anywhere, a sailor's always ready to 'sail consort,' or to ' splice the main-brace !'

"Why, you don't think, Mr. Britton, that Walter would be guilty of polygamy? " cried Rose, blushing and laughing.

"Poll-higomy or Sall-higomy, he's guilty on 'em all ! Here, dame, fasten this bucket to my button. Ah, there's no parsley among it ; you don't understand how to make a posie."

The good dame fixed a large nosegay of strikingly contrasted flowers in the old blacksmith's coat.

"Hey ! Jess, this makes us feel young again, old lass," he said, chucking his wife under the chin, and giving her a smacking kiss. "How these chimes do ring up old tunes in our hearts, sure-ly."

"Oh, ain't they charming?" cried Nelly, clapping her hands, ecstatically. La! I could fancy them speaking, and this is what they say." And she sang in accompaniment with the clashing bells—

' Now, may all joy betide
Rose, pretty blushing bride—
Marriage is holy !'

There was a general laugh.

"Bah! Nell, that's a false varsion. What have the wedding bells rung for generations ?

' Turn again Whittington,
Thrice happy single man.'

"But the moths *will* fly to the candle, the ships will run in the shark's fin, and men will rush into church, to the loss of their peace of mind and their blessed liberty. Here come the blue-jackets !"

A cheery shout was heard, and soon before the window appeared a crowd of sailors, dressed in their Sunday ducks, with new ribbons streaming from their straw hats : the jolly fellows, moreover, wore ruddier cheeks and brighter glances, in honour of the "auspicious event." Conspicuous amongst them were the worthies, Joe Juniper and Bill Hawser, and the gigantic Tom Truepenny.

After giving three hearty cheers they passed on, for it was arranged that they should join the wedding party at the corner of the street.

The door was hurriedly opened, and Walter Halliard rushed in.

He gallantly saluted his bride, and blushing and tremblingly she lightly touched his arm, and, supported by Nelly, the pair moved towards the door.

Wild Thyra entered suddenly.

The couple started slightly, as the girl scattered some flowers on the threshold, and, raising her strange weird blue eyes, bent them with a vacant wistful stare upon the face of the young sailor.

Thyra wore a wreath of sea-bine, and strange herbs she had gathered, and, along the edge of her bodice, and upon her snowy bosom, she had strewn some wild flowers.

The crazy girl smiled upon the bride, and touched her dress admiringly ; then she clutched the sailor by the arm and said, in a tone of entreaty—

"Walter, you cannot refuse this to Thyra—let her be bridesmaid too ?"

The flush deepened on Halliard's cheek : he smiled, and nodded assent.

Wild Thyra drew him aside, and said, in low and earnest tones—

"The spirits have whispered me many secrets of you and your bride, Walter. Your path is dark—mine is barren and dark too ; for the light that sometimes shines on it is but a halo of unearthly light, through which I see coming things dimly floating. The mortal light of sunny life is very, very pale with me ; but I would not speak of myself—I think little of myself. You will say my dress is queenly—that these herbs and flowers are chosen with all the skill and care of a wise rune-kenner. But, then, I am not thus adorned for my own sake, but for hers about whom you will twine those strong arms gently, that strike like thunderbolts when there is war on the sea ; for her to whose ear you will soften the ringing voice that out-calls the tempest when the storm-fiends play madly with man's frail handicraft ; for whom you will husband all your thoughts and all your love, when you have forgotten poor Wild Thyra, or laugh at her runes, and say she is possessed with a lying spirit !"

The strange girl sighed heavily.

Halliard grasped her hand tenderly. A thrill ran through him, and, despite his reason, he looked on the beautiful, frail, and fay-like being, so wild, yet so refined—refinement is more often the gift of nature than the effect of art — who stood beside him silently weeping.

Wild Thyra raised her hand to her head.

"It is here," she said, in a hollow tone ; "but it began here !" and she pressed her hand against her soft rounded bosom.

Rose drew to her lover's side.

The cheek of the bride was flushed, and there was a gleam of jealous anger in her large brown eyes.

Halliard looked confused.

Wild Thyra, with touching simplicity, snatched hold of the bride's hands, and upon the bride's shoulder nestled her head, with its veil of misty hair, the hue of which resembled the soft tints of the sun that gild a light cloud.

"You will love me?" said the girl, entreatingly. "You will not scorn Wild Thyra, dear Rose, and Thyra will tell you all the spirits show, even though she angers them. Do not despise me!"

Rose pressed the girl to her heart.

"We will be sisters!" she said, softly.

"And your husband shall be my brother!" murmured Thyra. "Oh, I will love you both; but you must not tell Hylda or Thorkil of this compact. Come, the sailors are shouting. Poor fellows, if they could know! And the bells are singing the marriage runes. Come—come!"

The bride and bridegroom walked to the door

The bridesmaids followed.

They were received on the step with a hearty cheer from a crowd of rough but honest-faced fishermen and farm lads, with their wives and sweethearts.

Halliard acknowledged the salute with a gallant bow. The bride kept her eyes fixed on the ground, her cheeks glowing like a blooming peach.

At the corner of the street the procession was formed.

It was a strange party, quaint and droll.

First, with stately walk, swaying his huge, shaggy head with comical gravity and self-importance, Neptune pattered along.

Behind him came a sailor scraping a fiddle with more vigour than melody, yet infusing a wondrous amount of spirit into the "Wedding March," then followed the bride and bridegroom, after whom came several officers from Halliard's ship; a merry party of sailors brought up the rear.

Round the door of the church another group of the villagers were assembled, who also received the young couple with a hearty shout.

Behind a sombre yew tree in the little churchyard, and apart from the rest, two men were looking on with bent brows and sullen faces.

"Humph! she's a bonnie bride, heartie; her face is fresher than the sky on a spring morn—a beautiful craft, I must say; and not such an ugly hulk, her convoy," said one of the fellows, with gruff cynicism. "Why don't you shout with the rest? why don't you wish the couple joy?"

"I wish them joy—thrilling joy, a happy home, a bounding love, a fair child; I wish it from my heart!" cried the other, hoarsely.

"How? What do you mean?"

"To poison their cup when it is sweetest; to cut the fleshy tendrils when round their braced hearts they twine the tightest; to crawl like a serpent into their home-garden when love has made it an Eden; to snatch from their arms the child of their union when it is fairest and dearest; to murder their peace; to crush out their hearts—that's what I mean!"

"Phew! you are bitter. Well, you have great provocation; they are in the church now. Hark! they are singing; listen, Black Will!"

"I will turn their songs into a death-wail!" cried the violent Trelawny, shaking with passion. "Oh, Thorkil, I am poisoned with the venom of my own hate!"

"A pretty strain, that; I like music. Did you notice Wild Thyra was with them? She will give the bride a love-philter, and rune the roving sailor-Jack into a steady, good man. Ha! ha!"

Trelawny dashed himself against the tree.

"Whist! it's all over! they are hand-fasted; only he who breaks the chord of life can unbind the link that braces them. You've lost her, Will, and she will tease her husband when she is shrewish by reminding him how much you loved her, and how she jilted you for his sake. I understand the creatures; mated myself, you know."

"Will you drive me mad?" cried Trelawny, seizing him by the collar.

"I should not have to drive you far!" returned the other, laughing. "There, there, hearty, in your ear—a wild night—black as a rover's bunting—a flaring beacon—a frigate on the reef—the head-waves shivering her to splinters—a handsome skipper high and dry, and ready to pass muster with the quartermaster of graves—a fair girl rending her hair on his life-deserted hull—Black Will triumphant! Stop, we'll see them come out of church."

"No! no! come away! come away!" cried Trelawny, pulling the wrecker forcibly from the spot. "Hark at the 'Royals,' they're shouting as if this skip-jack were an admiral. Bless your soul, Will, it's the prettiness of the prize he has captured that makes them sing out so lustily; none like your true salt to appreciate beauty."

Trelawny seized the speaker, and shook him roughly.

"What the devil are you about?" growled Thorkil. "I'm not a lieutenant in the king's service, am I? My eyes and limbs, Will, you're mad!"

"Aye! mad with spleen. I shall never have patience to wait my turn; I shall kill him!"

"Eat him, you cannibal; but don't shake me to splinters! Well, well, mate, we'll go, that cheer doesn't please you; fancy it the roar of a chopping sea. Trelawny, we're out of hearing, or, at least, the shouts come faintly as the boom of a minute-gun from a distant fog-bank. Now, Will, I'm off to-morrow to meet the Dutchman, Michael Guldenhoff. I want to know my bearings; am I to look upon you as a partner in my schemes of money-making and vengeance-taking for, mark ye, lad, I hate this skunk as much as you do, though I know how to mind distinctions between friend and foe, and am not disposed to fire a broadside into my consort because I'm not within range of my enemy? Are you determined to play out the little game you planned so deftly? Do you intend to stick to the plough like a chaw-bacon swab, or do you mean to leave the coulter for the keel, and plough the seas instead of the fallows, and find your harvest on the stony beach rather than on the stony land? Speak out! have you any British metal? Will you be flouted by this slut, and bear it with a grin, or do you mean to wreak a wrecker's vengeance?"

"I would wreck every craft on the four oceans, so his ship were amongst them!"

"Then you will join us?"

"Join the devil, and live in flames, so I might help to torture these hated enemies."

"Give me your hand then. What will you do with the farm?"

"Sell every acre."

"Now, you're the man I like; the man I want; the man who deserves me for his backer, for, mind you, Black Will, I mean to lengthen my hawser, to sail a longer cruise in a craft of heavier burden, and you shall share all with myself, and the band and the sea will bring you more treasure in one foul winter than the land in twenty-five summers. Is it a bargain?"

Trelawny grasped his hand.

"Good! this is better than a slant of wind due-north, with a fat merchant off the Lizard. You'll never regret this, Black Will Trelawny, till guineas are hot coals and vengeance without sweetness. And now to our chief cave at the Seal's Cover."

CHAPTER VII.

ROSE HALLIARD'S NEW HOME—THE STORY OF WILD
THYRA—NEPTUNE IS ROUSED—IT IS HARD TO WAIT
FOR VENGEANCE.

"AND on our wedding-day! Dear Rose, these tears distress me; I could not have thought you so weak and foolish, my own, as to attach importance to the idle wanderings of the disordered mind of poor Wild Thyra. Wild, indeed! she is quite insane. I cannot help wondering that she should be so refined and interesting, but there is something of genius that lends a romantic glow to her strange fancies, and I like to take her in a prophetic mood. She seems so earnest, so self-convinced, so mystic, yet so graphic; but we should be mad as she if we could put any faith in her oracles. And for my being a sailor! Wife of my heart, reflect; there are two sides to every condition, to every event in existence—a bright side, and a dark one. Now, all our chance of earthly happiness consists in looking on the bright side of things; you must not think of sad partings, of the anxiety of absence—you must remember how sweetly the days will spin round, that hour by hour bring me nearer to you; you must picture the deep, deep joy of our re-unions; you must realise the pride of hearing of my advancement in a profession to which I was born, and soon, very soon, I trust to reach the post of captain, and then you shall be with me in all my wanderings, or, most probably, I shall resign, and you and I will live like mated birds in our lone nest, happy in each other, and seeking no other blessing than our mutual love and home-sweet joys."

The newly married pair were sitting at the door of the pretty cottage which Halliard had bought and furnished for his young wife.

It was situated about half a mile from Seawardine, in a lonely but charming spot, shielded by long, low hills, and from a distance overlooking the sea.

It was a glorious night. The multitudinous stars spangled the solemn vault till it twinkled in one mild blaze of astral brightness.

The dark blue sea murmured caressingly, and spread to the misty horizon in gentle-moving wavelets.

The cheerful light, shining through the diamond panes, glistened on the dewy leaves of the whispering trees in the sleeping garden.

The dog lay dozing at the door.

For some moments Rose did not answer, but clung fondly to her husband's breast.

"Oh, Walter, if it must be so," replied Rose, tenderly. "If you *must* leave me, and so soon, I will trust you to Him who stilled the waves of Galilee, to Him who holds the seas in the hollow of his hand. The All-merciful will keep you, and give you fair winds and prosperous voyages. I am not your wife to perplex when I should comfort, to wear you out with useless plaints when I know that, though you love me best, you are bound in duty to serve your country and your King; you have not married your own Rose to be paralysed from active service, to become a worthless drone. Forgive me; teach me to think how you are mine, at least, for a little while, and let me not shudderingly look beyond the little golden space that we shall be together.

"My own wife!"

"And, Walter, let me ask you a question?"

"Only let me hear you speak. What is it, Rose?"

"This Thyra."

"Aye, Rose, what of her?"

"Did you—you will be angry?"

'Angry! nonsense, speak plainly and boldly."

"When my father was killed in battle, and my poor mother came here to die, I was young, and I knew little of you then, Walter."

"Well, dearest?"

"Wild Thyra was your playmate in those early days."

"Yes, Rose!"

"You have not answered my question, Walter," said his wife, leaning her brow on his shoulder, blushing, and speaking in low tones.

"No?" "What was it?"

"Did you,—did you ever love Wild Thyra?" asked Rose, with a little gasp.

Halliard's breast heaved, but he answered quietly and firmly.

"No, Rose, never!"

"You will forgive me for asking the question."

"My darling, it is wrong of you to think that you could offend by asking me a fair question. I am only too glad that you should understand me thoroughly. I will tell you the story of poor Thyra; it is composed in a few words. Like the little one we have sworn to protect, Wild Thyra is the child of a wreck—a foundling from the sea. She was found by some of those monsters, the wreckers, and was brought up with Hylda Penreal. It was discovered, as she grew older, that she was subject to occasional fits of aberration, and for days she would, with strange fearlessness, wander about the perilous brinks of the tallest cliffs, or along the groins and waterbreaks when they were lashed by the roughest seas; and when in such moods she could not be prevailed upon to eat or sleep, and was wont to chant and mumble the traditional nonsense that these Cornish gossips believe so profanely to have power to raise or still tempests, to induce good or ill-luck. Those old Norse 'runes,' I suppose the ancient Britons of these parts learned from their great enemies the Danes. The sages of Sewardine began to think that Thyra was no mortal child, but a changeling of the water-wraiths, and as the little girl had been much persecuted and annoyed by the coarser youngsters of the village, even the more sensible people in the place encouraged the notion that Thyra was "eldrich," so she was much protected by her questionable reputation, her young tormentors standing in awe of her, and even treating her with propitiating respect and kindness. As a boy I was very fond of Thyra; many and many an hour we have played together on the beach, and I have laughed to see how gleefully she would shout at the great tumbling billows and say she was making them angry, and if the wind was in a bad quarter and the water really did roll up in increasing masses, if the sky grew wild and dark and the wolfish wreckers prowled along the strand watching with hungry eyes the distant sail, the strange little being would be wailing soothingly till the storm subsided, and then take credit to herself that she had hushed it—just as one might tug at the taffrail of a ship and fancy the exertion of one's puny strength was aiding the mighty ship in its course. As I grew older I went to school. I owe much to my old master; he was a thorough seaman and a perfect scholar. I often fancied that he had committed some great crime, or suffered some great sorrow, and that he had sought this outlandish part of our island as a sanctuary from his pursuers; however that might be, though he was a morose, eccentric man, to me he was ever kind, and he spared no pains to teach me all he knew. He is dead now; his secret, therefore, is literally a dead one; his crimes or sorrows are untold; the earth lies lightly on him. I was passionately fond of learning, as is often the case, I was fond of imparting the knowledge I had gained. An apter pupil than poor Wild Thyra no teacher need desire; mad or sane, she is a genius, and soon she became as erudite as her instructor. You perceive, Rose, how much finer is her accent than that of her associates; how much superior to them she is in manner. Her memory was wonderfully retentive; her chief fancy was for rhymes, and she was no mean poetess. I loved her as a sister, and, as I was the only person in the world who could appreciate her, could sympathise with her, I fear she loved me deeply. I do not say this in vanity, but in sorrow and regret. When I saw Rose Lavington I lived a new life, I lived to higher purpose; the sun was brighter, the world was fairer, life was sweeter, and I forgot poor Thyra, my wayward, wild pupil. Estranged from me, brought into closer connection with the wretches her keepers—I cannot call them protectors—Thyra grew worse and worse, and, as I am sure she is too good, too gentle, too highly gifted, to be a mere imposter, and as I have some belief in the infectiousness of madness and some faith in mesmeric influence, I feel convinced that she really does work upon the imagination or the sympathy of the weak and superstitious. I have told you all I know of this strange girl; I have answered your questions; and now, Rose, I, in turn, will ask you a question."

"What question, dear Walter?"

"Are you jealous of this poor girl?"

"You must not blame me for being a woman, Walter. I was, but I am so no longer," returned Rose, frankly.

"Indeed, you have no cause for jealousy, my own. I cannot think of Thyra without being moved by the tenderest brotherly affection and sympathy, for, were she not afflicted as she is, she would be a splendid creature, a genius, with all womanly charms to soften and exalt her. She was my earliest companion, and I am sure you will love her and be kind to her. You see how warmly I speak of her; should I talk so truly if I were guilty of a thought that wronged you, my pride, my prize?"

"Oh, Walter, I am sure I will love her as my sister, for her own sake, and as your childhood's companion."

At this moment Neptune, who had been quietly reposing by the side of his master, suddenly raised his head, and gave a low, fierce growl.

Halliard and his wife started.

The dog got up, scented the ground, and once more gave vent to his suspicions by a fierce howl.

"What is the matter with Nep?" asked Rose, clinging to her husband.

"Some one is passing on the road below, perhaps, or the rascal has been dreaming. Here, sir! what now, dog? Down!" cried Halliard, stepping after the creature, as he ran towards the garden gate.

Neptune barked furiously.

Catching him by the collar, and forcibly holding him back, Halliard looked over the pales in every direction.

He returned to Rose laughing, and dragging back the dog.

"It is a fancy of our canine friend's. Perhaps he wants to show his zeal for his new mistress, or, most likely, he caught the sound of a distant footstep."

"Walter, the wreckers!"

"Pshaw! a sailor's wife, and so full of idle qualms and fears. I am well armed, poor, and have mixed with the rogues when I was a boy. They must have a motive for their atrocities, either of avarice or vengeance; no such motives can influence them against me. Indeed, I think the scamps ought to

favour me for my forbearance; had I done my duty I should have handed over your precious uncle, Murdoch Polruth, to the revenue officers. Down, Nep! down, sir! I'll thrash you!"

The dog reared on his hind legs, and growled and barked savagely.

Halliard pulled him into the house, and, throwing him off, chid him into a corner, where he lay crouching and whining, and displaying every symptom of restlessness and uneasiness.

Rose closed the door and half drew the curtains.

A man stepped from the shadow of the garden wall out into the starlight.

He lurked low, stealing along the wall; with one hand he clutched the ivy, in the other he grasped a long fowling-piece.

There was a satanic light in his eye, and his broad mouth was tight compressed.

His cheeks were flushed, and his eyes brilliant, as if from hard drinking.

He was muttering hoarsely,

"I will do it now! Thorkil Penreal shall not fool me out of my revenge. The hound may escape; I will give him no chance; jilted, slighted, married before my face! I cannot breathe the same air with the smirking maccaroni; arms entwined, eyes talking, lips silent and parted. The red lightnings strike me if he lives another hour! When he is dead! Yes, a brave thought! she will be in my power; that's something like a triumph, the disdainful minx! I'd rather dance upon nothing than lose my revenge. Good night; your honeymoon goes down betime; I'll not hurt the wench till I have killed him. Ya! now he moves."

Black Will Trelawny took a step backwards, raised the gun to his shoulder, and deliberately aimed through the window.

A loud barking shook the house.

Trelawny involuntarily started and lowered his piece.

"Blast the dog! I wish I had my knife in his throat!" growled the ruffian. "Humph! the bridegroom approaches the window; his last step is taken!"

Quickly as the gun was raised to the villain's shoulder there was time for him to catch a sound, a sharp light click.

He turned hastily, the blood rushing from his cheek, and the qualm rising in his throat.

Jauntily perched upon the low stone wall sat a young fellow, dressed as a sailor of the merchant service; in the clear starlight his handsome, regular features, and his bright black eyes, were distinctly visible.

He had just drawn back the fire-lock of a pistol, which he aimed at Trelawny's head, as the latter turned and crept back from the window.

The sailor beckoned the farmer to approach him.

Black Will answered only by half raising his gun.

The sailor tapped the fire-lock threateningly, and frowned, and made motion to indicate that he did not wish to alarm the inmates of the cottage; he then held up his hand and made a peculiar sign with his fingers.

Trelawny started, and answered the sign by another.

The young sailor nodded and grinned.

Trelawny stepped lightly across the little garden, and, vaulting the wall, walked down the slope of the cliff, the sailor following.

"Sorry to disturb you, mate," said the stranger, in a low, chuckling tone, "but I can't allow you to endanger the safety of the band by such an act as that you were about to perpetrate. Who lives in the bunk, hearty? it's as pretty a little berth as

I've seen since I returned to old England! 'Love in a cottage,' that's what I've dreamed about in the dog-watches of dark nights, when in the maintop the cold froze up my eyes, and my hair has rattled with icicles like a glass lustre."

"And who are you?" asked Trelawny, sullenly.

"Pshaw! don't you know me? Have you forgotten the brush we had on Druid's Mere, when I nearly doused one of your toplights with a long shot from my starboard bend; however, you made work for the surgeon and the lob-lolly-boy; you used your boarding pike, and the blood swamped my mid-hips; I've the mark on my bulwark to this day. Have you forgotten me, messmate?"

Trelawny paused in his walk and glanced at his companion.

"Paul Adair!" he exclaimed, in unfeigned wonder.

"Aye, mate, the 'Paul Adair,' run into this little harbour to re-freight with lead and saltpetre; though, to weather Brag Point, I was run right before the wind in the lee-shore, a mile below the Seal's Cover. I've heard you have a frigate moored in these waters."

"Aye, if all hands were aboard, and I had charge of the magazine," growled Trelawny.

"Avast, you swab! would you wreak the grudge you owe one man upon a whole ship's company? Have you no conscience? is human life no more sacred than the breath you vent in curses? is blood no more precious than the water with which you freshen your swedes?"

"You have a right to preach of conscience—you, forsooth, you value the life of enemies or friends—a cursed——"

"Hist!—I follow my calling; you do the same. But, tell me, Black Will, how long have you joined the wreckers?"

"Since this morning."

"So lately! and who is he whom you wish to wipe off the ship's books 'dead and discharged?' Shiver me, Black Will, if you gained the name by your black looks you deserve it, for, when I pitched the hatchway of the little garden, I was suddenly struck as with darkness—the air seemed fraught with sulphur, like a hot night off Jamaica before the ground shakes and the wind catches fire. When I could make out your figure-head I thought you the devil that had just lost a 'brand,' for your face was the living picture of malice and murder. What has the native in that caboose done to stir up such a mutiny of the passions?"

"He has robbed me of my sweetheart, and I will have my revenge in spite of the devil."

"And who is the fellow?"

"A cursed skip-jack from the man-of-war in the roadsteads."

"What, the Defiance?"

"Aye, he rates as second lieutenant, I believe. His name is Walter Halliard."

"Good God! I hove in sight at a happy time. You know me, Black Will?"

"For a——"

"A man of my word. If you attempt to overhaul the craft you were sneaking after just now, either in port or on the high seas, dam'me, I declare war against you, and will show you no more mercy than I would to a custom-house swab. Walter Halliard! Humph! Well, Master Trelawny, I have given you warning."

"And I give you warning, Paul Adair; if you think I am to be brow-beaten, threatened, or thwarted, by such as you, you are infernally mistaken!"

"Black Will, you have done a wise thing."

"Oh, indeed!"

"You have joined the 'coasters,' and are under the band's protection, or, blow me, if I wouldn't pay you off, and send you back to your legitimate skipper, Old Nick, before you did further mischief."

"You would, you lubberly powder-monkey?"

"It's no use trying to whistle up a breeze; I'm in no mood for a brush, to-night; I'm tired of 'War's alarms,' and have come land-cruising on business of more importance than clapper-clawing with land-sharks. Here's the road to Seawardine, and there's the path to your farm; so here we part company, Black Will. I wish you good-night!"

Before Trelawny could reply, the young sailor turned down the diverging path, and walked quickly away.

Black Will turned, with a scowl on his face, and played with the trigger of his fowling-piece; then, with a muttered curse, he shouldered the gun, and proceeded on his way.

CHAPTER VIII.

THE SAILORS ON SHORE — A DISCUSSION — A STRANGER—THE SMUGGLER'S RUSE—A LOVER'S MEETING.

THE liberty-men from the Defiance were carousing, with uproarious fun, in the tap-room of the largest inn of Seawardine.

The place was a great barn-like interior, lighted by flaring oil-lamps affixed to sconces in the wall.

The fire-place was as ample as an ordinary chamber, and though the summer was scarce past, a large fire roared up the chimney.

All manner of frolic was going on: here a number of jolly tars were singing interminable sea-songs, or twisting mendacious yarns over the grog-kid; there, a fiddler was playing a hornpipe, to which a well-made fellow was stepping with true seaman-like grace and agility.

In one corner of the room, Tom Truepenny, Joe Juniper, Bill Hawser, and the old blacksmith, Joel Britton, were seated in conclave, eagerly disputing.

"Stopper all, mates; don't think you can run your rig upon me, I've sailed round Cape Horn!" shouted Joe, at the top of his voice. "I've heard too many galley yarns to be bamboozled by methody. I say as Noah were the first admiral of the Blue, and if he warn't an Englishman, he ought to have been; not as I should think so much of the build and rig of that old commodore's transport, but to say that ever raal Britons paddled in canoes like Sandwich Islanders——"

"Well, dum it, my good fellow," cried Joel, puffing fiercely from his pipe, "isn't Sandwich in Kent? and isn't Kent in England? and arn't all those cockle steering niggers emigrants from that same port?—In coorse they are."

Joe subsided, his mouth wide open and his eyes starting with dismay.

"That's all a-taunto, Muster Clod-crusher!" cried Bill Hawser. "But how do you account, hearty, for their being black?"

"Do they use soap?" said the disputatious blacksmith, promptly.

"Well, not as I heard on, hearty."

"It's the work of generations," said Joel, conclusively; "you all knows what colour you'd be if you didn't use that same article."

"Why, you unreasoning lubber!" cried Tom Truepenny, greatly scandalised. "Why don't the niggers swab white, then? Do you think all the holy-stone used on deck of every man-o'-war would ever swab a black-a-moor white?"

"It's the work of generations," returned Joel, pertinaciously.

"Stand by!" cried Bill Hawser, "these book-larned lubbers, that never sucked the monkey at Barbadoes, nor shook hands with Yellow Jack, are not to be convinced by the best pilot as ever steered a wessel. I'm of Joe's opinion; and as for Britons painting their figure-heads, unless they were women, bless 'em! and paddling canoes, like Patagonians, I'd as soon believe that the whole fleet would strike flags to a French fisherman."

"And that's about as likely, hearties, as that the Defiance should send her crew ashore to get drunk and spend their prize-money when the saucy French privateer, the Hirondelle, sails out in the offing as if there were no such thing as a British line-of-battle in the Channel."

These words, spoken in a clear, rich voice, caused a general start among the sailors.

Joel Britton looked up at the speaker.

The man glanced him steadily in his face, as if they had never met before.

Joel drew back in his chair; every vestige of colour stole from his cheek, and he stared at the stranger with boundless surprise.

"Avast there, youngster," that's an assartion you ought to have good warrant for," cried Tom Truepenny. "Shiver your mizen! do you mean to spoil our leave? I see we must overhaul your ship's books, my little cheery. What's your name?—where do you steer from?"

"I've sailed under the British Jack since I was high enough to handle the top spokes of the wheel. My name is Jem Bunt, formerly a King's man, but since I was paid off on discharge at Gosport, I've been cruising these water's in a collier belonging to Masters Stoke and Poke, of St. Austle's Bay."

Joel Britton was suddenly seized with a violent fit of coughing.

"That look's ship-shape," said Bill Hawser, "and where does your barque moor now?"

"We lost half our freight in the storm, and have been crawling along with a jury-mast, all hands at the pumps. The Black Diamond has run into Mount's Bay for refitting."

"Well, mate, and how do you know the bearings of the Hirondelle?"

"Our look-out spied her about six bells, steering close by the wind, nor-by-nor-west, off St. Ives."

"What's this fellow saying?" cried an officer, who was playing cards with a middy at a little table apart from the men.

He was the third-lieutenant of the Defiance, and stepped briskly towards the little group.

"Why, sir, the youngster says that the Hirondelle has sailed out of harbour, and was standing off St. Ive's at six bells."

"It's true, sir," said the young sailor, doffing his cap. "We had been hard at work all night and had got the water a little under; I was in the forecastle helping the carpenter, when the skipper sings out, 'Grog ahoy!' you may suppose we didn't limp as we went aft at the call. While we had turned to, to freshen hawse, the chap at the fore-top reported a sail on our lee bow—the skipper clapped his glass to his eye, and says he, 'Jack'——"

"Why, you lying lubber, you said your name was Jem," cried Tom Truepenny.

"They call me Jack aboard. I sailed first under a purser's name. You see, I'm all fair and above-board."

"Go on, sir," exclaimed the officer, impatiently.

"'Jem,'" says he.

"Jack—Jack," cried Tom Truepenny.

"I thought you objected to my purser's name, hearty. Well, he said, says he, calling me by my name, 'By the great guns, that's the Hirondelle. I saw her at Toulon. I know the cut of her jib, and I could swear to her among all the masts of the French navy.'"

"What colours did she carry?" asked the lieutenant.

"A Dutch bunting, your hononr; but there was no mistaking her clean run, and rakish gear—there isn't a prettier craft in the high seas than that spanking privateer."

"Well, did she signal you?"

"Aye, your honour, and we were so near that we could see the fellow pulling at the signal halyard."

"Well, what did she say?"

"She ordered us to 'heave to.'"

"Did you obey?"

"No, sir; the skipper gave the word to 'make sail,' and we crept in shore as close as we dare in these confounded rocky waters, and, as the privateer sheered off, she opened a port and sent us her compliments with French politeness; however, her pretty billet draked along the surf within the length of a marlinspike of our head-rails, and sank with a souse."

"Mr. Bowline, had we not better go aboard, and take this fellow with us?" said the midshipman.

"I hope, sir, you won't require me to come aboard," said the young sailor, humbly; "I heard that you were lying off Seawardine, and the skipper gave me leave to come over to report the Hirondelle; but, as I'm chief mate of the collier, and shall be wanted, I hope you will kindly excuse me."

"Well, if what you say is true, and I cannot conceive what motive you could have to deceive me, we owe you many thanks for your zeal and loyalty. Here, my lad, is something to drink the king's health, and to us a successful chase of the troublesome cruiser."

"With pardon, your honour, I must refuse," said the young sailor, drawing himself up proudly, "my satisfaction in having done my duty is a sufficient reward."

"Well, Mr. ——"

"James Bunt."

"Ay, true; well, Mr. Bunt, I suppose you are to be heard of?"

"Masters Stoke and Poke, St. Austel's Bay."

"I will bear it in mind, my boy, and, if we take that wasp of a privateer, I will not forget you. And now, lads," the officer continued, addressing the men, "I am sorry to be a mar-sport, but I put it to you whether you would like the cursed French pirate to have the laugh of us for the sake of a few hours' tippling, when there will be prize-money and renewed leave for all of you if we can run down the Hirondelle. You are willing to return to your duty, I know, lads."

"Ay, ay! sir," cried the men, with alacrity.

"Mr. Armitage."

"Here, sir," said the middy.

"It's rather hard upon poor Mr. Halliard, but you must run up to his cottage, and tell him what has occurred, and bring him aboard directly."

"Ay, sir."

"I will leave Hawser and the boat's complement on the beach for you and him; we will put off in the jollies."

"Very well, sir," replied the middy, saluting and leaving the room.

"And now, my lads, fill up. Mr. Bunt, the kid is by your side. Here's 'Long live the King, and may his Majesty's true-blues soon sweep the seas clear of England's foes!'"

THE MURDER OF WALTER HALLIARD

"Hurrah!" shouted the sailors, honouring the toast by draughts of the deepest. "God save the King—hurrah!"

There was something impressive in the silence that pervaded that quaint, ungainly place, when the last seaman had swayed out from the door.

Nothing broke that silence but the ticking of the old case clock in the corner and the flaring of the log fire.

The young sailor stood, with his arms lightly folded. gazing abstractedly on the blaze.

Joel Britton still sat in the chimney corner.

He seemed to be stricken speechless with astonishment at what had transpired, and looked at the handsome youth before him with awe, and perhaps alarm.

The young sailor turned towards him, a bright, merry smile lighting up his fine, daring face.

The old man burst out at last.

"You intolerably imperant, seditious, high-treasonous, unpardonable, unparalleled young scoundrel"

"I see you know me, Mr. Britton," said the young sailor, laughing.

"Know ye—Paul Adair!"

"And I knew you at first sight. But, you see, I was sailing under false colours, and dared not exchange friendly signals. How's Nelly? 'Oh! Ianthe, what a treasure had'st thou!' I have called my new cutter Nelly of Sewardine."

"You unmitigated——"

"And Mrs. Britton, how I long to shake hands with her. You did not thing to see me again?"

"I hoped you had walked the plank, been keelhauled, flogged round the fleet, transported, dismasted, or hauled up at the yard-arm, years agone."

"Humbly grateful, I'm sure, Mr. Britton," returned the young sailor, laughing. "But my cruise is not over yet. Hark! there's a gun; that's a signal for poor Wat Halliard. I'm sorry for him. It's a burning shame. That pretty Rose, too. Well, they won't run this gull's chase over a se'nnight, and by that time, my friend Letourier will have flown his Hirondelle out of the channel. But, you know, Mr. Britton, a frigate is too expensive an ornament for my preserves; my herring-pond must be kept clear of such craft; I can have no men-of-war in my waters."

"*Your* waters?" cried Britton, throwing back his head, and flinging up his arms, with a groan.

"Aye! *my* waters—

'Shall I tell you my trade?—Ah! you look at my sign;
The freight I have paid for, the flag is not mine;
I've a store in the hold that was won by the bold,
To warm jolly hearts that should never grow cold.

I've pipes and I've puncheons, and bottles a store,
A cutlass or two, and of guns three or four;
I honour the king; but I don't see the fun
Of paying high dues, so I risk a sly run!'

Another signal! They're weighing anchor; so I'll just take a rest, for I have a hard night's work before me. Joel, I've better champagne than you can distil from your parsnips, not to speak of schnapps and cognac, liquid fire, and Promethean to boot."

"You precious villain! And you have bamboozled the men-of-war's-men, in order to run ashore a cargo?"

"Right, Master Britton; your grog-kid shan't be empty till I return to replenish it."

"Do you think I'll have dealings with smugglers?"

"No; but you may spoil the Egyptians, and drink the king's health in liquor that won't disgrace the coast. Tip us your fin!"

"My fin?"

"Ay, give us your hand, hearty, and tell me how I wear. There's not a shot in my hull, though I have been through a leaden hailstorm; there's not a flaw in my heart, though it has been strained by treachery and sprung by oppression. I have gone in for repairs, and now I'm thoroughly seaworthy—ready to mount any flag—even the black one; ready to face any foes—even the 'Royals.' I'm all taut, and am making a purser's fortune. Give us your hand!"

"What! shake hands with a smuggler?"

"Aye; you haven't the heart to refuse to shake hands with Paul Adair."

"Well, durn'ee, I'd be the last to blow the gaff on yer, though I'm as loyal as a Whig; and, as the dame is rather weakly, why a nip of *eau de vie* is not a bad cordial—and, dash it all, a man can't be

responsible for the way good things come, when he don't seek for em'. Well, Master Paul, I'll shake hands wi' you, on one condition, lad."

"Ha! give us your flipper; why, I could shake this honest old hand as long and lustily at if it were the pump handle, and there were six feet of water in the hold. Come, come, you're glad to see me, though you pull a phiz like a skulk at the gratings; confess it now!"

"Lord love ye, boy, you'll not tell anybody?"

"No."

"Then, daum it, I *am* glad to see ye. You mustn't breath it to a soul; but, you cursed rascal, I—am—mortial glad—to see ye—surelie!"

The blacksmith shook the sailor's hand as if he meant to dislocate his shoulder.

"But there's one thing, Master Paul."

"Aye! Aye!"

"My darter, Nell; it would break her mother's heart. There's a sort of honour about you, you scamp, and you mustn't think of splice——" The door was suddenly opened, and the blacksmith's daughter bounded in.

"Are you not coming home, father?" she exclaimed, in a pettish tone, "the very sailor fellows are gone aboard, and——" She paused and started back with a bright blush; she took a sly look at the young sailor, started, and drew timidly to his side. He snatched her to his arms.

She murmured gently, as she feebly struggled to disengage herself, "Paul Adair!"

CHAPTER IX.

A LAPSE OF TIME—A HAPPY HOME—THE BIRTH OF OUR HERO—ROSE AND THYRA—ROSE HALLIARD'S FOREBODINGS—THE CHILD OF THE WRECK.

Four years had passed away since Paul Adair had deluded the officers and crew of the Defiance, and Halliard had been torn from his wife within a few hours of their marriage.

It need not be stated that the man-of-war failed to overhaul the Hirondelle.

After a week's fruitless chase of the phantom ship the captain of the Defiance received authentic intelligence that the privateer had made his escape to the German Ocean.

Halliard obtained leave, and spent four months of bliss with his pretty wife in their humble but happy cottage at Seawardine.

Stimulated by the desire of gaining a position which would enable him to have his wife almost continually by his side, and impelled by his attachment to the service, and his thorough seamanship and tried courage, Halliard had risen rapidly to the post of captain, and now commanded the Thetis, a splendid frigate, engaged in Channel service.

Within a year of their marriage was born to Walter and Rose Halliard a fine little fellow, whose beauty and sweetness of temper endeared him not only to his parents, but to all their friends, and everyone, with unfeigned heartiness, declared they had never beheld so sweet, so handsome a babe as OUR HERO—HARRY HALLIARD.

His eyes were soft blue, his hair flaxen, and his complexion as delicate as the tender tint of a white rose.

The little foundling who had been committed by Wild Thyra to the care of Rose Halliard, and who was nurtured by a good-hearted woman of the village, had been christened Helene, and Nelly Britton, at her own earnest request, had, with Rose, stood sponsor for the poor, parentless child.

Helene grew a lovely creature, with large, lustrous, pensive black eyes, and dark, flowing hair.

She was timid and gentle, yet lovely and warmly affectionate.

Rose was intensely happy, her husband's absence being the only thing that caused her feelings of regret, and even to that there was some counterbalance in the great joy of their meetings, when, for a short time, the mariner returned to spend the happy hours in his love-blessed home.

Rose saw little of Wild Thyra; the strange girl occasionally visited her protegé, and on all occasions demonstrated her strong attachment to the child and to Rose herself.

Black Will Trelawny had sold his farm, and had bought a barque of some burden, in which he performed several voyages round the coast, and report spoke darkly of the traffic he was engaged in.

Young Harry was now a merry prattler three years of age, Helene a year older, and the two children already appeared wonderfully fond of each other.

Captain Halliard had received orders to cruise round the coast on the look-out for privateers, smugglers, and other nefarious characters, and had prevailed upon Rose to trust little Harry to his care for one voyage, and, as he promised, for one voyage only.

As the weather was fair, and the service not one of danger, the young mother, though loth to part with her darling, even for a short time, consented without misgiving.

The months passed rather wearily with the sailor's wife, and she anxiously counted the days for her husband's return.

The summer was waning, the wind blew fitfully from varying quarters, the waters rolled turgid and vicious upon the rifted shores, and the spray wreathed and chafed about the fatal Shark's Fin as if restless for mischief.

Rose sat at the door of the cottage.

From time to time she would raise her eyes from her work, and gaze wistfully over the world of heaving waters, and then, with a little sigh, resume her work.

Little Helene and Old Nep were merrily gamboling upon the little green without the garden.

Suddenly the little girl gave a cry of joy, and bounded forward to meet some one who was advancing from the cliff.

On looking up, Rose saw that the little one was clasped in the arms of Wild Thyra.

The girl presently rose, and, leading the child by the hand, drew near to Rose.

Rose received her warmly, and together they entered the cabin.

"It is long since you have visited me, Thyra," said the sailor's wife, in a tone of affectionate reproof; "you said we should be sisters; is it sisterly that you should come so seldom?"

' I am not welcome now!" said Thyra, sadly. "I mean you would not welcome me if you knew what I have upon my heart.'

"What do you mean, Thyra?" said Rose, with a start, and turning very pale. "No evil news of my husband? I know that the bearings of important

ships are well known to the people along the coast; has anything happened to him?"

" You will smile at my old news," returned Thyra, quaintly,

'E'er the sun is setting, gorgeous is his shining;
Stars clearest beaming, nearest their declining.—
Rose, brightest blooming, round the oak entwining—
Life is a shadow!' "

Rose smiled painfully.

The wild girl said, with a grave look,

"You do not think that Thyra can hold converse with the water-sprites. Perhaps you believe that beneath that great sea which covers mighty forests of strange plants; where there are high hills, and rocky mountains, and low weedy valleys, as upon the land; gardens of sea-flowers; pavements of pearl, that flash like moonlight-mansions of corals, that glow like rubies and glancing armies of silver-mailed fish, ever scutling through the pure cold depths—perhaps you believe, Rose, that there are no intelligent beings there, who can behold and admire the awful wonders of two-thirds of this globe—no spirits that wander the golden sands among the spars of wrecks and the bodies around—feel pity for us helpless, hapless mortals, and seek to warn us of the rising storms; aye, and are moved to rage, terror, or obedience by man, who knows the mysteries,—who of creatures the frailest, holds the highest place, as, among the spirits of the mines, the dwarfs and pigmies rule the giant gnomes. You do not believe these things, Rose, and you think your unbelief is wisdom."

The sailor's wife took the wild creature by the hand, and said softly,

" My sister, there are other spirits of whom you should think more—angels!—viewless legions of the blessed, who keep watch about the righteous, to shield them from the barbs of the Tempter. It may be there is a spirit world beneath the boundless wastes of water, but there is also a heaven above—beyond—among the glittering stars, or in that great orb of day shedding its generating warmth to bless our little planet with joy and abundance! You should think of those bright spirits, the angels! of that great and glorious world, Heaven!—and believe me, Thyra, your humble prayers will better move the Eternal Spirit than your arrogant rhymes and 'runes' can influence the wraiths of the dark sea."

Thyra shuddered and clung to Rose,

" I think of them too," she said, quietly; " but the world is the stepping-stone to Heaven, and I have nothing to do with the world. I have no father, no mother, no husband, no lover; I am a child of the sea, and its voice surges in my heart like the roar in a shell. I have one link to bind me to the earth—my little sister," said the poor girl, tearfully, embracing Helene, " and she is a foundling of the great ocean."

" Lena love 'Tara'," murmured the child, caressingly.

The wild girl kissed her passionately, and then sprang to her feet.

" I must begone, Rose!" she said, quickly. " Hylda has forbidden me to come here, and I must be cautious now. Hear my words; the wind is rising; Hylda is runing; the stars are in threatening conjunction; the Thetis is off the Lizard!"

" Good Heavens!"

" Hush! The spirits will tell Hylda! I will save the great ship if I can, but the stars are against me. Rose must not forget the lesson she teaches. There is a bright world far up, beyond! There are no storms there; no rocks, no shoals, no wreckers, but there the calm is eternal.   Do not go to sleep to night. I will come to you again."

" Stay, Thyra, tell me——"

But the wild girl was gone; waving her hand she fled out of the cottage, As Rose watched from the window, she felt her heart thrill with a strange feeling.

Her eyes bent on the ground, her dress and her long misty tresses fluttering in the shrill sweeping wind, Wild Thyra looked indeed like some weird being, half mortal, half fairy, some Ondine of the sea.

Rose walked quietly into her bedroom, threw herself upon her knees, and prayed with silent fervency.

Little Lena came into the room.

Her beautiful eyes dilated with childlike graveness.

She placed her tiny dimpled hands together, and, sinking on her knees by Rose's side, she lisped some simple prayer she had been taught.

Rose looked at the guileless little one with brimming eyes.

She thought of the words of Wild Thyra; she thought how the great ocean had cast this weakling, motherless and fatherless, upon the cold earth.

She thought of her own darling, of her own husband.

The rough gales from off the restless, surging waters, struck the house, and whistled savagely past, fiercely scattering the petals of some wallroses in at the open window.

A qualm of deadly terror overwhelmed the sailor's wife, and she nervously clutched to her palpitating breast the little orphan of the wreck.

———

CHAPTER X.

THE WRECKER'S RENDEZVOUS—WILD THYRA'S BAN —THE MINUTE GUN.

THE wind blew fresher as the evening advanced, the sea roared hoarsely on the stony strand, the bluish-grey clouds thickened and grew darker, and the surly breakers played savagely about the cruel rocks and raved for their prey.

A man walked along the beach ; from time to time with malicious joy he glanced across the heaving billows.

There was a wild and rocky cove about a mile from Seawardine ; this the man reached, and, rounding the bluff that jetted rudely out at the point of the curve, he made for a cottage which looked like a limpet-shell imbedded in the cliff.

" Ahoy !" shouted a voice from a distance.

The man leaped through the cloud of spray that foamed up at the edge of the bluff, and, crashing onward over the shingle, took off his hat and waved it.

The broad-built, handsome-faced rascal, Thorkil Penreal, approached.

He clutched the man by the hand, and said, in his mellow, deep voice,

" The day and the hour, Black Will ! I have kept my promise. Hylda has conned her most potent spells for the occasion. Did the sea ever look more ugly ? Now you will have your revenge !

Harlock and Agger are off the Lizard with their blue lights ; the fog is blowing up, and the Thetis will heave in sight before night-fall. But there's one thing we must look to, mate."

" Aye ! and what's that ?" asked Trelawny.

" That devil's doxy, Wild Thyra ; she is out runing down the storm, and, may I be keelhauled, if the fog does not seem to sweep back from her breathings, and the surf growls like a lashed hound half cowed and half enraged."

" You are superstitious."

" Belay all that ! I don't want the young hussy to fetch half Seawardine to man the life-boats for the rescue. Our task is one of difficulty ; the skipper of the Thetis is an old coaster, and we must use more than ordinary craft to decoy him."

" The fog thickens. Ah ! this is brave work ! Now it comes back to me. I loved that girl, and set my hopes of possessing her above all else, for what is the worth of life but that a man should gratify his inclinations ?" cried Trelawny. " I remember the sting of slighted love, the fury of thwarted passion. Do you recollect my wishes for their happiness, Thorkil, when we stood beneath the old yew in the churchyard, and heard the bells ring and the villagers shout ?"

" Ay, mate ; and, blow me, if I don't feel half strangled as I recall the grip you gave my winds'l," returned the chief of the wreckers, laughing. " I mind it well ; you wished them abounding love, and a fair child."

" I did—why ? It is mercy that kills the miserable ; but, now my revenge will be complete—my hate will be satisfied. Come on, mate, we must get the boats off the Deadman's Point, and light up the——"

"There she goes along the brow of the cliff !"

" Who ?"

" Wild Thyra. Let us catch the young witch, and shut her up in the hut till the work is done."

Thorkil led the way up the side of the cliff.

Black Will followed him.

Trelawny was dressed in a guernsey, wore a scarlet cap, and high boots.

They reached the summit of the precipice.

The girl stood on the brink of the cliff, her white arms outstretched, her eyes raised to the lowering clouds, and her hair wildly flowing. She seemed to be propitiating the storm-spirits, and was chanting a strange and plaintive melody.

The two ruffians stole behind her.

She turned, and crouched down with a scream.

" Now, lass, you've no cause to be screeching like one of Mother Cary's chickens in a squall. We don't mean harm to you, Thyra. Home, lass ; this is no night for you to be out breasting the gale," cried the chief of the wreckers.

" Away from me, Thorkil Penreal, or I will smite you with a curse that shall cleave to you like a leprosy, shall haunt you like the memory of a deed of blood ! What would you do, wretch, more remorseless than the treacherous waves? Four years have gone—for this is the very night—since you wrecked the barque that bore home your father !" cried Thyra, wildly ; "and now you would destroy a man who never wronged you, an innocent the very tempest would spare——"

" Spawn of a sea-devil ! be quiet, or I will fling you over the cliff !" cried Penreal, fiercely, seizing her arm.

Thyra laughed, and struggled in a fit of insanity.

"Pitch her over the brink!" growled Trelawny. "Are we to be clapper-clawed by a blasted witch, that ought to be burned in a tar-barrel?"

"*You* kill me!—you, Thorkil Penreal!" cried Thyra, shrieking. "Do you think my kindred would suffer me to be murdered by such a miserable ground-shark? Let me go, parricide!"

The beads of sweat started to Thorkil's forehead; he trembled like a reed.

"Stand out of the way. I'll soon stop her 'conjuring.' I'll rip out her black heart with my knife—the ogress!" shouted Trelawny, savagely.

"Aye, Penreal, I spared you for your father's sake—for your father, who meant kindly when he brought me up, and kept me from those who are beckoning me now. Listen to their voices, and harm me if you dare!"

As she spoke, an immense tide-wave thundered dreadfully up to the foot of the cliff, as if it would sap the earth beneath their feet, and a bursting squall of wind and rain howled wildly past them.

"I have borne much—very much," cried the mad girl, in a thrilling voice; "but the cup of my endurance is full. And now, Thorkil Penreal, I will put my darkest ban upon you! Listen, while I curse!—

'Branded with a father's gore;
Rockier-hearted than this shore;
Darker-souled than this dread night
Falser than yon luring light;——'"

"No curses! no curses!" cried the superstitious Penreal, in deadly terror, placing his hand over her mouth.

"Let me get at the rip!" cried Trelawny.

"No, no, Black Will; she is 'eldrich,' she is protected. Let us get her to the cabin. But I would rather lose the plunder of a whole fleet than suffer a single hair of her head to be touched."

"Anyhow I'll stop her croaking," cried Black Will.

Rushing upon Thyra, he clutched her slender throat with his hard, strong hands, and, before Thorkil could tear him away, the poor girl sank on the ground insensible.

A vivid blaze of lightning quivered around them. Then came an awful crash, just above their heads.

"If you have killed her, I wash my hands of this night's work. I'll quench the beacons, and send home the men!" cried Thorkil, in a faint voice, paling, and trembling like a craven.

"Killed her! No, she is silenced for an hour, that's all; the hag will recover soon enough to ban and beshrew you to your heart's content," muttered Trelawny. "Come, lend a hand; we'll bear her off to the cabin."

The two ruthless villains took up the girl, and carried her down the cliff by a winding path-way.

The storm increased.

Thorkil opened the door of the low hut with a key.

They lifted the insensible girl over the threshold.

Penreal piled some tarpauling and sail-cloth in a corner, and laid the girl upon it.

"A wreck! a wreck!" shouted voices without.

The heavy booming of a distant gun sounded across the sea.

"Ha! ha! so soon!—that's well!" cried Trelawny, with brutal glee. "Now we shall have the ringing of the fog-bell instead of the wedding chimes; the death-shriek of the bridegroom instead of the shouts of his friends, and me bride, the happy bride, and the pledge of their union, the cherished first-born. Come, Thorkil, I aim no share in the salvage; all you can snatch from the waves is no more worth than the seaweed the surf flings ashore compared with *my* treasure, the corse of him who dared to rob me of my love. Oh, revenge is sweet to the slighted!"

CHAPTER XI.

THE WRECKING OF THE THETIS—THE PERIL OF ROSE HALLIARD AND HER CHILD—BLACK WILL THINKS HIS VENGEANCE COMPLETE.

THAT awful cry, "A wreck!" ran dismally along the fatal shore, and was re-echoed by the cliffs and rocks. As it rose above the storm it swept to the ear of the lonely wife, as with pale face and clasped hands she stood at the window of her cottage looking out upon the wild face of the lurid sky.

Rose hastily threw a mantle about her, and rushed out into the stormy night.

Still came the cry, "A wreck! a wreck!" but the haze upon the sea was so thick that she could discern no hull in the offing, and the blinding gusts of rain and sleet nearly hurled her to the ground.

Behind her she heard the rattle of a chain, and the piteous howling and angry barking of a dog.

It was Neptune struggling for liberty.

The noble brute was eager to accompany his mistress, and, for an instant, Rose paused, half resolved to set him free that he might go with her; but warned by another shout from the beach, and the sound of distant guns, she dared not pause, even for an instant, but hurried through the storm towards the shore.

Upon reaching the strand Rose looked wildly across the raging billows.

She shrieked and shrieked again.

A stately frigate, her bow-sprit shivered, her toproyals gone; every inch of canvas, every shroud and every shred of tackle stripped from her masts; the foam glittering in white curls, as it dashed over her, from hull to trucks, the mighty frigate was seen drearily drifting.

Through the fog, glaring bewilderingly, shone the treacherous beacons.

Along the shore ranged groups of the fiendish wreckers, laughing and shouting in their hellish triumph.

Rose sank on her knees upon the rain-drenched shingles; her heart stood still; she heard not the bluster of the winds; she recked not of the thunder of the billows; her soul was concentrated upon one object; her strained eyes beheld but one spectacle—the drifting wreck. Her lips were frozen with horror; her face was rigidly fixed with an expression of intensest agony; like a statue she knelt on the wild and dreadful shore, as if she had been struck into stone by the greatness of the awful calamity.

She was not startled even by the gruff laugh of a tall dark fellow, who had taken up his position by her side.

It was not till a heavy hand was laid rudely on her shoulder that she looked up.

No words could paint the fiendish leer that light on the fierce dark face that gloated upon her misery.

She tried to speak, but her lips only fluttered,

and again she turnd her eyes, aching with agony, towards the fearful object before them; still she watched in mute despair the dreary, drifting wreck.

"You thought, Rose, when you jilted me, that you would hear of my having hanged or drowned myself, or died of a broken heart; you thought I should slink through the world a sighing, snivelling maunderer, for you knew I loved you hotly; you thought to insult me with your pity, or to injure me with your scorn. You knew me not. I should have made you a manlier husband than the dainty spark you chose; I should have loved you with deeper, stronger passion; but, when you jilted me, you turned my love into hate—poisonous deadly hate! But, I waited my time; I gave you grace; your life was nothing. I did not cut the worthless stem till the rich fruit was grown. You have a husband whom you prefered to me, you have a child your richest boon on earth; where are they now? tell me, scorner, where are they now? You are sulky, and will not answer; well, there is no need. The fierce squall, the shouting billows, the forked lightning, the tempestuous shoals, the false beacons, the thick fog bank, the Shark's Fin, the water-logged carcases of drowned sailors, the handsome form, but dead, dead! of an 'exemplary husband,' the alabaster corse of a lovely child——"

The infernal villain was interrupted by the wild shrieks of the agonized wife and mother.

"Trelawny!" she cried, "from whose hand come these swift lightning shafts? By whose breath are these mighty waters heaved against this shore? Think of Him—think of His vengeance, and repent, for if there be justice above us, your doom will be so awful that I could weep and pray for you, though you have tempted me to curse bitterly the hour that I was born! My husband!—my little one!—my life!—my comfort!" cried Rose, distractedly, extending her arms to the raging, cruel sea. "Oh! let me die with you; bind me in your arms, husband mine; let the sea take us both with our little one; but, oh! do not let us be parted by death, even for the briefest space. I am sure I shall go mad, and shall rebel against the Almighty's decree. I cannot, cannot bear it—anything but that! My husband, my darling, let us live or die together! Oh, grant it, Heaven! if there is any sanctity in another's love do not refuse me this little, little prayer—let me die, let me die with my husband and my child!"

Rose Halliard caught the wrecker by the arm; she pointed at the distant ship.

"Trelawny," she said, in a voice so impressive that the villain stood paralysed and unable to collect his thoughts, "in that shattered hull are my husband and my first-born; wave by wave they are nearing the Shark's Fin; a few moments, I shall be a widow and childless! The wild storm in this dark sky does not rage more cruelly than will the pangs of desolated love sear and madden my brain; the stones under our feet are not colder, harder, heavier than my heart will be when I look round upon the peopled world, and murmur in my anguish—I am quite, quite alone! But, Trelawny, mark me, my unspeakable misery is unutterable joy compared with the just agony you will suffer for your unnatural, monstrous cruelty to one who never wronged you, one who has shed many bitter tears for your vile sake. Farewell, you have no power to kill me, even if you had mercy enough to end my misery. I stand here, and I lay upon you a wife's—a mother's curse!"

Black Will Trelawny could not reply; he was thunderstruck by the vehemence of the simple girl

whom he had so often brow-beaten and insulted, and who had shown but an occasional spark of indignation at his persecutions, and generally broke down in her self-possession and threw herself upon his mercy, pleading her weakness with a flood of tears.

The heartless villain did not think of the divine instinct that raises a woman above her womanly frailness—a mother's love.

He extended his hand to grasp the arm of his upbraider; but she was gone.

Black Will walked moodily along the shore, and as the devil never gets perfect mastery of the human heart, and though human nature uncontrolled is bad indeed, it is in the worst at times affected by better emotions. The fiendish wrecker could not quell a sense of regret and remorse as he saw the splendid frigate with hundreds of gallant lives aboard, drifting hopelessly on to the fatal rock.

Rose rushed wildly along the beach.

A glare of torches caused her to arrest her steps.

She was surrounded by familiar faces.

A girl threw herself into the young wife's arms.

"Oh, Rose! my dear, darling Rose!" she sobbed, "pray—pray don't despair! Father and the rest of them will put off the boat from the end of the break, and your husband and your sweet child will be saved. I know—I know they will. Oh, I would give my life—a hundred lives for them. But, dear Rose, think, a great frigate, with lots of boats, you know; of course, they must be saved."

"Nelly," said Rose, kissing her friend affectionately, "you must pray for me till I am lost in that raging sea, and then you must remember me, for I dare not hope to save my husband or my child, but I will die with them."

"Thank ye kindly, I'm sure, Mrs. Halliard," cried Joel Britton, cheerily, "as we're all going together, why we shall all go down together. My love to your mother, Nell, and tell her to brew the punch hot for I shall come home as wet as a mop. You see, Mrs. Halliard, that's my anxiety; I'm afeard of catching cold, but not of keeping so; it's old Gout and not Davy Jones I'm afeard on. Now, Tom and Ben, and all the rest on ye, heave and a weigh. Cheerily ho! Good-night, Nell; good-night, Mrs. Halliard; we'll not board the prize without bringing home a taste of the cargo. One, two, three; take the third wave, Bill; now we go."

"Stay, stay!" cried Rose, running into the receding waters; "I will go with you."

"No, no, lass; I say you shan't. Bide ashore, like a good girl."

But Rose had leaped into the boat.

"You shall not refuse me," she said firmly, at the same time lightly springing into the boat.

"I never knew a woman yet as didn't have her own way," cried Britton. "Now, my hearties, pull away with a will; I'm coxswain."

*   *   *   *   *

Black Will Trelawny stood sullenly looking over the sea.

The fog had cleared off, and the Shark's Fin stood so near in-shore that, by the red glare of the beacon the villains had erected on a sandy shoal, the hull could distinctly be seen.

The light boat that carried the dauntless villagers who had so nobly ventured their lives to save the husband and son of Rose Halliard danced over the dreadful waves like a walnut-shell; the boat lived in a sea which would have assuredly swamped a heavier one; its very frailty was its preservation.

Trelawny did not move, but still kept his eyes gloomily fixed on the vessel.

"Now are you satisfied, Black Will?" said a gruff voice in his ear, while a heavy hand clapped him on the shoulder. "This is revenge with a vengeance! My God! a three-decker, a king's ship with all hands aboard; if a man escaped to tell the tale ours would be a sorry scrape; his gracious Majesty would send the whole standing army to hunt us out of our gull's nests, and, curse it all, Will, you don't look grateful."

Trelawny did not reply, but turned sullenly away.

Still the storm raged.

"Eh, mate, there's a soft spot yet in your heart for the scornful wench. Well, suppose we save the interesting family, fancy what will then come of your vengeance—the ecstacy of the re-union, the hugging, the kissing, and the blessings they will heap on your head for your kind but baffled intentions."

"No," muttered Trelawny, savagely, "I will not quail at carrying out my plan; I won't shrink from my own work; I will have my vengeance on the jilt. I have not sacrificed all for nothing."

"Look how distinctly one can see what is going on," cried Thorkil, grimly laughing. "The boat tosses alongside."

"Some one leans over the bulwark."

"Yes, it's the fond father; he hands over the heir apparent. Ha, ha! shiver me, hearty, but she reaches up to him and throws him kisses. Ha, ha, ha! there's a sight for you at such a moment; why don't you sing out 'victory?' What the devil are the sailors doing?"

"Seems as if they were trying to push the skipper overboard."

"Aye, mate, they want him to get into the boat to his wife and youngster, but, to give the devil his due, he's true to his ship. You see he won't leave her, though his wife spreads her arms like a dying martyr invoking the saints and angels."

"Hark at that shriek! Breakers dead ahead, not half a bower hawser's length from the Shark's Fin! Why don't they put down the boats?" cried Trelawny, in wild excitement.

"Our pretty captain knows the coast too well. How could he land on the lee side of the reef? No, he means to stand the shock—take the chance of the ship's stranding fairly on the Fin, then he'll put off in the boats; but they won't live, mate, so you needn't look flabbergastered. Hylda decidedly improves, and we shall have now little cause to set false signals, for no barque but the Flying Dutchman can ever weather a breeze in these waters. Ha! she strikes!"

"And the boat with Rose and the child?" cried Trelawny, breathlessly.

"Will never reach shore! That Harleck's a jewel. See, he has doused the beacon on Sandy Point, and the lightning seems quenched by the awful sea. Phew! how this sou'-wester rackets. I wish we could see the boat."

"She can never live in such a sea, she can never weather the breakers," whispered Black Will, in a hoarse, low tone.

"Not possible! Well, I think if you're not satisfied with this night's work you are no reasonable creature."

"Well, the girl and the fellows on the shore are screaming and shouting; I suppose the boat has gone down."

"Let us get out of the way," growled Trelawny.

"Ah, I see you are not yet a wrecker," returned Thorkil, with a laugh. "But I'm off; you have had your vengeance sated; I must look after my salvage."

Black Will Trelawny was alone; he walked a little distance up the beach in an opposite direction to that taken by Nelly and the other villagers who ran along the shore holding aloft their torches and following the course of the unfortunate boat, which had been swamped, and was drifting keel upwards at the top of the breakers.

He heard a shriek.

He glanced at the water.

A woman was struggling in the waves; a little child floated on the strong swell a yard or so before her.

A billow washed it up on to the beach.

A demoniac flash darted from the wrecker's eye.

The child was unhurt, and not insensible.

The mother rose on the crest of a wave, tossing her arms and shrieking wildly.

The monster stooped and picked up the child, and clutched it savagely in his hands.

The rattle of a chain clinking along the pebbles caused him to start; he heard a fierce growl, and heavy paws pressed on his shoulder.

In great dismay the wrecker held the child aloft, and flung it into the waters; he then took to his heels and fled after the torch party, panting and sweating with fright.

It was the brave dog Neptune had broken his chain and had rushed down to the beach in pursuit of his mistress.

With a sharp, honest-toned bark the dog fearlessly plunged into the thundering breakers; struggling through the surging brine, he reached his mistress, who was sinking, the child in her arms.

The noble dog fought fiercely back to the shore, having seized the cloak of the drowning woman.

Dragging Rose and the child far up the beach, the sagacious animal set off at wild speed to bring some of the party who had gone in pursuit of the drifting boat to the assistance of his mistress.

Joel Britton had clung to a spar from the wreck and had been got ashore, and, most happily, every one of the gallant crew of the life-boat were eventually saved.

The dog leaped upon Nelly.

The girl screamed; so intent was she in looking over the waters in a hopeless search for Rose and the child, that she had not perceived the Newfoundland was behind her.

The dog barked and ran away towards the spot where he had left his mistress, and, seizing the girl by the dress, tried to drag her in that direction.

As the noble creature shook off the brine from his shaggy hide like water scattered from a trundled mop, the party divined the true state of the case, and, with a joyous shout, hurried after their canine guide.

Soon they found Rose.

Nelly and her father raised the girl; the child was soon restored to animation and seemed but little injured.

Rose returned to consciousness, and raising her hand to her head, murmured softly,

"My husband!"

Leaving the men to bear the poor girl along in

their strong arms, Nelly Britton snatched up the child.

"Father," she said, "I will carry the poor child to the cottage, and prepare a fire and the bed to receive poor Rose. Some of you go along the shore in search of her husband, for the villanous gang of wreckers are prowling about. I will have all prepared for you."

With this the kind-hearted girl ran off to the pathway that led to the top of the cliffs.

She reached the height.

The little one clung about her neck.

Yet young as he was he did not evince much terror, but only stretched his hand towards the waves and called to his mother.

Wild and dreadful the scene around. Dark night overhanging in frowning clouds; the sea raging far below; the wind rushing along on its death-wafting wings; the rain drenching down in its pitiless fury

There was a cry from the ocean below.

Nelly, clasping the child to her bosom, peered fearfully over the horrible chasm.

The long boat of the man-of-war was capsized, and the men were struggling in the surf.

Away down the beach glared the torches of her father's party.

Intent upon their care for Rose Halliard they had not continued their pursuit of the man-of-war's boats.

Nelly placed the child on the ground.

"Harry, darling," she said, "will my pet stay here? is Harry afraid?"

The little one did not seem to understand the question, but only smiled through his tears.

Nelly placed him on the sward at some distance from the edge of the cliff.

"Is Harry frightened?" again asked the girl, smiling, and smoothing his flaxen curls. "Will he stay here?"

"If Nelly bring mamma," returned the child, earnestly.

Nelly walked away.

She turned: the little one sat quite patiently, and, though he was sobbing bitterly, did not seem the least alarmed at being left alone.

"If that dear child lives—but I'm afraid he is too sweet and good for life—if he lives," murmured Nelly, who was also weeping bitterly, "he will be a brave man—a hero."

She ran down the zig-zag rocks and gained the shore.

The storm was abating, but the wind still soughed fitfully along the cliffs; the fury of the waves was too much aroused to be soon appeased, and the darkness was deep and solemn.

Little Harry sat crying on the ground, but still did not appear in the least terrified at being left alone in the gloom.

A tall fellow sauntered along the edge of the cliff.

He had not perceived the child.

Suddenly he started back, uttering a fearful oath.

A sound was heard, as if the falling of pieces of stone and rock.

Then over the brink of the rocks a head appeared.

The man, who was Black Will Trelawny, stepped back into the darkness.

The other who had clambered over the edge of the cliff, threw himself upon his knees.

He clasped his hands and seemed engaged in fervent thanksgiving to the Almighty.

Black Will advanced towards him.

He sprang to his feet.

"You are Walter Halliard!" said Trelawny, in a hectoring tone.

"And you, accursed villain, are William Trelawny, and a wrecker!" cried the other, sternly. "Mark me, you sent aboard the Thetis one of your gang, who pretended to be a channel pilot. That wretch perished the first of those who were destroyed by your atrocious strategy; he escaped a more shameful death which you and your fellow monsters are doomed to. My ship is strewn in the waters; my gallant crew have perished; thus far you have triumphed; but here your triumph ends——"

"It ends here, Walter Halliard!" cried Black Will, fiercely; "and it ends to my heart's satisfaction—you had a fair wife, and a beloved child; the boat to which you confided them was swamped amid the breakers. I would not separate child from mother, so I flung back the little one into the waves were the mother was struggling, and they perished together. Be my witness, this little belt; that was round the youngster, and which when I flung him into the surf it remained in my hand. It remains now only to kill you, as I have killed them, and my vengeance is accomplished!"

The silence of a few moments followed this speech.

Walter Halliard stood almost on the brink of the cliff, gazing in a stupor of wildness at the miscreant whose boast of what he had done to his wife and little one was like molten lead falling to his heart; then his teeth set hard together, and his hand closed on the hilt of his sword.

No word to indicate his agony, no word to speak his purpose; silently, swiftly, he made ready to cut his foeman to the earth.

Black Will, laughing an ominous, hollow laugh, marked the action. He, too, was prepared for deadly work, but his villany gave him the advantage.

He drew a pistol from his belt, and, as his coarse laugh grated on Walter's ears, he aimed point blank at him, and fired.

The flash shone on Walter's sword as it bared in the air; it gleamed upon his ghastly face, as he staggered back; its glare played a moment on the fitful waters, moaning and chafing at the base of the hollowed cliff, and then flash and echo died away.

The gurgling cry of the falling man, and the brutal scoff of his murderous enemy, mingled with the roar of the moaning sea. A startled sea-gull shrieked hoarsely by. But, above all these sounds, the shrill cry of an agonised woman rose shrill and wild, then a child's terrified voice, speaking his father's name. These last two sounds reached the ears of those two men—the doomed, and the slayer.

Black Will, with a furious oath, turned round. Walter Halliard, paused, reeling on the cliff.

Nelly and the child were hastening to the scene, horrified at the frightful spectacle. The young girl had consciousness only long enough to see Walter's haggard, bleeding face, lighted up by the instantaneous glare of the pistol—to see a powerful form, the face wrapped in impenetrable shadow, standing before him, ere she fell to the earth senseless at the feet of Black Will.

The child ran forward crying, and putting out its little hands.

The ruffian uplifted his weapon to strike the

NOTICE.—The next Number of the Boys' Library will be Published on Friday, June 27th.
Order early of your Bookseller.

No. 3, New Series. Price One Penny.

BOYS' LIBRARY

HARRY HALLIARD;
OR,
THE YOUNG BRITISH TAR.

NEPTUNE ATTACKS BLACK WILL.

father down; but Walter Halliard was already falling; as if stricken by lightning, he tumbled back from the rock, and passed from the murderer's sight.

Black Will peered over the butting brow of the cliff. A dull murmur came from below: the sea ebbed and chafed: the white foam bubbled up the sides of the steep shore: the cold waves flashed and trickled and splashed—splashed over the form of his victim, and, as it seemed, tore him away from the rugged beech, away and away, and out of sight.

CHAPTER XII.
THE NELLY OF SEWARDINE.

THREE hours had passed; the storm had in a measure subsided; the wind lulled; the agitated waters still heaved mountains high, but the mountains rolled in less heavily, and not with such powerful impetus.

The beach was strewn with dead bodies, and with spoils from the wreck.

The sea-vultures were eagerly searching for treasure.

As the wind changed and the tide turned favourably for calm, a boat put into a little cove a mile or so to the west of Seawardine; seven men leaped ashore.

They walked along the beach keeping close under the cliffs.

They carried no torches.

One of them turned towards the others, and said, in a low tone, with a side glance at a cluster of wreckers who were swarming round a large haul from the wreck,

"Of all the cursed services that ever a man followed, who took the devil for his skipper, there's none, to my mind, so damnable as this, what say you, Blane?"

"I say a blood-thirsty pirate is an angel of mercy, and an honour to society, in comparison with these infernal wreckers. Look at the kites and ravens, they have found a dead carcase, and they hover round it as if they would eat it. It makes me feel like a lubber on his first cruise. I feel sea-sick," returned the other, with a growl of disgust.

"Well, hearty, whatever may be our private opinions of the pretty trade our friends follow, we must not pipe too loud about them."

At this moment, a party of wreckers were seen advancing round the bluff of the rocks, conducted by a stalwart fellow, and a youthful woman.

"Ahoy there!—what cheer?" cried the wreckers.

The men replied by a shout, and he who appeared to be their leader advanced, and held out his hand.

Thorkil Penreal, for it was the chief of the gang whom the sailor saluted, laughed gleefully, and shook the proffered hand with great cordiality.

"Fair welcome in foul weather, Paul Adair. Have you come ashore to share with us the spoils of the enemy? A frigate of the line, hearty. It seems impossible; but there she is, astrand on the Shark's Fin."

"And who was her skipper?"

"Captain Halliard."

"The devil!"

"If he is that black rover, he's safe moored in port in his own regions," returned Thorkil, laughing.

"Then he is drowned!"

"Aye, mate. Is he a brother?" cried Penreal, with a leer.

"Of my soul!" returned the young sailor, wringing his hands for a moment, in great chagrin and sorrow.

"Well, hearty, if we find his body, we'll sew him in a hammock, tie a shot to his feet, and give him a sailor's funeral, as if he were one of the band. But, what news from St. Ives?"

"All's well, Thorkil."

"And Michael Guldenhoff?"

"Will run a cargo into the Seal's Cover before one bell to-morrow."

"He shall be welcome!" cried Thorkil, laughing. "And now, whither do you steer?"

"I thought you were my convoy, and carried ship's orders," returned the young sailor, smiling; then a dark shadow swept over his face, and he asked,

"How was it, Thorkil, that Halliard run astern of the 'Shark?' He ought to know his soundings in these waters; he was born at Mount's Bay."

"I sent a fellow aboard as a pilot when I saw the ship crawling over the shoals to lee-ward. The skipper was thoroughly bamboozled, but the poor fellow, my pilot, was drowned with the rest. They took to the boats, and were swamped."

"It is an infernal act!" cried Adair, with unconscious vehemence.

"Halloo! what say you?" cried Penreal, fiercely.

"The less we say about this affair the less chance there will be of our running athwart hawse with each other, messmate. But, now, since we've spoken, I will send Blane and half the men back to the Nelly, and we will steer her quietly into her old moorings beyond St. Michael's Mount."

"Aye, mate, so do."

Paul Adair ordered four of his men to return to the boats, while he proceeded with the wreckers towards the Seal's Cover.

Though the swell was still heavy upon the sea the wind had lulled, and the morning was breaking brightly.

Blane and his three companions hurried along, conversing upon the events of the past night, and expressing in no measured terms the disgust they felt at the treachery of their allies, when suddenly Blane stumbled against something that lay beneath the cliff.

He stooped over it, and said, in a tone of pity,

"One of the Thetis's men; and, blow me, an officer!"

"Perhaps it's the skipper?"

"Is he dead?"

"Shiver me, mate, if I can tell; but, as I'm no doctor, it seems to me that he hasn't slipped his anchor, for, do ye mark, here's a patch of blood clotted on his forehead, and it looks as if it had but just ceased flowing."

"Some of the blasted wreckers have scuttled his hull."

"Think not, Ben," returned the other. "Most like he was thrown up by the waves, after skimming about in the 'under tow.' Perhaps a breaker caught him in the swell and flung him against the side of the cliff and so smashed his forecastle."

"Well, what shall we do with him?"

"We'll not leave him adrift, hearties, to have his throat cut like a pig by one of these cursed landsharks. Lend a hand."

"What, take him aboard the Nelly?"

"Aye, Ben."

"To blow the gaff on us!"

"What, for saving his life? I've no very great opinion of human nature myself, but, dam'me, I wouldn't wrong my feller creeters with such a dirty suspicion for all Mike Guldenhoff's guilders. Lend a hand."

The sailors lifted the body from the ground, and bore it away towards the boat.

They placed it in the bows, and then pushed off.

As they pulled strongly through the rough, rolling waves the mist curled up from the surf that was tinged pale-gold by the slanting beams of the rising sun.

More than one floating corpse thudded hideously against the prow of the boat, causing the little barque and its crew to shudder as if their revulsion and horror were mutual.

Soon they floated under the side of the Nelly.

A man leaned over the bulwarks.

"Why, Blane, where's the skipper?"

"Off with the blasted land-sharks, Ned, to the Seal's Cove. But, quick, hearty; throw a rope and lower a chair—we've brought a cabin passenger."

The men from the boat scrambled on to the deck, and the insensible man was drawn up in a chair.

"Off with him to the hospital bunk; there's no time for sick-nursing," cried the man who had first spoken. "Don't you see, Blane, what's in the wind?"

"What are the chaps at aloft there—not making sail?" cried Blane.

"Aye, mate, making sail it is," returned the other.

"What, do you mean to sail without orders, messmate, and leave the skipper ashore?" asked Blane, with a laugh.

"A fellow I can trust has reported a revenue cutter on the look out to overhaul our cargo," returned the man. "She is now dodging about in the mist off St. Michael's, and we shall have to make a run of it before the haze clears."

"But the skipper?"

"Must wait his chance. I'll fire the gun twice, and then we must 'take to ourselves wings,' as the parson says, my hearty. Who is this poor devil, shipmate?"

"A fellow we picked up on the beach, one of the ducks from the wreck; but get him below, and lay him in my bunk, physic him with schnapps, and if that don't put the spirit into him, he's had his call from aloft, and it's all no use to try to keep him. Now, lads, on deck; lower away, put the helm up."

"Aye, aye," responded the man at the wheel.

At this moment the gun was fired.

"Down-haul, rig the boom in!" shouted Blane.

A second shot.

"Starboard a little!"

"Starboard it is."

"Whose in the chains?"

"Plummet."

"What does she draw?"

"Seven by the deep—sev-en!" sang out the leadsman.

"Helm's a lee; ease off the jib!"

"Now, she makes way; fire the last gun!" cried Blane.

This order was obeyed.

The first mate of the Nelly went below.

The sailor whom he had brought on board was lying in a hammock; a negro stood by his side, wetting his lips with the cordial.

"Well, Mingo, how's the patient?"

"Yo sar, yo be quiet; I'se not want nuffin to say to no one jist now; doin' berry well, sar, dis patience," returned the black, shaking his woolly head with great solemnity.

"Does he breathe?"

"Wal sar, his breff come and go like catspaws afore a white squall, but he *drinks* mirac'lous. I'se pour'n down his troat 'nuff s'quealin' hot stingo to make him burn blue. Please don't come a near wid de lantern, or we all burn to glory; I'se gib 'im a little more."

With this the darkie dropped another stream of the strong cordial upon the clenched teeth of his victim.

The man's breast swelled, he gasped and spluttered, he opened his half-glazed eyes with a wild vacant stare.

He closed them again with a shudder.

"What cheer, hearty! open your ports, lad, you're in good hands."

"Halloo there, Jack, the skipper's come aboard, and the cutter has hove in sight to windward," shouted a voice down the hatchway.

Blane rushed on deck.

Paul Adair stood on the poop, eyeing the cutter through his glass.

"We shall have a stiff run for it, Jack," he said.

"We'll skulk the muster yet, cap'en."

"I hope so."

"How did Mike Guldenhoff's lugger weather the gale last night, cap'en?"

"Well nigh foundered, Jack. How that cursed craft hugs the wind."

"I ventured, cap'en, to do something without orders; I'm sure you won't object to it."

"Ha! what's that?"

"I have a poor fellow below that we picked up on the shore half water-logged."

"Who is he?"

"An officer from the Thetis, that struck on the Fin last night."

"Eh, I'll go and have a look at him."

"Sail ho!" shouted a man in the ratlings.

"By the Lord, Jack! another cutter!"

"The hulks for all on us!" groaned Blane.

"Bah! our log is not run up yet, hearty; clap on every stitch of canvass; if we can but keep to the leeward without running on the shoals, we'll soon take the wind out of their sails."

"That's the Gannet, of Helstone, and a trim little cruiser she is, I confess, cap'en."

"Aye mate."

"And the other is Dan Bradford's Dreadnought."

"Aye Jack, there's no mistaking her build, hearty. Look, she falls off from the wind. The current strikes her, and she reefs her topsails. What is the Gannet about, Jack; she is making signals?"

"Aye, cap'en, to some one on shore."

"We shall have tight work to clear the island," said Paul Adair. "Well, we might fire a parting salute to the Dreadnought; she hauls her wind and lags in our wake like a blown porpoise."

The Nelly was now steering between an island formed by a high rock banked up with sand, and the revenue cutter, which was fast bearing down upon her.

Just as the Gannet was about to run into the smuggler's barque a cross wind took her right athwart ships, she gave a lee lurch, and, before she righted, with a hearty cheer the crew of the Nelly found themselves forging ahead at a spanking rate as they ran along the sides of the sandy islet.

Paul Adair laughed derisively, and tossed up his hat.

"Boom!—bang!"

A cloud of smoke curled up from the summit of the rock.

A heavy shot crashed through the rigging and shivered the foretop of the smuggler's ship.

Topmast and rigging crashed down upon the deck and with a loud cheer three boats were put off from the island, manned by a number of determined looking fellows, armed with cutlasses, pistols, and boarding pikes.

CHAPTER XIII.

THE LAW TRIUMPHANT.

PAUL ADAIR turned for a moment towards the shore.

The boats were pulling fast towards them.

"My lads," cried the smuggler captain, "we must strike our flag; the game's up with us, for the present, at least, as I see no valour in a useless resistance, and no glory in a swing from the yard-arm. Well, as I'm the chief loser, and run the worst risk, I hope you will profit by my example ; the true test of a brave man is this, he can always stand reverses without grumbling."

The boats ran along side.

A revenue officer came on board with a number of stern-faced myrmidons.

"So, you have run aground at last, my hearty," said the officer, with a laugh, and clapping his hand on the young smuggler's shoulder.

"Aye, sir, fortune's as fickle as a chopping wind that blows round the compass before you can bout ship," returned Paul, cheerily, yet turning his eyes with a glancing regret upon his gallant little barque. "I'm sorry for the Nelly, sir ; I have run many a cargo with my little schooner, as you know ; but, I trust my cruise is not over, Mr. Badger, for all that."

"No, my fine fellow," returned the officer, "there's promotion and prize-money for you yet ; it maybe you'll have a month or two on leave in the goal at Penzance, and then you'll go with your heroes ; you will serve the king on board a man-of-war."

"Look you, sir, you will find a man below whom we picked up half drowned on the beach ; he is not of our crew, he is a king's man. I thought it best to mention it, lest you should clap him into irons and send him off to Penzance with the rest of us."

"Well, my hearty, I'll investigate. Sampson, the darbies ; when you get ashore keep to your orders, and avoid Sewardine."

A dry smile curled the lips of Paul Adair at these words.

The handcuffs were fixed on the wrists of each of the men belonging to the crew of the Nelly.

While a dark, sinister-looking fellow was fixing the manacles on Paul's wrist, the young smuggler whispered in his ear.

"Couldn't save ye," muttered the man, in reply.

Paul whispered again.

"Too late, I tell ye."

"Will they break ?" asked the smuggler.

"Like glass ; there's a flaw in the steel."

"Right ; send word to Penreal, do you hear, mate ?"

"Aye, aye !"

"Mark ye, mate, no pulling the bow-oar in an admiral's galley for me or mine ; no tender-ship, no back-scratching, no oakum-picking. Do you hear ?"

"Aye, aye !"

"Tell Thorkil what I expect of him. I've friends in Penzance."

"Avast ! old Badger is watching us."

"Very good. But see that you don't forget what I've told you."

"And now, as everything is clewed up," said the officer, with a laugh, "take the prisoners ashore, clap them into Penzance gaol, and join me at Seawardine."

"Aye, sir."

"And now I'll go below, and overhaul the stores. Good morning, Master Adair. I trust you'll do your duty to your king and country, and steer clear of the gratings, and the yard-arm. Sampson !"

"Aye, sir."

"Rendezvous at the 'Anchor,' at Seawardine."

"Aye, sir."

The men put off the boats with their prisoners.

"I wish," muttered Paul Adair, "I had seen that sailor chap. I wonder what the rev hawks will do with him."

CHAPTER XIV.

SHARING THE PLUNDER—THE DUTCH SMUGGLER—THE WRECKERS' SPY — STRANGE NEWS — THE WRECKERS RESOLVE TO RESCUE PAUL ADAIR—TRELAWNY'S MISGIVINGS.

BLACK WILL TRELAWNY, Thorkil Penreal, and the rest of the wreckers, were assembled in an immense cavern beneath the rocks, in the recess of the little creek called the Seal's Cover.

The magazines of these rascals were very extensive, and their stores heterogeneous and valuable.

Light was admitted to the cavern through a large hole in the rocky wall on that side of the cave which gave upon the sea.

This outlet was carefully masked by a pile of loose stones, arranged in such a way that the light streamed in through their interstices.

A heavy gun, mounted on a rude, unwieldy carriage, was run back on its breechings, and pointed across the room ; by the side of it was a heap of shells and grape-shot.

The men had met to receive their sharings from the plunder of the wreck.

The proceedings were conducted by Thorkil with much dignity and great impartiality, and the men seemed to be perfectly satisfied with his distribution of the spoil.

At the foot of the table, sipping from a glass of the strongest Schiedam, a short, broad, fat, red-faced man was sitting.

He was very corpulent, and waddled in his walk, had a voice harsh and husky, and wore a great black beard.

He was dressed in a blue guernsey, wore high and heavy boots, a scarlet cap, and had in his belt a couple of monstrous pistols.

At a little distance from him sat a broad, freckled-faced, sandy-haired German, with faint blue eyes, and expressionless features. His dress was similar to his companions, but a long knife was the only weapon he wore.

These worthies were Michael Guldenhoff, master of the barque Der Adler, of Rotterdam, and his mate, Hans Berthold.

Black Will Trelawny sat moodily apart, his raven hair hanging down upon his forehead, his arms folded, and his wild, black eyes fixed on the ground.

Both the Dutchmen were smoking pipes, with bowls about the size of tea-cups, from which the smoke clouded up like the smother from a lime-kiln.

"Aye, Mynheer, a good haul, I assure ye ; and only to think, a frigate of war !" said Thorkil.

"Ach ! zat ship go down, also. No von vos save ?"

"Not a soul, as I think, and we got all her stores and ammunition, mess-chests, spars, canvass, cot-clews, and even her guns !"

"Och Himmel ! zat vos vonderful, zat. And vot for a skipper had dis ship ?"

"A fellow who knew his way aloft—a friend of my partner's, Black Will."

"He vas drown also ! and vat does Mynheer Redfearn ?—how goes it mit him ?"

"Lost the pretty cargo he bought of you—run down by the infernal revenue-cutters. I suppose he had paid you for the freight ?"

"Nein ! Mein Gott ! lost ze cargo ! Zavanzig—

tventy barrels of de best branty, to zay not von vord of ze Schiedam! Pay me! Nein, nein! Herr Thorkil, not pay me von dam kreutzer!"

Penreal laughed.

"Well, such are the fortunes of war! Come, Mynheer, freshen hawse. Don't spare the black strap. To-day we lose and to-morrow we win; such is life's cruising. Drink, Mynheer; remember what the old song says—

'Every Dutchman's draught should be
Deep as the rolling Zuy der Zee.'"

"Tonner and blitzen! I vish dat I vas roll in de Zuy der Zee when I trust ze cargo to zis Eselkopf, dis head of a jackanass!" roared the Dutchman, in great wrath and vexation.

At this moment a voice was heard without the door which surmounted some rudely carved steps on one side of the cave.

A challenge was given by a sentinel without, and was gruffly answered by another voice.

The door was opened.

A man, closely mantled, entered.

He came down the steps, and, as he advanced towards the table, he pulled off his fur cap and shook back his cloak.

He appeared dressed in the uniform of a boatman of the Preventive Service.

Thorkil started up, and looked at him inquiringly.

The Dutchmen took their pipes from their gaping mouths, and peered from under their shaggy brows at him with surprise and curiosity, evidently astonished at his appearing in the wreckers' stronghold in his Governmental uniform.

"What cheer, Lacon? What news from Penzance?" asked the chief of the wreckers.

"Bad enough, Master Thorkil—very bad!"

"Well, let's have the worst of it?"

"Paul Adair——"

"Taken?"

"Aye, he and all his crew!"

"Phew!" whistled Penreal, with a blank look.

"Vat you call zat? Taken! Anoder cargo lost also! You not tell me zat?"

"Every cask! the craft seized, the men in bilboes, and the revenues boozing their jibs and forecasting their prize-money."

"My timbers! and where are they, Lacon?"

"At Penzance, I tell you."

"And where are the Gannet and the Dreadnought?"

"Off the Lizard, looking out for Mynheer's barque, the Adler."

The fat Dutchman started up, his broad face flushing scarlet, his limbs trembling with rage.

"Zay look for me! Vot for men are zay dat tink they can take my cargo, ha? Do zay know I have on board of Der Adler two swivels and a stern-chaser, ha? I swear also, if zay vill take me, I vill blow zem to der teufel!"

"And what does he expect us to do for him, Lacon?"

"To rescue him out of the hands of the revenues."

"Cool that, certainly."

"He says it may be done."

"By a King's warrant or a press-gang?"

"By you."

"By me! Am I a Sampson, to carry away his prison-doors?"

"No, but you may be the rat to nibble away the lion's net."

"What do you say, Black Will Trelawny? I never was one to desert a messmate when run down by the law-sharks. What's to be done?"

"Curse me, if I care!" returned Black Will, roughly. "Paul Adair is no friend of mine."

"While he is in league with the band you are bound to befriend him, partner," returned the chief of the wreckers, quietly.

"Be it so; I'm ready for any work; the more dare-devil the better. Suppose we go in a body to Penzance, and make a bold stroke of it—tear up the hatches, and let the birds out of the hold."

"Shiver me, Will, but it does me good to hear you hail the deck so cheerily."

"Well, mate, let us call the men together."

"Ay! Where's Harleck?"

The ferocious-looking wrecker, who was lying as if asleep in a corner of the cave, raised himself on his arm.

"Here, cap'en," he said.

"Go round to the cabins, turn in at Polruth's kiddleawink, fire the long gun off the Black rocks, bring the men together to the Seal's Cover, and let them come armed. Be alert, my hearty; trip anchor at once."

"Aye, cap'en," responded Harleck, as he rose and left the cavern.

"And now, Thorkil, I must be off," said Lacon; "mine is a service of danger; it's hard to serve two masters."

"And they were all taken?"

"Aye, cap'en, all but the man they had aboard; the revenues left him in his hammock when they fitted a jury-mast and sailed off with the cargo."

"What man was that?"

"A chap they had picked up from the wreck of the Thetis."

"Ah!" cried Black Will, "did you see him?"

"No. I believe, though, he was one of the cocked hats; he was dressed like a skipper."

"Did Paul Adair speak of him?"

"Yes. He explained to the officer that took him that the man below did not belong to his crew, and that he was one of the ducks from the frigate."

"Where did they find him? Was he adrift on a spar, or did they pick him up under the cliffs?" asked Trelawny.

"Hang me if I know; but the barque is in the hands of my mates, and I will get full particulars of this fellow. I fancy they will run her into Plymouth harbour. The Dreadnought is her convoy."

"Mark ye, Lacon, we must save Paul Adair if we can; the men must not lose confidence, and Paul is a useful ally."

"And how do you mean to manage it?"

"In this way. Mynheer's men shall go to the different inns and kiddleawinks in Penzance, and shall pretend to be a crew on leave from some Dutch merchantman; the band will go severally, or in very small parties, to visit their friends in Penzance, and, as fortune ordains, there's a market-fair to day."

"Nothing could be better arranged, Thorkil. I see what is intended; at night there will be a riot, and the crew will break into the shanty of a prison and let out the captives."

"Even so."

Harleck entered the cave at this moment.

"Cap'en, the men are mustering," said the wrecker.

"That's well. Come, Mynheer, you will render us your assistance," said the chief of the wreckers.

"Yah! I vill send for ze hands from zeer Adler," replied Guldenhoff, "and ve vill cut ze throats of ze swines zat rob me of my cargo; and when I have zet Mynheer Paul free, I vill make him pay ze debt of zat dummelkopf, zat blockhead, Redfearn; for I vill not lose my guilders for all ze revenue-cutters in your island of Britain."

A man rushed hurriedly into the cavern.

"Cap'en!" he said, breathlessly, "the revenues have taken the Nelly of Seawardine!"

"Avast! you skulk; a precious look out you," growled Thorkil, "she is in dock by this time. One of the revenues brought us the news of her capture while you were sleeping on your post or boozing in some kiddleawink. You must keep your weather-eye wider open, hearty, or it will be worse for you."

"But he didn't bring you news, cap'en, of her being run down and retaken together with her convoy?"

"Is it so?"

"Ay, cap'en; that's all fair and above-board, I do assure ye; I heard the guns myself off the Lizard, and, after a time, three ships hove in sight. I made out the Dreadnought and her prize the Nelly, while close astarn a French schooner, I should say she was a privateer, was raking the Dreadnought with a starboard broadside; the revenues cut the tow-rope and tried to sheer off, but lost her mizen-top, and was forced to strike her flag; she will be snugly moored in Brest before six bells first watch to-morrow."

"And what privateer do you think it was that overhauled the cutter?"

"I should say, from her rakish build, she was the Hirondelle," replied the wrecker.

"Then there will be no news of the Thetisman," murmured Black Will.

"I heard of him from one of the revenue men."

"Ha! had he seen him?"

"No; none that came ashore had seen him; but they say he was one of the officers."

"Was he wounded?"

"Can't say."

"Paul Adair knows the skipper of the Hirondelle," said Thorkil. "And if we are lucky enough to rescue him he will find out all you wish to learn concerning this poor devil you seem so curious about. Meanwhile, I'll step out and speak to the men. Meantime, messmate, do you look up some barkers and boarding-pikes, for I'll have young Paul, dead or alive, though I storm the town of Penzance."

CHAPTER XV.

THE PRISONERS—PROSPECTS OF A RESCUE—AT-
TEMPTED ESCAPE OF PAUL ADAIR—THE PISTOL
SHOT—A BRUTAL OFFICIAL—A DISCREET MAGI-
STRATE—THORKIL HARANGUES THE MOB—THE
CITIZENS PROCEED TO VIOLENT MEASURES—THE
RIOT.

HANDCUFFED in couples, the crew of the Nelly, about a dozen men, exclusive of the captain, were marched along the road that, winding over the cliffs, led to Penzance.

The chief boatman walked ahead of the party, a drawn cutlass in one hand, and a loaded pistol in the other.

On either side of the prisoners walked the crew of the boats which had overhauled the smugglers' barque, each man having a flashing cutlass in his hand and pistols in his belt.

Paul Adair walked erect with a bold step, a firm look resting on his face.

Blane was by his side.

From time to time the men conversed in low whispers.

Two revenue officers were at the rear.

The party passed a row of hovels.

The half-barbarous natives of the sterile coast rushed out from their doors or thrust their heads from windows.

Their sympathies were with the smugglers, and they saluted the preventives with ironic jeerings.

The prisoners nodded at the cottagers, and laughed, as if being taken prisoners and put in irons with the certain prospect of penal confinement in the hulks, or what, to most of them, was quite as distasteful, on a man-of-war, were nothing but a matter of sport.

The Cornish lads who hung before the doors of the kiddleawinks, fellows who had all at some time or other been engaged in smuggling, hooted the escort, and were only restrained from attacking them by their formidable display of deadly weapons.

The stern-visaged preventives took no notice of the taunts by which they were assailed.

"Cap'en," whispered Blane, as they neared the town.

"Well, mate?"

"Shall we try a run."

"What, with our arms lashed akimbo?"

"It might be done."

"How?"

"Hush! the fellow on our lee-bow eyes us like a ferret watching rabbits."

"There's a fair to-day."

"Aye, there's a fellow aboard a land-lugger, see how he pulls up the tiller-ropes and heaves too as we passed. Did you notice how he signalled me with his weather-eye?"

"What, the fellow on the shaft of that waggon?"

"Aye, he sits on the jib-boom with a one-tailed cat to keep his crew from skulking."

As Blane made this remark a heavy wain with a couple of fine black horses with jingling bells on their heads and necks rumbled by; an evil-looking fellow, dressed as a carter, but with a swart and villanous countenance that gave him more the appearance of a pirate or a highwayman, sat on the shaft, and touched up the horses with a long whip.

This fellow stared earnestly in the faces of the luckless captain and mate of the Nelly.

He winked his eye, pointed his thumb significantly over his shoulder, as if to intimate that his load consisted of something else besides the two trusses of hay that were covered so carefully by such expansive tarpauling, and then clapped his whip to his left side and laid his right hand on the top of it.

"Do you make out his signals, cap'en?"

"Aye, mate."

"Cutlasses!"

The carter had passed on with his waggon whistling the tune of an old sea-song.

Paul Adair gave a low, chuckling laugh.

"Hearty!"

"Aye, Cap'en."

"Did you think old Thorkil had so much pluck in him?"

"I should scarcely have thought it."

"Can you guess what he means to do?"

"I think so. It's a desperate venture."

"Every man that's not a preventive along this coast is a smuggler, and half the preventives are smugglers themselves."

"Then the odds are not so long as they look."

"No!"

"Cap'en."

"Well, Jack?"

"What sort of hulk is the prison-ship to which they are towing us?"

"Not seaworthy, mate; a chap with a tolerably solid brain-cap might jump through the bulkhead like a harlequin through the milliner's window, without damage to his figure-head."

"But these cursed bilboes! if either of us was free from these cable-chains we might manage to steer round the bluffs of one of the houses and sheer off. I wonder that skunk Lacon should have clapped you into darbies."

"Avast! mate, as our convoy has fallen a point astarn I will put you up to a secret. There is a flaw in this pretty chain work, and I can snap the iron as easily as Sampson rent his doxy's seven strong hawsers."

At this juncture they arrived in the town.

The place was densely crowded.

All the streets leading to the market place were crowded with the inhabitants of every neighbouring village. Carts, horses, cattle, sheep, mountebanks, musicians, farmers, clod-hoppers, sailors, screaming women, and squalling children blocked up the way.

It was not without the greatest difficulty that the preventives could get their prisoners along through the yelling, bustling crowd.

It was very plain that the town's folk seemed anxious to throw every possible obstruction in the way of the escort.

And nothing but the determined air of the men, and the fact of their being so effectively armed, deterred the mob from attempting a rescue.

At length the party reached the prison. It was a small grey stone building, in a dilapitated condition, and did not appear to have many inmates.

There was a good deal of delay before the party were admitted within the walls.

Meanwhile the crowd without groaned at the officers, and cheered the prisoners.

Paul Adair turned his handsome face to the people—tossed back his head, shaking his rich curls from off his clear brow, and laughed and nodded at several of his acquaintances.

Several men held out their hands to him.

He glanced down with a dry smile upon his handcuffs and shrugged his shoulders.

Several of the bystanders tried to grasp him, but the revenue men pushed them back, brandishing the cutlasses in their faces.

The doors at length were opened; the governor of the gaol and some of his people appeared on the scene.

The mob still yelled and hooted.

Paul Adair stood a little on one side.

His men passed in file before him.

The last who entered the prison door was the black, Mingo.

The negro turned his ebon face to the mob, he ducked his head, rolled his thick lips and showed his huge yellow fangs in such a comically hideous grimace, that the mob screamed with laughter.

It was at this moment that Paul Adair whispered Blane,

"Now, mate, as I can have the advantage of free hands, I'll make a run for it. Tell my lads that if ever they carry powder, or swab the main-deck of a man-of-war, while they serve me, I will give them leave to say that there is not mettle nor honour in Paul Adair."

With this the captain of the Nelly stooped a little and made a dart between two of the preventive men. They slashed at him with their cutlasses.

Paul had wrenched his wrists round in such a manner that the flawed steel shattered like broken glass.

The daring smuggler leaped into the arms of the mob.

They received him with a hearty cheer.

One of the revenue officers fired.

Paul Adair staggered and fell on his face.

Some of the mob gathered round him, and lifted him in their arms.

The yelling was terrific.

Wielding their cutlasses, the preventives made a charge.

Paul Adair was recovered.

The handsome face of the young smuggler was very pale.

His eyes were closed.

The blood welled from a wound in his shoulder, and stained his guernsey crimson.

Two of the men lifted him.

They bore him up the steps.

Just as they were passing under the arched door a wild shriek was heard.

A girl flew up the steps.

She flung herself upon her knees.

With a bitter sob, she extended her hands to a red-faced, stout, irascible-looking officer.

"Oh, sir!" she cried, between her sobbings, "one word, for human pity! Is he—is he killed? Let me look in his face—I shall know in an instant. Do—pray—pray let me have one little glimpse of him."

"Pooh, pooh! ridiculous! Stand back, young woman; you *look* respectable; but, to go mad about a smuggler fellow! He is well enough, and will live to be hanged, as he deserves. Go home, do; go away, I tell ye, or I'll turn you over to the beadle, you young hussey!"

The girl had clung pleadingly to his arm.

Greatly irritated, the officer pushed her back.

Her foot slipped, and she fell heavily on the steps.

It was well for the officer that he had quickly entered the prison and clapped too the door, for some one in the crowd fired a pistol.

The bullet thudded into the oaken door just at the spot which the round, fierce face of the blustering official had occupied.

The people yelled and hooted around the prison.

Stones were thrown at the walls and windows.

The people seemed worked up to a high pitch of excitement.

In the midst of the hubbub a number of the more orderly sort tried to appease the wrath of their companions.

This minority, however, was sadly ill-treated, hustled, and driven off the field.

Enraged by this usage, and not sufficiently strong in numerical force, they made a general rush to the house of an illustrious tallow chandler, who enjoyed the dignity of the city's mayoralty.

They found, to their surprise, that the patriotic magistrate, feeling that example is far better than precept, had shut up his shop, and retired to bed.

They were, moreover, informed, somewhat shrewishly by the wife, from the battlements of the first-floor window, that so much shocked and disgusted had the chief magistrate felt himself by the scandalous behaviour of his rebellious fellow-citizens, that he had virtually abdicated his civic throne, and was resolved in no way to meddle with the rabble or its disputes.

Around the prison prevailed a scene of terrible confusion.

A tall, handsome, though sinister-looking fellow, dressed in a guernsey and high boots, with his arched and black brow bent in a dark frown, his rolling black eyes flashing with anger, dashed through the crowd, and leaping on a barrel in the middle of the market-place, held up his hand for silence.

From all points, evil-looking fellows, with ugly knives and savagely-clutched fists, stole towards the orator, and gathered round him in a thickening phalanx.

"Men of Penzance ! brave Cornish lads ! listen to me !"

So stately and commanding was the attitude assumed by the chief of the wreckers, that a sudden hush testified the respect of the crowd for the handsome and daring-looking demagogue.

"You have all seen to-day an act of injustice," cried Thorkil, in his clear, deep voice, "a deed of black and brutal cruelty, perpetrated by the revenue officials, mark ye, the *revenue* officials, the publicans that take tithes, which would not be tolerated by the tamed and slavish Turks in the streets of Algiers. Let us be thankful we have a strange king sent to us, a foreigner of whom we know nothing ; and, to fill his coffers and those of his outlandish parasites, heavy imposts are laid on the drink that makes our hearts merry ; the spirits that give Dutch courage to the very coward, and makes the half-starved, toil-worn Cornish poor forget how the wind is bad for fishing, and the soil is barren for sowing. Is it such a crime to run a cargo, my Cornish lasses and lads, and to snatch a few tubs of good stingo from the clutches of the custom-house sharks ? Are ye not sea-born sons of those real ancient Britons, who chose this stony 'Land's End' of the island that they might be free and do as they liked ; might make amends for a sterile soil by taking what the sea sends them, and keeping the fog out of their hearts by a dram of good spirits. Is the crime of running a cargo, which is charged, but, mind ye, not proved against a handsome, jolly Cornish lad like Paul Adair, to be punished by being shot down like a mad dog in the street, and his gentle sweetheart stunned to the earth before your faces, while pleading for a glance at her murdered lover ? Dam'me, are ye Cornish men and will stand that ?"

"No, no, no !" roared the mob. "We'll sack the prison first !"

"There is no chance for ye, Cornish lasses ; you must fight for the few old or crippled that are spared you, for every saucy, bonnie lad is snatched from your arms to be lashed to the gratings and flogged at the orders of every cursed Saxon gold-scraper that struts the quarter-deck of a man-of-war—is set up to be shot at by foes that never injured you or me, and if he escapes with the loss of his limbs is sent to crawl about the land to beg for charity, or die if he is too proud for that. Will you stand this, sons and daughters of Caractacus, with the Druid-stones and the logan-rock always before your eyes as monuments of your lost freedom ? Where is the good old spirit ? If you have any blood in your hearts—if you are not lily-livered skunks, only fit to be slaves to your Saxon masters, for what the devil have they to do with us ?—I say, if you are strong men and kind women, and not fawning dogs and silly sheep, up, up, and revenge this poor lad and lass, and set his mates at liberty !"

"We will ! we will !" shouted the mob. "Down with the sharks ! down with them !"

A zest for mischief spread through the crowd like wild-fire.

Men rushed home and armed themselves.

Crowds rushed round the prison, roaring for the liberation of the captives.

Sticks and guns, and hatchets and knives, were furiously brandished, and the stones and other missiles poured against the windows of the gaol like hailstones.

CHAPTER XVI.

WITHIN THE WALLS—THE SIEGE—THE STORMING— THE RESCUE OF SMUGGLERS—THE WRECKER AND THE CHILD—THE FAITHFUL DOG TO THE RESCUE.

WHILE this scene was enacted without, one of scarce less violence was passing within.

The captives had been removed in a body into a stone room,

The warders and officials connected with the prison were few in number, and greatly over-awed by the turbulent, lawless populace of the town.

The revenue-men, as before stated, were, many of them, directly or indirectly connected with the smugglers.

The roar of the people without, the thudding of the stones against the walls, the crashing of glass from the windows, all conspired to fill the revenue-men and the prison officials with dread.

When, pale and passive, the blood streaming from his shoulder, Paul Adair was borne into the stone room, the rage of his crew knew no bounds.

They stamped and cursed, and struggled with their handcuffs.

Even the revenue-men looked darkly on the officious fellow who had fired the shot.

Paul was laid upon the ground.

Blane leaned over him.

The young smuggler opened his eyes.

He looked up into the face of his comrade, and faintly smiled.

"What cheer, cap'en, the sharks have not cut your cable yet ; you will live to run many another cargo, in spite of the sharks."

"I hope so, Jack. I thank the skunk for one thing," murmured the smuggler, gently ; "I did not think poor little Nelly loved me so much."

THE COCKNEY FINDS HIMSELF IN A STRANGE PLACE.

The goaler raised the young smuggler, and the prison doctor came to his side, and kneeling down felt his pulse.

"How is he, doctor?" asked the man who had fired the shot, with a pale face, for the mob without were howling and hooting frantically.

"His wound is serious," returned the physician, curtly.

A man ran into the stone-room, his eyes staring, his arms extended, his hair on end, the picture of dismay.

"Mr. Shackles; where is Mr. Shackles?" cried this fellow, in trembling tones.

"Here, here; what is it?" cried the governor of the gaol, turning quickly.

"Oh, sir, deliver up the prisoners; the mob will tear down the place as the Jews did Jericho, and sow the ground with salt. I'm wounded already, sir; here's a bump on my head as big as a cocoa-nut; I got it by running foul of a turn in the passage, when a bullet smashed through the window. O lord, sir, do surrender, we shall all be murdered, and my wife has just weaned my thirteenth child ! We're all married, sir, or ought to be. Pray give up the smugglers, sir, or the wretches will burn us alive !"

"Hold your tongue, fool !" cried the governor, stamping his foot ; "I trust I shall do my duty to his Majesty, and not give up these felons to the lawless ruffians till I have resisted to the last. Revenue-men, you are armed, go on to the roof and threaten the people by a show of weapons."

Every face was pale, every limb trembled, nobody stirred to do their superior's bidding.

Paul Adair slowly opened his eyes, and feebly raised his hand.

The roar without was tremendous.

"Blane, are you near ? It's the leak, I fancy ; I faint like a wench in a crowd. Are you near ?"

"Aye, aye, cap'en !" murmured Blane, with a sob. "Lord love you, close along side."

"Who shot me ?"

"Ben Penrowen ; but, rest quiet, we'll revenge you ; we'll have the scoundrel's life, never fear."

"Blane, there's no mutiny, eh ? I'm skipper !"

"Aye, cap'en, you can't complain of us."

"No, no ; I don't mean that, Blane. All of you protect Penrowen, he only fired at his man ; I don't blame him. Promise, Blane ; I'm so dizzy—I—I—am going to sleep."

"I promise, cap'en, though it's hard."

"But, Blane ?"

"Aye, cap'en."

"Who struck Nelly Britton ? I can't say I saw it ; but I know it. Who was he, mate ?"

"Wat Tredegar."

"Cut his throat some of ye, will ye ? Good night ; if there's a rescue, don't tow me along too roughly. Lord, I bleed to death, Blane !"

"Cap'en ?"

But there was no reply ; the young smuggler sank back and swooned.

An awful crash at the outer doors was heard, followed by a triumphant yell.

There was a door in the stone-room opposite to that which opened upon the passage leading to the gates.

Through this door all but the governor and the prisoners made a headlong rush.

Penrowen was the last to fly to the door.

His foot slipped.

He fell prone.

He was immediately surrounded by the smugglers.

The opposite door was burst open.

Black Will, Trelawny, and a throng of desperadoes rushed in, brandishing weapons and torches.

When they beheld the prisoners they set up a wild huzza.

"There is the villain who killed him, messmates !" cried Thorkil, who, upon glancing at the pale face of Paul Adair, believed him to be dead.

"There is the spy, for I know him for a smuggler, like the rest of us," he went on, pointing to the trembling Penrowen, who crouched in a corner. "Upon him, mates, scuttle his hull ; down with him !"

With a yell of execration a dozen fellows rushed upon the cowering wretch.

Blane threw himself before him.

"Hands off, my hearties ; it's the cap'en's orders that he shan't be hurt. Queer orders, you'll say ; but I'll see 'em carried out, though I shiver to pistol him. Stand clear, hearties ; sheer off, I tell ye, you shall not reach him without shoaling over my carcass."

"This is infernal stupidity, Jack ; the skipper is skipper no longer ; we'll do ourselves the pleasure

of revenging his death," cried Thorkil. "If you are dying for pleasure of that sort, give chase to the Wat Tredegar, and when you've overhauled that craft, burn or sink at your good will. He struck Nelly Britton, the skunk, and it was the cap'en's last wish that he should be keelhauled."

"Where is he, where is he ?" roared the mob, athirst for mischief.

"He's gone through that bulkhead up the gangway, hearties ; set sail, and run him down some on ye, while the rest knock off our darbies."

With a shout a number of the ruffians darted through the door.

The rest soon set the smugglers free of their manacles.

The governor interposed.

The intrepid fellow was struck down.

The blood-thirsty Penreal pointed a pistol at him.

He was, however, pulled back by several wild-looking men, with short cropped hair, and dressed in prison clothes.

"No, no, mate ! let him bide," shouted the new comer ; "he's a humane man ; we like him."

When Thorkil saw that the governor's deliverers were the convicts under his charge he laughed roughly, and turned away.

"Mate, what stores aboard ?" he asked of one of these men.

"Darbies, whips, stocks, skilly and oakum," returned the fellow, with a laugh.

The wrecker gave a growl of disgust.

"We'll set the place a-fire, eh, cap'en ?" said the savage wretch, Harleck, with a leer.

"No, mate," returned the wrecker ; "we've raised enough smoke already ; we shall have the yeomanry burning their noses. We must weigh anchor while the wind's in our sails. Some of you look up Adair, and all of you follow me ; and, remember, lads of my band, there's the same protection for the humblest among ye, that serves me faithfully, and I'm as ready to punish treachery ; remember that also."

The rioters were received on the steps with a deafening cheer from the surging crowd without.

CHAPTER XVII.

THE SMUGGLERS AT THE KIDDLEAWINK —A COCK-NEY ON HIS TRAVELS—A DRINKING BOUT, AND ALL ABOUT IT.

A LARGE party of the wreckers and smugglers were collected in the tap-room of Murdoch Polruth's kiddleawink.

They were carousing with great enjoyment, and discussing the late events over their grog.

"Yes, hearties," said Agger ; "there never were a king of the wreckers more fit for his post than Thorkil ; he's as hard as the Fin and as true as the compass ; but, I'm thinking, that they won't take the rescue of Paul Adair and his men so easy as might be wished at head quarters. You may depend on't ther'll be a fine bobbery, and shouldn't wonder if they sent a whole company of the jollies to drive us out of our stronghold."

"But you were speaking of Bradford's, saying it had been run down by the Hirondelle prize—the Nelly. Why don't you keep to your tack ?" rejoined Harleck, gruffly.

"Well, mate, I arn't the fust as has ' missed stays ;' but what I wants to remark is the perwention of Providence : a whole crew of revenue-sharks, their cutter and prize, fallen into the hand of Johnny Crapand."

"'Providence disposes, man proposes,'" Murdoch Polruth joined in, with gravity. "This Bradford thought he was going to seize my house, and all Nat Redfearn's last cargo."

"He's lucky," growled that smuggler fiercely, dashing his fist on the table till the glasses leaped and jingled; "it's four year agone since he robbed me of the prettiest little cargo ever I run, and I mean to pay his reckoning."

"But who's the land crab that was seen at Penzance, this morning? I saw him in the market-place, hearties, and a queer fish he seemed, and no mistake," said Polruth.

"Hist! talk of the devil—and here he comes!" cried Agger, holding up his finger.

The door was opened, and an eccentric-looking personage peeped in.

He drew back for an instant, and then entered timidly.

He was a short fellow, dressed in a suit of plaid cloth of a large pattern; he had a knapsack on his shoulder, in his hand a little hammer, such as used by geologists, in the other an umbrella, while upon his nose was a large pair of green spectacles.

"Come in, yer honour," cried Polruth, winking at his companions. "You'll find us rough and ready, but leastways quite at your sarvice; we arn't much used to gentl'em of the hadmiralty, but we're old salts, and knows our duty; and if yer honour's disposed to freshen hawse, why all I've got to say is as there arn't a kiddleawink, from Falmouth to Mount's Bay, which offers safer anchorage, or better spirits than the 'Jolly Mariners.'"

"My dear fellow—extwemely obliged; I'm bound to confess myself weally vewy ignowant of nautical phraseology; but I study the pictuwesqueth," said the stranger, with a smile, half-nervous, half-patro-nising, "and the vagabond pictuwesqueth is my *penchant*."

"I say, Nat, you speak the language. Why don't you exchange signals with mounseer," said Polruth, addressing the smuggler, Redfearn.

"That *ain't* French; don't know his lingo," returned the other gruffly.

"French! now weally, you quite supwise me; but I'm often told that I've the air of a foweigner. Sowwy to say I have not travelled vewy much; I've visited Bologne, and I wead a little French, and should like to understand it better. Monsoo vous etes Français?" he went on, addressing the smuggler.

Redfearn blew a long whiff from his pipe, waved his hand oratorically, and answered with profound solemnity.

"Nong, Mounseer, qui vive! Vin ordinare, il fait botong; sacré pommes de terre, honi sworki-mally-pens."

"Well, Nat, your laruments nat'ral, I s'pose," said Agger, admiringly; "but, shiver me, if your jawing tackle is'nt well rigged; them long words tells out like a greased rope through a hawse-hold."

"It's practice, hearty," returned the other, with a smile of gratified vanity. "I'm reckoned one as could puzzle a lawyer; even the Frenchers them-selves don't understand me, unless they knows me, and then I signals the lubbers with my fists, or my fingers; just listen to this—mon ami junky parlky tray-poo."

"Is that some baby's name? 'junky' sounds like a Chinaman," said Polruth, deferentially. "Lord! what it is to be a scolard!"

The stranger looked upon the rough fellow with much awe.

"You have a vewy fine accent," he said, taking off his green spectacles, wiping them carefully with his silk handkerchief, and once more deftly balancing them on the small fulcrum of his little turned up nose. "Your pwonunciation is twuly we-markable."

"Yes, yer honour, I'm told so; but speechifying in foreign lingos always has a remarkable effect upon my speaking trumpet."

"Pwobably you mean the asophagus."

"I arn't got sich a thing; I mean my winds'l."

"Your windpipe, I suppose?"

"Ah, well, a werry good name too, yer honour. Windpipe is it? French allers makes me dry."

"A vewy seasonable hint—I'm dwy myself, and we must 'fweshen—something.'"

"Freshen hawse, yer honour," cried the smug-glers, in chorus.

"Wemarkable expwession! Well, landlord, pway be good enough to bwing us something to 'fweshen hawse.'"

"Aye, aye, sir; what's it to be?" said Polruth, readily.

"Pewaps, gentlemen pwesent will favour me by allowing me to fill their glasses all wound," cried the traveller, with his weak eyes twinkling through the green gig-lamps, and his cheeks crimsoning.

"Your honour's a trump!" cried Agger, smiting the table emphatically,

"Aye, we ain't proud, none of us," growled Har-leck. "Fill up the grog-kids, Murdoch. And, do ye hear, messmate, be alert and bale from the best punche n—heave ahead."

"Have a quid of 'baccy, sir," said one of the smugglers, extending his tobacco box,

"Extwemely obliged; don't smoke."

"My limbs!" growled Harleck, "what a lubber!"

Murdoch Polruth returned with a couple of cans of the best and most potent spirits.

The men filled their glasses.

"Messmates, we'll drink his honour's health, three times three," said Redfearn, with a knowing look at his companions.

"Aye, mate, in his honour's name," returned the smugglers.

Redfearn looked at the stranger inquiringly.

The little man rose, and glanced round the circle and bowed with a complacent smile.

"Gentlemen! weally! I won't say 'unaccustomed as I am to public speaking,' because that can't be called owiginal; but, pewhaps, you may wish to learn who I am, and where I come from, and, as I am pwarticularly interwested in the county and people of Cornwall, I will exchange confidence with you, and begin by giving you some account of an illus-trious ancestor."

"What's he mean, you sea-lawyer?" asked Agger of Redfearn, in an eager whisper.

"He's a goin' to tell us what port he hails from, hearty."

"But, who's Ann sister?"

"His other sister, in course, you lubber! Stopper all."

"My ancestor, from whom I am pwoud to claim descent, was a distinguished patriot."

"What trade's that?" asked Harleck, surlily.

"And—a—I should expwain, gentlemen—a fish-monger."

"Hear! hear! heave a-head, your honour."

"A patriot's a fishmonger!" remarked Agger to Redfearn, as if greatly delighted with the "wrinkle."

"I twig!" returned Nat, "Thorkil's father had a smack as was called the Masan'ello, and a school-master-swab told me it was named arter a Naples' fishmonger as was a patriot. He were called a *Patriot* 'cos he got up a Irish row."

"But he says he was Ann's sister.''

" Avast heaving !"

"My ancestor was a man of large views——"

" 'Cos he wore green goggles as big as fighting-lanterns," muttered Harleck.

"His views were so large that they extended over the universe ; his experience was limited, because it was restrained to the narrow bounds of St. Nemo's the Needless in the City—he was a churchwarden of that parish — but, alas, gentlemen——"

" There's allus a 'lass' in the case," whispered the loquacious Agger.

" That he was a gweat man the gweatest own !"

" Eighty stone ! Blow me ! a craft of heavy burden, messmates," cried Redfearn.

" My sainted welative was my godfather, gentlemen, and bequeathed me his name, and enough money to keep it in good odour. His name was Theophilus Lobb—excuse my emotions, but man is a worm !"

" A lob-worm," assented Redfearn.

" I wepeat it, gentlemen ; well, I pour a libation to his ashes," and he drained his glass, "for he has long gone the way of all flesh."

" And fish and fishmongers," rejoined Polruth, refilling the glass which his guest had emptied. " Well, sir, he did not drink enough to freshen his clay, or he would have skulked Davy Jones's muster, and would now be as taut as the best on us."

"Pway, don't pwess me to dwink," cried Mr. Theophilus, in great alarm. " I weally must decline ; stwong liquors have the wemarkable property of turning my spectacles into multiplying glasses, and when I imbibe a little too fweely I am guilty of the most widiculous things. I wemember once at a dwinking party I twied to sing the Old Hundredth !"

" Aye, aye, yer honour ! A song ! a song ! belay the speechifying ; let's have a song !" shouted the smugglers, collectively.

The rough fellows clinked their glasses, and simultaneously burst out into an uproarious chorus,

"Fill the can, my jolly, jolly boys,
To him who first gets mellow
We'll drink a toast, my jolly, jolly boys,
And call him the jolliest fellow !"

The roof of the kiddleawink rang with boisterous laughter.

"His honour is fond of music," cried Polruth. "Order ! order ! some of ye sing a stave."

" Aye, messmate, well said ; "give his honour summit real Cornish," cried Agger.

"Harleck's trying to right himself on his pins," rejoined Redfearn, with a laugh ; " he's got a voice as loud as a boatswain's whistle, and deep as the bark of a forty-pounder ; let's hear the sea-dog howl. Silence, fore and aft ; he looks at the moon, and is going to bay."

The atrocious-looking fellow had, indeed, staggered to his feet.

Mr. Theophilus Lobb drew back his chair with an instinct of terror as he caught a glint of the red and hyena-like eyes of the ruffian, who was the very personification of untermable ferocity and brutish malignity.

His face was broad, and had something Asiatic in its shape and swarthy complexion ; his eyes were black as polished jet, and his hair lank and elfish, and coarse as the mane of a bison.

Many a basso profundo on the lyric stage would have envied the rascal the depth, thrilling cl ness, and power of his voice, and there was so thing in which he rolled out the dark words of strange, wild song.

Nothing but the whirling of the wind witl broke the profound and involuntary silence preceded

The Song of the Wrecker.

" When the gale from the north bellows loud on the coast,
When the mist o'er the shoals drifts along like a ghost,
When the sea-gulls fly homeward, the sea-wraiths are c ing,
Then the wreckers are gathered, the water-hag's runing.

" 'Tis a wreck ! 'tis a wreck ! Hark, the hard rocks rebou
To the cry, and I start like a wolf at the sound ;
Like a wolf, when he first scents the prey from his lair,
Or a vulture that swoops at a taint in the air.

" O'er the loud crashing beach, through the bluster and sq
'Mid the hooting of breakers, the hail-arrows fall ;
With my red-flaming brand, like a fiend of the night,
I revel and rave as the ship heaves in sight !

" Ha ! she strikes ! and the strand with rich booty is strew
What is thrown by the sea on our land is our own ;
I heed not death-peals from the prayer-mocking sea,
What is ruin to others is but riches to me !''

When Harleck reseated himself, there was on face a leer so satanic, that, contrasted with thorough good faith of his enunciation and his spectable sentiments, it was some moments be his audience could realise the fact of his ha ceased.

After a moment, however, the silence still prev ing became too oppressive.

A sound, much resembling a heavy sigh, pa round among fellows neither over scrupulous particularly impressionable, and looks of mingled and aversion were cast upon the villainous wrec who showed no particular desire of applause, lifted the can to his lips, and relieved the comp of the uncomfortable spectacle of his glittering and close-set cruel lips for some considerable t by burying his entire face in the grog-kid.

As if to shake off some unpleasant impres the ruffians gave vent to another chorus, and Theophilus, upon whom the "enemy he had into his mouth " had began to assert his sway, g more and more communicative.

" And what I tell you, of course, gentlemen, I you in confidence ; wouldn't mention it, but we I esteem you so much—hic—and my mamma, is to shay, my mother, gave me this advice— shays to me, she shays,

'A fwog he would a wooing go.'

" Thash a wemarkably pwetty little song ; what the deuce that ash to do with what I wa saying—

'Whether his mother would let him or no.'

"Ah, vewy good ! I wecollect what I was sl ing—' my mother would let me or no.' If please, Mr. Polruth, one more glash ; not too sl Weally, I wouldn't be guilty of the disgwac beastliness of intoxication, for I'm study ge-olo-gy, all about stratas and foss-fossils minewals, you know. This is my hammer, bweak—to bweak something ; but, weally, head—there's something the matter with gwasses. It seems, gentlemen, that either I or are walking on the woof, with our heads do ward, but which of us is acting in that widicu manner I can't shay. If you please—but only glash more, Mr. Polruth. P'waps it will give nerve, and sh-shettle my intellects, for, weall

shtop, I'm all wight, perfectly wight. I was a looking for some pebbles I put in my pocket ; p'waps
you can tell me if—no, that's my p-pocket-book,
whe-where I ke-keep my wemittances."

Harleck whispered hoarsely across the table,

"Nat, that's his swag ! grab it ; the lubber's as
helpless as a shoaled porpoise."

"Avast heaving, you shark !" growled Redfearn,
in reply. "If the lubber is his mammy's pet,
without his bib and tucker, he's not a bad chap, for
all that; so, if you don't want your raven's claws cut,
keep 'em on your own side of the table."

Harleck snarled like a dog from whose jaws a bone
has been snatched.

"What cheer, hearty ?—three sheets in the wind,
eh ?" cried Redfearn, slapping Mr. Theophilus on
the shoulder. "Put the helm up, cheery, I shall
sheer off ; it's four bells, and I must run into port,
and you'd better let me convoy you, there's pirates
in these waters. Come, messmate, are you ready to
trip anchor ?"

"Weady for anything. Bwess you, I'm all wight.
But, I shay—scuse me—not formally intwoduced
you. What'sh—hic—I shay, what'sh name ?"

"My name is Nat Redfearn, at your sarvice. But
I say, young chap——"

"Wewy well, Mr. Wedfearn, I'm all wight ; why
I've got in my p-pocket-book five or six bank-notes
and half-a-dozen soweigns."

"Clap too, you fool !" cried Redfearn, fiercely,
catching his arm.

"Strike my top-lights ! Did ye hear that,
Agger ?" whispered Harleck. "Real flimsies, and
a handful of beans !"

"It's quite twue, Mr. Wedfearn ; I'm not without pwoperty," continued Mr. Theophilus, maunder-
ingly, as the smuggler dragged him out of his chair,
" and crowns and half-crowns."

"Bull's and half-bulls !" interpreted Harleck to
his comrade.

Mr. Theophilus was once more upon his legs, or
rather upon the smuggler's arm, for, as in the old
fable, his limbs had rebelled, and the first to strike
were his " pillars of state."

"Mr. Wedfearn," he whispered, confidentially, to
his Samaritan, "what an awful thing is dwunken-
ness. I wouldn't mention it, but all these fellows
are as dwunk as pwinces ; they're all a wheeling
wound and wound, and what seems so pwepostewous
is to see that disgwaceful old clock staggering about
and making the most insultin' grimaces, and telling
infamous lies about the time, wunning his hands
wound the dial, to make a fellah believe it morning,
noon, and night, all jumbled together like my ideas,
for weally——"

"Avast heaving ! " roared Redfearn, administering
a dislocating shake.

"Heaving ! I do feel inclined to heave ; and,
weally, it's enough to make a fellah sick to see all
these poor, weak-minded cweatures a pwey to intoxication."

Amidst the shouts and laughter of the smugglers
and wreckers Nat Redfearn dragged his protegé
into the open air.

No sooner did the poor fellow feel the fresh sea-
breeze blowing upon him than he was so overcome
by the sudden change of atmosphere that he stumbled, and would have fallen to the ground but for
the support afforded him by the smuggler.

However, as he was quite powerless, the men
placed him on a low settle before the door.

As they gathered round him he looked so pale
and seemed so perfectly insensible, that they looked
upon him with some dismay.

"Clear the gangway, mates," cried Harleck ; "let
him get some wind in his sails. Stand back ; I'll
loosen his neck-cloth. Nat, run for some water."

With this the rascal threw himself before the
patient.

With his right hand he fumbled at the necker-
chief, the left he thrust into the capacious side-
pocket.

Some one had gone for water.

Redfearn had placed his finger on the patient's
pulse.

In an instant Harleck had sprung away.

"Stop that thief !" roared Redfearn, to the others.
" Knock him down !"

Harleck turned.

Five or six of the men belonging to Redfearn's
craft rushed after the fugitive.

They suddenly stopped and drew back.

In one hand the rascal held aloft a large pocket-
book, with the other he pointed a pistol at the men
who were advancing to seize him.

By the side of the wall lay a coil of rope-yarn, to
which was attached a heavy block or pulley.

Redfearn seized this as the weapon readiest to his
hand.

Rushing through the vanguard of the smugglers,
he whirled the rope round—the block crashed down,
striking the pistol out of Harleck's grasp.

The weapon exploded.

Nat Redfearn sprang upon the wrecker.

Ding dong and right and left, the two men struck
at each other with their fists, the blows ringing
out most crushingly.

Harleck, however, seemed to have no taste for
this thoroughbred English kind of encounter; and as
he felt his nose spreading across his face, his jaw
receding into his cheek, and was entertained, as to
his eyes, by the most beautiful pyrotechnic fountains
of sparks, he conceived it wise to "assist nature "
by the defensive appliances of art—to this end he
sprang back, warding his face with his left arm, and
gripping at a bone-handle on one side of his belt.

Nothing daunted, Redfearn flew upon him.

The smugglers ran up to the spot.

Harleck was seen running along through the
darkness, something flashing in his hand.

With a stifled groan Redfearn staggered and fell
heavily backwards into the arms of his comrades,
who received the dull weight with a cry of horror
and execration.

All was not over yet.

Redfearn was left in the charge of two of the
men.

The rest ran off in pursuit of the wrecker.

Soon they sighted him.

He was once more engaged in a struggle.

This time with a stalwart youth, who, though
displaying great strength, and having already gained
the advantage over the murderous ruffian of having
disarmed him, showed some awkwardness in the
wrestling.

Soon, therefore, Harleck contrived once more to
break away.

His pursuers followed him close.

He contrived to elude them.

Upon reaching the cliff, at fearful risk, he dashed
over the brow, and scrambled like a cat down into
the darkness.

More than one random shot was fired at him by
his exasperated associates.

But he was lost to sight, and had made good his
escape.

Upon re-collecting around the fainting Redfearn,
who was being softly borne back to the kiddleawink,
the youth who had vainly attempted to arrest the
flight of the assassin appeared, with his left arm

bound in a sling, and his face was pale, as if he were but just convalescent from some bodily injury.

It was Paul Adair, the young adventurer whom Thorkil Penreal had rescued in such a dashing manner from Penzance gaol; he had been carefully tended by Wild Thyra, and nursed by his sweetheart, and was now, with the exception of the temporary powerlessness of his arm, fast recovering from the bad effects of the pistol-shot fired by the revenue-officer on the occasion of his attempted escape.

Redfearn, groaning faintly, was rested for a moment at the foot of a solitary tree, a few yards from the kiddleawink.

He opened his eyes, and feebly beckoned Paul to his side.

"Hark ye, mate," he whispered, painfully; "this infernal brush arose through my taking the part of a silly land-lubber chap, with whom we were boozing our jibs at Polruth's. The infernal wrecker-sharks wanted to pick his bones; I took his part, and, oh lor; that blasted skunk, I'll—I'll roast him alive. And what I meant to say was, take care of the chap, will ye?"

"Aye, mate, I'll take him in tow. Are ye much hurt?"

"Oh, Lord! I—I don't know; don't talk to me; here's the kiddleawink. Curse ye, you mutton-fisted swabs, do you haul a wounded man as if he were a bundle of hammocks in a netting? Easy, and be hanged to ye; so lay me down softly. No good ever came of an honest smuggler's sailing consort with a gang of blasted wreckers!"

Paul Adair went to the settle, where the unfortunate Theophilus still was reclining passively in a stupor of intoxication.

The youth turned to the men.

"Some of you carry this chap to my bunk, below the Puffin Rocks. And, look here, you Thorkil's fellows; who's the biggest thief amongst ye? Oh, you're there are you, Master Agger? A pal of Harleck's, and, by consequence, the greatest robber present on this occasion. Here's this poor chap's money-book; you have charge of it, Agger—you, you thief, and take it with him to my bunk; and if every stiver is not where he left it when he comes to his senses, imagine the consequence, for I never threaten. Make sail, and remember ship's orders!"

CHAPTER XVIII.

ROSE HALLIARD'S ILLNESS—A WILD HOPE—ONCE MORE FACE TO FACE—THE ATTEMPTED MURDER OF THE BOY SAILOR—THE NOBLE HOUND TO THE RESCUE.

UPON the fatal night of the wreck of the Thetis Rose Halliard was carried home to her cottage.

Joel Britton and his daughter had found her lying senseless upon the brink of the cliff from which the murderous Trelawny had hurled her husband back into the waves.

For several days the poor young wife lay in a dangerous state; a raging fever consumed her frail form—her eyes glittered with fiery brilliance, her cheek flushed hot with a scarlet brightness, and on her panting breath, as it swept from her parched lips, came the plaintive moanings of her horror-maddened spirit.

She raved of her husband, she shrieked of Trelawny, she pleaded for mercy, and was almost momentarily asking to be shown the child, which she would clutch to her bosom with nervous tenacity, and could only be separated from it by the use of gentle compulsion.

But Rose Halliard, in spite of her girl-like form and feminine softness, was strong and healthy by constitution, and though so severe, the attack was not of long duration.

Left alone in her cottage after her recovery, Rose Halliard sank into a listless condition of the profoundest despondency.

Even the innocent pratlings of her little son, and the infantile graces of the adopted Lena, for by this name the foundling was generally called among the villagers, failed to rouse her from these fits of gloom and depression.

Sometimes a wild hope sprang up in her heart. She would dream that her husband had not perished—that Trelawny was a murderer in intent, but had not consummated his dreadful purpose—that, though Walter had been cast from the rocks, he might yet have escaped by some miracle; he might have been picked up by some boat's crew—his body had not been found.

So terrible was the agony of her desolation, that sometimes hope would call imagination to her aid to cheer the lorn one, and at such moments the poor girl's eyes would gleam with the ecstacy of the blissful though delusive vision, and her breath would stop as though the very pulse in her heart would jar away the fond imaginings. Then she would give way to uncontrolable grief, and would find solace in a flood of tears.

But Rose Halliard was poor, and she was a pious and sensible girl; she was a mother, and had sworn to protect the orphan of the wreck.

Oft times she had thought of denouncing Trelawny, but, probable as it seemed that it was he who had murdered her husband, so dark was it at the time the fatal deed was perpetrated she could scarcely have identified him upon oath.

The sight of her husband's pale and bleeding face had petrified her—congealed her blood—deprived her of her senses; she knew not how the deed had been done. Like the final pang of a hideous nightmare, the whole catastrophe was felt rather than seen.

But her husband was dead, dead! and the world was a desert.

Yet she was not alone in that desert; she could not sit down in the arid waste and starve. The stock of money her husband had left her was fast dwindling away, and she knew not which way to look for assistance.

She was still possessed of a little, and struggled with mute and exquisite sorrow to keep up the appearance of ease and respectability which had excited the admiration of her friends, and had roused the envy only of the very malignant, for Rose Halliard was universally beloved.

Unfortunately, in the wild and lawless part of the island on which her lot was cast, the people were either half-barbarous outlaws engaged in nefarious traffic in contraband goods, or in the most heartless of all the works of villany, the wrecking on the coast, and there was little chance of her obtaining any other than the most humiliating employment amongst the inhabitants, yet she shrank from the thought of abandoning Seawardine: she would not confess even to herself the true secret of her unwillingness to leave a place in which she had met with such fearful calamities; she would not admit, even to her own heart, the mad hope that sometimes inspired her, notwithstanding the dictates of reason.

One day as she sat in her cottage pondering on the prospect that lay before her, she was suddenly startled, not by a sound, but by the hush which succeeded the musical laughter and the patter of tiny feet that bespoke the presence of little Harry.

Lena was away at the Brittons', and Rose turned to look round the room ; her eyes fell upon the portrait of her husband ; a strange fear arose in her heart, and a thrill of undefined terror ran through her veins.

She ran out of the cottage.

The child was not in sight.

She paused and leaned faintly against a tree.

She pressed her hand tightly upon her throbbing bosom.

Again she moved onwards.

She reached the brink of the cliff.

She started back and threw up her clasped hands with a cry of horror.

It was the first time she had visited the place since the night of the apparent murder.

She quelled her dreadful impulse to fling herself over the precipice, and put an end to the maddening sensations which were almost too much for endurance.

She threw herself on her knees for a moment and prayed.

As she lifted her tear-streaming eyes to Heaven and breathed a few words of supplication with the most fervent devotion, the dark-lowering cloud that hung over her seemed to be rent, and a pale, and then brightening ray of light burst through, and her eye travelled down its oblique pathway, spanning from earth to Heaven as in the angelic dream of the patriarch.

She saw, golden flashing in the sunbeam, the snowy sail of a little barque sailing landward, though still far, far at sea.

Perfectly calm, and with a face touchingly expressive of heavenly resignation, the poor widowed girl rose to her feet and looked once more from the height.

She soon perceived her child ; he stood at the end of one of the water-groins, the great waves tumbling and shouting about him joyously, while he waved round his head a long ribbon of seaweed as if in his childish sport he were signalling the sun-lit sail in the offing.

Neptune was gambolling along the cliffs at a good distance from his young master, and was running in an opposite direction, intent upon the chase of a wounded sea-fowl that screamed and fluttered along the beach.

Rose walked down by the rough path that was hewn in the cliff, and drew near to the child.

She called him to her side.

"Harry, darling, you must not wander to the beach ; you must not come here unless I am with you," said Rose, gently.

"Harry is not afraid of the sea," said the child, gravely ; "but if mamma is frightened, 'spose Harry must wait till he's big before he goes alone in the ship with papa."

" Oh, no, dearest boy ; you must never go to sea —never again, my birdie," cried poor Rose, clutching her child to her bursting heart, and sprinkling his flaxen curls with her bitter tears.

" Bad man hurt papa ; it was not the sea," said Harry, weeping silently, and looking up into his mother's face with childlike awe. " But isn't papa well yet ?—will they cure him very soon ?—will he get up and see the waves again, as Harry did when *he* got well ? Mamma, when will the 'captain' come home ?"

In their happy hours of artless mirth Rose had sometimes taught the little one to call his father "captain."

Rose smiled bitterly, and kissed the child—her heart was too full for speech.

Not old enough to be initiated in the dread mystery of death, Harry could not realise the thought that his father would never more return.

" Will my boy know that bad man if he see him again ?" asked Rose, somewhat eagerly.

She almost started at the strange fire that glowed in the child's soft blue eyes, as he answered, curtly,

" When he is big, Harry will know him."

" We are taught to bless and not to curse," murmured the bereaved girl, with a shudder of suppressed passion ; " but the lesson is hard to learn."

" Rose, look up and speak to me," exclaimed a deep voice at her side, in a husky tone. " Don't stare, don't shriek, I am not a ghoul, nor do I mean mischief."

Tightly the poor girl clasped the child in her shielding arms. She sank on her knees as she turned towards the speaker with a face white as the foam the billows left in long wreaths by her side.

It was Trelawny who stood before her. His arms were folded across his broad chest, and his bearded chin was drooped upon them ; a single black elf-lock fell from his scarlet cap and hung upon his iron brow.

There was a look of sullen contrition on his dark face. He stammered slightly as he continued,

" There must be an end to everything in this world, and there's an end even to my vengeance."

The young mother trembled violently, yet she could not overmaster her feelings of indignation, and she said bitterly—

" It need be so, Black Will Trelawny ; you have done your worst !"

" And I am satisfied ; but, look you, Rose Lavington, if I had not loved you, I should not have done what I have done. That sounds strange ; but, if you reflect, you will see that it's true, and so I'd advise you to let bygones be bygones, for, after all, I love you," he went on with unquailing effrontery.

" Love me !—my husband's murderer !" gasped Rose Halliard, still clinging to her child.

Harry burst into tears.

" Do not cry, my own treasure ; God, who protects the fatherless, will protect us," murmured Rose, soothingly.

" He is a bad man, and—I—I—am a little boy and cannot fight for you mamma. Oh, if I were a man. Go away !" he cried, fiercely struggling to escape from his mother's arms. " Wild Thyra told me of one who was young too, that fought a great giant, for God helped him."

Black Will Trelawny scowled upon the child and receded a step.

" A precious whelp to father," he growled, " always to be yelping at one's heels; but, if its for him you're afraid, you may take my word for it, I'll not hurt him, and, more, I'll do a good part by him, if you don't make a fool of yourself, Rose Lavington."

Rose could only mutter brokenly—

" Murderer !"

The blood tinged the ruffian's face, and he turned savagely.

" Why, in the name of the fiends, do you taunt me with that lie ? He drew his sword on me ; can ye deny it? Why should he cut my throat while I can defend myself? I knocked him off the cliff with my pistol-butt ; I might have blown his brains out. He threatened and attacked me ; but let all that sink to blazes ; I say it again, love for you was at the bottom of all of it. I couldn't brook a rival; I always told you so, and now you see the truth of the saying. Let us refit for a fresh cruise, Rose. What are you going to do for a living, eh ?"

Receiving no reply, the scoundrel burst into a scoffing laugh.

"I see there's many a question easier asked than answered. What are you going to do to feed this fledgling? he won't live upon worms and insects, pretty bird as he is. Does the widow of the late Captain Halliard, of the Royal Navy, intend to turn drudge, to milk farmer Barren's starved cows—or keel the pot in blacksmith Britton's kitchen, eh? What are you going to do, Rose? can you live upon love and recollection? can you dream of playing the admiral's lady while young hopeful breaks your sleep by wailing for hunger? What do you mean to do?"

"Ah! still no answer," continued the ruthless scamp, laughing mockingly. "Well, I'll tell you what you shall do—and then say if you have not mistaken me, and stoop on your bended knees and ask my pardon for flouting and jilting your best friend, and he'll forgive you. You shall have a fine house of your own, servants, and, if it pleases the captain's widow, a coach and horses; jewels shall twinkle in your ears, and silk shall rustle round you when you walk; for I can promise these fine things, Rose Lavington, and warrant performance; for now I follow a better trade than farming. Come, lass, if you've any motherly feeling for the youngster, we'll bury the past in the deep sea, and there's my hand. Say the word, and choose your bridesmaids, for to-morrow we will be married in all due form and ceremony."

Rose Halliard stood erect, her gentle breast heaving, her eyes alight with scorn, and her cheeks crimson with passion.

She cried, in a thrilling voice,

"If I were not the wife of one now in Heaven; if I were unmarried, free, and loved you; if you were king of this rich island, and I starving to death, I would not take that hand, Black Will Trelawny. Why?—because I could not clasp it without wetting my own with blood, because ermine and purple could not conceal the festering leprosy of your awful guilt! As I am the bereaved wife of one whom you murdered in cold blood, the woman whose helplessness you have persecuted with a meanness of cruelty that Satan himself would blush for, in the right of my great wrong, I appeal to Him from whom man shall not arrogate vengeance, to punish you to the full measure of your over-brimming crimes!"

For a moment the villain stood appalled by the vehemence of the wronged and defenceless woman.

Then he gave a forced, gruff laugh.

"Soho! then there's no striking a bargain? No fair sailing, no pardon for the man who would make a lady of you, and keep your beggar brat out of the workhouse or the kennel. Ha! is it so?" cried Trelawny, in a bullying tone. "And my vengeance is satisfied, eh? We shall see, we shall see, you minx!"

He caught her by the wrists, and forced her backwards against a rock.

"My hand is wet with blood, is it? Good, good."

He relinquished his hold, and stepped back, and deliberately unsheathed a glancing knife.

"Rose," he panted, in a paroxysm of fury, "I see now my error; I have *not* done my worst. You are a woman, and if you fancied me would have me, though I had killed a score of husbands. You loved him for his epaulets, as you spurn me because I cannot cut capers like a dancing ape. Well, we will see if there is not a way to reach you yet. Every woman loves her own puling brat. But, curse me, if I do my work by halves; I will not be fooled, by the living thunder! And so——"

He caught the struggling child from the embrace of his mother.

He threw back his arm.

The knife descended like a lightning flash, it's keen point grazing the soft neck of the innocent little one.

With superhuman strength Rose threw her arms round the murderer, and parried the blow.

"No, no, not the child, Trelawny! not the child!" she shrieked. "I was wrong; forgive me; I will pray for you—not the child, spare him. Kill me, if you will. Mercy, mercy, mercy!"

A growl like the roar of a strong lion, a scattering noise on the shingles, a heavy crash.

The next moment showed the monstrous ruffian tumbling and battling on the ground with a huge beast. The struggle was furious; the animal had fixed his strong fangs in the throat of the wrecker, and pell-mell they wrestled together, savage curses and more terrible growlings commingling.

Rose snatched up the child; she fled with the feet of Atalanta along the wild shore, which roared its echoes of the fray.

Thus a second time had the Newfoundland saved the life of the Boy Sailor.

CHAPTER XXIX.

THE COCKNEY TRAVELLER DISCOVERS HIS CONDITION, AND REFLECTS THEREON.

An amalgamation of all that was nauseous, terrific, sickening, head-splitting, and chaotic troubled the visions of the sleeping Theophilus.

Fierce brigand-like faces revolved as if they had been stuck on the spokes of a Catherine-wheel, and were speeding round with such velocity that they either exchanged places, or blent in one hideous distortion; a number of cannibals with flaring torches seemed dancing along a coast, every rock of which was cast in the shape of some gaping monster, and not content with awaiting their "roast" from the wreck, the man-eaters seemed running over the shouting billows and clambering the hull and seating themselves along the jib-boom and yards, severally munching at some dainty limb that had been torn from their living victims. All that was absurdly horrible, and horribly absurd, mingled together in queen Mab's carnival, held in the capacious, and not otherwise cumbered cranium of the unfortunate Cockney in dreamland.

With a sudden jerk and a bilious sense of falling down an unfathomable abyss, Theophilus awoke and opened his heavy, burning eyes, and his furred, fouled, and parching lips.

Surely nature might almost be called an unnatural parent for the severity with which she punishes certain delinquencies. She visits no offence against her wise and noble laws so stingingly as the breach of temperance; she is, indeed, terribly "strict" in chastising those of her children who descend from the place of honour she has assigned them in her well-ordered household, to make beasts of themselves.

But we will leave Theophilus to moralise on his own account.

"Wh-where wam I?" cried this delinquent, raising himself upon his arm, and staring wildly about him while making this remark, so original in such cases. "I weally should be wewy glad to know where I am; in some wemote pwace, I'm conwinced. Wichard, bwing me my hot water, and tell aunt Wachel I shall want some more of them

NOTICE.—The next Number of the Boys' Library will be Published on Friday, July 4th. Order early of your Bookseller.

BOYS' LIBRARY

HARRY HALLIARD;
OR,
THE YOUNG BRITISH TAR.

THE COCKNEY ADRIFT.

camomiles, for I'm expiwing. What the deuce! Yes — no — yes, I weally think I'm aboard the Bologne packet, and the steward's wan away and left me to my fate, awfully sea-sick. Yah!—but I must not talk about that, even to myself, or welse—.''

The poor fellow closed his eyes, and groaned piteously.

Again he opened his "burning orbs."

He passed his hand about his breast, and found that he had all his clothes on except his boots and coat.

He peeped over the side of his hammock.

It was hung rather high, and the floor below seemed whirling about like a quick-shoal.

"How wam I to get out?" he cried, distractedly. "Evewy time I move the widiculous thing cawies me away like a swing-boat at Gweenwich fair. Well, I'll twy; I can't do more than twy."

With a great deal of difficulty the two ropes that swung the hammock were grasped, one in each hand. The result may be anticipated.

The ropes being drawn close together, the bed

collapsed, and, as the lines twined round the wrists of the "sleeper awakened," he hung suspended by his hands, like some victim of the Inquisition undergoing the torture of the cord.

Theophilus kicked and roared lustily.

"Help! help! Won't some Chwistian come and help me?—I shall be stwangled! Oh, lor! it's beginning to bweak, and I shall come down with an awful cwash!"

This was a tolerably safe prediction, and soon verified.

With a shocking concussion the philosopher found where to "sit," and the earth was moved.

With many a mournful moan Theophilus raised himself in a sitting posture.

From such objects as he could detain sufficiently long on the camera of his brain to photograph upon the tablets of his memory, he perceived that he was "cabined and confined" in a sort of boat-house, or store-hut, built in the cover of the cliff, and from a narrow window over-looking the sea.

He rose, and contrived to creep to this outlet.

He looked about for his coat, and eagerly thrust his hands into the pockets, and then let fall the coat with a cry of alarm.

"I've been wobbed! Five pounds and thwee shillings, my lucky sixpence, and a Fwench fwank!"

This balance of the ex-exchequer may somewhat start'e the reader, who remembers the sum mentioned by the traveller, the amount of petty cash on the previous night; but human nature is weak, and the greatest have their failings; Theophilus was addicted to romancing.

"The best thing I can do is to fwy!" he murmured, in great consternation, as reminiscences of last night's orgies and the company with whom he had mingled, recurred to his confused mind. "I wish I could fwy literwally, for I wealey can hardly walk, and I'm dying for my bweakfast; pwaps some fellow has bwought me here for chawitable motives, but more like the wascals mean to detain me for a hostage to get some of their fellow wogues out of pwison by tewifying the government about me. But what shall I do without my specks? if the wetches have only left my gween gwasses I forgive them evewything else."

This unkindest cut of all was spared, and having once mounted his green goggles, he tried the door, but it was locked without.

"I told you so," cried he, addressing himself. "Theophilus Fwederwick, you're a pwisoner!"

He now proceeded to examine the place; the walls were covered with fishing nets, bolts and tackle, floating corks, a harpoon, two or three keys, and some hanks of rope yarn.

A large sea-chest stood in one corner of the room. Theophilus opened the lid, for it was unlocked; to his dismay, he found it full of cutlasses and pistols.

In one corner of the locker was a glossy roll of black silk, round the folds of which appeared a white streak, that looked as if intended to represent a human bone, and just the edge of white skull peeped out among the wrinkles of the black field on which this strange device was broidered.

Just as Theophilus was about to unfold this suspicious bunting, voices were heard laughing without, and there was a rattling at the door.

He dived into the chest and seized two immense pistols that were placed apart from the rest in a separate compartment, and were loaded.

"The wuffins will kill me!" he cried, "but I'm bwave enough to fight when I can't wun. I'll twy to intimidate them." With this he shouted right manfully, "Hulloa there, who are you? Don't you come near me if you've any wespect for your wives, I'm a wegular fuwy!"

Both pistols exploded at once, their charges lodging in the roof, and bringing down a very shower of miscellanies that depended from the rafters.

Paul Adair and Jack Blane rushed in.

Theophilus tried to escape by the window, but found himself checked midway, and held fast.

"Why, you graceless and ungrateful lubber," shouted Paul Adair; "is this my return for picking you up, and giving you cabin passage when I found you a castaway, all adrift among a shoal of ground-sharks that wouldn't have left you the ghost of a mag, or, perhaps, would have stripped your masts of their last bit of canvass? Here, take your purser's bank," he went on, flinging the pocket-book at the feet of Theophilus; "count over your guilders, and see the logs clear, and then sheer off, for, dam'me, if ever I saw such a piece of infernal pirate's trick to fire upon a chap that befriends you. Brush, you swab! you must shift your moorings, I can tell you!"

"My dear sir, now weally," cried Theophilus, in a tone of eagerest apology, "if there's one sort of dewavity I hate more than another it's ingwatitude. Wecollect, if you please, the wewy peculiar pwedicament I was placed in. Upon tumbling out of bed this morning, which is not a vulgar way of expwessing the manner in which I wose, I found myself, to my wewy gweat surpwise, in an unknown wegion; I had a confused wecollection of the events of the past evening; I thought I was entwapped by some wetches for tweasonable purposes; I found the door was locked, and inhewiting something of the fewocity of my wenouned ancestor, I couldn't wesist the weckless impulse to pull the twigger; but, if I had known the weal state of the case, I would have wather turned the weapons against my own bweast!"

"That's all a-taunto, messmate," returned the young smuggler; "but, let me counsel you not to be too ready with the barkers if you don't want to get your own fingers bit. And now where are you going to steer to?—whither bound, my hearty?"

"Weally, sir, if I understand you wightly, you wish to know where I am going to bweakfast?"

"Aye, mate; though, if you like to mess with me this morning, you're welcome. I've some eggs and a pullet, and a loaf of soft-tack my sweetheart gave me, and a bottle of schnapps that I bought cheap for myself. Will you come?"

"Weally, sir, you're wewy polite" returned Theophilus, "and I can't refuse such a good offer. Will you permit me to inquire what is the matter with your arm?"

"Winged by a revenue, hearty."

"A wevenue! Oh, then, you're a smug—a wine-merchant."

"Right, a free-trader; but we can exchange salutes without over-hauling ship's books, and the fewer questions of that kind you put, the more likely you are to receive true answers. Lock that sea-chest, Jack," he went on, addressing Blane, "and we'll weigh anchor, for I must meet Black Will in an hour at the Seal's Cover."

Blane locked up the chest, replaced the pistols, and, with Theophilus, followed the young smuggler from the hut.

"And where do you lay by, shipmate?" Paul asked of the stranger.

"Lay by what?—my money?"

"Aye, mate, and your hulk and tackling."

"I weally don't compwehend!"

"What's your port?"

"My port! Thirty-five shillings a dozen; perhaps you can sell me a bawel cheap, as you wun it free of customs."

The smugglers laughed.

"No! no! hearty. I mean, what are your bearings?"

"My 'beawings!' Ah! I see; you mean 'my beawings as a gentleman.' Well, you know, all my family are distinguished fishmongers, and our cwest is a 'wed hewing passant.'"

"Did you ever see such a queer lubber?" cried Blane, much amused.

"Anyhow, where do you cast anchor?—where do you lay in dock?—what harbour do you put in? —where do you moor?—do you lay off Penzance?"

"Now I compwehend; you speak figwatively, as if I were a ship?"

"Aye, aye, mate, and a queer craft, and no mistake—broad in the beam, and of devilish rum build and rig," said Jack Blane.

"Well then, gentlemen, I cast anchor at Penzance, at a little tavern they call the 'Wose and Cwown.'"

"I know it; it's kept by Jacob Panton, and a sweet pretty pinnace, his daughter Luce. Tell you what, my hearty, you'll want a pilot while you're in these roads, and I'll send one of my chaps to run you safe into Penzance; and, if you'll take a fool's advice, you'll steer clear of these waters, or you will be run down by pirates."

They had now reached a curve in the cliffs, from which they could see the few straggling cottages around the kiddleawink of Polruth.

A smack lay at a little distance from the end of a long sandy promontory, and a boat was dancing over the rough waves towards the shore.

"Cap'en, that's the Dutchman; he is sending his men to know whether the coast's clear, for he's going to run in the cargo from the Adler," said Blane.

"Aye, Jack, they're hailing us from the boat."

"Ahoy!" shouted the men in the boat, as they grounded on the sand-bank.

"Hilloa! what cheer, hearties!" responded Paul Adair.

"Iz das all vell, mein friend Paul?" asked a huge fellow, the second mate of the Adler. "Mynheer Guldenhoff vill run in ze cargo, if all zat be vell."

"All's well," returned the young smuggler. "But, can you tell me, Claus, if the Defiance is cruising off Cornwall? I heard so; but it can't be true."

"Ach, mein Gott! dis is sehr true; dere iz not miztake about zat. Von man-of-var, mit a teuflish freight of guns and shots, and mit a crew of five hundert men. I vish also dat Mynheer Guldenhoff vos now in ze harbour of Rotterdam!"

"Well, I wish you a safe run. I'm off to the Seal's Cover. We shall meet to-night."

While this conversation was passing between the smugglers, Theophilus had sauntered on,

Lost in thought, and not a little apprehensive for his safety, for he began to think that the kindness shown him by Paul Adair could scarcely be so disinterested as it appeared at first sight, he pushed on through the whistling breeze that seemed to waft away the fumes of the last night's debauch, and to brace up his nerves for any fresh adventure.

He had not proceeded far before he was brought to a stand by the sound of pealing shrieks among the rocks ahead.

He looked back for his companions.

A turn in the cliff concealed them from view.

A few roods before him on the beach, he beheld a sight which caused the blood to curdle in his veins, and raised each particular hair on his head.

A man was fiercely struggling to snatch a child from the arms of a woman, who pleaded on her knees; a knife glanced in the ruffian's hand.

Theophilus plucked up what courage he could muster, and dashed forward to the rescue.

He was forestalled by the Newfoundland. As we have seen in the last chapter, the noble brute had saved the life of child and mother, who were fleeing fast along the shore.

So terrified was Theophilus by what he had seen, and so keen were his suspicions of his late companions, who, by their dress and appearance, seemed to follow the same calling as that of the ruffian whom he caught in the very act of murder, that he paid no heed to the shouts of Paul Adair and his comrade, who had arrived at the spot where Trelawny was struggling with the hound, and had driven the animal off his foe with much difficulty, and at no small risk to themselves.

Onward he sped, panting and trembling, his head and heart throbbing in unison; slipping over the slimy rocks, toiling over the stony beach, and often stumbling on his hands and knees.

At length he spied the yawning mouth of a dark cave, into which, in his fear, he took sanctuary.

Plunging recklessly into the gloomy cavern he rushed along what was seemingly a beaten way.

There was a heap of stones on one side of this hollow at the top of which appeared a glimmering of daylight.

He scrambled up this pile of flint and chalk, and, wriggling his body through a hole, found that he had entered a long, narrow passage.

Down this he sped in such haste that he did not perceive that there were three or four steps at the end of it which led down into a lower passage until he had tumbled headlong.

"Cwikey!" he moaned, as he lifted himself upon his seat of honour, "if this is twavelling, I wish I was at home in Finsbuwy Square. I've been knocked about like a pantaloon in a Chwistmas pantomime, and the widiculous figure I make is twuly deplowable; here's my shoes cut to the vewy sole by the cwuelty of those hard-hearted wocks, and I'm smothewed with lime like a journeyman plastewer!"

Limping, and groaning in spirit, the luckless adventurer threaded the passage till he came to a wide opening.

On passing beneath the frowning brow of this entrance he found himself, to his utter amazement, in a place that reminded him forcibly of the treasure cave of the "Forty Thieves."

On either side of the long tunnels in the rock were rows of vats, casks and barrels, bales and sea-chests.

"This is pwepostowous!" he exclaimed, holding up his hands and staring about him in an ecstacy of astonishment. "I've been weading the Awabian Nights, and this is all a dweam."

The sound of voices was heard re-echoing down the sounding vaults.

"It's the Forty Thieves appwoaching; I shall be murdered! Oh, where shall I hide."

Creeping between two of the barrels, he fell upon his knees, and, nervously fiddling his spectacles, peeped over the top of one of them, and looked down the dark passage in the direction from whence the sounds proceeded.

He spied a broad-chested, obese, red-faced, black-bearded fellow, waddling along under the weight of a heavy barrel of spirits; he was puffing, and grunting, and growling at the weight of his burden.

This man, who was evidently of Dutch build, staggered along directly to the spot where the valiant Theophilus was crouching in ambush.

He let fall the barrel with an awful crash, and starting back, roared out in a deep growling voice,

"Tausend teufels! dere is zometing behind ze barrel—von beast mit green eyes!"

The shuddering Theophilus crouched low in the shadow, and pulled off his tell-tale spectacles.

"Ach! Berthold, vere are you? vill you come and look at zat?" screamed the Dutchman. "It is von teufel—von goblum, von spectre! He has taken out his eyes mit his own hands! Tonner and blitzen, I vill kill de beast!"

Savagely the irate Guldenhoff, for it was that worthy, pulled out a huge pistol, and aimed between the barrels.

"Murder! Police! Wobbery!" shrieked Theophilus, leaping up like Jack from his box. "Pway don't shoot!"

"Ach! vot for a man is dis?" cried Michael, lowering his pistol, and stepping back.

"A wespectable, wetired fishmonger, from Finsbury, quite weady to go back to his home and family," stuttered Theophilus. "Pway don't cut me to pieces. I am not an 'Awabian Knight,' and I only wan in here for wefuge, and as for your tweasure, I had enough spiwits last night to depwive me of any wish to dwink for the west of my life. Pway don't kill me!"

"Vat does ze dummelkopf zay, Berthold?" asked the surly captain of the Adler 'of his mate, who had just come up with another barrel.

"Speak you—vat you do, sare, in dese place, vere no von shall come?" asked Berthold, more mildly.

"He is von revenue—von spy; I vill kill him! I zee dat he is von teufel of a revenue shark," roared Guldenhoff.

"My wevenue is vewy small," cried poor Theophilus, his teeth chattering, "but you shall have evewy coin in my purse. If you won't destwoy me I'll turn smuggler myself."

"Blitzen! Who tell you dat I vas a smuggler—ha?" cried Guldenhoff, fiercely. "He is von spy, and I vill cut his troats!"

With perfect deliberation the Dutchman drew out an immense knife, strapped across his broad horny palm and run the edge along his thumb, with all the coolness of a butcher about to slaughter a sheep.

The terror of the unfortunate Theophilus was boundless. He threw himself on his knees, in his distraction, as he stammered incoherently,

"I pwotest; pway don't weak your wevenge upon an innocent wespectable twaveller, who will pwomise to emigwate to Jewicho. Here's my watch, my purse, Wosina's portwait, my—my gween eye-pweservers."

The wretched victim extended his glasses with a last fond look at them from his weak grey eyes, and an imploring glance at the ruthless smuggler, that might have moved a heart of stone.

"Hulloa! what's this, hearty? who have we here? what land-crab has crawled into our magazine?" exclaimed a deep rolling voice, in a tone of surprise and displeasure.

The speaker and several other men had entered the cavern, and had gathered round the Dutchman.

"Mynheer Thorkil, it is von revenue shark; he zay so. I am glad you are come; ve vil cut his troats and trow him into the zea."

"Ha! a custom-house hunk? What! have you the daring to beard the wolf in his den? Well, my beauty, we will show you the danger of such cruising. Speak out; who are you? where do you steer from?"

"I can't expwess my delight at being able to communicate with a wational being," cried Theophilus, nervously; "I pwotest against your pwoceeding to violence. I am weally what I pwofess to be."

"A custom-house shark, eh?"

"No, no! I'm—a—a wetired fishmonger. I was fwightened into this place by a bwute of a dog, that I found dewowering one of your weputable associates; I was tewibly afwaid of the cweature, and wan into this place for pwotection; pway be merciful, I entweat you."

"Harleck," cried Thorkil, with a sneer of his lip and a cruel gleam in his eye, "bring a rope."

"Aye, cap'en," responded the fellow, readily.

"Now, my beauty, you came into our secret stores from motives of curiosity; examine the place well, it ought to interest you, for its the last you'll see in this world; clap your glass to your eye, and take your last look, for I mean to give you a dance without music."

The blood-thirsty scoundrel took the cord from the wrecker, and making a running noose, tossed it deftly over the head of the luckless intruder, and drew it tight.

"Murder! Police! Oh, Wosina, I shall be wetchedly murdered!" screamed Theophilus. "Will nobody wescue me from this wascal?"

"Hullo! Hullo there! What are you doing, you cursed cowardly skunks? Don't you see the poor crow is an inoffensive, shore-going creature, and no 'jolly,' or revenue at all? Let go, I tell ye, Thorkil, or, by the blazes, I'll rip your liver out!"

It was Paul Adair who spoke.

"Oh, my genewous pweserver, if I had not mistwusted you I should have been safe," moaned Theophilus, "but by my widiculous suspicion I have not only lost my bweakfast but pwetty near pewished."

"And so, Master Paul, you dare to threaten me, do you?" cried Thorkil, leering fiercely upon the young smuggler.

"Dare to threaten you? Phew! do you think you can make the earth shake with that black frown? May be you can; but make me shake, you can't. Why, dam'me, you blood gorging raven, you're only fit to be cook's mate in a cannibal island. Do you think I'm to be scared like an infant by a pitiful grimace? It's well for you I'm disabled."

A bright smile broke over the handsome, generous face of the youth, as he added, with a laugh,

"Aye, but, mate, that reminds me that I'm 'disarmed;' you saved me like a true comrade, and risked your neck for my sake. Blow me if ever a man could set forgetfulness of a kindness on the black-list again Paul Adair!"

He held out his hand.

The lowering cloud lifted from the dark, fine face of Thorkil, and he grasped the hand extended with the air of a man whose tried courage and known power would put this show of conciliation beyond the suspicion of its being prompted by fear.

By nature and habit Thorkil was utterly remorseless, and even blood-thirsty, but he was too brave and self-confident to be sullen and morose.

"Well, hearty, you know it's one of our strictest rules," he said, "that an intruder into our secret magazines should never leave them a living man. The dead tell no tales!"

"You must waive that rule, Thorkil, for the sake of evading another," returned Paul, laughing. "That devil last night stuck a knife in the ribs of our brother, Nat Redfearn, and by a rule of our order, he is bound to stand his trial and pay the penalty of his offence against the unity of our band."

The wrecker pondered.

"Well, hearty, thus far I'll compromise. Shiver

me, though, if I can tell what interest you can have in the life of such a lubber as this," said Thorkil. "Don't press your claim for Redfearn, and I'll spare your favourite, but, on this condition, as no intruder must leave our caverns a living man, he shall stay here a prisoner till he is summoned by the quarter-master of graves, in the usual form, for when he leaves the Seal's Cover it must be in his hammock, with a shot at his feet to find his next birth in Davy Jones's locker."

"Be it so," returned the smuggler.

The wreckers laid their hands on the shoulder of the prisoner thus condemned to perpetual captivity.

CHAPTER XXX.

WELCOME FRIENDS AND PLEASANT NEWS.

MANY weary days passed over the head of the unhappy Rose Halliard, each bringing her nearer to that from which there was no escape.

Day succeeded day, growing more gloomy than its predecessor, and the time when she would have to relinquish her home and its comforts, and throw herself upon the charity or the bitter exactions of the world, grew nearer and nearer.

She lived in terror of her deadly enemy ; other localities offered her better chances of obtaining suitable employment, yet she could not, perhaps, dared not, stifle the wild, fond fancy—for hope it could not be called—which made her cling eagerly to the Cornish village where she had spent so many happy hours with her lost husband.

One evening she stood by the table, counting the few guineas that remained, and then closed the little, strong box with a heavy sigh, and throwing herself into a chair, wept long and bitterly.

There was a timid knock at the door.

She bade her visitor enter.

With a little cry of joyful surprise she started up as she recognised in the two men who entered, her old defenders, Joe Juniper and Bill Hawser, of H.M.S. the Defiance.

"We axes pardon, madam," said Joe, pulling his forelock and scraping his foot, "me and my mess-mate, Bill, we axes pardon, as is no offence meant, but cruising in these parts we thought it our humble duty to perform, jest to put into this port to pay our humble respects to the widow of our late gallant cap'en, Cap'en Halliard of the Thetis, which is gone aloft, where he will be received with all honours as a man who did his duty on sea and land, and can go through his court-martial with honourable acquital and desarved permotion."

Joe had evidently prepared this speech, and grew red in the face during its delivery.

"I cannot tell you how very welcome you are, my dear, good friends," said Rose, tearfully ; "my husband esteemed you, and I shall ever remember most gratefully your former kindness. Oh, pray sit down," she went on, placing chairs before the cheerful fire, "and let me know how you have fared since the far away time when we last met."

Joe twiddled his straw hat round and round on his fingers, and looked sheepishly at his companion.

Bill Hawser returned the glance with another, expressive of similar bashfulness, and slightly coughing, nudged his companion.

"Don't you hear young madam?" he said, in a boatswain's whisper, "Behave."

Rose placed upon the table the best of her scanty store, with a bottle of rum, some pipes and glasses.

"And do you still serve on board the Defiance ?" she said, bustling about the room, with an assumption of cheerfulness, though she had much ado to choke her rising sobs.

"Well, you see, madam—Lord love your eyes—it arn't our fault ; there was'nt a chap, afore or abaft the mast, that wouldn't have been stopped of his grog and his leave, for the whole voyage of his life-sarvice to have saved poor Mr. Halliard, or even for the honour of going down with him ; but, when the chaps were draughted from the Thetis, for a north'n cruise, we, Bill and me, we were kept aboard as being old and steady hands, as could teach the a'kard squad we got from the tender-ship their duty. Cap'en Halliard tried very hard to get us transferred to the Thetis, but the scrapers at the Hadmiralty wouldn't hear on it."

"How happy I am that you should have escaped my poor husband's terrible fate."

"And how is the cap'en's son, ma'am ?" asked Joe, drawing the back of his hand across his eyes.

"Well, you shall see him," returned Rose, with a gratified smile, "but you must tread softly, for he is asleep, and I do not want him to be awakened."

"Aye, aye, madam, we knows the orders—'Stand steady '—'silence fore and aft '—don't we, Bill ?"

Bill Hawser nodded assentingly.

With ludicrous awkwardness the worthy tars stepped softly across the room to a little curtained bed.

Rose knelt beside the cot, and gently removed the coverlet from the sleeping child.

His flaxen hair strewed the pillow, his long lashes interlaced, the rose softly tinged his delicate cheek, and his tiny hand lay on his light-heaving breast, and he smiled in his sweet and peaceful slumber.

"My jib, Bill ! isn't he a beauty ?" whispered Joe with intense admiration. "Nothing personal, you know, ma'am."

"A reglar hangel," responded the other.

"Ah ! but his eyes are closed now," said the mother, with a beaming smile of love and pride ; "he has beautiful eyes."

"So had the cap'en ; 'scuse my remarks, which is not formal," returned Joe ; "his toplights were as bright as them two big stars in the South Pacific—you know's 'em, Bill ?"

"Aye, mate, and he's a reglar true-blue kind of figure head."

"The werry moral of the cap'en, and I know he'll be a sailor—I know it by the cut of his jib, Lord love him."

"Aye, mate," rejoined Joe Juniper, "he's got a sort of 'spressive countenance, as can show every signal except one, and that's the white bunting of fear ; there's no fear there, hearty."

"Bless your poor soul, not a bit on it," rejoined Joe Juniper, and then raising his voice, in his enthusiasm. "Tell you what, ma'am——"

"Avast, yer lubber !" muttered Bill Hawser, shaking his fist.

"I'll tell you what, ma'am," continued Joe, dropping his tones to the most cautious of whispers, "he's reglar ship-shape fore and aft, and blow me, a regular BOY SAILOR."

"Oh, I trust not !" exclaimed Rose, in a tone of sadness and terror. "He is all that is left me—Heaven is too good to deprive me of the only stay and solace of my widowhood and sorrow."

The two sailors looked at her with manly sympathy, and then rising, trod softly back to their seats.

At Rose's pressing invitation they partook of

supper, and afterwards lighted their pipes and mixed the grog.

Joe Juniper, as he imbibed the cheering spirits, and puffed the long blue curling wreaths from his peaceful pipe, became more confident, and winked at his messmate.

Bill Hawser acknowledged the signal by a grim smile of awful significancy.

Joe took his pipe from his mouth, and "stoppering" it with his finger, shook his head gravely, and began—

"When a seaman falls at his post, madam, it is a comfort to them as are his relations and friends to know that he died while doing his duty to his king and country ; they can brace up their wounded hearts by that conviction, and they may feel as proud of his memory as a young mid of his side-arms ; but sich pride and sich comfort, ma'am, arn't sufficient ballast to steady the keel when the wessel has lost its rudder and compass, and me and Bill, was agoin' to say, madam, leastways, your two humbles was agoin' to ax you a favour, which is quite conformable to ship's orders, and should be werry obligated if you could grant it accordin' to your nat'ral good natur' in sich cases. Its your hinterest with the hadmiral as we wants, for, shiver me, ma'am, if there's anything but hinterest as can cut a cocked hat out of the Board of the Hadmiraly ; we wants hinterest, what say, Bill ?"

"Aye, mate," returned the other, in a tone of deep gravity.

"Interest, my interest ! I never saw an admiral in my life," Rose replied, with a smile of amusement.

"In course not—lor love your blessed peepers—nor we arn't seen him neither," exclaimed Joe, in a tone of biting sarcasm, and winking tremendously at his companion.

The sailors laughed expressively, till their eyes brimmed, and their faces out-glowed the cheery fire.

"Not dizactly, ma'am," Joe said, when he could find breath ; "it's a good man as can take the quarter from the main-deck at one leap, though any lubber can jump no end of fathoms from the foretop, but that's down'ards ; sich is life ! Lord, Bill, my timbers creaks with larfin." Joe pointed his pipe to the cot where little Harry was sleeping. "There's the hadmiral, ma'am, there's his lordship. May God bless the son of Cap'en Halliard ; may his cruise be long and prosperous ; may he never strike his flag to an enemy ; and never relinquish his post till he is summoned at last by the word of command from one aloft who rules all !"

"But I must tack about, ma'am, I'm falling off from the wind."

"Aye, mate ; put the helm down ; you're missing stays. About our future hinterest ; heave ahead, hearty."

"Well, you see, ma'am, a sailor's life is a werry hard one—not as I'm complainin' of the sarvice, quite contrarywise—and we poor sea-goin' chaps is not proverbial for bein' graspers ; aboard a man-of-war it arn't 'the things of this life' we has to look to, but only just this life itself ; and, whether we're reefing sail on the foreyard, or at diwisions, at the guns, or boozing the kid and spinning yarns under the lee of the weather bulwark, it's all one and the same thing ; we have got our 'food and raiment,' as the chaplain calls our purser's allowance, and we're content ; arn't we, messmate ?"

"Aye, Joe ; 'ceptin when we lies becalmed in a tropical sea with the Yellow Jack at the mast-head, and a shoal of sharks sculling round and axing for their daily rations."

"And, you see, ma'am," Joe went on, "when we're ashore we falls into the hands of land-sharks, crimps, Jews, and jezebels, and they fleece us till we're as poor as Spanish dons when our leave is over ; and if so be we escapes the sailmaker, our weather-beaten hulks get too old and shattered for sarvice ; if we arn't lucky enough to have our legs or arms blown off and so get moored for life in Greenwich dock, we're forced to crawl about the land like crabs out o' water with nothing to depend upon but that kind of charity as only keeps a fellow from starving. Now, we wants you to help us."

"I ? Oh, how can I help you ? You must help yourself, Mr. Juniper, by taking care of your wages and prize money ; by foregoing a little skylarking while you're young that you may be able to pay harbour dues, and moor out of the reach of tempests when you're old," returned Rose, pleasantly.

Joe looked at the speaker with much admiration and deference.

"Well, ma'am," he said, "Bill and me has just taken our wages and prize money, and we wants you to keep it for us, to use for our hinterest, by and by, when the young skipper gets his first command on a man-o'-war ; in the meantime you may find it werry useful, and, God bless you, we shall only get boosed and spend the werry last doubloon among the crimps of Falmouth. You've got such a kind face, madam—no offence, you know—that I'm sure you won't refuse this favour to men who had the honour to sarve under your husband. That log's run up all fair and square ; ain't it messmate ?"

"Quite, hearty," returned Bill Hawser. "And I hope as madam will obligate."

Both the worthy fellows drew from their fobs heavy purses, and laid them chinking on the table.

Rose could not speak ; tears choked her utterance.

"Avast, you swab ! don't you know as we've got to make the next port afore fust day watch. We must trip anchor," said Bill Hawser, rising, "and take our leave with humble duties, if so be as madam will kindly excuse us ; we're under sailing orders."

Joe Juniper rose, and, taking up his stick and blue bundle, walked towards the door.

"Stay, stay !" cried Rose, springing after him, and catching him warmly by the hand, "you are too good and generous ; I know not how to speak my thankfulness, but I cannot, I must not, accept of your offer ; it would not be right—it may never be in my power to return you your own. Take it back, I beseech you ; if you leave it here, I shall not touch it ; but with it take a widow's thanks and blessing."

She pushed it into the hands of Joe Juniper, and retreated to the other end of the room, waving him away, smiling through her tears.

The two seamen looked at each other in consternation.

Joe Juniper bent his eyes and looked much chagrined.

Bill slily slipped a quid into his mouth, and rolled it in his cheek reflectively.

Joe started.

"Well, if I don't desarve three dozen at the gangway for neglect of orders," he cried, with genuine self-reproach. "Why, here am I running my rig and forgetting that one of the officers, an old friend of the cap'en, gave me a despatch for you, madam."

"A letter for me ?"

"Aye, ma'am, shouldn't wonder but it's a letter of condolorence, as Cap'en Randall, of His Majesty's frigate Orestes, was a werry intimate friend of Mr. Halliard."

"Yes, of course, he knew of the loss of the Thetis," said Rose, with a sigh, "at the time he wrote this letter. I see it is directed to me; it looks official."

She seated herself by the fire, and, with quivering lip and trembling fingers, began to peruse it.

The worthy tars did not perceive the look of blank astonishment and the flush of pleasure and gratitude that passed over the poor girl's face as she read.

They were enacting a little bye-play.

Bill Hawser slipped his purse into Joe's hand with a mysterious look.

Joe took it, and quickly passed it, with his own, behind some books upon a little sideboard close at hand.

He then folded his arms, and seemed to be intently criticising a picture of a schooner that hung against the wall.

Bill Hawser at the same moment discovered that his bundle was not sufficiently secured, and with great diligence began tying knots in the blue kerchief.

The letter fluttered from the hand of Rose Halliard, and she started up.

"Oh, my dear, brave friends," she cried, joyfully, "you are indeed bearers of good tidings; this letter comes from some officer of the Admiralty, I suppose. The noble gentleman, Captain Randall, has memorialised for me, and I am to receive a widow's pension, the first payment to be made in three months."

The good-hearted fellows faced about on their chairs, and stared at each other with looks expressive of their sincere delight.

Joe Juniper brought his hands down upon his thighs with a spanking clap.

"Dam'me, Bill!" he roared. "Three cheers!"

Rose held up her hand deprecatingly, and, with a sunny smile, pointed to the little bed.

Bill Hawser shook his fist at his comrade reprehendingly.

Joe was subdued in an instant, but indemnified himself by holding his sides and giving vent to a convulsion of smothered, chuckling laughter.

"And now, hearty, we must hoist the Blue Peter," said Bill, tossing his kerchief over his shoulder. "Signal for sailing, you know, ma'am."

Rose filled their glasses; they chinked them together, once more drank the health of the "young hadmiral," and, shaking hands with Rose, passed out into the wild dark night.

"Well, Bill, that was a lark!" cried Joe, still chuckling; "didn't we land our cargo in face of the flashes of her lovely orbits, which is worse to stand than the flame-spurts from the ports in a raking broadsider? Why, mate, she were reg'lar bamboosled. Three months! its a long time to live on her prospec's, poor soul—though I'm glad that, for once, the Hadmiralty have done the right thing; and, as we shall go aboard to-morrow, there can't be any fear of a restitootion. Hearty, this was a wictory!"

"Joe, it were!" responded his messmate, sententiously.

CHAPTER XXXI.

ROSE HALLIARD'S GRATITUDE—A SUDDEN ALARM—THE RETURN OF THE SEAMEN—THE WOUNDED STRANGER — WILD RAVINGS — THYRA — THYRA IS SUMMONED—THYRA'S SPELL—ROSE HALLIARD'S RUSE.

LEFT alone, Rose threw herself upon her knees, and, with tears of bitter sweet emotion, poured out her fervent thanksgivings to the All-bounteous for her timely succour, and invoked a blessing upon her simple, but worthy, benefactors.

When she rose it was with a feeling of calmness and resignation she had not before experienced. At least, she would now be preserved from want, would be spared the pang of parting from her little one, and would be able to afford him those advantages of education so essential to his future success in life. She kissed her sleeping darling, and hung over him awhile with yearning fondness. She then drew near the little side-board to take down the book from which she derived, from the highest source, her widow-comfort and Christian solace.

A look of such gratitude, as was almost painful in its intensity, lighted her face as she took up the two purses hid together, and concealed with such gentle cunning by the kind-hearted seamen.

She placed them in the cupboard, and locked them there.

She seated herself to read, for, though it was growing late, she felt disinclined to retire until she could ensure rest by first exhausting or diverting the exciting train of thoughts into which she had fallen.

The fire began to expire.

The silence of midnight reigned around, broken only by the hoarse murmers of the distant sea, and the tic-tock of the clock in the corner.

Rose closed the book and replaced it on the sideboard.

She was about to bolt the door before retiring to her bed when she was suddenly alarmed by the rattling of Neptune's chain and his deep baying without the cottage.

She thought of Black Will Trelawny, and her heart sank.

The sound of footsteps was heard.

She clasped her hands as she knelt by the bed of her sleeping child.

A boding of evil oppressed her mind, and she regretted that she had not detained the seamen.

"Raise the hatches, ma'am," cried a voice without, "it's only me and Bill. We've found a poor gentleman who has struck on a rock or been boarded by pirates. Please let us into the cabin."

In an instant Rose had opened the door.

The two sailors entered, carrying the apparently lifeless body of a man.

Rose shudderingly lifted the candle, and led the way into the little chamber where she slept.

The wounded man was laid upon the bed.

He was very handsome, and richly dressed in a suit of fine black cloth, and a cloak lined with costly fur; he wore high boots with spurs.

It was plain that he had not been robbed, for, if he had been attacked by thieves, they would scarcely have spared his valuable mantle and the heavy gold guard and watch which hung loose from his pocket.

His face was ghastly pale, his features perfect and patrician, his hair beautifully glossy and rich with heavy curls; he had a pointed black beard.

On one side of his forehead was a wound occasioned probably by a heavy fall.

"As I takes it, ma'am, he is some big-wig as cruising aboard of a horse and got swept off deck by a lee-luch, or by striking agen a reef," said Joe.

"Avast heaving, messmate; he opens his peepers," muttered Bill Hawser.

Rose had torn some soft linen to shreds, and dexterously bound up the wound on the stranger's pale high forehead and was wetting his lips with the brandy flask.

"The horse will break his neck! Where is that

cursed groom ? and Falcon, too, the best hunter in my stables ; a guinea to any man who will thrash that varlet. I've broken my wrist."

These incoherent words were muttered in fierce and haughty tones, as the stranger opened his bright black eyes and glared wildly about him.

"Am I at home, or is this some confounded market inn or kiddle-a-wink ? Give me more brandy, and send for a surgeon, my right hand is disabled. I shall never again be able to use my pistols, and every knave may insult me with impunity. Where's Amos ? Why the devil did he trap the horse with a rotten farthingale ? It's a conspiracy. By God ! you shall all pay dearly for it. I'm not dead yet, as some of you shall find, you villains ! Yet more brandy, and hurry the surgeon."

The stranger closed his eyes, and sank back with a deep groan of pain.

"A pretty Chris'en creetur, Bill," whispered Joe Juniper ; "this is pretty sort of talk for a chap with the sailmaker's needle tickling his nose, arn't it now ? I should like to be his coxsw'n or his wally de chambers."

"Stopper all," growled Bill. "Lord, how he stares at you ; he looks like the ghost of old Jaw-bones, that cut his throat with a belaying pin."

There was something appalling in the fixed look with which the wounded man regarded the little group beside him.

"Is he dying ?" asked Rose, breathlessly.

"Well, madam, the sharks gets all," returned Joe, stroking his chin ; "and if there's no more rain falls on the land-hole where they buries these shore-going chaps than tears shed on it, the grass as grows won't be much of a nibble for the parson's sheep."

"You are wrong—very wrong, to speak in that way !" cried Rose, indignantly. "He may have a wife, or a mother, who loves him as we love ours—for shame."

The stranger moved and writhed as if in great anguish.

Bill Hawser threw his sinewy arms about him, and lifted him upon the pillow, and placed him in a more easy position.

"If you're the surgeon, attend to my hand first. I will not grudge you a thousand pounds if you can set my dislocated bones ; this hand is wanted ; there's work for it. What's your name ? do you belong to Penzance ?" Again he sank back, hoarsely murmuring, "I tell you, Stanley, that I will never rest till I have satisfied my vengeance ; I will kill the scoundrel. Brow-beat and sermonise me, the dog ! Lady Beatrice shall marry whom I please ; she is my ward ; there are convents and mad-houses, and I hold control over her fortune, and can strip her of her last shilling. Everybody plays the fool with me, and I'm a cursed fool to be played with. You, sir, what are you ? are you a surgeon, or a horse doctor ? You precious clown, I shall lose my hand."

"A patient for a cockpit that," cried Joe Juniper.

"If I was the lop-lolly-boy, I don't think I'd commence by cutting away some of his jawing tackle ; I don't think I'd give the *tourniqeut* a hextra screw. Did you ever hear of such a catamountain ? I hope he's got his billet."

"What *shall* we do !" cried Rose. There is no doctor in Seawardine, none nearer than Penzance. Now, I bethink me, Wild Thyra is staying with Lena at Joel Britton's ; will one of you run to the village for assistance ? Stay, I will write a few words, if one of you will bear it to the forge in Seawardine, and tell the girl you saw with me when—"

Rose paused, and wrung her hands distractedly. "The thread of my life has become one tissue of blood and horrors."

"A frail little craft, slight built, with a pennant of silken gold, and top-lights as blue as the Bosphorus," cried Joe. "Aye, ma'am, I remember her, she was your bride's—well, ma'am, if she can cure by conjuring as the natives do, she knows her duty like a full-rated A. B., and we shall have this commodore wielding the rope's end, and swearing at the fo'castle as if he'd never run a-stern of the rocks and splintered his bow-sprit ; I'll clap on all sail, and return in the twirl of a handspike."

Joe took a little note that Rose hastily scribbled, and rushed out of the cottage.

Bill Hawser and the girl carefully tended the patient, or rather the "impatient," smoothing his pillow, chafing his arm, and binding his swollen wrist with all the skill they were possessed of.

In an incredibly short time, considering the distance he had to traverse, Joe Juniper returned, bringing with him Thyra, who was accompanied by Joel Britton the blacksmith.

The party gathered round the bed where the stranger still lay moaning, and fiercely whispering all manner of savageries.

The blacksmith recoiled, and threw up his hands with a cry of consternation.

"'Sdeath ! it's the Earl of Penalvon !"

The stranger opened his eyes and frowned at the speaker.

"Who calls my name so rudely ?" he cried, in a tone of intense passion. "Let me get up ; this is some den of thieves or wreckers. Oh, oh, my brain is touched, and my right hand is shattered." Again he sank back, groaning piteously.

"My toplights, Bill, that's a earl ! Well, I should like to be his heir happarent ; it's a rough gale that blows no one good."

Wild Thyra approached the bed-side.

She folded her hands and looked calmly upon him.

She touched her forehead, and smiled significantly.

"It is brain madness," she said ; "his heart is too hard to be touched by the grief which poisons the mind ; he will recover soon, though he is so near the dark line that spirits are here who yearn to know if he will cross it ; they are not all wise alike; there are many who know little more than we, and dark ones are never far from the path of Penalvon of Fenwold. Get a little water; I will see to the child ; steep these herbs," she went on, drawing some simples from a pouch that hung by her side. "I will see to the child, but I will not delay an instant."

The party looked at the strange girl with no little awe.

Rose brought a vessel of water and soaked the leaves.

The rest of the party made way for her with deferential obsequiousness.

The sturdy sailors who had looked death in the face with beaming eyes quailed and quaked under the influence of her superstitions.

Joel and Rose knew Thyra too well to venture to interfere with her movements ; they knew she was an excellent "mediciner," and were content to let her manage things in her own way.

Thyra walked to the little bed.

The child was broad awake; he had been roused by the noise and bustle that had followed the return of the seamen with the wounded man.

She knelt by his side.

"Thyra, is it papa ? could they not make him well ?" whispered the child. "Is he ill now ? will

THE BOY SAILOR'S FIRST BATTLE.

you cure him as you did Harry? That is not my papa; he looks evil."

Thyra clasped a little necklace round the child's neck.

She whispered something to him in a gentle, soothing tone.

The child looked at her gravely with his large, thoughtful eyes, and lay quite still.

Thyra stood between the cradle and the moaning patient.

She remained for a while, muttering some quaintly foolish and poetically wild charm, and seemed to stand between the child and the dark agencies, the spirits of ill her disordered imagination pictured as trooping the room.

She then approached the bed on which the Earl of Penalvon lay writhing.

She took the herbs from Rose, and, having murmured over them a charm of wondrous efficacy, as she sincerely believed, bathed the wound with the water in which they had been steeped, and bound them about the patient's brow.

She then took his hand.

He moved as if stung by an adder.

He gazed at her dreamily.

"I perceive you are an angel, a spirit," he said, in a low, faint voice ; "but I know you not, whoever you are. I have done *you* no wrong—away, do not haunt me with your wild eyes and your filmy hair. What is it ? what have I done ?"

"Hist !" cried Thyra, in her wild and weird manner, raising her fingers, "I will sing him my 'runes,' and you shall hear what he will say."

The girl then broke into a low, soft and monotonous chant, so hollow and clear sounded the notes of her strange rhythm—

> "When the sands of life run low,
> Then the soul's eyes clear'st glow ;
> Light on mortals' eyes is thrown,
> Spirits' light is all their own.
> And it shows the darkness clear
> As the noonday : then so'f-near
> Distant deeds to present fear.
> Time knows not the eternal soul,
> Sees no part, but feels the whole.
> Lingering on its last farewell,
> Let the tortured spirit tell,
> All that's conjured by this spell."

The little group drew back as if awe-stricken and moved by dread and respect, unwilling to hear the Earl rave of his closest secrets.

His eyes were glassy bright ; that ethereal light which often illumines the face of the dying, broke upon his rigid countenance ; he seemed indeed to be under the influence of mesmerism, or in some way spell-bound, but his lips breathed no oracles, at least to mortal ears, he only muttered brokenly ; he stretched out his clasped hands as if beseeching pardon ; he then extended his arms as if to clasp some fleeting shadow, and then let them fall heavily by his side ; he breathed thickly.

Thyra made some rapid passes above his face, and his breast heaved more lightly, and in a few moments he had sunk into a deep, quiet slumber.

Wild Thyra seated herself on the bed ; turning towards her companions, she broke into a harsh and eldrich laugh, and pointed at the Earl with a smile of triumph.

"The girl is mad," exclaimed Joel Britton, drying the sweat from his brow ; "mad as the March winds, and she deals with the wraiths and the spirits, and ought to be burnt for a witch."

Thyra motioned Rose to bring her some linen, and then quickly and dexterously swathed the wrist of the sleeper, poured some of the water upon the bandages, and laid the passive hand on the coverlet.

"It is done," she said, rising, with a smile ; "when he wakes he will be well ; but let me give you yet another rune of warning."

Joel Britton, however, had enough of this performance, if these displays of the poor girl's insane enthusiasm deserved no better name ; so he drew her away, and engaged her in conversation.

All this while the seamen looked on in bewilderment.

Rose looked round to see if she was unobserved.

The blacksmith and the sailors were too much engrossed in trying to extract something from Thyra, who stood mute and peevish, as if much offended at being prevented from inflicting her magic rhyme.

Rose snatched up Bill Hawser's blue bundle ; she took the purses from the cupboard, and ran into the next room.

She opened a sea chest that had belonged to her husband, and drew from it two rolls of tobacco of choice quality, and two bright tobacco boxes ; these she slipped with the purses into the bundle. Her grief lay too deep, and was too heavy to be always rising to the surface. With a low silvery laugh she returned to the sick man's chamber, and unperceived by the rest.

Another actor now appeared on the scene—Nelly Britton, wrapped in her cloak and hood, entered the cottage.

She kissed Rose, who embraced her warmly, and told her what had happened.

"I couldn't rest at home, father," said the lively girl, "and here I am, in spite of your parental authority ; but, then, you know, I fancied poor Rose might want a nurse as well as a doctor, and I thought of little Harry."

"I'm glad thou'rt come, lass, thou thou'rt a little rebel, and I shall have to read the riot act to thee ; thou shalt stay here with Rose till my lord recovers, and I will at once go over to Fenwold Castle and summon assistance from my lord's folk."

"And, blow me, madam, if we shan't get our backs scratched for out-staying leave," said Joe Juniper ; "we must weigh anchor without further parley, and so we leaves you, ma'am, with a good night, all's well to one and all, and our humble duties and sarvices ever to command."

Rose smiled as Bill Hawser took up his bundle, and, having heartily shaken hands with her kind friends, the seamen and the blacksmith left the cottage.

Wild Thyra lingered a moment.

"Rose," she said, in her low, impressive voice, "do you remember that I told you truths, too sure, too sad, before you became his wife from whom you are now parted ?"

"I remember them," returned Rose, sadly, "they came too true, indeed."

"Yet you despised my warnings ; you thought they were dictated by jealousy and malice !"

"No, not so."

"Well, that is all past ; you believe in me now ?"

"I believe that you are kind and good—the best, the kindest," said Rose, softly.

"Yes ; but that I would deceive."

"Only yourself."

A flash of scorn darted from the wild blue eyes of the rune-kenner.

"Well, we are sisters now," she said, after a pause, and tenderly clinging to Rose.

"Yes, dear Thyra, heart and hand."

"Then do not neglect the warning I am about to give you."

"Not to-night, dear Thyra ; you are excited, you will be ill ; some other time."

"Some other time is never, or too late !" cried the girl, passionately stamping her foot.

"Quick, then, for I must return to my lord."

"My lord ! Ha ! ha ! Oh, it is cruel to see—to tell, and not to be believed ; it is of him I speak !"

"Indeed !"

"Yes ; Rose, do you love your husband ?"

"He is in Heaven."

"I did not say that ; do you love your child and my foundling Lena ?"

"Yes, Thyra," returned Rose, with vacant impatience.

"Then beware of Edgar Penalvon, of Fenwold ; he will lay siege to your soul, Rose Halliard ; he will tempt you as the devil tempts men with lies and the offer of desirable things ; he will tempt you through your womanly weakness, through your motherly love. Black Will Trelawny is a friend compared with this enemy ; pray, Rose, beware of him !"

"Thyra, I cannot tell you how much you grieve me ; I know and I appreciate your soul of benevolence ; I pity and even respect your strange assumption of mystic knowledge," said Rose, in a tone of serious reproof; "but I cannot help feeling angry with you for the indelicacy with which you carry out your foolish and capricious fancy by solemnly warning me of dangers which cannot threaten anyone who is worthy the name of a wife.

Thyra threw her arms about Rose with timid entreaty and affection, and burst into a flood of tears.

"Woe is me, unhappy one!" she sobbed, bitterly. "Shall I see the snake in your nest and not warn you of his fang?"

"Indeed, I thank you, dear Thyra, for your caution," returned Rose, gently kissing her. "But you do not reflect; I am but a sailor's poor widow, he is an earl. He is dangerously ill."

"I have cured him. Will you not believe your own eyes?" cried Thyra, fiercely; she then lowered her voice to a thrilling whisper. "One crime may save many," she hissed forth, between her gnashing teeth. "Kill him while he is asleep! I will give you the means; I have deadly poison in my bag, sure and beyond detection, and I will bear all the blame!"

Rose started with horror.

"Thyra, you are mad! You can have no such wicked thoughts of your own nature; you are possessed by an evil spirit!"

"I did not mean what I said," returned the girl, wearily; "if we could look into the future we should often be tempted to kill our very dearest friends to save them from after crimes and sorrows. Farewell, I warned you before; you did not heed me then, you will not heed me now."

"Do not look so vexed, dear Thyra," said Rose, smiling sweetly; "you must fight against black thoughts by prayer; and, as for this enemy, why, as you have restored him, Thyra, to-morrow he will be gone."

"When he leaves your house," said the rune-kenner, wildly, as she swept through the door, "he will leave his shadow behind him!"

It was very late when Thyra left the house, and the darkness soon broke into light.

The Earl still slept deeply.

Dark fears took possession of the heart of Rose.

She drew to the side of the child's bed, and gazed on him as he lay smiling in repose.

"Heaven," she murmured, with pride, "makes the fatherless and the widow His especial care; and as I look upon the calm, sweet face of my darling, I see that it wears the brave look of his father, and I feel, infant as he is, that I am not left in the world without a true defender; and not my motherly fondness, but with something of the spirit of that kind, foolish, fortune-telling, wild Thyra, I can predict a long and bright career to the widow's son, the Boy Sailor!"

END OF PROLOGUE.

Book the First.

LIFE ON BOARD A MAN-OF-WAR.

CHAPTER I.

THE BOY SAILOR AND HIS CHUM—OUR HERO ALREADY A DISTINGUISHED CHARACTER—A KIND OFFICER—THE PROSPECT OF A BATTLE ROYAL—THE BOY SAILOR THRASHES A BULLY.

THE BRITISH FLEET lay off Cadiz.

Nothing imaginable could be grander than the splendid panorama of sky, sea, and land, that was beheld with such exhilaration by a couple of handsome-faced, bright-eyed, russet-cheeked, merry, mischievous, plucky-looking urchins, perched like monkeys on the foretop of H.M.S. Thunderer.

"Harry, my chum!" cried one of them, with a merry laugh, his words struggling against the bluff breeze, that, blowing stifly from land, seemed to drive them back into his bright grinning teeth and roguishly curved lips, "what do you think of your new life?—what do you think of being a Boy Sailor?"

There was a strong contrast between the speaker and the companion to whom these words were addressed.

The former was a pale, straight-built fellow, with raven black hair, large, round, merry twinkling black eyes; he was a tall lad, about fourteen years of age. The latter was about twelve, not quite so tall, and frailer looking, with rich, curling, flaxen hair, and bright blue eyes; his face was extremely beautiful, his cheeks softly flushed, and his expression was one of mingled intelligence, drollery, and thorough courage.

Harry drew a long breath.

His blue eyes sparkled, his lip dimpled, and he sung out in a ringing, chuckling tone, which seemed to come from the very core of his stout little heart, "Jolly!"

"Ain't it? Bless my heart, Hal, who wouldn't be a British Sailor Boy? who does not like the SEA! Lor, I should die if I was a shore-going lubber, to see nothing of life—to live without sky-larking—to have no spice of danger to brighten up one's work. Ain't it supreme when the officers give you a pat on the head and call you 'a little Briton?' Don't you remember kicking the live bomb overboard? You are a real plucky chap, Hal, and every man, fore and aft, knows it, only you've got a most awful fault, you have! You see, I'm your elder, and, of course, your superior, and, don't you know, your duty, you little lubber, is to 'order yourself lowly and reverently to all your betters?' Very well, then, profit by my instructions—

"'When first, my boys, I went to sea,
    I thought the life was rough;
A bigger swab did bully me,
    But soon he cried ' enough,'

Says I, old chap, I like a spree;
    But when it falls to spite,
There's but one plan that I can see,
    A Jolly stand up fight!'"

The young philosopher emphasised this opinion by punching the mast so vigorously that, if he had not been blessed with knuckles of iron, they must have been smashed.

"There's no good ever came of quarrelling, Frank," returned the Boy Sailor, with a good-humoured laugh; "and there are some lubberly chaps who couldn't breathe if they didn't brag. So long as they keep their hands off, hard words never shivered the mizen."

"No; but that's all very well, Harry, my chum," returned the other lad, shaking his head, and speaking fretfully; "you're such a good-natured little beggar, that you don't know when you're put upon. Look at that surly bully, Dan Crawley."

"Bosh! He's a poor crow" returned Harry, contemptuously.

"My little chum, poor crow as he is, I can tell you he croaks about you behind your back, and some of the rough waisters laughed at you rarely."

"I'm sure they're welcome to do that," said Harry, carelessly. "My mother has taught me what *true* courage is; there's a good deal of mistake about the thing; it is more in bearing disagreeable things than in doing desperate ones. I don't *like* to be laughed at, Frank; but if I got riled at a little chaff, my pluck wouldn't be worth much."

"Your mother!" murmured Frank, thoughtfully, a shade of sadness falling on his sunny face, "I have no mother, Harry; perhaps it's as well, though, that my mother has gone aloft, and is with the angels; I'm only a rough, careless sea-boy, and I'm afraid I shouldn't be half kind enough to her; but there," he added, with a burst of fire, "its the jeers about that which make me so awful wild!"

"About what?" asked Harry, wonderingly.

"Well, I suppose you won't blame me for telling you; but that young beast, Dan, is always gibing about your 'mamma,' and the smuggler raffs and other pressed men in the fo'castle laugh and encourage him. He always fawns upon me, the dirty skunk, because he knows I give him more of my toe than my tongue; but, you see, we're about the same size and age. I *should* like; but there, Hal, I don't want to set you on, God knows."

Frank looked at his companion.

He could not help starting.

The ship lurched at the moment, and he was forced to catch the stay to save himself from tumbling.

The gentle face of Harry glared with the anger of a young lion.

"Hurrah, Hal!" cried Frank, laughing merrily, as he wantonly swung in the tackling, "but when you show such a face as that, I'd rather be your chum than your enemy."

"There will be fun to-night," said Harry, rousing himself from the thoughtful mood into which he had fallen, his cheek still richly flushing; "the admiral is going to attack the Spanish gunboats, and I shall be in the captain's pinnace."

"You're a lucky dog, Hal," returned the other; "but since you got that cut on the wrist when saving that Cockney pug-nosed mid, that always bullied you out of sheer jealousy, everybody seems to make much of you; but, be alert, we're hailed on deck," he cried suddenly, looking from his swaying perch down the dizzy depth below.

"Aye, aye, sir!" sung out the boy sailors, and down the quivering ropes they glided and leaped upon the deck.

The men were at divisions.

The captain, a fine-looking seaman, stood on the quarter reading a letter.

An officer from another ship stood near him in respectful silence.

The captain went below with the officer.

Presently he returned, talking eagerly with the messenger from the flag-ship.

The order was given to "pipe the side."

With all honours the officer was passed over to the gig.

The men were dismissed.

Harry and his comrade sauntered to the bulwarks.

As they looked over the side their eyes were gratified with a noble scene.

The English fleet were blockading the town.

The Thunderer belonged to the inner squadron, engaged in this blockade of Cadiz.

The flag-ship was flying her signals to the rest of the men-of-war, which were grandly soaring closer in upon the forts, foaming through the glancing waves.

On board the flag-ship was the Rear-Admiral, HORATIO NELSON.

The town had ceased firing.

It must not be supposed that the boys on the foretop had enjoyed such a quiet watch as might be imagined by the free and easy manner in which they had been conversing.

For an hour they had enjoyed a respite, and were enabled to look about them on the truly sublime scene without apprehension; but, prior to that hour, they had been in instant danger of cruel death.

The town had been enveloped in a cloud of fire and smoke.

The sea had seemed to tremble under the heavy roar of the thundrous cannonade.

A long row of vicious-looking gun-boats were chained along the fortress.

All was now calm and still.

It was the general subject of debate on the forecastle whether it was intended by the great ocean warrior to make a night attack upon the troublesome gunboats.

Frank and Harry stood leaning over the bulwark, gazing upon the town, rich-glowing in the crimson haloes of the sunset.

In the sweet carelessness of blithe boyhood they were gaily chatting.

A grave and gentlemanlike officer approached them.

He was the second lieutenant.

The boys drew back respectfully.

They touched their flossy forelocks, and with downcast eyes were about to move away from the side.

"Stay, my lads, let me have a talk with you," said the officer.

The sailor boys paused.

The officer laid his hand kindly on the head of our boy hero.

"My lad, your face is not strange to me. What is your name?"

"Harry Halliard, please, sir," returned the Boy Sailor, naively.

The lieutenant seemed surprised.

"Halliard!" he murmured, "and there's a likeness, too. What was your father, my lad?"

The young ship-boy drew himself up to his full height, quite unconsciously, but with touching grace.

"My father, sir, was lieutenant on this ship," he said, simply, but with a proud light shining clear in his brave blue eyes.

"Halliard! Just God, how strange!" muttered the lieutenant. "Are you sure there is no mistake?"

The boy coloured.

"Mr. Juniper, the coxswain, or Mr. Hawser, the boatswain, will tell you, sir, that it is true," replied our hero.

"But, my dear child; why, you seem a boy of talents and refine——Is it possible?—and your mother, where is she?"

"She lives in Cornwall, sir."

"Ha! true; but your mother," the officer hesitated, "may I ask?—she received a pension from the Admiralty, did she not, my boy ?   I ask—that is—of course, I knew your father very well, Harry, and you will do well if you follow in his footsteps, for he was perfectly a gentleman, who knew his duty well, and, gifted as he was, would have performed it as nobly before the mast as in the quarter-deck. Did not your mother receive an annuity from the Admiralty ?—there is a reason that justifies the question. Tell me, my boy ?"

"No, sir," returned our hero, with a deep blush. "The Earl of Penalvon, who is a black villain, robbed my poor mother of her rights. I found that out, sir, myself. My mother did not tell me."

"You are right—you *must* be right. I remember the circumstance," said the lieutenant, speaking rather to himself than to the boy. "Lord Penalvon had great influence ; his representations to the Admiralty—an unsuitable match—the daughter or niece of a wrecker. I remember the whole circumstance. Harry !"

"Aye, sir."

"Come into my cabin after six bells."

"Sir, I am going in the pinnace with the bo'swain, Mr. Hawser," returned the boy, eagerly, as if fearing he should lose the treat of danger.

"Then you are the little fellow that tossed over the shell; that was hurt by the langrel at St. Vincent ; that was wounded in defending a midshipman ?"

"Yes, sir," replied the Boy Sailor.

"Harry, if you are steady, and fortune does not frown very darkly on you, you will win honour. And you are going in the pinnace to attack the Spanish gun-boats, eh ?"

"Yes, sir."

"I understand. Humph! they want to get the urchin a midshipman's warrant. Too bad, though—much too bad. Harry, I'll get you off this duty, if you like."

"Oh ! please not, sir," cried the ship-boy, eagerly.

"But, your mother, Harry——"

"Teaches me to love my country first," said the brave child, with perfect simplicity.

The officer cast an admiring look on the little hero.

"Well, Harry, 'there's a sweet little cherub that sits up aloft to take care of the life of poor Jack.' And you will enjoy an honour that many great men will envy you, in engaging in such a dangerous service, under such a great commander as NELSON."

The officer paused.

"What a noble thing it is to be beloved, Harry," he re-commenced. "That flag-ship was engaged in the mutiny of the Nore, and every man on board the Theseus was discontented and rebellious. But Nelson had not been on board her ten days before all the crew were as eager to do their duty as the brave genius who was placed over them. They dropped on the quarter-deck the best sort of 'round robin'—a memorial of praise and devotion to England's greatest naval hero. I remember the words ; they are very memorable, as coming from stern men, whose bitterness of heart was turned into sweetness by the impartial justice and gentle kindness of this great man. I learned the words contained in this paper, which I have seen. Shall I tell them to you, Harry ?"

"Thank you, sir.

"It was in this way they showed their duty to their zealous and nob'e superiors : 'Success attend Admiral Nelson ! God bless Captain Miller ! We thank them for the officers they have placed over us. We are happy and comfortable, and will shed every drop of blood in our veins to support them ; and the name of the Theseus shall be immortalised as high as her captain's.' What do you think of that, Harry ?"

"I think, sir," returned the boy, with glowing cheeks, "that the men were heroes as well as their admiral ; that there are as many great men before the mast as on the quarter."

"Well said, Harry Halliard ; and what would the skill of the officers avail but for the faithfulness of their gallant lads ?"

"The men only do their duty, sir, and are quite satisfied ; I've heard them say so," returned our hero, simply.

"Yes, and the more honour to them, poor fellows."

"The common soldier or sailor ! Those for whom they shed their blood often turn up their noses at the 'common' soldier, and the 'common' sailor. Officers have the praises, and the rewards of their country to uphold them ; while the commom soldier or sailor fights and dies with the mass of his comrades, and has no reward but the approval of his own conscience."

"And my mother says, that conscience is enough for any true man, sir," replied the Boy Sailor.

"You have a good mother, Harry Halliard ; honour and love her, and you will be happy. 'Bye, for the present ; we'll have a chat some other day." The officer walked aft and left the boys together.

"A nice gentleman, Lieutenant Armitage ; I always liked him," said Frank.

"I wish I could die for him !" returnd our hero, warmly.

"And I could die for you, chum Harry," returned the elder boy, griping his companions hand, "only I wish you would give that bully, Dan Crawley, a glorious licking ; but here he comes. Well, I'll be off; he won't say any thing to you if I am by, and if you stand any of his humbug, won't I whollop you?"

With this Frank turned away, and walked towards the forcastle.

Our hero leaned against the bulwarks, and fixed his eyes on the clear fleeting waters, and seemed lost in boyish reverie.

An ungainly, low-browed, surly-looking lad, much taller and seemingly much stronger than our hero, came swaggering along.

He stopped opposite our hero and burst into a sneering laugh.

"Well, younker," he said, in a mocking tone, "and how's mamma ?"

The Sailor Boy turned, and fixed upon his tormentor a calm disdainful glance.

"Dan Crawley," he said, in a quiet tone, "for what you say of me, or for your stupid chaff, I don't care ; but, if you speak to me again of my mother, why, I shall have to knock you down."

"How ! what ! you imperant young blackguard ! say that again !" cried the bully, clenching his fist, and standing on tip-toe to make the most of his superiority in height.

"I don't want to say it again," returned the Boy Sailor, quietly, "but I'd advise you not to forget it, for all that."

"Why, you infarnal young swab ! do you mean to tell me that I arn't to talk about who I choose, and what I likes ? Your mother ! what's your mother ? Yah ! I knows all about her, my pretty skip-jack, and if you don't take to show me a proper respect I'll tell all I knows on her."

The Boy Sailor kept his eye fixed on the bully.

His lip compressed, his colour heightened, but he did not speak.

"There's a fellow in the fo'castle, some relation of

yourn, I expects ; he was pressed for smuggling, and his name's Harleck. Know him ?"

Still no reply.

"A sort of pirate hunk, I fancy. He told me all about you and your father and mother, and the wench that came from nowhere, but must belong to somebody. You're a beggarly lot, and, for all your fine airs and graces, your 'mamma' is obliged to ply the needle——"

The Boy Sailor drew back his arm, and then shot it out with an impetus little to be expected from his age and size.

His fist reached the coward full between the eyes with a hearty thwack.

He was knocked heels over head on to the deck.

A number of the men who were passing gathered round the boys.

Some of them were rough and evil-looking fellows.

Others were of kinder and more genial aspect.

Among the latter were Joe Juniper and Bill Hawser.

"Hulloa, youngsters ! what's all this ?" cried the boatswain, sternly. "Hey-dey ! are you the chap to get up this breeze, Harry ? Behave, you young dog !"

The bully scrambled to his feet.

"Please, sir, he's been and hit me unawares, sir, and all for nothin', sir," snivelled Dan, drawing his sleeve across the bridge of his nose.

"He insulted me about my mother, and if he speaks of her again, I'll serve him so till he gets tired and gives up the fun," said the Boy Sailor, fiercely.

"Stand by, you young reprobate !" cried one of the seamen ; "let us have *his* report on it. You'll both run astarn of the bo'swain's cat, I can tell ye, ye quarrelsome imps. There can be no brawling allowed on deck, either between men or monkeys."

"No, sir, nor more I don't, sir," whined the elder boy, a thorough cur. "I didn't go for to hurt nobody's feelins'."

"You'll find *your* feelin's hurt, sir, I assure ye, if you get kicking up a bob's-a-dying aboard this wessel," said the seaman, who was a petty officer.

"May I never die, sir, if I said anythin' to offend him, sir," protested Dan. "I axed him if it warn't so, that's all, sir."

"Warn't so ! What 'warn't so,' you baboon ?"

"Why, sir, in coorse, nobody can't help their relations. I says to him, quite soft and gently, sir, 'Harry, didn't your mother used to go for to take in needlework ?' And as soon as the blessed words was out of my blessed mouth, his fist was in my eye, sir, quite unawares."

"I say, Master Hal, you look here, young chap," said Joe Juniper, angrily. "I promised as I'd look arter ye—werry good ; but, blow me, if there's anything worse than big lads playing the skipper over little ones, it is for sich small fry as you bein' imperant to their elders."

"Yes, sir, he's so wicious ; he knows as I don't like to hurt him, sir. I'm sure I wouldn't harm a fly, which my parents told me not——"

"Why, dam'me, Joe," cried one of the men, stepping up, "every man aboard, with his eyes open, knows as this young devilskin is the most bullying tyrant on earth. I hit him a crack this morning for pulling a poor little chaps ears."

"No matter for that, I hates imperance," said Joe, with a wink at the petty officer.

"So do I, and I won't allow it, no ways."

"Sir, I wasn't impudent," said the Sailor Boy, boldly. "I have borne a good deal from Dan, and

should have borne a good deal more, if he had not jeered me about my mother."

"Oh, lor ! sir, what a lie !—which I ought to say a story. *He's* always a badgering *me*, sir."

"Well, then, he shall be punished."

"Oh, sir, I'm sure—I did not wish—but, really, if you could get him to leave off—it's very bad for me——"

"Box his ears at once !" said the petty officer.

"Sir, do you expect me to stand that without resisting ?" cried Harry, briskly, his eyes flashing.

The seaman did not reply.

"Do you hear, sir ?" cried the petty officer to Dan.

The young bully looked up at his prompters to see if they were in earnest.

He gave a sneakish leer, and turning back his cuff, peered down at the little fellow with his small, deep-set eyes twinkling with malice.

"Well, sir, many's the time I've thought, if it warn't agen orders, I'd give him a reg'lar good hiding."

"I give you leave ; you're big enough to eat him."

"Werry well, sir, if you wishes it. He wants bringing down, he does ; all the boys is annoyed with his fine airs and graces."

"If he touches me I shall knock him down again," said Harry, quietly.

"*Will* you, my boy ; hey ? *will* you ? we'll see. Mind your eye ! I ain't got to put up with your imperence, you little beggar ! Mr. Stiff *says* I ain't," shouted the bully, tumbling to the fray, butting his head, and flinging his long arms about like the sails of a windmill.

Harry's eyes flashed and his lips quivered, but with admirable coolness he walked right "into" the braggart, not heeding his wheeling arms, which were easily eluded.

Harry drew himself up and quietly hammered at his opponent's nose,

The men roared with laughter.

Dan slipped away with his face red and his nose vermilion.

Harry did not follow him, but leaned back against the bulwark, his delicate chest heaving, his face immobile, but his eyes flaring like a young tiger's.

Dan stood bewildered with fright, and, though removed full two yards from his "man," elevated first one elbow and then another in quick succession, as if warding off the blows of an imaginary foe.

The rough tars held their sides with mirth at the odd figure the young dastard cut in his paralytic manoeuvering.

The petty officer seized the defeated tyrant by the back of the neck.

"How, sir ; do you dare to disobey me ?" he thundered.

"Oh, no, sir ! I'm sure, sir," Dan snivelled, most piteously.

"Did not I tell you to thrash that lad ? he's but a little one. Pay him well, sir ; if you don't thrash him till he gives in, I'll thrash you."

"Werry good, sir," returned the cowardly fellow, trembling in every limb, yet screwing his courage to the sticking place. "Now, younker ; I'll smash you !"

With this terrible threat again he butted his head, swayed round his lank arms, and charged furiously.

This time the Sailor Boy sprang forward to receive him

Throwing out his arm he caught his foe full in the face.

Dan fell flat on his back and was knocked completely "out of time."

"Now, you young sycophant," cried the petty

officer, leaning over him, "let that be a lesson for life ; learn that a coward will be sure to find a match where he little expects it, and that cruelty always brings its own punishment."

At this moment the second lieutenant, Mr. Armitage, quickly advanced.

"Can I believe my senses, Mr. Stiff?" he cried, in a tone of extreme displeasure. "Is it possiblet hat I find you inciting the lads to fight?"

"Sir," said the petty officer, "I don't know what to say in answer, except this: I have charge of these troublesome youngsters, and am responsible for their conduct. I find that there is no sort of vice so hard to deal with as this of ' bullying;' the victims of it are afraid to complain ; they know that they can't be always grumbling about ill-treatment ; besides, every boy has an aversion to telling tales. One way to cure it is by such means as I have already taken. I have had my eye on these lads for a long time, sir, and I must say that a quieter lad than Halliard, and a bigger bully than this Crawley, never trod the decks of a man-of-war.

"A bully, is he ? we'll bully him ; send him to the trip deck, and let him be soundly chastised."

Harry sprang forward.

"Oh, sir, pray recal that order," said the boy, earnestly; "I am to blame as well as he, and as I was allowed to fight my own battle, it cannot be fair that he should be punished now."

The officer smiled.

"Well, my lad, perhaps you're right ; but let him take warning ; and a word to *you*: don't presume upon the protection you have received to be impudent to elder boys, for, after what has happened, I should visit such an offence with tenfold strictness."

"I don't think I ever shall, sir," returned Harry simply.

"I do not think so either ; but, young or old, we easily fall astray."

The officer walked aft.

Dan sneaked off, blubbering.

The men dispersed.

Frank now returned to his chum, and having first administered a friendly slap between his shoulders, that was much harder than any of his foe's worst hits had been, performed around him a dance of triumph.

This gymnastic display was in the nature of a war-dance, if one might judge by the bellicose movements of the hands and arms.

"Now Harry, my son," he cried, dancing persistently, "you have given him the finishing touch (on Dan's nose) to your best achievements, for all wise philosophers (like your humble servant) hold that a chap who stands *too much* humbug will never make a hero."

CHAPTER II.

THE LONG BOAT OF THE THUNDERER—THE BOY SAILOR AN OBJECT OF INTEREST TO THE OFFICERS—THE NIGHT ATTACK ON THE GUNBOATS—ENGLAND'S GREATEST HERO—THE ATTACK OF THE SPANIARDS—PROUD DEED OF THE BOY SAILOR—THE IMMINENT DANGER OF LORD NELSON—HEROIC DEVOTION OF HIS COXSWAIN—THE TAKING OF THE LAUNCH—VICTORY !

THE waves of the Bay of Cadiz rolled black and turgid beneath the lowering sky.

The lights from the town, and the lanterns at the stern and on the mast-heads of the anchored fleet, glared round in the darkness red and dim, like the fires of a sorcerer's magic circle.

The silence of the stilly night was deeply oppressive.

Yet nothing could be more favourable than the solemn gloom for the purposes of the British admiral.

There are blades softly dipping in the rippling waters.

A long-boat pushed off from the dark high sides of the Thunderer.

It contained the captain, Sir Everard Brandon ; the lieutenant, Armitage, and eight men.

A light and active lad was required for the service.

The election had fallen upon our hero.

The heart of the Boy Sailor beat wildly ; his lips quivered with intense excitement.

Perhaps he was somewhat awe-smitten by the intense darkness, by the silence of the ocean, and by the low whisperings in which the officers carried on their earnest conversation.

Yet his heart leaped with the romantic joy peculiar to fresh and glowing youth, and his hand clutched the short side-arms with which he had been adorned for the occasion.

"I think it rashness, Mr. Armitage," whispered Captain Brandon.

"It would indeed be so, Sir Everard, in any other man, but not in Nelson."

"But to risk a life so valuable. Well, you will see ; he must fall at last."

"Perhaps ; but it will be into the arms of victory."

"It is almost too bad to bring that mere child with us ; but he is his country's, and we can spare no sacrifice," said the captain of the Thunderer.

"Why did you not choose one of the midshipmen ?"

"There was not one of them in whom I felt able to place so much dependence as upon this lad. He is an extraordinary little fellow—nimble as a squirrel, lithe as an eel, docile as the ship to her helm, and brave as the British Lion. I must do something for him."

"Do you know who he is ?"

"The son of some poor widow at Cornwall, I believe."

"But his father ?"

"A sea-faring man, I should think, from the boy's training ; perhaps in the merchant service."

"Sir Everard, I made a strange discovery about this lad only this morning."

"Indeed !"

"He is the son of poor Halliard that went down in the Thetis, off the Shark's Fin."

"As supposed, there's some infernal trickery of the wreckers of that desperate coast."

"Most likely."

"How strange ; then the less said of his mother the better ; I understand she is a low-bred woman."

"The sweetest woman I ever beheld, Sir Everard."

"Ha ! then you have seen her?"

"I served as midshipman on the Defiance, of which he was in succession made lieutenant. I was present at the romantic and hasty marriage at Seawardine."

"But it was strange he should form such a connection."

"You would not say so, Sir Everard, if you had seen Rose Lavington."

"But I thought she was associated with pirates, wreckers, smugglers, or some such miscreants ?"

"That is strictly true ; she was an orphan, dependent upon an uncle, a smuggler, and everything else that is rascally ; a low-bred fellow who brutally ill-used her."

"Strange ; and she lost her pension ?"

"Through the villainy of an arch-villain, the Earl of Penalvou."

"My God ! is that possible ?"

"It is too true ; the lad ought to have a midshipman's warrant."

"In due time."

At this moment, dancing like a will-o'wisp over the misty wold, a lantern at the prow of a boat was seen ahead.

"Hold water !" whispered Sir Everard.

The men softly raised their oars.

An admiral's barge ran quietly alongside.

A lantern burned on the grating in the barge.

Its dim flare shone on the faces of the heroes that manned it.

The Boy Sailor rose eagerly to look at the great British Admiral, whom he had never before seen.

He was not much impressed by the first view of England's great Hero. A little pale-faced gentleman sat in the stern ; he was wrapped in a thick coat.

As he turned his head to the light it was seen that one of his eyes were dim ; but that defect was greatly compensated.

By his side sat Captain Freemantle.

His faithful follower, John Sykes, acted as coxswain.

The ten oarsmen were splendid specimens of true British tars.

The Boy Sailor contemplated the pale-face and emaciated form of that great little man as if he were some divinity of the ocean.

The officers in the Thunderer's long boat rose, and saluted their great commander.

"How many are ye ?" asked Nelson, in a tone rather sharp and testily.

"Twelve, Sir Horatio, and the boy."

"You have brought him with you," said Captain Freemantle ; "is he of any use ?"

"A treasure, though I speak it before him."

"A midshipman, of course ?" said Captain Freemantle.

"No, sir ; a lad I have selected for his superior merit.

"All the better ; let him come into the barge."

The Boy Sailor stepped lightly from the boat.

Courage is of no age or condition.

Young as was Harry Halliard, he was purely brave. He had shouted with glee as he rushed through the smoke of the battle, and had recked no more of the pondrous shells, as they whizzed past or crashed at his feet, than if they had been so many shuttlecocks in a playground.

Yet as in that dark and stithy night he saw, by the dull gleam of the fighting-lantern, that glittering eye fixed searchingly upon his own, he felt every drop of blood rush from his cheeks, and a thrill of awe passed through his sensitive brain.

"Very good ; I like the look of him," said the admiral. "Sykes, take charge of the youngster."

"Do you wish us to commence the attack, Sir Horatio?"

"No; drop astern, and keep to the lee of the signal-buoy till the gun is fired from the Theseus."

"But, sir——"

"Outside the signal-buoy!" repeated the admiral, in a manner that would not be gainsaid.

The word was given, and, with a steady, silent stroke, the barge pulled through the parting waters.

"My lad, give me that night-glass," said the admiral to our hero. "Thanks. What is your name, my boy ?"

"Harry Halliard, sir," replied the Boy Sailor.

"Halliard ! I knew a gallant officer of that name."

"My father !"

The word had almost risen proudly to our little hero's lips.

As he checked it, and reflected on his temerity, he felt his cheek burn with a hot blush and his limbs to tremble.

The barge rowed on for some time.

They were nearly alongside of the gunboat.

"Can you climb well, youngster?"

"Yes, sir," replied the Boy Sailor, shuddering with joyous excitement.

"Give him a grapnel, Sykes."

At this moment a large boat was seen approaching.

The fog was clearing off, sweeping away seaward.

From the rapidly-advancing boat rose a deafening cheer.

"The Spaniards are upon us!" cried Captain Freemantle.

"Steady, men!" cried the admiral. "We must fight for it now or never."

A heavy launch, commanded by Don Miguel Tregoyen, and carrying twenty-six men, dashed alongside.

In the twinkling of an eye a furious encounter had commenced.

The Spaniards recognised the admiral.

So far outnumbering the Englishmen they made sure of victory.

They yelled and cheered frantically with exultation.

A volley of pistol shots were fired on both sides.

The heavy barques dashed furiously by each other.

Hand to hand with swords, breast to breast with blazing pistols.

The greatness of the issue depending on this fight nerved every arm with temporary strength, wrought every heart to the highest pitch of desperation.

Wildly shouted the Spaniards, and deep and stern rolled the cheer of this handful of England's greatest warriors in the frantic struggle against a foe double their number.

The Boy Sailor leaped up in the boat, and, drawing his dirk, flew upon a man who had jumped almost unheeded into the barge, and was rushing upon the admiral, his arm uplifted, his Spanish sabre gleaming in the pistol flashes.

With a wild cry our hero leaped or stumbled over the bodies of the slain and wounded that cumbered the boat.

The bullets flew past his flowing locks ; pikes and cutlasses clashed in his face.

All passed before him in an instant.

Throwing back his arm, and exerting all his strength, the Boy Sailor plunged his dirk to the hilt in the Spaniard's body.

The sabre fell from the relaxed grasp of the assailant.

It fell, and struck the shoulder of the admiral, who was still furiously fighting hand to hand with Don Miguel Tregoyen.

The Spaniard staggered round.

He grappled the boy with his dying fingers. The barge lurched, and man and boy rolled heavily into the sea.

Harry struggled to disengage himself from the seaman's clutches, but down, down he plunged, strangling through the engulphing waters.

NOTICE.—The next Number of the Boys' Library will be Published on Friday, July 11th
Order early of your Bookseller.

BOYS' LIBRARY

HARRY HALLIARD:
OR,
THE YOUNG BRITISH TAR.

THE BOY SAILORS' PRACTICAL JOKE.

Harry Halliard rose and clung to the gunnel of the barge.

The Spaniards fought with the fury of demons.

Through all his long career, up to this time, Nelson had never been in such imminent danger.

It is stated that the great admiral always considered that his personal courage was more conspicuous on this occasion than on any other during his whole life.

The numbers on both sides were decreasing from the effects of the shots and sword-thrusts, exchanged with such mad and terrible obstinacy.

The Boy Sailor had scrambled into the boat.

He took up a pistol that he found at the bottom of the barge.

He fired, and struck an officer who was about to fire upon Captain Freemantle, and then the daring boy snatched a cutlass, and setting one foot on the side of the Spanish launch, cut right and left with his small weapon, shouting for the boat's crew to follow him.

It was at this juncture that the faithful coxswain performed an act almost unparalleled in the annals of heroism.

Three several times he had parried thrusts made at the admiral which must have been fatal.

Twice he had saved his life by killing his assailants.

At length, seeing the sabre of one of the fiercest of the Spanish assailants glancing through the air, and descending upon his beloved commander, he actually opposed his own head to receive the blow.

There was a furious shout from the Theseus men as the gallant coxswain sank down in the barge.

A Spaniard, who had been struggling in the water, crawled over the gunnel.

His eyes ablaze with vindictive passion, he wrestled to get near the admiral.

The Boy Sailor seized him by the throat.

What the lad lacked in strength he made up in agility.

He dodged under the Spaniard's arm.

His antagonist growled and cursed.

He gripped Harry by the throat, and tried to push him into the water.

But the Boy seized a gun that lay in the stern-sheets, and striking the seaman across the head, knocked him into the sea.

Eighteen of the twenty-six Spaniards that manned the launch were killed.

All the rest were wounded.

The launch was taken.

The hearty seamen had not suffered the daring deeds of the gallant Boy Sailor to pass unnoticed.

They snatched the Boy up in their strong arms, and laughing and shouting in triumph that their admiral had been preserved through so much danger, leaped on to their hard-won prize.

CHAPTER III.

SYMPTOMS OF DISCONTENT—ANOTHER BATTLE AND GLORIOUS VICTORY.

UNDER the forecastle of the Thunderer, sprinkled broad-cast in every attitude of repose, the hardy fore-mast men were lying asleep.

Many of those deepest slumbering displayed on their heads and on their limbs bandages blood-soaked from recent wounds.

Strange and weird the gloomy scene, faintly illumined by the flickering light of the lanterns, the low arching beams of the upper deck, cramping the movements of the tired seamen, as, relieved from watch, they limp in, stumbling wearily over the prostrate bodies of their unconscious comrades, and then stretching themselves down by their side, and sinking into the same profound and sweet oblivion.

In the gloomiest part of the sloping cabin a knot of the roughest-looking fellows were conversing in low whispers.

They were apart from the rest of the men, perhaps on the old principle that birds of a feather flock together.

A wild group, indeed, they formed, as they lay extended on the planks, with bare feet and brawny breasts, their unkempt hair strewing their weather-beaten faces, for none of them were possessed of the long pigtail which betokened long service.

In the midst of them, and lying upon the floor, was a loose handkerchief thrown over some object it concealed.

This was a bottle of spirits, from which the conversers would take an occasional sip, and glance furtively round to see that they were not watched by the eye of superintendence.

Conspicuous among this ruffish set lay a massive, villanous looking fellow; his figure, which was but little, if at all, below the average height of man, at least, when he stood alone, appeared dwarfish, from the giant-like proportions of his huge, strong limbs. His face was broad, sallow, and stained; his eyes rolling and black; his hair, shaggy and coarse, hung on his bull-neck in long elf-locks.

His back was propped against the bulkhead, and his brawny arms folded across his broad chest.

The other ruffians seemed to consider him the oracle of their clique.

"Aye, messmates," growled this fellow, "though I was caught at last, you may believe me it was not till I had seen many a cargo run, and, between ourselves, hearties, more than one rich sea-chest hauled out of the foaming surf, in a channel gale. Those were the days, my boys, eh?"

"Aye, mate," returned another, "when a man might roll home like a porpoise every night, and skulk through the heat and sunshine of every day, without getting his back scratched. Bless yer eyes, mates, I knows the sweets of liberty, and the jolly fun and pleasure of free-trading."

"Right you are, my souls," cried a red-haired fellow, "and where was the risk, eh? Nine times out of ten, a cargo could be run without trouble; five times out of ten in open day, for there was agents all along the French coasts."

"Pish!" growled a fourth. "Why, dam'me, is there any risks like those we run on board a man-of-war?"

"None, mate," muttered a fifth member of this black club, looking around him and whispering, "not even—on—board—of—a—*pirate!*"

The men started and looked nervously round.

"Nor more there arn't, mates," growled the most influential ruffian, in whom, perhaps, our readers may recognise Harleck the wrecker, "where's the risk? Why, here we may all be blown up at any moment; half on us, I daresay, will miss their men afore this time eight bells to-morrow; and then there's scurvy and the 'Yellow Jack' in the cussed ports they sends us to rot in; and, more than all this, marn't we be flogged into ribbons for sleeping on deck, though our peepers be battened down by snow-flakes, and all the 'wake' in us froze up with bitter cold, and then there's allers the noose dangling for our necks, and yer knows what court-martial justice is?—its a safe wage; ten to one on us, that not a soul sees this Thunderer put into Gosport. What dangers, mates, lies under the black flag? Shiver me, if piracy arn't safety compared with this blasted pressed sarvice!"

"Vy, it weally air, pals," said a lanky Cockney fellow, as thin as a herring, and as clumsy as a lame bear. "Vy, the roarin' life of the mooching boys is nothin' to it; and, my vig, how jolly! It's all werry vell for you covies to crack about running tubs of swill through a fog, and boozing your jibs in spite of the pwewentive officer; but, cwiminy, my flash culls, fancy the sublimity of faking a bo'sman on the high-toby!"

"What's that, you land lubber?"

"Vy, my dimber pals, robbing a farmer on the high-vay."

"Oh, cuss all land-cruising!" responded Harleck, with savage contempt.

"Vell, vot's von man's meat is another man's pison. I'm fly to that, my dainties. But, I don't twig the use of sticking in a jug—vich I'll explain to your benighted ignorance, means a pwison, vether it's a stone jug or a vooden von—if there's hiver a chance to hook it, vich I don't mind confiding to you, I mean to do, venever I finds there's no von down, and the toby's clear. To enlighten the Hottentots, vot I means is, I shall *desert*, fust oppertoonity."

"So will all on us," muttered the pressed men, with a low growl.

"Aye, dam'me, or *mutiny!*" muttered Harleck; "it only wants pluck and sticking together. Oh, lord, I wish we had Thorkil Penreal, or young Paul Adair, on board this 'farnal wessel, the cocked hats would find they'd the devil among 'em !"

"Avast heaving, yer swab," murmured the men, aghast with fright, as the quarter-master entered the forecastle.

The malcontents stretched out their limbs, snored, and affected to be fast asleep.

Presently they roused themselves.

"To be watched by cats like rats in a cage ; ah, beastly !" murmured Harleck, shaking his huge shoulders.

As he spoke there suddenly arose on deck the brisk rattaplan of drums and the shrill whistle of pipes beating to quarters.

It was a strange sight to see the unlucky sleepers awake, start in their sleep, and blunder mechanically to their feet.

Still the rattle of the drums and the squealing of the pipes on deck.

Half-dreamily the poor seamen, robbed so ruthlessly of their scanty share of necessary sleep, hurried on to the main deck.

"Thunderer !" snarled Harleck, "I'd make it thunder, and lighten too, if I were in the magazine with a handful of blazing tow !"

Moodily he followed his messmates, arriving last on deck.

The roaring of guns was now heard from the town.

The forts around the bay of Cadiz also belched with smoke.

The grey streaks were broadening in the eastern horizon.

In the paling zenith a few stars still twinkled.

The breeze was blowing freshly from the open main.

The ships of the squadron were forming into a line.

The large flag-ship of the rear-admiral was flying her signal.

The officers were all at their posts.

The marines paraded.

The men formed at divisions.

Orders were given to man the sides.

The man and the signal-midshipman were busy at the halliards.

The guns were manned.

There was breathless silence.

It was an awful moment ; the bravest men cannot help feeling moved with awe when entering upon an action.

The excitement and clamour of the raging battle divert the thoughts from personal interests.

Orders were given to trim the sails.

The admiral had signalled for all the ships to bear up in line of battle.

The yards were squared, and the Thunderer soon had steerage way.

At one of the guns—a large bow-chaser—were stationed Lieutenant Armitage, a midshipman, and our hero.

Their duty was to fire upon the gun-boats cruising about the bay, their task being unshared by the rest of the crew, who were engaged in pouring their broadsides of shot and shell, round and grape, into the town.

Among the men at the bow-chaser was Harleck.

"Steady, my men !" cried Armitage. "Take fair aim—fire ! Stop your vents."

The ship shuddered with the thunder of the guns.

The blood started in the ringing ears of Harry, his brain swam, his head seemed reverberating with the dreadful din.

His lips closed, and he shook his curly head, his eyes smarting and his nostrils choked by the sulphurous smoke.

He laughed low and gleefully.

He clenched his hands and drew himself up to his fullest height, his chest swelling with the zest and joy of battle.

The heavy metal crashed past him.

Spars and tackling toppled down.

Heavy shots smashed into the vessel's hull.

Louder, more awfully louder, thundered the Thunderer.

Denser and denser grew the palling smoke.

Fiercer, intenser flitted the flashes of blinding flame.

A plank was stove at the Boy Sailor's feet.

He did not stir.

The men were busy as working bees, and quite as dingy in hue, as they drove home the charges of grape and langrel into the chambers of the hot-mouthed guns with their long rammer.

"Set that quoin, Harry," said the lieutenant.

A quoin, it may be mentioned, is a wedge that elevates the gun.

Harry obeyed.

He did not recede.

His eye was fixed on the boats.

They were visible as the smoke soared upwards.

"That was well aimed, Harry," said the mid, who was very partial to our hero.

"Yes, sir," returned the boy, respectfully.

"I should like to be a gunner," said the mid, with a laugh.

"Yes, sir," said the Boy Sailor, abstractedly ; "there's higher work ; but it's very amusing."

The roar of the guns was still deafening.

Men were shouting aloft.

Some excitement prevailed.

The Thunderer was suffering terribly from the furious cannonading from the gun-boats.

The lieutenant pulled the Boy Sailor back.

"Keep by my side, Harry," he said, kindly. "You are but a muff. Next to cowardice, rashness is most fatal."

The men at the bow-chaser huzzaed.

Four of the launches and three of the gun-boats had been swamped.

"Now, men, that heavy craft carries a freight of torpedoes. Phew ! I told you so."

A blazing shell dashed through the fore-top.

The fore-topsail and stays were in flames, and the foremast was shattered.

Men were hurled from their dizzy height into the waves.

Others crashed hideously down on the deck.

"Steady, my lads. Remember the saying of your great admiral, ' Victory, or Westminster Abbey !' Now, fire !"

Harry could scarcely repress a shout of exultation as the well-aimed shot carried away the mast and fore-sheet of the death-laden launch.

"Next time !" said the gallant mid, rubbing his hands.

"Aye, sir," responded Harry.

"Take your time, men," said the lieutenant.

The gunners paused, and swabbed their dripping foreheads with their sleeves.

"Make ready!"

"Aye, aye, sir!"

"Now, you landsmen," cried the lieutenant, "I am pleased with you; but attend; be careful. Lean well over the right knee, keeping the left foot well from the recoil."

"Aye, aye, sir," again answered the men, with cheerful promptness.

The little party at the bow-chaser regarded nothing that was passing on deck.

The old clock on the mantel does not tick more unheeded than the broadsides bellowed dumbly to those men, so intent upon their own task.

The shot struck the launch at the same moment that one of her torpedoes was playing "Old Harry" in the rigging of the Thunderer, firing her sails and stays.

"Stir them, my lads! another launch has put off!" cried the lieutenant, growing excited, in spite of his philosophy. "Stir them up! open their eyes! but—steady!"

"Hurrah!" shouted the gunners.

"Bravo!" returned the lieutenant,

"What a spree!" cried the Boy Sailor.

The launch was sinking.

Her freight of fire was quenching in the cold waves; her crew struggling in the surging waters.

Again the gun was loaded.

The gunner stood ready to point it.

A third launch steered out of the harbour.

Still roared the din, unheeded around them.

"Damn the smoke!" said the lieutenant, losing sight of propriety as he lost sight of the boat.

The gunner stooped down.

He placed one eye on a level with the cannon, closing the other.

"Now, sir," he said.

The words were his last.

Both he and the man who should have fired the gun were dashed, shattered and torn, on the deck.

A hot shot ripped by.

The Boy Sailor leaped forward, and snatched up the match.

He thrust the flame on the vent.

A body of smoke, like a thunder-cloud, stole from the muzzle of the cannon.

A swift, vivid flash!

A thunderous roar.

A moment's suspense.

The cloud floated and wreathed up.

The last launch from Cadiz lay disabled on the waters.

The bow-chasers had done their work for that day.

Then, as if suddenly startled by the sound, they were appalled by the rocking of the vessel, and the roaring of the flaming guns.

The men looked at each other and laughed.

The bantam midshipman shook hands with the gentle Boy Sailor.

Harry Halliard shouted with glee.

"Youngster," said the middy, "I hear that your father was a post captain."

"Nelson knew him," returned our hero, simply, and with characteristic unction and simplicity.

"I'll believe anything from you; if nothing happens to prevent, my boy, you will be a great man yet."

"If nothing happens to prevent it." The prediction was a safe one.

But what recked our hero?

A brave, gifted, happy English boy, there was no gloom in the bright future, no terror in the perilous present, that could daunt the fearless heart of the BOY SAILOR!

CHAPTER IV.

THE COCKPIT AFTER THE BATTLE—THE WOUNDED WRECKER—HARRY'S KINDNESS—TALK OF BLACK WILL TRELAWNEY—HARLECK IN DUDGEON.

THE wounded had been carried below.

The cockpit presented a dreadful spectacle.

On the table some poor fellow was undergoing the torture of the amputation of one of his limbs; the deck was strewed with the writhing and groaning bodies of the wounded.

Among the latter, but preserving the stolid fortitude of a red Indian, sat Harleck, his chin buried in his breast, his coarse matted hair hanging over his lowering brow, his teeth clenched, his sullen eyes gleaming with a threatening light from beneath his rugged brows, his arms folded across each other; the tight grasp of his iron hands on either shoulder being the only indication of the acute agony he was suffering with a manly endurance worthy of a better character.

His side had been torn by a piece of shattered langrel, and the wound was extremely painful.

Our hero was assisting the surgeon.

Very quietly, yet with prompt attention to the doctor's slightest sign, young Harry moved about among the patients.

He passed by the wrecker and stood for an instant looking at him.

A bright beam shone in his pleasant blue eyes as he contrasted the patience of the Cornishman, with the piteous demeanour of the whining, weeping, and wriggling cad, that lay twisting like a worm on a hook, by the side of the sturdy wrecker.

This was Tony Wilks, the ex-pick-pocket.

"A draught of water, lad, when you pass with the can," muttered the wrecker, huskily.

"O lor, O lor! stwike me lucky if I haint got my discharge and no mistake," groaned the Londoner. "O vy vos hiver I born to be massecreed in this vay? Oh, my dimber little pal, hif you 'ave got sich a thing has a 'art, be quick vith the vater; my hinside is burning hup like Wesuvius, and oh, my painful vound! I shall 'ave to be cut in 'alf, and trundle my hupper parts on four vheels about Vhitechapel, vith a pictur' round my blessed neck of this hawful scene, and a placard a statin' 'England's gratitood to her wounded weterans.' O lor, O lor! pray tell the willin I'm dying without benefit of clergy!"

"Avast, ye skunk!" growled Harleck, turning his evil eyes upon his companion in grief, "are ye a man to be screaming and twittering like a winged sea-gull?"

"Vy you hunfeelin' monster! its hall vewy well for you, vith jest a bit of a scratch hunder your harm, ven there's no counting my vounds; I'm squashed like a kid run over by a two-hoss 'ackney, and all my limbs smashed like a jewellers' vinder. Vill that little ruffin niver bring the vater?"

Harry Halliard returned with the can, and pouring out a hornful of the water stooped by the side of Harleck.

"O, lor! me fust; my vounds is 'scrutiatin'!" cried Tony, with greediness.

"Stopper this lubber first, youngster!" growled Harleck, "and I'll wait my turn when the lolly-boy comes round with the stingo—I was never a friend to you."

"We're shipmates, Master Harleck, and fellow county-men. I don't want your friendship!" returned Harry, with a smile, "but a cup of water wouldn't be refused to a wounded Frenchman."

The surly fellow muttered his thanks, and drank with eagerness.

The men assisting the surgeon now approached.

O lor! be gentle; I am dead already," moaned Tony. "O, *vill* you be gentle? I'd rather not hundergo the hoperation, my constitution is veak; I shall never survive."

"Dam'me, you cowardly swab, behave, and be thankful," returned one of his supporters, whose brawny arms were bare and blood-smeared, and whose general aspect was that of a butcher at work in the slaughter-house, "you'll never disgrace the service by walking the deck like a cat in walnuts, and, what's better, hearty, you won't be able to mount the treadmill."

"O, I vish I'd been lagged for life—werry much better than bein' maimed for the term of my nat'ral servitood," Tony groaned, as they flopped him on the table.

His wound, however, was by no means serious.

He soon gave place to other unfortunates.

Harleck's hurt was very serious, and he bore the cruel torment of the lancet and caustic with the firmest stoicism.

The men around looked at his dark wild face with softened glances.

Even the stern doctor murmured approvingly as the half fainting seaman was borne away.

As he lay in his hammock slung in the hospital berth he whispered hoarsely in his fevered trance.

He opened his wild, red eyes, and glared upon the face of a boy that stood beside him.

"Ha! what do you want, youngster?" he said, in a thick harsh tone.

"I want you to drink this, Harleck," returned Harry, holding to him a cup, containing a soothing draught which he had just fetched from the doctor's room.

The man grinned.

"Well, I'm not Black Will Trelawney; I suppose it's not poison?" he said, gruffly laughing, though his broad sallow cheek twitched with pain.

The Bay Sailor shuddered, and then his eyes darted a gleam of fierceness.

"Harleck," he said, "what has become of that villain? he is never heard of now at home."

"No, he has gone to sea!" returned Harleck.

"Well, and for a long cruise?"

"I should 'spose so!" returned Harleck, with a meaning leer.

'Smuggling?"

The wrecker did not reply, but lay in his hammock, his arms folded, his wild eyes fixed vacantly, a satanic smile lurking on his lips.

"There's a higher game than that, lad, for men with Cornish mettle," he answered.

"What, has he, then, turned pir——" gasped Harry.

"Hulloa! I see what your steering for, young viper," cried Harleck, with a sudden burst of wrath; "sheer off, or it will be worse for you."

"You have no cause to be angry, Harleck," returned the boy calmly.

"How do I know that? I want no talk with you, lubber's brat! Brush, I tell ye."

"But, Harleck——"

The wrecker hurled the cup at the boy's head.

"There's nothing atwixt us. Do you hear, you infernal young spy? Be off; I have nothing to say to you."

The wrecker turned his back, rolled himself up in his hammock, and closed his eyes.

Harry lingered a moment, and then went on deck.

CHAPTER V.

SKY-LARKING ON BOARD — MR. KONKS, THE BOATSWAIN'S MATE—THE BOY SAILORS IN TROUBLE—THE BALM OF SOFT SAWDER—A PRACTICAL JOKE —A TALE OF A TUB AND A PIGTAIL.

"Come here, you sirs; come here, you scamps," roared a fat, pompous-looking boatswain's mate, with a bottle-nose of ruby hue, to our hero and his chum Frank, who were larking about the main deck.

"Aye, sir," responded the boys, looking at each other, with faces expressing their mutual roguishness, mingled with trepidation.

Hot and panting, they stood before the officer, and screwed their smirking countenances into an expression of awe and reverence.

"You young dogs; do you show no more respect for your betters than to be skipping about like kids at Gibraltar, and in my presence, eh? Come here, you baboon-behaved rascal; what's your name, you ape?" shouted the scandalised officer, catching the elder boy by the ear.

"Frank Rayner, sir."

"Do you know who I AM, sir?"

"Yes, sir," returned Frank, lowering his eyes, and murmuring humbly; "boys will be boys, sir, and I and Halliard didn't mean any disrespect." Harry smoothed his handsome face with his hand, and looked the picture of penitence.

"Dam'me, sir, that's immater'al to me!" cried the boatswain's mate. "Do you, sir; I repeat, do you know who I AM?"

"Very well, sir; heard the first lieutenant say, sir, there wasn't aboard, sir, a more valuable officer than Mr. Konks. Didn't mean to mention it, sir; hope no offence," replied Frank, with touching humility.

"Very well, sir," returned the boatswain's mate, in a tone rather mollified; yet, notwithstanding, applying his rattan smartly to the young rogue's unmentionables. "Take that, sir; and that sir, and larn to behave for the future."

"Thank ye, sir," returned Frank, breaking loose, and clearing away.

"And now, you," the mate went on, catching hold of our hero.

"Oh, if you please, Mr. Konks, I really didn't——" cried Harry, writhing in his grasp.

"I repeat, sir, that's all immater'al to me. Do *you* know who I am?"

"Oh! yes, sir; heard the captain tell the admiral—"

"Hey! what?" cried the irate seaman, releasing the boy.

"That you saved the ship, sir, in the last gale."

"That's all immater'al," returned the mate, though evidently much flattered, "only let it teach you to pay me proper respect."

"Always do, sir," returned Harry, with great apparent sincerity.

"Very well; you may go for this once, you monkey; but, remember, that next time I catch you sky-larking and running athwart my dignity, I'll make you sit on hot coals for the whole cruise, you scape-grace."

Thus enfranchised, the chuckling boys darted forward.

When they had reached the forecastle, they sat down and laughed merrily.

"I shall owe old Blowhard one for that," said Frank, applying his hand to his smarting nethers, and making a wry grimace; "he's a precious deal too fast with the rattan and the rope's end."

"You see, you don't know how to manage him," returned our hero, with a grin; "he only wants a little soft sawder."

"Anyhow, I should have been skinned if I had not thought of the lieutenant," returned his chum.

"Ah! but the captain, Frank; the captain got me off scot free."

"Lucky for you; my notions were not so high. What would you have done if I had thought of the captain?"

"I shouldn't have suffered, Frank; I should have appealed to the admiral. Did he hurt you?"

"Rather; but never mind, 'its immater'al to me.' I'll pay him out somehow, I'll warrant," returned Frank.

"There he goes, with his nose glowing like the red lights off Land's End," cried Harry.

"Yes, and now he sits down against the carronade," rejoined the other. "Something twinkles between his sleeve and his lips."

"Yes, he's pouring in oil for the beacon. You'll see it shine redder and fiercer as the night gets darker,

'The tulip's rich stains
No such glories disclose
As the toper's bright tip
On his jolly red nose,'"

sang Frank.

"Stopper all," chuckled our hero, administering an admonitory punch in his chum's ribs; "he'll hear you, and if he does, you'll think the cross-trees red hot when you perch aloft, my hearty; lor, can't he lay on?"

Frank rose and stole off.

He returned.

His eyes gleamed with fun and mischief.

"Such a lark," said he, "the old buffer's fast asleep, and the pride of his heart, that's his pig-tail, lies along the top of a barrel against which he's leaning; he sits with his back to the after hatchway; and, look here, the carpenter has left his hammer and nails on the grating, he's been caulking up the shot-holes of yesterday's row."

Frank showed a small mallet, and a bag of nails.

"How's your heart?" he asked, with a knowing wink, and using a by-word common among the crew.

"Tough," returned the Boy Sailor.

"And how's your legs, cheery?"

"Taut."

"Well, if you're game, so am I?"

"But what's the game?"

Frank touched the back of his head to indicate Mr. Konk's pig-tail, and then pantomimed striking a nail through the cherished adornment into the top of the cask.

"Twig, Hal?"

"Aye, Frank, and we can bolt down the companion-way, before he has time to unclose his peepers."

"So we can."

Frank walked softly aft.

The Boy Sailor followed him.

A little barrel was lashed by the ledges of the hatch-way.

Against this the boatswain's mate reclined.

His long pig-tail was stretched along the top of the cask.

The Boy Sailor crept behind his comrade and drew the hammer from his hand.

He motioned Frank to hold the nail.

The two urchins looked fore and aft.

They were not observed.

Frank applied the nail.

Harry gave it a sharp, straight tap, and drove it through the bunch at the end of the pig-tail into the head of the tub.

The boatswain's mate snorted, opened his lips, and murmured,

"Dam'me, sir, its immater'al to me!"

The boys writhed about in a convulsion of smothered mirth, and then darted down the gangway.

The second lieutenant walked forward from the captain's cabin.

"Pass the word for Mr. Hawser," said Armitage, to a midshipman.

"Aye, sir,"

The word was passed forward.

The boatswain walked aft to the officer.

"Pipe the men up to divisions," said the lieutenant.

The boatswain lifted his hat with the eternal response,

"Aye, sir."

Soon the pipes sounded shrilly, and the drums tattooed briskly.

Swiftly and noiselessly the well-disciplined seamen formed at divisions.

The officers gathered on the after-deck.

The boatswain's mate started from his sleep like a war-horse at the blast of a clarion.

Woeful his case.

Bound like Prometheus to the rock, he wrestled in vain with his pigtail.

Madly he struggled to free himself from the cask.

"Mutiny!" he roared; "somebody come and free me; I'll bring the villain before a court-martial. Oh, dam'me, it's immater'al to me, but if I don't have him keel-hauled, I'm no Christian."

It was dusk.

Before the cask was the heavy carriage of the stern-chaser.

On either side were the shot-racks, bolted to the crampions.

He was completely concealed.

The wind was whistling through the rigging.

The drums and pipes still kept up their squeal and rattle.

All things conspired to prevent the appeals of the captive from reaching the ears of his shipmates.

Driven to desperation, the boatswain's mate, whose name had been twice called, threw all his strength into a final effort and started up.

The lashings of the cask gave way.

He rushed forward.

The tub flew after him, bumping and dragging on the deck.

There was an irrepressible shout of astonishment as he blundered into the arms of a stout and starchy sergeant of marines, his novel and weighty appendage trundling from his "queue."

Even the lurid scarlet of his jolly nose was almost eclipsed by the indignant blushes that dyed his cheeks.

"Mr. Konks! are you mad, sir? What does this mean?" cried the captain.

"Dam'me, sir, it's immater'al to me!" shouted the boatswain's mate, beside himself with fury. "A joke's a joke; but whoever played me this infarnal, lubberly trick, he shall pay dearly for it, sir, for the sarvice is all going to pot, and I'm——"

In his wrath he sprang back, shaking his massive fist.

He tripped over the tub, his heels soared up in the air, he was pitched bodily and barrelly plump down the main-hatchway, and his former place knew him no more.

This was too much even for the stern decorum of the man-of-war's men.

There was a universal roar of laughter, in which none joined more lustily than Frank Rayner and the Boy Sailor.

CHAPTER VI.

OFF MALTA—HARLECK'S RESOLVE—THE DESERTERS IN THE GUN ROOM—A NARROW ESCAPE—AFLOAT IN A SHORE BOAT—FOILED.

TWELVE days after Nelson's perilous encounter with the Spanish gunboat, the squadron sailed from the Bay of Cadiz and steered its course for Teneriffe.

The Thunderer was detached from the rest of the squadron, and sent with dispatches to Malta.

For many days the man-of-war lay off the island.

Both the wrecker Harleck, and the respectable personage, Mr. Tony Wilks, had recovered from the wounds they had received during the blockade of Cadiz.

The Cornishman and the knight of the road found their life on board a man-of-war so intolerable that they, in conjunction with other desperate foremastmen, had resolved at any risk to effect their escape.

The plan determined upon by Harleck was to take advantage of the darkness of the autumn nights, and slip from the ports of the gun-deck into one of the shore boats always floating alongside of the anchored vessel.

What was to follow their reaching shore had not been resolved upon.

The wrecker, however, although he knew that such a course would render him liable to be hanged at the yard arm, had made up his mind to desert to the enemy.

The night appointed by the mal-contents for their hazardous venture had arrived.

The hour and the weather were propitious.

It was midnight.

The night was very dark, the sea was mantled with a thick fog.

The lanterns at the binnacle and under the quarter gleamed faintly along the wet and shining deck.

It drizzled rain.

The men had been hard at work all day.

Troops had been embarked, and the crowded state of the ship was rather favourable than otherwise to the purpose of the deserters.

An extra allowance of grog had been served out.

The men, worn out with fatigue, had retired to their hammocks.

The captain, and a major part of the officers, were on shore.

The lieutenant who had been left in charge of the ship had received a hurt while in the boat alongside.

Some of the baggage of the troops, which was being hoisted by blocks, broke from the tackle, falling into the boat, swamping it, and crushing several men, inflicting upon several very serious injury;

among the rest the lieutenant had suffered by this accident.

Not finding his hurt very painful in the first instance, he had not thought it necessary to send for assistance from shore.

His pain and weakness, however, increasing, he was obliged to keep his cabin.

During the earlier part of the night, boats had been passing backwards and forwards from the ship.

On deck a very careless watch was kept.

The absence of the captain caused some relaxation of discipline.

The weary officers of the night watch, drenched with rain, and pierced with cold, paced the deck in spiritless silence and dejection.

A little knot of men were gathered at one of the ports of the gun-room.

They were crouching beneath the shade of a huge gun.

"Are ye all ready?" whispered Harleck, who was the ring-leader of the party.

The superior tact and courage of the hardy wrecker had induced the men to place implicit reliance on his generalship.

"S'whelp my davy! you knows we are. I say, Harleck?"

"Well, now, land-lubber?"

"Hif anything vos to 'appen, vy in coorse you von't forgit as I'm only a wictim; I pertest agen' the whole thing."

"Then stay behind, you whelp! we don't want ye. By the blazes, I wish I'd stuck my knife in your weasand, for you'll blow the gaff on us all," growled the wrecker.

"No, I won't! I never peached on a pal, and I hopes I never vill; but, hif so be, as ve gets diskivered, vy, ve shall all be flummexed, vich don't blame me, 'cos vy—I pertested."

"Avast heaving! where's the boy?"

"Here he is, mate," returned another seaman.

The boy Crawley came slouching along, casting an alarmed glance behind him.

"Lie close!" he muttered, "here's the master coming!"

"O lor! I vish I'd stuck to my dooty; sich vays niver prospers."

"Think of your wound, Tony; think of this hell upon earth. If we get free, we've a chance; if we stay here we've none," whispered a pressed man, hoarsely.

"Vell, I do think of my vound, but I have a 'art and loves my country, and hif ve should go to git diskivered——"

"Down!" growled Harleck.

The men crouched low in the deep shadow of the gun.

The boy walked to the larboard side.

A stout man, wrapped in a thick coat, came down the companion-way.

He stamped his feet and shook himself to get rid of some of the clinging moisture.

He yawned wearily, and advanced along the deck.

He stopped suddenly.

"What are you doing there, youngster?" he asked of Crawley.

"Jest off duty, sir," returned the lad, touching his hat.

"Oh! what duty, boy?"

"Been into the top, sir, with the lamp man."

"All right; and now tell me where's the bo'swain."

"Turned in, sir."

"Good! but I want to see him," said the master,

seating himself on the side of the very gun behind which the deserters were crouching.

"Shall I go and call him, sir ?' asked Dan.

"Aye, boy," replied the master ; "he's wanted on deck."

The boy touched his forelock and went on the errand."

The master still sat on the gun-carriage, listening wearily to the dull lapping of the heavy surf, the moan of the wind through the cordage, the dripping plash of the rain, and the measured tramp of the watch above.

Little did he know the deadly danger that menaced him.

Harleck crouched in the intense gloom close at his side.

With a gleam of snake-like malignity in his evil eye, he clutched a broad, shining knife.

The master buried his head in his hands, and sat waiting the return of the boy.

Silently the wrecker raised himself on his knees.

He lifted his arm to strike.

A seaman clutched his wrist.

Harleck knew that the slightest movement would betray him.

Suppressing the oath which rose to his lips, once more he lurked down.

The boy returned, bringing with him the boat-swain.

Bill Hawser touched his cap to the master.

The other returned the salute.

"You're wanted ashore, boatswain."

"Indeed, sir !" ·

"Yes ; call up some trusty fellows, and man two jollies."

"Werry good, sir."

The master retired to his berth.

Bill Hawser presently crossed the gun-deck with a score of men, whose looks betrayed their unwillingness to leave their hammocks after their day's hard toil.

"We're not missed," said one of the deserters, when the boatswain had left the gun-room.

"No ; there's not a man in the fo'castle that does not wish himself out of it, whatever they may say," replied another.

The boy returned.

"Dan," said one of the men, "you're a Briton. Won't you come with us, lad ?"

"I'm afeard," returned the boy.

"Nonsense ! it's a safe game. The fog's as thick as a blanket, and they're keeping a dead-man's watch on deck."

"Hist ! they're manning the davits," said another.

The boats were lowered.

The men went over the side.

The steady plash of the oars died away.

"Now's the time," said Harleck. "Steady, boys ; I'll get into the boat first, you follow. This land-crab next to me, mark ye ; I don't trust him."

"Vell, these insinivations is painful to the feelin' 'art. Hif you can't trust me, vy, I'll go back to the fo'castle."

"Too late. We might have provided ourselves with arms, messmates," said Harleck.

"Better not ; if we're taken it would tell worse agen us," returned one of the others.

"At all events, I'm all right that way ; its no good to do things by halves."

"Silence all, and stick together !" muttered the Cornishman.

"I say, Harleck ?"

"What do you say, Will'em ?"

"This lad——"

"Same opinion ; he must go with us."

"May I never die if I goes for to desart this yere ship. If I was taken—they owes me a grudge—and I should be flogged by that devil of a Konka till my beams was peeled of every bit of paint, like the starn-rails in the tropics. Don't you go for to suppose sech a thing," cried the boy, in great terror. "Aint it enough, you ungrateful fellows, as I runs sich risks to get ye off, but you wants me to suffer ?"

"He's right, let him bide, Harleck."

"Very well ; no more palaver ; here goes."

The dauntless wrecker swung himself out from the port.

The men peeped through the outlet, and could just discern their ringleader steadying the boat against the dark side of the vessel.

Tony Wilks was handed out.

Clumsily he scrambled into the chains, thence into the boat.

One by one the men followed.

They were all afloat.

"Make way," muttered Harleck, striking the long oar against the dark hull of their prison-ship.

"Softly !—now pull—so she goes—steadily ho !"

Dan Crawley was leaning out of the port.

The darkness masked his sneakish features.

Light would have shown the gloating leer of delight that sat upon him.

He rushed upon deck,

He hastened to the midshipman of the starboard watch.

"Oh, please, sir, something most impertinent I has to communicate," he gasped, taking off his hat.

"The devil doubt you. 'Impertinent,' eh ?"

"Yes, sir. There's twelve of the waisters, pressed men, sir, and other sich, has been and gone and deserted, sir." ·

"What ! are they on shore ?—broke leave, do you mean ?"

"No, sir, which it wouldn't be my duty to mention ; but I seed 'em do it, sir ?"

"Do what ?"

"I seed 'em all get out of a starboard port in the gun-room, sir. Which one of 'em is a perfect monster, and threatened me with a pistol, sir ; but I knowed my dooty, and when they axed me to go with 'em, I says I'll see you——. Which means for to say, I'd rather die fust !"

"Why, you little scamp, is this true ?"

"May I never die, sir, but I saw 'em with these blessed hies !"

"You're a good lad——"

"My parents, sir, always told me to do my bounden dooty. And I told 'em ; I sez, you may kill me, you pirates ; but inform agin you I am resolved ; not as I looks for any reward, sir, because I likes to do my dooty."

"Go forward and bring here the quarter-master !"

"Aye, sir. I knows which way they was steering ; hope you won't tell 'em as it was me informed agen 'em ; I'm only a boy, sir, and they'll jist kill me."

"Come, youngster, fetch the quarter-master ; you need'nt fear the rascals."

"I am humbly grateful, sir, but do take care of 'em yourself, sir, I heard 'em say as they hated that something naughty young Fraser worse than any officer aboard, and they what-you-may-called your eyes, sir, in a most awful way, sir ; indeed, they swore as they would have your blood, which made me shiver as never was. But I made up my mind, and sez I, I'll do my dooty, cos my parents is poor people, sir, and it would break their precious hearts, sir, if I had anything to do with sich wickedness."

GALLANT ACT OF THE BOY SAILOR.

"Fetch the quarter-master!"

"And sorry I am to say, sir, one of the boys as is always molestin' us, and which curries favour with the officers, all the while he laughs in the most disrespectfullest manner, and mocks 'em behind their backs, sir; he act'lly said, sir, as it was wasting oil to use dead lights while Mr. Konks was aboard, all along of his poor nose, sir."

"Fetch the quarter master!"

"Yes, sir; directly, sir! and this Halliard waited on that werry Harleck when he was wounded, sir, which is some kind of relation, sir, as used to smuggle and murder poor sailors after they was washed ashore, dead and drownded"

"You little villain, will you fetch the quarter-master?"

"Oh yes sir! I knows my dooty."

And away ran the young hypocrite to summon the officer, and to spread the intelligence of the escape of the wrecker and his companions.

Meanwhile the deserters were gliding in their bark through the black and turgid waters.

"And vhere are you a goin' to steer to, my pal!"

asked Tony Wilks, looking about him with livid cheeks and tottering limbs.

"If we get to the island, hearties, we shall find a berth in some privateer craft, or we might steal a yawl, or perhaps a pinnace, and make the land to-morrow."

"We're sure to be taken," said of one the seamen, despondingly.

"They won't take me, any how," said Harleck, fiercely.

"Oh! I vish I hadn't wentured," sighed Wilks. "It's allers the vay with me ; I am the most unluckiest cove as ever had a misfortin'. I'm led like a hinfant, I'm so hunsuspectin'. But I purtested; you know I did."

"Ugh, you lubber! do you want your back scratched? do you want to marry the gunner's daughter—to be swung at the fore-yard?" Harleck hissed out, at the same time seizing Tony by the collar.

"Sich is not my haspirations——"

"Hark!" cried several men.

The throbbing strokes of strong oars were heard in their wake.

A gun was fired from the ship.

It was the signal that some of the hands had deserted.

It was answered by a shot fired from a frigate moored at a little distance.

"Steady, lads! don't be flurried!" murmured Harleck.

"Bolts and timbers! it's all up with us, my hearties; that's the long-boat; we can't escape her."

"Hold water! You fools," growled Harleck, "you scum of tailor-swabs! have ye got any grit in ye? Whist! the fog's so thick that we might lay by till they ran astern of us, or we might cut and run into the offing."

"O dear! O lor'! you vorship, I svare I can prove a halibi! I purtested; I vos led hon! I'm as hinnocent as a suckling hinfant; it's all this villain, Harleck!" mumbled Tony, trembling so violently that the frail boat quivered beneath him.

"Men! a word," whispered the wrecker, hoarsely, "better drown than be lashed like curs, and fettered like mad beasts. It is to be done; we can run into and sink her. Give me hold of the tiller; will you fight?"

"No, no, no!" whispered the men, "no, for the Lord's sake! Harleck, have you any arms?"

"Aye, mates, two barkers, and half-a-dozen cutlasses that I threw into the boat to-night."

"Over with 'em! throw them into the sea, we shall all be hung," muttered the seamen.

"Here's 'hearts of oak,' with a vengeance. 'Fore George! if I only had Thorkil, Paul, or Black Will, we three would take the cursed ship by the board!"

At this moment they were hailed by the boat.

It dashed alongside.

Harleck straddled over the gunwale.

He had a pistol in his hand.

Tony saw it.

He trembled for the consequence of a shot, in the penalty of which they would all be involved.

He snatched at the weapon.

Harleck was pulled down in the boat.

A file of marines levelled their guns.

An officer had leaped in among the deserters.

He had seized the luckless Tony with the pistol in his hand.

Harleck drew his knife and with a fearful oath rushed upon the officer.

He was felled by a blow from behind dealt by the hand of one of his own party.

Half an hour had scarcely elapsed ere the whole gang of deserters were lying helpless and heavily ironed in the hold of the Thunderer.

CHAPTER VII..

THE COURT-MARTIAL — FLOGGING IN THE NAVY — DAN CRAWLEY'S TREACHERY—THE BOY SAILOR BRAVES THE WRECKER.

THE next day Captain Brandon, and the rest of the officers of the Thunderer, returned to their ship.

A court-martial was held, at which Harleck, Wilks, and ten others were tried for attempting to desert.

The court was not a little amused by Tony's special pleading.

Though suffering from the agonies of terror, he showed himself quite a master of defence.

Nevertheless the fact was incontrovertible that he had been caught with the rest, and it was scarcely likely that the poor fellow's assertion that he had wrested the pistol from Harleck to prevent mischief would be believed.

The wrecker did not bear him out in this statement, and being quite callous as to his own fate, seemed to take pleasure in the sufferings of his less courageous mate.

The sentence of the court upon Harleck and Tony Wilks was that the wrecker should receive five and the knight of the road two dozen lashes.

Sentence was reserved with respect to the other men.

They were removed and placed in the hold.

The next day the sentence of the court upon the two deserters was executed in the presence of the assembled crew.

The prisoners were under charge of a guard.

Marines were drawn up with fixed bayonets.

Every man and boy turned up to witness the punishment.

The boatswain's mates stood near, with calm, passionless faces.

The shirt was pulled over the head of the hapless Tony, and, half fainting with terror, he was lashed up to the grating.

Harleck stood with folded arms, his shaggy brows overhanging his scowling eyes, his chin buried in his breast.

The officers were assembled in uniform about the captain.

When all was ready the captain read the crime for which the men were about to suffer, and the article of war under which it comes.

The solemnity with which the whole ceremony was conducted was very impressive.

The craven Tony sobbed and wailed in a piteous manner.

Then through the stillness that reigned around the "cat" was heard sweeping.

Tony shrieked, writhed, and besought pardon.

The Boy Sailor gazed on, his brows knit, and his colour deepened.

He knew that the men had been pressed; he could not help sympathising with them to some degree.

Frank Rayner looked grave.

Dan Crawley rolled up his eyes sanctimoniously, and crossed his hands with saintly meekness.

Very slowly the lashes fell—very deliberately.

Soon the man's back was terribly seamed and scarred.

His flesh was white and delicate, for he was a landsman, and, besides, had never hardened his frame by wholesome labour.

He was cast loose.

The shirt was thrown over his head, and he was led away.

Harleck was next lashed to the gratings.

His punishment was very severe.

However, the whole number of lashes was not inflicted.

The wound in his side, caused by the splinter of langrage, was opened.

The blood gushed out upon his back.

The ship surgeon interfered.

He was cast loose.

He had endured the torture of the cat with indomitable fortitude; only when the cruel knots of the cord had torn open his wound had he evinced any symptoms of quailing.

A visible tremor shook his huge frame, and an involuntary moan, hollow, and thrilling from its deep burden of anguish, fluttered from his burning lips.

When the shirt was thrown over his bleeding shoulders he turned upon Lieutenant Fraser and upon the captain such a look of covert, but demoniac ferocity, that neither of the usually dauntless officers could repress a shudder.

The hands were piped down.

The men having suffered their punishment were removed to the hospital.

Harleck lay passively in his hammock.

Dan Crawley entered the room.

The boy had entreated the lieutenant so earnestly not to mention the fact that it was he who had informed of the men, lest the many rough fellows on board, who took part with the deserters and pitied them, should wreak vengeance upon him, that the officer had taken good care not to let it be generally known from whence he had obtained the intelligence which led to the detection of the offenders.

Harleck turned a fierce glance upon Dan.

"Oh, jest arn't you kind, Harleck, jest arn't you. I'm much obliged to you; that little beggar were near finding me out, and shouldn't I have been larruped?" said Crawley, in a whining tone.

"What do you mean?" cried the wrecker, savagely.

"I means how kind it were of you and all the rest on yer, not to peach as it was me as helped you to get off. I'm afeared that Lieutenant Fraser's got his eyes on me; but I don't care so long as you sticks to me. I am werry glad I didn't wentur' into the boat with you, though I means to hook it as soon as I does get a chance. This here life is torful, what with bein' half flayed by old Konks's rattan; beat about by a little beggar, with all the crew to back him agen me, so as I darn't defend myself—I wish I was right down dead, I do. O lor, do pray take care on that little 'sinevatin' blackguard; he's got a tongue to cajole the very devil—which Satan, I should say—take care on him, that's a werry dear feller, or, lor love you, he'll get you hung. All the officers is on his side, and he don't stand for no lies, however tremendjous."

"Whom do you talk of?"

"Why, in coorse, who but the young willen that blowed the gaff and told the officers about you and the other poor chaps, which was to curry favour."

"Let me mark him; was it one of the boys?"

"In coorse it was; old Joe Juniper's little pet lubber, him as the coxsw'n calls the BOY SAILOR, as if there wasn't no other sailor boy in the British Navy. Phew, it's reg'lar 'nough to make a chap sea-sick."

"What, young Halliard?"

"Yes, the 'significant little sea-lawyer swab; vy, he looks like a hangel, don't he? I used to be nat'ral fond on him, which my parents would be grieved if they knowed I kep' sich company; his mother and uncles and aunts, and all his lot, are reg'lar gallows birds. But the hawful things as he put me up to do, and I'm sich a stupid, easy sort of a youngster; why, he used to twiddle me round his finger like a bit o' buntline and laughe'd in his sleeve, and laid all the blame of everythink on to me."

"Ho, ho! that young wolf-cub, eh?"

"You'll be hung, Harleck. You see if my prophesies won't come true, if you don't take care of that young wicious brute."

"I'll see to him; and now brush, I've had enough on ye for the present. A pretty thing for me to be swung here in my hammock, through the tyranny of these cocked-hat rascals, and the sufferin's of a sarvice which is all slavery. I wish I was sewed up and pitched down the gratings. Be off, you little fool; don't you see I'm roused? I shall knock your brains out for want of some one else to vent my spite on; I am sheer mad with fury."

The wild wrecker raised himself in his bed, and scowled at the boy with indiscriminating and insatiate vindictiveness.

"Well, if you wants some one to ease your feelings on, here's that cussed young spy."

With this the little sneak slunk off.

Harry Halliard ran down the hatch-way.

He advanced towards the wrecker with a light springing step.

In his hand he carried a glass of grog.

"Harleck," he said. "I've begged you a dram from the grog-kid. I know the doctor's rather against your taking spirits till the fever's all past, but this can't be enough to hurt you, and may be sufficient to cheer you up, old chap."

The wrecker fixed his cat-like eyes upon our hero.

"You take a 'varsal interest in me, youngster, how's that?"

"You're the only man aboard that comes from Seawardine, and not that I see you have any reason to think I am trying to get into your good graces, any more than to win the favour of all the men, which I own I should like to do; but still, Harleck, you can do more for me than ever I can for you—you can tell me something I would give half my life to know."

"I suppose I can peach on you, when you try a desperate trick to get out of this hell of a sarvice. Ha, I can get you flogged or hung, eh?"

"Well, Harleck, if I had been on watch I should have sung out when you got over the side, I can tell you that; but, if not on duty, I'd rather have been flogged round the fleet than split on ye."

"Then you own it, thunder and devils! you own it to my teeth!" cried the wrecker.

"Own what?" returned the Boy Sailor, calmly.

"That you informed against us."

"I did not, Harleck; you know that very well. I was fast asleep in my hammock when you were taken."

"Look me in the face."

The boy raised his glance, and bent it steadily on the bloodshot, murderous-looking eyes of the barbarian; the lad smiled quietly.

"You did not tell the lieutenant, then, that I and the rest had got away?"

"Of course not."

"Say so again; it's good for you."

'See ye hanged first !" cried the Boy Sailor, jumping up, and turning away with disgust and impatience.

"Oh ! I have not made out your colours yet, Master Hal ; see that you carry true ones, or woe betide you ; a hound may be lashed with safety, but, dam'me, a wolf will remember the injury, and keep his fangs sharp to revenge it !"

"I have never injured you."

"Best not, I can tell you. Yon lad, Dan Crawley, told me that you peached——"

"He's a contemptible liar, and you're a fool not to know it !" said the Boy Sailor, disdainfully.

"Come, come, better language."

"On both sides ! but you make me wild, Harleck ; I'm hot tempered, and won't be threatened."

"Of course, my little hero, you think I'm a chained growler and can't bite ; but look out for my teeth."

"And you, mind you that I don't break 'em !" shouted the fiery sea-boy.

"You little whippersnapper, with that wasp's waist and baby's mug. Yah ! an imperant age !" cried the wrecker, choking with spleen.

"You make me forget my age," said the boy, fiercely.

"'Fore George, I'll teach you to remember it when you talk to me, young cheery !"

"A bulley is always a coward. I don't wish to be impudent ; but because you are older and stronger than I, it's the more shame you should abuse me. Good bye, Harleck ; don't think I want to be insolent ; but, if you declare war against me, very good, you'll find, little as I am, I can nail my colours to the mast ; for, let me tell you, Master Harleck, you may crush, but never conquer Harry Halliard !"

CHAPTER VIII.

HOMEWARD BOUND—THE CLIFFS OF OLD ENGLAND
—THE BOY SAILORS MORALISE ON THE SIGNS
OF THE TIMES—OUR HERO OBTAINS LEAVE—
HARLECK THE WRECKER.

UPON leaving Malta the Thunderer steered her course for England.

On her way home the man-of-war fought several brisk actions.

More than one French privateer was run down, and two corvettes had struck their flags to the British "Jack" before the Thunderer had reached the channel.

Much to the delight of Harry Halliard the ship was ordered to put into Falmouth harbour for refitting, and in order to convey from thence a number of transport vessels.

Soon they made the coast of Cornwall.

Harry and Frank, seated on the foretop cross-trees, uttered a hearty hurrah as the cliffs of old England rose dimly through the clearing haze.

"Home ! home !" cried Harry, gleefully. "Oh, Frank, what a word is home ! I shall be with mother and Lena once more ; I shall walk among the peaceful cottages, and shake hands with the old friends."

"And dig your knife into the softer tack !" added Frank, with unction.

"Old friends——"

"Fresh meat and potatoes !"

"Green fields——"

"Green peas !"

"Every tree and bush familiar."

"And freighted with apples and gooseberries !"

"Warm embraces, sweet kisses——"

"Hot grog, and sugar candy !"

"A talk of old times."

"A glass of old ale !"

"A walk round the garden."

"And a land cruise on the gardener's donkey."

"Oh, the joys of home !"

"And soft tommy !"

"No more hard duty."

"Nor hard biscuits."

"No more rough words."

"Nor maggoty bilge-water."

"Home, sweet home, and England for ever !"

"Rule Britannia !"

Both the boy sailors joined in a hearty laugh, and a lusty hurrah.

The droll curve of Frank's lip fell, and his eyes softened, a tear dimming them.

He was silent a moment.

"Harry, my chum," said Frank, after a pause, "you're a queer chap."

"Am I ?" asked our hero, dreamily, for his mind soared away in the eager glance that yearned from his glowing blue eyes towards the bold cliffs of his rough, but native strand.

"Yes ; sometimes I don't know what to make of you."

"You ought to know me by this time, Frank."

"You know, I am a philosopher, Harry ; I study mankind, and, though I'm only a boy, I like to find out peoples' characters. Now, you pride yourself on being plucky ; don't you now ?"

"Every true British boy thinks himself born brave. Courage is a Briton's birthright."

"That ought to be put in a book, with all the big B.'s."

"It's found in a good many."

"Stopper all, and hear what I am going to say."

"Preachee, preachee ! as black Sambo says, when the chaplain jaws the men about the swearing and smoking," cried Harry, laughing, and shaking his head impatiently. "Don't bother me. I want to see if I can make out the Shark's Fin. I wish I had a glass."

Frank pondered, and was silent.

An expression of acute pain swept over the face of the Boy Sailor, as he beheld afar the deadly rock jutting out from the deep blue sea.

He sighed.

"Heave ahead, philosopher," he said, presently. "I like to hear you lecture."

"Well, then, to return to the subject. Don't you think, Harry, that to be brave one ought to be rather unfeeling, rather 'hard' like."

"There's two sorts of courage, I think," returned Harry. "Some fellows 'harden their hearts,' as the saying is, and make themselves insensible brutes. They pride themselves on being callous to pity and fear ; but that's wolf's courage. True, manly bravery is tender-hearted. The boy that would strike his sister or insult his parents may bluster and brag, but he has not one grain of real pluck in him."

"That's my sage opinion, too," replied Frank ; "and some boys are ashamed of the very words 'love' and 'religion,' and, I believe, sometimes even of 'home' and 'mother.'"

"Oh, to be sure ! The 'guv'nor,' the 'old woman ;' being in love is being 'spooney ;' a good son is 'soft' or 'mammy-sick.' But, I say, Frank, do you know what those little shore-going lubbers try to pass off for manliness ?"

"Don't know."

"As they've but little true steel in 'em they try to make up with plenty of brass."

"I suppose so."

"Yes; they're ashamed of themselves."

"Well, that's modest, anyhow."

"It's a fact, they're ashamed of being 'boys;' and how do you think they make 'men' of themselves?"

"Don't know."

"Why, they smoke short pipes, spit, swear, talk slang, sing dirty songs, carry walking-canes for show, drink swipes, lay a 'tizzy' on the favourite, and talk about their 'gals.'"

"What lubbers!"

"They wan't a missionary, don't they?—not to give 'em tracts, which they won't read, and to teach them that a bit of mischief is an awful crime—but to show them how to thrash big bullies, and protect little cripples; to let them see how noble and plucky it is to help their parents, and put up with their father's cross ways; to look their masters in the face with a proud sense that they've done their duty; to keep the smoke out of their mouths, and the filth off their lips; to be up to any spree that doesn't mean harm or annoyance to others; to give their money to a blind beggar, or to spend it on a jolly book of knowledge, poetry, or honest romance; to be rough-and-ready, bonny British boys, with bright dreams of pitch battles and rattling adventures, with hard hands to knock into hard work, and warm hearts to love and honour their father and mother, their little brothers and sisters, and their chosen chums."

"Ah, well, they're true Britons after all, poor, silly chaps; and they'll soon find out what bosh all that sort of thing must be; and they're not all such noodles."

"No; and right's always stronger than wrong, and those brave chaps that can stand a little chaff are curing the others as fast as need be."

So ended the philosophic discussion of our boy sailors.

That night the Thunderer anchored in Falmouth roads.

The next day many of the crew obtained liberty for a fortnight.

Among the rest the Boy Sailor, and his inseparable companion, Frank Rayner.

Before narrating the startling adventures of our hero on his "land cruise," it is necessary to say a few words about Harleck.

The wrecker was not permitted to go ashore.

He had been picked up from a smugglers' yawl, off the Lizard, and was known to have a number of evil associates along the coast, and it was to be feared that they would persuade him to desert if he were allowed to leave the ship.

Harleck's conduct would have puzzled any ordinary observer.

Since his recovery from the effects of his severe, or, it might be fairly called, his cruel punishment, he seemed a changed man.

It is true that he spoke less, that he maintained the most impassable taciturnity, but he seemed at the same time to have lost much of his former sullenness.

He now showed no dislike to the service, testified no desire to regain his liberty.

Born on the roughest of coasts, innured from his earliest childhood to the hardships and dangers of a seafaring life, a skilful pilot, and, a thorough seaman, he was in all respects a valuable hand.

His conduct for steadiness and promptness was unexceptionable.

This reformation in his character was observed with much satisfaction by the officers, for he had gained their respect by his fearless courage in battle, and dogged fortitude under suffering, and they encouraged him the more, because the favourable change relieved them from no trifling anxiety, for before he had been a dangerous man.

He had been promoted to the post of captain of the maintop.

More than once Captain Brandon had instanced his amendment as a striking example of the good result of a discipline the judiciousness of which was often called in question—corporal punishment.

Little did his superiors know what a volcano of hellish passion was gathering its forces in his cankered heart; less could they anticipate how swiftly, surely, and completely, he would work out his merciless revenge.

CHAPTER IX.

THE BOY SAILORS ASHORE—A SHOWMAN'S ELOQUENCE—A STRANGE MONSTER—THE MONSTER BROKE LOOSE AND THE SHOWMAN TO PAY.

THE Boy Sailor and his friend Frank were strolling among the quays of Falmouth Harbour.

The busy scene around them seemed to confuse their senses, unaccustomed so long to the bustle of cities.

Many of the passengers cast looks of interest upon the bright-faced sea-boys, as they swayed along with streaming ribbons and sunday ducks, gaily laughing and chatting.

"What a pity these shore-going folk don't always feel as we do when, after being so long rocking about on the deep, we first set our feet on *terra firma!*" cried Harry as he peeled his third orange.

"You see, my little chum," said the philosophic Frank, as with his elbow he polished the smooth and rosy cheek of his tenth apple, "man was made a restless animal; he can't remain long contented with anything. Why, if we were to stay ashore for six months, we should be fit to hang ourselves! there's nothing on land that gives any lasting satisfaction. Just look at me now! the first apple I bolted as the shark did the round shot; I've only eat nine, and now I'm looking for the juiciest place to set my teeth in. I'm getting dainty already."

"And I wonder, as people can't always keep jolly, whether they can be always miserable?"

"Bless your innocent eyes, not a bit of it," replied Frank. "Look at that poor convict chap that's picking stones for the new dock with his hair cropped round like a fellow with a fever, the irons clanking at his heels, and no prospect before him but sailing in stays for the rest of his life, perhaps; there he sits, taking a rest on his heap of stones, blinking at the sun, and, I dare say, thinking he's much better off than he would be aloft on the main-top-gallant in a white squall, or down in the cockpit with old Sawbones' knife scraping his thigh-mast."

"Any how we'll have as much fun and as much change as possible while our leave lasts; won't we, Frank?"

"'It shall go hard but we will!' as the rusty lieutenant said when he ran into the teeth of the big battery. But, hulloa! what's in the wind? there's a fellow beating to quarters on a drum like an empty keg, and squeaking on a double row of yellow jury teeth; men and boys are all mustering before a painted mainsail, with an alligator swallowing two blackamoors and a sea-serpent. Here's a rum go!"

"It's a show," cried our hero, excitedly.

"What's to be shown?"

"The alligator, I suppose."

The boys joined the crowd about the caravan.

At the top of the steps stood a stout, red-faced man, with a huge spotted muffler about his neck, a cocked-hat on his head, and a long wand in his hand, with which he was indicating the most interesting and awe-striking details of the magnificent tableau on the "painted mainsail," as Frank had styled the gorgeous cartoon.

He was addressing the crowd in a voice hoarse and much worn, but with a delivery deeply impressive.

"*The* hanimal vich *his* pourtrayed before you in *this* division of the hilustrations, ladies and gen'lemen, *vas* diskivered *hon* the hisland of Pokajoko, in the Southern Hocean!"

"Latitude marked uncertain," whispered Frank.

The lecturer continued.

"*Hintelligent* friends *vil* diskiver that this *most extr'ornary* creetur *his* a kinder freak o' natur, *vich* his 'ed resembles a monkey's, *vhile* his tail terminates in a flaky pint like an 'arpoon. *Hon* his back may be seen *a* pair *hof* vings, like a heagle's *or* an 'awks, *vich* the creetur' cannot fly, as he got injured *a* crossing *hof* the line. His natur's gentle, '*cos* his usage *his* humane, notwithstanding *hon* occasion he has done terrific damage, *for* his tail is deadly wenemous, *hand* he killed a whole ship's company by dipping of it in the reservoir of fresh water *vich* supplied *the* wessel, *has* above. His food is heggshells finely powdered, *hand* his drink is bitter haloes. Nat'ralists calls him the Longtailarus Wenemosus. *Hall* alive, *hand* to be seen for the small charge of *vonpenny*!"

The satyr below struck on the tabor and blew on the Pandean reeds.

Up the steps rushed an eager throng to behold the *lusus naturæ*.

Our ship boys, intent upon fun, were the first to "board."

They entered a dark compartment, and in the centre perceived a cage on a table.

Within this small den paced the terrible nondescript.

He certainly had a monkey's head and a scaly tail, while on his back appeared a pair of black and clumsy-looking wings.

It was too dark to examine very minutely, but the spectators were evidently fully satisfied as to the creature being a genuine monster, for he looked so monstrously absurd.

The Boy Sailor and his companion stood looking with the rest at the monster, as he meekly paced about in his cage.

"What sort of fish do you think it is?" asked Frank.

"A dog-fish, I should say," replied Harry, with a grin.

"Avast, you little lubber. Can't we have a lark with the 'wenemosus?' Suppose we let him loose?"

"But the skipper, he keeps too sharp a look out," returned Harry.

"If I divert the old chap's attention, couldn't you manage to raise the gratings?"

"Nothing like trying. Lor! to see what a bobbery there would be among the people, it would be glorious fun."

"And shouldn't I like to bamboozle that long-winded chap with some galley yarn," Frank rejoined, laughing. "Now if we had anything to bait the animal with."

"Well, as we've no pounded egg-shells, suppose we ask this butcher chap to lend us his leg of mutton. We can tantalize the freak of nature and make him bark."

"Leave it to me. The worst will be to take off the showman's attention," Frank replied. "You get close to the cage—have a long and steady look at the fastenings, and then try them with your knife. The door's at the back of the cage, and it's as dark as dogwatch.

"All right, you manage the skipper; I'll talk to the butcher boy; he looks the right sort. If I can open the hatch I'll show the poor dog, for I'm sure it's some wretched mongrel, the best side of a leg of mutton, and if he don't jump out and make off with it, I'll believe in the island of Pokajako."

Frank walked straight up to the showman.

Beg pardon, sir," he said, with a look of immense gravity; "but may I ask if you ever had in your collection such a thing as a real mermaid?"

"Had a many," returned the man in a surly tone.

"Well, you're lucky then, sir, for at sea they're very scarce; but the captain of our ship, the Thunderer, ninety guns, Captain Brandon——"

"Has he got a real one?—is there hany real mermaids?" stammered the "caterer for the public taste."

"They're very rare indeed."

"Well, mine, you know, warn't quite the right sort; they is rare; but a real live one?" asked the man, with breathless eagerness.

"If Captain Brandon hasn't got one, nobody has."

"And—and what does he mean to do with it?" asked the showman.

"Well, it's a ticklish thing to do. A mermaid is half a woman, and it's not quite right to kill it, you might get tried and half-hung; of course, it would be only half a murder, it can't be even manslaughter to kill fish. You might escape by cutting the fish end; but, perhaps, that wouldn't be mortal. I see the cap'en's game; as he doesn't like killing the creature to stuff it, he stuffs it just to kill it, and that's why he puts rum in the sperm oil it drinks by the gallon."

"But why don't he give it away?"

"Well, you see, none of his friends like to undertake it; and the mermaid has got so fond of him that she sticks to him like a leech. If he throws her into the sea, she always crawls home again."

"How wonderful!"

"Not a bit more wonderful than your 'wenemosus.'"

"But where did you find the stron'ary hanimal?"

"In the land of Nix, beyond the mountains of the Moon."

"S'welp me never! Do you think he'd sell it?"

"No; but he would gladly give it to any one who would take care of it."

"Blow me if I don't apply to his honour."

"I would, and show him the 'wenemosus.'"

At this moment, a pealing yell reverberated through the caravan, and the spectators scattered as if a shell had burst amongst them.

The little rascals had accomplished their design.

Harry had opened the door of the cage. He placed the leg of mutton immediately under the nose of the "Wenemosus." The extraordinary animal emitted a sound remarkably like the bark of the "tykus domesticus," and with truly canine instinct, snapped, not at a shadow, but at the substance of the "piece of flesh," and dashed off as if he had seen the ghost of a street-boy, with his hands full of tin-kettles.

With shouts, and cries of direst consternation, the

crowd circled wide, and the weakest went to the wall.

The dog darted like a flash of lightning through the stumbling, scattering crowd, and, wonderful to relate, left his head behind him, or rather, his master's; or, should we say, the monkey's. "By the three-headed Janus!" it's a case of possession that might puzzle a lawyer.

"Stop him! stop the—the—'stro'nary! stop him!" shrieked the showman.

"Clear away!" screamed Harry and Frank. "Mind his tail! You'll all be poisoned!"

"Hi, sir! Here, dog! Cost me five pounds to 'get him up.' Phew!—phew!—phew! Bingo, Bingo, Bingo!"

Balked by the people in the crowd, that tumbled over each other in all directions, out-run by the butcher-boy chasing for his mutton, pursued by his frantic exhibitor, eager to recover his properties, the little monster turned, and doubled.

"Stop thief!" bawled the butcher-boy.

"Kick his brains out! My scaley tail and ostrich feathers!" yelled the showman.

"Mad dog! mad dog! Let him run!" roared the young Thunderers.

The dog darted between his master's legs.

The showman stooped, and caught him by the tail.

The butcher-boy ran to recover his meat.

"Ahoy! the cutter 'Wenemosus!'—slip your cable, and run," shouted Frank.

The dog profited by this excellent suggestion, and leaving the "scaley tail" in the hands of its owner, tightly gripping his prize in his hungry jaws, he flew (literally, for he was yet winged) along the high road, and soon was lost to view.

In distant parts of the county it was recorded by many that they had beheld the apparition of a winged-dog, flying along the earth, with a leg of mutton in his mouth.

Those who were wise in auguries, declared it to be a very bad omen, and a sure sign of a rise in the flesh market.

One misfortune never comes alone, and the poor showman had not only lost his performing dog, so expensively "got up," but had lost his credit with the fickle mob, who resented the trick that had been played on them most ferociously.

The luckless exhibitor and his musical assistant were driven into the caravan by a shower of stones, and a whirlwind of hisses.

Profane hands rent the glowing canvas, with its faithful picturings of the sublime and terrible in and out of nature, basest of missiles were hurled against the wooden walls of the museum of wonders.

The hubbub was terrific.

Frank drew out his purse, and gave the blubbering butcher-boy more than the worth of the leg of mutton, and did not think the lark too dearly paid for; but, seeing several officers from the Thunderer mingling in the crowd, both he and our hero deemed it advisable to "sheer off."

CHAPTER X.

THE BOY SAILORS AND THE HIGHWAYMAN.

THE boy sailors retired to a tavern, and ordered a dinner.

As they sat shelling nuts and drinking small ale after their repast, they laughed long and heartily over the practical joke they had played on the showman.

"And now, Frank," said our hero, with beaming eyes, "we must consult the chart, and lay out our plans for our next cruise."

"Of course, you are anxious first of all to put into your home-harbour. Well, that's the best and the pleasantest port to make. But, how far are we from Seawardine?"

"Some leagues, Frank; and I've thought of a plan by which we can get there before midnight."

"What, on board of a land-ship?"

"Yes."

"Oh, that'll be jolly!"

"Can you steer?"

"Well, I can handle the tiller-ropes a little."

"All right, then, we've agreed upon that point; but there's a sweet little craft we must convoy."

"The Lena of Seawardine; she's in dock at Falmouth."

The Boy Sailor blushed, and laughed.

"Yes; but hang it, Frank, while we're ashore let's talk like landsmen, or folks will think we're a couple of sea-calves that don't know a tree from a turnstile."

"All right; heave ahead, mate; that is, get along wid ye."

"Well, then, you must know that if ever there was a dear, pretty, gentle——But, you'll see her presently. Lena is at boarding-school in Falmouth, and, I don't mind telling you, the expense of her education is partly defrayed by the rector of Seawardine, now mother is very poor."

The boy stopped.

A faint sigh rose to his lip.

"Never mind that, my cheery; as we're both born to be port-admirals, it can only matter for a time," cried Frank, cheerfully. "Make weigh!"

"And we cannot, neither mother nor I, injure Lena's prospects. Well, I wish I could find a sack of sovereigns in a shark's belly, like the sailor in Tom Truepenny's yarn."

"Still, never mind; but I see the mark, and will take aim. This feminine commodore, this school-mistress; what's her title?"

"Miss Tabitha Tingles."

"What a name! it makes one dance to think of it. She's a bit of a martinet, and keeps strict discipline aboard the tender ship!"

"Just so; but she's a thorough good teacher, and our Lena would forgive her anything if she didn't snub her about being a poor orphan foundling."

Frank's cheeks reddened, his eyes flushed, but he smiled immediately.

"Never mind; little Lena will turn out to be a princess, and the old witch will be changed into a screech-owl. I've read it all in the fairy book."

"Well, I must grow a man some day," said the Boy Sailor, sighing.

"Tossing bombs over the quarter, storming the gun-boats with Nelson, and, best of all, licking Dan Crawley, you're getting on, and decidedly growing—up. But does Lena complain?"

"The little cherub does not know how to complain; but I know the cause of her sad, wistful look; it's the wormwood, and not the birch, that makes her cup so bitter."

"That old faggot. Go on Harry."

"Well, I rather doubt whether she will let the poor little thing go with us."

"What! after storming Cadiz, can't we take the fort of that she-commodore? Birch Hall or Westminster Abbey!"

"Well, we'll order the chaise to wait here, and walk over, it's not far, when the afternoon studies are over, and signal for a parley. But I've not much hope. If she does let us in, you'll do me a favour. Do you like cats?"

"I should, if it wasn't cruel to brickbat 'em!"

"Well, she's got two cats, awful beasts, and a parrot that swears like a bo'swain. You must make much of them if you want to conciliate their —mother, I was going to say."

"Why, Hal, I'll ask her for the next litter of blind kittens, and teach Poll to pipe Jack Robinson."

A man on horseback rode past the window.

"There's a fine pad, Frank," cried Harry; "admire its rakish build and clear run."

"I wonder if its a race-horse," said the sea boy, *naively*.

"No, you muff; men don't ride such young racers as that. Its a hunter, and a fine one."

A man stalked into the room.

He was a tall fellow, manly and handsome; his hair was raven black, and hung on his shoulders in ringlets, long as a woman's; his eyes were fierce, and looked like sparkling jet.

He was dressed in a red rug coat, wore high boots and long spurs, a belt and pistols.

He rang the bell sharply.

A maid entered.

"Dorothy, a bottle of wine; mind, blue seal, as before."

"Yes, sir," returned the girl, as the boys thought, rather tremblingly.

The stranger threw himself into a chair, and spread wide apart his booted legs. He flung his heavy, lead-loaded riding-whip on the table with a bang.

He laughed, and the oaken panels quivered with the reverberations of his deep and ringing tones.

"What, my young sea-pups!" he cried. Come ashore, eh? to booze your jib, ha! ha! Glad to see you; you're England's best babbies; young hopefuls, that turn out old heroes! Well done! This is fortunate! We must have a little confab' about wars and warriors, ha! What are you drinking? Bah! The hog's wash! Won't it run to something better than this liver-shrinking swill?"

The stranger made no more ado than to snatch up the jug, and fling its contents across the oak floor.

The girl entered with a bottle and glass which she set on the table rather nervously.

"Dorothy, my duck, I've changed my mind," said the cavalier, in the same deep ringing voice; "leave the bottle for these young gents; bring another glass, and make me some punch."

"Yes, sir," responded the girl, humbly.

She left the room.

Frank rose.

"I and my partner, sir, are much obliged to you for your kindness; we are not much skilled in shore-going manners, but we can't accept favours from one we have never had the pleasure of seeing before. If you'll excuse us, sir, we'll refill the jug; and, as for the wine, it is too strong for us."

"I like your grit, dam'me, I like your grit," cried the horseman; "but I shall think ye no free, jolly sons of the brine, if you don't act fair and square with a comrade, whom, if you've never seen before, you may never see again. Your health, my dimber lads! don't act the cautious swab-like jacks without jollity; for, I repeat, to-day up, to-morrow down; you may never see me again!"

"Swinging in fetters, perhaps," muttered Frank, who had already conceived an antipathy against the swaggering cavalier.

The girl brought in a large glass of steaming punch, and made a hasty exit.

'Frank, don't be crusty," whispered our hero,

"we're not afraid; shan't stay long, and there may turn up another jolly lark."

"As you like, only don't drink more than you can help; the less the better," replied Frank Rayner.

The stranger drew his immense pistols, clapped them on the table, and unbuckled his belt.

"And so my little hearties, you are man-of-warsmen, eh? and, youngster, you have a cut on your cheek. Seen service, I suppose?"

"All aboard see service now, sir," returned our hero, laughing lightly.

"Your health, sir," said Frank, sipping the wine.

"Ha! good toast, but old and common-place. I'll give you another. Here's the main-toby!"

"And whose the man Toby?" asked our hero, laughing.

"Refreshing innocence! The HIGH ROAD!"

"Rayner frowned; he snatched up his glass, and said, in a tone of sternness that startled his companion—

"Here's the King's High Road May his Majesty's trusty officers soon sweep it clean of foot-pads, mounted robbers, and other vermin that now infest it, to the danger of his lieges and the disgrace of his reign!"

The cavalier flinched.

"A — very — good — toast!" he growled out. "Dam'me, I like your grit!"

And he liked his punch, too, by the dip he made into the glass.

"A fine pair of pistols, sir; will you permit me?" said the dauntless sea-boy, taking up one of them with the easy heedfulness of long usage, "but it's a pity you should be obliged to carry fire-arms."

"Hem, well, so it is; but, as you say—

> 'The foot-pad lurks behind the pale,
> The gipsy haunts the glen, sirs;
> And where the road winds down the vale,
> We meet the toby-men, sirs.'

"Give us your purse, Hal."

Our hero complied.

"Take it back; I've filled it with buttons."

Our hero obeyed, and slung it by his side as before.

"A very good song, sir; is there any more of it?"

"Oh, it's a stave of my own composing. I'm a bit of a ranting rhymer—

> 'But men must live; they get the least
> That labour most, I think, sirs;
> And when poor hunger gets a feast,
> I feel inclined to wink, sirs!'"

"But poor hungry people shouldn't pick each other's bones, should they, sir?"

"That's just what you sea swabs do to your best messmates; when you get cast away on a raft, you draw lots to drink each other's blood; ha, my lad, are you answered?"

"Such cases are extremely rare, sir, and greatly exaggerated, and their existence does not justify cannibalism," returned the gallant Frank, with charming boldness.

"Hey, well, right you may be. I've been robbed again and again to the amount of some thousands. I own I'm too benevolent," grunted the fellow."

"Hal, get this chap to the window," whispered Frank, quickly; "the shark's *a highwayman!*"

"I knew there'd be a lark!" chuckled our saucy young rascal.

"Hulloa! there she goes! That's a fine sight, sir, isn't it?" cried Harry, jumping up and approaching the window. "That's our cap'en's pinnace—see how gracefully she trails her colours in the surf—that boat was nigh swamped, sir, in the action off Cadiz."

The cavalier arose, his spurs loudly jingling. He followed our hero to the bow window.

NOTICE.—The next Number of the Boys' Library will be Publish Order early of your Bookseller.

BOYS' LIBRARY

HARRY HALLIARD;
OR,
THE YOUNG BRITISH TAR.

THE BOY SAILOR STEALS A KISS FROM LENA

Harry kept the fellow's attention directed by pointing out and commenting upon different parts of the hull and gear of the Thunderer.

Frank fixed his eye steadily on the pair.

Quickly and softly he took up the heavy pistols.

They were stoppered with small phial corks.

These he drew.

He still kept his eyes fixed on Hal and the stranger.

He took up the wine bottle.

He filled each barrel half full with the liquid.

He tightly re-stoppered with the corks.

Very cautiously he replaced the weapons.

"Avast, mate, why do you pester the gentleman with things that can't interest him, as a landsman?" cried Frank.

The cavalier turned, and walked up to the table.

"Oh, but they are things which interest every true patriot," yawned the stranger; "but I must be off, lads," he added, buckling on his belt, thrusting his pistols into their rests, and taking up his riding-whip.

"Adieu, my hearties; come, a stirrup-cup this time, a bumper to the last toast—

"The main-toby!"

"With all my heart. Once more—the main-toby —and may every toby man choke on a gibbet!"

The fellow set down his glass with a black scowl, laughed snarlishly, and, humming a flash tune, stalked out of the room.

"Now, Hal, my boy, give us back your purse."

"Why!—how!—my toplights!—it's gone! I must have lost it as I stood by the window."

"And so you would have done, Hal, if it had been full of bullion instead of brass."

"Hang me if I don't run after the thief and fight for my buttons!" shouted Hal valiantly.

"Stay where you are; he's a strong man; his whip is loaded, and, no doubt, he has a dagger in his pocket. But what a dirty skulk to rob a poor ship-boy of his paltry liberty-money."

The girl again came into the room.

"How much, ma'am, do we owe you for the wine?"

"Oh, that's settled, sir; he always pays us."

"We cannot suffer ourselves to lie under obligation to a thief who has no one but what he has filched; but why do you suffer such a villain to haunt your house?"

"What is my father to do?" said the girl, sadly; "the last landlord was shot dead in the road for peaching on Jerry Barker."

"Well, ma'am," said the Boy Sailor, "I'm sure you won't refuse to sell me the pistol that hangs on the wall. If I meet the scamp, I'll give him another button to put in his pocket!"

The girl handed it to him with a flask and ammunition.

Harry offered her the money.

"Not a farthing!" she said, firmly; "I would not give it you but that I know you belong to the Royal Navy, and may be trusted with arms; but, dear little fellow, do not be so rash, or you will never wear white hairs under your bonnet; and if you have a mother you will bring sorrow on her head."

The boys thanked her, and ordered the chaise to be got ready for their return.

"Oh," cried Hal, as they left the house, "if we meet the man, Toby, won't it be a lark?"

CHAPTER XI.

FRANK'S FOREBODINGS—THE OLD GIPSY—THE BOARDING-SCHOOL—THE PRISONER—SAILOR-BOYS AND SCHOOL-GIRLS—LENA'S TROUBLES—THE ABDUCTION OF POLLY—A RUSH TO THE RESCUE— THE BOY SAILOR HAS A DUCKING AND GETS AMONG THE DUCKS—A TRIUMPH OF DEVOTION.

WHEN Frank and Harry had left some distance between them and the tavern, the former spoke.

"I wish we were at Seawardine, Hal; I don't like the idea of meeting that land shark when the night falls, especially if we have Lena in the chaise."

"Confound him," cried the Boy Sailor, "I wish I had him in chase now. You say you stoppered the mouths of his barkers, made 'em drunk and unfit for action. Well, I've heard of many an odd ruse; but I never yet heard of stoppering pistols with port wine."

"Yes, unless he finds out the trick; and the pistols, when thrust into his belt, were in good order, barring their extra charge. It's likely he won't examine them till the moment before he wants to use them; but, be that as it may, my little cheery, we shall have warm work if we meet him on a lone heath in the dead of the night."

"Oh, it'll only be a lark. I was never born to die in that fashion. Wild Tyra would tell you better than that."

"And who is she?"

"A wonder! Bless your heart, she knows everything; she is acquainted with all the 'good folks,' the fairies. When we get home she will tell you your fortune; she is such jolly company, and will tell you some fine yarns."

They were proceeding along a road skirted with fields of corn and spinnies of hazel and larch.

They rested by a gate.

"Yonder is the school-house; let's go across the fields," said Harry, vaulting the gate.

"Is this your fairy godmother, Hal?" asked Frank, as an old gipsy woman advanced. She had risen from a bank of fern and hare-bells, and was tottering towards them.

She carried a basket of laces, thread, and other such trifling wares, and was puffing the smoke from a little black pipe. She mumbled between her broken teeth.

"The heavens bless ye, young gentlemen," she whined, "and keep your vessels from storms, and your lives from danger; only cross my hand with the line of silver, and I'll tell ye both a pretty fortin'."

"O, that's all humbug, you know it is, mother," cried Frank, impatiently.

"I'm real romany, sir; real gipsy," replied the old woman; "and I can read your fortin in the lines of your palm as plain as in a book."

The sea-boy laughed frankly.

"You're right there, mother, anyhow; if my fortune lies anywhere it lies in my own hands."

"And I see that both you young gentlemen are born to be great and rich; you are—oh, yes, I can forecast."

"Come, come, you cannot forecast for us one hour of safety. We are mad, brainless boys; but we lead solemn lives; the hot breath of death sweeps over us even while we sleep," returned Frank; "but here's a shilling, mother, and, if you're going our way, let me carry your basket awhile."

The old woman mumbled her thanks, but seemed more displeased at the sea-boy's want of faith than grateful for his charity.

As they walked on, Harry looked at his companion thoughtfully and respectfully.

Frank seemed to show more self-assertion, deeper feeling, and stronger sense now he was ashore.

The fact was, Frank being older, and having suffered more from bitter reverses, he had more stability of character than our hero, or, rather, more fixedness of purpose and consistency of manner.

They were both intelligent, well-educated lads, placed by circumstances below their natural level, but joyous and free of heart as the exulting larks then darting up and down with swift quivers through the evening sunshine.

They clambered the hedge, and stood before Birch Hall.

It was a square, white-stuccoed, prim, and rigid-looking house, with snowy blinds, green shutters, and spotless door step; the knocker and bell-handle were of shining brass, as also a large door-plate, which bore the inscription, "Miss Tingle's Establishment for Young Ladies." There was something repelling in the severity of neatness that pervaded the place.

"My jib! our lady skipper keeps clean decks, and, at all events, she doesn't grudge elbow-grease or holy-stone," said Frank, laughing.

"No, she doesn't spare the skulkers," returned Harry, twitching up his trowsers, and looking nervously at the gaunt, stiff house, as if he didn't much like to tackle the work before him.

"Pretty Polly, what's o'clock? Past nine; time for lessons! Ten bad mar—rks; oh, dear! oh, dear! oh, dear!"

"That's the parrot; how I should like to wring it's neck!" cried Harry, starting electrically with boyish instinct for mischief.

They looked at each other rather uncomfortably.

"Now, you man-of-war's-man, board there!" hallooed Frank, laughing and nudging his companion in the side.

"Blow me, hearty, but I'd rather face all the gun-batteries in Spain and Portugal than that old rip! Do I look pale?"

"Rather; do I?"

"Rather. Well, my lad, we will stick to our colours, and listen to nothing but the 'woice of dooty!' as the old boatswain said when the cannon shot whistled his head off. Here goes; charge for glory!"

With looks of mutual encouragement they advanced on the green.

The parrot in a brass cage, which hung by the window, screamed distractedly.

"Murder! horrid boys! tell gov'ness. Cr-r-ah, go away, you r-r-ragamuffins!" hideously shrieked the indignant parrot, at the intrusion of the sons of Neptune upon the sacred threshold of Minerva's temple.

"Blow me, Frank," gasped Harry, swabbing his forehead, "if I'm not reg'lar nervous; that beast of a bird!"

They timidly approached the door.

Harry gave a faint smile.

"I vote we reconnoitre," he said; "let's take our bearings before we begin in the action."

Daintily stepping along the prim and narrow gravel path, between the precise parallels of close cropped box-border, they turned the acute angle of the house.

He drew near a window.

Harry advanced a step.

In a small study, hung with maps, and adorned with globes and book-shelves, a tall, gaunt woman, with a beaky nose and cold grey eyes, her hair gathered up in a bird-like crest, a very parrot humanised, was terrorising over a little trembling prisoner, a pretty blue-eyed girl of six years old.

"My eyes, Frank!" gasped Harry, "Mother Tickletoby is teaching some little duck to box the compass."

They could distinctly hear the shrill voice of the preceptress.

"Now, Clara, I ask you, for the last time, what is meant by 'the spherical aberration of luminous particles?'"

"Please, ma'am, I don't know, ma'am," whimpered the trembling culprit, pleadingly.

The sharp rustle of a stiff-starched taffeta dress was heard as the governess crossed the room and opened the door.

"Miss Wincer!" she screamed, harshly, through her thin blue lips, "Miss Wincer; bring the rod!"

"Oh, dear ma'am, if you please, I will be good!" sobbed the desperate criminal, throwing herself on her knees.

Harry could stand no more.

His handsome young face glowing wrathfully, he gave a very man-of-war's-manlike thump with his fist on the window-pane.

The governess uttered a shriek.

She swept to the window, and threw up the sash.

"What do you want, boy?" she asked, sharply.

"I wish to see my—my sister Lena, if you please, madam," said Harry, fiercely, yet taking off his hat with some nervousness.

"There is no young lady of my establishment who bears that barbarous dissyllabic name."

"Well, ma'am, her full name is Helena," said Harry. "She is of Seawardine."

"Helen Foundling we call the pupil you mean," returned the governess, coldly. "You are the son of her—hem—her protectress, I suppose?"

"Yes, madam; and I hope you will kindly give me permission to see Helena," said the Boy Sailor; "and if you would grant her leave of absence for a few days, that I may convoy her home to my mother's, I shall be very grateful."

Harry blushed and gasped.

"I am sorry that I cannot comply with your request," returned Miss Tingles; "but it is impossible. It is against the rules of my establishment that any young lady should visit her friends during the term, except in cases of great emergency. Miss Foundling is at present in disgrace, and confined to her room, and, therefore, you cannot see her; besides which, let me assure you that, my seminary being conducted upon exclusive principles, I cannot permit my house to be invaded by disreputable persons, among whom I include common sailor-boys."

With this, Miss Tingles banged down the sash and drew the blind.

"She'll keep the prisoner in the hold; won't let us see her," said Harry; "and calls us commo sailor-boys!"

"That's uncommon civil!" said Frank, gnashing his teeth. "Never mind, Hal, when we get to Seawardine your mother will send for her. Meanwhile we'll have a peep at her, if we can; and if we can get in among the little cherubs, won't we just——!"

"Hurrah!" cried Harry, his face brightening, "won't it be a jolly lark?"

They moved away from the window.

As they passed round the house they were stopped by a sudden cry.

They looked up.

A window was thrown open, and a pretty girl, about thirteen years of age, with the purest and rosiest of complexions, the darkest of eyes and ringlets, looked out.

"Harry!" she cried, joyfully, "Dear, darling, Harry, is it you?"

"Lena," returned our hero, in the same ecstatic

strain, "can't you leap out of the window ? O, we will catch you safe, you little cherub !"

"I—I didn't know my geography ; I got wrong in my theology ; and now—now I have been punished ; and am kept—kept in," sobbed Lena. "Won't the old cr-creature let me see you ? Oh, I am so lonely and unhappy, and—and I thought you would be ki-killed, and I should never see you any more. Oh, I shall break my heart !"

"Never mind, Lena, my little beauty ; shiver my top-lights, if I don't cut you out !" roared the Boy Sailor. "Frank Rayner, my chum, Lena ; the very best fellow in the world ! he'll help me, and we'll take the fort and spike the guns and carry you off in spite of thunder !"

Oh, no, no ! run away. You will be turned off the grounds ; I shall be birched and put to bed, and have double lessons for a month to come. Oh, do go, dear, darling Harry ; but wait one minute, while I ask Fan Raymond—she's my husband, you know—for a bit of cake and some goodies, and then—stay a minute, I'll be back !"

The school-girl disappeared from the window.

"Oh, that old rip !" cried the wrathful Harry ; "only let me get alongside of her, I'll give her a broadside that shall shiver her timbers. Why, I've been all this while aboard a man-of-war, commanded by a lot of petty officers, no better than a set of raffs, and though I'm a young devilskin, I never yet came astern of the cat, while dear, gentle, good little Lena, is punished for nothing but spite."

Lena returned to the window.

"Here, catch these, Harry," cried the girl throwing out a piece of cake and a bag of sweetmeats. "Oh ! I wish you could come in; that dear little husband of mine, Fanny Raymond, has got a hamper of goodies and a bottle of such delicious cherry wine ; but good-bye, my dear boy, do pray run off, or you will get sent to prison for trespassing, and you don't know how I shall be punished. Do run away, like a dear good boy. 'Bye 'bye, 'bye !"

And kissing her hands, she darted back into the room.

"Lena !" shouted our hero, "stay one moment, you dear little cherub. I can't go. I won't till——"

"Oh ! pray—for my sake !" cried Lena, quickly returning, and waving her hands with earnest entreaty, her face betraying her dismay.

"Not till I've given you one kiss, in spite of Mother Broomstick. Give us your shoulder, Frank, and see how I'll storm the fort in spite of the old furies."

Frank laughed and stooped down, while our hero mounted his shoulders.

The Boy Sailor kissed his little sweetheart. She smoothed his glossy curls, and taking from her side a small pair of scissors cut off a rich lock and placed it in her bosom.

She shrieked, and suddenly sprang back.

The cold, stern face of the severe preceptress appeared at the window. Her grey eyes flared with wrath, and with vicious grip she brandished a birch-rod.

Our hero saw her but for a moment ; the next he lay upon his back on the ground and looked up to the close-drawn blind in semi-stupor.

Frank, who had been startled by the cry, stumbled aside, and our hero was thrown down.

Frank helped him to rise.

The boys looked at each other with mutual indignation, and shook their fists at the window.

Frank drew his companion away.

"Come, my little cheery, it's no use, we must sheer off," he said. "We will tack round the house ; perhaps we may find some chance of getting poor little Lena away."

The boys sauntered dejectedly to the end of the garden wall.

"What cheer, Hal ? Don't look so glum ; your mother must bring Lena home. I wish that old Hicate had given us a chance of palavering ; depend upon it we might have soothed her with a bit of blarney. I believe you might cajole Old Nick by admiring the sleekness of his long tail. Flattery is like oil, which makes the wheel of favour turn to your hand. Lor, if we could only have stroked the cat, or scratched the parrot, the old girl would have treated us like admirals. But, hulloa ! here's our fortune-teller. I wonder what sort of welcome she'll get ?"

The gipsy woman whom they had met on the heath approached the house.

The boys drew aside, and stepped behind a little clump of trees, in order to watch her movements.

She was muttering to herself as she passed them.

She looked up to the house with a dry, meaning smile, thrust open the gate, and walked straight up the prim path to the door.

She knocked.

The boys peeped from their ambush to learn the result.

The door was opened, and the servant shook her head at the woman, pointing over her shoulder to indicate that the mistress of the house had little sympathy with rogues and vagabonds.

The woman howled out something impertinent.

The wrathful "lady-principal" appeared.

A short, sharp, and pithy dialogue ensued between the governess and the suppliant, and then the door was sharply clapped to.

The boys laughed.

The woman passed along the side of the house.

She paused for a moment, and looked carefully round.

The boys were concealed beneath the shadow of the trees. The woman had not perceived them.

The parrot happened to be dozing.

She threw her shawl over the cage, and poor Poll was borne off in a state of unconsciousness. The woman carried the cage carefully at arm's length, and moved quickly across the garden, passed through a side door, and walked sharply over the fields.

"Hurrah !" shouted the Boy Sailor, "that old girl deserves to be made a queen ; anyhow, I'll give her a crown."

"What, you little vagabond ! would you aid and abet in robbery and abduction ? Now, look here, hearty ; do you love your Lena more than you hate Mother Tickletoby ?"

"I do love Lena, poor little thing, with all my heart ; and I'd put myself under the command of the she-skipper, and stand her worst usage all my life, to save our little cherub one punishment in a year. What a burning shame ! But she shan't stay here !"

"Meanwhile, there goes poor Polly. Ah, she wakes ! Hark how she shrieks for help ! Now, my cheery, we have the governess quite at our command. She can refuse nothing to the gallant deliverers of her representative."

"To the rescue! To the rescue! Stop thief! Stop, you she-pirate!"

An exciting chase commenced.

The woman turned and yelled, in shrewish derision.

With cruel violence she shook the cage.

The fluttering and shrieking of the frightened bird were terrific.

The boys laughed and shouted.

Though they gained upon the gipsy-woman, she showed no little agility and endurance, and dashed forward.

"Round in the weather braces—ware ship. She's run the headland and makes for the river. Hurrah! —heave and haul!"

Laughing, and panting with exertion, the boys kept the chase in sight.

On towards the river sprang the vindictive gipsy-woman.

The stream ran along under a steep acclivity. On this she paused with murderous intent!

Holding the prisoning cage of the hapless pretty Polly at arm's length, she swung it off, and it fell plump into the water.

With a piercing scream the woman indicated her triumph and derision by a gesture more expressive than elegant, consisting in the application of the tip of her thumb to the tip of her nose, and the distending and shaking of the remaining fingers. This mode of expressing contempt is, we believe, not strictly "romany," nor entirely confined to the class to which this woman belonged.

The boys set up a shout of consternation.

With faces flushed, the chivalrous youths dashed down the hill, resolved to peril their lives for the rescue of poor Poll.

Recklessly our gallant hero plunged into the rolling waters of the mighty rivulet!

Desperately he struck out.

He dived.

Soon he appeared, fiercely buffetting the rippling stream in full four feet of water.

With unparalleled heroism he fought his way to shore.

He landed, the cage in his hand.

Frank was by his side in an instant.

Poor Polly lay at the bottom of the cage, a bundle of drenched and ragged-looking feathers.

"Is she dead?" asked Frank, breathlessly, as if he was speaking of a human being.

The Boy Sailor shook off the water from his clothes and laughed gaily.

"I don't think so. No. Look, she draws the grey cover off her little round peepers."

"Now for a lark!" cried Frank. "We'll get into the fort by a stratagem. As I ran over the top of the bank, I heard a hullabaloo in the distance. I looked back. A man, I suppose the gardener, the skipper, her first-lieutenant, and a swab of a Frenchman, as I judge by his big moustache, were running along eight knots an hour; they'll be down on us in the snapping of a firelock. Now you must be drowned!"

"Drowned in fresh water? See you hanged first."

"Don't be an ass! I'll kick up the most tremendous bob's-a-dying. You lie here on the bank, batten your peepers and stiffen your legs. You will

be carried into the house, and laid in dock, alongside of all the sweet little pinnaces moored there. A little moaning and groaning will bring Lena to your side. If the parrot isn't dead, the old girl will be frantic with gratitude. I'll hug the cats (not forgetting to pull their tails, if I get a chance), and in a few hours we shall be cast loose, with dear little Lena to be convoyed, outward bound, and free as sea-fowl."

"Oh, it's glorious! I'm as dead as Julius Cæsar. Only lay me on my face, for I know I shall laugh."

Harry had scarcely stretched himself upon the ground when the party of pursuers dashed over the top of the bank, and flew down to the river-side.

Miss Tabitha's first, her only thought, was for her feathered pet.

Stumbling over the prostrate body of the boy, she seized the cage with a scream of positive anguish.

She drew out the bird, and fondled it in her breast, and when the creature feelingly persuaded her of its animation by fiercely pecking her fingers and emphatically blessing her eyes, she almost fainted with delight.

Meanwhile the valiant French-master, accompanied by the gardener, had set off full speed in chase of the gipsy.

Our hero did not receive the reward due to his duplicity.

Soft arms enfolded him, and a sweet, patient face looked down upon him with tender sympathy; and as he peered through his half-closed lids at the poor pale girl that bent over him, with her gentle eyes agleam with tender sympathy, a burning blush rose to his cheeks, and only the qualm of shame that rose in his throat prevented him from calling out that he was shamming.

"Oh, madam!—the poor boy—he is drowned!" cried the girl, raising him in her arms.

"Indeed, Miss Wincer; I am concerned to hear it. The boy deserves a better fate; he has preserved the life of my beautiful bird, and I should have given him a shilling, and perhaps a reward-book. The poor child may be insensible only. It is rather against the strict rules of my establishment to allow of the admission of a common sailor-boy into my house; but, under the peculiar circumstances, I think I may with propriety permit of his removal to the Hall."

At this moment the gardener and the French master returned.

"Ah, quelle horreur! the woman is echapé," cried monsieur. "'Scaped, madame. The mauvile! Ve shall announce to de magistrates—she vill be pursued. But de bird—ah, de pretty bird! I expire of anxiety; nothing has arrived to the bird?"

"I'm blamed, ma'am," cried the gardener, "if this boy beant drownded; he be dead as daisies in December!"

"And he's Lord Nelson's favourite, and the Boy Sailor; but the bird's such a beauty! that's the only consolation," rejoined Frank, his eyes twinkling and his sides shaking.

The young governess looked at him with a glance of alarm. There seemed something so awfully daring, so impiously presumptuous, in playing a trick upon the autocratic mistress of Birch Hall, that she at once dismissed belief in its possibility; yet her kind eyes flashed eagerly upon the light form of the mischievous urchin as the men raised him in their arms.

As our hero was carried softly over the fields

towards the house, Frank walked gravely by the side of the lady-principal, and poured his cautious flatteries into her willing ears with all the tact of a veteran courtier.

They had now reached the lawn of the house.

A bevy of pretty, excited faces beamed, a galaxy of bright eyes twinkled, from window to window. They were gone in an instant, as the school-girls scampered away, like fawns at the sight of the hunter, as soon as the grim form of their monitress appeared.

In a few moments our hero was lying on a bed, surrounded by eager faces. Even the stern governess was moved by the scene, and gave orders that he should be carefully attended.

The Boy Sailor was honest and ingenuous. The worst of practical joking is the almost unavoidable necessity of using deceit, which is always revolting in any shape—deception cannot be authorised to a true heart even by harmless motives. Harry was glad to get into the house; exulted in besting the arrogant, hard-hearted school-mistress, but was deeply ashamed of the trick he was playing.

He opened his eyes.

As the proud and cold-natured woman, the founts of sympathy in whose heart had been dried up by long and arduous labour in the most thankless of all toilful enterprises, the education of children, looked upon those bright, roguish blue eyes, a pang shot through her heart, and the sternness melted from her authoritative countenance, she laid her hand on the boy's shiny locks, and her hand trembled.

A piercing scream startled the bystanders, and little Lena rushed into the room.

"Go; you must leave the room at once, Miss Halliard," said the governess coldly, as she caught the girl's arm. "I cannot——"

"Oh, Miss, punish me as much as you please; but do, do let me stay with dear Harry. Is he dead? O dear, dear Harry!" She threw herself on the Boy Sailor's breast. The words rushed to his lips, "I'm a treacherous young scamp, and ought to be keel-hauled." He checked himself, and winding his arms round the little foundling, kissed her tear-dewed cheek with affection.

"Please Miss—I will be so good, Miss—do, pray, do let me stay with him," cried Lena.

"For twenty minutes," returned the governess curtly, yet with a softened glance, as she swept out of the room, and beckoned the rest to follow her.

Frank remained.

He looked on with a grave face.

"Lena, darling, don't be cross with me. I was determined to see you again. I am not hurt, my dear. I ran into the water after the parrot, and got a ducking—that's all. Who is that nice young lady who looked at me almost as pityingly as mother would have looked?"

"Oh, you mean Miss Wincer. She is so timid, so frightened of Miss Tingles, and the girls are so naughty with her," cried Lena, warmly. "I'm sure it's dreadful!"

"What, don't they like her?"

"Oh, yes; they love her with all their hearts. But she don't like to have them punished, you know. She is weak and good-natured, and they take advantage of her goodness, and sometimes they lead her a terrible life. She is the silliest angel, Harry, that ever you saw. I don't think she minds any suffering, though it makes her look

so sad. But she is very pretty; don't you think so?"

"I am quite in love with her."

"But isn't she pretty?—that's what I ask you."

"Very."

"You're a dear boy to say so. But poor people can't afford to be pretty; and Miss Tingles is always finding fault with her dress, though she looks like a Quaker, poor thing. Oh, I do so love her."

"You would love any one."

"Don't believe it. Very often I quite hate Miss Tabby, as we call the mistress."

"She is severe with you."

"I don't mind that; because she teaches well, and liberty will be so nice, and I shall be such a scholar when I leave this place. But I do hate her for being so unkind to Miss Wincer."

"And now, Lena, dear, let me introduce you to my chum, Frank Rayner; the best fellow in all the world."

Lena turned to Harry's friend, and held out her hand with a blush.

He caught it and kissed it gallantly.

"Hurrah—this is a jolly lark!" cried the Boy Sailor, chuckling and throwing up the pillow. "I say, Frank, this is better than the soft side of a plank, hearty."

At this moment Miss Tingles re-entered the room.

Frank, who was the soul of politeness, and had a most gentlemanlike address, assured the schoolmistress that Harry was quite recovered—spoke of Lord Nelson—said that Harry was half rated for a midshipman—all this in answer to Miss Tabitha's questioning; and hinting, in the most delicate manner, that Lena had spoken highly of the nature of her instruction, so cajoled the old lady, that she could not resist his entreaties to permit the girl to go with her reputed brother and his friend to Seawardine.

The boys were profuse in their thanks, respectful in their expression of them, and Lena was well-nigh wild with joy.

The Boy Sailor rose and dressed himself, his clothes having been dried by the fire.

Lena packed up a few things in a little bundle, kissed Miss Wincer and her school-fellows, and danced joyously down the stairs to join Harry and Frank in the hall.

In another hour they had returned to the inn, had got into the chaise, and were driving along at reckless speed through the darkening twilight, and down the wild and lonely country road that, diverging towards the cliffs that beetled over the sea, wound its long and dusky way to Seawardine.

CHAPTER XII.

THE ATTEMPTED HIGHWAY ROBBERY—EARL PENAL-
VON RESCUED BY THE BOY SAILOR.

THE Boy Sailor, Frank, and Lena rattled along in the chaise through the gathering darkness, and whirled past the flying hedges; the dark, deep, lone sea on one side, the rounded, treeless hills on the other. The horse tore along over the racing road, and every object swam wildly past them. Their spirits rose, exhilarated by the rapid motion; they laughed and chatted gaily.

As they were passing rapidly down a steep decline, which descended into a deep valley, the Boy Sailor sang out: "Don't you remember the highwaymen, Frank—

'And where the road winds through the vale,
We meet the toby-men, sirs——'

"If we meet him, Frank, it would be a lark; and I owe him a grudge for stealing my purse that you stuffed with buttons, brass, or bullion, as you said. The thief would not scruple to rob a poor sailor-boy of his liberty-money."

"Look out, Hal! Starboard there! Pull the laboard tiller. We shall be tumbled into the windward hedge."

"Starboard it is! But, halloa, whose ahead?"

Harry drew up the horse.

A narrow bridle-road ran into the main way a little below them; a lane ran off close beside on their left.

A sudden light shone brightly from before them.

A man was displayed by its gleam seated on the bank, lighting his pipe.

Steaming in the cold night air, a fine black horse stood beside him.

"Our highwayman!" muttered Frank.

It was very dark.

The wind soughed sadly past; dull, distant, the roar of the sea came faintly on its breath.

Their horse stood trembling with the fatigue induced by their rapid progress.

They pulled up.

"Frank," whispered the Boy Sailor, "I happen to know these waters, and we'll tack to the windward, and bear down on this pirate from another point, for I know he means mischief. Let's run up this roadstead."

He turned the horse, and dashed down the lane at a rattling pace.

Trembling, but quiet, Lena clung to the daring boy's arm.

Frank leaned over the back of the carriage and listened.

"He's after us!" he whispered.

"Let him come. *I've lost the pistol!*"

"Lucky you did, for I found it," returned Frank; "it slipped from your belt as you rushed down the bank to rescue poor Polly. It would have been of little use if it had been by your side when you plunged into the river."

"Shall we turn her head and bear down in his teeth?"

"No. Hark!—slower—put the helm down—he's away, Hal—he only followed a little to see that we had sheered off; depend upon it, he's playing a higher game. The yacht may go free when there's an Indiaman in the offing. Shouldn't wonder if the shark means to overhaul a stage-coach, as Turpin did."

The Boy Sailor laughed, and hummed with much enjoyment—

"The bold Dick Turpin, he took the road—
His little persuader first he showed,
And then the mail-bags did unload,
One werry cold frosty mornin'!"

"Avast!—you're an idiot. What can two such monkeys as we do against this ruffian? This is a dangerous service, Hal, and you ought to be steady."

"Aye, aye, sir! But now we shall get back into the road. Listen! 'tis the sound of carriage wheels—the craft he is on the look-out for!"

Harry guided the horse round a turn, which brought them back to the high road.

The carriage had passed the outlet, and was half way down that part of the road which they had avoided by turning off by the lane.

Harry drew up.

"We must leave you, dear Lena, for a few moments," he said. "I have a pistol, and it will be easy to steal along the hedge, and get within range of the villain."

"But there may be more than one on the road. Is there a farm house near?"

"Yes, within a few hundred yards."

"Then Lena will be safer on foot," returned Frank. "Let her get out of the chaise, and go over the fields. She will be unobserved in the darkness, and she can call up the people at the farm, and hurry them to our assistance. Are you afraid, Lena?"

"Yes, a little; but I can do what you tell me as well as the bravest, for it is so easy. I know the farm house, and the people there are very kind. I'll fetch some one directly. But, oh! pray don't be too daring."

Frank handed Lena from the chaise. She passed through a gap in the hedge, and hurried on her mission.

The boys threw the horse's rein over a branch, and crept down the road as quickly and stealthily as possible.

They soon overtook the carriage. In this part the road was full of ruts, and the coachman was forced to use caution, and drove at a gentle pace.

Suddenly the moon, which had long been hidden by a bank of heavy clouds, soared out from behind her curtain, and threw down her flood of silver upon the road.

A horse was leaped over the bank, and the rider reined full in the mid road, and presented a pistol at the coachman's head.

"Stand!" he cried, in a stern tone.

The coachman replied by blazing at him with a pistol he had concealed beneath the apron.

The shot did not reach its mark.

The man leaped off the box.

The ruffianly highwayman flew upon him, and hurled him to the earth with a downright blow.

The poor fellow lay quite motionless.

Catching the long reins in his left hand, and grasping his pistol in the right, the highwayman walked towards the door of the carriage just as a dark, handsome gentleman was about to leap out.

The highwayman pushed the pistol against the passenger's face, thrusting him back into the carriage.

"Come, sir, deliver! I've other engagements, and can't lose time."

"You precious scoundrel!" hissed the man, "I am not alone; I have a lady in the carriage, who must not be alarmed ; but I shall meet you again, and then we will settle the reckoning between us."

With this he extended his purse.

The robber gripped it.

"A lady ! Ha ! sorry to be troublesome, but the lady has also a purse, a watch, and rings. Come, I'm not on half-pay, but in full service ; I must have all."

"You shall have enough, curse you !" shouted the other.

A pistol flashed in the highwayman's face.

The bullet grazed his cheek.

He drew back.

"Now, dam'me, there's no quarter !" he roared.

He drew the plug of cork from the muzzle of his long pistol.

He aimed into the carriage.

He looked at his hand.

It was wet.

He thought it must be blood.

He pulled the trigger.

The flint flashed, but there was no report.

He growled savagely.

The lady in the carriage shrieked.

The robber drew the other pistol.

He did not wait to draw the plug, but pulled the trigger.

With the same result as before.

Uttering a fearful oath, he drew a gleaming dagger, and jumped into the carriage.

He seized the traveller by the throat.

The lady threw herself between them.

He spurned her brutally with his foot, and struck at the man over her shoulder.

In another instant he would probably have stabbed them both, but the opposite door of the carriage was snatched open.

A pistol was fired.

The bullet passed through the ruffian's cheek, and struck out two of his teeth.

Half choked, and utterly dismayed, he stumbled away to reach his horse.

He had been forestalled, however, for Frank sat in the saddle, though with less ease than he would have perched on the cross-trees.

The highwayman, half blind with agony, struggled to put his feet in the stirrup.

Frank struck him a fearful blow on the head with a stick he had cut on his way.

The traveller and Harry Halliard came upon the field, and attacked the enemy in the rear.

The highwayman wore a short riding-cloak.

Upon this the traveller and our hero fastened like limpets to a rock.

The robber was nearly strangled.

The button at his throat, however, at length gave way, and having freed himself, he blundered up the bank, and, pushing through the hedge, decamped across the country.

The gentleman turned upon our hero, and held the purse, which had been dropped in the encounter.

"Here, my brave lad, take this," he said, "as a little earnest of a greater reward I will hereafter bestow upon you for your gallant courage and kindness."

At the sound of the speaker's voice the Boy Sailor started back with a cry of surprise.

A dark shade fell on his face, his bright blue eyes sparkled and his white teeth clenched tight.

"Ha ! young Halliard !"

"It is I, sir ; and the sooner we part the better."

He turned quickly away and beckoned Frank to follow him.

"Where does this breeze spring from ?"

"That villain is the Earl of Penalvon," said the Boy Sailor, gloomily.

"Is it possible ? the man of whom you have told me so much, who has injured your mother so basely and cruelly."

"The same villain. I am glad I have fired the charge in the pistol," muttered the fiery boy in a thick tone of passion.

"Ha, my lad, will you serve me so ? will you not even deign to receive my thanks ? Well, I suppose you scarce deserve them," said the Earl with a sinister laugh, " for, had you known it was I that was attacked by the thief, you would have taken good care not to have done anything to save me."

"My lord, you are mistaken ; though I am young I am in the king's service ; and, besides, as British born, always his subject, and, however much I hate you, I would not see you assaulted by a thief in the high-road without doing my best to rescue you from his clutches. Good night, my lord."

"Stop, you little scamp ; stop, I say, and listen to reason ! Here, give me your hand, I can undo all that has been done amiss," cried the Earl, laughing, and drawing the boy away ; " but now we must see to the lady."

But the Boy Sailor seemed in no mood for conciliation ; he stood mute and unyielding.

Frank pulled his arm.

"Take a word, Harry," whispered Frank ; "never kick against the quarter-deck ; you'll only bruise your toes. Don't offend this port-admiral, and we'll sheer off as quickly as we can."

"Perhaps he may turn over a new leaf and make amends to poor mother. We can't always afford to be too dignified, I know ; but, as you say, we'll sheer off as soon as we can. Here come the farmer's people."

A crowd of men armed with guns, pitchforks, scythes, and similar weapons appeared.

They carried torches in their hands.

The carriage was surrounded in a moment.

A lady was lifted out.

She was wrapped in a thick fur mantle.

Her face was delicately fair, and now showed very pale from the recent fright, and her soft brown eyes shone with a mild sad light ; her manner and appearance were extremely refined, and in features she closely resembled the earl.

Lena, who had walked timidly among the men, drew to the lady's side, being the only other female present, and gently tendered her services.

The lady smiled, and, as they walked together towards the farm house, she leaned her jewelled hand heavily on the girl's shoulder.

The girl looked pleasantly into the lady's kind sad face.

The lady started.

"My child," she asked, in a tone of surprise, "what is your name ?"

"Helena," replied the girl, simply.

THE ATTEMPTED MURDER.

CHAPTER XIII.

ONCE MORE ON THE ROAD—THE ESCAPED CONVICT—
HIS STORY AND HIS DREAD RESOLVE—THE KINDNESS
OF THE SEA-BOYS—HOME, SWEET HOME.

"WHY don't you talk, little cheery; what's amiss
with your jawing tackle? silence is all very well
before an action, but when the brush is over it's well
to crack a little," said Frank to his companion, who
since his short interview with the Earl of Penalvon
seemed to be depressed and meditative.

The two sea-boys and Lena were still travelling
through the night, but were fast approaching
Seawardine.

The Boy Sailor roused himself, and laughingly
replied—

"I was thinking about the old times, and forget-
ing the future, Frank, and I know that's stupid;
but, mate, our land craft heels over to the blackberry
bushes; starn all, or we shall capsize."

"Here, take the tiller yourself, Hal, you're the
better steersman."

With this Frank handed the reins to our hero.

"Oh, Harry, how brave you are," said Lena,
"and what nice letters you write, only you never
say how you are, and you should always dot your
I's; if you were in our school and neglected that,
would'nt you catch it?"

"Lena's skipper is like our old boatswain; says

he, 'my lads, be great in little things, tie every clew line,'" rejoined Frank.

"Well, after all, it's very jolly to be free like this, I own," said the Boy Sailor "but order goes a long way to brace one up and make one satisfied; it is a fine thing to see every man at his station, and the captain at their head; but, I tell you what, my hearty."

"What is it, Hal?"

"Those fellows who write books are lubbers in many things; they've heaps of soft sawder for a hectoring commander, but they haven't half enough praise to bestow on a submissive foremastman; there's a quality they don't make enough of—Obedience!"

"Hurrah, Hal, you're getting quite a philosopher, and I love you the better for it, my chum."

"Well, I don't see because a boy likes to read of wild adventures, or to show his own pluck in a daredevil fashion, why he shouldn't listen to reason."

"Nor anyone else who has common sense; boys are not such fools as some believe. 'The boy is the father of the man,' says sage somebody, and, hang me, if I don't think that the boy-father could often teach the man-baby a good lesson, though it isn't his place to lecture his betters."

Harry yawned.

"Well, stopper all that, we're nearing port," he said. "Oh, mother dear, dear mother, my heart dances at the name of home!" he cried, joyously.

Frank sighed.

Lena looked earnestly into his face; with the delicate tact of her sex she read his thoughts at once; the poor boy had no parents, no home.

"And mamma often says, when she speaks of you, I have another son now," cried the girl, laughing sweetly. "Harry has a friend, and Harry's friend is always a son to me; but mamma is so clever, she knows how to say what she feels; now I don't. Oh, you will be so happy at home, Frank."

The tears sprang to the boy's eyes; those eyes which had stared death out of countenance.

"Hulloa, here's a castaway, let's overhaul his log," said Harry, suddenly pulling up the horse.

A man was crouching low on the bankside, seemingly asleep.

He started up.

The moonbeams flashed on something in his hand; it was a knife—a common table-knife.

"What cheer, shipmate? you've swung your hammock in a queer place; all adrift?" asked the Boy Sailor.

The man concealed the weapon.

He drew near, and leaned on the dash-board.

He lifted to them a haggard and hunger-pinched face.

His appearance was far from prepossessing.

He was a lean, gaunt fellow, dressed in a tight-fitting suit of grey, and wearing a sort of skull-cap, pulled close down upon his brow; around the edge of it appeared the short, blunt ends of his close-cropped hair, which he seemed attempting to conceal.

"Art'ee goin' to Penzance?" asked the man, in a hoarse, wheezing tone.

"No; but we're going to Seawardine, not far from that place," replied Frank. "We will give you a berth, if you like."

"Thou be'st good, lad, but I ha' nowt nayther in pocket nor in 'self, for nor matter o' that, lad—mortal hungry I do be," returned the man with a ghastly grin.

"Oh, you shall have a free passage if you'll tell what you are. We've met with one land-shark already, and we've had enough of his breed. Who are you?"

"Art'ee set to ask I sich questions? or are ye simpletons, as ye look von?" asked the man, suspiciously.

"We sail straight, my hearty; you may know us by our rig. We're man-of-wars-men. But come aboard quick, for we've had a long cruise, and want to run into port," replied Frank.

The man got into the chaise.

"We're pretty heavily laden for a craft of our burden, and this is rather a queer sort of supercargo," whispered the Boy Sailor; "but I wouldn't have left him on the shoals for any consideration."

"No, the poor lubber. But there's a tear in the wind's eye. We shall have rain directly."

"What a cherub is our little Lena! See, she is feeding the poor fellow with sugar and soft-tack," said Harry, in a whisper.

Such was the fact; and to judge by the manner in which the stranger devoured the rich fare, he had not tasted food for a week.

"And may we ask what port you steer from, messmate?" asked Frank.

"Thou'st a right to ax questions, lad, and I've a right not vor to answer 'ee," returned the man, curtly.

"We don't want to be inquisitive; and if we can help you, we're ready to do so," said the Boy Sailor.

"Thee'lt not suffer vor't, depend on't, lad; I be a bad un; they told un I'd come to the gallows; they did so, avore I could lift the vayther's spade. My mother did—she be buried down 'long side of my three sisters at St. Ives' church. I bean't vor-gotten un. They were kind to I, were my mother and my sisters, and the chaplain at the ga——, leastways a kind-hearted gentleman, said as there be a place, as you hears talk on, where there be no hard winters nor blamed game-laws, and where a chap's heart be allers soft and kind loike. He told I, the chaplain did, that One did become poor and lowly, and did suffer much to bring such as I to this vine, good place, where mother and sisters be at rest. He told I all about it; but I knows nawt. I be a reg'lar bad un, lor' bless ye."

"And you have been punished for some faults. Well, poor fellow! many escape who deserve death, and many suffer severely who are scarce to blame! But I suppose it can't be helped while we have but human judges, who can but do their best."

Frank sighed as he made these philosophic remarks.

"I be reg'lar bad un, I tell ye. Fust I got into trouble vor stealing Varmer Hardman's turmuts; but I was hungry, and when I asked him for bread, he swar at me, he did—he! he! Loard, but he be the very devil, Varmer Hardman!"

The simple fellow drew his sleeve across his eyes.

"But you should not have stolen," said the Boy Sailor, yet in a gentle tone. "You deserved the cat for that, hearty."

"Don't I tell 'ee I be a reg'lar bad 'un, 'nation bad. Well, I sure I got a month vor the turmuts; and now 'ee shall hear summut else as I did. I stole Squoire Trueman's bridle and saddle; vound 'em hangin' outside ov the stable; tuk 'em down, and hid 'em under a hedge, while I went arter a pardridge; and jist as I knocked 'un down, who'd come out ov the holt but squoire himself. He collared I. My garters! how he did lectur', and scowl'd; it was wuss nor swearin'! He tuk the pardridge from I, and axed un iv I was very poor. 'Nation poor I be, and mortal hungry, yer honour,' sez I. 'Why doan't 'ee work, lad?' said the squire. 'Since I be coome out of gaol nobody will give un nowt to do, yer honour.' 'Go into the tool-house, vetch a rake, and set-to with those fellows in vield down yonder.'" A sigh. "He was a kind measter, and I worked for 'un till he died."

"But about the saddle," said Harry.

"Thee'st right. When I'd got rake on to shoulder, and were jist a-startin' off to work, I sez to his honner, 'Squoire, there be thy saddle and bridle; there, 'long the hedge yonder.' 'And how came 't there, lad?' sez he. 'If thee'lt not ax that, maester,' sez I, 'I'll tuk 'un home; and I'm blamed if ever I touch nowt as beant my own in my mortal futur' born days,' sez I, jist like that, 'more nor I ain't ceptin' of hares and pardridges.' But, lor! I be a bad 'un, I be."

"And you have been in prison since?" asked Frank.

"Scarce ever out on't; everybody knows as I be a bad 'un, and I has to suffer for everything as is done; locked up for burning a varmer's hay-rick, when I was t'other end o' county side. I be in now vor snaring hares last winter."

"What! in prison now?" asked the three youngsters in a breath.

"Aye, sure; though I be a vule to stick out. But ye'll not split, I know. Look here, be my 'fractory."

With this he lifted his foot against the dashboard, and, pulling up his trousers, displayed an iron ring locked round his thin leg.

"It was all along of the blamed warder I got that sort of hay-band; but, durn'ee, I'll mark 'im! I ground a knife in the gov'nor's kitchen, and, if I'd met this warder chap as I were crossing of the gaol-yard to clamber the last wall, I'd have stuck it into his heart, like that!"

The half-wild fellow plunged the knife savagely through a large piece of seed-cake that Lena had set on his knee.

The girl drew shudderingly away from him, and nestled close to our hero, who was driving.

"My tops'ls, Frank! it seems our luck to run alongside of suspicious cruisers. What sort of a pirate do you call this?" said Harry, in a low tone, to his comrade.

"The poor fellow is ignorant; his passions are unsoftened by sympathy. A rude bore. He is little better in some things than a mere savage; and yet I fancy he has a good heart, he seems so simple and confiding."

"Anyhow, we'll lend him what tackle we can for a refit; he can never cruise along shore under those colours without being captured. I'll give him a shilling or so and so shall you, wish him a merry cruise, and leave him to the weather."

"That's the best plan, I think," returned the Boy Sailor. "Hearty! what do you mean to do? Where do you mean to cast anchor, now that you have got off the rocks?"

The chaise was rattling swiftly down a lane which led to Seawardine.

The sky was dark and wild; the country bold, weird, and barren.

Large drops of rain pattered into their faces, driven by a bleak wind from the sea, which was provoking the distant waves to incessant hoarse and angry soaring.

The escaped convict looked up at the lowering clouds, and answered, with a wild and naive simplicity,

"Thee'lt not tell, lad; but I be tired on't—always hunted, and always gettin' caught—and I beant gwine to bear nowt no longer! My limbs be sore, my back wealed, my belly pinched, thee see'st, and I'd be better dead! The brook that shines yonder in the dark grass, turns the old mill, thee know't; un' call't the Willow-pool mill-dam. There be an old bridge there—grey, moss-stained, pretty, and quiet like; the water be clear, too, deep, and runs fast. Sisters and I used to sit on side on't, and throw white stones down through the clear water, and see 'em sink deeper and darker, and go out o' sight. Sisters used to throw daisies into stream to see 'em swept under the reach, such we all loved the old Willow pool." The convict lowered his voice to a whisper, "I tell thee what I'll do, lad, I'll throw myself down the lock into the mill-stream, and there'll be an end on't."

"Oh, you must not do so, poor man," said Lena, looking into his face with gentle compassion. "The High One, whom your good teacher spoke of, he has borne so much for you, and can you bear nothing? Must you throw off that yoke of sorrow which will make happiness seem so sweet before you have carried it to the end of the journey? Oh, bear up; not for the sake of anything in this world—the best things here are sure to fail you—but for that good place where your mother and sisters are at rest!"

The girl's voice trembled with emotion, and the tears brimmed to her gentle eyes.

The sea-boys looked at her with simple awe and affection.

The convict listened with deep attention.

"I thank'ee kindly, young miss, I thank'ee," he said, with strange softness. "I don't quite mind the meanin' of all thy pretty words; I'm no scholard, but I know what thou'rt for telling me that my mother and sisters bore it all, and died patient. But, dang it, I be tired o' gaol; I've nowt to say at the food, that be good enough for a hungry man; beant afeard o' hard work; but to be used wuss nor dogs which ain't allers kep' in kennel, couldn't stand it at all, so I be broke loose the third time, and, now, as thou say'st, I be ready to die and to go to the good place chaplain told I ov."

A sudden, fanatical zeal lighted the wan face of the fugitive from man's inhumanity, for his punishment was greater than his offences, and his ignorance should have commanded some leniency.

"It be good what thee say'st. He fasted in the wilderness—I will starve, I will vind a lone dell, where I will sit and think I be praying till my soul be gone off into the air and zunlight, and be vreed; to eat I must steal, but that I'll not do. No! thank'ee kindly, miss, I know the way better, now; I'll not zet my foot by Willow-pool; but do'ee pull the rein, young master, there be Seawardine down yonder, and I be goin' t'other way."

The Boy Sailor checked the horse.

The chaise was stopped at the corner of a long winding lane which led to the village.

The man jumped out.

He shook hands with the boys.

"When I be *there*, I will remember 'ee; I will wait till ye come, lads; thou'lt not know me, lads, but I'll know ye. Good-night, miss, I be mortal 'bleeged to thee, thou'st taught me more nat'ral loike than the parson; I zee the meanin' clear, loike."

"Oh, no, no; you are mistaken. To come to that better land, you must work, not faint—strive, not starve. Oh, poor man, I—I wish I could teach you, I wish I could help you," cried Lena, bursting into a flood of tears.

"Thee musn't cry, durn it, I tell 'ee thee musn't; I be a bad 'un, thee musn't cry vor sech—fare 'ee well, miss. When I'm there, I'll find none kinder than thou'rt been. I were but a little one when mother and sisters died, and I beant used to it loike, it hurts me worse nor all—God bless 'ee, miss, and, lads, good night, and brave fortin' to ye."

The Boy Sailor leaped out of the chaise, and caught the man's arm.

"Avast, hearty; belay a moment. You must give up these mad-brained notions. Why not serve the king? Look at us, we're merry as gulls and fat as porpoises. Why not go to Plymouth, and serve on a man-of-war?"

"I can't, lad. Do'ee think I'd not be known in these clothes? Sartain there be a man along the cliffs az would give me something to wear if I'd money to pay vor't; but he won't give me the worth of one varthin without I lay down the stuff; it can't be done, ye see."

"It can be done well enough," said the Boy Sailor. "My chum, Frank, and I, will give you some money; you can get on to Falmouth, inquire for the 'Crown and Anchor,' and ask for Mr. Juniper, bo'swain of His Majesty's Thunderer. Tell him you are ready to enter the service, and say you are known to me—that I am a friend of yours—and that he may believe you, give him this, he will know that it's mine."

Harry took out a small pocket-knife, which he gave to the man.

The half-witted fellow thanked the boys in his artless fashion as they gave him as much money as they could spare, cheered him with a glowing picture of the manliness and jollity of life aboard, assured him that if he once got off to sea, and redeemed the past by good conduct, his escape from prison, even if discovered, would be winked at, as there was a great demand for men, and the officers were not over-scrupulous as to a man's antecedents provided he conducted himself with propriety in the service.

Lena took a kindly leave of the unfortunate, and he was sent on his way rejoicing.

"And now, hearty," said Frank, leaping once more into the chaise with our hero. "Clap on all sail, and let's get into harbour before the squall comes, for we shall have ugly weather."

"Heave and haul!" cried Harry, touching up their jaded steed. "Behave well you horse-marines, and you shall have a bucket of grog, you lubbers."

Away once more they rattled now through the darkness and the dashing rain.

They passed the quiet slumbering village, and in a few moments drew up before the cottage of Rose Halliard.

Long before they had arrived, the mother stood watching for her son.

The joy of their meeting was beyond expression.

The morning broke wildly on the sea; but still around the roaring blaze of the log fire, that happy group sat eagerly and lovingly conversing.

CHAPTER XIV.

THE OFFICERS ASHORE—EARL PENALVON—THE CAPTAIN NARRATES THE BRAVE ACTIONS THAT EARNED RENOWN FOR THE BOY SAILOR—A LETTER FROM THE ADMIRAL—HARRY HALLIARD A MIDSHIPMAN.

IN one of the principal taverns at Falmouth, and in a large, well-lighted room, a number of gentlemen, naval officers, county magistrates, and country squires were assembled.

At the head of a long table, on which was spread a dessert of fruit and wine, sat the Earl of Penalvon.

On his right hand were placed Sir Everard Brandon, the captain, and three lieutenants of the Thunderer, named respectively Norris, Fraser, and Armitage.

On his left were a number of officers from other line-of-battle ships.

The rest of the tables were occupied by the local gentry.

Hilarious mirth prevailed, for the wine circulated freely, and at the period of our story sobriety could scarcely be classed among the British virtues.

The topic of conversation at the table over which the Earl presided was his lordship's late adventure with the highwayman.

"It must have been Captain Travers—Black Tim, as he is sometimes called," said a judge who was present. "I once enjoyed the pleasure of passing the capital sentence on that outrageous ruffian, and suffered the mortification of its non-fulfilment."

"What, was the thief reprieved?" asked the Earl.

"No, my lord, he escaped—broke goal, and got off scott free, and within five days after he had regained his liberty he stopped the mail near Exeter. He is a sturdy rascal,"

"And yet no match for my young champion," replied Penalvon, laughing. "That boy is a wonder."

"That I can well vouch for, my lord," rejoined Captain Brandon. "Since he has been on board the Thunderer he has displayed a courage truly marvellous."

"But he comes of a bad stock, for all that," the Earl remarked, ungraciously.

"That is a matter of opinion, my lord. Circumstances often compel both men and women to associate with people of different nature to themselves. A more gallant officer—a more perfect gentleman than this boy's father never walked the quarter-deck."

"Ah, well, that may be."

"It is a truth that every one who knew Captain Halliard will make it their duty to maintain," returned the good officer, with a grave look.

"Yes, yes; I do not gainsay it; but of course I was alluding—regretfully, indeed—to the mother, and her connections."

"Mrs. Halliard, my lord, has been very cruelly traduced," cried lieutenant Armitage, with some indignation, "and whoever has been base enough to injure the poor and excellent widow of a brave officer deserves universal opprobrium and contempt."

All at the table looked with surprise at the bold speaker.

There was an awkward silence.

The Earl reddened, and bit his lip.

"I was, unfortunately, in some way connected with the affair of her being deprived of the crown-pension; but I acted under honest convictions, and believe I was justified in the course I took."

"I have no doubt, my lord, that such is your own impression," returned Armitage, coldly.

"Well, we will drop this subject," said the noble, in a curt manner.

Captain Brandon smiled.

"Not till I've told you a story or two of the Boy Sailor, as they call him, *par excellence*," said he; "and a thorough sailor he is, and an honour to the service. He was at first a cabin-boy, with the usual amount of devilry that characterises the monkey tribe, for

Harry Halliard is a genuine boy, and full of animal spirits as well as courage. The first act that brought him into notice was the saving of Captain Shand's little daughter. The gay little child was jumping upon the hammocks, crowing with delight at the novelty of all the objects around her—for she had just come aboard with the captain and Mrs. Shand, for we lay off Deal, where Shand was stationed—the careless nurse was chatting with one of the petty officers, quite regardless of the child, who peered over the bulwarks down the vessel's dark side, the ship heeled over, slapped by a tide-wave, and the child was thrown into the sea. A general consternation prevailed, for the tide was running fast and heavy, and the poor little fairy thing was fast drifting away. The Boy Sailor was aloft, but in an instant he shot down the rattlings, and bounded into the waves, at the moment Captain and Mrs. Shand rushed on deck.

"For a moment, the position of the Boy Sailor was very critical.

"But his coolness is as admirable as his courage. He had wound round his arm a coil of new rope with which the gunner was repairing the breechings of one of the carronades, to a ring-bolt of which it was attached.

"The captain could scarcely restrain his wife from leaping overboard.

"For a moment the most anxious suspense prevailed.

"The men at the davits were lowering the boat.

"Shand had a very fine Newfoundland which he had brought with him on board; the noble creature plunged into the surf and swam strongly towards the drowning child.

"The Boy Sailor had forestalled him, for, at that instant, he was working up the rope as nimbly as a squirrel, the child in his arms.

"The poor little thing thus gallantly saved was quite insensible, and it was feared at first that she was dead.

"We were all much affected by the mother's grief and followed her with our eyes as she carried the child tenderly in her arms towards the companion-hatchway.

"Despite his excitement Shand's first thought was to thank and reward the gallant boy; he took off his heavy gold watch and chain and was about to hand it to the little fellow; but, to the surprise of us all, he had vanished.

In the confusion that ensued upon the child's being brought on deck, he had slipped away, and flying up the shrouds to finish his watch, now appeared perched on the cross-trees as if he had taken no part in the exciting scene that had just been closed so happily.

"I hailed, and he came down from aloft with a look that betokened that he would rather have stayed where he was for awhile.

"He blushed and received very modestly the caresses of Mrs. Shand, who, poor soul, was half frantic with gratitude, and the praises of her husband, who was much struck by the ingenuous manners of the plucky lad.

"He would have made the boy handsome presents but they were steadily refused.

"Shand got over the difficulty in this way; he took young Halliard ashore with my permission, pretending that he required a boy to assist him in copying letters and the like. He would have retained him but the little chap could not be prevailed on by any inducements to leave the Thunderer."

A murmur of approval of the gallant little hero ran round.

"He certainly will be a great man some day," continued the captain. "I speak of him so warmly, perhaps, because he is the son of a gentleman whom we all respected. The boy is half rated for a midshipman for one of the most daring feats on record. It was after the battle of St. Vincent; our frigate was sent in pursuit of some of the enemy's ships, which had escaped from Collingwood; we were deceived by false reports, and missed them more than once. At last we fell in with two fine vessels in the Bay of Biscay. As you may suppose, our joy was extreme; Nelson's startling triumphs had rendered the admiralty exacting, and, as you may suppose, we thought nothing of odds in a battle with the Frenchmen. We fell to work, and warm work we found it when we had got into the 'middle of it,' and were pounded and being pounded in the most rattling style, the Crapands fighting most desperately, and making the most of their superior advantages. It was suddenly announced that two other large French ships were bearing down on us; we were in for it, but we were determined, after such a glorious victory as we had gained at St. Vincent, that we would not be towed into Brest harbour, though our alternative should be the destruction of our ship and our own general ruin; however, the crew had been fearfully thinned, and as the poor fellows remaining had had a rough watch the preceding night, and a tough tussle with the enemy since sunrise, it was not to be wondered at that they should begin to lose heart, and I daresay that there were moments when they would have welcomed the command to haul down the flag, not that they feared death, but were spiritless from fatigue.

"The fore and mizen top-royals were struck and crashed down, doing fearful damage.

"A division of men were ordered to go aloft and cut away the spars that were meshed in the tackling, and every moment threatened to crush us.

"As fast as the poor fellows ran up the rigging they were picked off by the sharp-shooters on board the Frenchmen, and ten or fifteen had fallen successively.

"The men began to get nervous.

"When a fresh division was ordered aloft they murmured and hesitated.

"I was in great perplexity; I rated the poor fellows, and blared out some fustian about nailing the colours to the mast.

"Harry Halliard, who stood near, snatched up the jack, which had come down with the fore-top. He seized a hammer, and stood with one foot on the rattlings.

"The action was one of pure enthusiasm, and not of presuming forwardness.

"'Men, let that child teach you your duty,' said I.

"In an instant the boy had flown up the rattlings.

"A shell rushed past him, firing the racqueting sky-sail.

"We thought he was killed.

"The men at the guns fired another broadside.

"The strained ship shuddered and lurched, and the deck was enshrouded in a dense cloud of smoke.

"As the cloud soared up it and dispersed the Boy Sailer was seen calmly hammering through the bunting at the mast-head—old England's broad flag rolling around one of the most gallant of her youthful heroes.

"The men uttered a deafening cheer, and tumbled over each other in their emulation, as they wildly flew aloft.

"The rigging was cleared, and the fight renewed with tenfold vigour.

"One of the French ships was sunk, the other disabled and silenced.

"We should have had hard times of it, however, with the other two had not three English men-of-war hove in sight.

"One of the Frenchmen sheered off, and though pursued, was not taken.

"The other hauled down her flag, being unable to get under weigh.

"I think, after this, that all will forbear making invidious remarks about the connections of such a splendid little fellow as Harry Halliard, the Boy Sailor."

Our hero's health was drunk with a cheer.

An officer entered the room at this moment.

"What news, Mr. Waters?" asked Captain Brandon, while the rest looked at the new arrival with inquiring glances.

"A despatch from the Admiral, sir," said the officer, bowing respectfully, and presenting a packet.

"As I came along I heard a piece of news that will give satisfaction to you, my lord," he said, addressing the Earl.

"Indeed! let's have it."

"Black Tom, the highwayman, who attacked your lordship, has been taken."

"I am glad of that. I hope they will hang the villain without delay," said the Earl.

"He is already sentenced," said the judge, "and will most probably be turned off with a whole batch of other crows of the same feather by next Monday."

"And what news from the Admiral, Sir Everard?" asked several of the naval officers, speaking together.

"In this letter he gives orders that the Thunderer should remain in harbour on recruiting service until further orders. And this paper—can you anticipate it's contents?"

"What is it, Sir Everard?"

"A midshipman's commission for the young hero of whom we have been talking—for Mr. Halliard," said Captain Brandon, with a dry and pleased smile.

"Hurrah!" cried the gentlemen, raising their glasses. "Here's health and honour to the lad, and may his example inspire the youth of England with emulative courage, and zeal and rectitude. Hurrah for Mr. Midshipman Halliard. Three cheers for the Boy Sailor!"

CHAPTER XV.

ONCE MORE AMONG THE WRECKERS—THE KIDDLE-AWINK—HYLDA, THE LUCKLESS CAPTIVE—HARLECK STATES HIS PLAN OF VENGEANCE.

As the Thunderer was to remain in dock for an indefinite, perhaps a long, period, most of the crew obtained extension of leave.

As before stated, Harleck, the wrecker, had acquired the good will of the officers by the palpable change which had taken place in his conduct.

He applied for leave.

There was some hesitation; but it was finally granted.

The wrecker came ashore with a party of men whom he soon abandoned to their festivities, while he wended his lonely way towards Seawardine.

Avoiding the road he walked along the coast and under the frowning cliffs.

The eyes of the savage miscreant shone with a strange light as he gazed over the tumbling billows, and rested them on the Shark's Fin, and the rugged rocks and boulders of the cliff-walled strand.

His teeth and hands were tight clenched, and his lips muttered.

He walked onward in abstracted mood.

The wanton breezes stealing over the fresh wide sea played with his raven-black elf-locks, strewing them over his dark and sinister face.

As he was rounding a bluff of land he perceived a party of six sturdy fellows hauling a boat along the sands.

His eye brightened.

His step quickened.

He hallooed for them to stay.

His order complied with, the men stood looking towards him with surprise and suspicion.

Chuckling with glee, he advanced towards them.

He held out his hand, with a deep, gruff laugh, to a tall, manly, and particularly handsome fellow, dressed in a rough guernsey and leathern kilt, high boots and scarlet night-cap.

The man stared at him in astonishment, and then warmly grasped his hand.

"Ha, ha, hearty, and its veritably yourself—old Harleck. We all thought you had gone to Davy Jones long, long ago! but you mean to prove that your flesh and blood—(slacken a bit, my hearty, my finger-bolts are starting!) — and your ghost would never sail in that rig."

"No, no; it's I, Thorkil, it's I. Dam'me, I am glad to see ye," growled Harleck, in a tone as gruff as it was hearty.

"And what news, messmate, eh?"

"You can see for yourself. I was picked up by the cursed jollies, and forced to slave in the service. Ha, Agger, and Dan, Elijah, Polreal, Trevallier!—what cheer, hearties? Dam'me, it's as good as grog to see ye all. What sort of cruising? How's trade, Thorkil?"

"Bitter bad, my soul; might as well skipper a bum-boat as be captain of wreckers and free-traders now-a-days. All's going to the bad, I tell ye. The times are changing, hearty," grumbled Thorkil Penreal; "what with new lighthouses, new stations, preventives, spies, and deserters, poor markets, and no reckoning of other devilries, I lose all pluck, and think I shall give up the profession, and take to dredging for shrimps and prawns."

"And Hylda—how fares she?"

"No change, hearty; except that her tongue sharpens as my patience shortens. But I suppose you've come among us to cast anchor—you've had enough of the service, eh?"

"Aye, Thorkil, but the sarvice has not had enough of me!" returned Harleck, savagely.

"Belay, then, time doesn't break our contract. You're mine, Harleck; and I'll protect ye."

"Aye, mate, but you can't revenge me," said the wrecker, with a meaning frown.

"Curse him for a fool who meddles with other folks' quarrels! Dam'me, I've had enough of avenging!" cried Thorkil, hotly. "I well-nigh ruined myself in righting the wrongs of that infernal rascal Black Will Trelawny, and what was my recompense?"

"Ah! Is there a split between ye?"

"Pshaw! I ought to have been keel-hauled for ever joining with such a beastly time-serving skunk!"

"Why, what has he done?"

"Done!—everything that's treacherous, Harleck. But, come along, shipmate, let's turn into Murdoch Polruth's kiddleawink, and overhaul the log together."

"I'm with ye, hearty," returned Harleck. "And where is Trelawny now, and Paul Adair?"

The captain of the wreckers looked around him nervously, though they were in such a lonely spot.

He lowered his voice as he answered,

"They're at sea, Harleck, cruising in the Black Eagle."

"Phew! Paul is the very devil," cried Harleck, much impressed by the intelligence implied in Thorkil's dark speech. "And where is he cruising now?"

"Can't say; I believe somewhere in the Spanish main."

They entered the kiddleawink.

Like the rest, Murdoch Polruth was much astonished at beholding Harleck.

The wreckers seated themselves at the table.

Murdoch brought black bottles of strong spirits, and pipes and glasses, which he arranged upon the table.

The rough fellows were soon enveloped in a cloud of smoke.

They carried on their conversation in low and earnest tones.

One by one the men left the little tavern, and Thorkil remained alone with the seamen.

"And so you hate the service, Master Harleck?" said the captain of the wreckers, refilling his pipe.

"Would you like it, think ye, cap'en?"

"No, Harleck, I'd prefer liberty in the hottest latitudes," returned Thorkil, laughing. "But, if you hate the service so much, why not desert? These rocks will offer you an asylum; they have been the cheerful cage of one poor crow nearly five years."

"What, do you mean the cockney chap? Shiver me! but it's useless expense and danger to fatten and foster a cursed spy because you're not man enough to slit his weasand! I should have settled him long ago."

"And so should I have done, Master Harleck," returned the captain of the wreckers, with a grim smile, "but I had given my word, and, if a man wants to be understood when he speaks, his word should be his bond."

"You have the credit of being fair-dealing, Thorkil."

"I deserve it, comrade; I never desert my allies."

"And are you primed for a daring venture?"

"In daring the devil, his imps and goblins——"

"You are afraid of nothing. Ha!"

"Except my wife!"

"Then, hark ye; I mean to return to the ship."

"What for, if you so hate the service?"

"I have a deed to do before I leave it."

"To leap over the fo'castle without falling into the water?" said Thorkil, grinning.

"I'll tell you what, my work in it is a work of vengeance!"

"Vengeance! to the fiends with such cant; I have paid dearly enough for other people's vengeance; work out your grudge as best you may without my assistance."

"How long since you've had a wreck on this coast?"

"Few of any kind, and none worth mentioning since the wreck of the Thetis."

"Ha! there shall happen a worse calamity to the Thunderer than ever befel that vessel," muttered Harleck.

"What do you mean?"

"You cannot guess?"

"No! unless another wreck."

"An utter wreck."

"Humph! it's almost too late in the day to attempt it, hearty; as I tell you the state's on the brink of ruin; everything is going to the bad, there's no trade thriving on land or sea. I hear the same complaints everywhere; a man must slave to death to earn scanty bread, and may be dismissed by capricious masters at any time they would rid themselves of his services; and yet a poor lad is not to pick up what he can on the highway or the high seas; it's infernal tyranny—impression. Look at the new lighthouse, now; and the mole, and the watchhouse right over the Seal's Cover; but that will come down some wintry night, its foundations are insecure," said the rascal, with a meaning leer.

"And the magazines aboard the Thunderer are also insecure, Thorkil. A spark might get into them at any moment, and where would the bullying, flogging officers and the fawning, treacherous men be hurled to? Such accidents as the fall down of the watch-tower, or the blowing up of the Thunderer might happen, cap'en, once or so in an age."

Penreal started to his feet in horror.

"There is reason in all things, Harleck; you don't mean to say that you would be such an infernal villain as to destroy every soul on a man-of-war, messmates and friends, to pay out the grudge you owe a single man?"

"I tell ye I hate the sarvice and all that belongs to it," snarled Harleck, savagely shaking his fist. "And haven't I reason? Why the devil should I load the guns to sweep off the French? Why should I expose my body to be made a target for those I care nothing about, who are nothing to me? and why, because as a free man I strike for liberty, should I be bound to the gratings and mercilessly lashed till I am bathed with blood—till the very wounds I bear for the ungrateful beasts I serve are torn open? Do you think I'll bear this, Thorkil Penreal? Do you think I will not for this great wrong wreak a great vengeance? Never believe it. I'm true Cornish. I have the old blood in me, and it will work, Thorkil Penreal, to the destruction of every living soul, as ye say—messmate or officer—on board the Thunderer. By the Logan stone, I'll make her thunder! But will you help me?"

"Never, never!" cried the captain of the wreckers. "It's well enough to destroy a ship by water. I've no objection to wrecking; in truth, I was born to it, and can see that there's no harm in it; for, as the old rhyme says,

' All that I give thee is thine,
And all that thou givest me is mine.'

If we trust our ships to the waves, they are at the mercy of the wind-spirits, and what we can snatch from the wraiths ought to be ours. But fire! fire is hellish; and the ship to which you return by your own free will—no, no; I must think."

Harleck made no reply to this vehement deprecation; he sat broodingly watching the light sails as they flitted along far, far at sea, and a satanic sneer played on his lip.

"Well, Thorkil, you refuse to help me?" said Harleck.

"Hearty, it seems too bad to think of."

"It was not too bad that I should be so clapper-clawed by those villains; but come, is it a bargain?"

"I don't see what I'm to gain by it."

"That I will show you."

"Well, I must think of it."

"Avast; why, Thorkil, you seem to have lost all your old spirit."

"Wiser, I am, that's all, Harleck."

"Well, cap'en, then I must look elsewhere for assistance."

"I tell you I must consider over the matter before I can give you a direct answer ; meanwhile we will be off to the Seal's Cover."

The two wreckers left the kiddleawink and proceeded to the caverns.

They entered the little hut on the shore, which we have before described, in connection with the adventures of the unfortunate Theophilus Lobb.

Thorkil lifted a trap very ingeniously disguised, and disclosed a deep, dark shaft, with a ladder descending into the regions below.

Thorkil lighted a lantern.

He led the way down the shaft.

Harleck closed the trap, and fixed the bolt with a mechanical air, as of one long acquainted with the place and its belongings.

The two ruffians reached the foot of the ladder and found themselves in a long vaulted passage cut in the living rock.

It was lighted by flaring oil lamps suspended from the stony roof.

It was curious to observe the beaten track in the hard stone, footsteps almost as plainly marked as if imprinted in snow ; on the rugged walls were other footsteps, the pronged claws of extinct birds of a far past cycle.

And yet these marks were on the sides of the wall, cut in the solid cliff.

A dim, pent, and dreary region the abode of the desperate gang.

Thorkil and Harleck walked side by side, for the passage was wide and ample, though irregular, here and there strange borders jutting out.

At the end of this passage was another crossing it, in the centre of which a glaring torch was fixed in an iron sconce on the wall.

Thorkil and his companion turned to the left and proceeded to mount a flight of steps, at a little distance from the angle where the rocky corridors met.

At the top of this flight of stairs another torch was burning.

Its light fell upon a piece of sail cloth which screened the arched entrance of another cavern.

Thorkil lifted this, and the pair passed through.

They were in a spacious and vaulted apartment.

The walls were hung with faded cloths and tapestries, adorned with shelves, on which were shining plate and glass, and various ornaments—spoils from many a wreck.

There were several mirrors, and even pictures.

The floor was spread with a rich carpet, and the furniture, though incongruous, was rich and quaint.

From the centre of the roof depended the bright brass branches of a sort of chandelier, from which long sperm candles distilled a mellow and cheerful light.

In one side of the room was a wide opening, used as a fire-place, and on a large slab a bright fire was spluttering and roaring right fiercely.

The place was by no means damp or chill. On the contrary, there was something pleasant and cheerful about this extraordinary abode.

One corner of the room was veiled by some rich hangings, which probably concealed a bed.

The walls were hung with divers sorts of weapons —guns and pistols, starry pikes, and glancing cutlasses.

Before the blazing hearth, the fire-glow beaming on her fine and haughty face, sat Hylda Penreal.

She rose as the men entered.

Thorkil was a step in advance, and as he was very tall, while Harleck, though broad and massive, was short in stature, the woman did not perceive the latter, for the rich piled carpet quite deadened all sound.

"Where have you been ?" cried Hylda, in shrewish tones, turning upon her husband. "Are these times when you can be wasting the hours with swinish companions, at Polruth's, when there is work in hand ?"

"You cursed screech ! and will you ever greet me with a scold's welcome ? I hate your voice, and I would rather be as deaf as these dead rocks, or as blind as the moles in the earth above them, than see or hear you, you eldritch sea-hag ! with a tongue as bitter as wormwood, and a temper that would disgrace the devil !" shouted Thorkil, stamping his foot and clenching his fists.

"A manly captain of Cornish wreckers—a brute and a bully, to victimise a weak woman that watches for his interest, and keeps him from the hulks or the gallows by her care, which is so vilely rewarded. Why did you come home ? Are you not valiant ? Do you mean to beat me ?"

The woman rose and glared upon her husband with flaming eyes, her fine form dilating, and her white arms stiffening with fury.

"Be quiet, Hylda. Some day you will drive me mad, and, by Heaven, I shall kill you !"

"As you did my father !" returned the woman, with a scoffing laugh of aggravation.

"You ungrateful harridan ! When did I strike you ? When was the time that I did not treat you gently ?" cried Thorkil, hoarsely.

"You have murdered me ! You have cut me to pieces, and stabbed my heart through by your rough words, your neglect of business. What do you care ? The band laugh at you and call you fool. I may slave, but there is no trade driving, and when we've a chance of doing something for ourselves, where are you ? Swilling your brains out, if they are not drowned in beastly schnapps already, with that idiot Polruth and the hogs that herd with him," screamed the shrew with intense fierceness.

"Come lass, come ! Be quiet, I tell you," cried Thorkil with quivering voice. "I can't stand much more of this. You will drive me into a frenzy, and I shall murder you !"

"As you did my father. Do your worst, I can follow him," retorted Hylda, in sneering contempt, and re-seating herself before the fire.

"Why, lass, what is in the wind ? What is this vast business that I have neglected now ?"

"There has been a message from Fenwold."

"What, from the Earl of Penalvon ?"

"Yes ! He pays well, does he not ?"

"Not in proportion to the risk, Hylda. What does he want ?"

"How should I know ?"

"Did he come himself ?"

"No, he sent for you to meet him in the village, at the house of one of his tenants."

"And was this the only cause you had for raving at me like a drunken fish-wife ? A man might just as well be in flames as linked with such a vixen."

"Cut the links and my throat at the same time. I wish you would ! I'm sick of the bondage."

"Then, curse you, go free ! I will give you all I own to rid me of the blight of your presence," cried Thorkil, wildly.

NOTICE.—The next Number of the Boys' Library will be Published on Friday, July 25th
Order early of your Bookseller.

BOYS' LIBRARY

HARRY HALLIARD;
OR,
THE YOUNG BRITISH TAR.

THE BETRAYED.

The woman looked at him with perfect coolness.

"I will take you at your word, Thorkil, and we'll leave you in peace."

"What infernal childishness is all this wrangling? Come, let us be at accord; there are miseries enough in the vile world, without our preparing plagues for each other. Look, Hylda, I have brought an old friend to see you."

Hylda turned quickly.

Harleck stood before her.

His eyes were fixed coldly upon her face; his broad, sallow face was wrinkled with a strange leer; his beetling brows met, and spanned his rugged forehead in one black line.

Hylda shuddered.

"And are you come back?—are you alive?" she murmured, in a low tone. "I thought you were dead."

"No, mistress, I live to serve ye yet," returned the ruffian, in a strange, hollow voice.

"Why did you bring him here? Have I another father for this monster to kill? Where are you sprung from? Are you a vampire, or a ghoul, and have you come from your grave?"

"Did you not know I was alive, then, mistress? You have not the skill of Wild Thyra; she predicted my return, as I am told."

"Any fool can prophecy evil; but I will venture this prediction—you will not live long, Harleck."

"If you could have your way, dame," rejoined Harleck; "but I am a king's man now, as you may see by my rig, and shall not stay here long to offend you."

"For that I am grateful," returned Hylda, contemptuously.

"Get us some supper, lass; I and Harleck are hungry as jackals. Smooth your brow for once in honour of his return. Come, Harleck, let us go and visit my new works below the watch-house on the cliffs."

Thorkil walked to the other side of the room, and lifting another curtain of sail-cloth, passed down another flight of steps, and threading a labyrinth of passages, came to a wider one, where a number of wild-looking fellows were busy in undermining the new station.

After Harleck had exchanged a few gruff words of recognition with the labourers they passed on.

Thorkil led the way to a sort of cell cut in the rock.

Into this they entered.

At a table in the middle of this cavern a man sat writing.

He was a queer-looking personage, with a full face, flabby cheeks, and dim eyes, that were peering through a pair of green spectacles at a rule with which he was drawing a map.

The captive started and looked up with much dread at the new comer.

It was our luckless geologist, Theophilus Lobb.

"Well, my hearty, hard at it?" cried Thorkil, laughing, "what entry are ye making in the log-book now?"

"Weally, Mr. Penweal, sometimes I am weally at a loss to know what is to be done with the leisure time that you have thought pwoper to bestow on me so libewally, so, to amuse myself, I am making a plan of the diffewent windings in the caverns."

"With a hope of finding them useful for making your escape, eh? is that what you mean?"

"'Pon my word, it's widiculous to entertain such a thought, Mr. Penweal," cried poor Theophilus, in alarm; "I'm very well content where I am; I shan't attempt to escape for the pwesent."

"You are right in that determination," returned Thorkil; "if you attempt again what you have tried before I will kill you on the spot; if you attempt it, you know I keep my word."

Agger entered the cavern.

Thorkil started when the wrecker announced the arrival of the Earl of Penalvon.

He then left the cell, Harleck remaining with the captive.

CHAPTER XVI.

THE BOY SAILORS AND LENA SPEND A HAPPY TIME AT HOME.

THE days passed swiftly and happily in the widow's humble home.

Frank Rayner had not for years felt such keen delight as he now experienced.

The morning was spent in rambles along the rugged and picturesque shore, in company with the strange and romantic Wild Thyra.

The evenings passed in mirth and comfort by the blazing hearth.

The autumn was advancing, and the nights were chill.

The term of their leave having expired, with aching regrets they tore themselves away from the scene of such dear delights. Lena sighed as she thought of hard tasks, cold treatment, and severe punishments, but she made no complaint.

Rose Halliard had been faithful to her trust; had little Lena been her own daughter, she could not have displayed more motherly affection.

The Boy Sailor had received no intimation of his promotion.

It was early in November when Lena left home; she was escorted to Falmouth by the gallant young sailors.

It might be considered unfeeling on the part of Rose Halliard that she suffered Lena to remain in a school where the pupils were treated rather as prisoned culprits than tender children; but the girl was shrewd and sensible; she loved her playmates and her kind and gentle under-governess; she dreaded, but in some respects, did not dislike the stern preceptress: for, though rigidly severe, she was impartial and consistent, and girls like the authoritative. Besides all this, Rose Halliard knew that her foundling was day by day becoming more accomplished, and she did not know in what other quarter to seek those advantages which she here obtained for her through the assistance of the good rector, who would perhaps be offended, and withdraw his support, if the girl were removed from the school where he himself had placed her.

The polite Frank had made a very favourable impression upon Miss Tingles, and there was something so delicate, yet so fearless, in the demeanour of our young hero that he, too, had made a strange impression upon her almost unimpressionable heart.

They were two interesting, handsome boys; they were full of life and nature; their presence as freshening as the breath of spring; they were particularly well-behaved, and profoundly deferential, and they had saved her parrot!

But those horrid blue jackets, paltry straw hats, and truculent ducks, that marked them common sailors!

However, they met with a more gracious reception than they had dared to anticipate, and left Lena in better spirits than they expected; but the brave girl cared little for herself, and was delighted that the boys received civil treatment from the awful queen regnant of Birch Hall.

Upon returning to the ship, Harry Halliard was summoned to the captain's cabin.

The latter jumped up, and caught the boy by the hand.

"Mr. Halliard, believe me that I envy your mother at this proud moment of your life," he said. "I wish you were my own son. Your distinguished merit, high courage, and good conduct have met their due reward. But, remember, that far more will be exacted of you now than when you were simply a lad before the mast. You may not be able to achieve sufficient for the high demands of our proud country, but I'm sure, Mr. Halliard, you will do your best, and more can no man!"

"Sir Everard!" gasped our hero, letting his straw hat fall to the ground, and starting back as if stunned by the intensity of the eager hope that struck his young, ambitious heart at these words.

"At the recommendation of Admiral Nelson a commission has been sent for you, and henceforth on board the Thunderer you will hold the position of midshipman. But, my boy, what ails you?

Why, Harry, you are fainting like a girl. Come' come, what nonsense !"

The boy had reeled against the side of the cabin. A smile of intense pride and joy flitted over his face, and he murmured the name ever foremost in his thoughts,

" Mother !"

He conquered his emotion, and though still very pale, drew himself up with firmness, and lowering his eyes, said, very quietly,

" Sir Everard, I don't deserve——Sir Everard, I will strive humbly, sir, to do my duty."

" I am sure you will. And now, my boy, you shall be the bearer of this good news to your mother, with this letter, and an extension of leave for two months, which will be granted to all those who have distinguished themselves and can be spared while the vessel is being refitted. You may go now." —

Harry Halliard bowed, and left the cabin.

He hurried to his chum, Frank, who stood leaning against the foremast, and looking wistfully towards the shore.

" Frank," cried our hero, laying his hands upon his companion's shoulders, and panting with excitement, " I—I am a midshipman ! "

The boy started back, with a cry of joyous surprise.

" It seems too good to be true ; but look, here is my commission—here a letter from the captain to my mother, and we've been granted two months' renewed leave."

Frank seized his companion's hands, and shook them ecstatically. He relinquished them and touched his hat, shook them again, and once more saluted.

Harry, my chum !—sir !—Mr. Midshipman Halliard !—you little brick ! you nice young gentleman ! Behave ! Aye, aye, sir, when I come to my senses; meantime, order the gangway to be cleared, sir ; here goes for a hornpipe ! "

And away sprang the light boy, his arms akimbo, and his feet bounding nimbly in the quick step of a sailor's dance.

When he had circled round the mast in this manner, he threw himself against the bulwark, and tossed up his cap.

" Hurrah for Midshipman Halliard !" he cried. " Oh, Harry, do not desert your old, faithful chum, now that you are promoted, or I shall lose more than you have gained. I'll be your coxswain, and many a glorious cruise we'll have together. Oh, what brave news for your mother ; what joy for little Lena ; what a satisfaction to Mother Tickletoby, that none of her boarder's brothers are common sailors ! The Admiralty have come to their senses, and that's more than I shall, till I see you full-rigged, and feel the wide space between us that parts the quarter from the fo'castle."

Harry fairly hugged his staunch friend, as he exclaimed, with great warmth,

" That's a shabby speech, Frank ; nothing shall ever separate us. Rather than be parted from your friendship I resign the post of High Admiral. You will gain honours too, old boy ; if right were might you would be in my shoes at this moment ; but it's my father's name, and the interest of Mr. Armitage and the captain."

" No, no ; your own courage, you heroic little brick. Well, I can be respectful, Mr. Halliard, but not till our leave has expired. Till then, we will be jolly together, and stand on our equality."

" 'Tis one or both of us goes over the gratings, cheery. Do not dash my pleasure. We are equals, and always shall remain so, till you get foremost in the race for glory, which you will, Frank, mark my

words, and no one then can say of you, as they might of me, that promotion came through interest; all the glory will be your own."

At this moment a sailor advanced.

He gravely touched his hat to our hero.

" Mr. Armitage wishes to speak with you, sir."

" Sir !"

As our readers will discover while they follow our hero's fortunes, Harry Halliard was born to honour.

Many an after triumph brought its commensurate pleasure, but never after, in his most brilliant hours of success, did he experience such a rapturous thrill of exultation as that which shot through every nerve at the simple " sir" and the respectful salute which confirmed him in his new position.

Frank Rayner sat down upon the deck.

He fell into a fit of abstraction.

His face beamed with sympathetic delight ; but yet again and again a shade of sorrow would sweep over it.

" No, Hal, it can't be !" he exclaimed, starting up impulsively, and striding towards the fo'castle ; " there is a difference between us now, which, however you may try to conceal, exists, and I will respect it. Well, there is no one in the world to love me but you, for I am all alone, and if I can enjoy your friendship on terms of equality, I can serve under you as a beloved commander with devoted loyalty."

He started back as Harry stepped quickly up to him, his eyes beaming, his cheeks aglow.

He was equipped in the full uniform of a midshipman, and his dirk hung at his side.

The boy had such a gentleman-like carriage, and seemed to accommodate himself to his new honours with such graceful ease, that Frank could not help lifting his hat as he said, gravely,

" Mr. Harry ; I think I had best not go ashore with you ; the men may hold you cheap if you associate too much with one below yourself in station, our friendship, meanwhile, suffering nothing by the change, dear Harry."

" The men would justly despise me were I the conceited puppy and upstart skip-jack to be puffed-up by a change which I can set down only to my good luck. I am prouder of your friendship, Frank, than of anything else in the world. Come, old philosopher, it gives me pain to see you look so glum ; the boat is waiting. We will pay a passing visit to Miss Tingles, take a bulletin of the parrot's and the cat's condition, kiss little Lena in spite of boarding-school proprieties, take a chaise, have another adventurous land-cruise to Seawardine, and if we can get another pop at another highwayman, *tant mieux !* as Johnny Crapaud says. Heave ahead like a jolly dog !"

He thrust his arm through Frank's, and forced him along to the accommodation ladder, down which the joyous tars were hurrying into the boats.

As he drew near, the men fell back, and when still keeping close to his trusty friend, he passed over the side, the true-hearted salts greeted the brave and generous little fellow with a hearty and affectionate cheer.

With throbbing heart the young mid placed himself in the stern.

He was the only officer in the boat, and with red-hot cheek and trembling voice gave the order to pull off.

They reached the shore.

As they walked along through the bustling streets of Falmouth the Boy Sailor showed just a tinge of natural vanity in the way he held his head aloft, and played with his glittering side-arms.

They betook themselves to the same inn where they had met the highwayman.

The landlord's daughter received them with a look of pleasure.

They ordered dinner, to which they did due honour, and after a dessert of nuts and ale, during which they laughed over their adventures with the showman and the robber, they ordered the chaise, as before, and drove off to Birch Hall, to pay a passing visit to little Lena.

Miss Tingles received them with great condecension.

The pride and delight of the school-girl at Harry's promotion were quite boundless.

She seemed beside herself with pride and joy, and expressed in the most extravagant terms her admiration of his elegant uniform, kissing him with affectionate enthusiasm.

Each boarding-school miss in the establishment, at incalculable risk to herself, ventured to take a peep at the middy, and kissed her hand to him through the door of the reception-room.

In a short time, Harry and Frank took their leave of Miss Tingles, and once more getting into the chaise, dashed off towards Seawardine.

Arrived at home, Harry enjoyed another ovation, on the part of his mother, Nelly Britton, and Wild Thyra. And the gratitude of Mrs. Halliard may be imagined when upon opening the letter from Captain Brandon, she found herself reinstated in her rights as the pensioned widow of the lost captain of the Thetis, and raised above indigence for the remainder of her life.

Frank and our hero spent many an hour of unshadowed pleasure in wandering the romantic coast, or mingling with the genial country people of the neighbourhood.

The Boy Sailors were cordially welcomed by every one in Seawardine, excepting the smugglers and wreckers whom they studiously avoided, though Murdoch Polruth was particularly gracious in his manner towards the Boy Sailor, and often invited him to mingle with the roughs that frequented the kiddleawink, who attempted to gain the boy's favour by offering him drink, and bestowing on him their most fulsome flatteries.

But our hero was unyielding, and would have nothing to do with his grand-uncle, or any of his disreputable associates.

The time passed on—the days grew short, the weather cold and dark, and wintry.

Christmas was at hand.

Day by day the boys looked forward to the time when Lena should come home from school.

The day at length arrived.

The boys went to meet the girl at Penzance, whither she had come by coach from Falmouth.

And now the happy family were once more assembled in their happy home.

Harry had set aside his uniform and accoutrements, and was dressed in a sailor-like suit of clothes, and in no way offered any ungracious contrast with the less fortunate, but equally deserving, Frank Rayner.

It was Christmas eve.

Around the cheerful fire, in Rose Halliard's pleasant cottage, a number of guests were gathered.

Among them were old Joel Britton, his daughter Nelly, his nephew Reuben, a channel pilot and a fine, frank young fellow, and Wild Thyra.

As they sat in the ruddy glare of the bright blaze, merrily talking and jesting, and sipping the punch which Rose had concocted so exquisitely, it was proposed that each in turn should tell a tale for the amusement of the rest. The proposal was agreed to, Wild Thyra consenting to take the lead in

A ROUND OF CHRISTMAS STORIES.

"I do not ask you to give credit to the legend I am about to tell you," the rune-kenner began. "I do not expect you to believe in the existence of wraiths and spirits of the ocean. You may consider the tradition of the Nymph's Well as an idle but pleasing fairy tale. Neither must you blame me for cleaving to a faith in the existence of beings with whom I have myself had frequent communion.

"You all know the well of the lone cavern in the rocks of Mount's Bay. It is a deep and sluggish pool, overhung by the lowering roof.

"It is more than a century since the old cottage that stands in ruins upon the top of the cliff, in which this cavern has been hollowed by the waves, was inhabited by an old man and his daughter.

"The man was a hardy, weather-beaten pilot, who had steered in the roadsteads since his earliest boyhood, and knew every hidden reef and rocklet, every shoal and quicksand, along either coast of Cornwall.

"His daughter, Elfie Brail, was a fay-like child. Beautiful as a naïad, light as a wind-spirit, she darted hither and thither like a sunbeam, and her voice was sweeter than the music of mermaids.

"No one could remember Elfie's mother. Many say that Japhet Brail, who was a man by nature reserved and taciturn, had brought his wife home from some part in another county, and had kept her in his lonely cottage, aloof from all the inhabitants of that part of the coast, through a whole year, at the end of which time she died, within a few days of Elfie's birth, and that Japhet himself had buried her in the sands. A more probable version of the case was, that Japhet's wife remained among her friends in her native home, and that he visited her occasionally.

"However, when Elfie first appeared, flitting about the cliffs and rocks of the bay, or gambolling with Japhet's rough and savage retriever,—a dog so surly and ferocious to all but the child, that he was as much dreaded as if he had possessed a legitimate claim to the name he bore, Wolf—she was a sylphide little creature, at most but three years old.

"Japhet took the greatest care that the little one should not associate with any of the children whom she met rambling on the beach.

"Perhaps it was from a jealous fear that another should share her love, which, stern and cold as he seemed to all who knew him, he fondly cherished, and would have kept in its fullness to herself.

"The pretty, gleeful fayling seemed to have a bounteous share of the commodity which she lavished freely upon her morose and solitary parent.

"The villagers often tried to catch a chance of speaking with the little fairy thing; but she was shy as a fawn, and though she would sometimes peep over the hedges when the men were mowing grass, or peer at them as they were hauling in their nets on the beach, and express by her looks that whatever report might say of her eldrich nature, her sympathies were human and affectionate; then she would spring away, and vanish into some hollow or cavern in the cliffs in a fashion that, to say the least, was mysterious.

"Time passed on, and Elfie ripened into girlhood.

"The spirits who fill the air and people the sea,

the very demons that dwell in the mines and the bosom of the earth, love the earth-born while they are children, and as Elfie wandered by the speaking waves she heard many strange voices in their murmurs or their ravings. A weird woman, who lived on a little island far off the shore, had taught her the runes and spells, which she could use more potently than her instructress, because her heart and mind were purer.

"Old Japhet would often take his daughter with him when he went for a cruise round the coast, which he sometimes did in a little launch, his business calling him to different ports, where vessels had put in under stress of weather. The skippers would never, if they could help it, employ any other pilot than Japhet Brail, who was reputed to know the waters better, and to be more skilled in seacraft than any other man along the coast.

"In one of these voyages, however, the launch was capsized in a heavy sea, and floated keel upwards in the foamy surf.

"The old man clung to the boat with one hand, while, with the other, he grasped his daughter, and kept her from sinking.

"Every instant they expected to be engulphed by the dashing billow-mountains, or torn from their hold by the savage wind that swept wildly past them.

"The grey morning broke with a sickly pallor on a night of the most dreadful suffering and appalling danger.

"Father and child still clung to their frail support in the midst of raging seas.

"The storm had somewhat abated, but as the tide was rising, the waves still raced along in swelling mountains, dashing with frightful force against the boat.

"A sail appeared in the offing.

"Japhet Brail made signals by waving a scarf at the top of an oar.

"The signal was made out by those on board; a gun was fired from the ship, and a boat sent off to the rescue.

"Exhausted, and half drowned, Elfie and her father were carried on board the vessel, which proved to be a small brig engaged in the coasting trade.

"The mate of the vessel, whose name was Miles Logan, evinced the tenderest care for Elfie, with whom he had already fallen deeply in love, although she had not yet unclosed her bright eyes, nor had charmed him with her siren-sweet voice.

"The next day the old man wished to return to the pinnace, which was towing astern of the brig.

"But Elfie still kept her cabin.

"The girl seemed spell-bound. She had exchanged a timid glance with Miles Logan; no words had passed between them, but she felt an ineffable dread of being separated from him.

"Perhaps it was for this reason that she did not appear to recover very rapidly.

"Old Japhet was wild with anxiety. The girl was frail and delicate, and a vague fear which he dared not give shape to, froze the soul of the stern and lone man. He dared not admit even the possibility that she might die; he was crushed at the very thought. How, then, could he bear up against the reality of such a bereavement?

"Japhet was not a demonstrative man. He preserved his ordinary demeanour of chill taciturnity though his heart was torn with all the pangs of torturing suspense.

"Elfie did not dream that her father was suffering so much. Miles visited her frequently, and ad-

ministered to her comfort with ever thoughtful care and delicate attention; he was respectful to bashfulness, and the girl trembled with agitation when he was in her presence, and though she shrank from him with maidenly reserve, felt in her heart a yearning impulse to tell him how dearly she loved him.

"At length the light broke in upon her. She was startled at her own heartlessness when she saw her father growing haggard and careworn, and she blushed at her own thoughtlessness and want of propriety in allowing herself to be so suddenly enthralled by an attachment her father would never sanction.

"Her recovery was rapid—abrupt. Her father wondered much when she came on deck; but she was so pale with agitation, and seemed so eager to go on shore, that he set down her rallying as an effort made to gratify his desire to leave the ship, and as the brig was now making the Lizard, he thought it would be better to get her to land at once, where she could receive the attention so needful in her precarious state.

"So Miles and Elfie were parted.

"The girl seemed much saddened after her return home.

"She accustomed herself to lonely rambles, and long and listless musings, as she strayed by the haunted waves.

"Her father was seldom at home, but Elfie Brail was never lonely.

"Sometimes she would stand on the wild shore and utter her runes, then listen, but the spirits now were silent.

"One day as she was roaming the beach, she perceived that a boat was pulling away from the little island that showed like a mote in a sunbeam in the long streaks of flashing light that lay rippling on the quiet sea.

"Her heart bounded as the little boat ran up swiftly on the advancing waves, and was left stranded among the glistening shingles.

"A tall, dark, and commanding-looking woman stepped out.

"This was Lorna, the witch of the island. The woman had a basket on her arm, which contained hose, and other wares that she knitted, to sell at Penzance; the sale of these, with eggs and little phials containing love-philters that the credulous girls eagerly bought of her, was her means of supporting life on her barren island.

"Lorna was reputed a witch, and, though the age had past when such a character was in danger of being dragged to the stake, yet she dared not remain in the midst of superstitious villagers or townsfolk, who might, at any moment, when provoked by a failure in the crops, a murrian among the cattle, or a wreck of their fishing yawls, rise and ill-use, perhaps murder her.

"Besides, Lorna was a true rune-kenner; her heart was in the mystery, and dead to human passions; she spared no toil, no suffering, no wandering, to collect essentials or to learn the runes that have power over the wild, strange beings who sweep along in the grey mist, who exult or murmur as each plashing breaker heaves on the shore. Great, indeed, are these agencies, mighty the work they have to do; most of them are formless, yet living ever; the ocean is the mother of the land, which sprung from the bosom of the sea; the spirits of the waves are the most potent of all spirits, though the spirits of air and fire, some of whom are pestilential, are most respected, because most dangerous to man. You smile at me; you think this is jargon—man is a worm of a day; the living agents of nature live for ever ; they may not be swayed by the vile passions that burn up the perishable clay, of which mortals are made. As the blazing wick wastes the candle, they may not have that wild, and ill-regulated brain-spring, called the mind, but they are the living thoughts of the living Deity—they are spirits."

"Elfie drew near to Lorna with a timid air, and took her hand.

"'Mother, I am glad you are come, for my thoughts have been of you constantly,' she said. 'I have sad news to tell you.'

"The witch looked anxiously in her pupil's face, but smiled.

"'Well, Elfie, it is better,' she replied, cheerfully. 'Knowledge is not happiness, and for a woman to give up all the charms of life for the slight power to be acquired by acquaintance with spells and simples, it is all folly. I know what you would tell me ; the spirits of the sea, the gnomes in the caverns, are deaf to your charms; you no longer hear their voice, they have ceased to commune with you.'

"'Yes, mother, it is so,' returned Elfie, with simplicity. 'The spirits of my fancy are mute now ; but it seems that a spirit in my heart speaks louder to me than they have ever done.'

"'Yes, and it repeats untiringly one name.'

"'Mother !' cried Elfie, starting and blushing crimson.

"'Yes, and the same spirit speaks in the heart of your lover, Miles Logan.'

"'Do you know this, mother ?' cried the girl, breathlessly.

"'How could I tell his name ?' returned the witch, with a strange smile.

"'Oh, if I could know that he loved me ! But, mother, my father would never consent to this engagement.'

"'He will.'

"'And we shall be happy ?'

"'I cannot tell that, daughter ; dark clouds overshadow the brightness of the future, yet you must not murmur if they break into a storm, for I can divine that you will call down upon yourself the tempest whenever it falls ; your destiny is in your own hands.'

"'I ask no more.'

"Foolish girl, most of our sorrows are born of our own perversity ; but you look doubtingly ; let me convince you that I have power to know these things.'

"'Whither are you going, then, mother ?'

"'To the magic well in the cave of the sea-wraiths ; will you come ?'

"'Yes, mother ; but now that I am sure Miles loves me I will learn no more spells, I will no more lack to evoke the voices of the spirits.'

"The witch and Elfie walked along the lonely shore till they came to the cave among the rocks in Mount's Bay—the cavern that you all know so well.

"You have explored its dark recesses, and remember the clear salt pool that lies like a sheet of plate glass framed by its mossy border of rock and petrified shells.

"When you enter this mine-chamber of the nymph's grotto, you take a torch with you, for the place is dark and dangerous ; but Lorna took no light, but, followed by her pupil, walked boldly into the profound gloom.

"I will not tell you what charms they used, what runes they muttered—though I know them all, for they are secrets.

"When Lorna arose from her knees, and the witch and her pupil stood locked in each other's arms, listening and trembling, a strange sound, like the vibration of a bell when the hammer has ceased striking, boomed around the rocky chamber.

"The darkness waxed into a bluish, mellow light, permeating the weird cavern, and sparkling on the spray-drops that spangled the bright, green moss around the pool.

"The well itself shone like a sheet of lightning—intense, and bluish white ; but its pale splendour was fixed, and not transient.

"The spray from the dripping cascade that waved at a far end of the cave, seemed fused by this new and strange medium of unearthly light, and rolled round the cavern in mist-like wreathing ; so that the shining disc of the brilliant, glaring pool, and the tortuous weaving mist rolls, made it seem to Elfie that she was amid the clouds gazing upon the full fairy moon.

"Presently, like the reflection of objects on a mirror or a camera, appeared on the glassy surface of the pool, a driving sea, with its plunging billows and scuddy waifs of foam. Seagulls dipping on their glancing wings, black clouds rimmed with softening crimson, and a boat strongly rowed by two men, whose forms were so familiar—her father and her lover.

"Their faces were smiling, their lips moving,

"Still the panorama of sky and sea flitted swiftly across the disk of the magic pool.

"Presently, frowning rocks and cliffs appeared, St. Michael's Mount and the old sea-worn church.

"The boat was run on shore, the men landed, still laughing and talking, though inaudibly, to the watchers.

"The old man lingered a moment to adjust something in the boat.

"The younger moved slowy on.

"He paused, and clasping his hands, raised his eyes to the deep heavens with thankful happiness. He drew from his bosom a tress of hair which he kissed with rapturous emotion.

"Elfie threw herself on her knees beside the pool, and uttered the beloved name in a loud and yearning voice.

"The spell was broken.

*   *   *   *   *

"Through the profound darkness Lorna the witch and Elfie Brail, passed out into the windy entrance of the cavern.

"They emerged once again on the bleak shore, and drew a long sigh of relief as the fresh cool breezes wafted upon their fevered, throbbing brows, and the mystic haloes from the spirit world were exchanged for the free and honest blaze of the genial sun.

"'What have you got in your hand, Elfie ?' asked the witch of her companion.

"'When I broke the charm by that involuntary cry——'

"'Which was rash. Such conduct angers the spirits—betrays your mortal weakness,' interrupted Lorna, 'but go on.'

"'I have nothing to tell you but that I found this fossil in my hand,' said Elfie, pettishly. 'I suppose, in my fright at the sudden fall of darkness, I snatched it up unconsciously; however, it shall do me no harm, for here's to throw it into the sea.'

"'Hold ! The most potent talismen are discovered in this way,' said the witch, catching her hand and taking the fossil from her fingers in which it was already poised for a cast.

"'It is as I thought,' said the witch.

"'Nothing but a paltry shell, petrified by the action of the air and water,' said Elfie.

" ' Thus things are judged by seeming !' exclaimed the weird woman.   'This headless coil of a serpent is a dangerous possession, Elfie.   Give it to me !'

" ' What are its virtues, Lorna ?' asked the girl.

" ' When the image of your lover is brought by spells upon the mirror of the wraith's well, this fossil, dashed into the pool, would kill him as surely as death's launched javelin, were he in the farthest confines of this wide world,' said Lorna, solemnly.

" ' Then give it me back,' said Elfie ; 'it is not right that his life should be placed in the hands of any stranger who might find it, for we are not the only rune-kenners in Cornwall, and our dark art has many evil votaries.'

" ' Should you behold him reflected on yon faithful mirror in the arms of some other love, tell me, Elfie, would you use the fatal power you hold to destroy him ?' asked the witch, fixing her deep black eyes steadily upon the girl's.

" ' I would !' cried the girl, with hot cheek and flashing eye ; 'but no, no, no,' she muttered, hoarse with horror, 'it would be worse than mere murder.'

" ' Then give the ammonite to my keeping, for woman's jealousy is a madness,' said Lorna, gravely.

" ' No, I am its only rightful guardian,' returned Elfie, firmly, as she placed the fossil in her breast.

" She started, for it sent a thrill to her heart like a piercing arrow barbed with an icicle.

" ' Be it as you will, Elfie Brail,' returned the woman, gloomily ; 'remember, I warned you. I wish we had not tampered with the spirits, or that you had not rudely broken the spell. No good will come of it. But get you home, your lover awaits you.'

" And Elfie needed no prompting ; she flew lightly along.

" When she reached the cabin she found her father and Miles Logan arrived before her.

" The old man seemed in unusually good humour, and Logan's face was radiant with happiness.

" Elfie learned that in the mate of the coaster he had discovered the son of an old and beloved comrade, who had been the truest, and, perhaps, the only friend he had ever possessed. He added, that Miles had spoken to him of the love he bore towards Elfie, and further hinted that nothing in the world would more delight him than to see his child united to the son of his old and valued friend.

" Then began a reign of bliss to the young lovers.

" Perfectly simple and guileless, the ingenuous girl with tender yet modest frankness avowed her affection for the young seaman.

" Many sunny hours they wore away together on that happy shore.

" Their marriage, however, was put off for awhile.

" Japhet thought his daughter scarcely old enough to enter into the engagements of wedded life.

" Miles Logan was looking forward to obtain the post of captain on board a vessel outward-bound for India.

" His hopes were at length fulfilled, and he obtained the desired appointment.

" The voyage was to occupy eighteen months.

" With many mutual vows of increasing love and unswerving fidelity the lovers parted.

" Left alone Elfie felt that the stay of her life had been rent from her, and that, feeblest of the feeble, she was unfit for existence, now that her intended husband was absent ; she walked as one in a weary dream, counting every grain of the slow-sifting hour-glass that must be so often turned before her lover could be restored to her. She thought, too, of his

perils—the sky, which beamed so brightly here may frown in its darkest fury on his far-away track.

" Torn by anxieties she could not conquer, Elfie resolved to consult the mirror of the wraith's pool.

" As her father was absent, she stole from the house, and hurried on towards the cavern.

" Just as she had reached the gloomy entrance of the cave, a large raven suddenly darted from a cranny in the rocks.

" The sinister bird wheeled thrice about her, hideously croaking, and finally perched in the front of the cave's mouth.

" His red eyes rolled and sparkled, and seemed by their gleam to dispute her entrance.

" Elfie accepted this as a warning of evil.

" She returned home, fully resolving that she would consult the mirror no more.

" She kept true to her resolve for many days, and was rewarded by the receipt of a long and loving letter from the absentee.

" After awhile the restlessness returned.

" She could bear her suspense no longer, having the fatal means of relieving it.

" She hastened to the cavern.

" This time she received no warning.

" She plunged into the darkness of the water cave.

" The runes muttered, the mystic rite performed, the same strange harmony that she had heard before resounded through the echoing concave rocks.

" Again the black gloom softened into mellow ethereal light ; once more the pool shone out with electric brightness.

" Mirrored vividly in the pool was the slow swaying cabin of a large ship.

" A lamp slung from the arched roof was burning mildly, and far through the cabin window the glittering sun-streaks danced on the rippling waves.

" At the table sat the captain of the vessel—her own true lover ; by his side were strewn the gage lock of her hair, and many little presents she had given him—treasures to him, so priceless to him.

" He was writing a letter ; from time to time he paused, smiling happily, as if seeking some fresh term of endearment. At length he had finished the letter ; he sealed and kissed it, and laid it sacredly apart ; he then wrote other letters with haste yet attention, and at last throwing down his pen fell into a reverie.

" His eyes closed—he was sleeping.

" And then the shapeless dream-spirits came sweeping into the cabin.

" They assumed the forms of maidens decked in misty white, and with modest wreaths of lilies.

" A quick pang shot through the watcher's heart ; but the mistress of the dream fays assumed the form of the bride, and in the light graceful figure draped in snowy white and crowned with orange bloom, she recognised her own image, and she knew that he was happily dreaming of her ; she felt his thoughts, as doubtless we feel the thoughts of dear ones absent. She knew that she was beloved.

" A cry of joy rose to her lips, but she suppressed it, conscious of her danger. Very carefully she spelled back the runes, reversing the charm.

" The images on the pool grew more indistinct and faded away, and the light waned slowly ; it had not quite died out in the darkness when Elfie left the cavern.

*   *   *   *   *

" The day arrived which should have brought Elfie a letter from her lover, but no letter came.

" Sickening with anxiety, she waited until the time once more arrived when she might hope to receive intelligence from him who had taken her away when he left her.

"Still no news.

"Days passed.

"Elfie grew pale and thin, and her father looked grave, and was more indulgent with his daughter, whose gentleness seemed a thing of the past, for now she appeared quite altered, having become strangely restless and fractious.

"Elfie resolved to pay one more visit to the pool of the water-wraiths.

"She stood once more in the whelming darkness, her foot on the brink of the magic well.

"For the last time.

"The runes muttered, the rite performed, again she looked into the faithful mirror.

"She started back, and almost broke the spell with a cry of passion.

"Under the graceful fans of a lovely palm grove, her lover reclined upon a bank of gorgeous Indian blossoms.

"A fair girl was by his side.

"She could tell by their affectionate looks and pleasant smiles that they were speaking of love.

"Logan seemed smitten with a sudden enthusiasm, and raised himself on one knee.

"The girl by his side laid her hand on his head.

"A ring of plain gold encircled her finger.

"She bent down, raising the tresses strewn upon his head.

"She kissed his forehead.

"Tight clenching her teeth, stiffly drawing up her slight and supple form, Elfie snatched the ammonite from her breast, upraised her soft white arm, and dashed the fossil deep down, plunging through the broken waters of the fathomless well.

"For an instant the images were distorted as when a mirror is crashed.

"Soon the surface smoothed, and all appeared as before.

"The beating of her heart stilled, the breath pausing on her budding lip.

"Her eyes fixed and strained to watch what would follow.

"There was no change.

"Still beneath those beauteous palm-trees sat the unconscious talkers, whose words were inaudible, yet palpable, to her.

"Could Lorna have been mistaken in the power of the charm?

"Oh, how fervently prayed the repentant girl that so it might be, though she should live for ever to endure her agony.

"Amid a little cluster of bright-hued flowers that gemmed the bank on which Logan was once more reclining appeared a little green gold coil as of a sleeping aspic.

"Suddenly it untwined and a tiny serpent crawled into her lover's bosom.

"Another instant he started up, livid and convulsed.

"With a look of horror the girl started from the bank and caught him quivering in death into her embrace.

"The very stones of the wraiths' cavern shudder at the pealing shriek of Elfie.

"The spell was for ever broken, and the rune-kenner sank down in a gulf of darkness.

*   *   *   *

"When Elfie wearily unclosed her eyes she found herself without the cavern supported in the trembling arms of Lorna the witch.

"The wail of the lost could not be more piteous and despairing than the moan of the hapless one as she gazed up into the face of her associate.

"'Is it too late?'" muttered the witch, in a husky tone.

"Yes, yes! but, oh, he was perfidious. I loved him! I loved him!' wailed Elfie. 'There is nothing now for me but death—sweet, sweet death! Oh, take me home to die!'

"Lorna carried home the fainted girl.

"Stricken from that hour Elfie pined away.

"A few months passed, and saw Japhet Brail, the tears trickling down his stern, hard face, by the death-bed of his darling child.

"He was called from the room to receive a strange lady who had come from India with sad news of his intended son-in-law.

"Soon after the lady, dressed in deep mourning, entered the sick chamber.

"All was soon told.

"Had she struck home a knife to Elfie's heart it could not have inflicted more keenly the mortal pang as those simple words,

"'I am *his sister*.'

"At the very moment when the serpent had stung him Logan was breathing his loving rhapsodies of Elfie to her from whom he had no secrets; the ship by which he had transmitted his letters had been lost; the last word in his life was the dear name of her to whom he had never been untrue, whom he had loved to the last with the fondest devotion.

"Elfie died, and at times her spirit is still heard sobbing by the brink of the pool of the Water Wraiths."

A deep silence reigned around the circle gathered about the glowing ingle as Wild Thyra concluded her strange legend.

The excitable Lena shed a few tears. Joel Britton coughed nervously, and he and Nelly looked with much awe on the eldrich-girl.

Rose Halliard, with a glance of affection and pity, while Joel's nephew and the two sea-boys seemed somewhat grave and thoughtful, as if they felt in no mood to question the veracity of the wild tale.

As Harry's faithful comrade sat next to Wild Thyra, it became his turn to make an effort to amuse the company, as the phrase goes. And in the words were told,

FRANK RAYNER'S STORY.

"Perhaps it is not in very good taste that one sad story should follow another; but it is strange that when one is very happy, as we all are now, it becomes quite pleasant to tell a sorrowful tale.

"So as we are on this tack, I think I will tell you a ghost story, or, at least, something like one; but, before I begin, I would assure you that allowing for any lapse in my memory, or variation in my way of expressing, what if I told a hundred times and kept to the truth, would amount to the same thing— 'the facts,' as the scribblers have it, 'being all within the author's experience.'"

"Why, hearty, you ought to write a book yourself," laughed Harry.

"Perhaps I may at some time or other, and if I do I shall write your life, my little hero. And such a work; it will be full of jolly larks and exciting adventures—everybody will be sure to read it, and to recommend it to their friends; but, meantime, stopper all, Master Hal. Miss Lena will tell you 'interruptions are impolite.' And now to get under weigh."

THE BOY SAILOR AND THE CHINAMAN.

"Perhaps you may imagine that I am going to tell you something about a phantom Dutchman or a haunted ship; nothing of the sort. The facts, for such they are, account for them as you will or can, occurred before I took that most important and most sensible step—to step away to sea.

"A man, who after being transported for a number of years, and thereby learning what transportation means, gets sentenced to the same service for the rest of his existence, but is suddenly transported, in a better sense, by a free pardon, he alone can appreciate the great deliverance I experienced when the 'sweet little cherub who sits up aloft to take care of the life of poor Jack' extended his favours to 'poor

Frank' and whistled him to get aboard that stately ark of refuge from all, but bo'swains' kicks and Frenchmen's round shot—to wit, the Thunderer—to flee from the wrath that was coming in the shape of a life's penal servitude as usher in a large boarding-school.

"Well, you smile, but I—even I—Frank Rayner, being an orphan on the principal's hands, was destined to become his 'birch-binder,' as we called the poor scholar who taught us all that he was paid for instructing. Being a modest youth, I am never the hero of my own stories; as you have anticipated, my hero was an usher in our school; but let me relieve your kind hearts by informing you that he is now on a ticket-of-leave, employed as a day or weekly literary labourer in writing very small works (educational) for very small boys under the distinguished name of Wilberforce Wearyquill.

"Now we all liked Mr. Stephen Charlesbury, and he knew it, and was prouder of our affection than he could be of any honour or profit he was unlikely to gain in any other hard lines of business ; for he loved us as though we were his brothers, and he had a way of doing his best that gave satisfaction to the masters, and excused him to us for being very soft and a lubber at cricket or football.

"He was rather sentimental, and you could see by the gloom in his dark eyes, and the lines in his thin, swarthy face, that he took it hard when he was snubbed by the masters, pitied by the parents, imposed upon by the boys, and sacked by the girls, in spite of his warm affection and his thorough principles of anti-humbug—all because he was a poor assistant.

"If he had been a plucky chap he would not have cared for all this ; but I suppose weakness and vanity lay at the root of his heart, and he deserved all he endured not over-patiently ; but he was a regular brick, for all that, and I'll sound his trumpet till he gets a better herald.

"This Mr. Charlesbury having few friends was accustomed to make a confidant of one of the elder boys, and I was his special favourite.

"Now what I am going to tell you happened towards the end of the last half, on the 6th of November, and about six bells second dog-watch.

"It fell upon this wise—I was sleeping in Mr. Charlesbury's room when I was awakened in the night by a strange thrill, as if something extraordinary were about to happen. I was very tired, as I had been playing a hard game at bandy—so called, I believe, from the almost moral certainty that those who indulge in it will get lamed for life—I was very tired and in a state between sleeping and waking, but sufficiently conscious to be sure that Mr. Charlesbury was up and dressed.

"His eyes were fixed and he seemed to be walking in his sleep. If he had appeared by daytime sleeping in his walk, I should have considered that only a 'trick of custom,' for he was always brooding and dreaming, as most ushers are who have any sense of their position, poor mortals ! Well, it was plain that he was walking in his sleep.

"Now, it would not be for a man-o'-war's man, who has fought under Nelson, to confess himself a coward, but I must acknowledge to an instinctive horror of somnambulists. I would rather, any day or night, meet a jibbing ghost, in a white shroud, than a wall-eyed sleeper, walking in his bedgown, or his decencies, as if he were led like a blind man by one of Miss Thyra's spirits which are all the more horrible for being invisible, and there is a scene in one of Shakespeare's plays would put me in a fit to see presented.

"This being my only weak point, I hope you will not despise me when I own that this handsome figure-head, which never ducked to the whistle of a bomb-shell, was bobbed under the coverlet, almost to the dislocation of this swan-like neck, which pivots it so gracefully.

"How long I remained in the bowels of the bed I know not, but when I ventured to peep over the edge of my tuffy-sheet, and transparent regulation blanket, Mr. Charlesbury was gone, the door being still shut.

He used to lock it at night, and though it is true that I did not get up and try it, yet I could see my belt curled in a peculiar knot on the ground

and just across the crack of the door, where I had thrown it.

"Our window was blindless, and the moonlight streamed in.

"I looked towards Mr. Charlesbury's bed.

"He was certainly not in it, if the evidence of my eyes was sufficient to establish that fact, for I certainly did not rise to examine it.

"I trembled myself to sleep.

"The sun in my eyelids, and the twittering of the birds in the ivy outside the window, awoke me early.

"I looked first at my belt, curled in the figure 7 before the door.

"I turned my head towards Mr. Charlesbury.

"He lay pale as death but deep asleep on the outside of the bed with all his clothes on, even to the little Scotch cap that once belonged to Phil Frenchboys.

"The bell startled us from our beds.

"It was fiercely pulled by old Twigem himself, for it was just thirty seconds past six, and it was Mr. Charlesbury's duty to sound the alarm at six precisely, when Duncan was obliged to hear it or he would be summoned to the studio, which was quite as bad as the other place.

"Poor Mr. Charlesbury jumped from the bed, and, in his bewilderment, snatched up his discarded nightgown, thinking it his coat. There was something half ridiculous, yet awful, in the amazement with which he regarded his lanky limbs encased so mysteriously in the threadbare garments.

"He hurried nervously from the room.

"The silly, weak-minded chap was idiot enough to ring the bell again, in a snivelling, deprecatory way, which only inflamed the ire of the bullying principal, and aroused the contempt of the pupils.

"Keep me and mine from weak-mindedness !

"All that day Mr. Twigem was in high dudgeon, but the usher did not heed him so much as usual ; he seemed to be deeply absorbed in speculative cogitation.

"During lessons I had to keep watch over him, for he was making all sorts of blunders in marking lessons, and even in setting sums and writing copies. One that he set for me was rather curious—

"'Idle reports should never be credited, for —it never was Marian.'

"It was lucky the line was written in *my* book. I quietly cut out the leaf, placed it in my desk, and without throwing him into hysterics by telling him of his error, made him set me another, dictating with a sternness that made him stare at me.

"At noon, when we were in the playground, I sauntered up to him, hat in hand.

"He was standing in his favourite corner, the only square yard of sunshine on the 'north front,' where our stone pen was built.

"He laid his hand on my shoulder heavily, and said with a kind smile,

"'Frank, have you a good memory ?'

"'Yes, sir ; I can repeat the first book of Æneid without a pause," I said, promptly.

"'And so can I—so can I, and the first book of the Iliad ; but it's very queer I can never recollect what happened yesterday ; at least I don't think I can,' he said, in his shambling sort of way, for, like Moses, Mr. Charlesbury was no spokesman.

"He remained silent for a few moments ; I looked at the ground, and swung my hat about as if I could guess what was coming, and felt awkward.

"'Frank,' said Mr. Charlesbury, 'did we chat last night before we went to sleep ?'

"'Yes, sir, you finished the fine long story you have been telling me,' I answered.

" 'Aye ; true, so I did,' returned our usher, hesitatingly. 'Now, Frank, you know that I am, in fact, that I am often abstracted, and do odd things unconsciously, did you notice whether—I—in fact—I did as most people do in a general way, whether I undressed before getting into bed ?'

" 'Yes, sir, you did,' I answered, firmly, 'I could swear it.'

" 'My God !' exclaimed Mr. Charlesbury, evidently much perplexed.

" 'And, in the night, you were not aware of my—in fact, of my rising in my sleep, and putting on my clothes !'

" ' Yes, sir, in the middle of the night I awoke and saw you sitting at the bed side, full dressed, with your little Scotch cap on.'

" 'Great Heaven ! and did I leave the room !'

" ' I think so, sir ; but I don't know.'

" 'Why, how should I get out of the room, you stupid boy, except by the door ?'

" 'Well, sir, if you went by the door you must have passed through the keyhole, for my belt lay on the ground doubled in a queer knot, in such a position that you could not have opened the door without moving it.'

" 'Then, perhaps, I got out of the window, Frank.'

" ' I did not see you go near the window, and if you went that way you were lucky that you did not break your neck, considering that our room is on the third story.'

" 'Bless my soul !' cried Mr. Charlesbury, 'then it must have been by the chimney.'

" 'No, sir, for don't you remember that Sam Scampington got stuck half way up the flue when he tried to clamber it one night for a lark ? Since the governor has had two iron bars fixed across.'

" 'But, perhaps, I never left the room after all,' said Mr. Charlesbury, beyond measure surprised.

" 'I daresay you did not, sir,' I returned, though in a tone of doubt. ' I fancied that you were gone in an instant ; I looked for you and your place was empty. However, being tired, I went fast asleep, and did not see you return ; but when old Twigem rang the bell this morning, you were lying outside the bed with all your clothes on.'

" 'Extraordinary !' exclaimed Mr. Charlesbury.

" At this moment the bell rang for dinner.

" Two letters arrived by the afternoon post for Mr. Charlesbury. I handed them to him, and observed that they were both directed in female handwriting.

" One was black edged.

" The other, I knew, was from his sweetheart, and was aware that, instead of making the poor fellow happier in his lowliness and slavery, would deepen his despondency for many a day.

" This was always the effect of these communications, which came irregularly. How did I know they came from Mr. Charlesbury's sweetheart? Schoolboys are gifted with a penetration in matters that don't concern them proportionate to their obtuseness in their legitimate studies.

" The afternoon passed away wearily with our poor usher.

" The boys soon discovered that he was moody and abstracted, and took advantage of his humour to amuse themselves at his expense.

" 'Night came, and we' returned to our bedroom.

" Mr. Charlesbury took a letter from his pocket—not the black-edged one—and lighting it in the flame of the candle, burnt it and threw it into the fireless grate.

" At sea one looks for hardships, and meets them with cheer ; on the wet deck or aloft 'mid the slippery tackling there is no mockery of a home.

" But it was piteous to see the bruised heart, the aching head, laid upon that hard quaint pallet in that drear room as cold as an ice cellar.

" But sufferance is the badge of all his tribe, and quite thankfully Mr. Charlesbury laid his head on the pillow.

" The gardener had lent me two large pieces of matting, which I produced from my secret treasury, an upper cupboard, which was only to be reached by an awkward scramble on to the mantel-piece.

" I threw one of these pieces of matting over our usher's bed, and one upon my own.

" He wrung my hand and looked into my face with a wistful smile of affection and gratitude.

" I wished at the moment I could have been a fascinating young lady with ten thousand a year that I might have put my arms round the silly fellow's neck, and humbly requested his love and protection, for I could see that his tried heart was breaking ; his face was deadly white, and he was trying so vainly to appear 'all right.'

" ' You are very good to me, Frank,' he said, in a quivering tone, 'and I am the more grateful because your kindness is disinterested.'

" 'Not a bit of that, sir,' said I ; 'see what pains you take to teach me ; you never get weary of the work, though I am so negligent and stupid ; and I'm sure if you neglected me altogether old Twigem would like you none the worse, for I am a poor, fatherless, motherless brat, who has no right to the same advantages that are better paid for by luckier fellows.'

" 'Ah, it's hard for you my boy ; but perhaps it's all the better. The cold is bracing ; sunny temperatures are enervating ; the chill wind without makes the fire burn brighter within. You must look things hard in the face, work hard, and make yourself a warm and happy home,' said our usher, his teeth chattering from his plunge into the frozen sheets. 'Oh Frank, you'll be so happy in your independence and exultation when you have wrought good out of evil, and snatched the pleasant things which a man may desire by your own strong arms. Comfort and competence inherited are nearly worthless ; won by self exertion they are beyond all price.'

" Mr. Charlesbury was a fine philosopher ; the only drawback was his inability to swallow his own physic.

" 'It's a hard world,' said I reflectively ; my world at the moment being the bed on which I stretched my weary limbs, and superlatively a hard one.

" ' It is,' said our usher, with a deep sigh, 'and yet it's precious cowardly to wish one had never been born.'

" ' You have had bad-news to day, sir ?' I ventured to hint.

" 'The worst, Frank,' said our usher, who, in his loveliness, could not out of the fulness of the heart forbear speaking his wearying thoughts, half as to himself and half to me. 'Yes I have lost her, as I have lost everything before. She was not kind to me, and I acted like a fool, for I was haughty and resentful ; I had neither the grace tamely to endure her sordid tauntings, nor strength enough to leave her. Well, she is gone ; she was dear to me, but sorrows that have their rise in passion always wear out. She is married.'

" I lay very quiet as Mr. Charlesbury thus murmured to himself abstractedly.

" Probably he thought I was asleep.

" At length I spoke.

" ' And pray, sir, what did you dream last night? Was it of this false girl, who, I am sure, was never worthy of you, or she would have been true to the last?'

" I said this very sagely.

" ' No, no, Frank ; I dreamed a better dream, though one that I cannot recall without great emotion. How strange, how very strange! but sorrows are blackbirds that fly in flocks.

" ' I should much like to know what it was you dreamed, sir,' said I.

" ' Well, Frank, I scarce need remind you that these little chats are confidential. I shouldn't like you to retail these things to your schoolmates.'

" ' I am too proud of your confidence to abuse it, sir,' I replied.

" ' Then, Frank, you must listen first to a little preliminary explanation, that you may fully understand the purport of my strange vision.'

" ' About five years ago, and at the end of the summer "half," I found myself free for a month or six weeks, to take my pleasaunce in the outer world.

" ' My mother was at that time living at a town in Warwickshire. I passed the holidays with her. During these pleasant times I became acquainted with two young ladies, who were orphans, but had many friends in the quaint old city ; they were merry, amiable, English-hearted girls, who received me as a brother. I was then a lad of eighteen, and no doubt, an agreeable companion to such gentle girls, to whom it was pure delight to make happy a lonely, gauche, and unsophisticated fellow, with no other recommendation than his being keenly appreciative of pleasure so rare with him as the society of charming, gay-hearted, and noble-minded women. I was happy, Frank ! My two friends were named respectively Blanche and Marian. The elder sister was a tall and graceful girl, with soft yet bright brown eyes, and a wealth of heavy hair ; she was as light-hearted as the wild birds, and as kind and genial as a morning in spring. Marian was quieter, more retiring perhaps not quite so fascinating—not quite so pretty ; but she had been more carefully educated than her sister, and displayed such a sweetness of disposition that it was impossible not to love and reverence one so good and gentle.

" ' With aching hearts her sister and I would watch her at times when her face became etherialised by the pure death glow of consumption, for every one could see that the frail and delicate Marian was in a deep decline.

" ' There was something so spiritual in that glowing cheek and glittering eye, in the bright scarlet of the tiny arch of her child-like lip, the animation of that look so saintly sweet, and yet so warm and unaffected, that inspired one with a thrill of awe. But, Frank, I shall send you to sleep with my poetic prosings, and I want to tell you the rest of my strange story.'

" Mr. Charlesbury paused, and I listened breathlessly, for I began to anticipate in what way he was going to connect the persons thus introduced with the purport of his visions.

" ' We were accustomed to wile away the autumn evenings by long rambles through some of the most thoroughly English sylvan scenes that can be found and over spots the richest in historic interest of any in the island.

" ' Many a night we saw the moon rise behind the towers of Warwick Castle and dip its quivering arrow of silver in the clear, gentle-gliding waters of the Avon.

" ' We looked round on the darkening woods from our favourite seats on the step of the grim monument that marks the spot where the stern old barons beheaded the parasite of their feeble monarch beneath the cross of Piers Gavestone, on Blacklow Hill.

" ' And as the evening closed around us we sat and talked a great deal of pleasant nonsense, till Blanche would start with loving anxiety, as the air wafted a chiller breath, or the sky grew more sombre ; and then we returned to the pleasant cottage, where my friends lived with an old widow lady, their aunt, and my mother's early friend.

" ' Of course, Frank, being but a youth, and having so little intercourse with any but my boy pupil, I was rather romantic and sentimental, rather "soft," you know.'

" ' Yes, sir,' I responded, with the full emphasis of concurrence.

" Our usher laughed, and gave a little sigh before he continued.

" ' Well, I was sincere,' he answered, gravely 'and that is something. Now, one evening Blanche. Marian, and I were sitting by the fire-side in the dear old cottage, the darkness sweeping about us, but warded off by the red fitful glow of the crackling embers.'

" ' We had wheeled the sofa before the hearth, and Marian was lying dreamily, her head pillowed on her round white arm, her thoughtfully blue eyes shining so brilliantly, for she was suffering from one of those fits of exhaustion into which she often sank when worn out by the occasional exhilarated words which charmed and yet distressed us.

" ' Blanche was seated close by the mantel watching the invalid with sisterly care and affection.

" ' I sat by Marian's side ; a book upon my knee, from which I had been reading aloud till the increasing darkness had silenced me.

" ' None of us cared to light the lamp.

" ' There was something weird and yet pleasant in the mystic gloom and the bright comfortable glare of the fire, and we were talking on subjects which better harmonised with the obscurity about us than with the matter of fact garishness of daylight.

" ' In truth we were talking of spiritualism, of oracular visions, and "well attested" ghost stories.

" ' The little book I had been reading contained an essay, professing to account for such apparitions which have been seen and sworn to by many most trustworthy people.

" ' The theory propounded was ingenious enough ; an affinity of soul was supposed to exist between people closely allied by the bonds of relationship, interest, or love, and other such attachments, and that some mysterious connection, as that which impels the needle to turn to the polar north, some electric linking unaccounted for, but not the less impossible, because unaccountable, exists between the minds, the brain, the spirits, or whatever you may call the souls of parted friends, and that some are able (though unconscious, perhaps, of their power) when in a state of high-wrought mental excitement, to impress their thoughts upon others who are absent, and even to give those thoughts a vivid portrayal to the senses of the "medium."

" 'Mark me,' added Mr. Charlesbury, ' this theory is not my own ; whoever wrote this essay was a cautious fellow, trying to steer between the absurdity of giving the lie to the plain testimony of most reliable people, or of accounting for mental phenomena by connecting them with trivial and unsatisfactory causes. Well, Frank, Blanche and I were discussing this very theory gravely, and both my friends related some strange dreams and waking visions, too, that had been seen by some of our acquaintances, when we were suddenly startled by the hollow yet sweet tones of Marian's voice as she broke a long silence.'

" 'Mr. Charlesbury,' she said, ' suppose we experimentalise ; suppose we try the effect of a mutual vow to appear one to the other at the death of either of us ? You will outlive me by many happy years ; would you, if far away, be very frightened if I came to apprise you that I had left this mortal phase of existence ?'

" 'Oh Marian, how shocking !—how profane !' cried her sister, with warm indignation.

" 'I started in great pain at the words of the poor young lady, and would have gladly given my own life for the hope that her term might be a long and bright one, but as I looked upon her hectic cheek, and quick-panting breast, I could see that such hopes were unwarranted by probability.

" 'Why do you both look at me so seriously ?' she said. ' Why do you reproach me ? I do not suppose that my disembodied spirit would be visible to Mr. Charlesbury, even if it were present with him, for how can the unsubstantial be visible ? But our theory is that by intensely thinking of some beloved one far away we can conjure our own image before his very eyes. Is it not so ?' she asked, appealing to me.

" 'Yes, for the theory is suggested to account for actual visions,' I replied, and then added, cheerfully, ' but I am sure, Marian, my presence in the spirits would not cause alarm to you.'

" 'Oh, no, but if I thought you would die before me I should be so grieved,' she replied, ' Not that life is very desirable, but you have much work to do, and will see so much happiness in this world.'

" Mr. Charlesbury paused again.

" 'She was not a good prophetess, Frank, though a prophetess of good, you see ; but I will not weary you with our long conversation upon such vague, unsatisfactory topics. She made me exchange a promise with her to the effect that whichever of us died first should appear to the other, if possible, though whether by a mental optical delusion, or by a real revisiting the glimpses of the moon, we could not predetermine. Blanche rated us soundly for what she told us was disgraceful superstition and profanity, and when the subject had dropped it was never again renewed. My golden age was over, and I was forced to return unwillingly to school, not creeping like a snail, but jolted along in a fast train, which seemed panting with malicious anxiety to wrench me from pleasure and restore me to pain, for never before did I feel quite such strong reluctance to return to Gaunt House.

" 'A year passed away. My mother had left the pleasant town in Warwickshire, and had gone to London. Blanche had married, and Marian was away on a short tour for the benefit of her failing health, so that I did not go back to the sunny oasis, but set off to the great caravansary in search of some other employment than that which implied alternate imprisonment, and almost equally objectionable listless liberty. You might suppose, Frank, that with a portfolio of testimonials, a heart yearning with eagerest zest to get such work as would enable me to pass the evening hours in social converse with chosen friends—you may think, Frank, that it was my own fault that I did not get a clerkship. A little more " modest assurance," perhaps, might have helped me ; but perseverance was of no avail. I failed miserably—spending almost my last farthing, and exhausted my hopes and energies in vain. Schoolmasters are objected to, not without reason, I fear, as being either too clever by half or utterly superficial and incompetent—in fact, as being in most respects unfit for business. I was obliged, at last, to take another mastership, and I came hither.

" 'One word of advice, Frank—while you are a boy, determine upon some pursuit and follow it with fixedness of purpose, and so take time by the forelock, for I can tell you, lad, you may lay up a fair store of knowledge, and what is even better, a firm balance of good principles ; but genius itself will hardly help you into a chance berth—instance, my case. I am an usher ; I hate my way of life and cannot change it, and I am getting old and worn out.'

" Mr Charlesbury was twenty-four, I was his confidant, and grumbling is a grand institution. Let me tell you, however, our usher was not a swab to eat bread in bitterness that he only half-earned. No ; the poor chap did his best ; but his heart was not in the work, and there is always something distasteful in every line of business—whether in preaching doctrines you scarce believe in, being agent of some law that you think iniquitous, writing sensational morality, or the moral sensational, aye, my dear young friends, or even in the glorious trade of cutting throats for the good of one's country. A fine philosopher is always a bad story teller ; but I will go on quickly, as I am, at last, come to the pitch of my story.

" 'And now for my dream, Frank, if you are not asleep and dreaming for yourself.'

" 'Not quite, sir,' I replied, opening my eyes and mouth very wide, and stretching myself stiff to shake off the drowsiness that is always induced by philosophic disquisitions. ' I am all attention, please, sir, and very anxious to know whether you went last night.'

" 'There's the wonder of it, Frank ; we have all heard how spirits will haunt a man, but never yet did I hear of a man haunting a spirit.'

" 'Perhaps, sir, as there was a lady in the case, etiquette required——'

" I checked myself, for the subject seemed too serious for jesting.

" 'I awoke from sleep. I am confident I was awakened ; I seemed moved by an unquestioned impulse to rise and dress myself.

" 'How, I know not, but I found myself walking along a sylvan road near the old town where I had spent so many happy days.

" 'The night was clear, and the moon shone with intense brightness on the sparkling branches of the frosted trees.

" 'The road was hard with frost, and I could hear the ringing echoes of my footsteps, and even feel the cold bracing air wafting in my face, and could see the light puffs of congealed breath as they flowed from my quivering lips.

" 'At a point on the road, where a narrow path winds across the frost-sheeted fields, every feature, every curve of her gentle form, brilliantly illuminated in the clear, bright moonshine, stood Marian!

"'Her face was pale; the hectic flush had gone. But moonlight has a ghastly effect upon the countenance; and the night was bitter cold. Marian's face was not fixed or unearthly. She was not swathed in a shroud, but loosely wrapped in her pretty mantle.

"'She held out her hand, and welcomed me with her own sweet smile.

"'I did not feel any sensation of surprise or bewilderment. I accepted all that happened as if it were but a matter of course. I took her arm, and we walked across the fields and homeward, my heart bounding with pleasure, as it was wont to do when I was in her company.

"'I chatted buoyantly, and did not heed that we were approaching the quaint and pretty cemetery that lies to the left of the road.

"'It occurred to me at that moment that during our walk Marian had not once spoken.

"'She checked me suddenly.

"'She looked me wistfully in the face, and then turned sadly away.

"'I drew near to her; she threw her arms about me, and leaned her forehead on my breast.

"'A wild, vague awe oppressed me; a strange light broke in upon my mind; eagerly I questioned her of her health, of home news.

"'She only smiled sadly, as I drew her closer and closer to my agitated heart.

"'I trembled violently. Her yielding form was warm, and seemed to pulse with life; yet, I remembered now, what before I had failed to remark, her step was noiseless and printless. Around me, on the white hoar-frost, were clearly marked the traces of my own steps; but the prints of her little feet were not amongst them. She had not spoken! The moonbeam's that threw upon the white ground my shadow, so black, and so sharply defined, seemed to be unobstructed by her light form—she was *shadowless*!

"'As I observed these mysterious circumstances, I seemed frozen with awe, and, gently disengaging her arms, held her hands in my own, and looked her intently in the face.

"'Quelling my excitement, I reminded her of our compact, and implored her to speak to me.

"'I did not hear her speak, yet I felt her words, as when one recalls the tones and phrases of some familiar friend.

"'I knew that she was dead. I knew that all was but a dream, yet more than a dream—a manifestation; for, either my soul was worked upon by the strong influence of "thought-impression," or I really held the spirit of my kind and gentle companion in my very arms. She told me mentally that she had wished to fulfil her promise, and that she was with me then to tell me that she had passed through the great change.

"'I wanted to dispute this truth with her; I yearned to ask her a thousand questions; but I could not command utterance.

"'With a cry of despair, once more I folded my arms about her. They crossed upon my breast. She was gone, before in the clear moonlight shone out the bronze gates of the cemetery through the fretwork of which I could see the neat, straight paths, with their borders of white graves, but Marian was gone.

"'I sat down upon the bank, and as I watched the shadows change upon places as the moon went down, I fell asleep.

"'When I awoke I was lying upon my bed, dressed as you found me.

"'This morning I received a letter containing the news of Marian's death.

"'And so, Frank, you have the story of my vision.'

"How is all this to be explained you will say? You will ask me whether I can believe that Mr. Charlesbury was bodily transported from one end of England to the other, expressly to hold a *séance*. I answer most emphatically no, I do not hold any belief so absurd, but I do feel certain that Mr. Charlesbury was mysteriously apprised of the death of his cherished friend, and I leave the subject, reminding you that there are more things in heaven and earth than are dreamed of in our philosophy."

THE BLACKSMITH'S STORY.

"Stir the fire, Hal, and sit ye closer, Thyra; and dame, a trifle more lemon in the toddy, and I'll tell you my story, which is neither quite a love story, and it's not a ghost story, but none the less interesting for all that :—

"When I was a boy there lived in our village an old curmudgeon whose name was Knip.

"He was a lank and meagre rascal, with a face of parchment, and a heart of buckram.

"He was the most miserable object imaginable, but reputed to be possessed of a fortune sufficient to enable him to live as happy as a king.

"He was one of that numerous class who follow no particular trade, but who are ever ready to purchase everything that is offered at rack prices by those in difficulties.

"He was remorseless as a vulture in the pursuits of avarice, and was of a pitiful and complaining disposition, always grumbling about the hardness of the times, never content with himself, and, consequently, seldom with anybody else; whining and hypocritical, griping and implacable, and he seemed to be quite devoid of natural affection for his only son, and was harsh and exacting with his niece, who had been left in his hands by the early death of her parents.

"Never in the world lived there a better pair than Maurice and Lucy.

"He was a blithe lad, good-natured and manly while she was the sweetest little angel that ever wandered out of paradise to carry some of its light into the dark world.

"Maurice and Lucy led but a sorry life. Maurice was ill-trained, because his narrow-minded father grudged the paltry expense which would have secured to his son the unspeakable advantages of a thorough education.

"But Maurice found a chance of improving himself where he least expected.

"And as he pursued knowledge from taste and a consciousness of its beauty and usefulness, and not from compulsion only, as he probably would have done had he been sent to school, he made great progress. But who was his teacher? His cousin

Lucy! The girl was employed at needlework by a widow lady in easy circumstances, who had settled in a quiet spot at some distance from the village, in a little cottage which had been built for herself. This good woman conceived a strong attachment for Lucy, and took a world of pains to make her a fine scholar. All that she learned of her mistress she in her turn imparted to her cousin Maurice.

"The old man never associated his son with himself in any matters of business, but was content to see him loafing about at the forge, or in fields, turning his hand to any chance work that fell in his way, without well learning any branch of trade.

"He made no practical objection to Lucy's studies, because they cost nothing, and he was afraid of offending his niece's patroness, but he was always grumbling at what he called the waste of time in fiddle faddle.

"Old Knip was so penurious that he grudged himself and family the common necessities of life, and on one occasion when the widow lady I told you of had gone abroad for a tour, and Lucy was forced to return home, the old man's spleen found vent in the cruellest revilings, and he cursed the hour that she had been brought into his house to be a burden to him.

"Lucy bore all this with great patience, though at the same time resolving that she would, as soon as possible, free herself from her degrading thraldom.

"What made things worse at this juncture was a mishap which had befallen her cousin Maurice, who had cut his hand while chopping wood, and had thereby disabled him from work.

"Every day the lives of poor young Maurice and his pretty cousin were getting more and more unbearable.

"Do what he would, poor Maurice could get no regular work. Everybody detested his father, and he had not the character for ability in mechanical employments. At last things came to a crisis.

"One day, old Knip entered the forge as the men were taking a rest at dinner-time.

"'Master Britton, I am a great sinner,' he began, in his whining tone; 'I know my unworthiness (and so did every one else), but I am that overwhelmed with losses and crosses that I feel sure my poor weak brain must at length yield to the pressure, and I shall be gone, gone, sir, like those sparks that fly up from your cheerful anvil and vanish in the sooty atmosphere.'

"Mr. Knip heaved a piteous sigh, and my father heaved a hearty laugh from the depth of his healthy lungs.

"'Why, what's the matter, neighbour?' he cried, cheerily. 'Your embers will burn bright for many a day.'

"'I have a son, sir, a son,' said old Knip, fairly weeping.

"'And a good lad, too. I've six children, Mr. Knip; but I should be sorry to shed tears at being blessed with a large family.

"'Blessed! Ah, you are blessed!' groaned Mr. Knip.

"'Oh, ho! Oh, ho! Then you're crying, neighbour, at not having a large family. Well now I don't think I should do that either,' said my father, catching the infection, and with a sigh, thinking, perhaps of the first six pair of boots and the rise in leather.

"Old Knip heard the faint bellowsing of my father's broad breast, and it did his heart good.

"'Yes, Mr. Britton,' he continued, in the same lachrymose strain, 'we are all sinners, great sinners ; and where we shall all go to it is hard to say ; but our punishment begins in this world ! You have had a short gleam of sunshine, and now you will see a great deal of shade, for the clouds return after the rain. I hear the squire has removed his shed of horses to his new place, so you will lose his custom. You did not vote for Sir Tompkin Tunbelly, and his custom goes to the fresh man ; and then there's your Neddy's ducking in the brook, a cold so severe is never to be got over. Then there's Billy's meazles and baby's teeth, and I can't help thinking poor Mrs. Britton is looking peaky. Well, we're all sinners ; we must all go when we're called. And that reminds me the good rector spoke to-day about the tithes owing in the village, and in Job Johnson's cart I saw that tax-fellow.'

> "Hi, hi, hi,
> The sparks must fly ;
> Ho, ho, ho,
> The bellows blow ;
> Ha, ha, ha,
> And sing la la ;
> Ching a-ring a-ring
> Makes the anvil sing,"

lustily sang my father, smashing at a red-hot horse-shoe.

"'You don't see these things,' said Mr. Knip, in a tone of deprecation and pity. 'You do not feel the blow till it is struck.'

"'And time enough then, I should think, neighbour,' returned my worthy sire.

"The other sire shook his head and murmured,

"'Well, I'm a poor sinner, and I am resigned to this blow.'

"He blowed his nose resignedly.

"'Come,' says my father, 'what's the matter, neighbour?—something serious I'm afraid.'

"'My Absolom!' wept the old sycophant.

"'Your what—your abseds?' asked my father, who was a little deaf, as most blacksmiths are.'

"'My son, Mr. Britton—my first and last and only son.'

"'What—what, Maurice Knipp?'

"'Nipped in the bud.'

"'Heaven forbid!—de-dead!' stammered my father, who was very fond of the lad.

"'Worse—worse!" murmured Mr. Knip, ruefully.

"'All your own fault,' cried my father, fiercely smiting the anvil, and then, grounding his sledger with something like an oath, said,

"'If the boy's hanged, remember you spun the halter for him. I suppose he's been disgracing himself. Well, I am sorry for my hard words ; but what could you expect when you did not allow him a handful of shillings from New Year's day till Christmas-eve? of course he would help himself when he got a chance. Has he robbed you of much?'

"'Rob me? of what could any one rob me, poor sinner that I am?' wailed the exemplary parent. 'He may be a thief ; its likely, the heart is desperately wicked ; but his cunning has been too great for me there. I have never found him dishonest—it's worse than that.'

" ' You alarm me ?   Ha ! there's a wench in the case ?'

" ' Oh Lord, no !' cried Mr. Knip, eagerly ; ' there's no wench in no case. What could the beggarly boy do to support—Mr. Britton, you are unkind so to agitate me. I will tell you the worst at once—he has gone and 'listed for a soldier !'

" ' Ha ! that's bad—phew ! very sorry ; but it might be worse.'

" ' And it will be worse ; he will be shot, sir, if not by the enemy, by his own comrades.'

" ' Nonsense ; he'll be coming home covered with glory.'

" ' Or two wooden legs, a hopeless cripple, and instead of being my prop and staff in old age, I shall have to find him crutches, and support him myself.'

" ' And how does poor Lucy bear up ? Does she take on ?'

" ' I wish she would take off,' grunted old Knip, vindictively. ' An old man like me to be weighed down by such burdens ! It's quite unnatural.'

" ' Well, neighbour, I'll take that burden off your hands, anyhow. Let Lucy come to me ; the wife wants help with the children, and she can stay with us till her lady comes home.'

" ' God bless ye ! you're kind. But of course it'll suit ye, or ye wouldn't propose it. You've taken ten years off my shoulders, Mr. Britton. Well, we're all poor sinners. But I'll send her over before she puts more than my share into the saucepan. " Wilful waste," you know. Good day, good day.'

" And away hopped the old raven.

" Years passed away. Lucy's patroness never returned ; she died abroad. The dear girl still remained with us. She was a great pet in the family ; my father was very fond of her, and when poor mother died, the loss was softened by Lucy's affection and energy. I loved her with all my heart, and suffered, as young folk will, very bitterly, because she could not requite my love. She still clove to the hope of the glad return of Maurice.

" Old Knip rarely visited us, and even his niece met with such a rough reception when she entered his cottage that though she watched over him, and supplied him with many little comforts, she seldom ventured to intrude upon him.

" As Lucy was such an excellent controller of children, and so fine a scholar, my father advised her to set up a school, which she did, and prospered well.

" Every day old Knip grew more morose and more niggardly.

" It was reported that he was making a mint of money out of other folks losses ; but to judge by his appearance, one might suppose him to be a miserable wretch, without a sufficiency of food to support life.

" Maurice came home at last.

" The old man's prophecy had in a measure been verified. He had lost his right arm.

" Then Lucy's love shone out in all its brightness—shone in her sunny smile of welcome, in her fond endearments.

" She could earn enough for both—now she could work indeed. He would be cruel and unworthy if he could think that there could be any loss or gain on either side in worldly things between two hearts knit by love. She said it in her own way. I know

what she meant, but can't repeat the exact words for want of what you Boy Sailors call ' tophamper.' Poor Maurice, he was very sad—his pride was too great to suffer him to depend on her exertions for support ; and I had almost said ' of course' he had been robbed—remembering those fine dashing highwaymen the boys think such heroes, and who were such dirty, sneaking cut-throats—poor one-armed Maurice had been robbed by Dick Turpin, or some other such rogue of all his prize-money.

" My father and I—for I was getting a man then, I had begun to shave—we advised Maurice to apply to his father. Now, as ill-luck decreed, the very day when this poor prodigal ventured to revisit his father's house, the old man was laid up by a sharp attack of fever, brought on through his chagrin at having been bested in some ninepenny bargain with a Jew pedlar.

" The reception of ' the cripple ' may be imagined, and Maurice replied to the paternal taunts with certain words not very suggestive of filial piety, bounced off in a whirlwind, and swore by the great guns and small arms that he would sing ballads from Land's End to Berwick-on-Tweed rather than apply to his father for a sixpence.

" A short time after this an old miser, not Mr. Knip, was murdered most barbarously by Jack Sheppard, or Jack Rawn, or Tom King, Blueskin, or Devil-skin—of course by one of those handsome knights of the road—and all the victim's hoardings were captured by the robber.

" Perhaps this had the effect of frightening old Knip ; and, therefore, may account for what happened soon after.

" Maurice, who had not yet married Lucy, who was breaking her dear little heart by his pride and mistrust, had set off to visit the house of a certain general, whose interest he wished to solicit in order to obtain a pension.

" My father, myself, and the rest of the family, were seated round the fire, listening to the wind whistling past, for it was at night and in winter, and wondering why Maurice did not return, and not a little anxious about his stump of an arm, which the bitter winds wrung sorely, when there was heard a smart rat-tat, as if done with the loaded top of a whip. The visitor proved to be a dark, dashing—oh boys, rejoice !—a remarkably handsome man, but with a look so villanous one felt that there was but the alternative of springing at his throat or taking to one's heels. He tossed me a guinea. A highwayman !—no other would be so generous. Oh, it is so noble to fee a hostler with a golden piece (of other people's hard-earned money). He imperatively bade us open the forge and attend to his pad, which had slipped a shoe. I and my brother led the steaming, quivering thoroughbred into the forge. We noticed that a rug had been thrown over the saddle, but as the night was cold we thought it had been done for the protection of the noble, fiery, yet delicate—strong, yet frail creature.

" While we were at work in the forge, and when the stranger's looks were fixed upon some other object, a man's face appeared at the door. It was Maurice.

" He held a long pistol in his left hand. Leaving my brother at work, I stole out to him.

" ' My father has been robbed, perchance murdered, by this villain,' he whispered. ' Under his saddle is concealed a bag of money that my father was carrying, under cover of darkness, to deposit in the bank at Penzance.'

NOTICE.—The next Number of the Boys' Library will be Published on Friday, August 1st Order early of your Bookseller.

BOYS' LIBRARY

HARRY HALLIARD:
OR,
THE YOUNG BRITISH TAR.

THE BOY SAILOR'S FIGHT WITH THE SHARK.

"'What is to be done?' I whispered.

"'You had better run for the constables,' he answered, 'while I keep the door with the pistol.'

"'Keep quiet and I will manage the affair.'

"My brother was hard at work at the forge.

"I went up to him as he crossed to the furnace, and whispered him to delay the work as much as possible, for that our customer was a suspicious character.

"My brother gave a knowing wink.

"He contrived to make some mistake, which made it necessary to forge another shoe.

"The highwayman stamped and raved with impatience, declaring that he was on a mission of life and death, and that the least delay would ruin him.

"I found some excuse for leaving the shop.

"My brother alone remained with the highwayman.

"At this moment some fool of the party who were hurrying on to apprehend the robber set up a shout.

"The highwayman was startled

"He fired his pistols at my brother.

"With only this effect that the bullet crashed

through the only panes of glass that remained unbroken in the soot-begrimed window frame.

"With a growl of rage the beast of prey flung himself upon my brother.

"But armed with his trusty sledger my brother was more than a match for the wolf.

"Whirling round his heavy weapon he brought it down with such a crushing force that, though the highwayman warded the blow with his pistols, he staggered and fell like an ox.

"The party from the village now tumbled in, and the terrified constable, who had the uncomfortable honour conferred on him of being placed in the van, was sent forward like a stone from a sling by the quick pressure of the rushing crowd behind.

"He tripped over the prostrate body of the thief.

"On righting himself he perceived that the formidable rascal was dead, or, at least, insensible, and thereupon the worthy limb of the law grew valiant, and soundly abused his companions for their want of mettle.

"The horse was then taken into custody by the functionary.

"Under the saddle cloth was found a heavy bag, which proved to contain a little bank of gold pieces, notes and bonds.

"As it was made plain by signatures and the like that this property belonged to old Knip, Maurice and the constable together took charge of it—the former placing it in his knapsack, and the latter locking it in a chest at his house, which was close adjacent.

"Then we all started off in search of old Knip.

"We fully expected to find him lying in some ditch with his throat cut.

"I am afraid that few in the party who looked upon his gallant son, disabled in his country's service, and thought of the old man's inhumanity to the brave fellow, and to Lucy also—his kind and gentle niece, who was ever so ready to administer to his wants and comforts—cared much whether the old man was dead or alive.

"It was a very dark night.

"We pushed along the road, keeping close together and feeling a tremor of terror, for it was reported that the highwayman we had taken was the captain of a desperate gang.

"At last we came to a lone spot in a neighbouring heath.

"It is a proof of the utter callousness of this class of robbers, that very near the place where we found old Knip was a gibbet on which some wretched culprit had long swung in chains.

"We found him insensible and lying in a ditch, and we lifted him and carried him home to his cottage. He did not seem to be very much hurt, he had possibly fainted with fright at the appearance of the robber.

"By my advice Maurice did not tell him of the apprehension of the robber, nor the recovery of the money.

"When the old man came to his senses he looked about him with wild surprise at the number of persons assembled round his bed, for a large part of the villagers came into his room to have a glimpse of the last of the vile highwayman's victim.

"Old Knip did not receive these attentions on the part of his neighbours with any gratitude, but reviled them in a delirious style.

"He raved for his gold, anathematised the robber, abused the government that could suffer such marauders to infest the high road even for a single day.

"At last, having cleared the room of all but my father, myself, and Lucy, Maurice sat by the old man's bed, and spoke to him in a tone, firm but not disrespectful.

"'Father,' he said, 'this trouble has fallen upon you by the will of Heaven. You have lost what you made little or no use of, and you must be content.'

"'I am a poor sinner—a very great sinner, and judgments will come to such sinful mortals,' groaned the old miser, 'but if I can but catch that villain and have him condemned, I will go on my bent knees to the judges to be allowed to wring his neck!'

"My father shook his head, and said, seriously, 'Neighbour, such language is very unbecoming. Charity——'

"'Charity! Oh, lor! and I shall now have to depend on charity,' cried the miser, bitterly; 'but only for a grave! I am dying, and I shall trouble the parish only for a deal box, and a little bit of common earth.'

"The old man turned on his pillow, and moaned piteously.

"'And you—of what use are you?' he cried, harshly, to his son. 'When you were born, I thought you would prove a comfort to me, and, instead, you go off to cut foreign throats for the best years of your life, and then come home a hopeless, helpless wretch, to prey upon a poor sinner that has been robbed of his last penny. Oh, lor!—two thousand, three hundred and forty-seven pounds, eighteen and sixpence-halfpenny!'

"This enumeration of his losses was too much for him.

"He fell back in strong convulsions.

"The doctor was sent for.

"At first it was feared that the old fellow was in a fit of apoplexy.

"Towards the end of the day, however, his paroxysm went off, and he sank into a deep and quiet slumber.

"When he awoke, he looked wildly round the room, hissed at his watchers, and tried to get out of bed, raving for his gold.

"My father was very firm with him, and, at length induced him to remain still, while he spoke to him concerning the highwayman's adventure, and suggested some plans by which he hoped that it was possible to recover the stolen property.

"The old man listened very eagerly.

"My father told him, in general terms, that the police were in close pursuit of the criminal, and that there were good hopes of his being caught.

"Old Knip sighed and moaned despondingly.

"'Father,' says Maurice, 'you are always upbraiding me with that which should cause you pride, and bring me pity and indulgence, my disabling wound, received in fighting my country's foes; now, should I be able to regain for you the money you have lost, would you consent to my marriage with Lucy, and, in consideration of my misfortune, give us some assistance?'

"'I would give you half!' cried the old miser, his eyes brilliantly sparkling, his thin lip pursing, and his claw-like hands extended ravenously, 'that is, I mean I would bestow on you my rich, my richest blessing.'

"'And would help me, father?'

"'You are, my son, you would not devour your own parent, you would not lay your grip on too much; little can be spared from such a small reward for so many years of labour. But, as I am a poor sinner, I will faithfully promise to help you, and you shall have my best blessing.'

"'Then, it's a bargain, father,' said Maurice, taking Lucy by the hand.

" ' Stick to him, lad ; make him give you a share while he is in the mood,' muttered my father in young Knip's ear.

" ' But you can't do it. All my property—all my poor earnings, and gettings and savings ! Oh, the black, murderous, infernal thief ! why did they abolish racks, and thumb-screws, stakes and tar-barrels ? I'd have him impaled, minced into a million morsels !'

" ' Fie, fie !' interrupted my father, very indignantly.

" ' I'm a poor sinner !' whined the old man, again sinking back upon the pillow. 'But I can't hold it very unrighteous to wish such villains to be properly punished—for instance, say roasted alive !'

" ' Well, father, we'll waive that. Suppose the robber brought every penny back to you, would you give him free pardon ?'

" ' Oh, yes ! I—I think I could fall down and worship him. But why do you suggest such nonsensical things ?'

" To put a stop to this sort of talk, which disgusted us all, you may be sure, poor Maurice, little thinking what would follow, tossed the chinking money bag upon the bed, saying—

" ' There, father, and now I claim your promise.'

" The old miser uttered a choking cry, fastened his claws upon the bag, and with trembling fingers opened it.

" In an instant his experienced eye could perceive that the sum was intact to the last penny.

" He eagerly grappled the whole to his breast, and with the gold pieces oozing through his griping fingers and bowling away on the floor—the notes fluttering down like snow-flakes—he fell back with a wild cry.

" We tried to lift him.

" He was rigid in death !

" Excess of joy springing from such a sordid source had killed him.

" You may imagine that we were all much shocked at this dreadful catastrophe.

" The old man was buried ; the house was carefully searched ; five hundred pounds were found concealed in the wainscot, and a box containing a large number of watches and pieces of trinkery which he had taken as pledges for repayment of certain sums which he lent out at usurious interest.

" Maurice and Lucy had a quiet but happy wedding, and for many months enjoyed as much happiness as ever falls to the lot of man in this world.

" But it is useless to deny that some folks seem born to ill-luck. Poor Maurice was one of these; an honest man and a simple soldier, he had no suspicion of others' guilt, and some rogues made him their prey, induced him to risk his money in speculations which failed, and at the end of two years poor Maurice died, his wife remaining gentle and constant to the last.

" About a year after the death of my poor friend Maurice, his widow consented to marry me, and Lucy Britton is the mother of our saucy Nell, and so you have my story, and in reward for my pains I only ask that you fill up, and drink a toast to one of the best women that ever blessed the world, Mistress Lucy Britton aforesaid."

The toast was drunk with all honours, and it being his turn to spin a yarn, the audience were thus gratified by

THE BOY SAILOR'S STORY.

" Of all the queer places and of all the queer people in this queer world, without query China and the Chinese are the queerest. After St. Vincent, you know, I had leave and came home for a spell, and after my liberty-time was over, I sailed in the Boadicea to the port of Canton. Never in my life shall I forget the strange sights that I saw in that cruise ; very few of the crew had ever made this voyage, and the larks we had with John Chinaman were surprising.

" The men dressed like women, the women like men ; the river crowded with lubberly barks that looked like the gilded gingerbread gimcracks sold at the fairs ; chop boats, sanpans, junks, and every conceivable craft in every conceivable style of awkwardness and tawdry ugliness ; such a toy bazaar of painted lanterns, flags, gongs, palanquins, fans, and umbrellas. Fancy a marine in full rig fanning himself with one hand, and with the other shading his blessed peepers with a parasol !

" And then the mob of comicals, with their pinnafores, curved shoes, curly hats, and long pigtails ; and to see the old buffers flying kites, and the younkers looking on as grave as judges ; everything was so novel, so funny, that I laughed from morning to night at some fresh oddity.

" And what larks in the street, to say nothing of the processions, which are something side-splitting; the jugglers, tumblers, rope-dancers. And as I've come to that strand in my yarn, I'll tack about a little, just to tell you of a clever trick performed by two of those Chinese conjurors, one which you will only believe on the strength of the good character I've always borne for not running the rig on my messmates or friends. Well, now—

" Two fellows were brought before the captain and some of the officers, at the summer-house of one of the rich Canton merchants, situated on an island that must have looked, when viewed from a balloon, like one of those lacquered tea-trays, with little men and big birds and flowers, puzzle-chairs and stools, and apple-dumpling trees—in fact, like a willow-pattern plate. These two conjuring chaps were brought before our officers, who were dosing themselves with a coffee black-draught from little china thimbles.

" One of the tumblers handed to the other a large china basin.

" The man tossed it up above his head, caught it, and performed several other like flourishes.

" He then turned it upside down, that the spectators might be convinced that it was empty.

" All at once he let it fall from his hand.

" We all expected to hear a smash.

" But just before it reached the ground he caught it.

" This movement brought him into a position resting on his heels.

" The basin was now hidden by the folds of his dress.

" He stretched his arms out wide apart, and remained in the form of a cross for some seconds, in no way touching the basin.

" With a sudden spring he stood upright, and displayed to the astonished spectators the basin filled to the brim with pure, clear water, and two gold fishes swimming in their native element.

" Then the next man performed a trick which required great dexterity.

" He placed on his head a porcelain jar with a narrow mouth.

" He poised this on the rim at the bottom, in an angular manner, so that the least movement on the juggler's part—even the relaxation of a muscle—would cause it to fall and smash.

" In his right hand were several pieces of bamboo.

" While standing perfectly still, he threw these pieces of bamboo to a great height with his left hand, and in such a direction that they all fell into the jar.

"This manœuvre must require immense practice and steadiness.

"After this, the first-mentioned juggler drew from a basket the stuffed skin of a rat ; this he gave to the officers, that they might examine it and be sure that it was just what he represented it to be.

"By placing the throat of the supposed animal between his finger and thumb, and pinching it, the jaws of the rat were forced open, and so exactly did the juggler imitate the squeak of a choking rat, that it was almost impossible not to believe that the thing was really alive.

"He then tossed it about his person with a singularity, a quickness of motion altogether admirable, at the same time uttering such piercing and natural cries that, till he suddenly stopped, and tossed us the stuffed skin, we could not help thinking that he had substituted a live rat for the stuffed one.

"I could tell you other tricks which were played by this frivolous, clever chap ; but I must keep to my course, or I shall tack about till you get weary of such cruising.

"There was a grand parade on shore on the occasion of the arrival of one of the kwang—the mandarins—from the city of Pekin. He was a mandarin of the second class, and, by the deference paid him, I thought at first he was the Son of Heaven and Brother of the Moon in person.

"I had learned a little Chinese, and I could understand what the cock-hat and red buttons meant.

"'Haou, tsing tsing,' said the interpreter, on behalf of our bluff old commodore, who was red in the face, and frowned at me most villanously, for he caught my eye and could hardly help laughing at the pompous finical swabs.

"I thought he would mark me, for he was a rare stickler for his dignities, so I was obliged to pull a demure countenance."

"But your Chinese, Harry ; you can't expect us to understand the tongue of the Celestials," said Frank.

"Right hearty. Well, *Haou*."

"Don't bark, but tell us what it means in Christian English."

"It means, 'Are you well ? Hail, hail !'"

"And what did the mandarin answer ?"

"'Soo yang fang ming,' which means, 'I have heretofore thought with reverence of your fragrant name.' You may laugh, but I think it was preciouscivil. Well, I'm still tacking off the wind, so I shan't enter into details about this audience, nor tell you how the grandee sent the captain a card of invitation, crimson-coloured, and inscribed with gilt letters, in which the time was mentioned ; and the old chap was invited to bestow upon the sender 'the illumination of his presence.'

"Now the Boadicea only mounted half her number of guns ; we were on a peaceful errand, and had orders to freight with provisions and shipstores of various kinds, besides a quantity of Chinese curiosities for the captain.

"There was a 'hong' or merchant, whose name was Wang-i ; he was employed as an agent in making the purchases, and was always present when the coolies stored the goods—the natives' system of storing being so excellent that the captain always entrusted that work to them.

"Among other things recommended as proper objects for purchase was a large number of cheeses made by the Tartars.

"The Tartars and the Chinese bear the same relation to each other as the simple country bumpkin to the downy cockney sharper ; they are always falling, like great bumble-bees, into the nets spun for them by these little spiders of Chinamen.

"Now, the man who should have been employed was the Tartar, who brought the cheeses from his tents on the wide Steppes ; but he was bested by the Chinaman, who bought the stores at a low price, sold them at an enormous profit, and almost doubled his receipts in the charges he made for stowage.

"But this little Wang-i was the same fellow. Of him a very queer story is told.

"He was a dwarfish, insignificant fellow, sallow as a lemon, and weak as a rabbit ; and yet he had thrown one of the most formidable of the Tartar wrestlers.

"The Tartar, a huge fellow, with strength equal to his proportions, had challenged every comer to a wrestling match.

"No one could withstand him ; the strongest and most skilful entered the arena, and were successively thrown.

"Some of them were desperately injured, breaking limbs, and receiving all sorts of contusions.

"At last a little dwarf of a fellow, in fact, our Wang-i, entered the arena.

"Everybody was convulsed with laughter as they saw the little chap swaggering up, like Jack to attack the giant.

"The Tartar laughed like an ogre, and stooped down to toss the little Chinaman, as a bull would a poodle-dog, when the little fellow raised his face, and from his swollen cheeks squirted about a pint of water, with which he had filled his wide mouth, full into the Tartar's eyes.

"It was a dirty trick, but, like many other dirty tricks, successful.

"Quite stupefied at this unexpected style of assault, the Tartar staggered back, and, quick as thought, the nimble little Chinaman flung him over his knee, and threw him heavily.

"Of course, the concourse shouted their applause, and little Wang-i was a nine days' wonder.

"It's not always that the Chinese best the Tartars, though sometimes it happens that they're not to be 'got over,' though they do come from the country.

"In all the Chinese cities there are moneychangers' shops, where cash change is given for ingots of gold or silver, or *vice versâ*. Large sums are paid with these ingots, but they are scarcely admitted as being current coin, and a deduction is made by the changers.

"I knew a wily old Tartar who, I dare say, thought it the height of virtue to bamboozle a Chinaman ; he brought one of these ingots into a moneychanger's shop, at Pekin, and demanded change for it.

"The rascally Chinaman, seeing that his customer was a Tartar—and, therefore, of course, a simpleton—resolved upon a little 'sharp practice.' He asked the Tartar the weight of the ingot, and was told that it was equal to thirty rupees.

"The Chinaman laughed, scoffingly, and inquired in what scales the ingot had been weighed.

"The Tartar replied that he had weighed it at home, in his own scales.

"The Chinaman scouted the idea that the huge and inaccurate scales used by a shepherd for weighing fleeces could be fit to determine the value of gold and silver, and declared that the ingot was equal in value only to twenty-five rupees.

"The Tartar, after a little grumbling, consented to accept the twenty-five, and asked for the customary receipt.

"This was given him and he left the shop.

"In the evening the young Chinaman was boasting to his father, the head of the establishment, of the manner in which he had choused the Tartar of five rupees.

"The respectable parent laughed heartily at this intelligence, and asked to see the ingot. Upon its being shown him, his consternation was boundless, for it was counterfeit, and not real gold!

"The Tartar was pursued, taken by the police, and brought before a mandarin.

"The Chinaman stated the charge.

"The Tartar pleaded not guilty, and stated that it was not possible that he could have changed the ingot in question, for its weight was stated to be equal to thirty rupees, while the receipt he held was only for twenty-five.

"The case was dismissed, and the Chinaman received a paternal correction with the bastinado.

"Let us return to Wang-i.

"It was surprising how dexterously the rogue contrived to pack the cheese; he would allow of no interference from our crew, and kept a jealous watch over his coolies.

"Our first lieutenant suspecting something to be wrong set me to watch the rascal.

"At last his motive for such caution was made plain; a pile of the cheeses was over-turned by a lurch of the ship.

"I secured one of them.

"'Ayah! no touch no ting!' shouted the Chinaman, catching me by the breeks, and pulling me back.

"I was tripped, and struck my nose against the cheese, and my figure-head was nearly disfigured for life.

"'Cheese,' I reflected, 'may be hard, but stone is harder.'

"Whereupon I snatched it up, and carried it off to the lieutenant; the Chinaman shrieking after me, and half-a-dozen of our chaps hanging on to his pig-tail.

"Our cheese would have made a capital ball for knocking down nine-pins; for it was very similar in shape, and made of precisely the same material as those articles—that is, of wood. More than two-thirds of the cheeses were found to be of the same quality.

"The scene on board was terrific, and the poor rascal of a Chinaman was chased fore and aft by us barbarians, and at last, I am sorry to say, at my suggestion, was hung to the yard-arm by his pig-tail, which I cut off with my knife close to his bald pate.

"He dropped souse into the sea; but managed to swim ashore, and got off like a fox from the trap, to play fresh rogueries, but minus his tail."

CHAPTER XVII.

THE EARL AND THE WRECKER.

FENWOLD HALL was a fine baronial residence, situated at a distance of five miles from Seawardine.

It stood commandingly on a high and bleak hill.

It was surrounded by a coppice of dark firs and cypresses.

The house itself was embattled and built of grey stone.

During the civil wars it had withstood many a fierce attack.

In a large and noble room, adorned with anti-quated furniture, grim armour, and sombre pictures—before an immensely wide hearth on which a pleasant fire was flaming brightly, the Earl of Penalvon was seated in his ample and cozy arm-chair moodily watching the fire.

A servant in a rich livery entered the room.

"The seafaring person, my lord; he is come," said the servant with a bow.

"Tell him to come to me here," returned the noble.

The man bowed and left the room.

Thorkil Penreal entered.

There was something of dignity in the proud step of that wild and ruthless captain of the wreckers which was not without its charm.

He looked round the room with frank admiration, and then approached the hearth and stood before his employer.

"My lord, I have come as you directed, and I have brought my answer."

"That's right, Thorkil; but, hist! a moment; you are not the sort of guest that is common in this presence-chamber, and, no doubt, your appearance has excited the curiosity of my meddlesome dependants. Excuse me just a moment."

His lordship strode firmly from the room.

He ascertained that there was no one within ear-shot, and then he returned into the room, locking the door behind him.

"You see, Thorkil, to a man in my station what would be luxuries with you are positive necessities to me. A man who has never been thwarted as I have not, must follow out the bent of his will at any cost; besides, as I really admire this woman, and mean to treat her handsomely, there's no great harm done at all."

"Harm or no harm, my lord, what you say is true, a man considers himself first, and if he can gratify his own wishes, he will not care too much by what means."

"That's sound sense, Thorkil."

"It is, my lord, at least with such as us; wilful men are not over scrupulous in any way."

"And you think the affair may be managed to-night?"

"The sooner the better, my lord."

"If I could make it appear that she had fallen over the rocks."

"That may be done."

"In what way?"

"Why, by hanging her hat or scarf on a bramble, midway down the cliff."

"A good thought; but then search would be made for the body."

"It will be supposed that the tide has washed it away, for at high water the surf plashes half way up the cliff."

"And you have a launch in the bay ready to bear her off?"

"Yes, my lord."

"That's well; the son and his companion are gone, and the foundling Lena has returned to school, so that Rosa Halliard will be alone in her cottage."

"It will be easily managed."

"I think so."

"And you understand the rest of my plans?"

"Fully; the girl is to be placed in the lonely convent on the opposite coast."

"Yes; and you think that I am safe with respect to your band?"

"What do you mean, my lord?"

"Why, Thorkil, I mean that I hope I may trust them not to prate about this business."

"If my lord knew by what oaths of secresy, by what binding laws our band is knit together, he would know that such a revelation is impossible, even on the rack, to any one of the followers of Thorkil Penreal."

"Very good; I will take your word, and to-night I will meet you at the Seal's Cover."

"Has my lord any further orders?"

"None, Thorkil; but I would advise caution—you understand?"

"I do, my lord."

"And Hyda, is she safe?"

"My wife? she is faithful to the bond."

"Rest well, then, for a while; we shall meet again to-night."

"At the Seal's Cover."

CHAPTER XVIII.

ROSE HALLIARD ALONE—THE EARL OF PENALVON—ROSE OVER-MASTERED BY THORKIL—THE ABDUCTION—THE WRECKER'S FEARS OF WILD THYRA.

A STRANGE feeling of undefined awe oppressed the heart of Rose Halliard, as she sat in her lonely cottage, on the evening when Thorkil Penreal visited Fenwold Hall.

She set it down to her loneliness and nervousness, the place seemed so quiet and gloomy now that all its late merry inmates were gone.

Even Neptune was away.

Nelly Britton had spent the day with Rose, and when she left at sundown Rose had despatched the faithful creature as her escort.

Rose sat before the fire.

She leaned her cheek on her hand, and listened sadly to the wind without.

Wild Thyra's prediction had come too true.

Widowed and deprived of the companionship of her boy, she could not help listening to the rough voice of the cruel blustering wind that, in its fickleness at one moment caresses, and assists the labouring barque, the next dashes it to pieces like a frail toy.

Shaking off her gloomy thoughts, she timidly drew the bolt of the door.

She turned to behold a man standing in the middle of the room.

She uttered a loud cry, and would have escaped from the house, but the man swept between her and the door, and caught her by the arms.

She gazed wildly into that dark and sinister, yet handsome face, and with a cry of terror and despair sank on her knees.

"What folly, Rose; why do you give way to these school-girl fits of alarm, when there is no cause for fear. Look at me. Do you take me for some midnight robber?"

"Rather the most dreadful and ferocious ruffian, rather, a thousand times," cried the girl, with passion, "than the base, the treacherous and infamous Earl of Penalvon!"

"Do not spoil your prettiness by playing the virago. What fault do you find in me? That I love you—very good—to that great crime I plead guilty, and throw myself upon your clemency."

"Are you a suitor in honour?"

"Yes, and you are free, Rose; but the very greatness of my affection for you forbids that I should lose you for want of that boldness which fortune favours and women love."

"If you love me, surely you should respect me."

"And I do; but there is no better way of showing my respect than by removing from you all share in the blame, if there any be blame, in your elopement with me."

"Elopement? Villain! have you broken into the humble home of a poor, defenceless woman to carry her away by force? It is impossible. Even Lord Penalvon will not carry his villany to that length."

"Villany or virtue, Rose, you are mine, and must submit to your fate. Believe me, you shall want nothing your wildest wishes can aim at. You shall have all my gentlest devotion and most lavish bounty. Act like a sensible woman, then, and succumb to what you cannot escape."

"My lord, as a widow, as a mother, I implore you, by her who loved and nourished you as her son, to have mercy on me," cried poor Rose, flinging herself on her knees before the noble ruffian.

"I have borne far more than enough of this. Rose, I love you, and you shall be mine! I have sworn it, and I will not break my oath. When you are removed from the associations connected with this place, you will listen to reason; so come at once, like a charming, sensible girl as you are. Throw on your cloak, and let us have no more useless protesting."

Rose sprang away towards the chimney-piece, and snatched down a loaded gun, which hung from the wall.

"Earl of Penalvon, we are equal now!" she cried, with fierceness; "it is for me to dictate and threaten. I am no poor, trembling girl, no weak-hearted woman over whom you may triumph in your tyranny; from my earliest youth I have lived amid stern and even savage men. I do not shrink at the sight of blood; the harsh, hard lessons of my former life have left this much good—that they have nerved my heart to kill such a reptile as you without ruth or remorse!"

The Earl frowned darkly, and then said, with a faint laugh,

"You are a vixen, Rose, but you would not have heart to kill me; yet I swear my soul is so warped in my fervent passion for you that, indeed, I set no value on life, except for your sake; so you have a fair mark. Send the bullet through my heart, but do not wound me by such unjust reproaches."

"Begone! or I will take you at your word," cried the woman, fearlessly levelling the gun. "If you remain another instant in this house, you will not remain alive."

The Earl drew back.

Rose pointed to the door.

Her soft, white arm was pulled down to her side, and the gun wrenched from her grasp by some one from behind.

Upon turning round to see whence proceeded this new and dastardly attack, she stood face to face with the captain of the wreckers.

"Come, come, lass, let's have none o' thy woman's tongue; when my lord has heard as much of such music as I have he'll be satisfied to let you go, I'll warrant."

"Thorkil, you are a man, although you are a wrecker; you and Hylda have known me from my childhood; my uncle, Polruth, is one of your band; you can surely find manlier work than this—you will not, I am sure—you are too brave, you will not tear me away from my peaceful home, and deliver me into the hands of this titled scoundrel. If you want—and times are hard, I know—only spare me, and you shall have all in the house, and I will double the sum. Oh, pity me, for the sake of the old times, when we were children together!"

Thorkil made no reply.

He got behind the girl, and held her arms while the Earl placed a scarf in her mouth, and bound it in such a way that she could not utter a sound, and was almost stifled.

The Earl then snatched her up in his arms, and carried her through the door.

Thorkil followed, and closed the door after them.

First, however, he snatched off a hooded cloak that hung on a nail.

The two wretches carried the now insensible girl over the gravel path, taking care to tread softly, Thorkil removing the traces of their footsteps as far as possible.

The night was dark and gusty.

They reached the top of the cliff.

The tide was low, and the water comparatively calm.

The pale silver waves shone coldly round the black points of the rock rift that jagged the cruel coast.

"Thorkil, you have strangled her," cried the Earl, suddenly, as the cold, soft arm of the poor girl drooped passively over his shoulder.

"It's her own fault, then," growled the wrecker; "she should have kept her clapper quiet. I hate the sound of a woman's tongue more than a pilot hates the roll of a fog-bell."

The Earl stooped on one knee.

He untied the scarf.

Rose Halliard's soft breast heaved, and she drew a long breath.

"She is very beautiful; in the full blush of womanhood she has not lost one trait of spring freshness," muttered the nobleman.

"Aye, aye, my lord, a pretty craft enough, and there are folks who admire the build of my Hylda; I've heard my wife called a beauty."

"And she deserves the reputation, she is a fine creature," returned the Earl.

"To the devil with such beauty! It's no recompense for the loss of peace and quietness," growled the wrecker; "but, now, my lord, this is not the time to be talking such nonsense. About half a cable's length to the larboard of this place the land has slipped, the last heavy rains caused the fall. However, this morning Nat Redfern and another of our chaps were nearly crushed. I'll fling the hood over the cliffs, so that it will catch midway upon a point of rock or a bramble; and, stop, this will make the proofs seem more convincing."

So saying, he caught hold of Rose's dress and tore away a large piece of it.

"I'll be bound your lordship will make good this little damage," said the wrecker, with a grin. "My lady will walk in silks and satins when she puts into a French port to refit."

"Your plan is a good one; but make haste, Thorkil," said the Earl, impatiently. "I will carry the girl down the foot-path on to the beach; do you follow me."

The Earl carried his unconscious burden down to the ever-murmuring shore, and made for a bluff in the cliffs, behind which a boat was awaiting him.

Rounding this point, he hailed several fellows, who were seated on the gunwale of a boat.

They came to his assistance, and helped him to place the poor girl at the bottom of the little bark, on a pallet of the men's pea-jackets.

The Earl caused her to be carefully covered with his own cloak, and pillowed her head upon his knee.

Thorkil joined them.

"Hush!" said the captain of the wreckers.

"Are we discovered?" ask the Earl.

"I cannot tell, my lord; that eldrich hag, Wild Thyra—she knows everything, and it is possible that the water-wraiths have told her of——"

"What a fool you are!" cried the Earl, fiercely. "What idiotic stupidity!"

"Call it what you like. It will be a great wonder to me if she does not blow the gaff on us."

"Have you seen her then?"

"Off the Wraith's Cave. She has been 'runing' to-night, the faggot. Why they did away with the good, wholesome law for burning such rips is more than I can see."

"At all events, we will get our fair super-cargo to her berth in the Foam, and then let who will give chase; for, by Heaven, I will not lose her now!"

"Yo-ho! Cheerily, boys! Now she goes!" cried Thorkil, putting his strong shoulder to the boat, and heaving her into the surf.

He leaped in, and, seating himself in the stern, took hold of the tiller.

Through the bounding breakers, and over the rocking waves, sped the boat, the men pulling strong and quick.

Soon it ran under the bows of a pretty launch, and Rose was carried on board.

The Earl lifted her in his arms, and bore her into the cabin.

It was a beautifully-fitted saloon, with couches and tables; the sides were adorned with pier glasses and panels of rosewood, richly gilded.

The Earl placed the girl upon one of the couches, and leaving a boy to attend to her, for she was slowly recovering her senses, he hurried up the companion-way.

He stationed one of the crew at the top, by the hatchway, fearing she might contrive to make her escape, and, in her desperation, might attempt to rush on deck with a design to throw herself into the sea.

Having given a few directions to Thorkil, and a word or two of caution, he got into the boat, and pulled off to the shore, leaving the girl to the charge of the wrecker to be carried off to the French convent.

CHAPTER XIX.

WILD THYRA ON THE WATCH — THE SEA-NYMPH ABOARD THE FOAM—NEWS OF TRELAWNY—THE DESPERATION OF ROSE—THYRA TO THE RESCUE—THORKIL QUAILS BEFORE THE STORM-RAISER.

SCARCELY had Thorkil returned from the bluff landfall, over which he had thrown the mantle and the shred of Rose Halliard's dress, and had put off the boat to carry the poor girl aboard the Foam, when a slight and fay-like girl, with long, wavy hair, glided swiftly along the beach.

Crouched behind a pile of rocks, she watched the boat as it surged its way to the ship.

It has been mentioned that the tide was low.

The incline of the shelving beach was very steep.

At a few yards the water in places between the rocks was very deep.

A long bar of sand ran out far into the sea, at the end of which was a large mass of stone called the Shag Rock, from the number of those sea-birds which built their nests there.

Along this natural break-water Wild Thyra ran nimbly.

At the end of it she paused.

She looked across the gleaming sea.

The ship was swaying at anchor at a little distance from the rock.

The boat was returning to the shore with the Earl of Penalvon.

As the whole crew of the launch numbered no more than eight men and the boy, only three were left aboard waiting the return of their companions.

None of these appeared on board.

Wild Thyra, for it was she, did not hesitate a moment.

She snatched a bind of seaweed of a peculiar kind, and, muttering one of her insane spells, wrapped the clammy plant about her forehead.

She then deliberately walked breast-high into the foamy breakers.

She kept her glance fixed unflinchingly upon the little vessel.

She stood like some sea-nymph, the spray dashing around her as much unheeded as if she had been born of the waves and in her more congenial element.

Striking boldly out with her white round arms she moved bouyantly through the parting waves.

Her long hair streamed in the surf as she seemed to fly along the surface of the water, her head pillowed on her graceful extended arms.

Far from showing the least fear Thyra, the sea-born, seemed to revel in her native element.

She had been born on board a stately Indiaman wrecked by the fiends of the coasts, and, in her childhood, had undergone a severe training, being often for sport tossed by the rough fellows into the sea and forced to swim for many yards after their boats.

She reached the ship unobserved.

She deftly clambered the side.

There was a deck-cabin aft, behind which coils of rope, blocks, loose spars and sail-cloth were piled.

Behind these she crouched.

She had not long been concealed when the boat ran alongside.

Thorkil Penreal came on deck.

"Now lads," he cried, "this job will be well paid for, and the sooner it's completed the better. 'Way aloft!"

"Aye, aye, cap'en."

"Now, my hearties, heave and a-weigh. Set stu'nsels."

"Aye, cap'en."

The men were now busy at the windlass.

"Yo ho! heave, yo ho!" rang their voices clear and shrilly through the pure, fresh sea air.

Thorkil paced the deck and seemed to be bitterly ruminating.

"The hell-hag!" he exclaimed, bitterly, it is probably mentally applying the epithet to his anxious spouse, whose peevish exhortations still rang harshly on his ear.

Thorkil seemed refreshed, and inspired by the cool sweet breath of morning, and not a little pleased with his enfranchisement from domestic discord; at all events, he hummed, cheerfully—

> "Oh, the Norse King rode upon the waves,
> With a raven at his prow,
> The serfs ashore are ocean's slaves,
> And steel wins gold, I trow."

"Agger, do you know anything of Wyld Thyra?" he said, addressing that wrecker who was at the helm. "Is she still moored at Joel Britton's?"

"Aye, cap'en," returned the other. "Murdock Polruth was over there yesterday, and the girl seems to have deserted us altogether."

"A precious good riddance. Curse all women—barring our mothers—for women are she-devils that make life a hell.

> 'My wife, sir, owned by all it is,
> Is handsome, rich, and young,
> No end to her fine qualities,
> But—no end to her long tongue!'"

"This Rose Halliard seems to have a spirit, cap'en," said Agger, with a grin.

"A spirit! Well, well, it's mighty fine to be a great lord to carry your fancy lass away to a French convent, where she will be broken to harness, and where you can pay her visit or leave her to her solitude, just as the humour takes you."

"Hylda certainly gets worse and worse; she swings about like a chopping channel-gale, and her voice is as harsh as the scream of Mother Cary's chickens," remarked Agger, with a gruff laugh.

"Avast, ye lubber, she is my wife, and if I growl when she vexes me, others must not mention her name disrespectfully," said Thorkil, in a surly tone.

"Pard'n, cap'en, but she is—well, a girl of wonderful spirit!" exclaimed the wrecker, a little nervously.

"And how about Harleck? the look-out brings no tidings from him."

"Not as I hear on, cap'en."

"Ha! he is vindictive. Vengeance is such a fool's game. And is there no news of Trelawny at our agents?"

"Yes, cap'en. Paul Adair has taken a splendid prize, but spared the passengers."

"The idiot! I hope he'll swing for such a cursed piece of tom-foolery," cried Thorkil, in great contempt.

"And now," he said, "I'll go below and look to our pretty passenger."

Thorkil was about to descend the companion-way when Rose Halliard sprang on deck, having pushed the man on guard, who tried to stop her, prone down the gangway.

The captain of the wreckers seized the girl. She wrestled strongly and tried to tear herself towards the bulwark.

"Hark ye, lass. I'm not for this infernal child's play. My orders are that if you turn mutinous you're to be treated as mad; and you know that mad folks must be put in bonds to keep them out of mischief. Come, come, I tell you it won't answer. Go below, go below."

The ruffian tried to drag the half-fainting girl to the companion-way.

She raised her eyes despairingly, and then fixed them yearningly upon the clear, bright waves.

She seemed to gather strength from her very despair, and she desperately struggled to release herself.

Thorkil was more patient with her than many a less hardened ruffian would have been; for, though he was utterly reckless of taking life, and was even blood-thirsty, as we have before stated, he had some instinctive respect for woman, and amidst all his passionate revilings he had never yet struck his wife, though sometimes she aggravated him to the verge of madness.

"Help here, ye lubbers! I am not used to spoiled children, and can't stand women's tarmagency. Get her below, and lock her in the cabin. Rose, Rose, you young fool, you will fret every bit of bloom off your pretty cheeks, and make yourself look as haggard and withered as an old squaw. There, there, don't be so silly. Why, lass, there's no help for you; better take it easy, then. Come, now."

HARRY NAILS THE COLOURS TO THE MAST DURING THE BATTLE.

Rose had thrown herself on her knees, clinging to the hammock nettings.

The men, at an impatient signal from Thorkil, made a rush to drag her away, when suddenly between them and their victim swept the nymph-like form of Wild Thyra.

Her hair streamed elfishly on her shoulders, intertwined with the sea-bine.

Her clothes were wet, and clung about her supple but well-turned figure; her wild and glowing blue eyes shone with a weird glare, and her frail and pretty arm was extended, with an authoritative gesture.

Thorkil and the rest fell back.

"Wild Thyra!" they cried, in as much terror as if she were indeed a ghost or a water-wraith.

The strange girl laughed low and scornfully.

"And did you think you could deceive me, Thorkil Penreal?" she said. "Do you think now that you can escape me?"

"How came you hither?" asked Thorkil, in great awe.

"How came I hither! Ask Hylda, she will tell you. Is it much for a rune-kenner, whose spells can unlock the dungeons of the wind-spirits? 'Bout ship, Thorkil Penreal," she went on, laughing long, and heartily. "Put the helm up, for we are bound for England!"

"For France! in spite of every devil of sea, land, and air! Do you think I will be braved out of my common senses by a pack of hags and witches?"

Thyra bounded away towards the stern, and the man at the wheel started back, as she fixed her eyes freezingly upon him.

"Haul over the boom! The rip will capsize us!"

Thorkil sprung upon the quarter, and tore the girl from the wheel. She only laughed, and madly raved her spells.

It happened that a black cloud at that moment passed over the sun, throwing a deep gloom upon the sea.

Thyra pointed in this direction of the heavens, and laughed triumphantly.

"'Bout ship, for God's sake!" groaned Thorkil, wiping the sweat from his brow. "The she Jonah is in league with the sea-fiends, and if we don't obey we shall all be drowned."

CHAPTER XX.

THE "JOLLY MARINERS" IN FULL BLAZE—MEETING OF WRECKERS, SMUGGLERS AND SAILORS—ARRIVAL OF A CLOAKED UNKNOWN STRANGER—THE SURPRISE OF MURDOCH POLRUTH — JOLLY TARS SPINNING YARNS—THE YARN OF TIMOTHY SILENT —STARTLING AMERICAN MAIL ROBBERIES—STEPS TO CRIME — TRAGIC END OF THE ROBBERS — FRIGHTFUL END TO A YOUNG MIDSHIPMAN'S MAD CAREER.

"HOUSE ho!" said a voice, knocking loudly and impatiently at the door of the 'Three Jolly Mariners.'"

The night was dark and boisterous.

The whole county was wrapped in midnight gloom.

No sounds were heard but the whistling winds, which fiercely rushed across the heath, and screamed in wild violence round the old wayside tavern, which, with roaring fires and bright windows, seemed all aglow with comfort.

The roar of voices conclusively proved that all within were engaged in song and toast and tale.

"House ho!—open! Polruth! Murdoch Polruth, open to a friend!" shouted the stranger, as he knocked louder than ever.

The sound of voices grew louder within.

At last, while the stranger stood in the wildly beating storm of wind and rain, the door opened and the traveller entered.

"A bed for to-night, Polruth," he said, shaking the host by the hand.

"Who art thou?" asked Murdoch, narrowly eyeing the new comer from head to foot.

"Nay, friend Polruth, ye know little of me, ye shall know more anon. Let's to a private room, the noise of these jolly fellows prevents conversation."

"Follow me!" said Polruth, leading the way to an inner room. "Mind the steps, my friend; follow the dark passage, and don't stumble."

Reaching an inner room, which was a small and private one, in which a fire burned merrily, Polruth locked the door, produced bottles and glasses, and the stranger, throwing off his wet cloak, spoke.

But while Polruth and the unknown were secreted together, the jolly company in the tap were story-telling and song-singing with more zest and noise than ever.

It seemed that all were bent on exacting a yarn from one of their companions, who had hitherto maintained imperturbable silence.

Loud ringing of their jugs and thumping on the table seemed to wake up their silent friend, who had then and there been unanimously christened "Silent Tim."

This latter personage took all their jokes in good part, and filling his pipe from a well-stocked bag of smuggled tobacco he carried in his capacious pocket, puffed away vigorously, and, after much winking and blinking, seemed inclined to favour the good-tempered company with a story.

"Well, lads, you've all had your say, and spun rather tough, startling yarns."

"Hear him!—hear him, shipmates!" cried all, filling pipes, and tossing off their grog. "That's right, mate, you've been with us a long time, and never opened your clapper yet—now for a good'un. Listen, lads, to Timothy Silent, as we calls him."

"Nay; I can't promise ye much; but such as it is, listen—I tell it as I heard it."

"Aye, aye, mate, make sail, my hearty."

"Midshipman Ripper was once on board a ship as I sailed in. He insulted his officers, was dismissed the service, and brought so much disgrace on his poor old father, that they both went to New York and settled, where young Henry Ripper soon got into a responsible berth as one of the principal clerks at one of the best banks.

"He did not give up his bad habits; but went on from bad to worse, as I shall soon show. He fancied himself a great gun at a game of billiards, and made a bet of 5,000 dollars that he could beat one of the greatest 'sharpers' in all North America. How to get the money he knew not.

"The evil spirit of gambling had strongly tempted him; but he proceeded about his business as coolly and indifferently as a professional thief.

"There were no signs of fear, or of unsteady nerves with him. He had endeavoured to borrow, but did not succeed, and, as he felt certain of winning, he felt certain also regarding his ability to replace any sums he might manage to abstract from the bank. His plan was this:—

"In many of the American banks there are certain sums of gold or silver tied up in bags, and as these are daily passing to and fro from bank to bank, some responsible person is always sent on the errand of taking or bringing. Ripper knew full well that a day would not pass without some of these specie bags changing hands; and as he was known to be far more fond of out-of-door exercise than of desk work, it usually fell to his lot to act as responsible messenger.

"Knowing the exact size and colour of the 5,000 dollar bags of the Atlantic Bank, he had procured one to be made in every respect identical, and had placed therein silver of the exact weight of two hundred and fifty twenty dollars gold pieces.

"This he deposited in a friend's room, to which he had daily access, and when sent for specie to the Atlantic Bank in the morning, he simply exchanged bags, and placed it behind the counter of the 'Commercial' as coolly and indifferently as ever, nor did a muscle move of his good-looking face, as he said,

"5,000 dollars specie from the Atlantic."

"In the afternoon it usually fell to Ripper's lot to put the specie bags in the safe, and on this occasion his portion of the task was performed without asking, for the clock scarcely pointed to four before

Henry was unusually active in clearing away for the evening.

"When he had retired to his lodgings, pulled down the blinds, and covered the keyholes, he pulled forth the precious bag with emotions of delight, and although fully certain it contained neither more nor less than the usual amount, he felt such extreme joy at being able to meet his engagements on the following evening, that he lay down upon his bed in reverie, and hugged the bag with fondness and pleasure.

"'Now I've done it,' thought he. 'My fortune's made! I shall come out a clear winner of not less than 5,000 dollars, and that will set me on my pins for some time. As to the outside betting, I'll take all I can get, when they see me post up the yellow-boys none'll doubt my ability to pay, so that I shall not have occasion to stake cash in outside bets. Come on, you little devils; let's have a look at you. It does a fellow's eyes good to see so many sleeping together in that old leather bag.'

"He untied the leather thongs with which the mouth of the bag was tightly bound, and to his consternation found it to contain coppers.

"This first step was an awkward one. He lost his money and his match, and soon afterwards was dismissed from the bank, not from suspicion, but from disorderly conduct.

"His father had died long before, and what had been left him was squandered away.

"He had married, also, but left his wife after all her money was gone, nor would her merciless father —old Skinner—give her a home, for Mr. Ripper had almost driven him to beggary, through forgeries and ill-conducted business transactions, until at last both Ripper and his father-in-law gained a questionable living, but how, none could imagine.

"'I wonder how my dear son-in-law is advancing in life,' thought Skinner one day.

"From constant meditations on the most practical modes of 'making money,' Mr. Skinner had hit upon a plan which greatly pleased him, and he was often seen to smile when mentally working out some mysterious details.

"'I want an assistant though; where shall I find one? Oh, Ripper's the man! He's not nice to trifles—at least, I should *think* not, judging from his antecedents, and what I hear of him. If we succeed, all right; if not, *he'll* be the one to suffer, not me. He ruined *me*; I should not be so nice about *his* feelings.'

"Mr. Ripper, who figured so extensively in Mr. Skinner's hypocritical pious meditations, at home and at church, could be found any night at the 'Excelsior,' between the hours of ten and two o'clock.

"He had little money, less credit, and roamed about seeking for youngsters whom he could easily fleece.

"He had initiated many into the mysteries of billiards and fast living, much to their sorrow, but now his calling as a sharper had become well-known, and business was 'dull' with him.

"Of all with whom he had associated, he could not 'hang on' to any but one Augustus Fumbleton, Esq., and upon *him* he constantly levied contributions.

"There were reasons for this.

"Ripper perfectly understood the equivocal relationship that once existed between the young fool and Mrs. R., but considering it to be a profitable thing, he never seemed to be aware of it, or at all anxious to stop it.

"He frequently borrowed from Augustus, but in his borrowings spoke in the mysterious tone and manner of one who *demanded*, rather than begged favours.

"It was while airing himself and his new clothes in Broadway one afternoon, and smoking the best Havannahs, that he was suddenly accosted by Skinner.

"The old man was much altered, and his face was wrinkled and crossed with care. His eye had a bright twinkle, which indicated intelligence and cunning. His dress was so unprepossessing that he had stood looking at Henry several minutes without being recognized.

"'Go away, old man,' said Ripper, carelessly, turning aside, supposing him to be a beggar. 'Go away, I tell you, I have nothing for you;' but when he looked the old man fully in the face, he recognized him, and was much surprised.

"'Why, Henry, my son, how do you do? Why, you don't know me! I'm glad to see you looking so well; shake hands.'

"Mr. Ripper, it must be confessed, was not overjoyed to meet his shabby-looking father-in-law in such a fashionable neighbourhood, for he feared that his own delicate 'reputation' might suffer. He got out of the difficulty by going down a side street, where they both entered a drinking-saloon.

"Perceiving the old man to be intent on drinking deeply, Ripper primed him lavishly, and both father and son were soon in a blissful state of intoxication.

"'Yes, Harry, everybody is getting on in the world, except you and I,' said the old man in his cups. 'It seems that honest folks cannot get along,' sighed he.

"'Honesty! who ever heard of a man getting rich *honestly*, and by hard labour? Look at *me!*' Harry observed, triumphantly flourishing his glass of brandy. 'Look at *me!* honest as the day is long, and *I* can't get along! I only wish I had a good chance to "hook" a few thousands unobserved, that's all!' he added, laughing.

"There was a bright twinkle in the old man's eye as he listened and sighed.

"'Yes, yes, *everybody* is getting on in the world but you and *me*. Look at Carrington! see him, now, shoved up as chief clerk in the Northern Express Office.'

"'Ah,' said Harry, with a grim smile; 'just to think of it. I should like to pull Charley Carrington down. Even a common fool can get along, and here are *we*, grovelling in the dust, despised and forsaken because we are *honest* men. Well, come what may, I'm going to make a break for *something*, very soon—hit or miss. One might as well bear the blame as the name; one might as well die for a sheep as a lamb, eh? What think you?'

"These worthy, respectable, and honest individuals were loth to open their hearts to one another; yet each was bent on 'making money' by some means, and broadly hinted that they were not particularly scrupulous as to the mode of doing it.

"'Look at me,' said the old man, laughing and chuckling at old recollections. 'Look at me. Thirty years ago I was a stranger in New York, and had neither friends nor money. I joined the church, the first thing, because it looked "respectable" like, and after a year or two married a widow with a little property. I placed money in the bank, and soon had the air of a monied man. Half a dozen of us clubbed together, and farmed the "Marine Insurance Company, capital 200,000 dols." We could not muster more than 2,000 dols. between the whole six of us—ha! ha! I've had a great run of luck and few losses. Three years ago, however, we lost a heavy "risk." We were able to make up the amount except 5,000 dols.—is the door shut ?—are you sure, Harry ?   Well, what did I do ? I goes to the Commercial Bank and borrows 5,000 dols. in specie, and when I got home I substituted coppers for the gold and—' Henry looked astonished, and opened his eyes and mouth very widely. 'Don't look so frightened—and returned the bag next morning, with all the airs of one worth millions. I saved my credit ; and if that cursed bank had not broken so suddenly, I should have fooled all my creditors just as nicely as formerly.'

" ' Who'd imagine he was such a scheming old villain !' Henry thought, when they had parted. ' Well, I don't think his plan can fail—at all events I'll so manage it that *I'm* not caught ; it don't matter so much about *him*, though, the old rat.'

" Such, also, was the identical train of thought which passed through Skinner's mind, when alone. ' *I'll* not be caught, you may be sure,' he imagined ; ' if we succeed, all right ; if we are discovered, why, then, Mr. Harry will be the one to suffer. Ripper and Alick, eh ? Well, these ruined gamblers are not usually nice to trifles. In a month I exchange these old clothes for new ones.'

" Mr. Ripper and Alick, the bygone ' marker ' of the ' Excelsior,' seemed to have a far firmer friendship than was ever witnessed of yore, and were frequently seen walking, arm-in-arm, through the principal streets, well clothed and in the highest spirits.

" ' If I can only ring *him* into it,' thought Harry, ' the thing is all but accomplished.'

" Mr. Fumbleton now began to consider himself too high-minded to be seen conversing with any such person as Mr. Ripper. As he held a responsible position in the Continental Express Company he forsook all former acquaintance but Alick, and for old association sake they frequently had a quiet game together, and ultimately secured him a position in the office, and went heavy security for him as messenger, which frequently occasioned Alick journeys upon the rail of two or three hundred miles.

" Carrington disapproved of Fumbleton's kindness to Alick, and told him he wasn't a person to be trusted.

" But, in truth, he was so much occupied with responsible duties in the Northern Express Office that he paid little attention to Alick or Fumbleton.

" Alick, the Express messenger at Fumbleton's office, had greatly improved in appearance since his brief connection with that company, and whenever he returned to New York after his usual long railway journeys, he seemed to be always in the highest spirits, and soon adorned his person with rings and watch-chains of massive appearance.

" Privately, Alick and Ripper were fast friends, and they often met at some designated rendezvous, where they were sometimes joined by Mr. Skinner. In truth, there was much change for the better in both of the last-named individuals.

" Henry, like his companion, now donned jewellery, and frequently visited Skinner's farm.

" Whenever these three worthies met, however—and it always occurred at some out-of-the-way saloon—they ' engaged the parlour ' exclusively for themselves, and made merry over the best of wines and suppers.

" ' It goes on capital, doesn't it, Alick ?' Skinner would say, rubbing his hands.

" Rolls of bank notes were frequently produced between them, and equally divided ; but whenever Skinner left the company he would rub his old, cold, bony hands, and mutter, with a chuckle,

" ' They can't fool me, old as I am ! I know a thing or two ; the mail-bags fall into my hands first !'

" Not more than three or four social meetings of this nature had taken place, with such satisfaction to the associates, when newspapers began to rumour that mail-bags had disappeared from cars on the Schenectady railroad, and that no trace of them could be discovered. Detectives of the post-office department were placed upon the road, and rode in the same car with the bags, the car being likewise used by the Express companies for their small parcels and most valuable freight. Alick, as messenger of the Northern Company, was always in the car, and superintended the delivery of goods ; but, despite the most strenuous exertions of the officers, valuable bags were occasionally missing, and no one could imagine how they disappeared.

" When Alick, Ripper, and Skinner met on one occasion, and had divided a considerable sum of money between them, the first-named confessed that he should discontinue his operations, for the hazard was daily becoming more fraught with danger.

" ' Dangerous ! Yes, but see what we've made, my boy !' said Skinner. ' Stop it ! what nonsense ! A few more hauls such as the last one, and we are all made for ever ! They can *never* find us out. But suppose we do stop the " mail " business, there's another line open to us ; there's the Express companies—*that's* the thing to finish it up with, and then our fortune's made. How shall we do it, ask you ? Why, very easily ; listen.'

" The crafty old man explained his modus, and when he had finished, both said ' Capital !'

" But while these three worthy scoundrels were growing rich upon public plunder, the Post Office authorities were not asleep, but had called to their assistance the most expert detective in the country, Thomas Reeves, Esq., of St. Louis, than whom no better officer existed on that vast continent.

" After much consultation, the Post Office department employed this person to discover the hitherto successful mail robbers.

" Mr. Bramble sauntered along Broadway with all the manners of a country dandy, and strolled into the ' Excelsior ' billiard-saloons. Henry Ripper, as usual, was present, and discovering the new arrival to be particularly flush of funds, and exceedingly ' green,' was not long in making his acquaintance.

" ' He came up to look about him,' Bramble innocently said, ' and was desirous of purchasing a nice snug farm somewhere.'

" Ripper knew of one ' which would exactly suit him. There's Skinner, he's tired of country life, and would sell out cheap.'

" It was agreed that Mr. Bramble should be introduced to Mr. Skinner.

" On the appointed evening they met, and conversed very pleasantly, and it was arranged that both should ' run down by rail,' and view the estates.

" By mere accident the topic of late Post-office robberies was broached by the old man, and seemed to fill Mr. Bramble with surprise.

" ' Oh, sir,' said Skinner, contritely, ' we live in a very wicked age—rogues and vagabonds abound in our midst. It was only the other night I spoke of that very subject at our weekly prayer-meeting, and we all came to the conclusion that the whole world was fast passing into the hands of satan and men of sin.'

" Mr. Bramble remained for a few days with Mr. Skinner, and said the old gentleman's conversation was so pious and edifying that ' it was almost as good as going to church.'

"He inspected every part of the farm, but did not purchase.

"Skinner and Bramble parted at the railroad, which ran within a few hundred yards of his house, and the tunnel was only a mile down the road.

"Mr. Skinner went to New York, Mr. Bramble to Davenport.

"Within two days Mr. Bramble unexpectedly returned to the farm, and found that Skinner had not yet returned.

"He came by the afternoon train.

"The old man was in great spirits, and as evening approached he said,

"'Let's take a walk and see the express train pass; it always gives me pleasure to go down to the tunnel and see *that* train pass. What a wonderful thing steam is, isn't it?'

"While standing on an embankment near the tunnel, the train was heard to approach.

"'Here it comes,' said Skinner, rubbing his hands. 'It's in the tunnel now.'

"And within a few moments the engine gave a long, shrill whistle, rushed past the two observers with great speed, and was out of sight.

"'I thought I saw something drop,' said Bramble, 'as the train passed us. What can it be?'

"'Did you? Oh, it can't be much—a stick of wood, perhaps, from the tender. Let's go.'

"'Stay a moment,' said Bramble, and he went upon the track, but found nothing. When coming away he stumbled against a mail-bag.

"'A mail-bag?' asked Skinner, in surprise. 'A mail bag! you don't say so?'

"'Yes, there it is, and no mistake! Ah! what negligence to be sure. No wonder the bags fall out when the doors are wide open. What's to prevent 'em?'

"Mr. Bramble and Mr. Skinner had important business at New York the following morning.

"Bramble declined going to the Post-office. Skinner went and made a very long oration to the chief postmaster, to whom he explained everything regarding the bag, and was much thanked by the chief official, who bestowed many encomiums upon the grey-headed gentleman, and highly extolled his honesty.

"'So much for that,' thought Skinner, leaving the Post-office with many important airs. 'One can afford to be honest occasionally. I wish that d——d fool, Bramble, hadn't seen it; it was a fine large bag, and had no end of money in it, I know. Harry Bramble! the fellow must have eyes like a cat, for he sees a long way in the dark, and no mistake. The game's up now, we must stop it.'

"A few nights afterwards the old man, Ripper, and Alick, met at an old rendezvous.

"'Why couldn't you have dropped it in the tunnel as usual, and waved your lamp as you passed my door?'

"'For the simple reason, I had no other opportunity,' said Alick, gruffly.

Skinner, Ripper, and Alick desisted from their labours, and in the hurry and bustle of life, people had forgotten the mail robberies, and thought nothing more of them. Ripper had bought considerable property in Decatah, Illinois.

"Skinner followed his son's example, and invested largely in lands in the same neighbourhood, and, as it was a railroad junction of importance, purchased several houses in the town itself, and opened a draper's establishment there. He seldom visited the shop, but frequently sent large boxes there, and had full confidence in the fidelity of his clerk, who shut up shop at sunset every evening, and retired to his boarding-house.

"Alick, it must be confessed, still retained his situation with the Express Company; but often hinted to Mr. Fumbleton that he intended shortly to leave his lucrative situation.

"He began to appear restless and discontented; 'he wanted change of scene,' he said. 'There is no novelty, and, besides, there have been so many mail robberies upon my route, that I feel uneasy, unhappy—*not* that any one could ever suspect *me*, you know.'

"Within a few weeks Alick was appointed to superintend the company's light freight delivery, as messenger between New York and Decatah, and he was happy. Mr. Skinner and Ripper heard of the change with joy, and when the three worthies met they all retired to a private room, enjoyed a fine supper and wines, and appeared in ecstacies.

"If Messrs. Skinner, Ripper and Alick were enjoying the fullness of life, rapidly rising in the world, and posting large sums to their respective names at various inland banks, Charles Carrington and the Northern Express Company were in the greatest trepidation and alarm, for a very large sum of money, in gold dust, had been consigned to their care for transit to St. Louis, and, in answer to various telegrams, their agents in Missouri returned word that it had never arrived there.

"Strict search and inquiry had been made, but no tidings were received or inkling gleaned of the missing treasure.

"This news filled the office with much anxiety. It had been stolen, but by what manner or means the wisest officers could not divine.

"In order to guard against any such recurrent loss, Charles, as the most trustworthy employé, was asked to go as special messenger to escort very valuable freight as far as Decatah. To this proposition he willingly consented, whenever gold dust or bank deposits of value were to be passed along that line of railroad.

"To the astonishment of every one another heavy express robbery was reported to have taken place, in which the Continental Company were at heavy loss. Express messengers, mail-masters, and conductors on the road were all amazed.

"'How can it happen?' asked one of another, in surprise. 'I'm sure it can be no fault of ours, for we never leave the car, at least, there is *always* one in it, under all circumstances, and, without it is the Devil himself, I'm sure none can tell how it happens.'

"'Leave it all to *me*,' said Alick to his employers; and that same evening, when his confederates met, he disclosed the many plans suggested to catch them.

"'One more haul,' said Skinner, very humourously, 'and that will be my last. What say you?'

"'Yes, one more, and then let's cry quits; it's *your* turn this time, old man, *I* did the last two journeys.'

"Alick informed his companions that the Northern Express was going to send much dust and specie over the road within a few days, in charge of Carrington, and that it would be a 'jolly go' to fool him, 'for he's so stuck up and starched.'

"'Well, as this is our last trip, boys,' said old Skinner, much elated, 'I don't mind being chief operator *this* time.'

"'All the treasure is in my store at present,' thought Skinner, when alone; 'but when we've made *this* haul, I'll take good care of it. I shall be suddenly found missing, and leave Mr. Alick with my dutiful son-in-law to blow their fingers.'

"When the old man had left their company Ripper and Alick began to joke, and say, 'What a capital thing it would be if they could only fool Skinner out of his share,' at which both laughed immoderately, and arrived at the conclusion that 'the thing could be done very easily, particularly as this was the first time he was going to be chief operator.'

"When Alick took charge of the company's freight and valuables in the express car, he found that Mr. Carrington was in charge in the same car of the Northern Express Company's affairs. As they were not on very intimate terms each transacted his own business without conversing more than was necessary, yet there were so many boxes, large and small, to be taken in and handed out at different stations, that it was absolutely necessary to speak occasionally.

"'Well,' Carrington observed, 'if any of those light-fingered gentry come near this car with their tricks let them look out, that's all!' he said, pointing to his revolvers lying on the safe.

"At which speech Alick laughed heartily.

"All progressed properly, and soon the train was on its way roaring along the broad star-lit prairies of Illinois.

"'How far do you go, Mr. Carrington?'

"'Well, thank goodness, this long trip will end with me at Decatah.'

"Town after town, and village after village was stopped at; through forests and prairies, flying past farm houses, the express train sped on its night-journey with wonderful speed, and soon the express car was almost filled with bales and boxes.

"At one of the wayside stations a very large dry-goods packing-case was lifted into the car by two sturdy men, and was directed 'Mr. S., Decatah, Illinois. Care of Mr. Alick, Continental Express; this side up, with care.'

"Alick stowed the long case near the 'Northern Company's safe.'

"'It won't be in your way there, eh, Mr. Carrington? We are so pressed for room, I scarcely know where to place things.'

"'Alick, why not place it on end like that one of ours in the corner yonder?'

"The case was a very large one, and almost six feet long, proportionately broad and high.

"Charles lit a cigar and stretched himself upon it.

"Charles at times was very busy delivering goods, and this occasioned him to open his safe frequently. They were but fifty miles from Decatah, and, while the engine stopped for wood and water, Carrington jumped out, saying, 'Keep an eye for me for a minute, Alick.'

"'Ready?' said Alick, as if addressing some imaginary person.

"'Yes,' was the whispered answer from one invisible.

"Alick opened Carrington's safe for a moment, and then shut it.

"'All right?'

"The whispered answer was 'O. K.'

"When Carrington returned Alick was whistling and shuffling his feet in a jig in the highest spirits.

"'Stay here a little while, Carrington,' said Alick, 'I shan't be long; I'll go and have a drain! Won't we have a jolly pile? what I shaved him from the two safes will make us!' thought Alick.

"'Alick will persist in having this long packing-case on the floor, taking up more room than it's worth; he's a long time away, I'll lock up the car and stretch my legs a little.'

"Charles locked the two side doors, but, before he locked the end door communicating with the passenger cars, he stumbled against the long pack-ing-case, and in rage and pain, he lifted the heavy case on end, slammed the door and locked it.

"Tired with walking about Carrington unlocked the end door, turned the long packing case full-length on the floor, and lay down upon it. 'I'll take a cat-sleep till the train starts,' said he, and stretched himself upon it.

"At that moment he heard a slight, faint moan.

"'Where can that come from? Oh, it's only the wind.' He smoked a cigar, and the train was soon again in motion.

"'There it is,' said Alick, looking out of the car door, and pointing to a gas-lit town in the distance.

"The train had scarcely stopped when two express carts drove up.

"Mr. Carrington, I'll trouble you for that large packing case standing in the corner—it's for us.'

"With much trouble the case was carted, and the two men drove rapidly away.

"'This is Mr. Skinner's store, isn't it?' said the driver, stopping before that warehouse. 'All right, open the doors and let's put it in.'

"'Don't lay it down in the middle of the floor; place it on end in the back part of the shop.'

"The cart had scarcely driven away when another came.

"'Don't shut the door, Sampson," said a voice like Ripper's; 'here's some goods for Skinner. Lay it on the floor, men, There, there's a dollar for you; Mr. Sampson, you needn't stay, I will mind the premises. Good-night!'

"Ripper bolted the shop door. He rapped on the packing case, and said 'All right, governor, how are you?'

"There was no response.

"'The old fellow takes things very coolly, at any rate; more than I could. Here, old man; unlock and come out; don't be fooling there any longer!'

"There was still no response! Ripper imagined that perhaps the wrong packing case had been sent. He saw the direction which he himself had painted, and was certain there could be no mistake, and immediately commenced to pry open the top with chisels and a hammer.

"When he had opened it, he started backwards, as if shot.

"'Dead!' he said, in surprise; 'dead as a door nail!'

"He sat down, and was soon lost in thought.

"In a few moments a rap was heard at the door.

"'Who's there?' he asked, cocking his revolver, and listening. 'Who's there?'

"'Alick, O.K.!' was the whispered response.

"The door was opened ajar, and Alick entered.

"'Well, where's the old man?'

"'Did you bolt the door? He likes his berth so much he won't come out. Just have a look at him; the top is open.'

"Alick did look, and then started back with looks of horror.

"'Dead!'

"'As a herring!' added Ripper, coolly.

"The old man was dead.

"His face was completely black, and much besmeared with blood.

"His head was thrown forward upon his chest as if the neck had been broken, and his limbs were curled up as if he had expired in the greatest torture, and amid fearful writhings and exertions to free himself.

"Bags of gold and rolls of bills were in the case beside him.

"'How could this have happened?' asked Ripper,

of the astonished Alick. 'Was this *your* little trick ?'

"'I never dreamed of such a thing. The case was always lying full length ; I sat upon it most of the time. Carrington must have turned it on end, and then left the car. He couldn't get out, except on the side ; the top was fastened. Being turned on end, he must have been strangled.'

"'It's no use of standing here, looking at him. A lucky job I didn't undertake to be the "chief operator." How far is the river ? A mile ! Then we must bury him in the garden. Come, let's be quick and dig a hole for him.'

"The two worthies proceeded to the garden, and, finding spades, were soon engaged in digging.

The night was dark and cloudy, and the houses far apart.

"The task was swiftly and secretly accomplished.

"Well, he's now laid low,' said Ripper. 'The best thing we can do is to divide the spoil, and make tracks for California, Canada, Texas, or anywhere. The whole pile is in the house somewhere. Let's seek it ; the cellar is the place. Come, let's commence the search.'

"The words had scarcely passed Ripper's lips when he and Alick turned to go towards the back yard, but at that moment two sturdy officers jumped from behind the counter, and seized the villains.

"A desperate struggle ensued. All four were powerful men, and it seemed to be a case of life or death !

"The struggle had continued a few seconds, when a second party of officers entered.

"Ripper, drawing his long knife and pistol, cut and fired in every direction, as did also Alick.

"They fought like tigers, and more than one officer lay bleeding on the floor. Through sheer weakness Ripper fell, overpowered, and was tied both hand and foot. Alick had almost effected his escape through the rear door, but a blow on the head from an officer felled him to the earth like an ox, weltering in gore.

"An hour subsequent to this tragical scene, Ripper and Alick were lying in the police-station, helpless and bleeding. Several officers were wounded, and conveyed to the hospital.

"Skinner's shop looked as if some little army had been fighting there. Remnants of clothes were strewn in every direction ; boxes and packing-cases were turned over and broken ; marks of pistol shots were seen on every hand ; windows were broken ; pools of blood were on the floor.

"No one was permitted inside the premises but a single officer, and he, lantern in hand, was searching everywhere.

"Within half-an-hour the sounds of a hammer were heard, and shortly afterwards an express cart took away a box, which was accompanied by the officer.

"Before these scenes were enacted at Skinner's shop, others were transpiring in the offices of the Northern Express, near the station. When their safe had been landed, Carrington began to adjust his accounts, but, to his consternation, as well as that of every one present, he discovered that it had been rifled of its gold dust and notes.

"He was almost paralized ; he could not speak, and fell into his chair powerless.

"Some thought he had swooned, or died, for he looked lifeless and inanimate.

"He suddenly rose like a maniac, and would have committed suicide. The revolver was taken from him, and a guard placed over him.

"Some one arrived, and, almost breathless, reported the bloody encounter at Skinner's.

"'I am ruined !' Carrington said, wildly clenching his fists with rage, 'I am ruined !'

"'Not yet, quite, I hope,' remarked a mild-looking gentleman, entering. 'I go to New York immediately. Mr. Carrington, my friend, you can inform your company the whole affair is over, and that they do not lose one penny !'

"In due course the trial of Ripper and Alick came off. The indictment against them was a very long one ; but it appeared that 'Henry Ripper and Alexander Greyshaw, *alias* Alick,' were arraigned for robbing the United States mail, and for abstracting gold dust and notes to a considerable amount from the safes of various express companies.' The prisoners were defended by the best of counsel. The court-room was thronged almost to suffocation, and the lawyer for the defence remarked,

"'It is true that gold dust and notes *were* found in Skinner's shop ; but that does not prove that *my clients* stole it ! Who knows but that the old man Skinner, who has been so long and mysteriously missing, might not have done it and escaped.'

"Both prisoners exchanged intelligent and approving glances.

"'The last witness has spoken at considerable length about what he did with a large dry goods packing-box. As counsel desire it, let a packing-case of the dimensions described be produced in court, and placed where the jury can see, say, even on this table, I'm sure the defence can have no objection, and then let's see what the other side can make of it.'

"'With your honour's permission here's the packing-case before me ; I call the attention of all towards it. I would further say that—Where's my handkerchief ? has any one seen it ?'

"The prisoners looked at the packing-case before them, and appeared paralysed with fear.

"'I was merely remarking, your honour, that—really, where *is* my gold pencil case ?—has anyone seen it ?—that the testimony just given by the officer Hoskins, and which lasted exactly half-an-hour by my watch, was not worth——Where *is* my watch, who has seen it ?'

"'Your honour, I am afraid there are some tricksters about ; my handkerchief, gold pencil-case, and gold watch have suddenly disappeared from this very table, and I am *sure* they must have been purloined.'

"The judge smiled, and said the prosecution would bring the packing-case in as a witness, at which everybody laughed, except the prisoner's counsel, who looked astonished, for the side opened, as if by magic, and Mr. Reeves, the detective, rolled out upon the table, returned counsel his missing articles, and took his place in the witness-box.

"His story defied contradiction ; he had watched the accused both night and day, had prowled about Skinner's farm at all times, in all weathers ; he was convinced that Skinner, Ripper and Alick were the true mail robbers, the first-named the master-spirit of the whole. He had searched Skinner's farm, and discovered spots where papers had been destroyed. The robbers had invested their money in lands and houses so that their sudden possession of large funds should not excite suspicions in New York. In all manner of disguises he had followed first one and then another, and, observing Ripper in the habit of visiting a trunk-maker, had dropped in to order a trunk as if by accident. His attention was drawn to the long and singular packing-case by the trunk-maker ; the case was taken away unknown to me.

"'Knowing that Alick was concerned in their doings I redoubled my efforts. Procuring a packing-case of exactly the same description, such an one as I could stand or lie down in without fears of suffocation, I placed myself therein, and frequently travelled in the same car with Alick, the express messenger, and, through several holes, observed all his doings. I distinctly saw the mode in which the robbers fleeced the Mail and Express Company's safes. By shoving *their* packing-case near one of the safes, when open, they had simply to raise the side of the case, and the person inside could reach out his hand, help himself, and secrete the property with him in the case.

"'On the last occasion Alick waited until Mr. Carrington had left the car for one moment, he gave a signal to his companion in the box to open the side, and handed to him whatever he could expediently purloin from the Express Company's safes, which were left open.

"'The case in which I had secreted myself, as explained, was placed in the car at Chicago, and no one was in the secret but the chief of police, who personally saw that I was placed feet downwards with my eyes on the express agents, and in the corner. All around me were boxes and goods so that I could not move the case in which I was hid. It was my intention to capture *all* the conspirators at one time, but my design was thwarted.'

"'Were there *more* than two, then?' asked the judge, in surprise.

"'I will shortly explain. The robbery was committed, and I saw the whole manner of it, as explained, Mr. Carrington was left in sole charge of the car. Alick, as I afterwards learned, being drinking with Ripper, and as the long packing-case seemed to be in Mr. Carrington's way, and as he was tired of sitting alone, he locked the side doors of the car, placed the long packing-case on end, slammed the end door, and left.

"'Within a few moments I heard cries and groans issuing from the robbers' packing-case, but, being unable to stir, I could do no more than shout for assistance.

"'My cries were not heard, and soon the moans and groans subsided. I feared the consequence of my suspicions, and I was correct.'

"'What were they?' asked the judge, much surprised, and growing interested.

"'I will shortly inform your honour. When the cars arrived, two officers, according to instructions, took the case in which I was concealed, and placed me on end in Skinner's store. Shortly afterwards Ripper came with his case; he frequently called upon old Skinner inside to come out, and no response being given, he broke open the case, and found him dead! I saw all that passed from my place of concealment. He had been turned wrong side upwards, and, unable to extricate himself, must have died from suffocation or strangulation. I saw the bags of gold dust and rolls of notes beside him in the packing-case, and also that the old man had bled fearfully. When Alick came, they buried Skinner, case and all, in the garden. While they were thus engaged, I got out of my case, opened the door, and returned to it again, to make still further observations. Two officers entered and secreted themselves behind boxes. When Ripper and Alick were intent on dividing the spoil, I gave the signal, and we rushed upon them. The struggle was desperate and deadly. I opened the shop-door, and admitted other officers, but yet the robbers fought desperately, and wounded several with their knives and revolvers. They now stand there before you. I have secured every penny of the spoil.'

"When Reeves had concluded, there was a buzz of astonishment through the whole court. The jury were not a moment deliberating, and both prisoners were sentenced to irons for life!

"Mr. Carrington, who had given evidence in the trial, felt comforted that his character had been vindicated, but as Ripper passed him, heavily ironed, he smiled sardonically.

"A few days after the trial, as the jailor entered Ripper's cell, he was horrified to see him hanging dead, from the cell window-bars. Upon his table were notes addressed to various persons, but one for the Northern Express Company ran thus:—

"'I am tired of life; there is no more pleasure in store for me. I die, and by my own hand. My first crime was forging my father's name to numerous cheques, which doubtless caused his ruin. I drowned my father; the manner you may never know. I have been Carrington's evil genius through life. I make no amends. In an hour I shall be no more, but add that, had it not been for evil teachings, I might have died an honest man. Skinner has preceded me into the other world by a few days. I now follow him.

'HENRY RIPPER.'

"Alick did not survive. He attempted to escape, and well-nigh succeeded, but as he stood at midnight upon the lofty prison walls, in the act of leaping into the river that flowed darkly and sluggishly at their base, one of the guards in a look-out tower espied him through the mists, levelled his rifle, and the lifeless body fell with a crash into the prison-yard, an indistinguishable mass of bleeding, mangled remains.

"Such was the end of Alick and of Midshipman Ripper, the profligate son, once the hope and pride of all who knew him."

CHAPTER XXI.

MURDOCH POLRUTH'S SURPRISE—REVELATIONS OF THE STRANGER—WRECKING ON THE COAST—ATTACK OF THE COAST GUARD—ESCAPE OF THE DUTCH GALLIOT—THE BOOTY—DISCOVERY OF PAPERS—PENALVON IS CURSED—THE RESOLVE—THE MIDNIGHT STORM UPON THE HEATH—PARTING OF POLRUTH WITH THE STRANGER.

FOR some time Murdoch and the stranger sat silently before the fire.

Neither spoke, and at last Murdoch filled the glasses to the brim.

"Come, friend, drink. The night is stormy; drink, it will do you good."

The stranger lifted his glass, which sparkled brightly in the firelight, and quaffed it to the dregs at a draught.

"Good!" he said. "Cognac!"

"True," answered Murdoch; "not bad, is it?"

"Never paid duty, *I* know," said the stranger, still muffled up closely, and winking intelligently at the host.

"How know ye *that?*" asked Murdoch, gruffly. "No man knows that."

"Well, well, Murdoch, do not knit thy brows. Your looks portend a gathering storm. Here, help thyself to a dozen or two of these weeds, they are excellent accompaniment to that prime old brandy."

Both personages were soon smoking choice Havannahs, and the odorous smoke curled on high in mystic circles.

"Duty paid, of course?" said Polruth, drily.

NOTICE.—*The next Number of the Boys' Library will be Published on Friday, August 8th Order early of your Bookseller.*

BOYS' LIBRARY

Harry Halliard: or, the Young British Tar.

THE MYSTERIOUS APPEARANCE.

"Nay, my friend. I never trouble the Customs, nor *you*, I judge?"

"You seem to know me."

"I know no harm of you."

"Nor good, perhaps. Some would call me hard names, but 'tis long since a stranger complimented me."

"I know you, Polruth, but you know not me. There is much goodness of heart in all you do. You would never see a friend in need if it lay in your power."

"Not if he were a good man and true."

"I knew it, and to prove it I came here to-night."

"But yet I know you not. How can I confide aught to one I never knew?"

"Thou shalt hear. It concerns you deeply."

"How, I pray?" asked Polruth, eyeing his companion narrowly, and withdrawing his chair some feet from the glowing hearth; "how can it concern *me*?"

"Thus. The galliot that should have anchored last night, and for which those in the tap are impatiently waiting——"

"For which they are waiting!" said Polruth, in surprise. "What know *you* of a galliot and of the men in yonder?"

"I know more than you suppose. Nay, do not stir. You shall not move a foot till you have heard me."

"Am I not master in my own house? Shall a stranger intrude upon me, and bid me not stir? What know you of my affairs, young man?"

"It strikes me you are a spy!"

"That I am not, Polruth, or I should not have ventured hither among so many. List you again, and be calm; listen, and when you have heard all, tell me I am an informer, if you dare."

"I listen—go on!"

"This galliot, which you expect, sailed from Holland laden with cloth, spirits, tobacco, and sundries. It reached the coast, but stranded."

"Stranded! Where, pray?"

"Thirty miles down the coast. Myself and others were soon on the spot, and by the aid of the crew would soon have discharged the cargo, but——"

"But what?" asked Polruth, excited.

"But the coast-guard got wind of the affair, and before we could complete our work pounced down upon us."

"Well, quick, good friend, let's hear the finish."

"They rushed down to the beach, armed to the teeth; but myself and a few friends got between the officers and the galliot, and, as they attempted to board her, we drew our weapons and beat them back."

"Brave lads!"

"The fight was long and desperate, several were cut down; but, as luck would have it, the tide arose during the encounter, and amid the cheers of the crew, she put out to sea, and soon her white sails were lost in the mists, and far beyond the reach of the government cruisers."

"What became of the coast-guard?" asked Murdoch, highly elated at the narration of his companion.

"We were nearly overpowered, and must soon have been in their power, when the sounds of approaching footsteps broke upon our ears, shouting, 'Give it to 'em, lads, secure every one of the blood-thirsty scoundrels!'"

"Who were they?"

"We made sure our time had come at last; with the desperation and fury of dying men, we fought more ferociously than ever, our swords clashed and rung again with the quick, hard blows, when six sturdy wreckers rushed to the rescue, and beat down the officers."

"Brave boys!"

"We soon bound them hand and foot, and feeling sure that the affair would soon become known, we immediately had them conveyed, blind-folded, to our rendezvous, and after their wounds were dressed, treated them as brave men ever should treat brave enemies."

"Right!" grunted Murdoch.

"Some were unable to walk; these we placed in carts and drove them across the moors some thirty miles, and there left them to their fate, for we felt certain that those who were able would soon arrive at some village, and be far out of our reach."

"But the cargo!—what of that?"

"Be patient! I secured all among the rocks and caves, where no man but myself could find it, and in looking over the bales and boxes made strange discoveries."

"Discoveries!"

"Yes, stranger than you would e'er believe."

"Your tale is strange, young man."

"Yes, but it will be still stranger."

"Come, drink again, you are a good and true man, whoever you be."

"Good, I doubt, Murdoch Polruth, but true and faithful to you and yours."

"To me and mine? What mean you by that slow and solemn way of talking?"

"Answer my questions."

"If I can I will. What are they?"

"You had a niece—Rose Halliard?"

"Yes! What of that?"

"Know you Penalvon?"

"I do! Earl Penalvon."

"The same."

"What of him?"

"Much that you know not."

"Nothing that is bad, good friend; one so high and mighty in the land would never disgrace his name and station."

"Not so fast, Murdoch; you have lived longer in the world than I, but these high and mighty ones who lord it over us are not so good as many men who watch the coast as wreckers."

"You must not say so publicly, young man; it is dangerous work for any on this wild coast to get in the clutches of a powerful earl."

"I care not for all the nobles in the land, they are but men, and if one dared to do to me or mine what I fear is already done to thee and thine——"

"To me and mine?"

"Yes; to thee and thine; drink no more till you have heard me out."

"Nay I *must* drink, for I am all surprise and fearful of your strange words and still stranger manner."

"Among these boxes was found a desk filled with papers and letters, which, as well as I could decipher them, spoke of some who are now engaged to Penalvon in deeds of knavery."

"Deeds of knavery!"

"Yes! deeds of deep-dyed villany!"

"Were they written in French, say you?"

"Part in French, part in English, but still another part in cipher which I could do no more than guess at."

"But how can this concern me or mine?"

"Rose Halliard, Harry her son, and Helene are watched and guarded by more than *one* pair of eyes, Murdoch Polruth, and, if I guess right, an evil hour has befallen them. It was of this I came to speak to-night. I fear no officers on my track, they cannot harm *me*, but I came as a man to warn you and put you on your guard."

"Who art thou, then, that seems to know so much?"

"Thy friend," said the stranger, approaching the light, and throwing off his heavy covering, and smiling at the astonished innkeeper."

"Paul Adair!"

"The same."

"Some said you were dead, Paul, yet it was but the other night the wreckers told me you had taken a splendid prize but spared the passengers."

"So I did. I captured as fine a yacht as ever tipped the seas, the fastest craft, good Murdoch, that sails around these islands. The passengers were noble, and returning from Italy; they had much riches on board, both in gold and silks. I kept all; but, as I stepped upon the deck, they made sure myself and men were bent on bloodshed.

"Several noble ladies knelt before me and begged for mercy; one, a young and lovely girl of sixteen summers, clasped my rough, weather-beaten hands, and kissing them, begged the lives of all, while her grey-haired father, sword in hand, would have rushed upon me, but was withheld by my men.

"My heart was softened, for, as I looked at the young and tender form of Leona, with flowing raven ringlets, bedewing my hands with tears, I forgot all feelings of revenge for their stout resistance and spared them all.

"I landed them safely down the coast, and begged Leona's miniature, which she willingly granted. I repainted the pretty craft, and set sail for home, and had scarcely anchored her safely up No Man's Nook when I espied the stranded galliot which brought me here!"

"Strange adventures, Paul Adair!"

"Yes, and Paul Adair hath stranger work in hand. Listen!" said he, addressing Murdoch in whispers, which lasted some time; at the conclusion of which he said aloud, with clenched hand raised on high, "If I do but prove it, if Penalvon is what I expect, let him tremble, for I will watch him and dog him both day and night, and nought shall content me until I see the last of his upstart, merciless-ruling race."

"Paul," said Polruth, "this stormy night portends evil. I cannot rest ; methinks I hear strange wild cries upon the heath. My mind is restless ; there are weird forms passing before my eyes, struggling with the wind and waves down by the Seal's Cover."

"Nay, nay, good Polruth ; Wild Thyra's spells have not possessed thee? Come, drink again ; drink deep. Give me thy trusty hand. Seal thy mouth to all ; whate'er befalls, whate'er you hear, know nothing, say nothing ; and, until I return, be patient ; Paul Adair hath a part to play. Until I return, farewell!"

"Farewell," said Polruth, as he led him to the door, and saw him muffled up again, and go forth into the inky darkness and pitiless wind and rain that encompassed and swept the wild and dreary heath.

CHAPTER XXII.

EARL PENALVON AND HIS UNWELCOME GUEST.

"Who rings at this unseemly hour?" said Earl Penalvon, as he sat before his library fire, with slippered feet on an ottoman, and costly wines and choice viands at his elbow on a silver service. "Who can it be? I heard my hounds bay loudly in the court-yard and suddenly cease. It cannot be the trusty Thorkil, for he is now far upon the waves with my priceless prize, safely cabined, on her way to France. Ah, Rose!" he muttered, meditatively, "you know not how I adore you ; but a few days shall elapse ere I clasp you to my breast!"

And with infinite self-satisfaction this reckless nobleman sipped his costly wines, and smacked his lips, with all the gusto of a voluptuary and libertine.

"Come in!" he said, in response to a knock at the door. "Come in! Tranter, who was that who rang?"

"A stranger, my lord, who persists in seeing you."

"His name?"

"He gave none, and refused to say."

"How was he dressed, and what was his manner? that of a seaman?"

"No, my lord, he had the air of one above those in the village, and was heavily coated and muffled, with a slouched hat over his eyes."

"He would not give a name nor in anywise disclose himself? Then I cannot see him, Tranter. Tell him to state his business and call to-morrow ; if it be the good honest Thorkil admit him at once."

"'Twas not he! 'Tis quite a young man, who insists on seeing my lord, and takes no refusal."

"Was he armed, say you? Did he ride hither or not?"

"He came on foot, my lord, and was so wrapped up that I could not tell whether he was armed or not."

"Then I cannot see him, Tranter. Tell him to call at ten a.m. to-morrow ; I shall have risen by that hour, and will see him. 'Tis strange that any lowly-born stranger should dare to call at this late hour, and in this frightful storm of wind and rain. Go, tell him to begone, and look you well to this stranger, for one who could pass the park gates and approach my very door, despite hounds and servants, is no sort of person to let go unwatched. Dismiss him, instantly."

The servant departed.

The hall-door slammed, and the night wind whistled down the chimney with moaning sound.

Lightning flashed round the old baronial hall in fiendish fury.

Rain dashed in torrents against the library windows, and the window-frames rattled, as if countless spirits of the storm were shrieking outside and rattling them in unrestrained fury.

Penalvon moved restlessly in his capacious, luxurious chair.

Strange thoughts passed his troubled, though unruffled, brow.

Still the winds howled fiercely, more fiercely than ever.

Chimney-tops tottered and fell with crashing sound into the stone-paved courtyard, while lofty beech and ash trees swayed and moaned and rustled together.

Branches cracked and fell, and the fierce, unabating storm ruled with wild riot, until, as Earl Penalvon stood gazing through the window at the storm-beaten landscape, and heard the distant heavy moaning of the wild Atlantic, roaring and tossing in the heavy gale, a sudden gleam of lightning flashed athwart his astonished gaze, struck a Mammoth tree that swayed its lofty branches stories high, and the grand old tree was suddenly lighted with the stormy fluid, and shook and trembled, and fell crashing in the courtyard with the sounds of thunder.

"What a dreadful night," said Penalvon, restlessly pacing his cosy library.

At that same moment a terrific clap of thunder burst with deafening sounds over head, which seemed to shake the mansion to its very foundation.

He sank into his chair, over-burdened with conflicting thoughts.

"How fares the barque to-night upon the waters?" said Penalvon. "No, it cannot be that harm's befallen her. Ah, Rose, ere long thou shalt succumb to my long entreaties!"

"Never!" resounded through his chamber like an echo from the grave.

"Was that the wind that moaned so ominously? It must be, and yet that sound struck my heart as cruelly as steel. I will get me to bed, and to-morrow learn tidings of trusty Penreal."

He rose from his chair, and crossed the room ; he looked nervously about as one whose conscience was troubled with crime.

He saw no one, yet he felt the presence of an unknown indefinable power.

He paced the floor and stopped to listen.

All were a-bed, except himself; of all in his vast mansion no one stirred but himself.

The winds gradually died, and he heard the sounds of his own footfalls echo through the library.

He felt as if spirits of evil dogged his footsteps.

He turned.

There stood before him some unknown, whose slouched hat and muffled form filled him with alarm.

"Who art thou?" he tremblingly inquired, leaning on the table for support. "Be thou of the living or the dead that ye stand there motionless, unbidden here in the secrecy of my chamber?"

"Of the living, Penalvon! I know thy secret thoughts!" the figure replied, still motionless, and with solemn voice. "I go and come unbidden, as free as thought that keep thee sleepless at this late hour."

Penalvon listened in evident alarm.

He looked about the apartment for a weapon but none was at hand.

"Seek not your sword," the muffled stranger said, "stand as thou art on peril of life, and listen. Rose Halliard——"

"Well, what know ye of her?" the Earl breathlessly inquired.

"Whom thou wouldst decoy and destroy—is safe."

"In France, say you, in France?"

"In England."

"And, Thorkil, what of him?"

"Beware, old man, beware; there are those who know more of thee and thine than I do."

"Thou art not—nay, it cannot be Trelawny."

"How quickly the devil prompts thee, unhappy wretch. Far be it that I should be he; but still I am one, who, should I prove it on thee, will weigh far more heavily on thy mind than his blood-stained memory."

"Who art thou, then?" asked Penalvon, with livid face, biting his lips with rage.

"I am the 'Rover.'"

"If money you want, name the sum."

"Curse thee and thy money both, thou hast cursed some already with thy blighting coin. Can gold or silver buy me, think'st thou? I could give thee money as honestly obtained as thine. I come not for that, but to simply say, Earl Penalvon, 'Beware!' I come to warn thee. Remember me, 'The Rover.'"

Before the astonished nobleman could recover his senses the intruder had gone.

His sudden mysterious appearance was startling, the equally sudden and inexplicable disappearance was astounding.

As if waking from lethargy and stupor, the Earl looked first to the right then to the left, as one demented.

Suddenly aroused, he rushed to a cabinet, seized a long, bright rapier, and with lamp in hand he searched the room, plunging his weapon furiously through the window curtains, fire screens and arras, in every nook and corner where it was possible a man might hide.

"Not here!" he said, opening an adjoining apartment; "he was mortal and must be somewhere hid. I'll slay him like a rat!" continued he violently ringing the bell, and arousing his household.

"Bring lights! quick! arm yourselves to the teeth! There are thieves and cut-throats in the house; follow me," continued the half-frantic Earl.

The servants armed themselves as best they could with pokers, tongs, brooms, rusty swords, and followed their master, who led the way into every room and plunged his rapier into beds and couches, through and through.

The women folk screamed and rushed about from place to place, imagining a thousand horrors, and tumbling over each other in the dark, until—what with the infuriated master and his male servants cursing, the cries, and moans and groans of the females, and the barking and baying of dogs and hounds, now let loose into the house, frightening, chasing to and fro, and fighting numerous cats—there was a perfect Babel of confusion and noise.

After hours of excitement and search nought was found, and the breathless servants in their night-clothes retired once more, not to sleep, but to lie awake imagining a thousand horrors.

One valiant servant undertook to stay up all night on the watch.

Another one, fancying he heard stealthy footsteps, left his chamber, and poked about the long, dark passages on a similar errand, for my Lord Penalvon had offered fifty pounds reward for the capture of the unknown intruder.

These two worthies, unaware, fell foul of each other, and a terrible fight ensued between them in the dark, each pounding away for dear life, and shouting at the top of his voice until the entire household, again aroused, went forth to the rescue, and found both combatants tight in mutual embrace, struggling and kicking and cursing on the floor, until the arrival of lamps threw light upon the scene, when oaths from Penalvon and jeers from their fellows rewarded them for injudicious vigilance and imaginary horrors.

CHAPTER XXIII.

DAN CRAWLEY AND HARLECK DO A LITTLE GROWLING—EVIL RESOLVES—FRANK HAILS A FRENCH CONVOY IN SIGHT—IS COMPLIMENTED BY HIS CAPTAIN—JUNIPER AND HAWSER ON THE LOOKOUT—A MIDNIGHT CHASE.

THE Thunderer had been repaired and undocked many weeks, and her original ship's crew, with few exceptions, had all faithfully reported for duty, so that when the gallant vessel put forth to sea once more, all things progressed happily and harmoniously on board.

Some of the men, it must be confessed, were loth to go aboard, for the temptations of shore life were so great that many could scarcely be councilled to tear themselves from taps, dancing-rooms, and the smiles of Jezebels who, in truth, having now fleeced the honest tars of all spare cash, were willing to part with their whilom lords.

The vigilance and persuasion of petty officers had their effect, however, and, as boat loads of noisy tars put off from the jetty to the Thunderer that lay at moorings with the blue peter flying, they gave hearty and boisterous cheers for those they left behind.

Among the many pressed men who, by dint of much begging, had obtained short leave, none was more trusted than Harleck. Yet, dark and morose and unconfiding, he roamed about Seawardine unresolved and purposeless.

Suspicions began to attach to his uncommunicative manner, when, by command of Frazer and other officers, he was closely watched, and was one of the very last to report himself for duty.

Dan Crawley, the sneak, had contemplated desertion, as also did the cockney Tony Wilks, but Joe Juniper and Bill Hawser, like true tars, obeyed the orders of their officers, and kept "a bright look out" on them, and had them aboard long before any one else.

It was a calm night, and the ship under easy sail was cruising off the French coast, when Dan Crawley, sidling up to Harleck, began conversation by observing,

"Ah, Mr. Harleck, 'kissing goes by favor,' they say; don't it? It would be a long time before you or me could walk the quarter-deck if we hadn't friends."

Harleck looked over the side, and, squirting tobacco-juice, growled out some response, not very complimentary to officers generally.

"Yes, true, Mr. Harleck; it's just as I've always heard you say. Just to fancy that that fair-faced little skip-jack should be dressed up with a dirk at his side to order sech as you and me about!"

"Every dog has his day."

"True! so they has; and so shall we. I should like to jest trip him overboard some dark night when we're aloft reefing; it's too bad to think of the likes of him being over sech as we, and, I hear, he's no real gent's son, either."

"A wolf's cub," answered Harleck, between his teeth; "but we musn't talk too loud—he's an officer now," he added, "and I don't forget old scores."

"No, indeed; nor should I if I was served out as he served you."

Harleck shrugged his shoulders impatiently, as if the memory of his flogging rankled in his very soul, and grinding his teeth, he muttered, with an ill-suppressed oath,

"I'll be even with the whelp yet."

Conversing in low suppressed tones while on watch, Crawley, Harleck, and Tony sat crouched under the shadows of the weather bulwarks, while the bright, pale moon shed lustrous beauty on the splashing, flashing waves, that rose with majestic swell and struck the quarter of the noble ship, which rose and fell as gracefully as a swan to every undulation of the mighty deep.

"Sail ho!" sung out the look-out, high aloft.

The news seemed to awaken the curiosity of all the watch, for every one strained his eyes over the moonlit sea in search.

"Mr. Halliard, go aloft, sir, take the glass, and see what she's like."

"Aye, aye, sir," was the response, and the gallant, agile, and graceful young middy ran aloft as nimbly as a cat, and was soon lost in the snowy canvas that puffed and filled with the gently rising wind.

"What an active little devil he is, lieutenant," remarked Armitage to Frazer, who now came on deck. "He seems to require neither sleep nor rest, he's always wide awake, and ready for any duty. Such a lad cannot fail to rise rapidly in such stormy times as these."

"Pass the word, Juniper. What does Mr. Halliard say?"

"A Frenchman, sir, cruising off Havre. Mr. Halliard says, sir, he thinks there are more in company —it looks like a convoy."

"Ask him, Juniper, how far out they are, and whether they are making sail westward."

"Aye, aye, sir."

"Well, Juniper, how many, and what are their bearings?"

"Five in all, sir—twenty knots—sou'-sou'-west of the headland—steering west."

"They are ours, Mr. Armitage," said Frazer, rubbing his hands. "'Bout ship!" said he. "Thank goodness, it's getting cloudy. Now we can give chase without attracting their attention."

"'Bout ship! Make all sail. Frenchmen in sight," and with a hearty good will, the watch soon let out every reef, and the freshening three-quarter breeze filled the snow-white canvas, as the Thunderer dashed through the waves with increasing speed.

The Frenchman and his convoy were far to windward, and were perfectly invisible as the clouds gathered; but the captain and officers well knew whither they were bound, and trusted for the morning's light to take more correct bearings.

"Who was the 'look-out,' Mr. Halliard?" asked the captain, Sir Everard Brandon, coming on deck, and scanning the horizon with his glass.

"Frank Rayner, sir," answered Harry, with much satisfaction, feeling proud to have it in his power to say a good word for Frank.

"What a pair of eyes the boy must have," said the captain, wiping his glasses, and looking long and intently to the south-south-west. "Pass the word for Rayner."

Soon that young sailor approached the quarter-deck, where stood Sir Everard, Lieutenant Frazer, and Lieutenant Armitage, in subdued conversation, with Harry a short distance respectfully apart.

Taking off his cap with a low, sweeping bow, he scraped his right foot in the approved style of all jolly salts, and stood, blushing and embarrassed, before them.

"Bearing westward, do you say, boy; five sail, and one like a fifty-gun frigate? You are sure of that, youngster?"

"Yes, sir. I saw 'em but a moment, your honour. They looked as if they had just tacked from the south, for they were not under full sail until I saw them the second time."

"Very well, Rayner, if my suspicions turn out to be true, I'll make a note of it. I am glad to see our lads have their eyes open. I often think that Mr. Halliard, and his old chum, Rayner, are a couple of young hawks, for they can see in any weather," remarked Sir Everard, in subdued tones, to his lieutenant. And then, aloud, "Go to your hammock, Rayner. That will do. I shall leave the deck, Mr. Frazer, and if the chase proceeds satisfactorily let me know instantly. This may prove to be the important convoy which Admiral Nelson advised me of ere we sailed from Falmouth. Press on all possible canvas, and don't let them escape your vigilance. Place reliable men in the fore and main, and report as soon as possible.

"Pass the word for Juniper and Hawser," said Frazer, when the captain had gone below.

"I'll go, sir," said Halliard, advancing respectfully, with a smile on his face, "if you wish it."

"They've turned in, sir," said Konks.

"Never mind that," answered Lieutenant Frazer, tartly. "Go, Mr. Halliard, and rouse the old sea-dogs, and tell them to come to my cabin immediately."

"Aye, aye, sir!" said Harry.

And in a twinkling he was below, and slapping his old friends heartily, aroused them.

In a few minutes these two weather-beaten heroes, cap in hand, were in Frazer's cabin.

"Here, men, take a good stiff glass of old Jamaica, and go aloft. Keep a sharp look out for the French convoy. There's plenty of prize money in store."

Gulping down their grog, their faces, which before had worn an air of great concern and surprise, turned into a broad grin, and taking an enormous chaw of tobacco, those brave old salts mounted aloft quickly, and scanned the waters far and near.

"Did yer see him skipping about, Harleck?" asked Crawley.

"Aye, lad, I did."

"Well, it won't always be so, will it? I shan't Mister him, if all the rest do. Stop till I get him on shore one of these dark nights, and Mr. Halliard will be found——"

"Found where?" asked Harleck, grinning maliciously.

"Oh, nowhere particular," said Dan, with a sneaking, cowardly leer.

"You'd break his dear mammy's heart," said Harleck, gruffly, "and you wouldn't do that, I know."

"In course not. Hullo! what's the mast-head saying?" asked Crawley, as he heard a voice aloft.

"Five sail in sight, sir!" shouted Juniper, with stentorian lungs, to the officer on the quarter-deck.

"Fifty-gun frigate, two armed brigs, and two merchantmen, did he say, Mr. Halliard?"

"Steering sou'-sou'-east—ten miles!"

"Tacked again, have they? Then Hawser was right, for he said they looked as if bound for the Spanish coast. A point or two west, sir," said he to the sailing-master. "And, helmsman, we must not let them find out our intentions. Did Juniper see their colours, Mr. Armitage?"

"No, sir; but he knows them to be Frenchmen by the cut of their jib."

"Very well, we shall be close on to them before daylight, and if I am not much mistaken we shall have a tough job ere we make them strike their colours."

The chase was exciting.

It seemed impossible that the Frenchmen could make out the object of the Thunderer, for the night was cloudy, and it was but by fits and starts, when gusts of wind swept the ocean, that the look out at the fore and main could catch a glimpse of them, and by trimming the Thunderer's sails more or less like the French, and by standing off and on the coast, the cunning of Lieutenant Frazer's tactics were such as to mislead the ships ahead, if even they had discovered a chase.

"Let the guns be double shotted," was the last order given, "and at the signal let every man be found at his post; there's warm work in store ere long, and death or glory for more than one."

"Death or glory for more than one!" thought Harry, as he left the deck to snatch an hour's sleep.

"Death or glory for more than one," thought Frank, "well let it come, I'm ready, victory or Westminster Abbey, as our admiral says. Frank Rayner, it may be your turn to-morrow."

CHAPTER XXIV.

EARL PENALVON UPBRAIDS THORKIL — MIDNIGHT MEETING AT THE SHAG ROCK—ANGRY ALTERCATION—THORKIL TREMBLES AT UNKNOWN SOUNDS—PENALVON ENCOUNTERS A SPIRIT OF THE STORM—HE TREMBLES AT ITS WORDS, AND SINKS PROSTRATE—THE MYSTERY.

I dreamed a dream, and in this wise I saw
A sea that roared at midnight round a land
   Unknown of men,
And far above the surf a spar of rock
Stretched out, that trembled with the ceaseless shock
   Of thundrous waves.
And suddenly, from out the hollowed doom
Of night, in terrible succession, came
Three fierce, long-lingering, jagged streams of flame,
And by the first I saw that on the cape
Of those black rocks sat one that had the shape
As of a woman; tresses long and fair
   Of raven hair,
The storm wind never-ceasing, backward bore
Uplifted from a face and forehead more
   Than earthly fair.

         The Dream.

THE night was beautifully clear, and the stars shone out with unwonted brillancy.

The waves with moaning sound swelled and rolled upon the white pebbly strand, and the lights of the village twinkled forth upon the cliffs with romantic beauty.

Wild Thyra roamed abroad, restless and sad; none knew whither she had gone,—perhaps, few cared.

The girl's heart was beating with wildness and sorrow.

The spell was upon her, and she could not resist the impulse of her soul.

She was a waif of the sea, and thither "she flew to its billowy crest like a child that seeks its mother's breast."

Seawardine, the Seal's Cover, the Kiddle-a-wink, nor any other place had charms for her.

Upon the Shag Rock sat Thyra, in all her wild girlish beauty, looking forth upon the starlit sea, while the freshening breeze tossed her raven locks about her beautifully moulded and spotless shoulders.

With clasped hands she sat upon the Shag Rock, and, with a low moaning voice, sung snatches of songs.

Sometimes she leaned her head between her hands and sobbed convulsively, while again and again she looked furtively around towards the Seal's Cover, and seemed to listen.

It was nought but the winds, and still she listened.

No one was visible.

"It cannot be," she said; "they do not follow me! Yet, why do I tremble?"

As if assured of All-powerful protection, she knelt upon the sand, and, lifting up her hands, breathed forth a weird, wild prayer.

While thus she knelt the sound of footsteps was heard crumpling upon the shore.

She smiled with content and happy face, and with a graceful, girlish, agile motion, tripped to a hiding-place among the clefts rent in the rocks by the tides and tempests of centuries.

Two men approached.

The footsteps of the first were heavy, slow, and regular.

The other's footfalls were light and buoyant.

They stopped at the Shag Rock, and began to speak.

"It cannot be, Thorkil, that a man like you should fear the ravings of a silly girl. You are not the man to tremble at trifles; you, who lure ships on to destruction, and live on a wrecker's spoil ; you, who, as a part smuggler, have had your neck in the noose for the past twenty years, are not the one to quail at a maniac's ravings. I'll not believe it, and I'm sorely tried to disbelieve you."

"Nay, you are hard upon me, Earl Penalvon. You speak as though you could harm me ; yet, recollect, my lord, *I* did not commence this business ; *I* did not first call on *you!* 'Tis strange, if I am all you say, that a lord, that the great Earl Penalvon, should seek the aid and secret service of the 'man-killer, the ship allurer, half smuggler, half pirate,' that you would paint me !"

"I'll have no more of this."

"Nor *I!*"

"Nor *you?*"

"No, until I hear more of it. If it concerns you so much, it concerns me ; at least, a little, to know what you intend both to me and her ?"

"To deceive her, and hang you !" was Penalvon's thought; but he answered, "Nay, nay, good Thorkil, I was passionate ; I said too much. But, this I will tell you, the visit of the 'Rover,' as he styled himself, and concurrent incidents, makes an impression on me like one that's committed crime."

"A guilty conscience wants no accusers, I've heard," said Thorkil, doggedly, smoking a pipe, and ruminating. "But no offence is meant, my lord ; all I meant to say is this, my pretty Foam has been stranded, and the wrecked timbers lie all about the strand."

"Well, what of that ? Have you no friend to lend you one until I can get you another and a better ? Nay, I promise you, if you accomplish this one thing for me, I'll get you the fastest schooner upon the water, and give a thousand pounds beside."

"It's a bargain," cried Thorkil, wildly ; "consider the thing done ; ere this time next week she is caged."

"You promise ?"

"I do."

"Will not fail ?"

"If I do, if I take note once again of all the runers on the coast, then may Earl Penalvon hang me on the tallest tree at Seawardine for——"

"What makes you turn pale, Thorkil ? what strange sound was that I heard ?"

Thorkil spoke not, but as he gazed on the pale moon rising from the sea, he sank upon a ledge of the rock, and listened as if he heard voices from the spirit world.

Again and again a low, wailing, melancholy voice broke upon the air, as if communing with the other world.

Thorkil looked at Penalvon, who seemed awe-struck.

"Let us go from here," he said, impatiently.

"Don't go yet, my lord," said Thorkil, musing ; "I know that Earl Penlavon has nothing on his conscience to cause terror or reproach."

"I will not stay, Thorkil ; what are these strange unearthly sounds ? Why brought you me here ?"

"That we might be beyond the ears of any one ; but do not go yet, it is only some runer's voice. Come, stay."

"Not one moment, Thorkil. Come. I feel faint ; your arm. Curse the runers, whence come these plaintive soul-emitting sounds ?" but as he hurried away a fay-like form in white danced about the sands, and the moonlight, falling on her pallid face and form, shed a ghastly lustre upon her as she, witch-like, danced before them, fast disappearing in the shadows of the mainland.

"Stay, Thorkil, one moment, stay. Your pistol ; let me fire and kill the witch."

Instead of fleeing at his words, the wild form stood still with outstretched arms.

Penalvon faltered.

The more he gazed upon that spirit-like form the more he trembled.

He lifted his hand.

Biting his lips, and turning livid with anger and fear, he fired.

The form screamed out aloud, "Your brother !"

"Give me the other pistol, in mercy ; the other, Thorkil, or I shall stifle with rage."

He fired a second time.

The unknown, motionless form stood as fixedly as ever, and shrieked out,

"Your wife !"

Horror-stricken, he rushed forward.

He advanced a few yards, and his courage failed him.

He quailed before the pale, outstretched hands.

In desperation he threw the empty pistol forward, and sank with exhaustion upon the sand, when the voice shrieked out,

"Walter Halliard !" and amid peals of demoniacal, derisive laughter that echoed among the rocks, disappeared like a thing of air.

CHAPTER XXV.

THE WRECKERS PREPARE FOR A RICH HAUL—THE UNFORTUNATE COCKNEY ON HORSEBACK—HYLDA'S WARNING—THE PHANTOM SCHOONER—AWFUL EXPLOSION ON THE WHITE CLIFF—CONSTERNATION OF THE WRECKERS.

"Black as death the sky above,
  Black the sea below ;
Now and again the jagged flame,
Suddenly out of the darkness came,
  With a moment's purple glow ;
Now athwart the hollow dark,
Printing clear a lurid arc,
  A dread illumination."

THORKIL seemed possessed with dread.

Some unknown influence hung over him which he could not shake off.

Hylda's presence was repulsive to him, and he dreaded meeting her, for of late she had sat before the cavern fire, rocking to and fro upon a stool, and with a pot-stick made all manner of figures upon the wood ashes on the hearth.

"Runing again, wife ?" said he, gruffly, seating himself near the cheerful blaze ; "runing again ? By my soul, everybody is runing now ! Why, that goggle-eyed fool in the cave, there, has taken to it at last, and I daresay *he'll* try to frighten us next !"

"Penreal !"

"Why do you speak in that hellish, guttural tone ?"

"Penreal !"

"Well, how many more times will you repeat my d——d name ? What of him ? Speak, if you will ; not all the devils in Hell can frighten me now !"

"Thorkil, is there not blood enough on thy hands already ? Would you double dye, and eternally damn thyself and me ?"

Hylda stirred not from her stool, but looked up at him with eyes that glared with unearthly brilliancy.

He had never seen her look so haggard before,

and never had gazed on aught half so eloquent and terrible as the pale, calm agony that sat upon her brow.

He drank deeply, and doggedly puffed at his pipe.

"Go not out to night," she said, calmly gazing at the glowing embers. "There is a craft in sight that brings no good to thee."

"Avast with your hellish gag!" cried he, tossing off a horn of rum. "Wrecking is my trade, and so let's have no more on't."

"Go not out to-night, Penreal!" she again repeated.

"What would you have me do, she-devil? Must I put on petticoats, and mind the pots?—to stay here and hearken to thy runing, and hear strange noises, strange voices ringing through these stone vaults all night."

"Strange voices! aye, strange sights, too, Thorkil."

"Well, well, we're all going to the devil fast enough," said Thorkil, angrily; "when we're wanted I suppose we must go. Hullo! who's that calling? You snivelling swab!" (addressing the unfortunate emaciated Theophilus, in an adjoining recess) "don't you hear me? Who's that, I say? Answer me, or I'll trample your life out! Master Agger, is it? Then tell him I'll come immediately. How now, my hearty! It's many a day since we've had any business on hand; and say you that a richly-laden schooner is weathering the point? Then, ere many hours, we must try it she can't be grounded somewhere hereabouts. How does she look?"

"Oh, labouring—breasting and beating against it; but it's no use, she will be sure to strand, if we're careful."

"Why, what a land-lubber he is!" said Thorkil, looking through his glass from the top of the cliff. "He knows no more than that shrimp of a cockney, our powder-monkey. Well, well, blow winds; blow, and increase to a perfect hurricane. Aye, Agger, it's all fish that comes to our net!"

"True," said Agger. "I've told all the lads to be at hand, as we expect a job to-night."

"Good! but have you got those powder-kegs ready for shipping?—have you had them in the sun to-day?"

"Aye, sir, twenty of 'em, and they are now at the foot of the white cliff, covered, ready at any moment when the Dutchman can run in and take 'em."

"Right, Agger, and see that the horse and lanterns are ready, for the storm is increasing every moment; and let all the lads be on the beach by nightfall."

When Agger departed Thorkil's brow seemed to gather and contract in anger, as he gazed on Hylda crouching near him.

He would have spoken, but filling a goblet of rum he quaffed it off at a draught and went to the kiddle-a-wink to gather his men, muttering and half humming,

"A wind arose from out the west,
    At setting of the sun ;
A fair wind for the homeward bound,
    The voyage was nearly done.
The schooner answered to the breeze,
    The sails were full, and now,
At every wave, the silver spray
    Come sprinkling o'er the bow."

Darkness was fast closing in.

Heavy shadows began to muffle the labouring schooner.

The foaming track that she left behind was changing from purest snow to phosphorescent silver.

As minutes flew the night grew darker.

Sea and sky were wrapped in gloom.

Shadows intensified, and the air grew thicker.

There is something awful in the idea of a ship on the stormy sea at night, no matter how secure she may be thought to be—a small frail section of life floating in darkness, between sea and sky, death and eternity.

The winds were now thoroughly aroused, and whistled and howled through the rigging.

The captain of the schooner, as he neared the dangerous coast, was calm, and gave his orders lustily as the gale increased in vehemence, while his crew, with every confidence in their chief, silently obeyed, and with cheerful alacrity.

"Does she near the Shark's Fin?" Agger asked Thorkil, as he stood on the cliff, "then we must signal her."

"Where's that land-crab of ours? You, you lob? Come here, goggled-eyed imp of darkness. Can you ride?"

"Oh, Master Thorkil, be merciful, I beseech you. Incarcerate me, perforate me with cannon balls; but in your gweat might, pwease have mercy!" cried Lobb, the unfortunate Cockney.

"You know how to hunt, do you, you son of a retired fishmonger? Well, we've got a horse for you this time. Ah, Agger, that beats them all. Come, my lads, bring the lantern to the nag. Now, you long-legged sand-crane, mount, I say, and quick, there's no time to lose."

"But, pwease, Mr. Thorkil, there's no saddle, and the animal's wertebway is like a knife."

"I hope it will cut you in two, then; mount, I say, or I'll send a bullet through your noddle before you can say Jack Robinson."

Theophilus mounted the animal, and was immediately pitched into a pool of water.

He received sundry hearty kicks from Agger and Thorkil for his awkwardness, and was again mounted, and tied on to the bony, hobbling nag, while the spray dashed over, and thoroughly drenched him.

Up and down the beach the unfortunate Cockney rode, with lantern dangling before and behind him, while Agger and other wreckers were busy in decoying the schooner, which momentary flashes of lightning revealed to be buffetting the angry billows.

"How does she ride, Agger?" shouted Thorkil, full of excitement.

"Gradually drifting, sir. Shall I fire the rockets, sir?"

"Thorkil! Penreal!" shouted a voice, audible above the storm of wind and waves. "Thorkil! Penreal! On her mainsail she bears a large black cross. Thorkil, beware!"

"Curse the hag, whoever she be! Yes, Agger, fire the rockets; and if that whining hound won't force the horse along, why give him a dig and stop his mumbling noise for ever."

"How does she look?" asked Thorkil, shading his eyes, and peering through the spray-splashed gloom.

"Strange craft, sir; large black cross on her mainsail."

"Wave the lamps again. Does she strike?"

"Yes!" said some, "no!" said others; and still the winds blew with increasing fury, and the waves dashed against the jutting rocks, throwing up heaps of seaweed.

"Does she ground, lads?" asked Aggar.

"She does!" cried Thorkil, in ecstasy.

"No, sir," said others.

CROSSING THE LINE.

"She brought full up in the wind, tacked, and is weathering the point beautifully," said one, admiring the schooner-captain's splendid seamanship.

"Beautifully! does she?" growled Thorkil, aiming a pistol at the speaker's head.

The shot missed.

"Curse her! curse the schooner!" cried Thorkil, enraged; "fire our long twelve, Agger, and sink her. We'll have her yet, we'll sink her first. All's fair in war."

No sooner said than done.

Agger accurately pointed the cannon from the cliff; its booming report reverberated among the hills, and its shot went screaming through the darkness, towards the little white speck of a vessel, that danced like a nutshell on the waves.

"Struck her, Agger, or did you miss, curse you?" shouted Thorkil, stamping like an infuriated demon.

"Don't know, sir, yet."

"Does she sink?" continued Penreal, excitedly, perspiration flowing from his brow in sheer anxiety and anger.

"No, sir, she tacks," cried several, "and is bearing down on the point again, right in the wind's eye."

To the astonishment of all, the schooner had tacked, and when abreast of the Fin, she discharged her port gun, and the shot passed completely through the horse, knocking the Cockney fully twenty feet, but not hurting him otherwise.

"Hullo!" shouted Thorkil, "this is something new. Weathers the storm, weathers the point, tacks and opens broadsides, eh? It can't be the revenues—they haven't pluck enough."

Before he could utter another word—and as the wreckers, giving up all hope of gaining a prize, and sorely puzzled at the manœuvres of the mysterious schooner, sat in groups conversing at the foot of the White Cliff, and watching the movements of the wonderful spell-bound craft dancing on the waves a hundred yards away on the turgid waters—a second flash illumined her sides, and a shell went screaming over their heads, and fell among the twenty kegs of powder which Agger had placed there for shipment.

The explosion that followed can be imagined not described.

The sudden crash!—the fearful roar and the deafening sounds of falling rock and mounds of earth was appalling; yet, before the astonished, terrified, electrified, and stupefied wreckers could awake from the stupor in which they stood apparently transfixed to the earth, the crew of the little schooner gave three derisive cheers, hoisted some unknown colours, and sped away upon the black and stormy billows like a creature of life, and floated from the ken of eye like a phantom ship with a ghastly crew.

CHAPTER XXVI.

JOEL, LUCY, AND NELLY BRITTON HAVE AN IMPORTANT CONVERSATION—PAUL ADAIR AND THE MAGNANIMOUS EARL PENALVON — NELLY RUNS INTO THE SNARE.

"Young and lovely, sad and lonely,
    Watching by the dying fire;
Fair, but wan with waiting, dreaming
    Bygone dreams that never tire."

"Why, Nelly, my daughter, why hang thy head in sorrow?" asked old Joel Britton, as he sat by his cheerful fire, smoking.

"I did not say I was so, father dear," Nelly answered, looking up into his face, with a quiet smile.

"Nay, but I know it, for wife and I have had a long talk about it, and we've come to the conclusion to marry thee!"

"Marry me?"

"Aye! Is there aught very terrible in that, lass? All girls have more or less thoughts of that, much as ye blush, ye little saucy, rosy-faced minx."

"Nay, I shall never marry, father," said Nelly, putting her arms affectionately about his neck, and kissing him. "I could never think of leaving you and mother alone in this lonely house."

"Oh, yes you will, you little puss, one of these days, I know."

"No, father, I have vowed to be an old maid—that is my lot!" she added, with a sigh. "I am very happy and contented as I am."

"But wife and I know a man as'll make you more happy and comfortable than we can. Don't we, wife?"

"Nay, father," said Lucy, intent upon her knitting, "I knows naught about it. I think that Nell has more thought about sweethearts than she lets on, if old folks' eyes don't deceive 'em. I did hear that she was once moon-struck about that romping, tearing, smuggling fellow, Paul Adair; but I should think she has forgotten all about him by this time."

The colour rose and fell upon Nelly's cheek, as she sat silently looking at the glowing embers, and her heart beat quick and violently.

"Nay, let's have no tears, Nell, lass. Mother and I wouldn't force thee, thou knows; only we were saying t'other night, that there's more nor one youngster well to do, as would like to drop in once in a while, and have a chat wi' thee. Paul Adair has gone off, none knows where. There have been strange stories about him, down at Murdoch's."

"Has there, father?" asked Nelly, interested.

"Nothing good, father, I know," said the wife. "Thou'rt too fond of going down to the kiddleawink. No good'll come of it, mark my word; mixing among wreckers, and smugglers, and pirates, and cut-throats, ain't the thing for a respectable married man like thee to do. Thou knows what the great lord told thee t'other day, when thou fastened his horse's shoe."

"Aye, I do, wife; but I doesn't mind what he says. There's just as good men to king and country as drink rum at Polruth's, as he who swallows bottles of wine at the Hall."

"Well, that's neither here nor there, Joel Britton. Thou knows he said that a single twist of his thumb would hang all the wreckers to-morrow."

"Aye, aye, wife, he says more nor he means, does the lord; but I think he'd have a tidy job like in swinging up all Thorkil's gang. There be some big stout fellows among 'em as wouldn't stand nice about trifles if they know'd his game. But that's neither here nor there; we want to get Nell settled and comfortable, out of the way of everybody hereabouts, and so the sooner the better for us all, for she's only fretting and pining as it is."

"I don't want to be settled," answered Nelly, shrugging her shoulders.

"Come, come, lass, thou shalt choose for thyself; only let him be a good'un."

"There's the parson's clerk, now," said Lucy, laughing; "he's a very nice old gentleman, and I know that Nelly likes him."

Nelly frowned and blushed.

"Nay, nay, wife; jokes aside, lass, we've better than him. There's the Earl's butler; he's often asked after thee, and comes down here very often."

"I wouldn't have the Earl, nor the butler either!"

"Why not the Earl, lass? Why he came here no later than last week."

"'Good morning, Joel,' said he.

"'Good morning, my lord,' said I.

"'Just fasten on my horse's shoe,' said he.

"I did so.

"'Is that your daughter, Mr. Britton?' he asked, looking hard at Nelly, who rushed out of the forge into the house like a young hare.

"'It is, my lord,' I answered.

"'One of the most beautifully-developed girls I ever beheld,' he said, still looking at her standing at the house door. 'Magnificent eyes!' he said, putting up his eye-glass, and quizzing her for some time.

"'Yes, fine eyes, my lord; just like Lucy's, my wife's.'

"'And such luxuriance of hair,' he went on, walking about the forge as if in thought.

"'Yes, fine hair, my lord,' I said.

"And by that time his horse was ready; but still he stopped.

"'Mr. Britton,' said he, 'I never saw such symmetry of figure.'

"'Didn't you?' says I, pleased to hear him praise our Nell, for he's travelled all over the world wellnigh.

"'She carries herself like a queen,' he says.

"And, then, before he went, he gives me a five-pound note, and, says he,

"'Joel,' says he, 'give this, with my compliments, to Nelly, my Nelly,' said he, and smiling, waved his hand towards our lass here, and trots off.

"Two or three days after he comes down again to ask me about some cottages of his in Seawardine, and he invited me up there; and after we had some wine, and lots of good eating,

"'Britton,' says he, 'your Nelly is completely lost where she is; she can't improve herself at all.'

"'Oh, my lord!' I says, "Lucy teaches her everything!'

"'Yes, yes,' he says, 'I didn't mean that. You are not rich,' he says, 'and can't give your daughter anything in marriage; so, if you like, let her come up to Seawardine a few weeks to improve her in needlework and housekeeping. My housekeeper has taken a great fancy to her, and then she might go out to service, or become so accomplished as to be able to marry some respectable master trades-man.'

"'I'll tell wife on it, my lord,' says I; 'I'm very grateful.'

"'And if she is a good, wise girl, she shall stop as long as she likes, and I'll give her a hundred pounds to get married with.'

"I thanked his lordship and came home. Now, what do you think of that, wife?"

"I think it is a good offer for any girl to go and improve herself in such a grand house as that."

"Improve herself, wife; nay, you didn't see the lord's meaning, he's a widower and wants a nice wife, and he's clapped his eyes on Nell, and wants to get her up to the big house so as he can see more of her, that's it, wife, and marry her. What do you think of that, old woman?"

"Don't be silly, Joel," answered his wife, blushing, and slapping her husband gently in the face, "he don't mean naught about it. He sees Nell is a clean tidy girl, and he wants to improve her, like a good, kind gentleman, as he is, and if I was Nell, I should say yes, and go at once."

"What say you, daughter? Nay, don't blush, girl, there's no harm meant, either way."

"I should like to go up to the Hall for a few weeks, to learn under the housekeeper," said Nelly, thinking, in her secret heart, "it would be so nice to learn all kinds of things in needlework and cookery, for I know it would please Paul."

"But what did the folks at Polruth's say of Paul father?" inquired Nelly, with a blush upon her cheek.

"Say, lass! What didn't they say? All kinds of idle words, you may be sure."

"'He's gone wrecking on his own hook, down the coast,' said one.

"'No, he's been pressed into the navy,' said another.

"'I hear he has turned smuggler, and makes no end of money,' chimed in a third.

"'No, no, lads,' said some one, 'he's turned pirate; smuggling is too tame for the bold, high-handed, Paul Adair!'

"'Aye, he's turned pirate, lads, for certain, for one of the wreckers on the coast told me about it. He seized a schooner, and murdered the whole lot of 'em, so I heard.'

"'Nay, nay,' said Polruth, 'he's done naught of the kind. Paul never willingly shed blood in his life, I know, except in self-defence, and in that case, small blame to him, say I.'"

"Did Polruth say that?" asked Nelly, looking up with flushed cheek and sparkling eye. "I know he spoke the truth! Paul Adair would never stain his hands with murder. Let the world say what they will of him, they can only say that he's been a wrecker, at the very worst."

"Hillo! wench," said Joel, taking the pipe out of his capacious mouth, and rolling his eyes in surprise. "Hillo, Nell! dost thou defend him? I thought thou hadst better sense than interest thyself in such a scapegrace," and then winking significantly to his wife, added in an under tone, "Thou must forget all about the likes of him; thou'd better go to the Hall, and stay wi' housekeeper a month or two."

"Whether I go or stay, father," spoke Nelly, with a trembling voice, "it can never alter my opinion of Paul! He had no enemy but his own good-nature, and that shone forth on every occasion."

"Aye, he was a good-natured lad enough, lass; but he cared naught for thee, from what I've heard of his wild freaks."

"Nay, I did not say he did, father, dear," said Nelly, smiling.

"But he does care for somebody as I've heard of."

"Does he?"

"Aye, without doubt, and if he ain't careful he'll get himself hung ere long."

"Indeed!"

"Yes."

"To whom, then? Who is his lady-love?"

"It concerns not thee."

"I beg to know, father. Tell me do!" she added, changing colour. "What is her name?"

"I never heard only part on't."

"Where does she live, then?"

"That I don't know."

"Is she pretty?"

"Aye, so I've always heard."

"Indeed! And is she rich?"

"Ah, very rich; but he'll never get a penny of it."

"A fine lady?"

"Aye, an earl's daughter."

"An earl's daughter!" mused Nelly, scarcely repressing her tears from flowing.

"Aye, lass, no less; so there's no chance if thou loved him ever so much."

Nelly Britton sat, with her head between her hands, before the fire, and while thus shading her face, the tears flowed freely but unobserved.

Her thoughts were rambling, and she little heeded the conversation of her father and mother.

Her whole heart and soul were far away upon the sea, and when she rose she felt an altered girl.

A void was rent in her soul that could never be filled.

Her day dreams were shattered to the ground in one brief moment.

She loved and had been beloved.

All had proved false, and for the first time in life she looked upon the whole world as a wild, void waste, with no cherished spot to rest upon, with not a single heart in which to confide.

She retired to her humble chamber, and falling upon her knees, would have prayed as of yore for the absent mariner, but her heart was filled to overflowing with long pent and poignant sorrow, and bursting into floods of tears, she buried her head in the snow-white counterpane, on which the silvery moonlight fell, sobbing, with choking utterance,

"Paul, Paul! Oh, why have you deceived me?"

CHAPTER XXVII.

THE FATE OF ROSE HALLIARD—POLRUTH ALONE IN THE "THREE JOLLY MARINERS"—HE ENTERTAINS A SINGLE VISITOR—HE IS SPELL-BOUND, AND COMPELLED TO TELL HIS SECRET THOUGHTS ALOUD—THE WARNING.

MURDOCH sat alone in the tap of the "Three Jolly Mariners".

He puffed his pipe discontentedly, and hearkened to the wind and rain beating down the spacious chimney.

"Ugh!" he muttered, "another nasty night, and no company. The kiddle-a-wink is going to the dogs! Wonder what has become of all the lads? Not pressed, I hope."

Filling himself a good stiff glass of rum, he added slightly of boiling water from a miniature reservoir, which, in the form of a mammoth kettle, hung upon the hooks, steaming and spluttering away at a grand rate.

"Nasty night for travellers," he mused. "Who's that knocking at the door? Come in," he added, in a careless, boorish tone, "whoever ye are."

The latch was raised, and Thyra, more like a thing of air than earth, glided rather than walked to the fire, and unbidden took a stool and seated herself.

Thyra, beautiful Thyra, noticed nothing of Polruth's looks or words, but sat meekly looking at the blaze, her lustrous eyes and sweet pale face, contrasting in strange weird beauty with the raven, wavy hair which streamed over her shoulders.

With her romantic blue mantle thrown carelessly about her shoulders, exposing her faultlessly modelled arms, she sat musing, with a bunch of herbs in hand—sat, not like a thing of earth, but some strange, gifted, mysterious waif of another and a better world, doomed for a while to sojourn below to be scoffed at and unprized of men.

"Wilt eat, lass?" asked the rough landlord, charmed by the innocence and simplicity of the one before him; "if so, thou't welcome, Thyra!"

Thyra looked at him for a moment with a half wild, dreamy gaze, and shook her head slowly.

"Wilt drink, then?" Polruth continued, as if possessed with sudden generosity, or some unseen influence. "Here, drink this, Thyra," he said, pouring out a small glass of wine. "The wench looks pinched and starved. She belongs to all on us; we must all be fathers and mothers to her, that's all!" he thought.

"Thank you, Polruth," said Thyra, scarce wetting her lips, and resuming her steady gaze at the glowing embers.

"Any news at Thorkil's?"

"No; nothing of note."

"Hast heard of Paul?"

"I have."

"What of him?"

"Nothing; at least, not now."

"What news have ye, then, my lass? Don't be cross, girl, I can stand anything but thy cursed runing, and if thou wants to do aught of that, why then get thee on the heath, for I'll none of it in my house, Thyra. Thee and Hylda have turned all our heads with hobgoblin tales."

"Hobgoblin tales, Polruth! I could tell thee one you'd like to hear."

"Nay, I wouldn't, Thyra, so stop thy blab."

"Know ye, Trelawny?"

"Black Will?"

"The same."

"I do; what of him? We've never heard a word of him."

"I have."

"By post?"

"No."

"By coach?"

"No."

"By thy everlasting rune-kenning, I suppose, eh? Then I'll hear naught of it."

"But you must!"

"Must!"

"Aye, must."

Polruth took the pipe from his mouth with much surprise, and gazing round the tap, as if looking for a ghost, said again, "Must!" and sat like a dumb creature gazing at the sweet, pale, spiritual, upturned face, looking on him with expressionless child-like beauty.

"Yes, Polruth; you must hear me."

"Go on, Thyra; be quick."

"Heard you of the explosion at the White Cliff?"

"I did; and a pretty mess it made. Thorkil swears he's ruined. Twenty kegs of powder blown to the devil by a single shot; half the cliff tumbled down about his ears; his horse knocked into a thousand fragments; that Cockney land-lubber, blown to nowhere, and all through a single schooner."

"With a large black cross on its mainsail."

"Yes, so I hear; know ye whose or what it was? It couldn't have been a real craft, or she'd have gone to pieces a hundred times, so Agger says. It must have been the devil himself out on the spree, Thorkil says; for no ship in mortal hands could have behaved as she did."

"She only returned Thorkil's compliments in kind; he wished to lure it to destruction, and he was repaid for his pains. So may it always be," added Thyra; "it is an unholy trade."

"Be it so, girl; but I'd advise thee not to speak so to Thorkil."

"Yes to thee, or Thorkil, or any of them; none can harm me," said Thyra, scornfully and disdainfully.

"But what hath the schooner to do with Black Will?"

"Much."

"Is he captain?"

"No."

"Owner?"

"No."

"Is he on board, then?"

"No."

"Then how can'st thou know ought of him, or it?"

"Much you dream not of."

"I've had enough of runing, Thyra; I'll have no more of it in this place. I do verily believe that you and Hylda, by your spells and incantations, have robbed the 'Jolly Mariners' of all its good customers by this everlasting rune-kenning; I'll hear no more."

"You must. Black he is, by name and nature; for Trelawny is a houseless wanderer on the earth to-night, haunted and hunted by an evil conscience or winged spirits of the coast day and night. Last night, when you, Polruth, and your friends were making merry with songs, and tales and toasts, a haggard face looked in upon your revels through the window panes ! Do you remember, when you rose during an oppressive silence that suddenly came over all, and went to the window and started back ? What saw you ?"

" Who told you of this ?" asked Polruth, startled. " You were down by the White Cliffs."

" What saw you ?"

" The figure of one like Black Will: his hands were red with blood, and his face begrimed with dirt. But it was only fancy."

" Fancy ! Was it fancy what you saw the second time, in your chamber ?"

" Aye ; it couldn't be real, for he is dead and gone."

" Who ?"

" Walter Halliard; and there he stood beside my bed, as if in life. I know it was but a dream. Oh ! but so natural."

" Natural? Thou never saw'st him with a beaten brow, streaming with blood."

" Who told thee I did see him, then ; eh, Thyra ?" said Polruth, who seemed like one talking in his sleep, or charmed by the steady, earnest glare of Thyra's eyes.

" I tell thee."

Polruth drew back, but seemed spell-bound, nor lifted his eyes from the beautiful wild looks of her before him, as she said, with a calm authority he could not disobey,

" Well, and what saw you the *third* time ?"

Speaking as one unconscious, he muttered in suppressed tones, " I heard the barking of a dog outside. I opened the door, but none was there, yet, as I turned to look at the time of night, I saw poor Rose."

" Where ? Speak, quick, Polruth, where ?"

" I know not where. In dungeons deep below the earth ; not far, it seemed to me, but where I know not. But what of this ? why this silence ? Have you spell-bound me by thy cursed charms ?" cried Polruth, in alarm.

" No ! but listen. *I* have seen the same, so has Hylda. Trelawny has not yet finished his hellish career. Take heed and do not offend him ; his own crimes, like hungry bloodhounds, will run him down ere long, for he who hath wrought all this evil will himself fall into silken snares, and be helpless as a puling babe. The craft that baffled both wind and tide, that rode and rose triumphant with the storm, bears a spell-bound life ; it is The Phantom off this coast ; wherever it goes evil befalls evil doers, and good flows to the poor and kind.

" I can tell thee, Polruth, things that happen ; mayhap, things to come. I can but warn thee, I cannot prevent ; but, heed me," said the weird, wild girl in graceful attitude and childlike innocence of abandon, " heed me ! have no hand or voice in aught that Thorkil does. To night he is bent on deeds of blood, aided and abetted by several I could name, high and mighty in the land. But let them strive against fate, it will all come to naught, for this world is like a pebble in the palm of Omnipotence."

Noiselessly she departed.

Polruth, aroused from his lethargy, sat as if awakened from a dream.

CHAPTER XXVIII.

THE BOY SAILOR AND FRANK RAYNER DISTINGUISH THEMSELVES — THE CHASE — THE DENSE FOG — OPENING OF THE ENGAGEMENT—TERRIFIC BROADSIDES DELIVERED AND RECEIVED—LIEUTENANTS FRAZER AND ARMITAGE LEAD THE BOARDING PARTIES — JUNIPER AND HAWSER WITH TWO BOATS' CREWS MAKE AN IMPORTANT CAPTURE— THE LIFE OF SIR EVERARD BRANDON THREATENED —HE IS SAVED BY HARRY HALLIARD—FRANK IS WOUNDED—JUNIPER AND HAWSER ARE MISSING.

" How goes the chase, Mr. Armitage ?" asked Sir Everard Brandon, appearing on deck long before daylight.

" As well as could be expected, sir," was the reply, " in such murky weather."

" Yes, yes ; 'tis very unfavourable. Have the look-out descried them during the past watch ?"

" No, sir. Juniper and Hawser——"

" Surely, Mr. Armitage, you have not kept those men aloft so long ?"

" I would not have done so, except at the pressing request of Lieutenant Frazer, who has just left the deck, and of the men themselves. We have not better men on board, sir, than they."

" I have heard good reports of them ; after the action you must remind me of it. They have seen nothing then, Mr. Armitage, you say ?"

" No, sir ; but two bells since we heard their signal guns ; they have doubtless separated during the dense fog, and are recalled by the frigate."

" In what direction came the report ?"

" On our port bow, about ten knots."

" Excellent ; if we can only get a good berth between them at daylight we can soon finish the job for the frigate before the others come up to its assistance. Is all in readiness ?"

" Yes, sir ; every man is at his post. The word was passed to each, and all prepared for action without the least noise."

" What's that ?—another signal gun ?"

" Yes, sir ; I take it to be so. 'Tis the brigs answering each other to windward."

" In an hour then we shall be within broadsides of them. Clap on all sail, Mr. Armitage, for half-an-hour, and then shorten, by that time we shall be ready for the fog to lift. Let all proceed quietly as before, and let every man stand ready without a whisper being breathed."

Sir Everard went below.

The excitement among the younger officers was intense, every one felt that the Thunderer was over-matched, but for that no one cared.

Every man in the Royal Navy had long become used to fighting against odds, and since Admiral Nelson rose meteor-like from the lowest ranks, a British tar thought himself a match for any number of foemen, whether French or Spanish.

No one could sleep or doze under the circumstances ; even Sir Everard, who had seen service since his boyhood, and had inhaled the smoke of battles scores of times, felt a little nervous, and sat in his state-room writing letters, and giving final instructions for the coming conflict.

Noiselessly the Thunderer ploughed the waves, enveloped in dense vapors. No sound of a human voice was heard on board, yet above and below all was latent life and activity.

Marines were stationed in the tops, gunners in groups stood ready at the heavy broadsides, waiting for the word to deal death and destruction upon the foe, while Juniper and Hawser, with hawk-like vigilance, were straining their eyes through the gradually dispersing fogs of morning to communicate the exact position of the foe.

A gentle breeze now swept across the deep, and lifted the dense fog like a veil from the face of the ocean.

The enemy were descried but a short distance in the van, and the sounds of many voices clearly betrayed that they had perceived us.

"Bowled out this time, by jove!" said Sir Everard, coming on deck, smiling, buckling on his sword. "They are clearing for action, gentlemen; they seem to be in a devil of a hurry. What's become of the brigs?"

"The look-out reports them bearing up and clearing for action, sir. The signal is flying from the frigate, captain; they are hoisting it now."

"Every man to his post, then, and at the word let them have it with a vengeance."

The words were scarcely spoken, when a heavy shot, with screaming noise, flew, tearing through the rigging, while a heavy, booming sound rolled over the ocean with long reverberation.

"Thanks, Messieurs," said Sir Everard, "you are rather early with your compliments this morning. Lieutenant Frazer, return it."

Instantly the bow-chaser fired, and its shot was seen to crash through the enemy's stern, knocking out huge splinters.

"Well done. Let them have it, regularly and coolly, Frazer. No hurry!"

"Aye, aye, sir!"

The Frenchman was nothing loth for fight, feeling confident in his strength of numbers.

The armed brigs gallantly bore down, and all three foes began to pour in long shots at the Thunderer, which, by great tact and seamanship, was coming down full sail between them and the frigate.

One of them attempted to cross the Thunderer's path, and delivering a raking broadside, it was hoped could take up a position more favourable for tacking; but, from inferior seamanship, she missed her opportunity, and the Thunderer came crashing on to her amidships, almost cutting her down to the water's edge.

A boarding party, pikes and cutlasses in hand, leaped on her decks; but ere the grappling-irons could be used, she sheared off, with the British tars on board, fighting manfully for the mastery.

The English and French frigates were now broadside to broadside, and their dark sides were vomiting flame.

Cheers and counter cheers arose on either side, yet neither as yet could claim the mastery.

Broadside after broadside was fired in rapid succession. Shouts and groans were audible above the din of battle.

Nearer and nearing the flaming ships approached each other.

"Boarders, prepare!" shouted Sir Everard, with stentorian lungs. "One broadside more, and then the irons. Let them have it, lads! Strike home!"

Quicker than pen can describe the Frenchman was grappled; when, at that moment, a broadside from the armed brig raked it fore and aft.

"Treachery!" shouted the French.

"Surrender!" shouted Sir Everard, on the quarter-deck. "Haul down your flag!"

Yells were the answer given, when Frazer and Armitage, heading boarding parties, sword in hand, leaped upon the Frenchman's deck, and a fearful conflict ensued.

A counter boarding party leaped upon the Thunderer's quarter deck.

With a lusty cheer, they were received with vollies from marines in the tops and below.

Seamen and gunners, stripped to the buff, with cutlass and pistol, rushed to the scene of danger, where Sir Everard Brandon, sword in hand, seemed surrounded by ferocious, yelling Frenchmen.

A moment more, and he would have been struck down.

A sailor boy dashed into the melée, shot one, and cut another down, rushed in front of his captain, and saved him.

The next moment the brave lad was felled to the deck by a stunning blow.

Harry Halliard perceived his friend, and covered the body with his own; but firing his pistols right and left, cleared a passage for himself.

"The deck is cleared, Frank!" he cried. "Up, lad; there's more to do!"

Half stunned, Rayner rose from the deck, when, perceiving the gallant tars in deadly combat on the enemy's decks, he seized the French captain's sword that lay near him, leaped on to the main deck of the enemy, and with a pistol in his belt and sword in his mouth, he clambered up the rigging like a cat, cut away the colours, spliced on the English ensign, and slipped down again like lightning.

The action had been perceived by many anxious eyes, who thought, from the vollies of shot continually fired at him, that he must have been killed; but when the British flag unfolded to the breeze in haughty triumph, and the brave lad jumping untouched upon his own deck, presented the French ensign to his beloved commander, loud cheers rent the air, and the fight continued more angrily than ever.

Halliard, Frazer, and Armitage, with the men under their command, were in the thick of the deadly fray.

The enemy's main and fore mast were shot away.

The Frenchman was fast sinking; but, having overpowered all on deck, a party of men rushed below, secured and ironed the submissive foe, and caulked the frightful leaks through which the water was pouring.

Within twenty minutes from firing the first shot the noble-looking frigate Arrogante presented the picture of a perfect wreck, while the Thunderer seemed scarcely touched, except a few large gaps in her main and fore sail, through which shot had ploughed its way.

The Frenchman's decks presented a frightful picture of carnage.

Streams and pools of blood were everywhere; cutlasses, fire-arms, and over-turned guns, mangled bodies and broken spars were strewn about, while prisoners, well guarded above and below, crouched as if in abject fear.

The Thunderer had not yet completed its work; there were yet two armed brigs and two merchantmen to windward, and these Sir Everard determined to sink or capture.

Making all sail, he steered down upon them, firing long shots as he approached.

He thought at first to sink them, on account of the number of his crew distributed already on the Arrogante and the brig; but he afterwards changed his mind.

"Steady, men—steady! Let every shot tell; we've none to spare! Bring them to at the first broadside!"

And he did bring them to at the first broadside, for as soon as the heavy iron hail went whistling and crashing through the sides of both war brigs and merchantmen, they hauled down their colours, amid lusty cheers from the Thunderer, and squared sails.

"Mr. Halliard, go with a boat's crew to that brig-of-war, and bring the captain here!"

"Aye, aye, sir," said Harry, leaping over the side, followed by some well-armed, sturdy fellows.

"Where's Juniper and Hawser? Tell them to take a boat and go on board the other brig instantly, the wind is rising!"

"They are dead, sir," shouted some one.

"Sorry for it, then," said Sir Everard, moving hither and thither, giving orders.

"The other brigs are boarded, sir!" shouted Lieutenant Armitage from the Arrogante. "Lieutenant Frazer and party are now hoisting the royal."

"Are you able to make sail, lieutenant?" shouted Sir Everard to Armitage, over the side. "I can't spare more men."

"All right, sir!"

"I will signal if the wind rises. If we part company make all sail to Portsmouth. We are all short-handed. My compliments to every man, big and little! Watch the signals closely!"

And every British seaman on board the captured ships did watch Sir Everard's signals, which fluttered proudly from the battle-blackened ship, and read, "England is proud of her brave, lion-hearted Sailor Boys!"

CHAPTER XXIX.

EARL PENALVON IS HAUNTED—HE IS ROBBED BY MAN OR GHOST—HIS TERROR AND ALARM—BLACK WILL'S STOLID INDIFFERENCE—SUDDEN DISAPPEARANCE OF PENALVON'S PRIVATE PAPERS — WILD THYRA—THE FATE OF ROSE HALLIARD IS DECIDED — TRELAWNY IS EMPLOYED TO DO THE DEED.

"WHAT was the time when you saw this thing?"

"Nay, my lord, I know not."

"Thou saidst past midnight."

"Yes, my lord, and so it was; but at what precise hour I cannot tell, for I had no command over my senses."

"Nor senses to command, thou ninny. Were you not man enough to challenge it?"

"Indeed I did, and most valiantly, but it heeded me not; and still I followed, until my knees shook from under me, and I fell upon the floor in a state of pure exhaustion."

"Pure exhaustion! Why, churlish boor, did you not arm thyself, and follow it? It was not a spirit, but some intruder, such as annoyed me on a stormy night full a month ago. But who is the stranger that awaits below?"

"He gave no name more than that of Trelawny."

"Trelawny! Then admit him."

Within a few moments, heavy footsteps were heard upon the stairs, and in strode Black Will, muffled up from head to foot.

"Thorkil said you wanted me, Earl Penalvon," he began, striding into the middle of the room, "and I have come."

"I did not want you, Trelawny, on any special service."

"Then, why send for me?"

"To inquire if you wanted aught."

"Naught but peace."

"Peace?"

"Aye, my lord, peace of mind—peace of conscience."

"Surely you are not troubled with any qualms of conscience."

"The greatest villains have sober, thoughtful moments, Earl Penalvon; and, if truth be told, Black Will is not the only one whose mind is torn at times."

"What mean you? Would you dare insinuate?"

"Nay, I insinuate nothing, my lord. But he that pays for a thing and he that does it, sail in one craft—pull in the same boat."

"Come, come, Trelawny, you are not wont to be like this. Drink deep. I wish to speak of something that concerns thee."

"What is it—some other case of blood-letting? Nay, I've had enough of that. One ghost to haunt a man, both day and night, is quite enough even for Black Will."

"Ghosts! Nay, you are not childish enough to believe in such trumpery nursery tales."

"What frightened thee, then, Earl Penalvon, a month since, when you went stamping and raving through thy house, sword in hand?"

"Imagination!"

"Was it imagination that stole from thee your papers, and your private correspondence?"

"My private papers and correspondence, say you? It cannot be! I have lost nothing," said Penalvon, looking astonished at Trelawny, who sat like a gipsy king or pirate, in the earl's arm-chair, with his dirty boots thrown negligently on a rich damask-covered ottoman as he held up a deep draught of rum to the light ere he drank it.

"Then happy are you, if you have lost nought," the smuggler said, with a loud, boisterous laugh. "Look first, ere you are so sure, my lord."

Penalvon was excited, his suspicions were aroused.

He rushed from the apartment with a hasty stride towards his private cabinet.

Quickly returning, he looked pale, and trembled in every limb.

"Who told you of this?"

"Have you lost nothing, then?" continued Black Will, lighting a cigar, and puffing away with great nonchalance.

"Who told you of this?"

"Those who seldom err—Wild Thyra."

"How knew *she* this?"

"By her spells and charms, and rune-kenning."

"I *have lost* something, Trelawny, and would give thousands to reclaim it."

"Which you *never will*."

"Never will!—then thou knowest of it?"

"Nay; no more than you; but this I know, that man or ghost who braved thee and thy household in the dead hour of stormy midnight, would ne'er return what he took so much trouble to gain."

"Does Thyra know where they are deposited?"

"That I know not."

"Could she not be *forced* to disclose her knowledge?"

"How mean ye?—by whips, and dungeons, and starvation? You had best think no more of *that*, Earl Penalvon. You would not bring swift destruction upon us all?"

"You know not the importance of that which I have lost."

"Nor care."

"Nor care?"

"No," replied the smuggler, with dogged indifference, eyeing Earl Penalvon with stern and steadfast gaze.

"You know your promise?"

"Aye, and will keep it."

"Will you fulfil it?"

"Aye, and quickly."

"That is all I desire, she must be conveyed away at once."

"Who?—Thyra? I would rather encounter all the north winds in a single gale than touch a hair of her head. I *dare* not touch her, nor any of us, rough-handed, hard-hearted smugglers and wreckers that we are."

"No, not Thyra—Rose Halliard, I mean."

"Rose Halliard!" Trelawny said, gloomily.

"Yes, now, instantly!" he said, rising in anger, and muttering, inaudibly, to himself. "Once in my power, she shall know how Black Will can be revenged."

"You will sail to-night."

"I will."

"And when she is safe, Trelawny, let me see you; I will reward you handsomely."

The smuggler left the room with flushed face and clenched hands, and as he descended the stairs, the servants looked upon him with a sense of awe.

He looked not like a man; there was something fiendish in his leer as he scowled around him. And when the obsequious flunkeys had shut the door upon him, they heaved a deep sigh, held up their hands in serio-comic terror, and breathed hard as if suddenly rid of an unpleasant nightmare.

CHAPTER XXX.

BLACK WILL'S BRUTAL PROPOSALS TO ROSE—HE SEIZES AND CARRIES HER OFF TO SEA—HER ALARM AND SUFFERING—TRELAWNY SEES A GHOST—THE WARNING—THE PHANTOM SCHOONER GIVES CHASE TO BLACK WILL—THE DESPERATE ENCOUNTER—ROSE HALLIARD SAVES HER RESCUERS FROM CERTAIN DEATH.

'Twas evening; the wind was up and thunder-clouds gathered together.

Large rain drops fell at intervals, and lightning flashed, by fits and starts, between clouds and sea.

A ship, with all sails bent, was seen hovering off the coast, and buffetting among the waves.

Black Will Trelawny stood upon a cliff, and viewed the scene with folded arms.

"It must be done," he said, musing; "to-night is the last she will ever pass near Seawardine."

The weather was rough and portended heavy storms, yet in a neighbouring bay his craft lay moored, and all hands were ready and willing for the signal to make sail, and start for the opposite coast of France.

The bay in which his bark rode safely at anchor was a wild, sterile, unfrequented spot, shut in from view by a chain of lofty rugged hills.

The hills were unbroken, allowing no footpath for strangers to stray upon the scene, while a single channel, dangerous and tortuous in its windings, was its sole outlet to the sea.

"Is all prepared Otho?" asked Black Will, gruffly, of one who stood near him.

"Yes, sir; everything as you desired, and nought remains but your signal for weighing anchor and making sail."

"Get you to the galliot, Otho, and await my coming. Ere the moon rises we shall be away."

Waving his hand in motion of command, Trelawny moved away, and, descending the cliffs close by the sea-beaten beach, was soon lost to view among the crevices and fissures of the rock.

He had gone to his cave, whither we will follow.

Seated in a rude stone apartment that had been cut by countless tides, centuries before, sat Rose Halliard at a rude oak table reading by the light of a single lamp, and with scarce a vestige of comfort save a few smouldering embers that flickered on a rude hearth some few feet distant in a corner. A poor pallet of straw served as a couch, and, save a large jar of water and the remains of a lof, this was all that the prison vault possessed.

He entered by a pathway unknown to any but himself, and stole beside her ere the unconscious, pale, and sorrowing woman was aware of his presence.

Perceiving him, she started as if stung by an adder.

The dark villain smiled grimly, and pointed her back to the seat she had just left, and, leaning on the table, he gazed upon her downcast eyes with looks of demoniacal triumph.

"Again!" muttered Rose, almost inaudibly.

"Yes, again! Rose Halliard," was the slow, gruff, tyrannical reply.

"Why not let me die in peace?"

"In peace? Why, then, you shall."

"Why come you here?"

"Why?"

"Yes!"

"To see once more the pretty lady who has fascinated all hearts," he added with a loud, remorseless laugh.

"Is it not enough that you have hunted me through life like a demon, but you must fain come, coward as you are, to torment me in my prison cell?"

"Prison is it? nay, then, you shall not have to complain of your lodgings long, fair mistress."

"Mistress!"

"Aye, mistress! You could not smile on me, Will Trelawny—Black Will, as some would call me—but you can fawn and trifle with noble and titled ones, hereabouts."

"What mean you?" asked Rose, rising indignantly.

"What do I mean? Nay, Rose, sit down, and do not play the hypocrite. You know full well what Earl Penalvon means."

"I know not what he means, no more than I know why it is that you and Thorkil and the rest have incarcerated me."

"To keep you from further harm," he added, grimly smiling, exhibiting glistening teeth which shone in the lamp-light like the fangs of a ravenous wolf.

"And would you let me die here, far from my humble, happy home; far from all knowledge of my darling boy?" gasped poor Rose, sobbing.

"Nay, not that; you must exchange this vault for princely apartments, and become an earl's mistress."

"Never! Oh, Heaven, defend me!"

"Then if not his, why not mine?"

"Thine! As soon would I live with wolves or snakes."

"Oh! oh! my pretty one, don't talk so loudly, and stamp your foot; remember you are in *my* power now, and beyond all aid."

"Nay, Heaven is nigh, and God will protect me."

"Then let him," was the ironical reply. "Black Will believes in naught so childish."

BOYS' LIBRARY

Harry Halliard: or, the Young British Tar.

THE ENGAGEMENT BETWEEN THE THUNDERER AND THE FRENCH BRIGS.

"Came you then to murder me, villain ?"

"Not quite, but to tell thee this : you must come with me directly, on board ; we sail to-night, our sole cargo consists of the pale, pretty, Rose Halliard."

"Now ?"

"Yes, instantly, not a moment's delay ; the tide is high, and the galliot waits."

"Whither ?"

"I know not, wherever fancy leads me."

"Why not kill me at once, rather than dishonour me."

"Dishonour you ? Did you not disonour your-self years ago in refusing a good fellow like me, and accept such a skip-jack as Walter Halliard ?"

"He was inferior to none, thou hideous wretch ; his superiors were few. But now that I look at you, Trelawny, and gaze at the twin devils dancing in your wolfish eyes, the more I love and doat upon his memory, and thank heaven on my bended knees that it saved me from such a wretch as you, for if you dare to approach me, I will tear my very heart out and die at your feet, rather than be polluted by such fiendish, blood-stained hands as thine."

"So, so," added Trelawny, scowling and laugh-ing hoarsely. "You love his memory still ; but if reports are true, you love other's better than him."

"Fiend, thou liest! No one on earth can say that I ever said or did aught that savoured of forgetfulness of Walter's memory, and, to prove it, prepare all the torments that your malice can invent; burn me alive, if thou wilt, but never will I allow foul hands as thine to touch me!"

"Enough of this Rose; time is flying; listen to me."

"I do."

"I love you."

Rose looked scornfully at the swarthy form before her.

"Thy destiny is in my hands! Will you consent to my proposal, or shall I force compliance?"

"Never!"

"Never?"

"No, never! Use all the cruel force that a fiend can find, and then, I say, wretched murderer—never!"

"Then it shall be by force," he muttered, with an oath; and, rushing at her with a drawn dagger, he would have plunged it up to the hilt in her heaving, half-covered bosom, but she fell, fainting, upon the floor; and as he gazed, lamp in hand, upon her unconscious beauty, the knife glanced in the air; but, as if paralyzed, he dropped the weapon and stood listening.

His eyes were distended, and he gazed around him as if watching some unseen object.

"Again!" he gasped, in trembling wonder. "Again!" he muttered, still gazing on vacancy. "The same form! the same look! Blood upon his forehead! the same hour! And those sounds—what can they be? Not of mortals!"

Gathering himself up with a mighty effort, he drew his cutlass, and dashed it at some unseen object, and it broke, like glass, in countless pieces against the wall.

"It must have been!" he gasped, in terror.

Gazing at the prostrate form of Rose, he stood over her, gloating his eyes upon the form lying unconscious at his feet.

He approached to touch her, but seemed restrained by some unseen power.

By a convulsive effort he seized her, and, laughing like a maniac, bore her away, through subterranean passages, to the galliot.

Black Will bore his helpless burden on board, and, the night being dark and heavy, he was unobserved.

He placed her upon a couch in his cabin, and, locking the door, went on deck.

A person stood by the water's edge and beckoned Trelawny.

"Is she safe?" asked the cloaked and booted stranger.

"She is."

"Then all's well. Make all sail thither and return. I have not heard from the Dutchman for many weeks, but he promised to be on the look out, and have all prepared. He will keep his promise. Here, Trelawny," he said, putting a heavy purse into his hand, "when you safely land your precious burden, drink my health. There are hundreds in notes and gold. If all goes well your fortune is made. Keep your own counsel."

"Never fear."

"Does Thorkil know of this?"

"How should he?"

"'Tis well. Adieu! remember me—make all sail. Farewell!"

"Farewell!" muttered Black Will, when he had gone on board again. "Farewell, for the present, Earl Penalvon; we shall be better acquainted by-and-bye."

"Now for the coast of France, my merry lads," shouted Trelawny, drinking deeply of brandy. "All hands splice the main brace, and then make sail."

"Aye, aye, sir," sung the dusky scoundrels that composed his crew, as they helped themselves liberally from the pailful of liquor that stood aft.

"Get the craft under weigh, Barton," bawled Black Will, walking the deck, impatiently puffing a huge cigar.

"Aye, aye, sir!" was the gruff response.

"Up and down!" was shouted on the forecastle.

"Stopper your cable, and pull the capstan!" cried Black Will.

"All hands make sail!" was the next order, and, quick as lightning, the vagabond crew flew hither and thither, and swarmed in the rigging like bees.

"Away aloft, lads!" was the next command; and, after some short silence, "Trice up, lay out!" was roared out by Trelawny.

And soon the extended yards of the vessel, covered with cloud-like sails, were up, mingling with the sky.

The sails gradually filled, every rope and yard were all pulled taut, and soon the vessel glided from her unseen anchorage, and being pilotted by Trelawny personally at the helm, she safely ran the dangerous intricacies of the inland, hill-surrounded bay, and put forth to sea proudly, and "walked the waters like a thing of life."

With a steady breeze in his favour, Black Will soon exchanged dangerous pilotage and low water for fair winds and open sea.

Like a willing servant his craft soon took all work into her own hands, and laying herself well to the freshening waves, she suffered her crew to lounge about the decks, or lean over the weather-rail, with folded arms and half-closed eye-lids.

Trelawny resigned the helm to Barton, with whom he conversed in suppressed tones, as he walked the deck, with his heavy boots and jaunty gait.

"What strange sail was that you saw to-day, Barton, cruising off the Point?"

"Don't know, cap'en. Seemed to be a fast sailer, as far as I could make out."

"King's men, or Revenues?"

"Neither, I should judge, cap'en, from her rig. We took a good squint at her through the glass, but the weather was thick, fog hanging around her, and of course I can't say what she was. Some of the lads say they saw her bowling along under mainsail and jib, suddenly rising and dipping; but they couldn't make anything on her, and came to the conclusion that it must be a phantom, or a ghost, or summat."

"A phantom, Barton?" asked Trelawny, suddenly turning and stopping. "A phantom? Surely Wild Thyra, or Hylda, have not been runing among my crew, eh! d—n them. Did you see either of 'em to-day?"

"No, cap'en, I didn't; but some of the lads say they saw her on top of the White Cliffs, throwing up her hands like as if she war praying, or summat like it."

Trelawny bit his lip, and, despite the coarse, loud laugh and oath with which he greeted Barton's remark, he seemed annoyed, and stamped his foot, as if endeavouring to quell unpleasant fancies that flitted across his mind,

The moon gradually peeped from behind the

clouds, and except the watch, who sat sleepily grouped in dark shadows, all were a-bed.

Trelawny still walked the deck, moodily pondering.

He seemed haunted by some unseen spirit, for he would suddenly start backward, and stagger, as if struck by poignant pain.

"D—n it!" he cried, "I am not crazy, to be paralyzed by spells of rune-kenners, or remorse of conscience."

And he laughed it off.

"What makes you keep so silent, Barton?" he asked of the helmsman.

"Nothin' particular, cap'en; but I feel uncommon queer like since I've been on board, and don't know why."

"Why, man, you ain't the one to be frightened by Wild Thyra, or the gabbling of Thorkil's old woman?"

"No, cap'en, I ain't afeerd of nothing o' that kind, but, as I was observing to Dick Rattles last night, at eight bells, 'Dick,' says I, 'there's uncommon noises heard aboard here, ain't there?' and he says, 'Yes, mate, there be, and strange sights too, lad.'"

"Sights?" asked Black Will, retreating a few paces, "sights, Barton?"

"Aye, cap'en, sights, and no mistake, for Dick and me t'other night were keeping watch, and we heard uncommon noises near the cabin, and 'fore we could say Jack Robinson, there came aboard, out o' the sea, cap'en, a tall, big fellow, and he stands on the bulwark as if he war made of stone, like. Dick and me watched, and he comes off the bulwark, and goes straight into the cabin."

"Into the cabin?"

"Aye, sir; and more nor that, he comes out again, and passes over the side, and we sees no more on him till next night."

"Did it come again then, Barton?" asked Trelawny, drinking off some brandy, and handling his pistol convulsively.

"Aye, cap'en, it did; and this time he looked straight at Dick and me, and comes and stands right afore us, and said something like 'leave instantly,' but Dick and me war too trembling-like to remember things correct, cap'en. But, by heavens, there it is again!" said Barton, pointing amid ships, and trembling at the wheel.

Turning instantly on his heel, Trelawny stood like one transfixed to the deck, with beads of perspiration rolling from his forehead. He leaned for support against the mast, and his limbs trembled from under him.

Then he stood for several minutes, when, clutching one of his heavy pistols, he fired at the ghost-like apparition, which fell as if killed into the sea.

The report of fire-arms aroused every man, who tumbled out of bunks and hammocks, and rushed on deck armed to the teeth.

Trelawny heeded not the swarthy, excited group that gathered round him, but still stood gazing on vacancy with determined attitude, grinding his teeth in fury, and muttering vollies of curses as fast as he could give them utterance.

As if suddenly aroused from a dream, he looked around at his astonished crew, and then laughing as one demented, rushed into his cabin, and slammed the door behind him.

Rose lay in slumber muttering incoherently. She was dreaming.

Her mind was far away to the fair and sunny days of youth, when hand in hand, and hearts throbbing in union, she and Walter had rambled over the hills together, or sat beneath the shade of forest trees, where he had confessed his ardent love for her, and where also she had leaned lovingly, confidingly upon his manly breast, and breathed a virgin's prayer for her own fondly cherished hero.

Her face, even in sleep, was sweetly smiling as she murmured Walter's name, when again and again she sighed, and pressed her arms across her breast, as if fondly caressing her dearly beloved first-born.

Trelawny stood over her with fiendish scowl; his brows were knit in anger.

A dark cloud gathered on his brow, and he bit his lip in anger until the blood flowed.

"So the rune-kenners have thee in their keeping, eh?" he muttered. "Sleep on! sleep on, Rose! thou shalt never be another's, to-night shall seal thy fate."

"And *thine*!" whispered a voice.

Black Will started! He looked hither and thither, but saw nothing.

Rose still slept, as sweetly and innocently as a child.

"It was not her voice," he said, "and yet——No, no, Will, it was thy own imagining!"

Still gazing lustfully on the sleeper, he listened to her breathing, and then stealthily peering in every corner, felt satisfied that what he had heard was all imaginary.

"Yes, Rose," he thought, "I could not possess thee in thy youth by fair and honest wooing; yet can I now have thee by force, and in thy woman's prime; this night shall see my triumph."

"And *mine*!" whispered one unseen.

As if struck dumb with astonishment Trelawny gazed from left to right, and from right to left, clutching his weapons with determined grasp. He might have long stood awe-struck, wondering at the strange sights and sounds that followed him everywhere of late; but the noise of voices and busy feet overhead on deck attracted his attention.

There was something unusual transpiring, and from the lusty commands of Barton, Trelawny felt assured that there was sufficient cause for his immediate presence.

"How now, men!" shouted Black Will, leaping on deck, cutlass in hand. "What's the cause of all this rumpus?"

"A strange sail, cap'en," answered Barton, looking and pointing astern, "has been chasing for an hour."

"What is she?"

"A heavy-armed schooner, as far as we can make her out, and the very *devil* to sail; she's been gaining on us this two hours or more."

"Well, what of that? Are they King's men or Revenues?"

"Can't tell, cap'en, we've signalled her twice, but she don't fly the bunting."

"How many guns?"

"Can't make out any, sir; nor can we see a soul on deck."

"Yes, but *I* see something," said Trelawny. "Can't you make out that large black cross in her mainsail?"

"Aye, true, cap'en, so there is."

"I don't like her looks at all, Barton."

"Nor I, sir, nor any on us; it don't seem to move like any or'nary craft as ever I see. Best make all ship-shape, sir, and prepare for squalls, she may carry some heavy pepper boxes aboard, and so we might as well be prepared to give 'em a taste of ourn."

"Well said, Barton lad. Muster all hands to quarters, open the magazines, and tuck up your sleeves, for, if I'm not much taken in, that craft is heavy handed."

"Aye, sir, sure to be, for she couldn't run afore the wind as she does if she warn't."

Within a few moments after the order was given Black Will and his band were ready for action, and every man at his post.

"If she won't hoist colours, Barton, let us show 'em how—up it goes."

A jet black flag was immediately run up, and blew from the peak like a wreath of smoke.

"That's it, sir," shouted Barton. "They can't mistake us now ; there's no quarter for 'em, cap'en, if they likes to tackle us."

"Now, lads," said Trelawny, pacing the deck, and addressing his men, who were grouped around the four cannons, which were all double shotted, and only waiting for the match to deal destruction on all comers ; "now, lads, listen to me. It's no use of disguising ourselves any more, and hoisting false colours—we must fight ! There is no getting out of it, if we felt inclined. Let every man take a good pull at the grog, and when I give the word, fight like tigers. No quarter, recollect, on either side !"

The approach of the fast-sailing stranger was intently watched by all on board.

The bright moon shone on her canvas pinions, and she looked like an albatross skimming along the surface of the foaming waters ; while the vast amount of canvas that she carried keeled her over till her coppered sides shone like burnished gold.

Ploughing her way with the green sea hissing at her sides, she gallantly bore down upon the doomed ship, but although men aloft were busy with glasses, not a soul nor a single gun could be seen on her decks. Naught, in truth, gave signs of life on board, and save a large black cross on her mainsail, she looked like a snow-white phantom on the waters.

"She tacks, sir, on our lee-quarter," shouted Barton, who was full of strange excitement.

"If she will not hail, Barton, give her a shot athwart the bows, and make her say something."

No sooner said than done. A heavy booming report shook the galliot, and in an instant a shot glanced upon the surface of the moon-lit waves, striking the schooner in the fore-chains.

On the instant the stranger unfurled a blood-red flag at her peak, and a voice was heard shouting with stentorian lungs through a speaking-trumpet.

"Surrender ! Trelawny, surrender !"

A derisive cheer was the sole response, and Black Will giving the word of command, his guns vomited forth death and destruction on every side, and all was instant life and bustle among the crew.

The stranger was not loth for action.

Her ports suddenly opened, and, with a wild cheer that shook the heart of Black Will, a heavy and destructive broadside was returned, cutting away the spars and rigging, which fell in showers over the deck.

"Heavy metal that, Barton," said Trelawny, as he hurried hither and thither, "we have caught a Tartar, lads, but we must fight till the last, anything is better than the gibbet ! Let 'em have it with a will, my lads !"

Broadside after broadside was given and returned, but the superior gunnery of the stranger told with fearful effect upon the galliot, whose masts and spars and sails were so rent and torn that she could no longer answer her helm.

"If she comes broadside to, men, grapple and board her," shouted Black Will, rushing about from place to place, among the dead any dying like an infuriated wolf.

"Surrender !" shouted the stranger. "Trelawny, surrender !" was shouted with distinctness above the roar of battle.

"Never !" shouted Black Will, firing his pistols right into the stranger's deck, as she gradually approached broadside to.

"Hurrah for Trelawny !" shouted his men, in wild despair.

"Hurrah for Rose Halliard !" was the response, with lusty cheers.

"What was that they shouted ? Rose Halliard ! Ah, ah, my lads, you've mistaken your man this time. I'll soon settle her business," he said, cocking his pistol, "and then, if they conquer, they may throw me to the sharks !"

Rushing aft to his cabin, he darted down the door with a fearful crash.

With terrific oaths he darted forward towards the sofa !

Rose Halliard had fled !

Dashing about the cabin, firing his pistols, in the vain hope of finding and murdering her, he was unconscious of the flight of time.

Cheers upon cheers greeted his ears ; the rush of many feet, and clanking of cutlasses, and report of guns and pistols were heard in every direction.

A dreadful conflict was then raging among his crew and a numerous body of boarders, who had fought their way on deck !

"Where is he, where is he ?" was the sound which caught his ear !

"Ha, ha !" he gruffly laughed, "caught me ! have ye ? The bird flown, and a gibbet for me, eh ?" and rushing out of the cabin, sword in hand, he dashed among the combatants, and cut down on every side.

Yelling like a madman, he fought until he sank with exhaustion upon the deck ; when, seized with fiendish resolve, he caught up a port-fire, and jumped into the fore-hold, light in hand, and reached the door of the powder magazine.

"We shall all end together," he said, "the victors and the conquered !"

In another moment the magazine would have been fired, but as he lifted the fatal match, a heavy blow fell upon his temples, and he lay senseless at the feet of Rose Halliard, who seized the light and extinguished it.

CHAPTER XXXI.

NELLY BRITTON LEAVES HOME TO DWELL WITH EARL PENALVON—WHAT SHE THINKS OF HIM—NEWS OF PAUL ADAIR, BLACK WILL, AND LEONA—UNEXPECTED ARRIVAL AT JOEL BRITTON'S HOUSE—HE DRIVES A FEW NAILS FOR A NAVAL LIEUTENANT.

"And must thee return this evening, Nelly?" asked old Joel Britton, as he sat smoking his pipe beside his cheerful fire. "Why, thou hast improved wonderful like since last we saw thee, ain't she, mother ?"

"Nay, I don't say much about it, Joel," was the calm reply ; "she never had my real heart's consent to go there at all; it were all to please thee and thy trumpery notions of grand folk. I'd rather have our Nell at home again, a-dusting and scrubbing about her own father's house, than see her skipping about with such fine dresses and ribbons and falderals."

"Oh, thee wert young thyself once, mother, so let the lass improve herself. She can't do much harm up at the Hall, for the Earl is a very good man, as everybody knows, and thinks a deal of her, don't he, Nell?"

"Yes, father, and he has given me so many presents and nice things, that I don't know how to thank him?"

"Dost do much work, Nell?" asked Lucy, still busy with her knitting.

"No, mother; the Earl won't let me do much, he says it will spoil my hands to do hard work, so he won't let me."

"Does he ever come and talk to thee?"

"Oh, yes, very often, and he sits down near me sometimes in the garden, and shows me all kinds of books with coloured pictures of grand lords and ladies, and says I may be like one of them one of these days, if I'm a good girl."

Nelly's picture of her happiness in Earl Penalvon's mansion so pleased simple-hearted Joel Britton, that he laughed and slapped his thighs in great good humour, swearing to himself that he was a fortunate father in having such a lucky daughter that could attract an Earl's admiring attention; but had he known that nobleman's real intention, he would not have been so happy and self-confident of her future happiness and welfare.

"Thou hast forgotten all about thy old sweetheart now then, Nell," continued Joel, joking his good-looking daughter, who stood blushing before him. "Thou hast no heart, now, for fishermen or wreckers?"

A shadow flitted across her countenance.

"Have you heard anything of Paul, father?" Nelly asked, in a confused manner.

"Paul who, girl?"

"Paul Adair, of course she means," chimed in Lucy. "What other Paul do we know?"

"Yes; I heard t'other day that he was wrecked, and nought has been heard of him since."

"No, that was part of Black Will's galliot that came ashore," said Lucy, "and a pretty fuss Earl Penlavon made about it, so I heard."

"It wasn't Paul's vessel, then," asked Nelly, with much simplicity, betraying her gratification at the news by smiling and blushing deeply. "I'm so glad of that. I don't care what becomes of all the rest, so that *he's* safe."

"Don't thee? Well, then, I'll tell thee, lass, what it is—it won't benefit thee much, if ever the Earl hears you talking so of such a scapegrace, for he's awful put out against Paul Adair, for some cause."

"I don't care if he is," answered Nelly, boldly. "He can't say any harm of him, nor can any one in Seawardine."

"'Tis very strange that a sensible girl like you, Nell, should uphold such a lawless rascal as Paul Adair, for thou knowest he's on the high seas, pirating."

"Ah! well, father, people may talk as much as they please; but if all were as good in heart as poor Paul, there wouldn't be many bad folks in the world. And as to that story of his falling in love with a nobleman's daughter, it is all lies—he's never seen Leona once since he took her father's schooner-yacht."

"How dost thou know all this, I should like to know?"

"Because Leona and her father called on Earl Penalvon last week, and I heard what she said about him."

"No good, *I* know."

"Not much harm."

"He seized the schooner and cargo, and put all the folks ashore, far from any town."

"Yes, I heard them say that; but when they described him to the Earl, he said, 'It must be Paul and no other; I'll have that fellow hanged yet. 'Oh, he didn't treat us with any cruelty,' the young lady says; 'but was most polite and kind, saying, as he left them, that he was very sorry to take the yacht, and shouldn't have done so, except that, being a very fast one, he wished to use it for especial purpose.'"

"To outrun the King's-men and Revenues I shouldn't wonder. What else could he want it for?"

"Leona said to me, in the orchard the next day, that she had quite fallen in love with him, but that she had never seen him since."

"'Tisn't likely she has, or will. He ain't fool enough to go near them again."

"But she says she should like very much to see him once more, and if he writes, she'll do so, unknown to her father."

"A pretty girl, indeed! What next, I wonder, Nell?" chimed in the mother, indignantly. "What next, I wonder? *You'll* be falling in love with some good-looking smuggler next. Let's have no more about such nonsense."

"You *do* admit that he's good-looking, mother," said Nelly, laughing heartily. "It was only the other day that father and you were saying he was ugly and wicked."

"Never mind, sauce-box, what we said," Lucy replied, tartly. "'Tis enough for thee to know that he's no good to thee, or any one, and that thou should'st have no thoughts, let alone anything to, say, in favour of such a worthless fellow."

"Aye, aye, mother; thou speaks good sense, now; and look ye, girl, let's quit this talk, for it's time for thee to be off to the Hall, before it gets too dark."

With many embraces, both to father and mother, Nelly Britton took a last look at the mirror to see that her appearance was becoming, and, feeling assured that she looked remarkably well in her new clothes and ribbons, she tripped off, with a light heart, to Earl Penalvon's mansion.

Joel and his loving wife sat conversing for more than an hour, and in their fond imaginings thought they already saw their darling daughter perched high in society, with nothing less than a coronet encircling her brow, and were weaving all manner of pleasant fancies for the future, when a loud knock at the door was heard.

"Is this Mr. Joel Britton's?" asked a mounted stranger.

"Aye, it is, friend, at your service. What might ye want?"

"Several things, good friend," was the light-hearted rejoinder of the rider, as he alighted. "And, in the first place, I want a few nails put in my horse's shoe; he has come far, and been ridden fast."

"Aye, true, friend, he does seem to limp a bit. Whoa, mare. Where might ye have come from?"

"Falmouth."

"A good distance, truly. And where may you be going to-night?"

"That depends on what kind of reception you may give me."

"Walk in the house, and speak to my wife. The forge is closed for the day; but, as you are a traveller, I'll try to oblige ye. 'Do unto another,' as they say. Whoa, mare, ye skittish little devil; whoa, I say."

The rider strode into the house, and, bowing to Mrs. Britton, took a chair by the fire.

She looked very hard at him for a moment or so ; but, meeting his smiling gaze, she said,

"You'll excuse me, sir ; but, at first, I thought you looked very much like a lad we used to know in these parts years ago. I am mistaken ; you are a gentleman, he was a—a——"

"A sailor boy ?"

"No, not exactly."

"A wrecker's apprentice, perhaps ?" he continued, laughing, and lighting a cigar.

"No, nor that quite," said Lucy, very solemnly.

"Well, a good-for-nothing wreckers' lad, half pirate, half smuggler, I take it ?"

"Well, whatever he was, I know you are not he, so, therefore, I shan't say what he was."

"Very well said ; according to the proverb, 'Speak well of the absent.'"

"Nay, I can't say much in his favour ; but, in truth, am glad he's away roving, for he caused Joel and myself a deal of trouble, for he was always after our Nelly."

"Oh, indeed ! That accounts for your maternal solicitude."

"Yes, perhaps ; but he's away, and she's——"

"What ?" asked the stranger, with much evident curiosity. "Not dead, surely !"

"No, not dead, but——"

"Sick ?"

"Far from it, she were never better in her life. But I were going to say, she's far away from his coaxing now, for she's in a gentleman's family."

"Indeed ; but love laughs at locks, you know."

"But he can't laugh at *them* locks."

"Yes he would at any locks if he really loves her."

"But I defy him to get in where she is, for Earl Penalvon's house——"

"Is she there, then ?"

"But why are you so surprised, pray ?"

"Oh, nothing ; merely a passing thought."

His entire dress was that of the king's navy.

As he heard the last words his cheeks became deadly pale, and tossing his cigar into the fire with an air of impatience, he rose.

"You are surely not going yet ?" said the good-natured dame. "'Tis some distance to any entertainment for man or beast, you had better rest and refresh yourself."

"I could not eat now," he said, "for a whole kingdom. Ah ! here comes the mare ; whoa, lass !"

"You are not going so soon, art thee, young gentleman," said Joel.

"Yes, Mr. Britton, I must be off on the instant ; here's a guinea ; many thanks !" and, before good old Joel could recover from astonishment, the young stranger had gallopped off in the direction of Earl Penalvon's mansion.

CHAPTER XXXII.

EARL PENALVON MEDITATES—HE IS FAVOURED WITH NEWS THAT STARTLES AND ALARMS HIM REGARDING PAUL ADAIR, BLACK WILL, HARRY HALLIARD, AND HIS MOTHER, ROSE—NELLY BRITTON IN TEARS AND JOY.

EARL PENALVON had just dined ; feeling content with himself and all the world he sat before his library fire, cracking nuts and eating grapes.

The apartment was the same in which he received the strange and ghost-like visitor described in a former chapter.

His lordship was dull, he longed for something to arouse him from the languid state in which he felt.

He wished for some pleasant toy with which to amuse himself, and knew not what. He cared not for expense, but he wished to be amused.

His eyes twinkled mischievously as he smiled at a passing thought.

"Tell Miss Britton I wish to see her."

In answer to the servant's summons Nelly soon appeared, and being pointed to a seat, she modestly sat looking at the fire and playing with her fingers.

"Rather a nice girl," thought my Lord Penalvon, scanning her from head to foot with the look and smile of a confirmed voluptuary.

"So you find things pleasant, do you, Nelly ? And my housekeeper does not kill you with her tuition. Well, I see a marked improvement in you already ; so do your parents, I think ?"

"Yes, my lord, they feel very grateful for your kindness, and so do I."

"And so do you, eh, Nelly ? Well, tell me how many sweethearts you have," said Penalvon, rising and moving his chair closer to hers. "There, don't cry now, I've only kissed you ; many a lady in the land would only feel too proud to salute Earl Penalvon."

The action was so sudden that Nelly was astonished, and blushed deep scarlet.

"Then, my lord, let me say," began Nelly, stammering, "I care not how much those fine ladies might desire such attentions ; all I can say is, sir, that you had best not repeat it."

Poor child ! the innocent rustic !

"Well, well, Nelly, don't cry. Come, there's a guinea for you."

"Keep your money, sir. You have taken more liberty than any ever did before, not even—not even——"

"Your sweetheart, I suppose," continued Penalvon, smiling, with mock compassion on Nelly's tears.

"I wish that he were here," sobbed Nelly, with half-choked utterance.

"A gentleman, a naval officer—Lieutenant Blane, sends his card, and desires an interview," said a footman, entering, with a card on a silver salver.

"Blane, say you, John ? I know no such person ; but, at all events, show him up. I'm always to be seen by His Majesty's officers. Nelly, you had better leave me for the present. Come, dry your eyes, my child ; weeping might redden them, and spoil their youthful lustre."

Nelly required no second intimation to leave the apartment, for her heart was so full that she could scarcely speak, and left the room with downcast eyes.

The footman opened the door, and admitted Lieutenant Blane.

"Of the navy, I believe ?"

"Yes ; of His Majesty's Thunderer."

"Be seated, sir. Might I inquire the special object of this visit ? Will you take a glass of wine ? Oh ! I beg pardon ; perhaps you prefer Cognac—naval gentlemen usually prefer ardent spirits, I am informed. John, you may retire. Now, Lieutenant Blane, I am at your service."

"I should not, perhaps, have troubled you at this hour, but——"

"Oh ! pray don't name it."

"I thought it incumbent upon me to do so."

"You are very kind. Proceed."

"We were beating up Channel with our prizes, gained in the late engagement——"

"I have heard of it. The action did my friend, Sir Everard Brandon, great credit."

"When we fell in with a wreck."

"Quite an uncommon occurrence in these troubled waters," the Earl remarked, very sarcastically.

"This particular one was, as you may soon hear. It was of a large and powerfully-built Dutch galliot. We saw no signals flying, but immediately lowered a boat, and, though in great danger of being swamped, we managed to board it."

"Gallant action indeed! Dutch galliot, eh? Any one on board?"

"One man."

"Only one! poor fellow!"

"He was a pirate."

"You don't say so? Really, how very interesting your narrative is. Proceed, I pray," said Penalvon, sipping wine very coolly, and playing with a silver nut-cracker.

"A pirate, or smuggler, or wrecker, or something of the sort."

"Yes, a rogue or vagabond; true. No consequence. I am all attention."

"He was of a dark, forbidding countenance, and had commanded the galliot, which carried four guns."

"His name—did you learn that? It's of no great great consequence, though. Yet, did you hear his name?"

"Yes; he called himself Trelawny—Will Trelawny, or Black Will, or something of that kind."

"Indeed! How very singular! He was dying, I hope, and you decently buried him."

"Oh, no, my lord; he is alive, and heavily ironed."

"Was there any one else on board?" Penalvon asked, very collectedly, without betraying any emotion.

"No; there had been one, that he attempted to abduct——"

"The atrocious scoundrel!"

"At the instigation of some nobleman; but was thwarted."

"You don't mean to say so, lieutenant? To think that a nobleman should descend to league with a half-smuggler, half-pirate, and for such a foul purpose! Good heavens! and we live in such an enlightened age! You did not learn the lady's name, I suppose?" asked Penalvon, sipping wine, and affecting much mock-horror and Christian indignation.

"Yes; Rose Halliard!"

"Quite a pretty name, in truth; never remember to have heard of it before. But was she rescued then?" asked the Earl, petulantly, and with ill-disguised passion in his tone.

"Yes."

"How?"

"This nobleman's correspondence had been tampered with, and a smuggler knew of the plot to disgrace his deceased friend's widow."

"How very romantic!"

"He watched the doings of this Black Will and his noble ally, and when Trelawny, with his ruffianly crew, were fairly out at sea, he bore down upon the galliot, and fought her down to the water's edge."

Penalvon turned deadly pale.

"Did this woman—no, this lady, as you call her —how could she escape?"

"Her friends were vigilant. In a fast, well-armed schooner, of more than common size, and of extra-ordinary speed, they watched the Shag Rock, the White Cliffs, and the Shark's Fin both day and night. Some of the schooner's most trusty crew went ashore, and secreted themselves in the hold of Trelawny's galliot."

Penalvon turned a side glance at the speaker, in excitement of curiosity.

"When Rose Halliard was fast under lock and key in the ruffian's cabin, some of these trusty fellows found means to communicate with her. Black Will would have outraged her."

"It cannot be!"

"It would have been consummated, but the schooner bore down too fast upon him, and commenced the action, which was long and bloody."

"And the woman was killed, you say?" asked Penalvon, with beaming face.

"No, she was taken from the cabin, and when Black Will rushed thither, when all hope had left his carrion heart—when he rushed like a demon to put an end to his cruelties by killing her—she had flown he knew not whither."

"Extraordinary! And the crew were all secured and ironed?"

"Yes, and all his papers were found untouched."

"Did he not burn them, the idiot?"

"Not one."

"And did Trelawny tell you all this?"

"He did, and to a superior officer much more that I know not of."

For some few moments there was mutual silence.

Smiling very blandly, and with a great air of unconcern, Earl Penalvon rose, and standing with his back to the fire, mused a moment, and said,

"Very extraordinary affair, isn't it? And, in order to finish your very extraordinary smuggler story properly, have you the name, or do you know anything of the strange individual who commanded the schooner?"

"Oh, yes; the man, Trelawny, said his name was Saul something."

"Saul! Paul Adair?" asked Penalvon, now thoroughly aroused, and looking as one suddenly stung by a serpent.

"The name exactly."

Penalvon visibly shook in every limb; but, calming himself with wonderful self-command, he tossed off a glass of wine, and then, turning to the calm and collected young man who sat before him, he said,

"And may I be allowed to ask, Lieutenant Blane, what interest *I* can have in your strange story, that you favour me with an especial visit in order to narrate it?"

"Oh, certainly, my lord. I thought it would be a fitting and proper introduction to what follows. I know that, as you interest yourself very greatly in the suppression of smuggling and the like, you might wish to be informed of the sad discomfiture of one of the rascals."

"Oh, of course I do. Now I remember, I think there *was* one who infested this part of the coast, whose name was Trelawny."

"And there is another named Thorkil, I hear?"

"I don't know him; never heard the name before."

"And a third is named Paul Adair."

"Ah! he *is* a rogue and vagabond. Look you here, lieutenant. I would willingly give £5,000 in prize money to any of his Majesty's vessels that should capture him."

"You would?"

"Yes. If you promise to bring him to this house I promise that sum."

"The bargain is made."

"Here is a cheque for half, payable on the instant at Falmouth ; the other half to be payable on the production of the culprit."

"I accept the conditions. I know where he is, and will produce him within a week."

"Well, put that cheque in your pocket ; bring him here, dead or alive, I care not which."

"Should you know him if you saw him ?"

"Couldn't be mistaken. There is not such another hang-dog, cut-throat looking scoundrel in the three kingdoms."

Earl Penelvon was thoroughly aroused, and paced about the floor in undisguised passion.

"But what is your other news, lieutenant ?"

"Simply a message from Sir Everard Brandon, speaking eulogistically of your protegé, the young midshipman."

"My protegé ? I have none on board the Thunderer."

"Harry Halliard."

"Why, he is the son of the widow that Trelawny attempted to— No, no, I am raving. What of him, is he dead ?"

"Oh, no, not yet ; he will have another rise in the service, soon."

"He is surely not coming home ?"

"Oh, yes ; he is off Falmouth, and on board one of the captured brigs."

This last piece of news fell like a thunderbolt upon the Earl, who sat in his chair, thoughtful and silent, long after the lieutenant had departed.

All his schemes had failed ! He knew not what to do.

With Trelawny and Rose Halliard dead, he might have braved the storm ; but since they were alive, and might yet crush him and lower his dignity down to the very dust, this was more than he could well bear.

He buried his head in his hands, and sat before the fire for hours, until long after the dying embers had ceased to flicker, and the wax tapers to splutter, and burn dim and low in their silver sockets.

When Lieutenant Blane had left Earl Penalvon, he slowly descended the spacious staircase, and, as he proceeded towards the hall, he espied a light, agile creature entering one of the parlours.

He hesitated, and his heart beat violently. It could not be that that was Nelly Britton !

And yet it must be, he thought, and immediately followed her retreating footsteps. He stopped, she turned, and in a moment she flew to his arms.

"Nelly !"

"Dear Paul !"

Such were the simple words that each spoke. Their hearts were too full for utterances, and as she placed her arms around him, and felt his strong stalwart form supporting her trembling frame, she sobbed upon his breast, and her bosom heaved in an agony of long-concealed, long-dissembled love!

That was a happy moment to each, more precious and priceless because least expected.

He would have spoken of his trials and triumphs, but girl-like she divined the strategem that had gained him admittance to the mansion, and as her fond eyes ran over each well-remembered feature, when she heard her own name whispered in the tenderest accents, and felt his noble heart beating against her breast, she was speechless, but proud to think she possessed the love of the noble and lion-hearted youth.

"I cannot longer stay, Nelly, we might be discovered. To-morrow, on the beach or cliffs, or in the woods, meet me, darling, for I have volumes to tell you."

"Dear Paul, this is the happiest moment of my life. I do not love aught on earth but you. Oh take me away, I pray ; I have done wrong in coming here in the way of temptation, but they told me all sorts of stories concerning you, which made me very wretched and unhappy ; in despair I scarce knew or cared what I did, or what became of me."

"Say not so, Nelly. Your own heart should have told you that Paul was faithful ; but, I hear foot steps approaching. I must begone."

With a long and tender embrace the lovers were clasped in each others arms, until in an agony of regret, Paul kissed her tears away, and stole noise lessly from the mansion, unsuspected and undis covered.

CHAPTER XXXIII.

THORKIL AND HYLDA QUARREL—DESIGNS FOR THE FUTURE – HELENA'S DESTINY IS FORESHADOWED—ENMITY OF PENREAL TOWARDS TRELAWNY—THE CARGO FROM ST. JACO.

"Now are ye content, wife ?" said Thorkil, entering his cavern home, and gazing on Hylda, brooding over the fire. "Now, are ye content with your runing ? Ye have well nigh ruined me."

"Why were you not more thoughtful, then, with your goods ?"

"Why not more careful ? Who is more careful than I ? Think you that any mortal e'er dreamed of that schooner opening her ports upon us? All our powder gone ! our store rooms a perfect wreck that powder monkey of a Cockney swab blown to the devil, and our horse killed ! Don't talk to me of thy spells and charms again ; all thou dost is to bring woe and misfortune upon us. If I catch thee or Thyra herb gathering or making chaplets of sea weed, I'll pitch ye down the cliffs, and make an end of both !"

"Take care what you say, Thorkil," said Hylda warningly ; "but take greater heed of what you do Recollect your master at the great house holds your neck in jeopardy, and at any time might swing both thee and me to the tallest tree in Seawardine !"

"Has an hold on me, say you ? Nay, Thorki Penreal knows more of Penalvon than Hylda guesses."

"No good e'er came of it. Misfortune hath followed us fast, and a gloomy day it was for both that you undertook that job. Where is she now ?"

"Aye, where is she ?—at the bottom of the sea I hope, she and her brat Sailor Boy both, I hope."

"Thyra could tell thee a different tale, Penreal, if you did but ask her."

"What could she tell ? That Rose became food for sharks, I suppose, and that the vessel was beached and proved a total wreck ? What more could she tell me than what I already know ?"

"There are more spars upon the beach to-day Penreal, than ever floated in thy craft."

"Whose mean ye ?"

"Black Will's."

"I'll not believe it, he has not one heart to venture alone. He dare not move without me."

"Dare not, idiot ; he has, but where he is to night the Fates alone know."

"Sunk like lead to the bottom, I hope ; but should I ever meet him, there is more than one score he will have to settle."

"Thou hast often said that before, Thorkil," answered Hylda, derisively.

THE SERGEANT OF MARINE'S DISCOMFORTURE.

"Would ye aggravate me? Is it nothing that I am all but ruined, and that I see thee roasting thy shins before the fire, day by day, that thou shouldst gibe and sneer?"

"Well, why sit ye here then, like the old hag that you call me? Is there naught expected from St. Jaco that ye smoke and guzzle rum all the day? Look at Polruth, even *he* can run in cargoes, and good ones, while here are you skulking about the beach like a worthless hulk, fit for naught but to badger women folk."

"Polruth! aye, he's no fool, dame; but he has more than one to help him, and good ones too. There's Paul Adair."

"And whose fault was it that he left thee?"

"Thine!"

"Mine?"

"Yes, thine! Thee and thy ruining will soon ruin all. Why, Agger even seems inclined to leave the band."

"Nay, he never will; there's a stronger hand over him than thine or mine."

"Whose?"

"Thyra's."

"What hath she to do with him?"

"Ask him."

"Ask him? Ye might as well ask questions of a milestone as to get aught out of him."

"So much the better then; a still tongue makes a wise head."

"I wish thou hadst a wise head then, wife, if only for the sake of the still tongue."

"Dost blister thee."

"Aye, does it; 'tis worse than the cat when lashed up to the grating."

"Perhaps Harleck has told thee of his experience that way?"

"No; but he has told me something better than that."

"What!"

"That concerns men, not women."

"Yet I have seen the time, Thorkil, when both you and Harleck were glad to ask Hylda what to do, when you and your cowardly gang would stand on trifles."

"Trifles! You did not always think them trifles."

"No; not when you murdered my father upon the beach in cold blood."

"No more of that."

"No more of that! and you would have strangled the babe that Thyra saved; but she was too wise."

"And why not? Are we to be pestered with babbling tongues to prate of our nightly doings? Who or what is this babe, that you think so much of? Helena—I mean Rose Halliard's adopted daughter—is aught to be made of it?"

"That concerns women not men, Penreal."

"Thy tongue is sharp."

"Not sharper than thy knife; but if even that were in my heart's core, I would not tell thee a single thing concerning her. She is fast growing into womanhood, and at a proper time will be mistress of her own actions."

"And, perhaps, cause us to dance in the air on a tight-rope."

"No fear of that. I fear there is no such gentle end in store for thee."

"What mean ye, woman?"

"I mean this. You have bred up enemies all around us—there is not one now scarcely willing to run ye a cargo; and yet, while the revenues are dogging your footsteps day and night, you prate of knives and pistols, and let your enemies run at large, baying like hounds at your heels."

"Not always, Hylda. We'll see what can be done to-night. If the coast is clear, a cargo from St. Jaco will set us on our legs again."

"Look well to it then, and mind who ye have in landing. They are not all wreckers and smugglers who sit like vultures on the cliffs. Some are hawks—night hawks, mind ye."

"One word is as good as a thousand. Have the lanterns ready, wife; I'll go and gather the band. I'll know a little more of Agger and Thyra, as well as Helena, or my name is not Thorkil Penreal."

Hylda smiled with a bitter smile, and watched his retreating form disappear through the windings of the cave, when she slowly whistled, and Wild Thyra emerged from her hiding-place.

CHAPTER XXXIV.

AFTER THE ACTION—THE ARROGANTE, L'EMPEREUR, AND JOSEPHINE—PARTICULARS OF THE ENGAGEMENT—HARRY HALLIARD AND FRANK RAYNER COMPLIMENTED—WHAT BECAME OF JUNIPER AND HAWSER—COMPLIMENTS OF THE FLEET—LAND HO!

WHEN the action between the Thunderer and the French frigate, Arrogante, had terminated, and the two armed brigs, and the merchantmen had likewise struck their colours, tremendous cheers were given by the brave British tars, which again and again were repeated, with an earnestness almost deafening.

The wounded even seemed inspired, and forgot the acutest suffering in their joy at the successful termination of so unequal a combat.

Headless human beings lay scattered up and down the decks; pools of blood, severed limbs, ropes, tackle, bolts, bars, cannon shot, cutlasses, guns, and tattered clothing were scattered everywhere, giving eloquent tokens of the fierceness and severity of the fight.

Doctors were hither and thither, attending to the wants of the many sufferers, while regular gangs of tender-hearted seamen were carefully collecting and providing for the many sufferers, moaning and groaning in every quarter.

Now that the action was over, all animosity seemed to have ceased, and officers and men were active and willing to attend alike on friend or foe.

Foremost to show his feelings as a man, towards the maimed and suffering, was Sir Everard Brandon, who went from place to place, with a pleasant voice and manner, cheering all with kind words and still kinder actions.

Every sufferer seemed to bless him, and followed all his actions with an affectionate look. So that, being inspired with renewed confidence in their able commander, the crew of the frigate, thinned as they had been from various causes, redoubled their energy and activity, and soon the glorious, battle-battered frigate was trimmed again once more, and spread her snowy sails to the breeze, and her ensign flaunted gallantly as ever.

"What signal is that flying from the Arrogante?" asked Sir Everard Brandon, coming on deck, and scanning the horizon, which was dotted with swan-like vessels, gracefully rolling and nodding in the freshening breeze.

"Can't make it out, sir," said passed midshipman Tranter, using his glass. "It looks like land, sir."

"Perhaps so. We can't be very far off Plymouth."

"No, sir," said Harry Halliard, coming down from the tops, with the agility of a daring young monkey as he was, "it is the Arrogante, signalling answers to the fleet, which is cruising to windward. I read them all, sir, with my glass, quite clearly, in the tops."

"You must have capital eyes then, Harry," said Sir Everard, kindly. "What were they talking about?"

"Admiral Nelson's flag-ship had signalled one of the armed brigs which we captured, but couldn't get any satisfactory replies."

"Perhaps they haven't a correct code, sir," said Tranter.

"The admiral said, sir, he couldn't make it out at all, and was going to bear down; but the officers in charge made themselves intelligible at last by hoisting the Union Jack, with the French flag under."

But there is the leading ship of the squadron, sir !" said Halliard, almost simultaneously with the stentorian tones of Konks, who sang out,

"Sail ho !"

"Is that Konks ?" asked Sir Everard.

"Yes, sir."

"Tell him I want him."

Konks soon appeared on the snowy quarter-deck, bowing and scraping.

"Got hit in the action, Konks ?"

"No, sir ; but came within an inch of losing my larboard fin, your honour," he replied, with a good-humoured grin.

"Better luck next time, Konks, let's hope. You don't want to be laid up in ordinary yet, I suppose ? How did the lads behave in the action, Konks ?"

"Well, your honour, there wasn't much to complain of, nor much picking and choosing, for all acted very well, thanks to my many lessons with the rope's-end."

"Too much of that is worse than the opposite extreme, Konks. You must learn to rule with kindness."

"Aye, sir, true ; but there be a few on board this vessel as ain't worth their hammock room."

"You don't mean to say that any were downright cowards before the enemy ?"

"Well, your honour, I doesn't know how to word it like, but I caught one of 'em playing dead for a good while, till I woke him up with a kick or two."

"Why, how was that ?"

"Well, you see, cap'en, when them ere Frenchers boarded us, we were short-handed ; and instead of rushing to force 'em back, this particular joker lays himself flat on deck, alongside some of the dead 'uns, and didn't seem inclined to face the music until I caught him at his tricks, and then he began to blubber like a fool."

"What's his name, Konks ?"

"Dan Crawley, your honour. or 'The Crawler,' as some of the boys call him. I reported the case, your honour, and he's under arrest, along of a few more as wants tying up to the gratings."

"But the majority behaved well under fire, I hear. I'm told that Frank Rayner——"

"Aye, your honour, he's a boy as is a credit to any ship, and although I am only Konks, your honour, I shall always feel proud to own I taught that boy."

"Where is he, Konks ?"

"In the sick-bay, cap'en ; he got a nasty slap on the head in saving you, sir."

"Me, say you ? How was that ? I never heard anything of it before ?"

"Well, you see, your honour, when the Frenchers' boarded us you had as much as you could very well do to look after yourself—a little too much, young Rayner thought, so he jumped in between you and a very nasty blow from a musket, and that floored him."

"A good, gallant boy."

"So said everyone who saw it, your honour ; but he did better than that, for, when Mr. Halliard there picked him up and dashed him with water, he recovered himself, and, in five minutes, hauled down the French colours ; although how the lad escaped seemed a miracle to all."

"Yes, yes ; I remember that very well. He's sick you say, Konks ; see if he is able to step this way."

In a few minutes Frank Rayner appeared, looking very pale and weakly.

He was much excited and trembled in every limb.

"Rayner," said the kind-hearted captain, "I have the very best accounts of you from all sides. I am very sorry you are laid up, but, as a reward for saving my life—which, from all reports, you undoubtedly did—I make you a present of one hundred pounds. It is not enough reward, I confess, but I am not rich, or I would do much more. For your general conduct in and out of action, I myself will vouch ; 'tis true, you are a little too fond of skylarking, yet I am proud to see you know your duty so well, and take care to fulfil it. Your conduct in the late engagement is on every tongue ; it augurs well for the future of our navy to see British Sailor Boys acting as you have done. I have to inform you that in my dispatch to the Lords of the Admiralty, I have especially mentioned you, and warmly recommended you to their earliest consideration for a vacant midshipmanship ; for the present, you can go to the sick bay ; you shall be tended by my own physician and surgeon."

A murmur of approbation escaped from the circle of officers as the pale, brave, trembling lad bowed and went forward.

The first to gain an opportunity for congratulating Frank, was his old chum, Harry Halliard.

As he grasped Rayner's hand in a light grip of true friendship, he said, with a trembling voice,

"Frank, I am too happy to say anything to you now. We shall be as inseparable as ever, and be more than we have ever been as messmates and brothers."

Poor Rayner was speechless.

He looked bewildered and faint.

He went below, and, when he had gained a spot removed from all, he leaned his head upon his hands and hot tears rolled down his cheeks in streams.

The whole of his life passed in rapid review before his eyes.

Friendless, houseless, he had been too glad to join the navy, and yet, within a very few years, by dint of attention to tuition, he had thoroughly mastered all his duties, and was well able to perform an able seaman's part, young as he was.

Now, however, he was about to receive his reward and be rated on the quarter-deck.

How his heart heaved as he thought of the glorious career thus brightly dawning upon him.

How he yearned to embrace Harry, his old and faithful friend.

"So that I am with *him*," he thought, "I care not what becomes of me, or where I go."

Yet there was a something, an indescribable void within his heart that nought could fill. He yearned for some one, young as he was, on whose breast he could lean, and pour out his youthful hopes, and fears and sorrows.

Yet he had no one. He would willingly have resigned all hopes of sword or epaulettes, if his mother were alive.

Mother ! That word wrung his very soul with pain, and as he sat lonely leaning on a gun, far away from all bustle and noise, it must be confessed, the brave lad wept silently and bitterly.

"But what has become of those brave fellows, Juniper and Hawser, Mr. Tranter ?" continued Sir Edward, still questioning. "Is it true that they are slain ?"

"Some think so, sir, but we know absolutely nothing of either. The last seen of them, Konks says, was when they led the boarding parties on board the armed brig that we ran into when the action began ; they may be alive, sir, but considering all things I think it is highly improbable they could have escaped from the numbers opposed to them."

"Is that her with the mainmast gone, that lags astern?"

"Yes, sir, L'Empereur, as she is called."

"You don't know who is commanding, say you? Then signal and let's see; it is necessary to know all these particulars for my official despatch. Back sails, and let her come up within hailing distance."

"Aye, aye, sir!"

And soon the Thunderer manœuvred, so that within less than an hour the French brig-of-war came within gun-shot.

"Ship ahoy! Who commands there?" reared Tranter through the silver speaking trumpet. "Any officers aboard?"

"What do they say, Tranter?"

"I can't tell yet, sir, but I think I know some of the jolly faces on deck; they are smoking, and appear to be enjoying themselves hugely."

Sir Everard was not kept very long in doubt as to who the commanders were, for a large, round, jolly face, appeared leaning over the side, which roared out, "No commissioned officers, your honour; Bill Hawser and me is sailing the ship."

"'Tis Juniper, by Jove!" shouted Sir Everard, laughing, and slapping his thighs with delight. "Juniper and Hawser in command, by all that's good!" he said. "Brave lads, Tranter—brave lads. I'm sorry they're hurt, though," he continued, looking into the decks of the brig with his glass. "Why they've got a dozen yards of lint round their heads."

"Sabre cuts, sir," said Tranter, smiling.

"No wonder, no wonder," was the quick reply. "How many men have they? Hail them, and ask."

"Fifty!" was the bellowing response, from Hawser, who, with hand to his mouth, was keeping up conversation. "Hundred prisoners below!" came across the water like the sounds of a gathering north-wester.

"Hundred prisoners below!" said Sir Everard, in great surprise. "Fifty or sixty men to take such a ship as that! Well, they are heroes, Tranter. What do you think of that, Harry?" he continued, slapping our hero on the back. "What do you think of that Halliard, eh? What do you think of our jolly salts, now, eh? Hearts of oak, as everybody must confess. What's the name of the other armed brig, Tranter?"

"Josephine, your honour; the two merchantmen are called l'Industrie and La Gloire."

"Very well. Signal all to keep in close company; let's all sail into Plymouth together. The fleet will give us a rousing cheer, I warrant, as we pass the flag-ship."

"Yes, sir, particularly when 'tis known that we have captured the long-looked-for convoy."

"True! Look well to the prisoners below. How do they seem to take their losses?"

"Awful bad, sir. The captain of the Arrogante seems broken-hearted."

"Poor fellow! A brave man, Tranter; he fought his ship like a trump."

"Yes, sir, and the doctors are surprised at the number of his wounds. He seems to care nothing for eating and drinking; he longs to die."

"Let young Rayner tend on him till we get into port; he's a kind-hearted, good-natured lad. He'll have a rise shortly, or I'm very much mistaken. What says the main-top, Halliard?"

"'Tis Konks, sir—Land ho!"

"Land ho! my hearties," said the seamen, in jubilant chorus. "Plenty of grog, and prize-money in store!"

"Anything in sight?"

"Cruisers signalling us, sir."

"What say they?"

"Compliments of the Admiral and the fleet, sir, twice repeated."

Sir Everard could hear no more; his emotions were so strong that he trembled.

"I don't care much for promotion," he muttered, as he went below. "All I want is to shake hands with Admiral Nelson, and the Admiralty can keep all their compliments and promotion for others."

"Make sail!" said Tranter, passing the word to the anxious and jubilant crew. "We shall anchor in Plymouth before the morning."

"Aye, aye, sir!" was the ready and hearty response, as the gallant tars danced about the deck, pulling and hauling with unusual vigour.

"Pull away, my hearties!" shouted Konks. "Plenty of grog and guineas on shore!"

CHAPTER XXXV

SURPRISE OF EARL PENALVON—ARRIVAL OF THE THUNDERER AT PLYMOUTH—PENALVON COMES TO THE CONCLUSION THAT HE HAS BEEN COMPLETELY SOLD—HIS ANGER AND RESOLVES—THE SKELETON IN THE MUSEUM—THE NOTE—THE UNKNOWN SIGNATURE—HIS TERROR AND DESPAIR—NELLY BRITTON IS UNHAPPY, AND WISHES TO RETURN HOME.

"WHAT news did the postman bring?" asked Earl Penalvon, as he sipped his coffee, and untied a large bundle of letters.

"Great news, my lord! There has been a terrific action at sea between the Thunderer and——"

"Yes, yes, sir; but have you heard anything of that young naval officer who called here a few evenings since?"

"No, my lord; but, judging from his manner when he left the Hall, I thought he was no naval officer at all."

"What say you? Think you I could be so easily deceived?"

"Well, my lord, I received a letter from my brother this morning, who serves in the Thunderer, and he says that none of her officers came on shore until three days ago. 'Tis more than a week since the stranger called, my lord."

Surprised, Earl Penalvon looked at his butler in great dismay.

"Bring me the Navy List. No, I don't see any such name here. I begin to suspect that I may have been imposed upon. Why, I gave him a large sum of money to ensure the capture of that d—dable rascal, Paul Adair!"

"Adair, my lord? Why, it struck me at the time that the stranger very much resembled him, although I did not like to mention it."

"Me to have intercourse with such a villain? What mean you? Think you I have any doings with such people?"

"No, my lord, it never struck me in that light before; but I have seen the same individual prowling about the premises more than once since then."

"Impossible!"

"Nay, my lord, 'tis true. He called once when you were out, and, thinking him to be some friend of yours, I showed him into the library, where he remained for more than an hour waiting for your return, as he seemed particularly desirous of seeing you."

"Heavens and earth !" roared Penalvon, in rage. "Is my mansion to be made a rendezvous for thieves ?"

"He seemed particularly pleased with your museum, and poured over your anatomical sketches for a very long time."

"My anatomical collection ?"

"Yes, my lord, and he pointed out a skeleton which you always like locked up, and he said he'd give anything in the world to possess it."

Penalvon turned pale, and clenched his hands with rage.

"What said he of it ?"

"Oh, nothing more than that it was the skeleton of one who must evidently have been a beautiful creature."

"Death and fury !"

"He said he knew whose bones they were ; but in answer to my repeated questions he only smiled, and said he had forgotten the name, but that *you* knew it very well."

"Leave me," roared Penalvon, as if struck to the heart by an arrow, "he knows more than I wish ; but *I'll* soon put a stop to his prying, for I'll destroy all traces of the past."

Rushing into his museum he unlocked and unveiled the skeleton ; he was amazed to see the right hand slowly raised, and in its bony palm there was a note.

He staggered with amazement, but seized the note. It was written in a disguised hand, and read,

"*Earl Penalvon shall meet his fate when least expected. The secrets of the past are known, known to one he does not, perhaps, suspect. All the glory of Seawardine shall crumble and decay. Justice shall be vindicated. Penalvon's stone vaults have secrets to tell. Mystery shall be unveiled to the noon-day sun. The time is not yet.*   "HELEN."

The note fell from his hands upon the floor. He left the room, and locking himself in the library, sat crouched before the fire, pale and trembling.

For hours thus he sat, he was unconscious of the lapse of time.

When evening came some one knocked at his door. He unbolted it ; it was Nelly Britten.

Penalvon gazed on the pretty fragile figure of the maid with lustful eyes.

"Why come you here, Nelly ?"

"I come to say, my lord, that I should like to leave ; I am troubled with frightful dreams, and know not the cause."

"Nay, you must not think of leaving me, Nelly ; your chamber is near to mine, you know, and there cannot be the slightest cause for alarm."

"That is why I wish to leave, my lord, for several nights I have seen some one very like you moving about ; it seems to follow me wherever I go, until I cannot sleep."

"Like me, say you," said Penalvon, laughing coarsely, "and would you be frightened at seeing a man enter your chamber, say a dear friend, who loved you very much ?"

"Nay, my lord, I know not what you mean. I already have a sweetheart ; but he is far away, I fear, and I feel lonely, I should very much like to return home."

"Well, then, so you shall," he answered ; but as she left, he added, "not yet, I must have new emotions, new sensations, my whole life is a burden, my soul is heavy, I am hunted by unseen ministers of torture. Yes, you may go, my pretty maid ; but not yet !"

He rang the bell.

"Bring me some wine," he said ; "let's see what potency there is in the grape."

CHAPTER XXXVI.

WILD THYRA AND AGGER—THE PROPOSAL AND REJECTION — THORKIL'S SCHEMES REGARDING HELENA — AGGER THREATENS TO LEAVE THE WRECKERS — APPEARANCE OF THE PHANTOM SCHOONER—THYRA'S DELIGHT.

THE evening was balmy, and the stars began to peep from the azure sky. The broad ocean was calm, and sea birds soared lazily about the beach and cliffs.

Thyra bent her steps towards the White Cliffs, and sat down upon a lofty crag that overlooked the sea.

She was pale and thoughtful, and her bright eyes were moistened with tears.

She had not long thus remained, when the rough figure of a wrecker approached.

"Agger ?" she said, almost inaudibly.

"Yes, lass ; I have come to have a word or two with thee."

"With me, Agger ?"

"Aye, lass. I wish to speak to thee of many things."

"Of Thorkil ?"

"No ; d——n him ! I shall leave him, I hope, for ever ; but it all depends."

"What has he done, then, that vexes thee so much ?"

"Done ? Oh, nought particular ; but he's always grumbling."

"Didn't he land his cargo ?"

"True, lass, he did, at least, *I* did for him, for he was as drunk as a clown, and didn't know what to do."

"And didn't that please him ?"

"No, lass. The more he has the more he wants."

"He wants you to do something, then, Agger, that you will not ?"

"True, lass ; but how knew you about it ?"

"I know it, and that's sufficient."

"About Rose's foster-daughter, Helena ?"

"Yes."

"Who told thee ?"

"It matters not ; and you will not do it, Agger. Promise me you will not."

"How could I lass, she never harmed me."

"Nor any one."

"Then why should I go and run off with her, and perhaps plunge a knife into her young bosom ?"

"Good, Agger, I love you for that," said Thyra, taking his rough hands and kissing them.

"Love me, Thyra ! You do not mean it !" said the wrecker, exultingly. "You can't mean that in earnest !"

"I mean that I love you for refusing to follow the commands of that wretch Thorkil."

"Don't speak so loud, lass, there may be ears that catch all your words, and then I wouldn't give a penny for your life. He hates you."

"I fear nothing from him, the monster ; but what has poor Rose, or Helena, done to him or his, that he should feel so remorselessly, so cruelly towards them ?"

"I don't know, wench. All I know is, that Agger will never lend a hand to harm the girl; but tell me, Thyra," continued he, softening his tone of voice, "what makes thee shun every one so much? I'm sure that I do not hate thee."

"I know you do not, Agger; I have known it long ago."

"And you know *more* than that, Thyra; you know that I——"

Her eyes met his with a long steady gaze, as she muttered,

"No, Agger; *not* that."

"Do you mean, then, that it can *never* be?"

"Yes!"

"Do you mean it?"

"Yes, Agger; I love you as a friend, perhaps more than a friend, but what you mean can *never* be. Ask anything but that and I would willingly grant it, but do not press me now, my heart is already given away."

For some moments they sat silently, occupied in watching the horizon, without exchanging a word.

"There it is! there it is!" said Thyra, at length, rising suddenly, and clapping her hands for joy.

"There is what?" asked Agger, in a gruff voice, looking out upon the calm blue sea. "I thought you had ceased your runing for ever, but I see that the fit is on thee again."

"There it is, Agger! there it is!" she continued, clapping her hands and pointing to a white speck that danced and leaped upon the distant waves.

"'Tis the Phantom, Agger; I knew it would come again."

"And it never comes without brewing mischief to some one hereabouts."

"And she is on board."

"Who is on board?"

"Rose Halliard and Will Trelawny, and——and——"

"Who?" asked Agger, doggedly. "Thy lover, I suppose," he added, with a rough, revengeful oath. "Who told thee that Rose and Black Will were on board? Trelawny sailed away more than a fort-night ago for France."

"Which he never reached. But look, look how gracefully she rolls."

"I wish she would roll and capsize, that's all the harm *I* wish her," said Agger, "for Thorkil will never forget the night she fired and blew up his powder. I must tell him of this, for he expects a craft in to-night. If the schooner ever comes within range again she won't get off so easily, take my word. We've made preparations for her, or for a dozen such as she."

Wild Thyra laughed and sang and clapped her hands.

"Harm her? sink her? ha, ha! Agger, you might as well try to drown the tall White Cliffs as injure her. She has a charmed life, so has her commander; he is the only true man that ploughs the deep."

"Oh, he is, is he? and what may his name be, then, wench, as you seem to know so much about him?"

"The Rover."

"The Rover! I'm just as wise as ever."

"And so must remain for the present, good Agger; but know he sails about the coast in search of something, and you'll hear of him sooner than you or Thorkil expect; he comes to-night."

Agger swore roundly about rune-kenning in general, and walked away to Thorkil's cave, in a sullen, revengeful mood of disappointment.

Thyra still sat upon the cliff, gazing below, and as she stretched out her arms towards the sea, she seemed to mutter something like a fervent prayer for Rose Halliard, and the schooner which was now fast sailing and tacking towards the shore, while the numberless stars shone forth with unwonted brilliancy, and the rising moon shed a belt of silver upon the white tufted waves.

CHAPTER XXXVII.

BLACK WILL TRELAWNY IN THE SICK BAY—HE IS CONFRONTED BY THE ROVER AND ROSE HALLIARD, AND UPBRAIDED FOR HIS VILLANIES.

"WHERE am I?" asked Black Will, rubbing his eyes and waking to a full sense of consciousness. "Where am I? Oh, give me something to drink, for mercy's sake!"

"Where are you?" said a seaman beside him, in an angry tone, "why, where you don't deserve to be, for if you had your deserts you would be at the bottom by this time. Know, then, you black, ugly rascal, that you're on board the schooner, and a prisoner, but if I was the captain, I'd cut your rascally wizen."

"Prisoner! Schooner!" muttered Trelawny, gradually becoming conscious of the past. "Oh, I remember," and he sighed heavily. "What has become of the craft, and the—the—Is she dead?"

"No she isn't, and isn't likely to be yet awhile, if our captain can help it."

"Captain! What's his name?"

"The Rover! that's all the name we knows him by, and a brave fellow he is as ever piloted a craft upon the waters. Here he comes."

At that moment a tall, handsome fellow entered the cabin, and motioning with an air of habitual command, the seaman left him alone with the wounded man.

"You are the captain of the schooner, I believe?" said Black Will, leaning on his elbow. "I think I have seen your face before."

"Perhaps you have, Trelawny, and may do so again."

"Your name is——"

"Never mind my name; answer my question Why did you abduct Rose Halliard?"

"How know you that I did so?"

"'Twas self-evident. I know you did; and more than that, you were hired to do so, and, villain as you are, would have done any sort of unmanly, dirty work for a little gold, and to satisfy a mean revenge."

"You seem to know so much, I don't think it necessary to answer your questions."

"We shall see shortly. You shall be placed where not even your very noble friend can assist you."

"My noble friend! what mean you?" asked Trelawny, writhing in mental and bodily pain.

"Mean, you mean-spirited cur; you well know what I mean. You sailed away with a merry heart, did'nt you? Cash was not lacking, and you had a crew of hang-dog looking rascals like yourself. But *I* knew your plans long before you set out to accomplish them, and here you are."

"And my craft—"

"Down at the bottom, with half your crew; the rest are in irons."

"What mean you to do with me?"

"Take care of you. Keep you a living witness of Earl Penalvon's villany."

"Earl Penalvon! ha, ha!" laughed Black Will. "You may harm me, but he is beyond your power, whoever you are."

"Don't croak, Trelawny; your very life hangs upon a thread. One word from me, and you would swing from the yard-arm in five minutes, murderer as you are."

"Murderer!"

"Yes, murderer; and if it were not for Rose's prayers, you would be dangling like a dog long ere this."

"And did she beg my life?"

"She did and does. When you would have fired the magazine and blown all to atoms, know that *she* seized the torch and struck you senseless to the earth."

"But how did she escape from the cabin?"

"Through me. Some of my men secreted themselves on board long before you sailed, and following my directions, watched all your actions, both day and night."

Trelawny looked astonished.

"Was that the voice I heard?"

"It was, and had you attempted to lay a finger upon her, a knife would have bursted your vile heart upon the spot, unseen and unheard."

"How long is this since?"

"Three weeks ago. I have since landed, and spoken to your noble patron. Disguised, I entered his house, and know enough of him and his infamous past career, to hang him with thee, side by side on some road-side gibbet; but the time is not yet."

"Then who art thou?" asked Black Will, in surprise.

"My deliverer!" exclaimed Rose Halliard, noiselessly approching, and confronting the smiling villain, lying helpless in his bunk.

"Rose Halliard!"

"Whom you sought to destroy."

"'Tis like a woman to speak thus bravely. I knew the time when you could crouch and fawn."

"'Twas like a man to do as you have done; were it not for a merciful Providence, I should have been lost. But, know now, you remorseless coward, I am beyond your power and desires. Thank Heaven, I am free again; and if it be within the reach of law and justice, you shall be amply punished for your wrongs to me."

"Woman, leave me; your words and presence are wormwood. If you wish to kill me, do so; but leave me, I beg."

The scoundrel, remorseless as he seemed, quailed before the pure-minded woman who confronted him, and he turned restlessly in his bunk, groaning and cursing.

"I will leave you to your own thoughts, Trelawny," said the Rover, sarcastically. "We are rapidly nearing the shore; in a few hours you will be placed where none can know or harm you. Until then, farewell."

The cabin door was closed and he was alone, save the presence of a sturdy seaman, who, pistol in hand, watched beside him, ready and very willing to blow out the murderer's brains, should he be fool-hardy enough to attempt violence.

CHAPTER XXXVIII.

KONK'S YARN—HIS CAPTAIN'S MADEIRA—CROSSING THE LINE—A FAT SERJEANT OF MARINES COMES TO SUDDEN GRIEF.

THE Thunderer and her consorts were gradually reaching Plymouth harbour, each vessel that they met, whether of the Royal Navy or Mercantile Marine, saluted the veteran ships with hearty cheers.

They were dirty, powder blackened, and ragged looking; their sails were patched and rigging cut and torn, yet, for all their looks, betrayed what seamen loved most, namely, the appearance of vessels which had been in the heat and storm of battle, returning home victorious from foreign waters.

When the several vessels had cast anchor in the Sound for the night, and all had turned in, Harry Halliard, Frank Rayner, and Konk's, found themselves on watch together.

"Well, Mr. Konks," said Harry, "we are nearly home again. What makes you look so gloomy? I'm sure when we're all ashore you'll feel happy enough, and soon forget all the vexations of our past cruise."

"Well, lads, I never reach Old England without having a fit of melancholy."

"Melancholy, Mr. Konks; why, with your share of prize money in view, I think I should feel very comfortable; I should, indeed," said Rayner.

"Well, you see, you ain't as old as I am; when you've been to sea as often as I, you may think differently."

"How is that, Mr. Konks?" asked Harry. "You don't mean to say there is a story attached to it, do you?"

"That's just what I *do* mean, Mr. Halliard."

"Let's have the yarn then, I beg," said Rayner.

"By all means," added Harry. "Here, squat down beside this gun."

"And let's hear it out. Attention, Frank."

"Well," said Konks, taking a fresh chew of tobacco, and hitching up his trowsers, "my yarn is pretty square sailing, so I'll steer close to the wind, and tack as little as possible.

"You see, lads, when I was a young man, a little older than either of you, I entered the Royal Navy as a landsman, and a pretty clever, smartish one I was, so they said. In a short time I could splice a rope on the main brace, reef sky-sails, and dance a hornpipe with any one on board.

"The Hornet was bound on a voyage to the Cape of Good Hope, with troops and stores, and altogether we soon became as jolly a ship's company as any that ever exchanged broadsides with the Frenchers.

"When we neared the Canaries, our captain went ashore and bought some casks of Madeira, and several boats' crews were detailed to go and fetch them. Among the number was Bill Hawker, as good a boatswain as ever trod the deck, he only had one fault, he *would* have his grog, if he could, sink or swim.

"When we beached the boat, Bill proposed that all should go and take an hour's stroll in town, but although the others were willing, I remained with the boat.

"Several hours passed, and there was no sign of Bill Hawker or our boat's crew. The evening gun fired, and our captain signalled for the boat to return.

"Not knowing what to do, I shoves off, and, after a pretty hard pull, reached the Hornet.

"'Where's my wine, and where's the boat's crew?' shouted our red-faced captain.

"I explained everything, and two boats' crews were sent off to shore immediately.

"We landed, broke up into squads, and went to all the wine shops and dance houses, but nowhere could we find Bill Hawker or his party.

"In one or two of the places we had a glass of rum, and this, with a smoke or two, made us all pretty jolly, and we sheered off to the boats again about midnight, and, as we approached the wine casks, we thought we could see about a dozen or two fine fat turtle lying sprawling on the sand, but it turned out that it was Bill Hawker and his men who had tapped the Madeira with gimlets, and, what with drinking and waste, half a cask had gone, and all of them were lying on the moonlit sand, as tight as lords.

"We put them all into one boat, one on top of t'other, and took it in tow towards the Hornet, and when we gets alongside the captain shouts out,

"'Where are they?'

"'Here they are, sir,' I answered.

"'Haul away, boys; pull 'em up. Now, gents,' says he, to his officers, 'I promise you as fine a drop of wine as the islands afford.'

"But, instead of hauling up the casks, we hauled up the boat's crew, all as tight as bricks, when the officers began to laugh right heartily, and myself also, for Bill Hawker when placed upon his stomach on deck, began to kick and plunge as if swimming, cursing and swearing like the devil until he was carried below.

"The casks were brought on board next morning, and we weighed anchor for the Cape.

"I never heard the last of the wine adventure.

"If I was fool enough to suppose that the wine scrape had been forgotten, there were others on board who did not, and from the many hints I heard I began to imagine that they supposed I had 'blown' on them to the captain.

"This of course was untrue, yet Bill always looked sideways at me, and I thought I saw the devil in his eye.

"As we neared the line there were grand preparations going on among the crew for those unfortunate devils who had never crossed it, myself among the number.

"Knowing nothing about navigation I could never find out the exact time when we should cross it.

"The weather became hotter and hotter every day, until, at last, every breath of air seemed to have left us, and we lay upon the water like a painted ship upon a painted ocean; the sails hung from the masts like wet rags, and, altogether, we felt very much like so many loaves in an oven, without any prospect of a change.

"From the grinning going on I knew we were somewhere near the line, but, when the officers at noon, after their usual daily observations with glasses, announced that we were on it, there was a general shout among the men.

"If I had had sense, I might have known that we were on the line, for there was not the slightest shadow falling from anything.

"To my great surprise I saw coming over the side a very strange sight; Neptune, sea-nymphs and mermaids, all came trooping on deck, decked out in the strangest manner, like a show I once saw in a theatre.

"Seating himself on a gun, with a tremendous trident for a sceptre, all the old tars gathered about him, and then commenced the very interesting ceremony of all being presented to him.

"Those who had crossed the line before were treated to a shake of the hand, but those unfortunate devils who hadn't, had to pay the penalty, whether they liked it or not.

"I was below when the ceremony began, but they soon hauled me up on deck, and had me before old Neptune, who ordered me to be shaved right off amid a general roar of laughter.

"It was no use of kicking and all that, for three or four stout fellows soon tied me up, while one chap, with a large piece of rough hoop-iron for a razor, and another with a bucket of paste, stood handy.

"They lathered me all over, pushed the brush into my eyes, and when I began to curse and swear, they politely shoved the brush into my mouth.

"I thought I should go crazy; the more I kicked the more they lathered, and roared out laughing.

"The brush was bad enough, but when they began to shave me with the hoop-iron I thought I should go crazy, for it scraped and scraped until my whole face was raw as beef, and I fairly howled with torment.

"It didn't matter how much I cursed and swore, they *would* go on with the whole performance.

"I felt awfully mad, and was going to knock old Neptune off the gun; but was prevented. I made up my mind to have revenge, and particularly against the fat sergeant of marines, who seemed to take such pleasure in my torment, for to be laughed at by my messmates was bad enough, but I couldn't stand anything from such a lubber as he.

"It gave me no pleasure to see other youngsters go through the same ceremony, so I went below, and was brooding over my rough handling for many a day, although I could never find out who Neptune was, and I strongly suspected that it was Bill, who had it in for me through the scrape at the Canaries.

"I was sometimes appointed to help the butcher, and the sergeant of marines, expecting to get a tit bit now and then, often came to have a chat with me.

"I didn't let anyone know that I had it in for him, so one day, when I was killing pigs, one of the men called him over, and they began to talk and yarn very comfortably. The sergeant was dressed in bran new regimentals, and with a cane in his hand, looked fatter, and more pompous than ever.

"He was very particular not to get near the pig-stye, but stood several yards off, talking about who and what he was, and how many engagements he had been in. His men were mustering for duty, and he said he must be off; but just as he was turning to go, I let slip the pig I was about to stick, and it ran between the sergeant's legs, upsetting him among the dirt, and spoiling all his new clothes.

"We all laughed at the accident, and particularly because he was obliged to report himself at parade, and there he stood before his superiors, soiled from head to foot, while all the men were grinning, and the officers ordered him under arrest.

"It began as a joke, but ended very seriously, for the sergeant lost his stripes, and he began to look gloomy, and talked of 'settling' somebody. The voyage progressed favourably enough, but when he had to do duty as a private, it went against the grain because his time was nearly up, and he expected a pension. He swore he would have revenge on somebody; but he felt particularly angry against his captain for dishonouring him, as he thought, without sufficient cause.

"When we were entering Plymouth harbour in great good humour, he goes up to his captain to ask him to sign his petition for a pension; but he refused, and made some annoying remark, when the sergeant struck him. There was a great uproar among the red coats, and he was seized; but suddenly upsetting the two marines that stood guard over him, he levelled a musket at his captain, shot him dead upon the spot, and jumped over the side of the ship, and was never afterwards heard of. So, lads, that's why I feel melancholy whenever I enter this port, for I always said, and stick to it, that harm befalls some messmate or other of mine, who ever sailed with me into this port."

Konk's last remarks were prophetic!

BOYS' LIBRARY

Harry Halliard: or, the Young British Tar.

FRANK RAYNER REPRIEVED.

CHAPTER XXXIX.

FRANK RAYNER BECOMES A MIDSHIPMAN — THE FRENCH OFFICERS ARE RELEASED ON PAROLE—JOLLIFICATION OF THE TARS IN PLYMOUTH—THE QUARREL — THE DUEL—FATAL RESULTS — INNOCENCE TRIUMPHANT—HARRY HALLIARD TO THE RESCUE.

THE church bells rang out merry peals, flags fluttered from windows and house-tops, and heavy guns boomed out long and noisy salutes, as the Thunderer anchored in Plymouth Harbour.

The whole town seemed to have taken a holiday, and every person was decked in his or her best attire.

The news of the gallant fight was noised abroad, and discussed and magnified, at street corners, and in every beer-shop for miles around.

Captain Brandon's name was on every lip, and toasted with hearty cheers by all classes, from the highest to the lowest.

Those who were not drunk from drink seemed intoxicated with joy, and not one of the Thunderer's crew could pass through the streets without meeting with smiles from fair dames, or shakes of the hand from sturdy, patriotic men.

All the ale-houses were crowded, and dozens of the curious would gather round any single one of the crew, and listen for hours to his long, rambling, and highly-magnified and embellished account of the action, until the jolly tars were fairly worn out with answering the almost numberless inquiries and questions.

Harry Halliard's first task was to write a very long and affectionate letter to his mother, giving every particular of the late engagement, for he felt certain that a mother's heart would be anxious to learn that her darling and only hope was safe, and had carried himself through all danger in a manner worthy of his name and recent promotion.

Alas! he little knew where that fond mother was, or his smile of pride and gratification, as he sealed his tender epistle, would have changed to a sadness bordering utter madness.

Putting on his bran-new uniform, he was about to take one of the ship's boats, and land for a two days' leave with some fellow midshipmen, when he saw Frank leaning over the side looking very miserable and melancholy.

His heart smote him, and he gave up his intended ramble.

"What's the matter, Frank?"

"Oh, nothing, Harry; I feel rather low-spirited. I feel as if some horrible calamity were about to befal me."

"Won't you come ashore?"

"No thank you, Harry; you are an officer now, lad, and I feel proud of it, but it won't do for you to be seen walking about with a common sailor-boy, you know."

"I am sorry you are so silly as to have any such foolish thoughts. You know there is no change in me, and never will be; you must always be Frank Rayner to me, if even I ranked as an admiral!"

"I know that, Harry; I feel it, that's more. But here comes Sir Everard Brandon."

Harry and Frank stood beside the gangway as their brave and much-loved captain stepped upon the deck, and saluted him respectfully but heartily.

"Good morning, lads!" he said, with a good-humoured smile. "Why ain't you off to town, Mr. Halliard, nearly all your brother officers are there? Have you been up to any sky-larking, that your liberty is stopped? Never mind, my boy, I'll give you leave."

"No, Sir Everard, thank you, I have done nothing wrong, that I know of, and was going ashore, but I stayed to have a chat with my old chum Frank, here, sir!"

"Good, lad, I like your spirit! You won't go without him, and he won't go because you are a middy and an officer, eh? I see. Well, well, we can soon manage that little matter," he said, winking at his first-lieutenant. "Step this way, Mr. Rayner, I wish to see you in my cabin!"

"Didn't you hear him say he wanted you, Harry? He wants you in his cabin," said Rayner.

"Me? No he didn't; he told you. Didn't you hear him?"

"Me? No, I'm sure he didn't. I'm no Mister! He said he wished to see Mr. Halliard."

While they were talking thus a marine stepped up to Frank.

"Sir Everard wishes to speak to Mr. Rayner and Mr. Halliard," he said, smiling, laying particular stress on the "Mister."

Frank coloured up instantly, and trembled in every limb, as he entered Sir Everard's state cabin, where his brave commander sat at a very large loo table, writing.

"There lads," he said, throwing down his pen, "I haven't had a pleasanter line to write in my life than putting my name to that precious little document."

Rayner stood cap in hand, and felt faint.

Harry imagined that the precious little document alluded to was a commission for Frank, and smiled with vast satisfaction.

"Take a glass of wine, lads; help yourselves, there's a decanter and glasses. Now, I wish to say a word to you both. Mr. Halliard, I have spoken personally to the admiral about your good conduct, and if you continue to improve in your studies, and carry yourself as you have up to the present time, I see no earthly obstacle to your gradual progression through all grades, even up to that of an admiral.

"As to you, Rayner, I owe you ten thousand thanks for saving my life, and shall never forget your self-sacrifice and true heroism until the day I die. Here is a check for £200; take care of it, my brave lad, and," said he, rising and placing an official envelope in Frank's trembling hand, "here is something even better still—this is a commission, my boy, you are rated on the books as midshipman. There, now you can go on shore, both together; get your uniform as soon as possible, and may God bless you. When you are in town, call at my house and dine; my wife wishes to see you."

Halliard's eyes danced with delight at Frank's good fortune, but Rayner turned deadly pale, trembled, and fell helplessly upon a sofa.

"Why, what ails the boy? surely he hasn't fainted!"

He had fainted, however; the shock was so sudden that 'twas more than he could bear, and he lay as helpless as an infant. When he recovered he hung his head in great dejection, and tears flowed fast down his handsome face, and his breast heaved like a sorrowing broken-hearted maid.

"Come, come, lad; don't let the news kill you. Keep up your spirits, 'tisn't the last commission you'll receive by a good many, I know, if you study to learn and do your duty well. There, you are better now. You and Halliard go off for a little fun, but don't get into mischief."

The two young midshipmen were soon on shore, and as their leave extended, as Sir Everard termed it, "for a three days' run," they both took rooms at the "Crown," and ordered a capital dinner of beef steaks and onions, not forgetting to indulge in a bottle of Madeira in honour of the occasion.

They were not long in satisfying the cravings of the inner man, and soon sallied forth to a fashionable navy clothier's to select new uniforms, one for each, so that they might appear in good trim when they called on Lady Brandon.

When Frank had done with the barber and tailor, and put on his bran new uniform, he blushed and looked very sheepish at himself in the glass; yet came to the conclusion that he had seen many a worse looking fellow among the "reefers," as he termed midshipmen generally.

Halliard felt perfectly at home in his new clothes, and seemed to be in a great hurry to go out and strut about the streets for a time.

Frank, however, confessed that he felt very awkward, and wished to stay at home. After some little persuasion, however, he donned his cap and dirk, and both sallied forth as large as life, and carried themselves with a free-and-easy grace of manner that struck the attention of more than one young maiden as she peeped through the blinds at them strolling purposeless about the town.

"If we could only meet Juniper and Hawser," said Frank, puffing hard at a very bad cigar.

"Yes; wasn't it a miracle? we all made sure they were down among the dead men."

"Didn't you hear Armitage and Fraser yesterday talking about their gallantry? Just to fancy that fifty of them could have done so much; it was a miracle all were not slain, and just to think of the men making them their commander, and bringing their vessel and prisoners all safe into port."

"Yes, and Admiral Nelson ain't the man to forget such deeds, mark me if he does. What an awful cut Juniper got, though, across the cheek; didn't you see the deep scar?"

"Hawser says he has been deaf ever since a shot whizzed passed his head, and came very near spoiling his beauty."

At that moment they were passing a tavern euphoniously called the "Black Pig," and the sounds of a familiar voice roaring out—

> "And I've a commission from the King
> To kiss all girls that's handsome!"

caused both to stop and listen.

"Juniper, by all that's lucky," said Harry, slapping Frank heartily on the back in great delight, "let's go in and shake hands, what say you?"

Nothing loth, both entered and peeped through cracks in the tap-room door, and could scarce refrain from laughing at what they saw.

There sat Juniper and Hawser in clouds of tobacco smoke, puffing at long pipes and taking very hearty drinks of mahogany-coloured liquor and water, which was steaming beside their right elbow, while on the left there sat two buxom wenches, who seemed highly charmed with Juniper's vocal powers, as he roared out with the lungs of Boreas the popular song of the "Rambling Sailor."

"How jolly they are," said Frank. "See old Hawser chucking her under the chin. Look at Juniper, how he does puff to be sure; he looks like a volcano—all fire and smoke."

"Yes; they seem to be enjoying themselves greatly," said Harry; "but I don't think their companions are worth much. Let's watch, and see if they try to rob them; they are all land-sharks, as sure as my name is Halliard."

"By Jove! Harry, did you see that, eh? One row has hooked Juniper's watch and chain. See them wink at Hawser's girl; they are all a gang and league, or shoot me," remarked Frank. "We can't stand this, let's go in, or they'll rob the poor fellows of all they've got."

"Stay here a moment, Frank. Turn the key in the door; that's it. Wait till I return."

Rushing from the house, Harry met a party of the Thunderer's crew, some half dozen in number, going towards the dockyard. They bowed respectfully to the young middy, and in a few moments he had explained all to them.

"You don't mean that!" they answered. "Come, let's go to the 'Black Pig,' and give the d——d fellows a good overhauling."

Quicker than words can describe they reached the public-house.

"Stay at the door, men, until I give the word. If any attempt to escape, you know what to do."

"Aye, aye, sir," was the response, as one and all took a huge chew of tobacco, hitched up their trousers, and prepared for possible fisticuffs. "Aye, aye, sir, we'll stand by, Mr. Halliard. You give the word, and we'll sail in, won't we mates?"

"Well, Frank, what news?"

"News! Why Juniper and Hawser are getting stupified, and they have just robbed them of their wallets. Let's go in?"

"Just so."

While all was noise and merriment in the tap-room, the young midshipmen quietly turned the key, and walked in.

"Why, Harry, my hearty!"

"What? Frank Rayner!" were the joint exclamations.

"Yes, shipmates, here we are."

"Well, you must drink with us, or I'll say you're no friend of mine," said Juniper, rising staggering, and offering drink.

"We will have a quiet glass directly, Juniper," said Harry; "but, first of all, let me ask you both—have you lost anything?"

This question seemed to startle all present save those to whom it was addressed.

"Lost anything?" said one, indignantly rising. "What do you mean, you young skipjacks," asked the women.

"Do you take us for thieves?" said a red-nosed fellow in shabby attire. "If you do, why then I shall leave."

"No, don't go yet; not quite so fast. I command you to stay where you are a few minutes!"

"Command!" he said, contemptuously.

"Yes, command; and in the King's name. If you don't, I'll make you!" said Harry, valiantly, and colouring with anger.

"Make me?"

"Yes, make you."

The person addressed made a blow at Harry, but Hawser stepped suddenly between, and knocked him down flat upon the floor, with a blow which resounded through the whole room.

In an instant all was commotion and confusion. Several rose, and the fight became general. But just as several rushed to the door, in dashed the party outside, and overpowered them.

The surprise of all was great; but yet still more so when Frank and Harry had each one searched, and Juniper's money and watch, and Hawser's valuables, were found secreted upon the persons of this band of thieves.

"Well," said Hawser, when the whole gang were securely locked up in the station-house, "whoever would have believed it? Why, Juniper and me have been feeding and lushing them all day, and singing a pleasant song or two; and then, when no one ever expects sharks, up they turns."

"'Twas lucky that Frank and I heard your voices, or you might have been eased of everything."

"Well, Mr. Halliard, and you, Frank, my lad, let me give you both my hearty good wishes. Luck falls upon some, they say. Perhaps, if I had a bit of learning, I might have found the right channel out. No matter, lads, you are both bright boys; and all old Juniper says is, he's much obliged to you for signalling the shoals and sandbanks, and if so be's he can do you a turn or two—as he did when, like young bears, he had to lick you into shape, as on board the Thunderer—why pass the word, hearties, and Hawser and me will never be the messmates to say nay. Now, shipmates, let's order in plenty of grog; let's blow a cloud together, and drink nine times nine to Admiral Nelson, Captain Brandon, and the whole British fleet!"

The proposition was responded to with vociferous applause, and while Juniper and Hawser were chanting a very long and noisy song about "Tom Bowling," or some other naval hero, to a sailor audience, almost lost in tobacco smoke, Halliard gave directions to have them carried off safely to bed at a seasonable hour, and left the tap unobserved, just as the tables, and glasses, and spoons were making a terrible rattle, as the enthusiastic company were applauding and demanding a repetition of the last song.

"Let's go to Lady Brandon's," said Frank, each moment feeling easier in his new uniform.

"You should go; but I was not invited, you know."

"Oh, hang that, where I sail you must be in company, you know."

"Well, its scarcely the thing, you see; but as this is a time for general enjoyment and pleasure, I don't mind."

They soon arrived at Clarence Terrace.

A powdered footman opened the door.

"Your cards, gentlemen."

"Oh, never mind that, governor; say that Frank Rayner and myself, Harry Halliard, have called to pay their best respects to her ladyship."

"They were shown into the parlour, and stood gazing at and much admiring the many admirable and choice appointments of the apartment, when Lady Brandon noiselessly entered. They were unaware of her presence, and continued their critical remarks on all they saw.

"Here's Sir Everard's picture," said Harry; "fine-looking fellow, ain't he?"

"Yes, and here's her ladyship, I suppose, on this side. What a neat, trim, fast-sailing, dauntless little craft she looks," was the response. "The captain's a good judge of beauty, upon my soul; why *any* fellow could fall in love with such a girl as that."

"Yes, there's no mistake about it; such a pair of eyes, and such snow white shoulders. Why, she's as pretty as a fifty-gun frigate in full sail, stunsails set, and the wind on the quarter."

Lady Brandon coughed slightly, which caused both young sailors to turn very suddenly, and in crimson confusion.

"This must be Mr. Rayner," she said, intuitively approaching Frank, and before he could recover from astonishment the good, warm-hearted lady embraced him, saying, with tears in her eyes,

"Oh, sir, I can never thank you sufficiently for your gallantry and heroism in saving my poor dear husband from certain death."

Rayner was speechless, he knew not how to reply.

"And you sir, Mr. ——"

"Halliard, at your service, dear lady."

"I thought so; Sir Everard has spoken so much of you both, and I am so happy to see you, and thank you a thousand times for your noble behaviour in that late dreadful, fearful, unequal engagement with the Arrogante and her convoy."

She shook both youths by the hand, scarcely able to speak a word from emotion.

"And to think that all should have done such wonders; why all England is full of the news, and my poor Everard is crazed to know what all this great fuss is about, dear, good soul as he is, and to think that such youths as you have been baptized in the dreadful fire of battle. Ah! England, dear old England can never be conquered when she has such lion-hearted sailor boys. But come, young gentlemen, I have much company to-day; Sir Everard is busy with the admiralty officers, and cannot return until 7 o'clock; let me introduce you to my friends. Come, don't be bashful, there," she said, smiling good humouredly, "you need not blush and stammer when you are both escorting a lady. That's it, give me an arm each, and in my dear husband's pet phrase, 'we will sail in company' as far as the drawing-room, where you hear the music."

Arm-in-arm with Lady Brandon the two youthful midshipmen entered the drawing-room, many naval, military, and civil gentlemen standing in groups, conversing with fair and tivating ladies of various ages.

"I have the greatest pleasure, friends, in ducing to all, my dear young heroes, midsh Harry Halliard and Frank Rayner."

All present turned in great surprise at the pected introduction, but bowed and smiled young officers, who seemed very much embar at the stately, but at the same time affabl pleased demeanour of those present.

"We were just speaking of them, mother said a lovely girl, who approached Lady Br and bowed very low to the two young officers were remarking how kind Providence pro dear father in preserving his life through the interposition of young Mr. Rayner, and—o Mr. Halliard."

Those young gentlemen simply bowed and bl but after being warmly shaken by the han highly complimented by all present in earnest natured terms, they gradually acquired a c and self-possession of manner, little to be ex from their total ignorance of the manners of refined and fashionable society.

Gentlemanly bearing and coolness of nerve ever, are attributes of nature; they may be ac by education and usage, but the pure and r are found co-existent with life and existence— whether running in patrician or plebeian vein

Within one hour Frank was lost, firmly ent in Cupid's intricate silken meshes. He thoug Clara, with raven ringlets, white muslin, blu and streamers, and fairy fingers, who pla divinely upon the piano, and sang such p pastoral songs, must certainly be some god least, and so overcome was he that he sat up sofa, perfectly oblivious of a powdered foo attention, who carried about a silver tray, a peatedly proffered, wine, cake and ices.

His moments of silence and thought wer observed by the warm-hearted Lady Brandor came and tapped him on the shoulder, so th first embarrassment soon wore away, and bef could believe his own senses young Clar beside him, earnestly engaged in a pleasant tête, while Miss Annie, the younger daugh light-hearted, merry laughing, and witty took Harry's unsophisticated nature by storn he was naïvely recounting to her, and an ad circle of friends, all he knew of the Thu and her doings, in his innocence not forgetti extol to the skies the behaviour of Captain Br and his lieutenants, and the unparalleled gallan Joe Juniper and Bill Hawser, who, at that mo were oblivious and snoring soundly in a comfo chamber at the "Black Pig."

After passing an hour or two in this ple manner, the two young midshipmen reluctantly their leave, Lady Brandon very kindly inv them to call and see her whenever they ha opportunity.

"'Pon my soul, Frank," said Harry, "I sca know whether I'm standing on my head or my Who'd a thought of such a kind and warm tiou, eh? I feel I should like to have a goo to-night before we go home to the 'Crown.'"

"No, no, Harry," said Rayner, calmly, "we go straight to bed; besides it's getting late; come along. How dark the streets are, w scarcely see our way. Hillo, what's that? your pardon, gentlemen; it was purely accide assure you," said Rayner, apologising to two p who stood before them.

"Apologise, eh ?" was the response, in very bad English. "Who are you ?"

"English officers—midshipmen," replied Harry, nettled at the sarcastic tone and sneering manner of the speaker.

"English officers, eh ? ha, ha ! Go home to your cradles, children," was the taunting answer. "You must learn manners, if you are gentlemen. You pushed against myself and friend purposely ; if you were *men* I might have resented it."

"If we did push you, sir," answered Frank, "it was mere accident ; as it is we apologise. As to our being children, as you call us, you had better not put our juvenility to the proof, I can assure you, bombastic as you are."

"Insolent brat !" was the answer, half in French and English. "Some of the Thunderer's crew, I'll be sworn."

"True."

"True. And do you know who *I* am !"

"No ! nor care much."

"Well, I'll tell you. I am a parolled officer ; third officer of the Arrogante, which was lost by treachery."

"No, not by treachery, but by fair fight," said Frank, "and I myself tore down the colours."

"You !"

"Yes, me."

"You lie, you insolent young cur, you lie !" was the answer, and he slapped Rayner violently in the face, which made him reel. "You lie, you sea cur ! you never did ; never could do it. The flag of France was never snatched by such a whip-staff as you."

Halliard jumped before Rayner, and spoke, "If you are a gentlemen, you will give me satisfaction."

"Fight, you mean ? with pleasure. When ?"

"Now."

"Now ? Ha, ha ! The bare idea of drawing weapons with such as he or you."

"You must, if not I shall take it," he said, drawing his dirk.

"Hold !" said the Frenchman's friend, in very bad, almost unintelligible English. "This affair has gone too far. Alphonse, you are in the wrong, and must make honourable amends ; there is naught for it but blows. I will arrange with you, sir ; I stay at the 'Garter.'"

"We will meet on the London-road at daylight. Come prepared with whatever weapons you please. Your name, you say, is Halliard, and your friend's Rayner ; mine is Durange, my friend's, Alphonse Lepelliter. For the present, adieu."

For the moment both youths were silent.

"This is a nasty affair," said Harry.

"It was not of our seeking. They grossly insulted us ; we must resent it."

"True, but what do *we* know of duelling ?"

"Well, whether we do or not it must be done. I have not worn my jacket long, but, by Jupiter, I'll never disgrace the cloth, on board or ashore, in presence of one or a dozen. So say no more about it ; let's get to bed. I dare say the landlord will lend us his pistols ; say we want them for private practice. Good night, Harry. I don't seem to mind this affair in the least ; that blow in the face was quite enough for me, I'll let him see what I'm made of at daylight. There, dont sit brooding ; get to bed. All will come right, you'll find. Good night."

Harry did sit brooding, however, and felt, in his heart of hearts, expressionless sorrow for what had happened.

He knew Frank too well to suppose he would forfeit his word. When Rayner had made up his mind to do a thing he knew it was useless to argue with him, for, when once he thought himself right, he was far more stubborn than a mule.

Frank slept soundly ; but Harry was restless, and would have sacrificed half the world if he could see any chance of withdrawing honourably from the quarrel.

"Why, he can't be much of a man to act as he has done to us youngsters. I wonder if he'll apologise ?"

Lying wide awake he heard the church chimes strike the hours of three and four, and then dozed off into an unrefreshing, troubled sleep.

His dreams were gloomy ; he woke several times and looked at Frank, who was soundly sleeping with a happy smile upon his face.

"Come, wake up, Harry," said Frank, yawning as the early cock crowed his salutations to the morn, "wake up, shipmate, we've got business on hand, recollect, that brooks of no delay. Don't let us be the last on the ground."

Harry endeavoured to dissuade Rayner by every possible argument to forego for once his foolish engagement, but 'twas useless.

He felt that he had pledged the honour of the whole British navy in giving the challenge, and "would see the last of it," he said, "if it cost his life."

"Have you the pistols you borrowed from the landlord ?"

"Yes. Are you sure he will fight with pistols ? if not, we shall be awkwardly placed, for we have no other weapons save our dirks."

"I dare say he will come provided for in some way. Let us hasten."

Leaving Plymouth behind them, they struck upon the London-road, and had advanced about a mile at a sharp walk, but had not, as yet, seen the Frenchman or his friend.

"Surely we cannot be too late," said Rayner, impatiently. "I wouldn't miss them or let them to suppose I was tardy or chicken-hearted, no, not for a captaincy."

"I don't think they're come yet. Who is that approaching ? 'Tis they, by all that's lucky !"

"Mr. Halliard, good morning," said Durange, "you are out very early ; nothing like punctuality. Beautiful weather for our meeting, is it not ?" he continued, in his broken English or jargon of half-French. "I was speaking to my friend, Lieutenant Lepelliter, and he says it seems a pity to shed blood, particularly as your principal is so young. He therefore desires me to say that, as the insult came from your side, he is willing to settle the matter if Mr. Rayner publicly apologises, and recants his statements regarding the Thunderer and Arrogante, during the late naval episode."

"I confess, sir," answered Harry, stammering, "I should feel very happy indeed to get out of this difficulty if I saw the least chance of doing so honourably, but, as you are aware, though both of us are mere boys compared to you and Mr. Lepelliter, yet, sir, we are are officers in the King's Navy, and our word is our bond. As I do not see that your suggestion is just, I decline to entertain it on behalf of Mr. Rayner. Your proposal, I confess, is both unjust and ill-timed, for you must be aware, sir, that if by mere accident we ran against you in the dark, we amply apologised. Instead of its being accepted, insult is added to injury by his blow, and particularly in his strange request that Mr. Rayner should unsay what had fallen from his lips truthfully in regard to things that I myself saw."

"Words are useless."

"It would seem so."

"Then we must, as our last resort, appeal to arms."

Both seconds spoke for a moment to their principals.

Lepelliter seemed to be very pale, and gesticulated wildly.

He stamped his foot and made all manner of ugly grimaces as he shot fiery glances towards our hero and his friend.

"You don't mean that he wished me to tell a lie in order to contradict what I know to be true. He must be a whelp; no matter, it must be done. Look well to the priming of my pistol, Harry; I feel certain I shall wing him. Somehow, I feel awfully confident this morning. You have already measured off the ground; fifteen paces, you know; I shall therefore now take my position and wait for the word."

It was arranged that Durange should give the word in a loud voice.

Both should fire at the word two and not after three.

Before taking up his position, Durange once more spoke to Lepelliter, who smiled, and said,

"I will kill him."

"Mr. Halliard, one word, if you please," said Durange. "My principal up to the last moment wishes to act magnanimously; he is a dead shot, as you may have gleaned from many of my remarks last night and this morning. I know he means to kill your poor young friend if he does not apologise; therefore, let me beg of you to speak once more to Mr. Rayner."

"With all my heart, since you desire it; but it will not have the least effect upon him."

"Apologise! not if I know it. He's going to kill me, eh? Well, its very kind he told me so beforehand. No, Harry, let's have no more child's play; the word is *fight!* that is final."

The seconds conferred for a moment, when Durange spoke out loudly,

"You know the conditions. Gentlemen, are you ready? One——"

Contrary to all expectation, Lepelliter fired at the word.

Harry was filled with horror.

It must have been a mistake.

Rayner quivered for an instant like a reed shaken in the blast of the north wind.

At the word two, he fired according to arrangement.

A sharp, sudden cry rent the air.

Lepelliter fell on the green, dewy sward.

Frank sank upon the ground.

The two seconds were beside, and bent over the combatants in a moment.

Rayner was pale—a cold perspiration was on his brow.

Harry tore open his jacket and sought for the wound; he found none.

There were no signs of blood; but as he lay Frank's manly frame quivered as he opened his eyes and said, "Where am I, Harry? Alas, it is *not* a dream! would that it had been. I have killed him, I fear. I am a murderer, perhaps."

"Are you hurt?"

"Nay, I know not; but what of the Frenchman?"

"Can't tell yet; but let me examine you. No, thank God, you are not hurt. It was the sudden shock which unnerved you, and made you fall."

"Oh, he meant to kill me, Harry, I know he did; or why did he fire at the wrong word?"

"Never mind, so that you are well; there is blood upon your ear. Why, he has shot part of it away! Thank Heaven it is not worse. It was a near thing Frank, my boy — sharp practice. But stay, there must be something wrong with Lepelliter; see how Durange is stooping over him; let me go, and inquire."

Lepelliter lay upon the ground bleeding profusely from a wound in his side.

He opened his eyes. "Does he live?" he faintly asked.

"Yes," said Harry, "and is unharmed."

A bitter smile passed over the countenance of the dying man, as he groaned in intense agony, and with a look of wild despair, mingled with a sidelong glance of deep-seated hatred and disappointment, he turned upon his side.

He was dead!

"You will bear me witness, Mr. Durange, that there was nothing unfair on our part."

There was no response.

Durange gazed upon the lifeless form of Lepelliter as it grew rigid and cold, and sighed.

Harry gave Frank his arm, and both friends left the ground, after conveying the dead body to a neighbouring roadside inn.

"I would give all the world, Harry, if I could but undo this morning's work."

"It is a sad lesson for both of us, Frank. In the eyes of all honourable men you must be acquitted of every charge of foul play. He evidently meant mischief to you; but good fortune was on our side, and you came out of the terrible ordeal like a true British Sailor."

Frank and Harry returned to town again, but by the time they had arrived at their comfortable inn, the former was so depressed in spirits that Halliard was obliged to rally him.

"What makes you so moody, Frank? You look so pale and melancholy that it grieves me to see you."

"Oh, Harry, I have done wrong, I would give the world this moment to undo what I have thoughtlessly and foolishly done."

"It was not your fault."

"I should have refused the meeting; he was much older than I was; I might have begged his pardon, and then I shouldn't have had this weight, this inconceivable load upon my conscience."

"What, apologise! beg a French lieutenant's pardon, and you an officer in the King's navy? What would the world have said of you? What a laughing stock you might have made of yourself both to friends and foes."

"Nay, I care but little for my commission compared to the anguish I feel. See what I have done; robbed some dear one, perhaps, of their natural protector, perhaps sent a soul unprepared before its God."

"But see the provocation and repeated insult."

"I know, Harry; I feel, and did feel, that it was hard, nay, very hard to bear, but there is no excuse for duelling, look at it in whatever light you may."

"But, you know, you saw as plainly as man could, that Lepelliter thirsted for your very blood; his hate was apparent in every look, every word, each action."

"True, it looked like it."

"And he fired before the signal; suppose you had fallen by his knavery, what should I have done?"

"You would have lost a friend, Harry, a dear and a long-tried one, believe me, one you perhaps might never meet again."

"I know it," he said, grasping Rayner's hand warmly, "and if you *had* fallen, neither Lepelliter nor his second should ever have left the ground untouched, for, if I died for it, one or the other should have bitten the dust. But come, forget all about it; no man can blame you for *your* share in the transaction; if anything attaches to your name, it most be praise, for there was naught for it but fighting and blood on one side, or dishonour on the other. Take my word for it, when the truth shall be known throughout the fleet, there will be more than *one* right good bumper tossed off in health to Midshipman Rayner."

Despite all his words, however, Harry could not raise Rayner's spirits.

He eat no breakfast, he could not even touch a glass of grog, or smoke a cigar.

He sat thoughtfully in the bow window of the inn, looking vacantly at persons passing in the street, while Harry amused himself with writing a letter to Helena, in which he spoke to her in very endearing terms, informing her of his own and Rayner's achievements on board the Thunderer, promising, if he could possibly obtain leave, he would run over and pay a flying visit.

While he wrote an officer entered.

"Midshipmen Halliard and Rayner, I believe?"

"At your service, sir," said Harry, rising and bowing.

"I am extremely sorry to inform you, young gentlemen, that your period of liberty is suddenly curtailed; you must report yourselves on board immediately."

"Why, what's up?" asked Rayner, turning pale, and looked much alarmed. "Surely Sir Everard cannot have heard of the occurrence so soon?"

"Nay, young sir, I know not what the captain's reasons are for ordering you on board; all I know is, he asked me to acquaint you both with his wishing to see you. I *did* hear it whispered that you had both got into a very ugly scrape; I would advise you to delay as little as possible."

In great dismay, and with all manner of forebodings, the young midshipmen took boat and put off to the Thunderer.

As they approached the sides of the majestic, battle-battered frigate, Halliard espied the meagre face of Dan Crawley, who was leaning over the side with a satanic grin upon his cadaverous countenance.

"Look at that lubber grinning, Harry," said Rayner.

"There's another by his side equally interesting," said Halliard, alluding to Harleck.

"There is some mischief brewing, Harry; see how pleased they are."

"Yes. I'd as soon meet the devil as look in their ugly countenances, at any time."

When the young midshipmen had stepped upon deck, the officer in charge informed them that Captain Brandon was below, in his cabin, and desired to see Mr. Rayner immediately.

"What can he want of me so urgently?" asked Rayner.

"Oh, never fear; he *can't* have heard anything of the duel," replied Harry, carelessly, "and if he does, my testimony can soon exonerate you."

They entered Captain Brandon's cabin, and with great respect doffed their caps.

Captain Brandon looked up from his papers with a very troubled countenance.

"Mr. Halliard, you may retire," he said, with great gravity and composure. "I wish to speak alone with Mr. Rayner."

Frank trembled in every limb, and could scarcely stand.

His colour changed from white to red, and from red to white. He entertained every conceivable fear, and the more he gazed at the calm, untroubled

countenance of Captain Brandon, the more he feared, for it was well known to every man and boy throughout the entire fleet that when the gallant captain of the Thunderer looked the most composed, the greater was the surety that weighty matter troubled and possessed his mind.

"Take a seat, Frank."

Rayner felt a choking sensation as he did so.

"I little thought, Frank, when I placed a commission in your hands, that you would disgrace it."

"Disgrace it, Sir Everard!"

"Yes, boy, disgrace it, and so soon."

"What have I done, sir?"

"Done?"

"Yes, Sir Everard."

"Everything."

"For Heaven's sake, captain, please tell me all. Do not kill me with suspense. All I have done I am sorry for, and beg your pardon."

"Nay, that is now beyond my power. A court-martial must decide upon your conduct."

"For what, sir?"

"For what?—why, for murder!"

"Oh, Heaven help me!" gasped Rayner; "then you know all."

"All! Nay, I know little or nothing of the matter at present. All I know is that the body was found just as you had done the deed."

"Pardon me, Sir Everard. I assure you the quarrel was not of my seeking. I did not wish to kill him, but he tried by dishonourable means to murder me in cold blood."

"Sought to kill you?"

"Yes, captain. I never exchanged a cross word with him, until he provoked and insulted me beyond endurance. Halliard will bear witness that he insulted me grossly, repeatedly, and if I killed him, it was in fair fight, according to the approved code known among gentlemen, and if he fell, it was merely a chance shot, for I scarcely ever handled a pistol until that day."

"Pistols! duel! what mean ye?"

"Simply this, Sir Everard, that Lepelliter forced me to fight."

"Lepelliter, the lieutenant! you kill him? Why, you are dreaming or mad, Rayner."

"Indeed neither, sir; I assure you."

"Lepelliter! fight a duel! What mean you?" asked Captain Brandon, looking very much perplexed and surprised, "I do not understand you."

Rayner was about to make explanation—

"There, there, that will suffice; I did not call you here to waste words; all I mean to say is, that you are under arrest."

"Arrest, sir?"

"Yes; and you will be tried by the first court-martial that sits."

"Court-martial, sir! what for, I beg to ask, if not for that?"

"For what? nay, do not be so brazen. I did not imagine you were so hardened."

"For what, then, captain? Oh! Sir Everard, in mercy tell me what for; your cold, pitiless looks are worse than death to me; for what am I to be tried? Speak, I beg of you!"

"For murder, I repeat."

"Murder of whom?"

"Of him you should have attended; the French gentleman, captain of the Arrogante, whom I entrusted to your care."

"Murdered! Nay, in the sight of Heaven I declare I have had no hand in this foul crime; indeed, I never heard of it until now."

"I should like to believe you Rayner, but circumstantial evidence is against you. When you left the ship, he was found dead : strangled and robbed of everything valuable about his person."

" But he was alive and well when I left the ship, sir."

" So everyone 'thought. When the lad Crawley, and Harleck, were appointed in your stead to nurse and tend him, they immediately reported him dead, and foully murdered."

" Oh, Heaven, that such an affliction should have befallen me !"

" I am sorry, Frank ; you shall have every facility for clearing and defending yourself. I must say I cannot credit the serious charge against you ; but every circumstance in the case seems to point to you, and there is naught for it but await judical examination."

Two marines removed Rayner and placed him in irons.

Halliard, when he heard the news, was almost frantic.

He firmly believed not only that his friend was perfectly innocent, but felt morally certain that there was or had been some devilish plot concocted to ruin them both during their brief absence.

As he paced the deck with livid cheek, he cast his eyes on Harleck and Crawley, who, being denied liberty, were crouching beneath the bulwarks to windward, and casting malicious, fiendish, self-satisfied glances towards the quarter-deck, where Halliard, disconsolate and terror-stricken, walked with quivering lip and pallid cheek.

" Raythor a sudden change, ain't there, Mister Harleck ?" said Dan.

Harleck mumbled out something between an oath and a growl in reply, as he looked doggedly towards the shore.

" I declare to goodness, Mister Harleck, if the Frenchman wasn't black and blue in the face when I went into his cabin."

" Was he ?"

" Yes, and he seemed to be calling on some one in the French language that I couldn't understand, and when I runs for the doctor he was dead as a herring before I get's back."

" Well, who do you suppose did it ?" growled Harleck.

" Well, you know, Mister Harleck, it's rather hard for me to say, you know ; but considering that Mr. Frank Rayner—for, I suppose, all of us must mister him now—was the last to see him, it does look rayther suspicious-like, don't it ? and so I tells the captain. I don't think he'll like his berth much down below ; what say you, Mr. Harlick ?—what say you ? Pride *will* have a fall sometime they say, and it looks very much like it, don't it ?"

Harleck made some unintelligible response, which purported to be a wish for the speedy transportation of Halliard and Rayner to rather warm regions below.

" I always said they'd meet with their merits one of these days, didn't I ? and it seems they are getting it, so all I says is good luck to 'em both, that's all. I should like to see 'em both swing at the yard arm ; wouldn't it be jolly, though ?"

" Frank Rayner, accused of murder—to be tried by court-martial—the captain of the Arrogante found dead in his cabin."

Such were the words whispered by one and another among both officers and crew of the Thunderer.

Harry Halliard was inconsolable.

He wept and beseeched Captain Brandon not to believe one word of the report until a full judicial investigation had decided upon his guilt or innocence.

Not one of the officers could be make to believe one word of the cruel accusation.

Lieutenants Armitage and Fraser were indignant, and swore roundly, saying it was more than likely that Dan Crawley and Harleck had a hand in the foul transaction.

Joe Juniper and Bill Hawser fairly turned blue in the face when informed of the affair.

Hitching up their trowsers and cursing loudly, they " shivered their timbers," if such a gallant lad could ever be guilty of the deed.

" But what can we say ?" remarked Sir Everard " I firmly believe in the lad's total ignorance of the matter ; but all we know is that he was one of, if not actually the last person that saw the ill-fated gentleman alive. Many circumstances seem strong against Rayner ; why even his watch was found upon him."

" True, sir," said Armitage, " but Frank solemnly swears that it was given to him."

" But who is there to prove it ?"

" Rayner told Halliard so, and Harry swears solemnly that he showed it to him two days before he was promoted ; it was given to him by deceased as a mark of respect for his kindness and constant attendance during his painful illness."

" I sincerely wish that all this could be fully proved," said Sir Everard, kindly, " but in the meantime this sad business has caused much remark throughout the entire fleet, and Admiral Nelson himself, in a note of to-day, comments upon the whole transaction as disgraceful to the whole British nation, remarking that it more than sullies, if not totally obliterates, the Thunderer's recent achievements."

Days passed, and more dead than alive, poor Rayner was in close confinement, looking pale and anxious, but up to the last moment preceding his trial, no evidence was produced that could in any way exonerate and acquit him.

" 'Tis hard," he said, " to die like a felon for no fault whatever. I am guiltless of this charge in the sight of Heaven and earth. If I must die innocently, Heaven above protect me !"

He was constantly attended by the ship's chaplain, to whom he narrated, with childlike innocence, every incident and circumstance of his whole life.

He was constant in his devotions, and attended service, not with the manner of a thief or robber, but rather with the air of guileless unconsciousness becoming a martyr who goes forth to the stake, blameless of all crime.

In due time the Court was convened, and among those tried were Dan Crawley and Frank Rayner, the former for cowardice during the late action with the French and the latter for murder.

Konk's evidence as to the " Crawler's " conduct was unimpeachable, and he added in very strong terms that although he could not convict him of aught else, yet he believed him capable of any meanness that is common to rogues and vagabonds.

The Court were not long in deciding upon the question, and condemned Mr. Daniel to thirty lashes.

The verdict was received with applause by the whole ship's crew, and as the " Crawler," as he was termed, passed out of Court upon deck, in charge of a file of marines, he was greeted with groans and hisses by every man and boy.

MIDSHIPMAN HARRY HALLIARD.

Even Harleck felt a little pleasure in seeing the slimy, oily Dan receive well-merited punishment for his offences, for, say what they might of Harleck in general terms for being sulky, and grumbling, and entertaining a total dislike for his Majesty's service, his bitterest enemies could not but confess that in time of action he had borne himself like a man, and worked his gun with wonderful quickness, precision, and effectiveness.

When Rayner's trial was announced as just commenced, the whole crew, both officers and men, testified their anxiety aud alarm for his safety, and if a ship load of gold could have been of use in vindicating his hitherto irreproachable character, and fully exonerated him from all participation in the heinous crime for which he stood accused, the entire fleet would have willingly contributed a greater portion, if not the whole of it, for the circumstances of his manly behaviour in the duel with Lepelliter had won all hearts toward him.

They looked upon the lad as a true and genuine type of the British Sailor Boy.

Letters of condolence flocked in upon him from every quarter, and he shed many bitter tears as he perused the warm and cordial words in which unknown friends spoke of his gallantry, and hoped that he might come out of his present severe trial with credit and with his innocence fully vindicated.

Among the many pretty epistles and notes which in this his hour of trial flowed in upon the poor, pale, dejected youth, was one which caused the colour to mount his pallid features as often as he glanced at it. It was signed anonymously, but an intuitive perception told him whence it came.

It ran thus :—

"DEAR FRIEND,—There are few who rejoice more in your late well-merited promotion than myself, or who feels greater pain at the cruel, murderous charge, under which an unforeseen chain of petty circumstances have miserably placed you, far in common with all who have ever known you, if even for ever so short a time, I cannot but reiterate the opinion universally expressed, that a gentleman such as you are could never be found guilty of the least dishonourable conduct, let alone being found capable of perpetrating such a horrid crime as murdering the ill-fated captain of the Arrogante.

"I never cease to pray that Heaven may interpose its protection in this your severe trial and imminent peril, and the more I supplicate nightly for your preservation on bended knee, the more fully I feel convinced that some circumstance may yet transpire, even, perhaps, at the latest hour, that shall lead to the detection and punishment of the real culprit. Feeling assured I shall see you again, and shortly,

"Believe me, yours truly,
"MARIE."

The trial lasted for a day and a half.

Counsel pleaded eloquently in his behalf. Brave old weather-beaten sailors felt their eyes involuntarily moistening as they gave testimony in his behalf; but, despite everything, there seemed no earthly hope of escape for him.

Dan Crawley's testimony was the strongest for the prosecution.

He deposed, and with looks of evident satisfaction, that when Frank Rayner had been promoted and gone ashore with Harry Halliard, Lieutenant Frazer had ordered himself and Harleck to attend and wait upon the deceased; but that when they went to his cabin, they found him dead, with his watch, chain, seals, and other valuables missing.

Harleck gruffly corroborated the statement. He had never seen any one attending deceased all that day, save Rayner.

It was said that before the French officers and prisoners had left the vessel, they begged permission to pay their respects to their wounded captain, but that all passed out from his cabin in an orderly manner, and there were no sounds of any scuffle going on that the marine guard could hear.

It was in vain that he wept and protested his innocence.

He told the attentive and commiserating Court all he knew regarding the murder, that the watch, chain, and seals had been given to him.

As he trembled and turned pale at the prospective fate before him, he sank upon the floor, faint and exhausted with his very few feeble, and almost inaudible, words of defence.

The jury retired.

The time passed. Hour after hour had flown, and yet no verdict was rendered.

Rayner, with Halliard by his side, comforting him, looked anxiously and often towards the cabin door.

The jury returned.

All was death-like silence.

They handed in a written verdict, which the president read.

"GUILTY" was the only word that poor Frank heard.

He sank into the arms of Harry, who bent over him and wept like a child.

The Court dispersed, silently.

A file of marines stood by. Rayner slowly opened his eyes and looked wildly about him.

"Is this a terrible dream, or what is it?" he gasped.

Halliard wept but spoke not.

Rayner looked at him with a faint smile, but when he saw the file of marines at hand, he fully realized his fearful position, yet marched between them with a firm step, looking about him with an air of manly innocence that won all hearts.

Days passed, and yet not a word was whispered of pardon or reprieve.

Frank prepared himself for his doom with a meekness and resignation that charmed the ship's chaplains, and they stoutly averred their firm belief in his innocence and total ignorance of the crime.

Dan Crawley said but little; in truth he dared not do so, for the whole crew detested him for his part in the prosecution, and there were not a few who swore roundly that they believed he was the one, and none other, who had done the deed, and had fathered the crime upon Rayner.

"Well, what do you think of Mr. Rayner, now, eh, Harleck?" whined Dan to his old friend. "I think a few more days will see the end of one of our upstart young officers. I shouldn't mind to see the other going the same way, eh?"

"Don't talk any more to me, Crawler," answered Harleck, gruffly, and in disgust, as he moved away, as if fearing that Dan's words would infect him with leprosy or the plague. "I wish you were going to be swung up, you white-livered hound," he added, with an oath and gesture that made Mr. Crawley whine and wince with displeasure and surprise.

Time passed; the day of execution drew near; gloom was depicted on every face.

Harry daily visited his friend, to console and condole with him.

"Been on shore, Harry? Did you call on Lady Brandon, and assure her of my innocence?" asked Frank, closing a Bible he had been devoutly reading.

"Yes, Frank," answered Harry, with a flushed countenance; "and no one believes in your innocence more firmly than herself and family; but I have news for you!"

"For me?" asked Rayner, looking astonished, and with bright, flashing eyes.

"Yes, I met Durange."

"What of that?"

"I overheard a conversation between him and one of the French officers on parole in town."

"But, how can that effect me?"

"Much, perhaps, if we follow up the scent; listen—

"'So Lepelliter fell in a duel, eh?'

"'Yes,' answered Durange; 'who'd a thought such an accomplished shot would have met with that fate, at the hands of a boy like that British middy? It was a good riddance.'

"'How?'

"'Why, don't you know that there has been deadly hatred existing between him and the captain ever since the Arrogante was captured? Each blamed the other for it. Lepelliter said he did not surrender; the captain swears he disobeyed orders, and struck to the Englishman. Lepelliter never spoke to him, but he often said he'd give him something privately he could not digest; and I believe he did.'

"'There must have been more cause than this for the deadly feelings that actuated Lepelliter; for I have often seen him clench his fist, and scowl behind his captain's back, as if he were actuated by feelings of fiendish hatred.'

"'No wonder; he seduced Lepelliter's wife in Brest; so I've heard it whispered.'

"'Why not revenge it then like a man, and not brood over it?'

"'He hadn't sufficient proof. He rejoiced at the captain's wounds and bad luck, and often prayed he might never again see France.'"

"Is this all you heard?" inquired Frank. "I fear there is not much in that which can save me from the gallows."

"I shall report the case to Captain Brandon; he might obtain a reprieve, you know; and meantime who knows what may transpire?"

Halliard obtained an interview with Sir Everard, and explained everything he had heard, together with his own surmises.

"I fear there is not enough to warrant me in asking for what you wish, Harry."

"Will you grant me leave of absence then, sir, for three days?"

"Three days! why you surely do not wish to leave Frank to die without seeing you?"

"Nay, sir; no one loves him more dearly than I do, but I think, nay, I feel certain that I may yet gather such information as may yet save my poor friend. Give me three days' liberty, I beg, Sir Everard."

"I will; but do not buoy him up with false hopes, Halliard; I fear that every loop-hole of escape is closed to him. You may go; I will let Rayner be informed you are ordered away on duty, that may reconcile him to your unexpected absence.

Harry hurried below, shook hands with Frank, and with many bitter tears, the harbingers of mixed hopes and fears, took a boat, and was soon on shore.

He had but three days! three short, fleeting days were all that remained to Rayner.

The first dawned and passed; the second came and went; the third was ushered in with a golden sun, that dispelled all mists and fogs; and the Thunderer, as she lay anchored off shore, glistened and shone like a thing of white and gold upon the flashing sea.

No tidings of Halliard! no one had seen or heard of him! He had landed, but that was all; not a shipmate had seen him; he had vanished from view, and poor Frank Rayner, pale and emaciated, sat lonely and sorrowing on the eve of his death.

He seemed not now to care for life; it had no charms for him, young as he was and little as he had enjoyed it. He listened modestly, calmly, and resignedly to the chaplain's words, and reverently bent in prayer and poured out his sorrowing soul to God in fervent supplication, while the hot, scalding tears coursed down his pale, yet firmly set and handsome countenance.

"To-morrow, Frank, you die. There is little of life and not a gleam of hope that remains. Let me beseech you to use the fleeting moments to the best advantage. To-morrow's sun, my poor, repentant, innocent boy, will set upon your lifeless corpse."

"Do you? Oh, say again, dear, dear, kind friend, say again that you believe me innocent, and I shall die in peace," said Frank, kissing the chaplain's hand.

"I do. Before God, Frank Rayner, I believe you stand guiltless of this crime. Yet such is the will of Heaven. Providence wishes to snatch you away from the temptations and cares of life thus early. Perhaps it is a merciful and gracious dispensation. Good-night, my poor lad. Heaven have you in its keeping."

"Gone," said Frank, sitting on a chest, and heaving a sigh. "Gone! and Harry gone also! No friend to speak to; and yet, to-morrow! to-morrow!" he could say no more, but sank upon his knees and sobbed.

The night passed wearily, slowly on. The ship's bells tolled watch after watch; no sounds were heard save the ebbing tide dashing in sullen murmurs against the Thunderer's sides, and the measured tread of the marine on guard outside the cabin door.

The fitful twilight of the morning illumined the blackened sides of the ship. Faintly and slowly light stole upon the ripless waters, and as the sun rose upon the scene, Frank got up from his sleepless bed and prepared for execution.

In his much-beloved sailor boy's dress—for his sentence had degraded him to that level—he met the gaze of all with a firm but modest look.

Captain Brandon and his officers kindly visited the pale-faced boy and bade him good-bye, and it was observed that he, Frazer, Armitage, Juniper, and Hawser, looked much dejected as they did so; the latter two worthies actually shedding tears as they left him.

The chaplain was early in attendance, and Rayner devoutly accompanied him in the service, responding with a firm but earnest tone to the psalms.

The sad and sorrowful procession commenced, and slowly reached the deck. The whole crew were drawn up to witness the sickening sight, while the marines, with a commanding officer with drawn sword, stood under arms beside the gangway.

Without moving a muscle, Rayner permitted himself to be pinioned; and a rough, hard-featured, repulsive-looking boatswain placed the fatal noose around his white and delicate throat, which was bared broadly and bravely. At a signal he walked up a plank from the deck, and as he reached the bulwark top his own weight balanced it.

A step now, either side, would have launched him into eternity, for it needed but a touch of the main yard, to the end of which the rope was attached, and it would have swung round and dangled him, struggling and helpless, between sky and sea!

The burial service was now well-nigh finished. Sir Everard was observed once or twice to turn his head and look towards the shore, for he could not bear to see his officers' looks of sorrow and pain, as they gazed at the degrading, harrowing spectacle, for many a seaman and middy, who knew Frank, shed tears and buried their faces in their hands.

"What boat is that?" said Lieutenant Armitage, with looks of much surprise, pointing to one that was rapidly approaching.

"I know not," said Frazer. "It is coming towards us, and some one is waving a white handkerchief wildly."

"Can you make it out?" inquired Sir Everard, straining his eyes, and shading them from the strong sunlight that now broke through the clouds.

"Yes, sir," answered Armitage, with a flushed and pleased countenance; "it is Halliard, Sir Everard, and two police-officers; they are shouting to us."

"Stop that service, parson," roared Sir Everard, "this is Halliard, the brave lad. Boat ahoy!"

"Ship ahoy!" was answered in response.

"That's him, sir!" said Frazer. "He is waving a handkerchief in one hand, and what appears to be a large letter in the other. How the crew do row though! they are pulling for their very lives."

"Ship ahoy!" roared several voices from the fast approaching boat.

"Cast them a line, men," said Sir Everard.

"Aye, aye, sir," roared Juniper and Hawser, doing so instantly.

"We must delay this execution, sir," said Sir Everard to the chaplain in a confidential whisper; "the lad Halliard's flushed and excited face betrays that he brings news of some importance."

Before he could conclude his remarks, Harry had clambered up the ship's side with the agility and suppleness of a cat, and scrambling on deck, heated and excited, rushed towards Rayner, waving in his hand a sealed document!

' Saved ! saved !" he gasped, and to the surprise of all, sank fainting on the deck.

Rayner stood like a block of marble, pale and motionless, unconscious of all he heard and saw.

At a signal from Sir Everard, Juniper and Hawser jumped upon the bulwark and cut the pinions and rope from about the boy's neck.

'Twas well they were so quick, for Rayner swayed to and fro. Another instant, and he would have lost his balance, and met with that disgraceful death from which Halliard's timely arrival had miraculously saved him.

Juniper and Hawser jumped upon deck with the unconscious lad in their arms; the doctor was on the spot, and applied restoratives. Officers and men stood in groups looking on.

"The system is rudely shaken, sir—pulse very, very low, that's all ; he's perfectly unconscious. He knows nothing, I'm certain, of what has passed. When he recovers, it must be broken to him little by little ; it might otherwise kill him."

"Thank Heaven, it is no worse," said Sir Everard, turning from the group with a flushed and gratified look.

"Thank Heaven, he is saved," exclaimed all, as Harry knelt beside the body and bathed Rayner's temples.

"Hang me for a swab, if I ain't better pleased than if I was rated an admiral," roared Juniper.

"Is he pardoned ?" whined the Crawler, of one by his side.

"Pardoned, ye hang-dog looking cur !—pardoned ! —what should he be pardoned for, eh, ye unlucky shark, when the lad's done nothing ?"

"Oh, I beg your pardon. I only thought Captain Brandon got him transported instead of hanged, that's all."

"Did you ?" said the seaman, with a malicious-looking grin, "I've a good mind to knock you over-board, curse you. I would, only it would spoil fun."

The news of Frank's acquittal ran from mouth to mouth, and all were pleased, and expressed their great satisfaction by indulging in an extra allowance of swearing, and as they quaffed their grog, and puffed the pleasant pipe, hearty good wishes and long life to Rayner and Harry, were echoed and re-echoed by every man on board, both officers and men, save one, and that one was " The Crawler."

CHAPTER XL.

HARRY HALLIARD'S PURSUIT OF DURANGE AND HIS FRIEND—THEY ARE OVERTAKEN AND EXAMINED —THE RESULT—RELEASE—FATE OF RAYNER—THE PORT ADMIRAL IN A RAGE—THE NARROW ESCAPE —JOY ON BOARD.

MR. KONKS was in his glory.

The news of Harry's timely arrival, and the unexpected ending to the melancholy spectacle on board the Thunderer, filled all hearts with joy, and every tongue was busily engaged in discussing Frank Rayner's miraculous escape from a felon's death.

Officers at mess were full of the subject, and never ceased their inquiries and conjectures regarding it.

"Most strange affair, sir," said Armitage, sipping his wine after dinner.

"Very," said Frazer ; "the most marvellous part of all is, that none of us as yet know precisely either the beginning or ending of the strange affair. Every man has his own opinion regarding it, and I warrant when the truth becomes fully known, all of us will find ourselves very much mistaken."

"How glad all hands appear though ; that speaks well for the lad's popularity among the crew."

"I never saw such excitement in my whole life ; Juniper and Hawser, and Konks, are in perfect ecstasies, and capered about the decks like wild men. Didn't you hear their mess singing over it ? Lord bless you, they must have bought something stronger than water from the bomb boat women to day, or I am much mistaken."

"'Tis well that Sir Everard is in extra good-humour, or some of those noisy dogs would be hauled over the coals, if I am not very much mistaken."

"Well, it is a very good ending to what was a miserable beginning, for I feel certain that every man on board believed in his innocence from the first, although it must be confessed that things looked very ugly and awkward for him."

"Did you notice Halliard ?"

"Was pale as a sheet ; he looked more dead than alive."

"Sir Everard was not long in looking over the port-admiral's letter and stopping the execution. Didn't the chaplain look astonished when the captain stopped him abruptly at his prayers ?"

"Yes, and if some one hadn't given Halliard some brandy, he'd a been laid up in the sick bay for weeks to come ; he trembled and shook in every limb like a reed."

"A good lad, very ; both of them are fast friends, inseparable companions. A true case of Damon and Pythias, if there ever was one."

"He was closetted with Sir Everard for two hours, so I hear. He must have had a pretty long yarn to spin."

"Where is Rayner now, then ?"

"Under the doctor's hands ; it will be days before he's fit enough to report for duty."

"It was a very near thing, and no mistake ; much too near to be pleasant."

"Hullo ! there is Halliard passing the cabin window. Tell one of the marines to call him in."

"Hullo, Harry, my lad ! We've been looking for you for the past hour," said Armitage, rising, and heartily shaking Halliard by the hand."

"Yes, why didn't you drop in at mess time, my boy ?" said Fraser, making room for Harry beside his own chair. "I'm sure the middies would have spared you for once ; and as to us, you know we don't stand upon strict etiquette as to rank on such important occasions as this. You look pale and jaded. Here, help yourself to wine ; there's plenty of it."

"Well said," quoth Armitage. "A bumper to Midshipman Halliard, and long life to himself and his faithful chum, Frank Rayner."

The toast was drunk with applause, but Harry was too much excited to make any lengthy reply for the unexpected honour.

He rose nervously ; his mouth twitched as if in pain or sorrow, as he muttered,

"I am much obliged to you, gentlemen, for the honour conferred upon me. I have done nothing more than my duty to a friend ; if anyone else had been similarly placed I should have done just the same, and thought nothing particular of it. Shipmates ought always to stick together through thick or thin. As Sir Everard always says, ''tis the secret of all success, afloat or ashore !' "

"Hear, hear !" was the general response. "Hear, hear, lad ! glad to hear a youngster talk like that.

Here's your health, and long life to you, my boy !" said several in accord.

"I am particularly glad that Frank was saved, though," continued Halliard, momentarily becoming firmer in his delivery, "because we've always been together, and it did seem rather hard that such a brave boy as all know he is should have met with such a misfortune just when he was promoted."

"Of course, my boy, of course ; but sit down and tell us all about it."

"Well, gentlemen, I never made a speech in my life, but all I know about it is this :—

"When Frank was tending upon the French captain he often heard him talking in his sleep about the loss of the Arrogante, and although he couldn't speak much English he used to say in his few words that he thought she struck through the cowardice or villany of Lepelliter, his second officer. He spoke in French to himself often when half awake, and repeatedly kissed a miniature of his wife which was suspended from his neck, and cursed Lepelliter until he got red in the face.

"Frank said he never took particular notice of the bad feeling between the French officers until one day Lepelliter sent him from the cabin to the doctor for something, and when he returned he found the captain with a long knife in his hand, threatening his second officer, and motioning towards the door, bidding him depart.

"Lepelliter laughed scornfully, and as he went offered Frank some money, which was refused, for, from some unknown cause, he hated Lepelliter, but for what precisely he could never tell.

"They were never friends subsequently, and Rayner has since said that he never [met, or even saw, Lepelliter afterwards but the latter used to scowl at him, and show his teeth like an angry cur.

"On the morning of Frank's promotion he was standing beside the companion-ladder, at the port side.

"He often left his sick charge for half an hour or so, when he was sleeping, to have a short chat with Juniper, myself, or some old friend that chanced to be near.

"On that morning he stood talking to me, and, as you know, the French crew had been landed and placed in prison, but the officers, being on parole, were paying their respects to their captain before going off in the boat.

"While Sir Everard was talking to Frank and myself, Lepelliter visited his captain, and as I afterwards learned by overhearing a conversation going on between Durange and another, he was the last of the French officers who paid his compliments, and did so purposely, as you will shortly hear.

"Frank being promoted, he immediately got liberty for three days, and left the ship with me, for Sir Everard promised that some one else should be left in charge of the wounded man.

"We had scarcely landed, when we saw Lepelliter and Durange together conversing very excitedly, but we were too intent upon pleasure to take heed or notice them, but I couldn't help remarking to Frank at the time that Lepelliter had a most repulsive, revengeful look upon his countenance at the moment, particularly as he grinned and showed his white teeth in the old cur-like manner, as we passed.

"Regarding our reception at Lady Brandon's, you have all heard ?"

"Yes. And a pair of nice little devils you were," said Armitage, laughing. "I've heard all about it ;

monopolised the two young ladies to yourselves, and all that sort of thing. Rather pleasant, eh, Mr. Frazer? Us poor Luffs standing all alone while the Royal Reefers had all plain and easy sailing, convoying the Miss Brandons to and from the piano, as large as life ; all right, my lads."

"Never mind, Harry," said Lieutenant Frazer, laughing ; "go on with your yarn, my boy. Armitage is a little jealous in that quarter, you know. Let's hear the end of the story, for I begin to think that Lepelliter proved the ugly disagreeable cur I always imagined him to be."

"And you have also heard the particulars of Rayner's duel ?"

"Yes ; and a brave lad he was to rid the service of such an unmanly whelp," said Armitage, striking the table rather roughly. "It was shameful behaviour to pick a quarrel with such a mere boy."

"Well, we imagined that we should get into mischief through it ; but what was our surprise to find on going on board that Rayner was charged with nothing less than murder."

"Rather a tough charge, certainly."

"Yes, it was, but there was no help for it. Crawley and Harleck reported the Frenchman dead. He had been strangled ; and because Frank was supposed to have been the last person in his cabin, suspicion fastened on him."

"Very naturally it did ; but, thank goodness he, or rather you were able to clear him, for I confess circumstantial evidence was very strong against him."

"I was horror-stricken; particularly when the captain's watch, chain, and seals were found upon him, for although Rayner showed them to me several days before, and said they had been given to him, every one else, even Captain Brandon, maintained that they were additional proof, or circumstantial evidence, as he termed it.

"Despite all they might think or say, I felt certain that Frank was innocent, and my suspicions, from some cause, fell upon Lepelliter.

"This I told Sir Everard, and I obtained leave to go ashore ; but how was I to proceed ?

"Lepelliter was dead !

"Knowing not what to do, or where to go, I walked the streets inconsolable, praying fervently in my heart that Providence might assist me in unravelling the mystery.

"I took lodgings at the 'Cross Keys,' and next room to mine I heard a conversation going on.

"One of the speakers was Durange.

"The other was an officer of the Arrogante.

"'How lucky it was that I was his second,' I heard Durange say, in broken English—part in English, part in French. 'He had most valuable papers about him, one from the lady in Brest.'

"'You don't mean to say that ?'

"'Yes, and she says that she hopes that the Arrogante may rather sink to the bottom of the ocean than ever bring him (the captain) home alive again.'

"'A most loving and dutiful wife, certainly.'

"'You know, of course, that there was a deadly feud between her husband and Lepelliter ; if he had proved it Lepelliter would never have been second on board the Arrogante long.'

"'But they were guilty, though.'

"'Oh, there can't be a doubt of it. Read this letter she wrote to Lepelliter the morning he sailed from Brest ; there can't be the shadow of a doubt as to her infidelity. Why, she even wishes that some lucky cannon shot may rid the world of her loving and liege lord. What can be stronger than that ?'

"'Yes, but there is an expression even worse than that. Why, the witch even says that she loves

Lepelliter so much she would willingly bestow all her fortune, and kiss the hand of the lover who should make her a widow.'"

"Did you hear all that and not make a move of some kind?" asked Frazer.

"I heard that, and more.

"'Lepelliter once told me that he'd settle him,' said Durange, 'and the morning he came ashore he drank deeply, and swore that he (the captain) would never disgrace the French navy again, for he was dead.'

"'Did he say so?' asked the second Frenchman.

"'Yes, but smiled significantly, and observed he was the last of the Arrogante's officers to pass the compliments of the hour and wish him good-day.'

"'But *is* he dead? You don't mean to say that Lepelliter killed his own captain, on board an English frigate, too?'

"'I don't mean to say anything at all about it. All I know is that he was found dead, and a young English middy, the same who killed Lepelliter in the duel I spoke of, stands charged with the murder, and the report is that there are strong evidences of guilt against him.'"

"Well, you alarmed the house, of course," said Armitage, "you didn't wait to hear any more?"

"I scarcely knew what to do, or how to act; I thought of alarming the house and have them arrested immediately, for there was no doubt upon my mind as to who had done the deed. As it was late, I thought I would defer it until morning, when my nerves should be a little cooler, for the strange revelations I heard unmanned me."

"You were silly, Harry; you should have called in assistance on the instant. But in the morning, what then?"

"I was astonished to find that both had left the house, and gone none knew whither."

"Curse it, I wish it had been me," said Armitage, excitedly, striking the table and making the glasses jingle and ring. "I'd have put a bullet or two into 'em before they should have so escaped. Let that be a lesson for your whole life, Halliard, 'always strike while the iron's hot—spread all sail when the winds are fair.'"

"In the morning I went to the port-admiral, but he didn't think my confused and hurried statement was of sufficient weight to induce him to grant a reprieve.

"I ran to the police authorities, and when I had explained all, they promised to assist me.

"We tracked Durange and his friend.

"From some cause they had hurriedly and rather mysteriously left town; we found they had hired a post-chaise and four, and were miles upon their road to London.

"We hastened with all speed, but found they had repeatedly changed their proper course from the high post road, and were evidently desirous of avoiding all contact with strangers.

"We travelled as rapidly as horse flesh could carry us, and, when least expected, came upon Durange and his friend, for their vehicle had over-turned in the mud, and one of the horses was foot-sore and lame.

"They were evidently surprised to see the police officers, and much more to confront no less a person than myself.

"Our party were extremely courteous to them, and, after brief explanation, they made no objection to returning, particularly when assured that no bodily harm should befall them.

"The home journey was accomplished, if possible, with more speed and anxiety than the chase, for I

was fretful and overburdened with alarm for the safety of Rayner, whose life, I knew, hung upon a single thread.

"When we arrived in town the sun was just rising. It was the day of execution.

"Breathless and in haste, I rushed hither and thither before the authorities, in order to have Durange's deposition properly attested.

"His statement seemed conclusive as to Lepelliter's guilt, for when he stated the true cause of difference between him and his superior officer, and produced letters found upon the ill-starred duellist from the lady in Brest, none for a moment seemed to doubt his fully-proved culpability.

"The port-admiral stamped with rage when he heard the circumstances fully explained, and without awaiting any judicial test, hastily wrote to Sir Everard, taking upon himself all after responsibility for the instant and rather informal acquittal and reinstatement of Rayner.

"With this precious document, signed, sealed, and delivered, I rushed from the admiral's office, and dashed along the streets at headlong speed, accompanied by several detective officers.

"From appearances in the offing I knew that preparations were progressing for an execution on board the Thunderer, and briefly explaining my urgent mission to a party of seamen, we seized the first boat within reach, jumped in, and pulled away for the frigate with all the energy of men in despair.

"Oh, how violently my heart beat.

"At each stroke of the oar I thought my soul would sink within me.

"I might be too late!

"A single moment might avert his fate.

"Jumping on the bow, I urged the men to almost superhuman exertions, as the blade of each oar bent under the over-straining, powerful efforts of my gallant boats' crew.

"I promised everything and anything to them, and with hearty goodwill they bent silently and manfully to each stroke, and our boat danced upon the wave-tips, and rushed through the water at momentarily and ever-increasing speed.

"The nearer we approached the more delirious I seemed to become.

"My eyes became hazy.

"I knew not what I did.

"Shouting, and waving my handkerchief and official despatch, I stood, bareheaded, with the sparkling spray moistening my face.

"The dark sides of the frigate came nearer and nearer.

"At last we dashed under its shadow.

"Murmurs of applause reached our ears from the ship's sides.

"We gave a hearty cheer, unshipped the boat-hooks, and instantly made fast.

"How I got upon deck, I know not; I was perfectly insensible for some moments; but, with the concentrated energy of hope and despair, I clambered up the sides, tumbled on deck, and when I saw Frank on the opposite bulwark, with the fatal halter about his neck, I had strength enough to shout 'Saved!—saved!' but of all else I recollect nothing distinctly until some hours afterwards, when I found myself lying on a comfortable sofa in Sir Everard's cabin, with a medical man sitting by my side, bathing my temples."

"Well, hang me, if I didn't always take that Lepelliter to be a scoundrel," said Mr. Armitage, "for do what you might for him, he could never look you straight in the face like any other man."

"I'm deuced glad Frank gave him his quietus,

for if it hadn't been for his scrape, French folks would have sworn that the murder was committed by some of us, and not all the testimony of the world would have deceived them."

"And all the disgrace. It is all right now though, and I have no doubt," said Frazer, "when the story of the Arrogante's capture is spoken of in the fleet, there will be found some willing and able enough to finish the story, by relating the brave and manly conduct of the two gallant British Sailor Boys—Midshipmen Halliard and Rayner !"

"Here !—here !" said all in chorus, "and none can do better at the present moment than drink a good bumper to them, and with a right good will—'Long life and pleasant voyage to both ; plenty of prize money ; lots of lasses, and no harm to either !' "

The toast was responded to unanimously, and Halliard's hand was grasped in friendship and admiration by every officer present.

CHAPTER XLI.

THORKIL, HYLDA, AND AGGER AT LOGGERHEADS—AGGER LEAVES THE BAND—PAUL ADAIR AND HIS CREW—EARL PENALVON—THE MEETING AT THE KIDDLEAWINK — DIVISION OF SPOIL — THORKIL BENT ON MISCHIEF—HE PREPARES FOR A PERSONAL ENCOUNTER.

"Where is Thyra, Hylda ?" asked Agger, as he stood, pipe in mouth, before Thorkil's cavern-door.

"How should I know, I haven't charge of her. She is big and old enough to care for herself."

"Haven't you seen her of late ?"

"Not I. She doesn't come here as often as before. Thorkil hates the sight of her."

"Does he ?—and why ?"

"I know not, nor care ; and I would tell you, Agger, it would better become you to follow my husband's advice, and do some work, than go gadding about with that pipe in your jaw."

"Would it ?"

"Aye, would it."

"Well, if all comes to all, Hylda, I care but little for thee or Thorkil. I can do without either, and as to following out his bidding, I know a thing or two better than that, Hylda. Thorkil can tell folk what to do ; but he takes good care of his own neck."

"You had better not talk to him in that way, lad ; it would not be good for your carcase if he heard you."

"Well, tell him, then, if it suits you. I am tired of him and his business ; he always gets the shark's share of everything, and I'm tired of it. Perhaps he'd like to get my neck in danger, so as to have me always at his beck and call ; Miss Helena, to wit."

"He can't harm her."

"No, he can't ; but he very much wished to try. But there are far more powerful ones than Thorkil Penreal."

"Oh, that's it, eh, Agger ? You are going to change masters."

"I don't say so, exactly ; but I might do such a thing, if I took it in my head, or perhaps do a little business down the coast on my own hook."

"Who's to help thee ?"

"Oh, I could get a few friends together, that would help me just as powerful, ugly and fierce-looking as any of Thorkil's gang."

"Who's talking of Thorkil's gang ?" growled Penreal, advancing unobserved behind Agger, with the looks of a thunder-cloud.

"Oh, Agger is getting discontented with wrecking, and would perhaps like to set up smuggler like others that we've heard of."

"Paul Adair, I suppose ?" Thorkil growled.

"Well, yes, if you must know, I'd have no objection to do a little business something like his."

"Would you ?" Thorkil sneered ; " well, let me tell you, that it's very good he don't come much about these waters with his crafty ways or he might get something he wouldn't digest in a hurry."

"Well, I don't think he fears any one much—least of all such as I am."

"Well, Thorkil has something in store for him should they meet," added Hylda.

"Yes, something he'll remember me for, or my name ain't what it is."

"Well, I've heard it whispered that he's not many miles away from here, now, for, of course you've heard the news ?"

"News ! what news ?"

"Oh, nothing particular, except that he's captured a cargo destined for you, and both he and his men are right jolly over it, and have sold everything for hard cash, and are expected in the neighbourhood here shortly."

"Are they ?" said Thorkil, with a frightful oath ; " then I'll be even with him. I know a certain person who'd give something to lay eyes on him for a few minutes. I don't think that Paul Adair would swagger about much afterwards."

"He goes well prepared, I hear, for all comers."

"He seems to be a great favourite of yours all at once."

"No, not very much so ; only I speak as I hear of him. There's very few persons that can speak ill of him."

"I know one that does, if Earl——"

"Thorkil !" said Hylda, warningly.

"Oh, I dare say you mean Penalvon," laughed Agger ; " but if all be true which I've been told, that nobleman wouldn't like to meet him alone on a dark night."

"Paul Adair is a robber, and a cursed low-bred whelp," swore Thorkil.

"Well, he may be to some people ; but he doesn't desert his friends."

"Well, do I ?"

"Call it what you like, Thorkil ; all I can say is that his men fare better than yours ; they've always got some money in pocket, and a good job in hand that's worth looking after, so we'll say no more about it ; I'm off to Polruth's kiddleawink."

"Ain't going to be on the look-out, then, to-night ?"

"No, not to-night."

"To-morrow night ?"

"No, nor ever again, Thorkil, for you. I don't want to get in your blood-stained clutches any longer. I shall be found at the kiddleawink when wanted."

He departed, and Thorkil looked after him scornfully.

"That all comes of asking such a chicken-hearted fool to do a thing. You are going on at a pretty rate, Thorkil ; your men are all leaving one by one. You'll be high and dry on the beach, by-and-bye, all by yourself, a wreck of what you once were, with poverty like heavy sea swells and breakers tossing over you, with no one able or willing to aid or succour you."

"Silence, woman! your tongue is always wagging; you tempt me to cut it out."

"I would if I were such a brave man as you. A pretty fellow to call himself a chief of wreckers to be snubbed by such a sea-calf as Agger."

"Nay, not so fast; he has a game to play, and so have I. I know what is going on at the kiddleawink to-night."

"Well, you will go, I suppose, and look at 'em divide what should have come to you?"

"Not so fast. I'll divide them, though, you'll find. I know what Earl Penalvon wants. A few friends will call upon Polruth and his party when least expected.

"You haven't the pluck, Thorkil."

"A man shouldn't tell me so without a proper answer. Sit you here, and stir not till I return. Should any want me, I am out, mind. I go to Seawardine; but you know nothing of it, remember."

The night was closing in dark and hazy.

Thorkil filled his flask with brandy, and, secreting a pair of pistols and cutlass about him, he put on a rough, heavy, seaman's jacket, and strode out of his cavern door, smoking a glowing pipe, and, while emitting clouds of odourous smoke, he muttered,

"Paul left me, and despises me, does he? Agger follows suit; ha, ha! we'll have a pleasant chat and some hot grog together to-night; it matters little who pays the reckoning."

CHAPTER XLII.

THE WHEREABOUTS OF PAUL ADAIR—EARL PENAL-VON'S FRIENDS ARE ON THE LOOK OUT—TREACHERY OF THORKIL — MERRY MEETING AT POLRUTH'S—THE DIVISION OF SPOIL—THE QUARREL AND FIGHT—PAUL ADAIR AND THORKIL ON THE HEATH—DEFEAT OF EARL PENALVON'S FRIENDS—THORKIL WOUNDED.

THE parlour and tap of Polruth at the kiddleawink were all a-glow with fire light and candles, which cast a pleasant stream of light upon the dark and gloomy heath on which it stood solitary and alone.

Something more than ordinary business was astir within.

Many voices, loud in song, proclaimed that the visitors were bent on harmony and jollity as well as business.

Polruth's face was beaming with pleasure, as he moved hither and thither among his present comfort and pleasure seeking company.

"Now then, Polruth, don't be all night; let's have that old Jamaica as soon as possible; we're all dying with thirst, my lad."

"I'll take brandy, old man," shouted another, who was deeply engaged in a game at cards. "We can afford to have something extra to-night, eh, Polruth?" he added with a peculiar wink at the landlord, who smiled and put a finger on his lip, as if indicating silence and caution.

"Oh, no fear, shipmate," cried a third, who saw the sign, and laughed at the landlord bustling about. "No fear, my hearty, there's no revenues within hail, or I'm much mistaken."

"No, messmate, all's right and above board here. I pity the coastguard or spy that would poke his nose in here to-night."

"Then why look about so careful-like, old fellow?"

"Well, you see, one doesn't know exactly wh[at] might be passing the 'Jolly Mariners,' and if an[y] strange sail heard your hailing me about contra[-]band, you know, particularly as the present lo[t] should have gone to Thorkil, they might blow th[e] gaff, you see, my hearties."

"Thorkil! Oh, yes, I've heard of him; but no on[e] fears him or his gang, I know, eh, shipmates?"

"Not if we knows anything," was the unanimou[s] response. "No one will trouble us to-night; [if] they do, let 'em look out, that's all I say; there'[s] more than one pair of little bull-dogs in our belt[s] to-night, eh, mates?"

"Aye, aye, sure! Come, look alive, hearty, an[d] bring up some old St. Croix from the cellar. Non[e] of your four quarter grog, mind. We are not use[d] to that mild swill. Let's have it up, Polruth. Yo[u] needn't be stingy with it; there's plenty more wher[e] that came from."

"You needn't trouble, lads; you shan't want fo[r] anything to-night."

"Well said, Polruth. But where's Silent Ti[m] and his fiddle? We must shake our heels, f[or] once."

"True, shipmates, and so you shall. Here come[s] the very man. Now, then, Tim, rosin the bow, m[y] hearty; but, first of all, wet your whistle, and the[n] tune up your catgut, and give us the best hornpip[e] you've got."

Silent Tim, the person thus addressed, sipped wit[h] one, and then another, and while he screwed up th[e] strings, with many an ugly twitch of his not ver[y] captivating countenance, some of the compan[y] tossed the stools and chairs about, shoved table[s] still nearer the walls, and having, as they termed i[t] "Clear decks, and all ready for action," two burly looking smugglers stepped lightly into the centr[e] of the large, commodious tap-room, and shook thei[r] heels gaily in a very intricate nautical hornpipe greatly to the pleasure of the company, wh[o] applauded and commented freely upon the exertion[s] of both stalwart dancers.

"Go it, Bill; put on the double, my lad."

"Shake it out, Tom. Unreef them legs o' yourn[.] Let's have the real thing."

"Come, splice the main-brace, my fighting cocks[,] and tack again."

"Go it, fiddler; never say die, hearty."

Such and such like, was the running commentar[y] freely and good humouredly bestowed upon Bill and Tom, as they capered to and fro, until Tim and his violin seemed to be in an ecstasy of delight, as h[e] scraped away vigorously and with fast increasing rapidity upon his instrument, while the bystander[s] applauded, and shouted, and clapped hands in unbounded delight.

"That's it, lads," encored Polruth, holding hi[s] sides, and shaking with laughter. "Don't spare th[e] resin, Tim; and you, my lads, don't forget your grog[.] Everybody drinks at my expense to-night. I don'[t] forget my true friends, lads, and I know my tru[e] friends will never forget me."

"Take a turn yourself, Polruth," some on[e] shouted. "Put on your sea legs, and sail in."

No sooner said than done, for upon Polruth and another, "according to imitation," sailing in, Ti[m] struck up a merry reel, and the excitement increase[d] every moment.

All the company were in the height of merr[i]ment.

Tim and his violin were working right manfull[y] and instead of two or four, the number of dancer[s] had gradually increased to a round dozen.

The room was cloudy with tobacco smoke.

BOYS' LIBRARY

Harry Halliard: or, the Young British Tar.

THORKIL AND HIS FRIENDS IN DIFFICULTIES.

The air was redolent with the fumes of rum and brandy.

Shuffling feet, and loud laughter were the noises heard, which well-nigh drowned the rapid screeching notes of the fiddle, as Tim's arm passed up and down with a convulsive, spasmodic, jerky motion.

Polruth and his friends were red and heated with merriment, exertion, and spirits, and all promised to end harmoniously.

Thyra unexpectedly entered, and touching the landlord on the arm, whispered,

"He is coming. Thorkil is on the heath and means no good will to the 'Jolly Mariners.' Take care, Polruth; if the captain is here, warn him."

"What does the pretty lass say, landlord?" asked several.

"Oh, nothing, shipmates! The little craft has been on a short cruise, and thinks there are breakers ahead."

"King's men or revenues?"

"Neither, mates, I think; but don't stop the dance for anything under an admiral or a seventy-four."

"Well said, landlord. Scrape away fiddler, there's plenty of grog and silver in store for you, my lad. Clap on all sail, and let's go a good one, right afore the wind, mind you."

While all was jollity in the tap, and heedless of observation, a man stood outside, and peeped through the window with a malicious grin.

"So that's the way you do it, eh, my fine fellows? You can well afford to laugh and caper at my expense. That's some of Mr. Paul's gang, I'll be sworn!"

Beside him, and listening to his words, was another person, that slunk beside the gable out of view.

"Don't you enter until I give the signal," said Thorkil, addressing him. "Go back and stand as I have told you. Tell the Earl," he said, in a whisper, "that I'll capture him, or die."

The one addressed slunk off into the total darkness that wrapped the cold, cheerless heath, like a thing of another world.

Unannounced, Thorkil entered, and unperceived took a seat in the darkest part of the room, and from his disguise was unrecognised.

The dance abated in its fury.

Tim and his violin were exhausted ; two strings were broken. The interval in replacing them gave a seasonable pause for rest.

The perspiring dancers returned to their steaming jugs of grog with renewed zest, and enlivened the proceedings by singing sundry naval and smuggling songs with an uproarious vigour that shook the very roof.

"Why don't you sing, mate ?" asked one, addressing Thorkil, and passing to him a steaming glass of newly-made brandy and water. "Why not unreef your slaps, and cast anchor awhile ?"

"Because I don't choose !" was the gruff reply.

"Least said, soonest mended, then, mate ; don't want to cruise round your waters, you know, shipmate. All well intended, my hearty."

At that moment, two of the smugglers entered the back parlour, and returned jingling money in their pockets. Others followed, until all had gone and returned again.

"Ain't it your turn yet ?" whispered Thorkil to Agger, who had been sitting apart, quietly smoking his pipe.

"No, not yet, Penreal," was the sarcastic reply ; "it may be, though, soon."

"Come outside ; I want to talk to you, Agger."

"Very kind, I'm sure, Thorkil, all at once ; what you have to speak, say here, I am very pleasant and satisfied as I am."

"Dare say ; but if you dare whisper I'll cut your treacherous throat !" said Thorkil, half aloud.

"Hullo there !"

"Avast heaving, mate, who talks of throat-cutting here ?" asked several rough and determined-looking fellows, approaching Thorkil menacingly. "If you can't pass the bottle round with a good will, up anchor and away out of this."

"Thorkil," said Polruth, "you needn't sit there in the dark, I know 'tis you ; you come here for no good, I know ; but take my advice, you are on the wrong scent to-night. If you attempt any of your close sailing here, you'll be scuttled and sent to Davy Jones's quicker than a brace of shakes."

"Well said, landlord."

"You are very brave to-night, Polruth ; you have good reason to waste breath and feel jolly over your last trip ; but the reckoning has to come yet, or I am much mistaken."

"Well, you ugly-looking swab," said one, "you must overhaul that log and your back reckoning at some other time, and in some other place, that's all, for, hark ye, mate, if you don't take a reef or two in your sails, I will for you."

"Nay, no fighting, lads," said Polruth, fearful of bloodshed.

"You will, will you ? Take that," said Thorkil, aiming a powerful blow, which intentionally fell upon Polruth, and not the smuggler, and felled him to the earth like an ox.

In a moment all was confusion and noise, and the report of a pistol seemed to have been a preconcerted signal between Thorkil and his friends without, for the door was dashed open, and some dozen or more of Penalvon's servants rushed in, the fight becoming general.

"In the parlour ! in the parlour !" shouted Thorkil ; "he is there !"

Before Penreal could advance a half dozen steps he was tripped up, and trampled upon indiscriminately by friend and foe.

Finding that himself and friends stood no earthly chance of overcoming the strong, burly, and determined smugglers, and being satisfied that Paul Adair was not about the premises, Thorkil and his friends retreated to the door, and with loud oaths were scattered over the heath by Adair's men, who fired rapidly, but at random into the darkness.

Finding their assailants vanquished and running, the bold smugglers gave lusty cheers, which Thorkil heard with mortification and pain as he rapidly retraced his steps homeward alone and full of anger.

Of all who had assisted him there was no one nigh ; he fancied he was followed, and quickened his pace.

"Couldn't expect anything else from a pack of cowardly servants," he muttered. "Penalvon must have been mad to send such fools on that errand. If I had known it he would never have got me into such an ugly nest of thieves. All I've got for my pains are empty pockets and a sore head."

He listened again and again, yet, though he neither saw nor heard aught, he felt certain, from some intuitive knowledge, that he was watched.

"So that too many do not fall upon me," he said, "I care not for one or two."

Binding up his head with a handkerchief, he slowly wended his way towards his home at the cliffs, and stood gazing on the distant sea, when some one advanced into view from the deep mists and shadows surrounding.

"Halt, there !" shouted Thorkil, drawing his cutlass. "Who and what are you ?"

There was no reply.

"Speak, I say, or it will be worse for you."

Still there was no reply.

Drawing a pistol, he fired ; but the figure seemed to vanish in thin air.

"Damn it, it can't be a ghost ! I'll just take a good look, and satisfy myself. I have heard of ghosts about these parts ; to believe Hylda and Thyra there must be dozens or more, but I never yet saw one. There it goes again, down by the road to Seawardine. I'll follow it ! it may be some King's man or revenue, on the look out. If it be, I pity him. Halt, I say !" shouted Thorkil, walking briskly, and firing his second pistol.

The figure stood still, but was unharmed, whatever it was.

"If pistols miss, this wont," said Thorkil, with an oath, as he drew his cutlass and dashed at the unknown.

His thrust was parried by the stranger with such quickness, decision, and strength that Thorkil retreated a step to recover from the unpleasant twitch which it had caused his wrist.

"Curse me ! you seem to know how to handle a sword, whoever you are," Thorkil swore. "Oh, I suppose it is one of Adair's gang, following me from Polruth's. Look ye, mate, you had better sheer off. I don't wish to harm you."

"Harm me ! Thorkil Penreal ?"

"Yes, you, whoever you are."

"No man fears such as you are. Women, perhaps, might."

"What say you ?"

"Why, that you are an unmannerly, cowardly cur, Thorkil, undeserving to call yourself a seaman or wrecker upon this coast."

"You speak boldly, whoever you are. Who be ye ?"

"You thought to surround Polruth's to-night, didn't you, but the bird had flown, and what got ye for your pains ?"

"More than I wanted."

"But you will receive yet more."

"I should know that voice."

"So you should ; I will give you cause for remembering it. I am Paul Adair !"

"Paul Adair !" exclaimed Thorkil, stamping with rage.

"None other. Next time you lay plots to destroy innocent women and children you will think of me. Come, come on ; don't stand there gaping like a stranded porpoise."

In a moment their cutlasses clashed in deadly strife.

Thorkil thrust and parried with the strength and fierceness of a demon.

Paul Adair, agile as a cat, jumped from side to side, unharmed by Thorkil's many desperate, oath-accompanied lunges.

The fight had lasted many minutes, and from its fierceness had now abated much in quickness, though not in ferocity.

Finding himself baffled, and unable to strike Paul in any vulnerable part, he rushed desperately to still shorter distance.

With the quickness of thought Adair saw the movement, parried the intended thrust, and gave a desperate blow in return, which caused Thorkil to stagger with surprise, weakness, and pain.

"Don't laugh yet, Paul Adair, we're not finished quite," said Thorkil, making a sudden dash within Adair's guard.

It had well nigh proved fatal, but by a dexterous guard he received the blow full upon his blade, and it shivered in two.

With desperation he seized hold on Thorkil's weapon, and a fearful encounter ensued for its possession.

Thorkil struggled with the energy of a despairing giant.

Paul Adair was more lithe and active.

Throwing his whole weight upon Paul, he sought to cast him to the earth.

Suddenly twisting, Adair tripped the heavy ruffian, who fell like an ox.

In an instant Paul stood over him, and still endeavoured to wrench the weapon from the prostrate, furious, and blood-stained wrecker.

Thorkil swore with the ferocity of a demon, and kicked, and twisted, and struggled, until both combatants paused, and panted with fatigue and exhaustion.

The sounds of approaching voices fell upon Paul's ear.

He made renewed and repeated efforts to possess himself of the wrecker's cutlass, but in vain.

He had neither pistol nor knife.

To loose a single hand from its iron grip would have placed him powerless in the wrecker's power.

The buzz of voices grew nearer and nearer.

"I am betrayed," swore Paul Adair, with a desperate oath. "I would give all on earth for five minutes more to finish this villain, but they are upon me."

Before he could decide upon any proper course of action he saw himself surrounded.

Bestowing a final vigorous kick upon Thorkil, he slipped away, but had not gone more than a dozen yards when Thorkil shouted faintly,

"Seize him ! it is Paul Adair."

With a wild yell, Earl Penalvon's servants closed in upon him.

A blow from behind felled him to the earth.

"We've got him ! we've got him !" shouted half-a-dozen in ecstasy.

He had fallen, it is true, but was perfectly conscious.

Several sturdy fellows in hurry and confusion stumbled over him.

He seized his opportunity, wrenched a bludgeon from one beside him, and struck right and left with a vigour and effect that surprised and startled all, until howling with pain several ran from the conflict, when with a shout of triumph, Paul Adair dashed over the cliff, and was lost to view among the many fissures and intricacies of the rocks.

"Escaped ! escaped !" shouted Earl Penalvon's servants, in rage and disappointment. "Down to the beach, men ; get lanterns and search."

Hurrying hither and thither they knew not what to do, or where to look, but ever and anon the breeze brought back upon their ears the sound of loud and derisive laughter.

"Who is that ?" asked one, who leaned over the prostrate and blood-stained body of Thorkil, lamp in hand. "Whose voice can it be ?"

"Paul Adair's !" answered Thorkil, writhing with pain and mortification, "Paul Adair's. My curses on his head for this night's work !"

CHAPTER XLIII.

EARL PENALVON, ALONE IN HIS STUDY, COGITATES— THE SHADOWS OF HIS PAST CAREER — HE IS PLEASED WITH THE IDEA OF A SPEEDY MEETING WITH THE ROVER—HE IS SURPRISED—HIS SERVANTS ARRIVE, AND TELL THEIR LONG, SAD TALE —HIS PASSION, VEXATION, AND DISAPPOINTMNT.

"WHAT time did they start, John ?"

"Oh ! they have been several hours gone, my lord. The man, Thorkil, promised to return before midnight, and bring the ruffian with him."

"Excellent, excellent ! He said he'd find no difficulty ?"

"No, my lord ; laughed, and said it would be the easiest thing in the world."

"Not a doubt of it, not a doubt of it. Have supper prepared for them all, John. They deserve and need substantial refreshment, after such a desperate undertaking. You can leave me. Let me be advised on the instant the man, Thorkil, arrives with his charge."

The servant bowed, and retired.

"Things bid fair to end favourably," Earl Penalvon mused. "I must not let this rascal escape, if there is any mode of capturing him. I fear he knows more than he should know. How came he within the hall so frequently ? Besides, who could have prompted him to steal the title deeds of Leona's inheritance ? No mortal on earth, I thought, knew aught of that save me. How, then, came he to take them, and to leave everything—money, jewels, all, in fine, untouched ? I must remove and secrete certain things I have ; they are not fit for common eyes to see. But, where to place them ! I am baffled in all I do. Thorkil abducts Rose, and the elements frown ; she returns. Trelawny engages to do the same thing, is overhauled, and sunk, half his crew destroyed, and himself a prisoner now in some unknown unfathomable spot. Rose Halliard has gone, none know whither. Her brat of a son, despite all I do, will rise in the service, and as he grows older, may yet be a thorn in my side. This Paul Adair is at the bottom of all ! But to-night he meets his crew at Polruth's ; they will be drinking and jigging, and in the nick of time, my servants, with Thorkil, and a few trusty ones, will surround and seize the kiddleawink, and secure him. If I do but get him within my clutches once," thought Penalvon, as he walked about his apartment, and ground his teeth, "if I do but get him within these walls once again, he shall never see the light of day."

Thus musing, the unhappy, thought-tormented Earl sat uneasy in his chair, playing with his bony hands, and grinding his teeth in a manner plainly indicative of the suppressed annoyance, anger, and rage which the name and deeds of Paul Adair had caused him.

He sat down and dosed before the library fire.

Midnight had come and gone, yet no one had as yet arrived.

The winds whistled wildly without, and sighed through keyholes, with sounds like moaning human voices.

Penalvon frowned, and thought,

" 'Tis too late to repent. Such a night as this is, windy and boisterous, always unmans me. It was on just such a night, twenty years ago——But what changes! Who would ever dream of who and what I am, or what accomplished in my time? One thing brings on another ; one crime gives birth to a seed that is interminable."

He sighed deeply, and hid his face in his hands.

"And yet, if I could be but what I was, I would willingly resign all, and retire where none could find me."

"My very footsteps have an hollow echo, that awaken strange thoughts and sounds wherever I stray.

"But this once accomplished, all fears and misgivings are at an end. It must be done ; I care not what it costs. He may elude me, phantom-like, for a time ; but the end must be his death. His bones shall be ground to the finest powder, even ; not a relic of him shall remain. He is my evil genius ; I have never had rest since first I saw him ; I have tempted Thorkil and Trelawny more than once to slay him ; but still now, as ever, he is free, and dances about me like an ignis-fatuus, always seen and felt but never grasped. Time speed on ! a few more fleeting hours may decide all ; once within my power Penalvon is himself again. No one, even in thought, can point at or injure me, then ; but until I shall see his eyes fast closed in death, I must lay upon the rack both night and day."

Earl Penalvon sat long, deeply buried in thought, but the sounds of approaching voices aroused him.

He rang the bell violently.

"Admit them to my presence instantly," he said, while a gleam of pleasure lit his countenance.

A troop of servants soon entered, slowly and solemnly.

"Why, how is this?" he inquired, abruptly. "Where is your prisoner ?"

"Prisoner, my lord ?"

"Yes, your prisoner, and the man Thorkil ; where is he ?"

"Alas, sir, we have neither with us !"

"How say you, neither Adair nor Thorkil ?"

"No, my lord ; we fought well, twice indeed, but both times were unsuccessful. We were overpowered at the kiddleawink by Adair's men, and were treated very roughly. We were returning home again, but the sounds of men engaged in deadly strife reached our ears ; we rushed to the spot, and found that Adair had attacked Thorkil, and at the moment of our arrival was leaning on his breast, endeavouring to wrench his cutlass from him."

"Did you not assist and capture him, then ?" What, a dozen or more to a single man ?"

"The night was dark, my lord, and we stumbled one over another, until, in the confusion, the villain escaped us, and glided down the rocks, laughing in derision."

"Did you not fire ?"

"We did, my lord ; but the excitement and uproar were so great I fear we did more mischief to each other than to him."

"And Thorkil, what of him ?"

"He lies dangerously wounded, frightfully cut about the face and arms."

"All I can say, then, is that both you and he are well-tried poltroons, and deserve all you have received. Begone !"

The chap-fallen domestics and rustics left the apartment with rueful looks, swearing roundly that if ever they came across Paul Adair they would, by fair means or foul, tear him limb from limb.

"Failed again !" cursed Penalvon, as he paced to and fro ; "but it cannot be always so. My next attempt shall prove successful, if I lead myself."

Taking a lamp he glided ghost-like into his museum, unlocked the glass case, and uncovered the skeleton.

"Dead ones tell no tales," he muttered. "I hope soon to have *another* specimen to add to this collection," he chuckled, with a demoniacal laugh. "I should like to look upon *his* bones, and, cost what it may, it shall be done. One more deed cannot trouble me more than this one has done ; all I live for now is pleasure and revenge. But, Rose. Oh, would that she of all mortals else were in my power for one brief hour."

He looked intently about him.

A sense of awe and fear possessed him.

Armed with a poignard that gleamed in the lamplight, he trod softly about, and, entering a secret door, disappeared, whispering as he went,

"I will gaze once more on Nelly ; she leaves me soon. This is the hour for pleasure and revenge ; for if my suspicions are not dull, this pretty childish jade is in love with Paul Adair, a ruffian who would drag me to ruin, if not to the gibbet !"

CHAPTER XLIV.

ROSE UNDER PAUL'S CARE IS HAPPY AND CONTENT — THE PRISON OF BLACK WILL TRELAWNY — AGGER MEETS PAUL, AND SWEARS LOYALTY TO HIM — WILD THYRA IS THREATENED WITH DEATH — HER TIMELY RESCUE — HYLDA AND THORKIL — FAMILY JARS.

"WELL, Rose, I have saved you from those who meant you ill, and all I ask is, that you will feel, or endeavour to be happy in your new home."

"Nay, dear friend, do not think for a moment that I repine, for, under Providence, I own that my life and safety once did, as it now does lay in your hands."

"Never mind, Rose, do not weep, for the sake of your dear boy Harry ; and, in memory of the dear departed chivalric captain, your lamented husband, I would have done the same, and will, if aught of harm should threaten you. 'Tis true this cottage is not so nice a one as your old home, endeared to you, as it doubtless is, by happy memories and old associations ; but, in the name, and for the sake of friendship, I will do for you all a brother might, if you permit it."

"Thanks, thanks, good Paul ; you have done so

much for me that I scarce know how to thank you. I fear I shall never be able to repay you for your more than brotherly kindness."

"But how came it, Rose, that you should have incurred the displeasure or enmity of Earl Penalvon ?"

"Nay, I know not, nor do I know now that he really is an enemy."

"Surely, from the base, cowardly, and unmanly conduct of his hirelings you might form an opinion of his real feelings towards you."

"True, kind friend, and so I should, but, believe me, I know not the reason why he should seek to vent his malice and fury upon a poor defenceless widow."

"Did he ever approach you otherwise than gentlemanly ?"

"On the contrary ; he seemed to court my society by every means that lay in his power; always smiled——"

"The fawning dog !"

"Always spoke of my bereavement with condolence——"

"The hypocrite !"

"And always promised to befriend me in the hour of need."

"Ah, Rose, you know not what the world really is ; you are one of those rare beings so blessed as to pass uncontaminated, and unconscious of the wickedness surrounding you in life."

"Why, he even spoke religiously to me, and promised his lordly influence in promoting the welfare of my darling boy, dear Harry."

"You know not all, dear Rose ; 'tis meet that you should not do so yet. You have a son, the brave, lion-hearted Sailor Boy, who, when he arrives at maturity, will do more in vindicating and avenging you than the poor wrecker, smuggler, or pirate, as evil-minded tongues would call me."

"Nay, let them say what they may, dear Paul, I know what you are, a noble-hearted fellow, whom, had my husband lived, he would have loved you for your true brave heart, and thanked you a thousand times more than I ever can."

"Did Earl Penalvon never visit you ?"

"He did, often. Why ask you ?"

"And not open his mind on many points ?"

"No, never."

"Not speak of the Seawardine estate ? Nor say he once knew one you much resembled ?"

"No, never."

"He is a hypocrite and a vagabond, Rose."

"Harsh words, Paul, harsh words ! Why do you hate him ?—'tis unchristian to feel so."

"Tut, lass, don't preach, pray. Nay, no offence, Rose ; but I know more of him than you ever dream of."

"What then ?"

"Why, this ; he has no more right to the estate of Seawardine, or to call himself Earl Penalvon, than Paul Adair, half smuggler, half pirate as I am."

"Paul——"

"I have proof, Rose, and 'tis because your meek, pretty face, and simple manner stung him to the quick, whenever he gazed on you, that he sought foul means to decoy and destroy you."

"How can I be in his way ?"

"You certainly are, or he would not pay Thorkil and Trelawny such a price to forcibly abduct you."

"Explain then, Paul, dear friend, explain ?"

"I cannot now, it would only fill your sensitive mind with hopes and conjectures, which, for lack of influence and money in these troublous times, might never be realized."

"Think you, then, that Thorkil and Trelawny were parties to his plot ?"

"None can doubt it ; I have had ample proof of their guilt. Nay, I knew the very day and hour that Black Will set sail."

"Oh, what an unhappy being I am."

"Nay, don't weep, Rose ; Black Will will not trouble you in a hurry again. He is bound fast in a cavern beside the coast, where my comrades meet ; and, as to Thorkil, I gave him something of what he deserves t'other night at the kiddleawink, and beside his home at the White Cliffs, when, dastard as he was, he endeavoured to entrap me with his own and Penalvon's myrmidons."

"Surely Agger would not harm you ?"

"No, he is a brave fellow, and as staunch a friend to you as ever I could prove."

"How know you this, good Paul, for certainty ?"

"He came to Polruth's and warned me."

"He knew it, then ?"

"Yes, he and Thorkil quarrelled about Thyra."

"Thorkil hates Thyra, and Agger loves her."

"As to Thorkil's love or hate, Rose, it lies very light upon Agger's shoulders."

"One would suppose he had become so entangled in Thorkil's villanies that he could not break the trammels and free himself."

"He has done so, and bravely."

"How ?"

"By refusing consent to any plot that portended harm to you or yours."

"How kind are all to me ?"

"Nay, not more so than you deserve, dear Rose ; for if any one dared lift a finger against you, there are more than one who would willingly save you at the risk of their own neck, despite Penalvon, or a dozen such earls. I cannot explain more now."

"But, what have you done—what do you intend doing with Black Will ?"

"Keep him where he is, out of harm's way for the present."

"What does he in your cavern warehouses beneath the rocks ?"

"Acts as a slave to all who bid him."

"Have you no fears for his escape ?"

"None at all. He's too well watched within and without. Thorkil, nor any one on the coast, save myself and crew, know the whereabouts to our hiding-place. We go, and come ; set sail, or anchor, like a phantom on the ocean. Such is the name they give us along this dangerous, treacherous coast."

"If Thorkil should discover you, Paul, it would be an evil hour."

"No fear, lass."

"They could gather together such a formidable body as to storm this place, secure and strong as it seems. Earl Penalvon would inform the naval and custom-house officers ; his word would be law."

"If he knew what was best for him, he'd keep quiet, and not trouble us."

"You speak as if he were in your power, Paul ?"

"So he is. Poor and friendless as I now appear, I could raise such a storm as would shake down and crumble all Seawardine about his ears.

"It is a secret, then ?"

"It is."

"Then explain, good, kind friend—explain, I beg, what it is."

"I could not now, dear Rose, as I have before repeated. I am not personally concerned, although I know he hates me with a deadly hatred far more than any living being."

"He hates me also, if I understand your words aright ?"

"Not a doubt, not a doubt. He would have immured you in some French convent ; he would have dishonoured you first, and, perhaps, having satiated his beastly passions, might have done to you as he has aforetime done to others."

"And what was that ?"

"Murdered, then, perhaps."

"You do not mean it ?"

"I cannot prove it, truly ; but, from all I know, I consider him capable of that or anything."

"Oh, how kind has Heaven been to me in saving me from such a one."

"True, lass, it has, and all will prosper who has assisted in it, as will, likewise, all those miserably perish who attempted to assist him in his intended wrong-doing."

"How came you to know all this ?"

"Through Wild Thyra."

"Thyra ! Why. surely she knows nothing of Earl Penalvon, or Seawardine."

"These are few things, Rose, she knows not something of if it be ever so little."

"And how came this ?"

"She says through spirit voices round the coast, and rune-kenning."

"But you did not believe her ?"

"No, never, until repeated predictions, and their minute fulfilment, fastened conviction upon my incredulity."

"Did Thorkil suspect her ?"

"He did, and threatened to slay her for her ravings ; but I interfered, and we parted in deadly hate."

"He had not harmed me then, dear Paul."

"No ; but was brooding mischief pleasantly as he went to your cottage, and spoke in raptures of Penalvon's admiration for you."

"But Thyra ?"

"He aimed a blow at her with his dirk. I jumped between, and warded the blow. High words ensued ; blood would have flown ; but Hylda interfered, and you know he always stands in awe of her."

"You left him ?"

"Yes; and ever since have I believed in the truth of what wild Thyra wildly spoke to me, for all has been fulfilled to a single sentence."

"But where were you when Thorkil forced me away ?—when he concealed me from all view ?"

"Preparing for Trelawny's expedition, which I knew would follow."

"Singular coincidences of her foreknowledge, Paul."

"Yes, lass, truly ; and it is because I rely so much upon her aid and advice in all I do or attempt, that Agger clings to me with almost the affection of a brother."

"Good Paul, may Heaven be always kind to you, for your noble, chivalric devotion and self-sacrifice to me !"

"No thanks, lass. I did and will always do to the unprotected of your sex as becomes a Briton, let the world call me what it likes for my pains. But I forgot ; I have good news for you."

"What is it, kind friend ?"

"The Thunderer is in port again."

"And my son—my Harry—what of him ?"

"Safe, Rose, and hearty."

"How know you this ?"

"Thyra was sitting runing in your old cottage, now deserted, when the postman called."

"A letter for me, say you ?"

"I heard it at Polruth's kiddleawink."

"And the letter—tell me, pray, where is it ?"

"She gave it to Agger. He will be here to-morrow. Calm yourself, lass ; don't weep. Report does have it that he's a noble boy, and hourly finds favour with his captain and officers."

"May Heaven preserve him! But can't I see him ? Oh for wings to fly to him, that I might once more embrace him !"

"You shall see him, surely, dear Rose, before he sails again. You must go to Falmouth; but on your word as a woman, promise me to breathe not a syllable of all that has lately happened, for it would only disturb him from proper duties and studies, retard his certain and rapid promotion, and excite him to attempt your legal justification and natal rights long before the proper moment. Be advised. You shall be comfortable here in the cottage within the valley, and although your only protector for the nonce is rough and untitled, he will tell you the proper moment to seek that redress which any untimely action now might render for ever abortive."

"Aught that you say or advise, good, kind Paul, I will heed and follow. Nay, I cannot thank you in words for the more than brotherly kindness you have ever evinced since I placed foot on your noble schooner, and until the day I die I shall fervently aspirate good wishes and prayers for Paul Adair."

"Thanks, Rose; 'tis late, you must retire. Harry will meet you within a few days. Think no more of all your wrongs. Good night."

Such was the conversation that passed between Paul Adair and Rose Halliard in the latter's cot, which Paul had chosen and furnished for her in a calm, secluded spot beside the sea, many miles from the plots and schemes of Seawardine.

His schooner lay moored in an adjacent cove, within the shadow of hills that overlooked its mouth, and as the moon arose brightly in the cloudless sky and tipped the distant glassy sea, Paul Adair sat at Rose's cottage-door smoking, and revolving many a scheme that should afterwards redound to his own honour and Harry Halliard's welfare.

CHAPTER XLV.

THORKIL WITH A SORE HEAD GROWLS LIKE A BEAR—HE INVEIGHS AGAINST PAUL ADAIR, AND VOWS VENGEANCE—HYLDA WARNS HIM TO HAVE NOTHING TO DO IN THE ABDUCTION OF NELLY BRITTON—HE DETERMINES TO DO SO—PENALVON WISHES TO KNOW SOMETHING OF BLACK WILL.

"DON'T lay grumbling there, you heavy lump of good-for-nothingness."

"Prate on Hylda ; let that tongue of yours wag as usual to everlasting."

"Don't call yourself a man ever again, Penreal. Do what you may, you can never explain why it was that Adair defeated you."

"Never explain, wife !" Thorkil discontentedly grumbled. "Is it not enough that my head and arm are wounded and bandaged, to sufficiently explain why it was I failed ?"

"No, it is not. A man like you, large and powerful, should have eaten a dozen such as he."

"One of his sort is quite enough for any man living ; let him be even as stalwart as Goliath."

"Well, console yourself as you may, Thorkil ; all I know is, that you have miserably failed ; you get nothing from Earl Penalvon for your sore head, and here you are the laughing-stock of every wrecker who knows you."

"Am I? Well, let me recover a little, and you will see, wife, if I don't get something for my pain."

"How will you get it?"

"By more ways than one."

"You are too chicken-hearted to attempt anything bold and daring."

"Except for thy cursed rune-kenning, I should have done much, ere this; but, do what I may, I am always met by warnings from thee or Thyra; but as for her, I will strangle her, for I am certain she forewarned Polruth of my approach, and advised him of my intention."

"But how could she have done this, then, if she had not had foreknowledge, or had not been warned by storm spirits?"

"Don't talk to me of storm-spirits. I will raise such a storm about *her* ears ere long if she sets foot within my place again, as will astonish both you and her."

"Nay, I imagine Thyra cares as much about thee as I; she needs no assistance from you or me. Polruth is her friend, one of many who would see little harm befall her if they could help it."

"She will be down here shortly."

"I don't think so, Thorkil; she is now many, many miles away from this place and Seawardine."

"Where then?"

"Why, she has gone to young Harry."

"Harry Halliard?"

"Yes, and doubtless will tell him all the news, and then, Thorkil, if he comes this way, I advise you to be prepared. Forewarned is forearmed."

"I fear not the brat."

"He isn't much of a brat, now, I warrant you."

"He dare not lay a hand on me, I am in Earl Penalvon's pay."

"And pretty pay it is; promises for nothing. What has he given thee for all thou hast already done?"

"Truly, not much; but he will."

"You know not that even."

"If he does not I'll wreak my vengeance upon him and his."

"Bravely said, but not bravely done. What would you do?"

"Do! why burn the mansion above his head."

"And hang thyself besides. That would be pretty vengeance, truly."

"Laugh on Hylda; let me be but well again and you will see I shall prove good as my word."

"If your word is worth anything. I have heard enough of promises. Have you heard what Polruth made?"

"No, I have not; but something handsome."

"Handsome! you may well say so. And will you allow him to enjoy it in peace and quiet?"

"Not if I can help it. But what did he gain by his villany?"

"Gain! why everything. The French brig that had signalled you night after night fell into the hands of Paul Adair. He boarded her and would have let her run her course unharmed, untouched, until he learned it was originally intended for you, when he seized the whole, and safely disembarked the cargo, and was paid, partly in money, for portion of it."

"Of what did the cargo consist, then?"

"Wines, brandy, tobacco, arms, clothing, and odds and ends, that would have ensured a ready market anywhere."

"Curse him! I'll be even with him yet. And Polruth, say you that he had any hand in it?"

"I know not, but this—that Paul paid his crew

at the kiddleawink, and that all of them are heavily laden with money, and are running up and down the coast bent on fun and frolic."

"It will not be difficult, then, to find out his whereabouts, and have ample revenge."

"If Earl Penalvon took an interest in the matter, I see no reason why you might not, with his aid, pounce down upon him, and have ample revenge."

"How my heart would leap with satisfaction."

"But know, Thorkil, he is as cunning as you. Yes, far more so; and I doubt whether you could ever manage to surprise or capture him. Polruth's friends would never allow you to obtain your desire, if they ever got wind of the affair."

"I fear not him. Who should warn him?"

"None that I know, save Thyra. She knows everything—nothing seems hidden from her knowledge."

"The only thing that remains, then," growled the wounded wrecker, "is to stop her breath."

"You would not do that, Thorkil."

"Why not?"

"Why not! She never harmed you. Why should you vent your spleen upon a harmless, half-crazy girl?"

"Half crazy! Nay, Hylda, she has more sense and cunning than either of us, and if something be not done our business on the coast is gone for ever, and I shall be pressed into the navy. Anything but that."

"Nay, there is plenty of business to be done even yet, if you will be advised by me."

"Advised by you!—in what way?"

"Why, leave Penalvon to his own plots. Attend to thy own, and make friends with Thyra, Paul Adair, Polruth, and Rose Halliard."

"Do you take me for a child, wife?"

"No; but that is the only course, at least, the safest one that is open to you."

"I could not, if I would. I am bound hand and foot by Penalvon. I can not do what I would; even now I am in league with him. There is still another job to do—a nasty one, in truth; but money does not fall with the rain. He has laid eyes on——"

"Whom?"

"Oh, no one in particular. Suffice it to say he has a wench in his eye he would like much, nay, give thousands to haste away from Seawardine. You know not, could not, even dream who it is."

"I do."

"How knew you it?"

"The spirits told me. I was runing yester-night."

"Enough, wife, hold thy tongue; I'll not believe in such childishness more."

"Whether or not, I know her; 'tis——"

"Who?"

"Nelly Britton!"

Thorkil was silent for a second, when Hylda resumed,

"Is there nought else in the world for thee to do than league thyself with a profligate nobleman to despoil honest men of the best and most loved ornaments of their homes and firesides? If I were a man, my cheek would blush to own it!"

"What has Joel Britton done for us that we should consult his feelings in aught we do?"

"Nay, don't say 'we,' for I shall have naught to do with it. But, mark me, young, pretty, and frivolous, as Nelly is, as much as she has thrown herself into danger unconsciously——"

"Unconsciously! Why, you are not such an idiot as not to plainly see the bent of her wishes and desires! She would wish nothing better, it seems to me, than be the petted and fondled mistress of a nobleman !"

"Foul-hearted fool, you know nothing of women ! Know that a girl would rather be the very slave to a man she loved than rule as empress with one she had no affection for ?"

"Tut, tut, prating, waggle-tongue ; women are but fools at best !"

"I was, truly, in having thee ; but, let me say, once and for all, you must have no hand in this, Penreal ! Know you not that she loves Paul Adair devotedly, ardently ?"

"Does she ?" said Thorkil, with a loud, rough laugh of triumph.

"I hear so."

"Hear so ? But I know so ; and, think you, that is not something that should urge me on ?"

"I would not revenge myself in that way."

"What other could be sweeter ? Once I have that girl in my power, I can dictate any terms to Paul Adair !"

"Don't flatter yourself too much. You are a pretty one to lie there concocting schemes of revenge, when you are not stronger than a kitten."

"You used once to boast that Thorkil Penreal was as strong, and bold and brave as a lion."

"True, I did, but that was when you did something to deserve the name ; but not for having round thee men—nay, not men, but fiends—who would shed the blood of helpless ones tossed ashore by angry waves !"

"Speak no more, Hylda ; it was Harleck that——"

"Yes, speak it out plainly, who foully murdered my father ! May vengeance follow him !"

"Well, well, he may be hung, drawn and quartered for aught I care, so that you leave me in peace. Who is that I hear approaching ?"

Hylda went to the door of the cave, where a youth in sailor garb stood waiting.

"Could I see Thorkil ?"

"Aye, wife, show him the way in. I know his voice ; it should be Donald. I thought so. Well, my lad, what cheer ?"

"Father and I were launching our boats to go a fishing, when a gentleman on horseback rode down the beach, and asked me many questions."

"About whom or what ?"

"About you and Will Trelawny."

"What of us, Donald ?"

"Oh, nothing in particular. He said he'd like to see you, and told me to say it was the gentleman at Seawardine."

"I know. It was—well, never mind, an old friend of mine, Donald, no one else—a person who once did a little in my way, you know, lad," said Thorkil, winking significantly. "What had he to say of Trelawny ?"

"He said he had gained information that he was in trouble, in prison or something of that sort, and that the Rover, as they call the Phantom schooner's captain, knew all about it."

"Ha, ha ! that villain again ! Oh, oh ! I wish I were well again."

"He told me to tell you that he had a plan for capturing him, schooner and all. He said you knew the 'Rover' well ; the same gentleman who met you at the kiddleawink lately."

"A friend of mine, eh ? did he say that ?" inquired Thorkil, sarcastically.

"Yes ; and told me to say, that as soon as possible, he wished to see you."

"Thanks, Donald. I fully understand him and if you see him again, say that Thorkil expects to be well again for business in less than a week. Nay,

don't go without taking a drain. Hylda, fill a bottle of the best Jamaica. That's it, lad ; I hope to be well again soon, and I know that at any time you'd lend a willing hand to sink the 'Rover,' for he has lately become the plague and terror of all the coast, so that honest men, like you and I, can scarcely get a living."

When left alone to his own guilty thoughts and speculations, Thorkil lit a pipe, and, despite his wounds, drank freely of brandy, until he become in a maudling, half-drunken state, in which condition he lay grumbling and growling, and swearing, until almost red in the face.

"I don't care a pin for life, wife," he grumbled. "All I want, is revenge ! revenge on somebody, I care but little who it is ; and revenge I shall have."

CHAPTER XLVI.

EARL PENALVON INTRUDES UPON THE PRIVACY OF NELLY BRITTON—SHE TALKS IN HER SLEEP—PENALVON RESOLVES TO ABDUCT, SEDUCE, AND DESTROY HER.

THE bright, pale moon shone with silver rays upon the snow white cot of Nelly Britton.

Unconscious of all harm, or the presence of any one, she lay as quietly and noiselessly as a child in slumber.

Her hair in long silken bands lay loose upon her pillow.

He neck was bared and heaved in sleep, while again and again a soft sigh escaped her lips as she inaudibly murmured.

Her spotless taper fingers twitched with nervous motion.

Her arms, all bare, lay upon the counterpane.

The moon, with full flood of silver light, illumined her countenance, and faint smiles played over her gentle face as her mind wandered far away in dreams.

A side door slowly, noiselessly opened.

No sounds were heard.

A dark figure of a man emerged from a secret closet, and, cat-like, crept towards her bed.

Hiding behind the heavy damask bed curtains he gazed upon the innocence and beauty unconsciously dreaming and murmuring in sleep.

It was Earl Penalvon.

"How beautiful !" he thought, as his beastial appetites shone forth from his lustrous eyes.

He drew the curtains aside, and gazed long and ardently.

He looked upon the virgin-innocence before him, and like the mirror of clear, placid waters, he saw his own guilty soul reflected.

He saw in her what he had been, and what he should be.

He heaved a stifled sigh, but strangled every feeling of compunction and remorse, which, like spectres, rose unhidden from the depths of his guilty soul, and frowned upon him.

"How lovely !" he murmured still.

He stood gazing as if entranced.

He felt that the sleeping girl was beyond all his craft and power.

A sense of awe fell upon him; he saw, or imagined he saw, angels kneeling beside the bed, or heard the rustling of wings as they flitted to and fro.

EARL PENALVON AND NELLY BRITTON.

His eyes were strained; he felt spell-bound, and could not stir.

The memories of the past hung about him like heavy chains.

He felt numb, and cold, and petrified; but still his guilty soul, like a seething fire, glowed and burned within him, and his brain, the seat of all past villanies, was active, alive, and full of dark resolves.

His feet seemed fastened to the floor.

He could not move, but heard his own heart violently beating against his guilty breast like an unwilling captive, forced to dishonour and degraded, knocking for egress from its prison walls.

The sleeper stirred.

Her disordered tresses fell in exquisite folds and delicious abandon upon her white and swan-like neck.

She murmured.

Penalvon listened attentively to every word.

"Oh, that I could see him once again, for one moment, I would give worlds. I know that he loves me. Nay, mother, do not chide me; I feel that he loves me, and always did. Brave lad, my blessings go with you."

"Of whom can she be dreaming?" thought Penalvon, his eyes glowing with rage.

For a few moments all was still again.

The winds softly sighed beside the latticed window, and the ivy rustled sweetly and harmoniously low.

The dreamer muttered.

Her lips moved, yet naught but a sigh escaped her beautifully-chiselled and coral lips.

Ever and anon she smiled, and her matchless teeth glistened like polished ivory, inlaid in a light, carmine-tinted cupid's bow.

"Oh, that harm might ne'er assail him. The companion of my childhood, my brave defender, who battled like a man for my school-girl rights. Ah, where is he now?"

"Curse him, whoever he is," thought Earl Penalvon.

"Away, alas! far away upon the stormy waters! Oh, never, never doubt my lasting, steadfast love, dear Paul—my own dear Paul Adair!"

As if stung by an adder the nobleman quivered in every limb when he heard the fatal word.

His eyes gleamed with unholy desires and keen revenge.

But the helpless one before him was so beautiful, there seemed such an halo of purity and holiness surrounding her, that he felt powerless to proceed to the accomplishment of the hellish resolves which then burned within his soul.

"She shall be mine," he thought; "but I cannot now—no, I cannot now!"

It was not pious promptings which held his heart and hand.

It was the curish fear of being heard or discovered that chilled his hot blood.

"If I should be discovered, if aught suspicious were to hang upon my name, this house, and all it contains, might be revealed to the curious and astonished gaze of open day. No, no, it must not be; at least, not now—not here. I will entice her, abduct her, take her far away, where no familiar eyes or ears can see or hear me!"

Thus he thought, and still he gazed.

"To-morrow shall see her mine! Sleep on, gentle one; your lover, Paul, shall never kiss those ruby lips again, nor place his dastard arms around your polished neck! To-morrow's eve will see you far from this; but, ere I go," he thought, "I must steal one soft kiss from that incomparable brow."

Noiselessly he approached the bed.

He leaned over the sleeping maid, smiling in her girlish dreams.

His head bent low, and he felt her pure, warm breath touch his face.

His cheek was all aglow with shame; it felt as if touched with a sting from some unseen, unearthly hand.

His heart was still, and the blood stagnated in his veins.

Nelly opened her eyes in horror.

She was speechless with surprise and fear.

Her rosy cheeks faded into lily-leaves, and her eyes, lit up with mingled fright and indignation, started from their sockets like avenging angels, withheld from slaying some myrmidon of Satan.

She screamed, and fainted.

Penalvon vanished; his form was lost in dark shadows as he touched the spring of the closet, and disappeared as he came, like a dark thing of night, or a vapoury being of the nether world.

CHAPTER XLVII.

POLRUTH BEFRIENDS THYRA—SHE SPEAKS OF AGGER AND PAUL ADAIR—AGGER IS EMPLOYED BY POLRUTH—WHAT THE KIDDLEAWINK CONTAINED, AND WHAT POLRUTH INTENDS TO DO.

"COME, Agger, don't look so blue and dull, lad.

I'm sure you're welcome to the 'Jolly Mariners' whenever it suits you to drop in."

"Thanks, Polruth, and between ourselves the kiddleawink isn't such a bad place to blow 'bacco in after all, with its bright fire, cosy tap-room, out of the wind and rain that blows so unmercifully to-day upon the heath."

"True, and although I say it, there are few places on the coast where a lad can get a better drop of rum, or a gill of good old Hollands, for we don't generally deal in four-water grog, eh, Agger?"

"No, Polruth," said Agger, sipping from a steaming glass of brandy-and-water, "thanks to Paul Adair, and the likes of such good-hearted fellows as he is; but if it lay with Thorkil and his crew a man's mouth might parch before he'd give a dram of right good stuff to anybody, for he casts all he don't want for himself into the country, bad luck to him!"

"And stick to the coin, too, if all be true I've heard."

"Just so, Polruth, but I've done with him for ever. He must get some one else to do his dirty work, not me, in future."

"Why, what was the fuss between you, then?"

"Oh, nothing; all about Thyra," replied Agger, with a sigh. "He's treated that girl worse than a dog; but he won't do it again in a hurry, while I've got a fist to help her."

"Why, what has she done, then?" asked Polruth, smoking and stirring up the bright coal fire.

"What has anybody done, then, if it comes to that? Why nothing that one could blame her for. She simply tells him what she thinks, as I do, or as any honest body ought to do. True, she has told him of nasty, unpleasant things that would come to pass, but if he'd been any sort of a man he should have thanked her for it."

"All I know is," said Polruth, blowing clouds of smoke around him, "all I know, lad, is, that while I've got a meal's victuals to eat Thyra is welcome to a share, and no mistake."

"Have you seen her lately?" asked Agger, with a reddening cheek.

"No, I haven't, Agger, but I heard she had gone on a journey somewhere."

For a moment both speakers relapsed into silence, and sat smoking, wordless, before the sea-coal fire.

"I did hear that Thyra was in love like," said Polruth, at length, with a sidelong glance at the manly, stalwart wrecker beside him.

"Did you? With whom, pray?"

"I forget his name, but I also heard that somebody else had a sneaking kind of liking for her," added Polruth, with a good-humoured smirk about his countenance.

"Daresay. Thyra ain't a bad sort after all, you see, Polruth, if she is called Wild, and is a sort of rune-kenner."

"No, that's true, Agger; and if she took a fancy to a fellow, I don't think the wench would make a bad sort of wife. But, at all events, let's drop the women folk, and talk of business. What do you intend to do with yourself now, Agger?"

"Scarcely know, now I've cut Thorkil."

"He'd be awful fiery if he thought you had anything to do with me, although, as far as that goes, I care little for him, or any one like him. I don't forget his dirty tricks. He tried to break me up more than once, but now he's got in tow with the big folks at Seawardine, there's no knowing what he intends towards the 'Jolly Mariners.'"

"Never fear, he won't do much."

"Oh, I don't fear much, so as he don't call in the Revenues upon us."

"And, if he does, there be some as can call 'em in, too," added Agger ; "and for more than stowing away a few barrels in their cellars."

"Well, if they were to come down now upon me they'd find a deuced more than I'd like 'em to, for we've got any quantity of things on hand. If them dealers in the country come up according to promise and take some away, I shouldn't mind much, but we've got a leetle too much on hand to be safe or pleasant."

"Anything that I could dispose of?"

"Well, I don't know. There's ten barrels of brandy, fifteen of Hollands, several hundredweight of prime tobacco, and many kegs of powder. Paul has sold much already, and distributed the proceeds among his crew."

"But what if Thorkil and his gang were to come upon you when unprepared, for you know the cargo was originally intended for him."

"So it was, but if Paul Adair likes to take the responsibility, and seize it, that's *his* business, and not mine."

"I don't imagine that Penreal would ever attempt any mischief, while Paul has such a powerful crew cruising about."

"It was well Thorkil escaped as he did on the last occasion, for had he stayed five minutes longer, he'd have been dragged out a dead man, for Adair's men were desperate beyond measure."

"Did they stay?"

"Of course they did, and enjoyed themselves more than ever. You never heard such singing, and never saw such dancing in all your life ; a braver, finer lot of fellows never stepped on deck than Paul's men, and they'd go through fire and water to serve him."

"All speak well of Paul, except Earl Penalvon's servants and Thorkil."

"Yes, because he is much too clever for either or any of them. I hear that Joel Britton hates him."

"Well, I don't know as he does. He says he don't like wreckers, and such as we, you know, but I think that Nelly might seek far and wide before meeting with a better-looking or braver fellow than Paul."

After some time spent in silence, Polruth bluntly asked the question,

"You are in love with Thyra, Agger?"

A few moments of pause, and he answered, equally as bluntly,

"I am."

"Then why not tell her so?"

"So I have, but it's of no use?"

"Why?"

"She loves another, that's all."

"And who is he, pray?"

"Why, I know not, Polruth, and you might as well endeavour to move the rock of Gibraltar as to draw that secret from her."

"But yet she speaks favourably of you always—nay, in very high terms."

"I know it, and believe she would almost lay down her life for me."

"True, lad ; she is a courageous girl, wild and foolish as some may call her. She has been to Seawardine."

"Seawardine!"

"Yes, and where else has she not been?"

"But what wants she there?"

"I know not, but there must be something very attractive, or she wouldn't go so often."

"What, to Earl Penalvon's place?"

"Yes, why not? They say he is very fond of her."

"So much the worse."

"So much the worse, Agger! Why, 'tis something worth talking about to boast of having such a powerful friend. So Thorkil thinks, at all events."

"He means no good, nor Thorkil either."

"Fear nothing, he will never harm Thyra. She knows more about Thorkil and Penalvon than either think for, so she tells me."

"What mean you—that they are in league? Then that accounts for all his past treachery."

"Thyra told me she has roamed all over the house, for she knows other entrances than by the door."

"By the door! What other mean you?"

"Why, through the woods, and a secret passage that opens there."

"You surprise me."

"But it did not surprise Paul Adair in the least, for he knew it long before her eyes discovered it."

"But what use could he make of such a discovery?"

"Simply that he wished to satisfy himself from time to time of how things were progressing there with his sweetheart, Nelly Britton."

"But that was merely idle curiosity. He must have had something else in view."

"I know he had. His love for, and interest in, Rose Halliard prompted him."

"But what can she avail him? He does not love her."

"He does, more than any mortal breathing, but I do not pretend to say he intends marriage, or anything of that kind."

"Does he consider her interests so important, then, as to jeopardize his life in her behalf?"

"He does, and has done so more than once. Thorkil will remember him for many a day, for he bears scars upon his head and shoulders that ointment can never heal."

"He has been a true friend to me."

"And to many beside ; he has engaged me in his interests, and I would not, could not serve a better master."

"Why, 'twas said he loved a nobleman's daughter."

"'Tis true that *she* loves him, as I know ; but 'tis doubtful if ever he thinks of women at all, his mind is bent on other things. In case of an attack from the Revenues, though, how would you act ?—you have none of Adair's men to help you, you know."

"I should have to blow up the kiddleawink altogether, that's what I should be obliged to do, for it would be much better to use powder and do that than be caged and transported for smuggling. I hope they may not make a descent, however, for I expect something valuable from France soon. Some French officers have promised to pay enormously to run across the channel ; they are spies, I believe."

"You would not land French spies on our coast, Polruth, to roam at large, and spy out our military and naval resources?"

"No, lad ; nothing quite so bad as that. I act with the full knowledge and concurrence of Paul Adair."

"What are your plans, then, for I know no dishonourable proposition could come from such a source?"

"Our plans? Why, simply these : they pay an extravagant price to come across the channel. This fact is told to Thorkil, who runs his sloop over at an appointed time, and when about to land will be attacked, and the Frenchmen handed over to the authorities, so that *we* are the gainers, and Thorkil the loser in every way."

" But will he do this ?"

" Never fear, he is base enough for anything."

" If this plot answers, Penalvon will have much difficulty in rescuing his friend from the gallows."

" I hope he may, for, at best, he's but a white-livered knave."

" It will be good for you."

" Of course, for all ; for government will commend, and, perhaps, reward us for our diligence and bravery, and never dream of sending the Revenues to watch us for a long time to come."

" Thorkil will be taken all a-back."

" True ; but it will be pay in kind for his attempted roguery with us."

" But who is to entice Penreal into this trap, he is artful and cunning ?"

" Leave that to us ; when he sees a good price in gold glittering before his eyes, he will grab the bait unthinkingly."

CHAPTER XLVIII.

JOE JUNIPER, BILL HAWSER, AND KONKS ARE LIBERTY MEN—THEY TAKE POSSESSION OF THE TAP AT THE "ADMIRAL BENBOW"—TELL SOME VERY TOUGH YARNS, AND DRINK VERY STRONG GROG.

" WELL, Konks," said the landlord, " I'm very glad to see you, and your shipmates ashore again, and am still gladder to hear that your young middy fully cleared himself from that ugly charge ; but of all the yarns I ever heard, I never listened to a tougher one than that."

" Every word true, hearty, every syllable, or I ain't Konks."

" Dare say it's all fair and square all concerning Konk's story ; but all I say, landlord, is, that it's rather dry work this, smoking and no drinking ; therefore, as I said afore, bring in your grog, and let's wet our whistles all round."

" Aye, aye, shipmate, well said," joined in Bill Hawser, rather gruffly, " and when it's all passed round, maybe, mates, as how I might give you one myse'f."

" Bravo, Bill ! Come, shipmate, drink, lad ; swig deep, my boy ; there's nothing like it, you know, and let's have that yarn."

" Give us the 'shark' story," said one.

" No, no, it might be personal, you know ; we're on shore now, lads, and not bawling afore the wind in the channel. Let's have 'Admiral Woodenleg.'"

" Woodenlegs ? Who's that ?"

" Oh, you'll hear soon enough, mates, if he'll only splice up, and heave a-head. Come, Bill, here's some real old Varginny tobacco, take a good chaw."

" Woodenlegs !—Admiral Woodenlegs ! whoever heard tell of such a man ? I have heard tell of Admiral Benbow, Admiral Nelson, and all the rest ; but I never heard of that chap. What ship did he sail in ?—what action did he win ?"

" Avast your talk, landlord ; there's more on board a ship than you'll dream of in a tap-room, as I've often heard say, leastwise, so our officers used to tell me."

" Take a swig all round, fair and square, mates, and you, Bill Hawser, begin to pay out your yarn

of 'Admiral Woodenlegs,' and I'll keep a bright look out for squalls. Heave a-head, my hearty."

Bill Hawser put down his pipe, took a huge chew of tobacco, had a strong pull at the the grog, and, after a preliminary cough or two, thus began :

" Well, shipmates, old Woodenlegs, as we used to call him, weren't a bad sort of old chap, but he had one idea above all others in that old head of his'n ; for he imagined because he had climbed aloft right smartly in the Admiralty's roll-book, that everybody else should be able to do the same, let the wind be fair or foul around the moorings of Whitehall. You see, shipmates, old Woodenlegs had entered the Navy as a poor friendless Sailor Boy under old Duncan, and had more than one brush with the Dutch and French, and soon got rated first luff, and soon after got the command of a tight little brig of war, and commenced to play the very devil with all foreign-looking craft as dare hoist a bunting in sight of Old England.

" He was the very devil for capturing prizes, and not a week scarce elapsed without Captain Billing was hailed sailing into port with something or other in tow, and what with prize-money and promotion, he soon became so well known that the chief Lords of the Admiralty sent him on a confidential cruise ; as some said, to get him into a trap, so as they wouldn't be troubled any more with the everlasting noise which his many captures caused throughout the length and breadth of the land.

" They took away his slashing little brig, and gave him an old tub to go cruising in, which couldn't make no more than six knots, with any wind or tide.

" This didn't suit old Billing, for as he had a nice little craft of a wife on shore, and a pretty daughter growing up, he wanted to go on getting rated higher and higher, so as he might retire from the service, and enjoy himself when laid up in ordinary, as any old salt would like to when they get bow-legged and of no use on board."

" Aye, aye, lad, just so," encored the audience, puffing huge clouds of tobacco smoke, and smacking their lips over steaming glasses of stiff grog.

" Well, as I was a saying, the Lords of the Admiralty gives Billing this old worn-out tub, and says they, 'Billing,' says they, 'you must cruise off the Hague, and don't let anything come out or go in.'

" 'All right,' says he, but he thought it rather hard and strange they'd given him so much to do, and such a good-for-nothing old craft to do it in. 'Never mind,' says he, 'some men can do things as well as others,' and off he goes to sea, with as strapping a lot of fine fellows for a crew as ever walked the deck.

" He hadn't been on his cruising ground more than a week, when heavy weather sets in, and the Porcupine—such was the name of the unwieldly old tub—was forced out to sea, and was tossing about and not expected to reach harbour any more, for she shipped a deal of water, and rolled about like a grampus when sporting under your lee.

" After three days of an awful rain squall, the Porcupine sighted two vessels making all possible sail for the Hague, and didn't seem at all inclined to make the acquaintance of the Porcupine, which was tumbling and rolling after them in chase, but with no more chance of overhauling them than I should of overtaking a half hungry shark.

" 'This won't do,' said old Woodenlegs, as we used to call him afterwards ; ' if the wind would only shift a bit, we might tumble against them in a fog.'

" The wind did shift a point or two, and heavy

fogs came on so that neither old Woodenlegs, nor his officers could take any correct reckonings.

"After a day or two they took soundings, and found they were close on to shore, and when the fog lifted, what should he see but a French frigate close at hand, and bearing down upon him ?

"'That's it, eh, Frenchers ?' said old Woodenlegs. 'Well, if they thinks they're going to run us down to the water's edge, they're much mistaken, if the old Porcupine does leak and make water faster than we can pump it out.'

"Without a word of murmuring, but with many a good oath in secret against the high and mighty Lords of the Admiralty for giving a good seaman such a worthless, leaky old tub to cruise in, Woodenlegs musters all hands, and, says he,

"'My lads,' says he, 'we're in for it, and no mistake ; we must fight while a stick of her holds together, and, although she is bigger and more heavily armed than we are, we'll give the Frenchers such a drubbing as they never got before, mark my words !'"

"Here's health to old Woodenlegs, mate !" said his pleased listeners, draining their tumblers, and jingling them approvingly on the table.

"Well, mates, no sooner said than done. Old Woodenlegs cleared for action, and every man jumped to his gun, and stood, stripped to the buff, ready and willing to do battle for the glory of Old England, and swore they would fight the old tub down to the water's edge before they'd surrender to the French.

"The Frenchman bore down upon us, right gallantly for lubberly foreigners, and when they comes within gunshot, we gives her such a broadside as made her shiver and shake from stem to stern. You should have seen the splinters fly, my hearties ; when that broadside struck her, the sea was covered with broken spars, which fell from her sides in showers. Our brave lads gave a cheer that made the old Porcupine almost shake again, while Captain Billing stood on the quarter-deck, laughing until red in the face again.

"'That's it, my lads,' said he ; 'once more. Aim low ; let 'em have it with a vengeance !'

"And so we did, for every man had full confidence in their commander, and was ready and willing to sink or swim with him.

"The Frenchers weren't long in returning the compliment, and they sent such a hailstorm of lead down upon us as made every lad stare with surprise. They almost cleared the quarter-deck, and among the first to fall was the captain, for his right foot was shot clean off.

"'Never mind, lads ; no time for compliments now. I'm all right,' said Captain Billing, while the surgeon was binding up his leg. 'Never mind me, lads ; fire away, my hearties. I'll never leave the deck until the Frenchers strike.'

"He was such a genuine trump to all of us, in action or out of it, that his wound worked up his crew to a pitch of desperation. Talk about working guns, my boys ; you've seen Captain Brandon's crew do a trifle in that line, not long ago, but when the first luff comes down among us, and passes the word to pepper away at will, the sides of the old Porcupine seemed one mass of flames.

"At it we went, hammer and tongs, for a full half-hour. Spars and yards and blocks were tumbling about our ears like hailstones.

"'Never mind them, lads,' roared our officers, high above the noise and confusion. 'Never mind them, lads ; pepper away while there's a shot in the locker. The Frenchman is sheering off ; don't let him escape.'

"When we heard that the enemy were thinking of cutting it, and making for port, we gives three cheers, and works away like a lot of devils.

"Not able to stand, Captain Billing got some of the officers to lash him to the mainmast, and there he stood, speaking-trumpet in hand, giving orders as lustily as ever. What crew wouldn't fight well, my lads, when they had such an old sea-dog to command them ?"

"True, messmate, true ; here's health to old Billing," was the unanimous response, as they drank the health of the Porcupine captain. "On with the yarn, my hearty."

"Well, sir, I never saw officers dash about as ours did, for there we were, fighting a bigger and a better craft than our own, but every moment we saw that our ship was leaking fast, and the Frenchmen trying to hook it.

"We double-shotted our guns, and fired like furies, but the Porcupine was fast settling down, and all her boats had been carried away.

"When the Frenchers saw what a pretty pickle we were in, they cheered like madmen, changed their course, and bears down to board us.

"'Hullo, lads, this won't do,' said old Billing, cursing and swearing. "Why, we've fairly thrashed 'em, and now they're going to board us. Double shot 'em, lads, and let every man prepare to board.'

"We all gave a cheer, and, putting pistols and cutlass into our belts we waited until the Frenchman came within distance, and then sent our shots clean through and through him.

"This surprised the lubber more than enough, but they returned fire very handsomely, and took away old Billing's good leg, as he was lashed to the mast, and unable to help himself.

"'Never mind me, men ; board, board, lads !' he roared, with loud curses, and in much pain.

"We didn't wait to hear him give the order a second time, for directly the Frenchman came broadside to broadside, and yardarm to yardarm, we grappled him and swarmed on to his decks, cutting and slashing like fiends, for we knew that the Porcupine was gradually settling down, and that it was now death or glory for all of us.

"We were all so anxious to do the work quickly and well, that scarcely a single one of our crew that could crawl or handle a boarding pike, but we had on board the Frenchman's decks, and a pretty hard job we had to clear them, my lads, for they yelled and fought like tigers. We did clear them, though, but not without losing many officers and dozens of brave messmates ; but when we hauled down their colours and run up our own, there was such a yell of delight, that it rings in my ears even now ; and so, when I've wetted my whistle, boys, with some grog, I'll tell you the rest."

"True, lad ; drink deep, and here's health to old Billing and his Porcupine and confusion to all our enemies," roared several half-tipsy seamen, knocking the tables with their huge, brawny fists in intense delight.

"But to continue, messmates. When we had cleared the decks, and thought that all was over, about fifty stout, hearty fellows rushed from the state cabin, and for a time things looked squally, for it seemed as if they were going to beat us from the deck again.

"They didn't succeed, however, and from the way we cut and hacked them about, the rest of the crew took a wise lesson, and remained very quiet.

"But during the fight, the Frenchers made so sure of capturing all our boarders, that they soon broke the Porcupine's grapplings, and the two vessels were now adrift again.

"Some of our lads flew aloft, and soon made things ship-shape; untangling the fouling of rigging and spars, and made all possible sail to overhaul the Porcupine, which, water-logged as she was, was drifting before the wind, and far to leeward.

"Now that the fight was over, and the thirty-gun frigate was fairly and honestly won from the French, our lads, or such as were able, seemed to redouble their efforts in making things comfortable for the conquered and chop-fallen foreigners. A good many were clapped into irons and sent below, while gangs of others, more peaceably inclined, were huddled together here and there, under guard of strong parties of marines.

"As we neared the Porcupine she looked as perfect a wreck as mortal ever saw.

"The sails were torn and shot through and through; an endless cobweb of loose and tangled ropes and rigging hung from her yards and spars; tremendous holes were through her decks; splinters lay thickly scattered on forecastle and main-decks, yet, though she hadn't many to man her, my lads, her colours still flew freely and bravely to the breeze, tattered and ragged as they were, while a faint cheer now and then fell upon our ears, as we tacked and bore down upon her.

"That was the proudest moment of my life, messmates. No man can feel the emotions which a seaman has in such a moment.

"There were we, a handful of hardy devils, masters of a fine frigate, bearing down to save our captain and messmates from the deep. The decks of both vessels were strewn with dead and dying, lying about in pools of blood; tattered garments, overturned guns, broken gun-carriages, tackle-blocks, cocked hats, swords, epaulettes, all were everywhere in bloody confusion, while we, a mere handful of British tars, were standing on the Frenchman's decks, and cheering the old Porcupine till nearly hoarse with shouting and bawling.

"When we got alongside, all were sorry to see brave old Billing lying on a heap of sails, pale and motionless.

"'Dead,' said one; 'he's dead!'

"'Dead be damned!' said old Billing, opening his eyes in an angry mood and tone of voice; 'dead be damned! Who could die now? No, no, lads, both legs are off, but I shall live to fight many a good battle yet, if I am rated on the books as Admiral Woodenlegs.'

"When we found he wasn't dead, every man gave a hearty cheer, that made each sail shiver in the wind, and we commenced with a right good will to pump out the Porcupine, and get her into port again.

"This we did at last manage to do; and when our prize crew sailed into Plymouth, with the old Porcupine in tow, you never heard such shouting in your lives.

"Old Billing was promoted to an admiral soon afterwards, but he was always called Admiral Woodenlegs, for when he got well he used to go about town on crutches, and swore he was good enough to command the best fleet that ever floated, if he did go on stumps; but the great lords didn't listen to him, so he had to lay up in ordinary for the rest of his life."

"Bravo, for old Woodenlegs!" was the general chorus, as one and all emptied their glasses in drinking to his health and memory.

CHAPTER XLIX.

HOW "OLD ADMIRAL WOODENLEGS" WISHED NANCY TO MARRY—SERGEANT HOSKINS GOES A WOOING —HOW SAM BARKER WON AN ADMIRAL'S DAUGHTER—THE STORY OF LOVELY NANCY.

"But that ain't all, shipmate, if I don't mistake the glisten of your weather-eye," said one.

"No, it ain't, lads. There was on board the Porcupine a harum-scarum middy called Sam Barker, a youngster that was as brave as a lion, and with a hand as soft as a woman's. Well, this lad had fallen in love with Nancy, the daughter of old Admiral Woodenlegs, but Pegs, as Sam used to call him, wouldn't listen to such a thing as give his consent to their marriage. Sam was a poor fellow, and had nothing but his good looks and brave heart to help him through the world, and he got along so fast with Miss Nancy that old Woodenlegs determined to put him out of the way.

"He was rated a lieutenant soon after in capturing the frigate, and was sent to the West India Islands in command of an ugly old hulk of a troop-ship called the Raven.

"He didn't like his commission much, but go he must or else leave the service.

"It wasn't a very bad move for old Woodenlegs, for Sam couldn't possibly return under six months, by which time it was thought Miss Nancy might fasten her affections on an old lawyer of the town who was very wealthy, but as sallow-coloured an old flint as ever breathed, and altogether devoid of pluck, although he had plenty of bounce.

"Sam went off with his ship, was chief in command of her, such as she was, and hadn't fairly got to sea before old Woodenlegs invites the lawyer to his house and makes much of him. Miss Nancy was told how rich and mighty he was, and that he was sure to be made a lord of, one day; and old Pegs didn't forget to tell her how many fine houses and how much money he had.

"'But, Sergeant Hoskins,' says old Woodenlegs, one day after dinner, as the admiral sat talking about the Porcupine, and all his other scrapes in the service. 'But, Sergeant Hoskins,' says he, striking the table, laying the law down to the lawyer in fine style——"

"Was he a sergeant? why you said he was a landshark of a lawyer," said one old tar, taking the pipe out of his mouth, and looking in indignant surprise at the speaker. "Surely old Pegs wouldn't run foul of an officer in the king's navy for a lubberly sergeant. What regiment did he belong to? Not a marine, I hope, or, dash my figure-head, if old Pegs oughtn't to be scuttled!"

"A sergeant of lawyers, eh? Well, now messmates," chimed in another, in breathless surprise, "you take all the wind out of my sails, and no mistake. Sergeant of lawyers, eh? Well, you don't mean to say they've got regiments of 'em, and all that sort of caper, shipmate? Why don't they press 'em and send 'em aloft with the marines, then, than have 'em lying rotting in port, and cutting out the King's craft, eh?'

It was some time before the speaker could explain to his indignant audience the difference between a military and civil sergeant, for one and all seemed to entertain such a bitter dislike to the "landsharks," as they unanimously termed gentlemen of the legal profession, and they thumped the tables so vigorously that it was with difficulty the speaker could continue.

"Well, mates, when old Pegs had shipped more than an ordinary cargo of grog after dinner, one day, he seizes hold of one of his crutches and flourishes it about so vigorously while describing one of his many fights, that the lawyer shifts his moorings once or twice out of harm's way.

"'I tell you what it is, Sergeant Hoskins,' says old Woodenlegs, 'although you're rich and a great man among parchments and wigs, and expects to be a lord and all that's high and mighty, I should like my daughter Nancy to marry a first-rate fighter.'

"'Fighter!' said Hoskins. 'Why, Admiral, what do you mean?'

"'Mean, Hoskins?—mean? Why, my lad, I mean this, I should like my daughter to marry a fine fellow that wasn't afraid of anything or anybody, a man that could take the wind out of the sails of anyone that dared to cross his bows!'

"'You don't mean to suppose I am not brave, Admiral Billing? As far as moral courage goes——'

"'Moral courage,' says old Pegs, pricking up his ears, and scratching his head. 'Moral courage, Hoskins; I don't know, nor pretend to know, much about your legal definition, Hoskins,' says he; 'but what I mean is this, you may have a ship load of moral, or any other courage I never heard of; but I mean pluck, my boy, true British pluck. A fellow that will run up his colours and strike them for nobody while a plank floats under him—that's my sort of courage, and if Nancy don't agree with me on that point, she ain't no daughter of "Old Admiral Woodenlegs," as the saucy youngsters and middies call me.'

"'Well, Admiral, as to that, allow me to say, that although only fifty odd, and in the prime of life, as we may say——'

"'Ahem! go on, Hoskins,' coughed Pegs.

"'I do not think there are many who would dare dispute my courage in the field, and to prove it I would here remark that, although I have your full consent to pay my devoirs to your lovely daughter Nancy, I could not stand by coolly and allow another to attempt to supplant me—in truth I should call him out.'"

"What's that?" inquired one of the seamen. "Call him out! What, to have a glass of grog like?"

"No," was the answer. "That's a word your gentlefolk on shore have for coming broadsides to."

"Aye, aye, mate! Heave a-head, my hearty!"

"Well, shipmates, while this lubbering old shark was tacking around Miss Nancy, Sam Barker was making the best of his way to the West Indies. But he fell in with a French squadron from St. Dominica, and he was wise enough to show it his heels, and returned to port within two months after sailing. Old Woodenlegs was not aware of his return; and while out one evening he saw Miss Nancy walking along the street with some dark-whiskered officer, and before he could overtake them, they had disappeared round the corner.

"The first fellow he chanced to meet was Hoskins, to whom he told everything.

"The lawyer was in a terrible passion.

"'Admiral,' he says, 'I'll seek him out immediately, and demand satisfaction on the spot.'

"'Do, my boy,' said Pegs. 'I'll lend you a pair of capital pistols. You can't miss your mark at twelve paces.'

"'Done!' said the lawyer.

"And away they went to the admiral's house. The first persons both saw, on entering the drawing-room, was Miss Nancy and Lieutenant Barker.

"'Thunder and lightning!' roared Woodenlegs 'Who the devil ever dreamed of seeing you here? Sam Barker, how dare you come across my door?'

"'That's him,' said the lawyer. 'The very man I wish to see. How dare you, sir——'

"'Nancy, leave the room. How dare you, sir, address my daughter when you know she is already engaged to Mr. Hoskins?'

"'Yes, sir!' roared the lawyer, 'how dare you speak to one I am legally, and with parental permission, addressing?'

"'Satisfaction, sir!' roared Woodenlegs, hopping about. 'Sam Barker!—satisfaction, sir! This gentleman demands it; and if he don't fight, why then, dam'me, I will!'

"'Yes, sir, satisfaction!' roared the lawyer, very valiantly. 'Legal proceedings, admiral, or satisfaction.'

"Just so, Mr. Hoskins. I owe you five thousand pounds. Legal proceedings, or satisfaction,' said Woodenlegs, who owed the lawyer the sum stated.

"'Satisfaction!' said Sam reddening. 'Pistols, you mean? Oh! certainly, with pleasure; nothing could give me greater satisfaction than to drill holes into a lawyer or two.'

"'How, sir; drill holes into a lawyer or two—into me?' said Hoskins, turning pale.

"'Certainly,' said Sam, laughing. 'The admiral, I know, will take great pride in accommodating us with weapons. We can fire across the table.'

"'Just so,' said Pegs, hobbling out of the room, and soon returning with a pair of pistols. 'As your quarrel is so deadly, I have but loaded one with ball.'

"'What's that?' asked Hoskins. 'Only loaded one with ball! Why, where are we to fight?'

"'Why, across the table. There, there is one each. You shall draw for the first shot. Hoskins, you have won it. Steady now, my lad!'

"Sam Barker and Hoskins faced each other across the table, and the lawyer shook in every limb.

"He fired. Barker stood smiling, but was untouched.

"'Death and damnation!' roared the lawyer. 'You have the loaded weapon.'

"'I have,' said Sam, coolly, 'and give you five minutes to arrange your affairs.'

"'Give me five minutes!' said Hoskins; 'how kind you are! I willingly avail myself of your kindness,' and he returned to an inner apartment.

"Sam Barker paced the room in which he stood, pistol in hand.

"'I think the time has passed, Sam,' said old Woodenlegs, eyeing the young officer narrowly.

"'Perhaps so, but there's no hurry, admiral; give him plenty of time.'

"The admiral said nothing until fully half an hour had passed, when he left the room to seek Hoskins.

"He had fled!"

"Bolted!" shouted the seamen, in disgust; "slipped his cable after firing the first shot."

"Aye, lads, he had."

"And what did old Pegs do?"

"Do? Why, when he found the lawyer had gone, he burst out into roars of laughter. He had put ball in neither of the pistols. It was only his little game to try the lawyer's pluck, that was all."

"And what became of that brave sergeant of lawyers, Hoskins ?"

"Why he sent a note next day, saying he was suddenly called away on urgent business, and declining to have any further claims to Miss Nancy, stating to old Woodenlegs that he'd willingly give him £5,000 he owed if he'd never mention the duel."

"And what became of Nancy ?"

"Why, Sam married her, of course, and received the lawyer's £5,000."

CHAPTER L.

THORKIL CONSPIRES WITH EARL PENALVON TO FOR-
CIBLY ABDUCT NELLY BRITTON FROM SEAWARDINE
—OTHO IS SENT BY PENREAL—HE MEETS AGGER—
THE SECRET IS KNOWN—COMBAT BETWEEN OTHO
AND AGGER—HE ACCOMPANIES PENALVON AND
NELLY, UNRECOGNISED BY EITHER — NELLY'S
PRISON.

THORKIL was some time under Hylda's care before he was able to appear among the wreckers.

In explanation of his many cuts and bruises, he gave out that he had been attacked, single-handed, by the whole of Paul Adair's crew.

Hylda, however, would not credit any of his wild, improbable tales regarding the night's proceedings, and told him, bluntly, that she believed he might attribute all his sufferings to cowardice.

This accusation exasperated Thorkil, who more than once rushed from his bed, cutlass in hand, and would have immolated his better half ; but she very wisely left him alone during his self-consolatory musings, and sat upon the cliffs beside his cavern-door, until his dangerous and moody fits had left him.

As to Agger, he vowed eternal vengeance against him. Wild Thyra equally shared in his half-wild malediction and threats ; but both were far away from all harm that Thorkil could do them, and, if the truth might be expressed, they secretly laughed at his threats and menaces.

Thorkil, in truth, was not the man he used to be. Agger had left him voluntarily.

Harleck had been, unwillingly, pressed into the King's service.

Polruth was doing a flourishing contraband business at the kiddleawink on his own account, and cared nothing now for Penreal, and his once power-ful gang of wreckers.

Of all towards whom Thorkil felt the bitterest animosity, there was no one he more sincerely detested than Paul Adair.

He determined upon having signal vengeance upon the rover, but was in a quandary as to what method to pursue.

If Black Will Trelawny had been at hand, he might have consulted that bold, bad man ; but he knew not where he was, nor could he imagine what had become of him.

While he sat musing, beside his cavern-fire, smoking and drinking deep of Cognac, Hylda entered, and sat herself beside him, but at sufficient distance to escape any lunge that anger might prompt him to make at her.

"So you've come back again, I see," said the wrecker, angrily, and with an oath far from complimentary to his wife.

"Back !—yes. You would not have me sit out there all day, would you ?"

"Yes, and freeze to death, for all the good you are," was the morose response.

"You must have somebody to talk to and swear at, or you could not live."

"Must I ? Well, I curse the day that fortune ever threw me into your path."

"And so do I, for all the happiness I've had."

"And whose fault has it been ? Not mine."

"Not yours ? Whose then, pray ? What woman could have been truer to Thorkil than I have ?"

"Many. If you cared much for him you'd have strangled that witch, Thyra, long ago ; she is the one who has caused us all the mischief with her damned rune-kenning !"

"It is no easy matter to do. Would you have me embrue my hands in an innocent's blood ? No, no, Penreal, I have seen too much blood shed since I've lived with you on this accursed coast !"

"Oh, ho ! that's it, eh, Hylda ? How long is it since you have so suddenly grown repentant ?"

"How long ? Why, many a-year. Is it nothing that I've seen you and your remorseless gang decoy ships upon the coast, and seen dozens of lifeless bodies floating upon the beach ?"

"Well, no more of that ; 'tis enough that wreck-ing is our business."

"A pretty business it is, then, from the looks of it ; we shall not have a gallon of rum or a pound of tobacco in store shortly, if things prosper with us as they have been doing of late. All your able men are leaving you. Why, you can't count upon a dozen trusty fellows now ; whereas, but a short time since, Thorkil Penreal could boast of fifty, or more, ready and willing to lend a hand on a stormy night. Where is Trelawny ?"

"Where ? Why, dead, if all reports be true."

"No, not so."

"How know you that ? How should you know more of him than I do ? Think you I have not inquired for him daily along the coast ?"

"True, but without success."

"No, not without success, you haggling, nagging she-devil, not without success ! I know where he is, and, when able to move abroad, you'll see that Paul Adair does not confine him long."

"You attempt to rescue him from Paul Adair ?" asked Hylda, with an ironical laugh.

"Yes, truly ; I, your husband, will rescue him. Think you that Thorkil requires more insult and injury from Adair than he has already received ?"

"I would warn you to go well armed, and have many in your gang, for I fear me he stands too well with the wreckers of the coast to lose many friends among them when the time comes."

"The time has come, then, Hylda, and ere many days, I and Penalvon's servants will rescue him from Adair's clutches, whether dead or alive, mark my words !"

Thorkil smoked on in silence, frequently taking hearty draughts of brandy.

Hylda sat upon a stool, looking at the glowing embers, but spoke not.

NOTICE.—The next Number of the Boys' Library will be Published on Friday, September 6th.
Order early of your Bookseller.

BOYS' LIBRARY

Harry Halliard: or, the Young British Tar.

THE ABDUCTION.

While they thus sat a stranger entered unobserved.

He was muffled up to the throat in a heavy cloak.

He noiselessly approached the wrecker, and laid a hand upon his shoulder.

Thorkil started as if stung by an adder.

The entrance and greeting were so sudden and unexpected, that he turned pale and grasped a cutlass by his side.

He was too weak with wounds and hurts to rise, but his eyes shot forth looks of angry flame as he hoarsely demanded,

"Who are you?"

"Your friend," was the calm and reassuring reply.

"Friend, say you? Then, friend, be seated, and welcome to my rough abode. Your business, pray, and your name?"

"Both at your service, friend, when we are alone."

Thorkil motioned Hylda to be gone.

She eyed the stranger inquisitively askance as she left the cavern, but held the outer door ajar, and listened.

"My friend, you say," said Thorkil, handling a pistol very threateningly.

"Yes, Penreal, but place your weapon aside; there is no need of that with us."

"Who are you, and your name, I ask?" said Thorkil, angrily. "Once more I demand your name and business. Strangers are not wont to visit me so unceremoniously as you have done."

The stranger threw the long cloak from off his shoulders.

"Earl Penalvon !" said Thorkil, reddening. "I ask your lordship's pardon, but you see it is necessary for me to know all who would dare pry into the secrets of this cavern home."

"True, and it is right I should also know the name and purpose of all who would dare pry into the secrets and ins and outs of Seawardine."

"How say you, my lord ? Surely none dare——"

"Yes, but there are those who dare, Thorkil, and do."

"But, surely your lordship would never dream—could never imagine for a moment, that Thorkil did so ? I, who am your very humble of the humblest of your servants—a very slave, in truth, whose life is in your hands at any moment !"

"No, Thorkil, I did not mean that. I know that you are a good and trusty fellow, and the last to cast inquisitive glances round the vaults at Seawardine."

"The vaults at Seawardine, my good lord ! Why, who could have done so ?" asked Thorkil, in pale amazement. "The slimy vaults, far below tide line, at Seawardine ! Who could have been so bold ?"

"An enemy of thine."

"Of mine ?"

"Yes ; and mine."

Thorkil looked fixedly at Earl Penalvon for one moment, and rather whispered than expressed the words,

"Paul Adair !"

"The same that I suspect."

"And what can I do, Earl Penalvon ?" asked Thorkil, with half-choked utterance. "Anything I can do you have but to command ; you know that these blows and scars are due to him."

"I heard so, Penreal ; and knew you would be only too willing to seek revenge."

"And how may this be ?"

"Be ! Thus : I have had one in my mansion this many a day whom I have treated more like a daughter than a worthless plebeian maid."

"What, Nelly——"

"Yes, Nelly Britton ; she is the one I long suspect of having used her eyes to my disquiet and disadvantage."

"But surely such a girl could have found nothing that might injure you ; for, in truth, Earl Penalvon has never yet done aught that fears the light of day ?" added Thorkil, deferentially.

Penalvon spoke not for a moment, but added, with a sarcastic leer,

"Men in all stations, Thorkil, high or low, have secrets to keep ; you will aid me to keep mine ?"

"I am sworn to that, and more, my lord, long ago. Aught that I can do to punish Paul Adair will prove a labour of love."

"Know you, then, that this same Adair has been lured to Seawardine by Nelly Britton. I have reason to imagine, nay, in truth, I know that they are and have been in confidential, if not secret correspondence for a length of time."

"How gained he admission, then ?"

"By means of an outlet known but to three. I once supposed that no one knew it but myself ; Nelly Britton has discovered it, and Adair has used it."

"And what do you propose ?"

"This. If we cage this little inquisitive minx in some distant part he will be sure to find her out and follow, in which case we have but to watch a favourable opportunity and secure him."

"And I have to——"

"Have to assist me in secretly abducting her."

"But her father and mother ?"

"Need know nothing of it for months to come."

"And when is this to be ?"

"To-night."

"It cannot be to-night, my lord. I would willingly assist but am unable."

"You could send me some one, then ; it must be accomplished secretly."

"Truly ; and are there no fears of detection ?"

"None that I can foresee. The carriage shall be in waiting in the park when she is hurried away. I have already found means for placing her where she will soon become the willing slave to all my desires, and extract from her all that she knows regarding our common enemy, Paul Adair."

"But Hylda and Thyra, what of them ?"

"Surely, Thorkil, you are not such a child as to be thwarted or intimidated by the untimely croakings of two half-crazy women ?"

"Half-crazy, my lord, if you think so ; but did you know half so much about them as I have just cause to do, you would think twice ere offending either of them once."

"Tut, tut ! Drink some more brandy, Thorkil, and don't sit there playing with your thumbs, like one half-resolved. I took you for a man, Thorkil Penreal, the chief of wreckers."

"And am I not, Earl Penalvon ? Do I not carry wounds in token of my faithful service ?"

"You do, and shall be amply rewarded."

"Reward I want not. All I ask and seek is ample revenge."

"You shall have it."

"Though I cannot go myself, I will send one on this errand as trusty as myself. If I only had Agger !"

"Agger ! who is he ?"

"You know him not, my lord ; one who used to be as faithful as my own right hand. He has deserted me of late."

"Then who will you send ?"

"Otho, one of Black Will Trelawny's faithful crew."

"Is he reliable and brave ?"

"None more so."

"Then let the hour be midnight. He meets me in the park, mind you, at eleven. The carriage shall be in waiting. The sign shall be, 'A friend,' the countersign, 'Paul Adair.'"

"Agreed, my lord, and ever as I have proved faithful, rely on me."

Earl Penalvon muffled himself once more in his heavy cloak, and glided from the cavern like a shadow, and was gone.

For some time Thorkil sat before the fire, hugging thoughts of sweet revenge, when Hylda re-entered.

"Some other plot, I suppose, Thorkil ?" she said, at last ; "something that a woman mustn't know, eh ? Who was he ? not a wrecker, nor a foreigner, I should judge."

"It matters little to thee, woman, who it was; mind your own business. Stir up the fire, and make that pot boil ; that's the best thing you can do."

"It was some man of wealth, I could tell."

"Could you? and how, pray?"

"From his regular step and creaking shoes. Wreckers and smugglers and pirates don't wear silver buckles in their shoes."

"You are very wise, wife, I dare say, in your own opinion; but take my advice; ask no questions, or maybe you'd tempt me to make thy bones creek. Go out and find Otho, I say."

"Otho! and what may you want with him, pray?"

"Go out and find him, I tell you, or, if I rise, it will be worse for you, wench."

Hylda reluctantly rose, and went in search of Otho.

That worthy was found sunning himself upon the beach, dressed in his guernsey and cap, heavy boots, and belt, smoking at his ease, listlessly gazing out upon the ocean, where various craft, like things of life, were disporting gracefully upon the snow-capped waves.

Without occupation of any kind, save an occasional job at wrecking or smuggling, Otho felt at perfect ease with all the world, and was so eaten up with laziness that he could scarcely afford the exertion of breathing free enough to expel clouds of tobacco-smoke from his capacious mouth.

His interview with Thorkil was a long one.

Hylda endeavoured, by every means in her power, to glean something that was passing between them, but without success.

When Otho had received his instructions from Thorkil, and a trifle of money withal to regale himself on the road to Seawardine, he sallied forth from Penreal's cavernous residence, blowing immense clouds of tobacco-smoke on the evening air, and strode forth on his errand with a grim smile of satisfaction and determination upon his weatherbeaten visage.

He had not proceeded far when he met Thyra.

"Why, who'd a thought of seeing you, Thyra?" he said. "Why, every one thought Polruth made so much of you at the kiddleawink, that you wouldn't scarce trust yourself out at this time of day."

Thyra made no answer, but looked pale and thoughtful, as was her wont. She looked at Otho fixedly for a moment, and then asked,

"Where are you going, Otho?"

"That's none of your business," was the wrecker's gruff, ungallant response. "I should have thought you wouldn't need ask that question, as you pretend to know everything by your rune-kenning."

"Where are you going?" still inquired Thyra, innocently and girl-like, sideling up to the small, but heavily-built and compact smuggler. "You will tell me, won't you?"

"Well, I don't know as I will; but, if you must know, Miss Busybody," said Otho, anxious to rid himself of her company, and of her deep-set, searching, inquisitive eyes, that fixed their glance immovably upon his twitching features; "if you must know, then, Thyra, I am going to Seawardine, to take this note from Thorkil to Earl Penalvon. So good-bye, lass, and go home to Polruth's."

"Is that all?" still asked Thyra, with a quiet smile. "Are you sure that is all, Otho, for I shouldn't like aught of harm to befall you?"

"Harm befall me; what do you mean? Are you going to bewitch me, then?"

"Nay, Otho, I never harmed you, nor anyone;

but I fear you are in league with a bad man, who wishes and designs evil to those who never wronged him. If it be that you have aught in hand to injure the innocent, forego it; leave him, as Agger has done, and do nobly by yourself."

Otho said nothing, but continued his journey towards Seawardine.

Thyra stopped, and looked after him anxiously.

Her pale face and flowing raven tresses bore marks of great mental suffering.

Her features were calm and girl-like, and her eyes possessed more than their wonted lustre.

With the simplicity of a child she closed her hands, and looked towards the sky as if invoking heavenly aid for some friendless one.

She sat upon a jutting rock overlooking the turbid sea, and while she murmured strange weird incoherences of speech, there approached one who sincerely loved her.

It was Agger.

He spoke not, nor did he advance.

Apparently struck dumb with the paleness, simplicity, and innocence of the one before him, he stood speechless and transfixed where he was.

"Thyra!" he at last exclaimed, and fell at her feet.

Wild Thyra turned her head and gazed with much astonishment on the unexpected figure before her.

He clasped her not unwilling hands and kissed them.

"Agger!" she faintly murmured, as tear drops bedewed her eyes.

"Yes, Thyra, it is Agger, dejected, dispirited and aimless. Oh, Thyra, you know not, neither can you ever know, the love and affection I feel for you!"

Thyra spoke not; but as she saw the brave and stalwart wrecker kneeling at her feet, clasping her hands in an agony of devotion, she sighed and leaned her head over his, as tears fell thick and fast upon his neck.

"Oh, Agger!" she at last exclaimed, "thank Heaven I have met you! Of all men on earth I wished to see no other!"

"Oh, Thyra, say that always."

"Nay, good Agger, I must not say it always; but now I can. You are brave and trusty; I have even prayed to Heaven that I might so meet you this night. There is doubt, treachery, and ruin in the air, the spirits tell me so. Thorkil, Earl Penalvon, and Otho have resolved on a fiendish plot. It is you—yes, you, Agger, that must unravel and thwart it!"

"I?"

"Yes, Agger; even now has Otho gone by this path to Seawardine. He bears a letter to Penalvon, and I fear you may be too late to prevent their fiendish mischief; it is a blow at Paul Adair, your friend and mine. Oh, Agger, hurry, hurry, I beg, nay, pray, hurry! I ask of you ten thousand times, by all that is sacred and holy, hurry, I beg, and prevent this consummation of their unholy designs!"

The wrecker looked at the weird, pale-faced girl, half in wonder and surprise.

She spoke not with the air and manner of one who begged, but of some supernaturalist that imperiously commanded.

Scarcely knowing what he did or said, Agger rose, with a flushed cheek and quivering lip, and followed the path indicated by Thyra's pointed finger.

He stopped one moment to look behind, but still the pale-faced Thyra stood in queen-like attitude, pointing in the direction of Seawardine, and intuitively he followed.

He had not long departed from Thyra, filled as he was with strange forebodings, misgivings, and anticipations, when he overtook Otho, who was seated on a rock, smoking and resting.

"Otho," he said.

"Yes. What brings Agger here ?"

"I might ask again what brings Otho here ?"

"Business."

"And so might I, also, say."

"Agger, from your looks I see you are bent on mischief. Your speech is angry."

"And why not ? Think you that Otho goes to Seawardine on a manly mission ?"

"Manly mission ! What mean you ? Did I ever prove less than a man, when called upon ?"

"Never, until now."

"And never until now has man ere dared to say so."

"Then, you see, I do."

"And what wish you with me ?"

"The possession of that letter."

"What letter ?"

"The one you bear from Thorkil."

"Who so told you ?"

"Thyra. Nay, deny it not. And if it costs my life, Otho, I must and will possess it. If you refuse me, draw your cutlass as a man ; I would not take unfair advantage."

Otho answered not a word, but slowly retreated several paces.

Observing Agger's determined looks and attitude, he drew his cutlass.

He made a fierce, sudden, and unexpected rush upon Agger, but the bold wrecker was fully on his guard, and parried the blow with ease and dexterity.

The combatants paused for a moment in silence, and eyed each other as if judging the sword play and capability of his opponent.

Within a few minutes their swords were crossed in fierce and determined fray.

For a moment they cut and parried with such rapidity and violence that sparks flew from their weapons in showers.

Another pause.

Otho felt he had met one fully his master, and ground his teeth together, inaudibly muttering a volley of smothered oaths.

He rushed to the contest once more, but a rapid cut from Agger sent him reeling and senseless to the earth.

Agger flew to his side and searched him.

Beneath his guernsey was found a note secreted.

By the light of the rising moon, Agger read,

I have fully instructed the bearer of this : the sign, "a friend," the countersign, "Paul Adair." He will disguise himself as one of your grooms, and await your pleasure at the mansion gates in the park. You may fully trust him in this business.

                    Your servant,   THORKIL.

"Oh, oh," softly whispered Agger ; "so there is more devilment afloat, and Thorkil, as usual, is at the bottom of it. What can it be ? So he has to disguise himself as a groom, eh ? Why, I can do that as well as he ; but how ? I have no livery.

Still I will journey on to Seawardine, and trust to fate."

Leaving Otho bleeding and senseless, rolling about in agony on the turf, Agger directed his steps hastily towards Earl Penalvon's mansion.

It was now getting late, and when he entered the park at Seawardine, he heard dogs begin to bark.

He stopped, but ere he could resolve what to do, a mounted servant espied him and galloped towards him.

"Who goes there ?" was the challenge.

For a moment Agger knew not what to do or say.

The challenge was again repeated.

He remembered what he had read in the note, and boldly answered,

"A friend."

"Approach, friend, and give the countersign," was the horseman's response.

Without intimidation, or second thought, Agger did so, and answered firmly,

"Paul Adair."

"Right," was the ready response. And are you Otho ?"

"Yes ;" answered Agger. "I want my disguise."

"You shall have it."

The horseman whistled, and a servant appeared with a large bundle.

"Give them to this man," he said, in tones of command. "There, that will do ; return to the hall."

Agger knew not the person speaking to him, for he was heavily muffled up.

He took the large bundle and undid it.

"Dress yourself in that livery, and follow me; attend my orders, and say nothing until I first give you leave."

Agger did as commanded, and, having attired himself, followed the nameless horseman to a thicket that grew near the hall gates.

"Stay here until I return," said the horseman. "If you do not know me, seek not the information ; if you do, either now or in the future, know me, keep silent, on peril of your life."

The horseman left him.

"Who can it be ? and what is my business here ?"

He knew not what to conjecture, but resolved to act coolly, and with circumspection.

His attire of a groom fitted him exactly, but the tight-fitting garments and belt constrained and retarded his wonted freedom of attitude and motion.

Presently he heard the sounds of carriage wheels coming from the rear of the mansion.

It stopped about a hundred yards from him in the carriage drive.

There was but one servant, the driver of the two-horse carriage, in charge, who sat in the moonlight with an ease that bespoke that he knew not the errand on which his master was bound.

Within half-an-hour, and just as the coach-house clock struck the hour of midnight, Agger heard footsteps on the gravel walk, and, peeping through the trees, observed two persons approaching where he stood.

Their voices were plainly audible in conversation.

"Believe me, it is true, Nelly," said the gentleman, who Agger now recognised as the muffled horseman, although he had changed his dress, and was now attired in the latest style of fashion, "believe me, it is true, Nelly; your father sent me a note not an hour ago."

"Alas, sir," was the feeble response of the maid, "my heart fails me; forebodings tell me that this night's journey portends evil to me."

"Forebodings of evil, Nelly child? Why, what strange thoughts possess you. You know that I would, and have befriended you; you could never dream of evil while I am by to protect you, for you know I love you."

"Love me, Earl Penalvon? Is it nothing that I am a plebian, and you a noble of the land? Is it nothing that I spurned your base proposal this very day; that I flew from your touch, left the apartment and buried myself all day long in my lonely chamber? Alas, I wish I ne'er had entered Seawardine's gates!"

"Speak not foolishly, Nelly, dear," was the pettish response. "'Tis true you did shun my company, and fly my presence, but you have too much reliance on my honour to doubt me now. Your father is sick, nigh to death's door, and calls for you. My love for him and you is so strong I accompany you myself, even at this late hour. There are not many in the land upon whom Earl Penalvon would smile so flatteringly."

"Nay, speak no more, my heart tells me that you mean me false; your smiles are withering, Earl Penalvon; my soul sickens in your presence. Unhand me; hinder me no more. Let me go alone; I will not trust myself in your keeping; I fear you!"

Penalvon smiled triumphantly as he felt the maiden's form quivering on his arm.

He passed his arm about her waist, and almost carried her towards the carriage.

He gave a preconcerted signal.

Agger approached, and with much well-affected roughness, seized Nelly by the arm, and assisted Earl Penalvon in forcing her to the carriage.

Fully assured now of his evil intentions, Nelly Britton gazed imploringly at Penalvon and his accomplice, but found no sympathy in the gaze of either.

Penalvon's face was lit with a look of fiendish malice and licentious satisfaction.

Agger looked downward, and dared not meet the maiden's looks of despairing innocence.

She struggled.

Earl Penalvon's hold on her was like that of an iron vice.

Her brief, girlish, weak, and feeble struggle to free herself ended fruitlessly.

She wept, she implored, promised all manner of wild promises; but all were of no avail.

She screamed.

Penalvon's hand was upon her mouth.

She swooned.

For a moment the earl gazed upon her with looks of lustful gluttony.

Pale, and tearful and helpless, she lay in his arms unconscious, while her sweet face was upturned, and in speechless beauty was lost to all remembrance or feeling.

They carried her to the coach.

They placed her within the vehicle.

The door was closed.

"Jump in, Otho," said Penalvon. "You must go to-night alone, I may go to-morrow. My coachman knows whither to drive. Stay you in the cottage with her until I come. Let her speak to no one."

Agger did as commanded.

The coach started down the carriage-drive, and rolled rapidly through the park.

The gates were opened in readiness for their exit.

Earl Penalvon returned to the hall, but for a moment stood as if undecided whether to return or accompany Agger.

The stately and superb carriage rolled rapidly along the moonlit roads.

Nelly was still unconscious, and lay upon a pile of soft cushions, while fitful rays of moonlight played through the half-open window, and kissed her pale cheek, cushioned on silken velvet.

The carriage rolled on with increasing speed, and fitful night winds, sighing through the trees, stole in upon her feverish brow, and played with the rich and luxuriant mass of auburn hair that rose and fell dishevelled on her white, heaving and throbbing bosom.

Earl Penalvon's carriage had proceeded but a few miles upon its moonlit journey when the cool air and jogging of the vehicle along rough country roads awoke her to a sense of consciousness.

For a moment she seemed as if recovering from the effects of lethargy.

Slowly she opened her eyes, and timidly gazed.

Agger sat beside her, supporting the trembling maid with his stalwart arm.

"Where am I? Who are you? Unhand me, villain! Let me return home once again to my father!" said Nelly, in renewed alarm.

"Nelly Britton," Agger replied, calmly, and with emotion, "fear not me!"

"Who are you, then, that speaks so familiarly? I should know that voice, I have heard it before; it sounds unlike one who would harm me!"

"Yes, Nelly Britton, mine is a familiar voice; you have heard it often, even in childhood, when I sat at your father's smithy door, and dandled you on my knee. You cannot forget Agger," replied the wrecker, with emotion, hiding his face with a large brawny hand.

"Agger!" exclaimed Nelly. "Then it is a dream! I am not betrayed by Earl Penalvon! Oh, assure me, Agger—tell me truly, that I am not in fear of danger or dishonour!"

"Speak slowly and softly, Nelly. I am your friend, I am not what I seem. These clothes I wear are supposed to conceal no other than Otho, one of Black Will's late gang, who sold himself to do this dirty work."

"What work? What are you about to do? Why do they spirit me away from my father and mother?"

"For no good. But, Nelly, fear naught, harm can ne'er befall you while I and Paul Adair watch over you!"

"Whither are we going?"

"That I know not; but rest assured the coach will stop at some out-of-the-way place. All you have to do is to submit to your confinement and fear nothing. The rest is to me—rely on me!"

Feeling thus assured of safety from all dishonour, poor Nelly burst into tears, and, knowing that some mystery was attached to Earl Penalvon's acts and intentions, she trembled violently, and leant her head confidingly on the rough wrecker's shoulder.

"Don't cry, Nelly," said Agger, with much tenderness. "This business is as much a mystery to me as to you."

"How came you, then, in such garb?" asked Nelly. "Were you not employed by the earl?"

"No, lass, no money could tempt me to injure Nelly Britton, or dishonour the honourable, manly Paul Adair. It was Thyra who first suspected the mischief brewing, and told me of it. I fought with Otho, and wounded him, found a letter upon him from Thorkil to Penalvon; I followed out the instructions it contained, and my coolness has enabled me to prove your friend in this your hour of need."

"Oh, thanks, thanks, good Agger," sobbed Nelly ; "I can never repay your kindness and devotion."

"Nay, no thanks, Nelly. I know that Paul loves you, and I would willingly sacrifice everything to serve him."

"Don't say so, Agger. Paul does not love me ; he cares for others more than me, or else I should not be now as I am. He loves Leona."

"You wrong him, Nelly. The last words he uttered when we parted were, 'Love to Nelly, Agger; while I am away, assure her of my constancy, and tell her to fear nothing.' Earl Penalvon dare not harm you."

"Alas! I fear that wicked man has evil designs upon me."

"Whatever he says, heed him not. In the moment that he feels confident of success to his hellish designs, fear him least ; there are shadows encompassing him that he knows not of. You are more strictly watched and guarded than Earl Penalvon dreams of. But, hush! the coach stops!"

While the wrecker was whispering to Nelly, the carriage stopped, turned up a lonely lane, and drew slowly towards a lone cottage that stood a few yards from the road.

Though the hour was very late, smoke ascended from the chimney, and lights shone through the windows.

Agger jumped out of the carriage, and assisted Nelly to alight.

Trembling and agitated, she leaned on Agger's arm and entered the cottage.

They were met by an old dame, who was much haggard and worn, who smiled grimly, as Agger led in the pale and fearful maid.

Nelly sank exhausted upon an old sofa that stood beside the fire.

The old hag hung over her, and gazed long and ardently.

Agger stood by, but said not a word.

"My lord told you what to do, I suppose?" inquired the old hag. "You can send the carriage back ; we don't want it, I suppose?"

Agger ordered the carriage home again, and soon the rumbling of its wheels was lost in the distance.

"The little wench had better have some sleep. It won't do for her to look pale and fretful when my lord comes to-morrow, will it, young man?"

Agger said, "No."

"Just so, groom, just so. I have known the earl this thirty year or more, but I never saw a prettier girl than this one he's now got," she continued, grinning, and pointing to Nelly, who lay fast asleep upon the sofa before the fire.

"And such beautiful hair, too!—such masses of it!" She went on handling Nelly's dishevelled hair, with looks of great approval.

Agger took a seat beside the fire, and smoked in silence.

"Well, it's no use of her lying there all night, sobbing in her sleep. Suppose you carry her in your arms into the next room. There's a nice bed there."

Agger followed the old hag's advice, and, lifting up Nelly like a child, placed her on a bed in the adjoining room.

"There, that will do, young man. Now you can go into the kitchen again, and I'll cover her up comfortably, and then we can have a drop together."

Agger did not leave the bedroom until he had fully assured himself that the windows were safely barred and bolted.

When Nell was comfortably provided for, the old hag returned, and sat upon a stool before the fire, and commenced to smoke a short black pipe, and take frequent draughts from a bottle on the mantle.

Both sat for some time in profound silence.

The old hag eyed Agger frequently askance, as if to assure herself that he was perfectly trustworthy.

Passing him the bottle, she asked,

"What is your name?"

"Otho."

"Indeed! One of Thorkil's gang?"

"Well, yes ; one of them."

"I suppose the earl told you all about this affair?"

"No he didn't ; he simply said I was to remain here until further orders."

"Just like him, he always is secret about such matters as that," said the old hag, grinning and pointing over her shoulder in the direction of Nelly's chamber. "It isn't the first time he's had a job of this kind ; rich men and nobles, you know, will have their own way."

"Just so," grunted Agger, drinking from the bottle. "Well, so as he pays well, I don't mind ; would you?"

"No."

"But he's got a nice one this time. Well, we've all been young once."

"The earl isn't young."

"No ; not exactly in years, you know," said the old hag, "but he is in feeling, like many another that has no work to do, and lots of money to spend."

"When do you expect him?"

"To-morrow, I suppose."

"Then, when he comes, I must return, I suppose?"

"You may be sure of that ; but is there any fear of her friends finding her out? I shouldn't like to fall into the hands of a furious band of relatives."

"No ; it wouldn't be pleasant, perhaps."

"Particularly as this is not the first time I've had this kind of thing on hand."

"Has the earl often visited you?"

"Oh, bless you, yes, no end of times ; he gives me a good salary for doing nothing in particular, you know," said the hag, with a lascivious leer. "He keeps me in this pretty cottage, and all I have to do is to follow his orders, and keep a silent tongue."

Agger said nothing, but nodded assent, and helped himself freely of the old hag's tobacco and rum, of which she had much in store.

"You don't talk much, young man."

"No; the earl don't like people that talk much, he like servants that can forget the use of their tongues."

"Just so," said the hag, winking knowingly, "just so, you're the very man to serve Earl Penalvon; it wouldn't do to let everybody know our business, you know, because the law might have something to say occasionally about it, eh? Ha, ha!"

"Ha, ha!" laughed Agger, feigning to be much pleased, but, in truth, amazed at the old hag's heartless hilarity.

She smoked and drank until the cocks crew, and then dozed off in a heavy slumber.

Agger feeling assured the wretched old woman was fast asleep, noiselessly opened Nelly's chamber door, and whispered,

"Nelly, Nelly!"

"That you, Agger? Oh, pray take me from here, I am almost dead with fear."

"Fear nothing; no one can harm you. Paul will be here to-morrow."

"Nay, I know not why you wish me to stay; but if it is his wish, I willingly consent."

"I know it is his wish. But hush! the old woman stirs. Go to sleep, Nelly. Fear nothing; you are safe."

Agger had but scarcely regained his seat when the old woman awoke, and yawned.

"Had a good sleep?"

"No, not exactly. I dreamt I saw a man go to that room and whisper to that girl," she said, with a malicious grin. "It won't do for me to tell the earl of it."

"And if you did?"

"And if I did—why, then, my lord might suppose you knew a little too much about his business; and, in that case——"

"Well, what then?"

"He might be tempted to treat you as an enemy, and act accordingly. He isn't very particular what he does, if once aroused."

"Well, what I did was very simple. I only wished to be sure the girl was there."

"Ah! that is different. But when any of my lord's female friends come here, they are under my care, recollect. I can account for them without your assistance."

Agger made no reply; but he saw the old hag fumbling in her breast for something, and perceived the gleam of a dagger in the glare of the firelight.

For an hour or more they sat, and spoke not.

Occasionally Agger heard, or thought he heard, a tap at the window.

He rose to go and ascertain the cause.

"You needn't trouble yourself, young man," was the hag's quick remark. "Sit down, and don't mind it; it's only the wind—nothing more. Besides, no one can harm you here."

For the first time in all his life Agger felt fear.

He knew not precisely the cause, but still he felt possessed of fear, and eyed the old hag with close scrutiny, and with much perplexity.

"You don't seem to be at ease, young man. I suppose you would like to know the cause of those raps?"

"Well, I should feel more comfortable if I did."

"Well, I'll tell you. It is some of my friends, who are on the watch, and take that method to inform me from time to time that all is well and safe about me."

"How far are we from the sea?" asked Agger.

"Why do you ask?"

"Merely a passing thought—that's all."

"Well, we are only a mile from the coast. My best friends are mostly seamen."

"Indeed! but are they never troubled with that scourge of the coast called the 'Rover?'"

"The scourge, say you?" said the old hag, laughing. "Why, he's done me more good turns than any smuggler or wrecker that ever sailed the waters of this or any other coast."

"Indeed!" said Agger, colouring. "But did you ever see him?"

"No; but heard much of him. Nothing would give me greater pleasure than to see him."

"Did you ever hear Earl Penalvon speak of him?"

"No, why? How should I? I seldom see his lordship; and when he chooses to call or stay here for a day or two, I see but little of him. He has most of the cottage to himself, for his own use and pleasure."

Agger said nothing in reply, but inwardly chuckled as thoughts flitted through his mind, and felt inwardly assured that though she knew it not, Paul Adair knew more of the old hag and her doings than she might ever suppose.

What with drink and smoke, the old hag consoled herself to her heart's content, and as she sat before the cheerful fire twinkling her small, deep-set, coal-black eyes, she much resembled a ferret, ready to snatch at Agger's throat as he yawned in dreamy, sleepy drowsiness.

"I wish it was dawn," she said, continually. "I wish it was dawn. My lord will surely soon arrive; I wish it was dawn."

She little dreamed, as she sat catlike before the fire, what that long wished for morrow would bring forth.

Could she have foreseen the part that Agger had to play, she might have been tempted to stab him as he carelessly yawned before her; but in her half-drunken mood she thought of nothing portending evil, or a speedy end to her long life of iniquity and cruelty. It remained for the morrow to disclose to her horrified vision the results of her live-long sin, and to rid the earth of one who had long been the willing, remorseless instrument in Earl Penalvon's hands for the accomplishment of his bestial and wicked purposes.

CHAPTER LI.

POLRUTH AT HOME—THYRA LEADS A PLEASANT LIFE—ARRIVAL OF STRANGERS AT THE KIDDLEAWINK—HIS FEARS AND ALARM—SOME NAVAL OFFICERS VISIT HIM.

POLRUTH's business at the "Jolly Mariners," was flourishing more than ever.

His customers were well cared for, and nightly returned to the pleasant tap of the kiddleawink, where song and dance were the order of each evening.

Thanks to the good offices of Paul Adair and other friends, Polruth had a fine and excellent supply of liquors and tobacco upon the premises, but took great care that few should find the place of their concealment.

With all his faults, Polruth had one quality that redeemed him in the eyes of many, namely—his partiality and kindness to Wild Thyra, who, in her simple easy way, quite won his good opinion, and the hearty good wishes of all who frequented the tap.

He heeded not her little ways; her eccentric conduct from time to time elicited no more than smiles; yet, in all that tended to her peace and comfort, Polruth was not grudging.

"Well, Thyra," said Polruth, one evening as he sat before his cheerful fire smoking, "well, Thyra, what makes you look so solemn, lass? Do you see aught in the fire that forewarns mischief? Cheer up, lass, and tell us the news. How's Thorkil?"

"I don't know, neither do I care. Thorkil is no friend of mine."

"Well, then, don't fret that way, lass, cheer up. I never saw such a girl as you are, you seem always up in the clouds dreaming. What is your vision now?"

"You will have strange visitors to-night," said Thyra, musing.

"Strange visitors, say you? Then I must look after those casks of brandy, and put them out of the way of all prying eyes. How do you know that I shall have strange visitors?"

"How? How do I know everything? I tell you, though you scarcely believe me. Perhaps you begin to think as Thorkil does, that I am a spirit of evil or an impostor."

"No, I think neither, lass; spirit of evil you certainly are not, rather a spirit of good; for the kiddleawink has done better since you have been here than ever before."

"And do you think that I have brought you good luck?" asked Thyra, while a quiet smile of pleasure lighted up her face.

"Yes, lass, I do," answered Polruth, emphatically, "d—d if I don't, and there ain't a man, woman, or child that comes into the 'Jolly Mariners,' but all take to you, as I have done, and if you behave yourself, lass, and make things snug and ship-shape like as now, you can ask anything of me that's in my power to give, and Polruth ain't the man to refuse you."

"Thank you, Polruth, thank you," said Thyra, casting looks of gratitude at her kind protector, who, pipe in mouth, looked straight at the fire, and from some cause seemed to evade her earnest glance. He continued to gaze in the fire for some minutes, occasionally stealing a look at Thyra, who, relapsing into her usual abstracted manner, did not notice him; at length he said,

"No more thanks, girl. I think you feel comfortable here, and your altered looks give me much more satisfaction than all your speeches; but I tell you what it is, lass, as you have taken a deal of trouble in clearing up the kiddleawink, and try to make all my customers comfortable, I will try if I can't pick out some fine strapping fellow for your husband; and I hope an honest as well as a deserving one, too."

"Husband, Polruth?" said Thyra, blushing scarlet, and turning her face.

"Husband, lass Why, yes; is it such a wonderful thing for a girl of your age to think of getting a partner?"

Thyra was silent; but her pulse beat violently, and tears started to her eyes involuntarily.

"Yes, lass, a husband, nothing less. I'm sure, if Hylda, nagging as she is, could get a husband, I'm sure that *you* can."

"But would you wish me to have such a fellow as——"

"No, lass, not such a rum-drinking, idle vagabond as he is; but a good hard-working fellow like——."

"Like who, Polruth?"

"Well, like several that I could name; for instance, there is Agger."

"No, Polruth, you are mistaken; I do not wish to marry; not at present, at all events. While I have such a home as you are kind enough to give me, I shall never wish to change; I could trust no one but——"

"But who?" asked Polruth, violently puffing his pipe, and shifting about uneasily in his seat. "You know, I should like to know who it is you do like, for if I'm successful in business, and your kindness make me certain that I shall be, you shall not want for anything. But who is it that you can trust?"

"You," said Thyra, seizing his brawny hand, and kissing it gratefully. "I can trust you, for let the world say what it will, let it call you smuggler, wrecker, or what it may, I know your heart is good and true, and I could love you always as a brother."

"Could you, lass? Well, then, you shall have your way; you may remain here as long as you please, and neither Thorkil nor any of his vile, cowardly crew shall ever dare to insult or touch you. Come, lass, cheer up; take a sip of my rum, it will rouse you, and when you like, make the kettle boil, and let's have a good cup of strong tea, for I expect some of our old companions will drop in upon us before long, and then we shall have no peace until long after midnight. They will soon be here."

Thyra required no second bidding, but started up at once."

She stirred up the fire and made it burn brightly, and ere long the huge kettle began to hiss and bubble and boil, and Thyra was soon engaged in dispensing steaming cups of strong and fragrant congo, while the red-faced host helped himself to toast and eggs, and other pleasant edibles, which Thyra, with quickness and neatness had prepared and cooked for him.

"Come, lass, sit thee down, and eat, and drink, too. I am often surprised how you manage to live with the little you eat. Why, the sparrow pecks more in a day than you do."

Thyra laughed at Polruth's comparison, and, seating herself, joined him in the meal.

The tea-things being cleared away, everything was made comfortable for the expected visit of any who might chance to drop in to spend the evening with Polruth.

The burly host bustled about his house, and arranged his cups and glasses, and had not concluded his preparations when Tim the Fiddler entered with a pleasant greeting.

"You are early," said Polruth. "Are any of the lads coming?"

"Aye, true, more than you expect, Mr. Polruth."

THE QUARREL.

Tim, having fully adjusted his fiddle, gave a few preliminary scratches, and dashed off into a very lively jig, which made Polruth's heels tingle again with pleasure.

After tossing off a good jorum of rum, he lit his pipe, and jumped into the middle of the fire-lit tap, and began to caper away with alarming vigour and energy.

"That's it, Tim; let's have the same tune again; if nobody else comes, why then, hang it, Thyra, we'll do all the dancing ourselves. Come on, lass, we might as well be merry as sad."

Thyra smiled, but declined to exhibit her Terpsichorean powers, despite Polruth's and Tim's solicitations, but sat laughing beside the fire, and evidently taking much delight in Polruth's exhibition of good-humour.

"That's it, Master Polruth. Try it again, master; there ain't another man living along the coast can foot a jig better than the landlord of the 'Jolly Mariners,'" approvingly observed the fiddler, as Polruth threw away his pipe in an ecstasy of delight, and executed a "double shuffle" with great energy and vim.

Polruth's merriment would have been of long continuance probably, for fate and fortune seemed to be smiling upon him of late.

He was daily becoming more popular among wreckers and smugglers, and a large class of non-descripts along the coast. His cellars were cheaply and amply furnished with every sort of refreshment, and with every brand of tobacco and cigars known to, or required in the market.

Except Thorkil, indeed, he knew of no one who refused him the frank and cordial hand of good fellowship.

All in all, he felt extremely happy and content with himself and all the world, and, having completed his dance, a mixture of jig and hornpipe, to his own satisfaction, as alike to the approving opinion of Thyra and Tim, he concluded his self-exhibition by rushing forward and kissing Thyra, who sat beside the fire with radiant face and laughing eye.

"Well done! Couldn't have been better," said Tim, screwing up his face into all manner of contortions, as he adjusted his fourth string once more, and began to scrape an old-fashioned love tune. "But isn't there some one knocking, Master Polruth? I thought I heard a noise, master."

"Aye, sure, lad, and so did I. Thyra, open the door, that's a lass."

Thyra willingly did so, and three or four coasters walked in, and took seats, with many complimentary remarks to Thyra and Polruth.

"Not like some of 'em," said one; "you don't try to get all and keep all, Polruth. You like to give a little fun to the lads sometimes for nothing, and that's the right way to do business; so says I and all of us."

"Aye, aye, messmate, that's true. I met many a lad to-night that's coming here to shake his foot a bit. Good evening, Thyra, wench; give us half a pint of rum. Here you are, Tim, my lad; rosin up that bow of thine, and let's have it in right old style, hearty."

"I told thee, Polruth, you'd have plenty of company to-night. Here comes half a dozen more lads. I can hear them coming up the road."

Before many minutes, the kiddleawink was visited by several dozen wreckers, half-smugglers, coasters, and nondescripts, who seemed right merrily inclined, and, ere long, Thyra found herself very busy in preparing hot grog for the fastly increasing company which honoured Polruth on this occasion.

Cards and dominoes were in great request in one corner. Dancers were kicking up their heels to Tim's enlivening music, while, ever and anon, there were sounds as of a miniature broadside from the back premises, where some half-dozen or more stalwart fellows were vigorously engaged in knocking skittles about.

Polruth was in his glory. A drink with one, and then a sup with another, was the order of the evening. Disputes at cards, dominoes, and skittles were settled by him, and all things were passing off with great satisfaction to all concerned, when the hands of a tall, old-fashioned clock pointed to the hour of midnight.

Tim was tired, but every symptom of fatigue was closely watched by his own particular patrons, who were so liberal in plying him with liquors of all sorts that he could scarcely maintain his perpendicular, perched as he was upon a table in the corner, bobbing his head in a semi-somnolescent state of premature inebriation.

Polruth was unusually frolicsome.

Unlike most landlords, he was not averse to granting "tick," as he termed it, to all he knew to be honest fellows.

"Drink, lads, while you can," he said. "Never mind the cash; another time will do as well as now. Thyra shall be steward to-night, so sail away, lads, and never mind to-morrow."

Brandy, rum, gin, whisky, tobacco, and cigars were the order of the evening, without apparent stint or frugality.

Regiments of empty bottles decorated tables and chimney-piece, the atmosphere was heavily surcharged with narcotic fumes, loud words and laughter, song-singing and toast-giving were progressing amicably and sociably in little knots of fours and sixes, and Thyra, light-heeled and obliging, moved hither and thither with all manner of beverages, but scarcely discernable in the clouds of tobacco smoke.

Polruth's unexpected " assembly" was unexplainable.

His company had dropped in as unlooked-for as unasked.

One would ask another the reason why so many jovial faces and merry voices had met thus together, yet no one could explain the why or wherefore.

No vessel had been wrecked of late upon the coast; Thorkil's gang had not, as of yore, decoyed a vessel or two upon the Shark's Fin, or on to the reefs by the White Cliffs, and thereby replenished empty pockets.

Neither had Dutch nor French merchants successfully eluded the coast-guard, and run a cargo or two near by.

None of his Majesty's ships had been paid off at any neighbouring port; nothing of more than ordinary character, indeed, had transpired of late to account for the joviality of the coasters and wreckers, yet happy and jovial they certainly were, and dropped more than one bright guinea into Polruth's pocket that night for liquor and tobacco.

Tim, indeed, looked like a demi-god upon his musical throne.

His artistic exertions had so pleased his audience that they showered copper and silver into his hat until his pockets were grown suddenly corpulent with silver and copper treasure.

What with drink and excitement, he seemed to have outshone all his past peformances, and made the catgut twang and squeak again with all manner of improvised modulation and variation until his face was teeming with perspiration, and the rosin flew from his bow in milky, dusty showers, serving as snuff to all within the radius of Tim's right elbow.

Midnight had passed.

Merriment, and forgetfulness of every wordly care, was at its height.

Polruth was as red-faced as any of his lively company, when Thyra approached him, and whispered,

"Strangers are approaching, and are now near the kiddleawink. They are friends; go and meet them at the door."

"Who be they then, lass?"

"King's officers."

"King's officers, say you? Then they are no friends of ours. If I go out to meet them it will simply be to warn them of all danger arising from an intrusion on our company. My friends would rise as one against all King's men; they come for no good but to pry into our cellars and little domestic arrangements we want no Crown officers to know."

"Have no fear, Polruth; go as I bid you. Thyra has never yet commended aught that could harm you. Go, I say, shake both by the hand and bid them welcome as a true seaman and a Briton; they are but youths, youths truly, but with the service and hard experience of men."

"Youths! boys, say you, Thyra? Oh, that alters the case; none of our company would molest boys."

"Don't treat them as such. Mark me, they are king's officers, gentlemen by rank and bearing."

"Supposed to be, always," answered Polruth, with a sarcastic grin, "always supposed to be, not always proved to be so, for I've known some of the biggest rogues and rascals in the world who carried royal commissions in their pockets."

With this speech Polruth left the noise and glare

of the tap-room, parlor, and skittle ground and went out alone upon the dull, dark-looking heath.

For a moment he saw nothing.

After a few seconds he perceived two figures standing opposite the door; he knew them to be males by the red glow of fragrant cigars they smoked.

He approached the strangers in a friendly manner and bade them welcome.

"We intended to have proceeded onwards to Seawardine, but our footsteps were arrested by the sounds of merriment within."

"I knew you were coming."

"Knew we were coming! Nay, how can that be?"

"Oh, easy enough, young gents. I have a quiet, harmless girl living with me, that I treat more like a sister than a stranger; a weird, melancholy, pale-faced rune-kenner who pretends to foresee and foretell things."

"Rune-kenner, say you?"

"Yes; a girl, harmless and lovable in her nature, Thyra by name."

"Thyra! Wild Thyra, say you? It must be the same; then I am not mistaken, Frank, this is, this must be the kiddleawink."

"Kiddleawink, gents; nay, that's saying more than you know. I don't like the 'Jolly Mariners' to be so called by any but particular friends."

"Well, then, so are we, Polruth."

"Polruth! why, then you know me, although I cannot recall your voice or countenance."

"Harry Halliard, then, and his friend, Frank Rayner."

"Impossible! what little Harry, the curly-headed captain's son?"

"Yes, and Frank Rayner, his chum, more than brother, if you will, midshipmen in the King's service."

"Right welcome then, in the King's name, lads; but I fear me, my rough company will not relish your uniforms much; King's men are not altogether favourites of theirs, particularly when they are commissioned men."

"Quite sufficient, Polruth; while we are with you, and that will not be long, we are simply your friends."

"Well said, gents; why then, let's go into the kiddle —— I beg your pardon, gentlemen, I should have said the 'Jolly Mariners'—and take a glass of grog."

Without more ado, Harry and Frank doffed their heavy over-coats and stepped proudly into the tap, but when their uniform was perceived, the company rose as one man, and, with scowling looks and suppressed oaths looked threateningly towards the fresh arrivals.

"What's all this mean, Polruth?" asked one giant-like individual, approaching the landlord with angry, pugilistic gait and manner. "What means this, eh?"

"Aye, true, lads, what means this d—d treachery?" chorussed the whole assembly, slamming pots and bottles upon the table, in a determined, vindictive mood.

"What means it, my lads?" asked Polruth, stuttering, and clearing his voice for a very eloquent effort at introducing his young friends.

"Yes, speak, landlord, this moment, or you shall pay dearly for thus snugly caging us all."

"Well, lads," said Polruth, hurriedly, "it means this—that while we've been enjoying ourselves, these two young gentlemen, King's officers, have been standing out in the cold, listening to Tim's music."

"Yes, and I suppose with a couple of well-armed boats' crews at their heels, ready to nab every mother's son of us; that's it, I suppose?"

"No, nothing of that sort. This is a lad who left our parts some years ago, a gallant young fellow, who has risen up in the King's service, and is an officer, like his friend and companion. You must know one of them, or heard of him. Not know Harry Halliard, lads?" asked Polruth.

"Aye, aye, of course we do!" said some.

"Just so," answered others.

"Used to live near here; a curly-headed little brat, always paddling in the surf and climbing trees. Oh, yes, of course!"

The countenances of all assembled changed immediately when informed of things aright, and many rushed forward to shake hands with and welcome the young strangers.

Among the last to come forward with her hand in welcome was Thyra.

She hung her head, and blushed deeply.

Harry knew her instantly, and kissed her tenderly, even affectionately, for Thyra had often nursed him, and shared in his childish sports, in happy unconscious years then long passed.

Thyra leaned upon his neck, and wept freely; but as she gazed with pride upon his handsome, sunburnt face, she seized his hands with fervour, saying,

"I always knew you would be an admiral."

A remark which elicited laughter from many; but from none more so than Frank and Harry himself.

Polruth didn't know what to think of his youthful visitors.

There was an ease, and a gentlemanly grace of manner in all their movements, totally at variance with all he had been accustomed to meet or associate with, that charmed him.

He could hardly believe his own powers of vision. He looked and looked again at Harry, now sideways, now full in front, and again sideways, and repeated his ocular observation so often that at last he puffed out huge volumes of smoke, ejaculating,

"Yes, that's him, lads! Like two peas in a pot—his father and him."

Though young in years, his experience among seamen had taught him that a liberal manner, and honest straightforwardness were sure to conciliate the company, and he therefore entered heart and soul into the merriment and good feeling apparent on every hand.

He threw a guinea to Tim, which seemed to wonderfully revive that exhausted fiddler's energies, for his bow seemed to redouble in energy and swiftness.

He gave orders to Polruth to serve the very best to all assembled, regardless of cost, and irrespective of let or hindrance.

Bottles of Cognac, old Jamaica, and St. Croix were handed about freely, and pigtail, cavendish, and cigars were in great request on every hand.

After imbibing a palatable potion of liquor and hot water, Frank and Harry became exceedingly lively and companiable.

They essayed a capital hornpipe, to the great delight and approbation of all, including the fiddler himself, who swore it couldn't have been done better, and to wind up the hornpipe, Harry and Frank proposed a four-handed reel, and to the uproarious delight of all present, Polruth, pipe in mouth, handed forth Thyra, who, to please Harry and his boon companion Frank, did the best she could on the occasion.

Stalwart, noisy fellows in the skittle-ground

seemed intent on smashing the nine pins into splinters.

Card players were pounding the tables, and making glasses jingle in their warmth and enthusiasm, while some noisy fellows in corners, having tired themselves with dancing, were now delighting nobody but themselves individually by roaring out snatches of popular sea-songs with the lungs of Stentor.

Polruth was hither and thither fulfilling orders.

Everybody drank healths to the burly landlord, and that red-faced, perspiring individual, nothing loath, was drinking the healths of everybody in return, accompanying each toast with unintelligible remarks, interspersed with hiccups, and an accompaniment of little apologetic coughs.

Everybody was applauding everybody.

The merriment and noise was becoming fast and furious every moment, while Harry and Frank monopolised Thyra between them, and were vastly amusing her with tales of their scrapes, adventures, and misfortunes at sea.

With all her well-assumed gaiety and merriment, there was a shade of melancholy that momentarily flitted across Thyra's face which was not unperceived by Harry, who inquired the cause.

"You must not ask me now, Harry dear," she said. "To-morrow I may tell you all."

"But why not now?"

"Yes, why not now, Thyra?" asked Frank, with a winning manner that sat well and engagingly upon his habitual modest and unassuming bearing.

"I know not why, Harry. I have but one enemy in the world that I can call to mind."

"And who is that, Thyra?"

"Yours, as well as mine."

"Mine!"

"Yes, and Polruth's also, and your dear, darling mother's also. The enemy of all, I do believe, who wish to live well with their [fellow-creatures hereabouts."

"The more reason then, Thyra, why you should advise him of it," said Frank, smoking complacently, and smiling at the boisterous and merry men about him, who occasionally rose and staggered forward, glass in hand, to drink his "jolly good health!"

"Why what is she saying?" asked Polruth, taking a seat beside Harry. "Not kenning, I hope. You wouldn't spoil sport at such a merry moment, Thyra."

While he spoke Thyra went to the door, and hurrying back, hastily whispered,

"They are coming."

"Coming! Who are coming?"

"Why the revenues."

"It can't be!" answered Polruth, in amazement. "But stay, I'll tell the tale."

After much ado Polruth obtained a hearing, and explained that his old enemy Thorkil, had conspired with the revenue officers to disturb the company for the purposes of search.

The scene of excitement that ensued baffles description.

The rough and half intoxicated company vowed vengeance against the landlord, whom they accused of having entrapped them.

They vowed death to Harry and Frank, for they fully believed that being King's men, they were in league with the revenue officers.

It was some time before Frank or Harry could obtain a hearing.

Harry asked a few questions of Polruth, and the latter gave an emphatic negative to all his questions.

"Listen to me, men," said Frank jumping on a table; "there has been treachery at work somewhere

to disturb all of us in our merry-making, but believe me, we are both totally ignorant of the origin of it. To prove it lads, if violence is threatened to any of us here to-night by the sneaking hounds who are coming at such an unreasonable and unlooked-for time, you will find that Harry Halliard and myself will be the first to retaliate."

This speech seemed to pacify the company, and calm the terrible storm that threatened to break forth.

"Shipmates," said Harry, following Frank's example, and jumping on the table, "one word to you. If these lubbers come simply to search, why let them do so quietly; there is nothing about the kiddleawink at this moment that they can find without a proper Government certificate for."

"True lads, every word," roared Polruth, "you have just drunk the very last bottle, and smoked the last pound of contraband I had in the place."

This speech was received with roars of laughter and applause.

"'Tis true, shipmates, and that's why I beg of you, my lads, to be guided by me," said Harry. "No seaman loves a revenue less than a royal does in his heart, but as they haven't got a haul this time, let them come and go peaceably; its no use shedding blood uselessly. If they show fight, you know that's a different thing altogether, lads; but let me pass the word to all when to give a broadside."

This speech was received somewhat favourably, but the majority growled very much, and seemed greatly inclined to break the head of the first revenue officer who dared to show himself across the threshold.

Tim's violin was silent; the skittle-players and cardsmen were all attention to aught that might transpire, while some drank more than deeply, and swore roundly that they'd break the skull of the first man that showed the white feather, or struck their flag to the revenue officers.

Harry and Frank, with a coolness beyond their years, stood in the midst of these infuriated men, and calmly awaited the approach of the revenue officers.

Presently a knock was heard at the door.

Polruth opened it.

"We demand admission in the King's name," said the voice of one who stood in the shade.

"Have it in the King's name, friend," answered Harry. "Advance! your business?"

"We are revenue officers, and demand the right of search."

"You shall have all you demand; your claims are just and legal. It might have served the ends of justice to have postponed your unpleasant visit to a more fitting time, I think."

"That's our business, young man. Who are you that dares to dictate to the King's officers in the execution of their duty?"

"I do, sir," answered Harry. "King's officer like yourself, and of equal rank."

"A King's officer in such company, sir!"

"I might have been in worse company, if in yours, perhaps."

This sally was received with roars of laughter by the rough and impatient company, who stamped their feet, and struck the tables with violence and passion, as some half-dozen officers or more entered, and began their search.

It was with the utmost difficulty that Halliard, Rayner, and Polruth restrained all present from resorting to violence.

After half an hour's search the officers returned without discovering aught that could criminate the wily landlord of the kiddleawink, who laughed b isterously at their futile attempts to unearth aught that was contraband.

"You haven't looked here, my hearty," said one rough, loud-spoken wrecker.

"Where?" said the eager, ferret-eyed officer of customs. "Where?"

"Why here," was the answer, as the wrecker upturned an empty glass. "Here, lad, smell it ; you can tell what's been in it, *I* know. Smuggled, wasn't it ?"

The officer was annoyed, and particularly at the roars of derisive laughter that greeted him as he turned away disgusted at his fruitless attempts to discover aught illegal.

One by one the officers returned to the tap.

"Satisfied, gentlemen ?" asked Polruth.

"Yes ; you've been extremely lucky, Polruth," said the chief man. "You may not be so again."

"Let us hope he'll always be so," was the noisy wish of the company.

Harry and Frank whispered to Polruth, who reddened, and said,

"Well you're work must have fatigued you, men. Will you take a drop of anything ?"

"Don't mind if we do," was the response.

"What shall it be, then ? Name whatever you like ; I daresay *I* can find something hid away that you've not seen yet. What shall it be ?"

"Brandy."

"I'll take rum."

"I prefer Hollands."

"Give me a pound of tobacco," said one or other of the custom's officers.

"Well said, gentlemen," answered Polruth, with a comical leer in his eye. "Bring out half a dozen glasses, Thyra."

They were brought out and placed upon the table.

"Don't treat 'em," roared numerous voices.

"I'd see 'em choked first."

"You shan't treat 'em, Polruth," cried many.

The noise now became deafening.

"Hold a minute, lads," said Polruth, with a laugh. "I shall do as I please in my own house."

The custom's officers anticipating a taste of something good, waited patiently, until Polruth returned and looked with scorn upon the numerous scowling faces around them.

Polruth presently appeared and filled the glasses from a large stone vessel covered at the top,

"Now then, gentlemen, take hold and drink to your own good health."

They took the glasses eagerly, and raised them to their lips, but placed them on the table again with looks of evident disappointment, annoyance and disgust.

"Why, that is water, Polruth," said the chief, indignant at the insult.

"Of course it is. Did you think I was going to give any better to beggarly revenues ?"

Nothing in the world could have tickled the company more sensibly, for they laughed and roared until the very roof shook with their terrific noise of shouting, stamping, thumping the table, and yelling, until, in the confusion, the revenues retreated discomfited, and humiliated to the cold, biting air on the heath.

Polruth's stratagem was encored again and again, and the merriment of the evening was resumed until long after chanticleer had bid defiance to the dawning morn.

Bottles and kegs, and rolls of tobacco and boxes of cigars, were mysteriously produced from places of deposit unknown to any but Polruth himself,

and freely handed to the company, who were drinking and rioting at Halliard's and Rayner's expense.

Tim, the fiddler, had enjoyed a nap during the recent visit and search, so that, when awakened once more, he resumed his bow with pristine vigour and ability, until at last most of the company succumbed to fatigue.

Some departed to their homes, shouting and bellowing, making night hideous with their songs and yells.

Others, who could not maintain the perpendicular, collapsed on benches or under the tables, and among the wreck of jugs and bottles, tobacco pipes and sawdust, until at last all subsided into slumber as they were, remaining faithful to their post in honour of Bacchus. A charming chorus was maintained during the night by the score or more of inebriated snorers, who, clasping empty bottles or glasses, sat or lay huddled together in the charming confusion of democratic equality, among the dirt and debris of the past evening's orgies.

Polruth, in truth, was not much better than his guests, for he sat bolt upright, prop-wise against the entrance-door, bottle in hand, and a broken stem of black tobacco-pipe in his mouth—the guardian genius of all present ; determined, with commendable pride, to detain all who remained safely within the portals of his thrice famous kiddleawink.

Harry and Frank had long retired to rest. Thyra sat sleepless in her neat little room, waiting for the dawn, to resume the offices of kindness which had so endeared her to Polruth and all who truthfully and faithfully knew and appreciated her.

CHAPTER LII.

LIEUT. FRAZER IS APPOINTED TO THE BRIG OF WAR, SCORPION—HE ASKS HARRY AND FRANK TO JOIN HIM—HARLECK AND THE CRAWLER—OPINIONS OF HAWSER, JUNIPER AND KONKS, AND SIR EVERARD BRANDON—HAWSER TAKES A CRUIZE.

THE Thunderer lay in harbour for several weeks before the Lords of the Admiralty thought proper to have her examined.

In truth, notwithstanding the severe shaking she had received in the late action, admiralty officers thought her fit to go on another cruize, and issued orders to Sir Everard Brandon to prepare his old ship for a long and dangerous voyage.

There were motives for this.

Authorities at Whitehall were sleepy officials, and somewhat jealous of the popularity and fame which Captain Brandon had already acquired, and of the high opinion and expectations entertained of him by Admiral Nelson, who publicly and privately spoke of him as one of the most promising officers of his day.

Had Admiral Nelson's encomium been passed upon any of the admiralty favourites—men with great titles and monied influence, but lacking in innate energy or talent ; or had the popular clamour fixed upon some other officer more compromising, and who would pander or truckle to the gross ignorance or negligence of many on shore who are supposed to govern and dictate to officers afloat— why then, Sir Everard Brandon would, perhaps, have been raised to the honour of a peerage for his late gallant deeds.

As it was, however, Captain Brandon was too much of an unflinching British seaman to wink at the system of gross and inefficient contracts existing in his day to expect much favour at the hands of those who were cognizant of, or parties to, the degrading system of "jobbing" which was resorted to by many high and mighty in office, desirous of, and willing to descend to peculation, to retrieve fallen fortunes.

If Captain Brandon had a good ship, he would acknowledge it, and modestly promise to give a good account both of himself and it, as this story has often shown.

If, on the other hand, purse-proud officials wished to foist upon him and the country generally, unseaworthy vessels, ill manned and badly armed, he was the very man, and the first, to complain of it so publicly that, in many respects, he won for himself the credit of the country's willing ear, who, through the press, took up the key-note, and raised such a storm of indignation as forced them into energetic measures, becoming and worthy of a great nation engaged in gigantic and portentous wars.

Hence, when the Thunderer was ordered to refit, and report for further arduous service off the coast, Sir Everard Brandon loudly and justly complained that his ship required extensive docking and repairs that would demand months of labour and much expense.

His ideas were scouted by high and mighty ones on shore, who knew little of, or cared much less for, service afloat, and he was accordingly commanded to cruize off the south coast on an experimental trip, but this Admiral Nelson would not permit.

He ordered the vessel into port again, as unfit for general service without extensive repairs.

It was well that Admiral Nelson had such foresight, for a storm arose when in sight of Plymouth, and the vessel proved so leaky, that it was with the greatest difficulty that she was kept above water, despite unceasing day and night labour at the pumps.

When the Thunderer, therefore, after a week's cruize, returned to port again, she was paid off, and put into dock.

Through the interest and exertions of Collingwood, Sir Everard was promised another ship at an early day.

Owing to official dislike and petty bickerings, he knew it would be some time ere he should be afloat again, and what chagrined the brave officer more than aught else was the reflection that, by the time he might procure another ship, all his crew, highly disciplined as it undoubtedly was, would, in all probability, be assigned to other vessels, and thus lose that unity of action and oneness of purpose which he had been so remarkably successful in instilling into both his men and officers, and which had proved of incalculable value in the real hour of trial, in displaying the superiority of British ships and British crews over all others with which, in those stormy and troublous times, they came into weekly, if not daily contact.

Perceiving that little could be done to advance his own individual interests with an acrimonious, selfish, envious Admiralty board, he next endeavoured to obtain eligible and desirable commissions for those of his young and well-tried officers who gave the best promise of undauntedly and unflinchingly upholding the flag under which he had served and fought since boyhood with so much courage and distinction.

Among the first of all his officers he selected Lieutenant Frazer, who had for years been rated on the Thunderer's books, and had never deserted it for any other vessel, despite all and every temptation of rival and ambitious commanders.

For a wonder the endorsement of Admiral Nelson, Collingwood and Captain Brandon had weight with the Admiralty, and, at an early day, Lieutenant Frazer was gazetted as commander of the brig of war, Scorpion.

It was not a new vessel, by any means, but one of the merchant service, which, years before, had been captured from the French, and had been doctored up at Portsmouth for the purpose of a channel cruiser.

So that he had "some kind of an old tub to sail in he didn't care," Frazer jocosely remarked to his many friends; "so that it was warranted watertight, that's all; if I want a better one I dare say I shall fall in with some Frenchman or Spaniard who can afford to let me have his after an hour's brush or so."

"That's it," said Hawser, who, paid off, was cruising about, hands in pocket, disconsolate for something to do. "That's it, lieutenant, nothing like fighting for a good ship, and exchanging property; exchange ain't no robbery, so they says."

"But will you sail with me, Hawser?" asked Frazer, who met and had comfortably cornered the jolly old salt in an ale-house, and had put rather a stiff glass of grog under the old hero's nose.

"Well, you see, lieutenant, that there all depends," answered Hawser, stroking his nose very wisely and slowly puffing at his pipe; "you see, sir, I've sailed so often with Captain Brandon, and he's got such a capital knack of falling in with plenty of prize money and short cruising that I should feel rather awkward like, treading decks with a strange commander, all respect to you, you know, lieutenant."

"But Konks and Juniper have promised to ship with me, what do you say to that?"

"They have?" said Hawser, surprised. "Why, then, shiver me, sir, if I ain't one, too."

"Well said, Hawser; and see if I don't make all things ship-shape and comfortable for you all."

"No fear of that, sir; but, as I was saying only t'other day to Captain Brandon in this very street, 'Sir Everard,' says I, 'I should like very much to sail with you again, for there's nothing like going in company with old hands you well knows.'"

"'True, Hawser,' he says, 'but I fear it will be some months before I get another ship, for the old Thunderer is all going to pieces, and is now in dock.' Lord, lieutenant, the old man almost shed tears as he shook hands and says, 'Hawser,' says he, 'whoever you goes with, don't forget to give the first hand to my lads, Mr. Frazer or Mr. Armitage.' Lads, he called you, sir, and so you are like, for you've been long together, and I know he feels to all of us like a father more than a fighting sea-dog of a captain."

"True, Hawser; so he does."

"But you ain't going to have Harleck and Crawley, and all that kind of stuff on board with you, are you? For, 'pon my soul, I can never make up my mind to sail with pressed men; you can't much depend on 'em, that's my opinion; one volunteer to twenty pressed men. That's what Juniper and I always say."

"No, Hawser. Dan Crawley has been flogged for cowardice, and Harleck for other offences. They are now on board the receiving ship and not allowed liberty. There are a few out of the old ship I would like to get, Hawser, old boy, if you and Juniper could manage it—two lads in particular."

"Who, sir?" asked Hawser, impatiently, withdrawing the pipe from his mouth and looking up to Frazer's face with much anxiety.

"Why, Halliard and Rayner."

"Just what I was thinking, sir. Two better lads never breathed the sea breeze on board the

King's ships ; both promoted, you know, for good conduct and gallantry. You couldn't have better men, for men they are, you know, in every sense of the word."

" True, Hawser, but they are off on leave. I don't know where to find them."

" Ah, but I do, lieutenant, and if you only gives me and Juniper and Konks, three weeks clear run of it on shore, I warrant we'll not only get those lads to join us but such a bonny lot of hardy sea-devils as will make the Scorpion a scourge to all the French and Spanish coasts. Plenty of prize money and lots of fun, say I."

Before parting Lieutenant Fraser gave Hawser full instructions, where to go, and how to assist in collecting a good ship's crew.

" Here my lad," said he, " here's a £50 note. Have a jolly cruise, all of you, and be sure to report for duty, well and hearty, within three weeks. The brig will be ready and willing to weigh anchor and cruise by that time."

" He's a brick, and no mistake !" mused Hawser, when Frazer had left him ; " and if there's a good glass of grog that Juniper, me and Konks can get at within the next three weeks, well then we'll christen and drown the Scorpion in rum, or my name ain't Bill Hawser !"

Thrusting the £50 Bank of England note into his watch-fob, Hawser refilled his pipe, hitched up his trousers, and, as he termed it, " took a cruise," in search of his messmates, Konks and Juniper.

CHAPTER LIII.

EARL PENALVON PREPARES TO FOLLOW NELLY BRITTON — HE CONFRONTS HER INDIGNANT FATHER — PENALVON'S BASENESS AND COWARDICE — HE SLANDERS PAUL ADAIR — JOEL'S AFFLICTION AND DESPAIR.

ON the morning following Nelly's Britton's abduction from Seawardine, Earl Penalvon rose from his sumptuously garnished breakfast-table self-complacent and ready for travelling in his commodious coach, which stood ready for departure at the hall door.

The earl was pacing his breakfast-room self-satisfied and remoreless.

He was bent upon an errand to irreparably destroy a maiden's fair fame and name.

He had done such a thing more than once, and looked upon the matter as an ordinary transaction in the easy, aimless life of a nobleman.

He considered the crime, for such it really was and is, in the light of a mere freak, common to the whims and ways of so called patrician's blood.

The maid was merely the offspring of an unknown, untitled boor, perhaps upon whom he might confer honor even by forcing an illicit intercourse.

The world, he thought, might consider his actions in whatever, under whatever guise it might think proper, it would simply pass among the rich as a nobleman's freak or folly, and among the poor—oh, as to them, it mattered to him almost as little as he valued the opinion of heaven—nothing.

He paced his breakfast-room, and pulled on his gloves.

He gazed at the costly exotic that decked his button-hole, and having, by careful study at the life-sized mirror, arrived at the conclusion that he was " a deuced fine-looking fellow," slowly paced up and down, when a servant noiselessly entered and announced a visitor.

" Who may he be, pray ? You know, Watkins, this is no time to disturb or detain me. I have state affairs of moment at present on my mind. If it is any of the tenantry—in fact, it matters not who he may be—refer him to my steward."

" It is the blacksmith, my lord, Mr.——"

" Blacksmith ! And what have I to do with blacksmiths, eh ? Have you so forgotten yourself, Watkins, as to permit such vulgar people to approach me ? You will consider it an honour, I suppose, one day to introduce, rather to obtrude upon my presence some vulgar tinker or other, gipsy, perhaps,'or strolling vagabond of a two-penny theatre. What next, I wonder ? I thought you had been in my service long enough, Watkins, to know who are, and who are not, fitting persons to trouble me with."

" It is Mr.——I beg pardon, my lord, it is Joel Britton, the ah—the ah—the person from the village, my lord."

" Oh, quite a different thing, entirely. Oh, of course, show him this way immediately. Quite an old friend, truly. Show him this way."

Earl Penalvon paced his breakfast-room, humming a popular opera tune of the day, and apparently as oblivious of Joel's real business as if an ambassador from Timbuctoo had been the person in waiting.

" Be seated, I beg, my friend," said Earl Penalvon, as Joel, red and perspiring from his long walk, entered the room. " Rather fine weather for walking, is it not ? And yet, you see, my friend Britton, I thought of riding. Differences in taste, you see, my friend ; and pray what might your business or pleasure be, that brings you here so early to day ?"

" Well, you see, my lord, the last letter I got from my Nelly, she complained of being very unhappy here, and so mother and I thought we'd have her back home again, my lord, that is all, and so I've come for her. We all say you have been amazing polite in keeping her so long."

" Thank you, Joel. And so she said she was very unhappy, eh ? Did she state any reasons, may I ask ?"

" None whatever, my lord ; not a word."

" How very singular !"

" It was, my lord."

" And still more singular when I tell you, upon my word as a nobleman and gentleman, that I was going to ride straight to your place to speak to you regarding the self-same matter. Singular, wasn't it ?"

Joel nodded, and Earl Penalvon, with a well-studied smile, proceeded with his catalogue of newly-invented lies.

" Of course, you know she   not here ?"

" Not here, my lord ! How is that ? Surely you don't tell me that any harm has——"

" Be seated, and calm yourself, my friend. You know I have always befriended you."

" Always, thank you, my lord."

" And have taken a great interest in the poor little girl from the first moment I saw her in your smithy."

" True, sir. What then ? I beg you will tell me instantly what has become of her."

" Well, sir, patience, if you please, and I will."

" Thank you, my lord. I'm sure her mother and I are under lasting obligations for——"

" Well, you see, my good housekeeper taught her everything that lay in her power, but she seemed to have gotten strange—in truth, wrong—if not highly improper notions in her head, and would not be guided by my housekeeper. In fact, you will scarcely credit it, she would not follow even *my* advice."

" But my lord, tell me quickly, I beg."

"Well, sir, among her many acquaintance she seems to have become attached to a vagabond who actually entered and robbed my house."

"Robbed you, my lord! And who in heaven could it be?"

"Some low fellow or other; a sort of half smuggler, half pirate, half cut-throat, half devil, I believe, for whose head, dead or alive, I would willingly, nay this instant, give £1,000."

"And his name, I beg?"

"From scraps of information that I picked up, I have reasons for supposing it was no other than the notorious, infamous Paul Adair."

"Paul Adair!" gasped Joel, weeping like a child. "And has she so disgraced us all as to——"

"Yes, exactly. She has run off, absconded, eloped, or whatever you like, with that scoundrel who infests our coasts."

For some time Joel buried his head in his hands and remained mute.

Earl Penalvon looked at him with a cold, passionless eye, and then smiling with inhuman satisfaction at the old man's tears, went on to say,

"This occurred, I am told, last night."

"Last night!"

"Yes, and as soon as it was discovered I ordered round my carriage with the intention of calling upon and apprising you of it. You will excuse me, I know, from saying more at the moment, but I have weighty matters that call me away at the moment. I may be absent a day or two; meantime, if any of my people can trace her, I will endeavour to restore her to you. My great respect to the worthy Mrs. Britton. I must bid you good morning. Watkins, give Britton a glass of wine, it may revive him," with which last injunction Earl Penalvon fell back upon the luxurious cushions of his carriage, which rolled away from the hall door and through the park at more than ordinary speed.

"Very neatly disposed of, I think," mused Penalvon, as the carriage left the park gates. "Very neatly accomplished, I imagine! Poor fellow, he seems to take it much to heart, though. Well, well, these little things must be; noblemen *will* have their foibles. Drive on, James; if those beggars approach us, whip them away," said merciful Penalvon, alluding to some poor travellers who looked anxious to ask a little relief of the heartless occupant of the richly emblazoned carriage.

"In a few hours I shall see this little creature," thought Penalvon, playing with a silver tooth-pick. "I wonder now if the old woman has tamed her yet. Ha! ha! We shall see, the saucy little minx!"

CHAPTER LIV.

THE CRAWLER AND HARLECK——THE CRAWLER RECEIVES TWENTY-FIVE LASHES FOR COWARDICE BEFORE THE ENEMY IN THE LATE ENGAGEMENT——KONKS GIVES HIS VIEWS TO LIEUTENANT ARMITAGE REGARDING THE IMPRESSMENT OF SEAMEN, AND ANTICIPATES A CAREER OF BALLAD-SINGING ON CRUTCHES——THEY MEET HAWSER AND JUNIPER.

DAN CRAWLEY, the Crawler, had much occasion to remember the Thunderer and its officers.

When the innocence of Frank Rayner was fully established, by events subsequent to the court-martial, the general opinion of all on board was, that his evidence had been given too hastily, and undoubtedly prompted by acute animosity.

Of all the officers who detested the busy-body, none showed greater dislike for him than Lieut. Frazer.

In truth, his life on board the Thunderer was anything but pleasant.

He had entertained and expressed very acrimonious feelings towards Halliard and Rayner, and vowed in secret that he would permit no opportunity to pass that might contribute to satisfy his great revenge.

It had been his great desire that Rayner might have been committed of murder; and he also insinuated insidiously among the crew, that if not guilty, he knew something regarding the foul transaction.

Harleck, in truth, was not the low-bred cur to do aught so mean towards two young officers, who, he knew, had risen to the quarter-deck through merit alone, and not by means of family influence, or money power.

He would have felt much pleasure, in truth, to see Harry "pulled down a peg or two," as he expressed it, and might have expressed pleasure if some other lad than Frank Rayner had managed to ascend the quarter-deck.

He knew too much of discipline, however, to express his annoyance or discontent aloud, for he full well knew that all the petty officers of the ship kept a close eye upon him, for he had never shaken off that repugnance to the service which causes "pressed" men to be suspected and distrusted.

None of the officers had to complain of him as a seaman, and a brave one also, when occasion presented fitting opportunities for the display of true and genuine British gallantry before the enemy.

But there was a forbidding moroseness in his manner, a hanging of the head, and downcast look, a sneering laugh about his mouth at times, and a peculiar sidelong leer in his eye, which gave token that there were feelings smouldering in his shaggy, hairy bosom, which might one day kindle into flame, and cause much mischief.

When, therefore, it became evident that the Thunderer would not be commissioned again, and that it would require months of docking and repair ere she could unfurl her ensign to the enemy, the officers determined to carry out the orders of the late court-martial, and so clear the books of all punishments against delinquents.

Among those who had not been punished for his misdemeanour was Dan Crawley, the Crawler, who, it may be remembered, was accused of cowardice before the enemy by Konks, and convicted on the united evidence of several officers, who were witnesses of it, during the late action with the French.

When the eventful day arrived there were very few on board the Thunderer who did not smile, for, despite all his endeavours to ingratiate himself into the good graces of both men and officers by acts of abject meanness and servility, there were few, indeed, who, having once seen him, would for a moment trust in his truth or sincerity.

He was lashed up to the gratings, and a strong-armed boatswain's mate laid the cat on his back with a vengeance; and two strokes of the whip had scarcely fallen upon him, as he stood writhing and howling, before, coward-like, he began to utter sentiments of the most servile, cringing nature to both officers and crew, begging to be cast loose and remitted his punishment.

Despite all his tears and prayers he received the whole of his twenty-five lashes, and as each stroke fell upon his bare back there seemed to be a murmur of applause involuntarily pass through the whole ship's crew then assembled.

NOTICE.—The next Number of the Boys' Library will be Published on Friday, September 12th Order early of your Bookseller.

BOYS' LIBRARY

Harry Halliard: or, the Young British Tar.

A GUILTY PURPOSE INTERRUPTED.

Had it been for any other crime than cowardice there would, undoubtedly, have been found some to express commiseration, or beg for a commutation of the sentence ; but the ideas of gross cowardice before the enemy are so abhorrent to a gallant tar that he would have considered it a lasting disgrace to whisper the slightest word of disapprobation.

" The Crawler," as he was called, fitly and justly, it would seem, from his past career, was so ostentatious and overbearing to the rest of the ship's crew of his own class of boys ; his mind seemed to be so much bent on fomenting quarrels, and creating disturbances where harmony might otherwise exist ; he was so treacherous and knavish with all, that the universal sentiment of the whole ship's company was against him, and many an old tar grunted with satisfaction when informed that the Crawler was to be sent to a receiving ship when the Thunderer was paid off, without liberty, and deprived of prize money.

A different feeling was manifested towards Harleck, both by men and officers.

They knew that he was a pressed man, and endeavoured to smooth away from his mind all unpleasantness that might arise from the degradation of a pressed man, and one who had been tied up to the gratings.

It mattered little what might be done for him or said of him, he was Harleck still, dull, morose, unforgiving, and vindictive.

There were other pressed men on board, truly, but they had gradually become reconciled to their lot, and made the best of seamen.

Such, therefore, of them, who had forgotten old sores, so to speak, and amalgamated fully with the crew, were treated with the same respect, and with the same chance of promotion as those who had been years in the service, and voluntarily entered it.

When, therefore, the Thunderer was paid off,

Harleck, the Crawler, and some few other malcontents were unceremoniously transferred to the receiving ship, there to await whatever calls the fleet might make upon it, making up the full complement of various crews.

"'Tis rather hard, you know, lieutenant," said Konks to Lieutenant Armitage, whom he met in the street. "Rather hard, sir, that, just come into port, you know, sir, with colours all flying, and prizes in tow ; rather hard, you know, sir, to be shipped off to a receiving hulk without liberty or nothing."

"True, Konks ; but what must we do ? Harleck, no doubt, is capable of becoming a first-class seaman and gunner ; but he is a pressed man. We have tried all we know to make him comfortable on board, but he's always that surly, sour-looking fellow that we saw t'other day. Discipline must be maintained, Konks, you know, and if the king wants men to man his ships, why, if we can't get volunteers, we must be content to go ashore and press a few ; most pressed men make capital sailors, I find."

"Yes, yes, lieutenant ; but I think the kings and all our admirals would get much better men, sir, and a great number too, if they'd only provide some snug harbour for them when unfit for service. Look at me, lieutenant, I know the time that you came on board the Thunderer quite a little lad—many a year ago. Well, sir, I was an ordinary seaman then, and I'm not much better now. If you liked, you know, sir, you could get rid of active service and retire ; if you were to loose a leg, or arm, or anything of that sort, why then you would receive a capital pension, and could lay up in ordinary for the rest of your life ; but look at me, if I were to lose a leg or two, why then they'd say, 'Konks, old boy, you ain't fit for any further service.' We'll make you a present of your discharge,' and with a silver medal or two, and a few pounds, they'd turn me adrift to beg, or go through the town chanting ballads, a penny each."

"It isn't always so. Come, come, Konks, you must not feel mutinous, and cry out against King and country, there's plenty doing that sort of thing already."

"Yes, true, lieutenant, ; but what I complain of, and a good many more too, is this here—why not follow the advice of brave Nelson, and provide something good for disabled seamen ?—why not dock the salaries of many a hundred who never face the enemy at all, and give it to them as do ? that's what I say, and so does Hawser and all of us."

"Isn't there Greenwich Hospital ?"

"Aye, aye, sir ; but how many of us get into such snug moorings as that ? If, instead of pressing men into a service they don't like, they'd hold out some prospect for them when they got old and shaky in their timbers, you'd find the King's ships wouldn't be long out of commission for want of jolly, and brave-hearted lads, ready and anxious to man them."

"Well, never mind grumbling, Konks, my old boy. If goverment don't take sufficient care of her gallant boys, I'm sure the nation fully appreciates us."

"Aye, sir ; but that's rather hard tack for a fellow to feed on when he goes limping around the country on crutches singing ballads penny each, and with no place to sling your hammock for the night without paying for it in advance."

"Well, well, my lad, don't let us grumble. Let's go into this public and have a stiff glass together. Who knows, you may be an admiral yet."

"Not very likely, lieutenant, there may be some chance for those on the quarter-deck, but very

little for those in the forecastle. But, split my sid if there ain't Hawser and Juniper in that the parlor, blowing tobacco like fury ; let's go in."

Armitage and Konks entered without being pe ceived, and that gallant young officer slapped old shipmates on the back with much cordiali which surprised both old salts very much, who ro and doffed their caps with every token of profou respect, at the same time proffering steaming glass of rum and water for their friend's acceptance.

CHAPTER LV.

EARL PENALVON PROCEEDS TO THE OLD HA
COTTAGE—NELLY BRITTON IN CLOSE CUSTODY
AGGER ON THE WATCH—THE COACHMAN'S SU
PICIONS AND REVELATIONS REGARDING EA
PENALVON, AND SEWARDINE—PENALVON'S COAC
MAN A MANIAC—THE REASONS WHY—WILD MI
THE HAG, AND AGGER—PAUL ADAIR RESCU
NELLY—DEATH OF WILD MEG.

WHEN Earl Penalvon's carriage had proceeded an hour or more at a rapid rate, he suddenly order his coachman to stop.

They had arrived at the lane which led to the hag's cottage.

Penalvon was not desirous that any of his or nary servants should be informed of his goings a comings, and for this purpose ordered them to aw his pleasure where the land intersected the ma road at right angles.

"John, stay you here until my return. I simp wish to walk along this pleasant lane for purpo of study and meditation ; if you are sent for, com

John the coachman looked at the footman in knowing manner.

They both knew, as, indeed, all the servants Seawardine did long before, that the movements the earl were very unaccountable, if not, in tru mysterious.

They also knew, of old, that any curiosity on th part would meet with instant dismissal from presence, for he would not even allow certain pa of his mansion to be explored, nor even clean except at certain times, and then only by the olde and most trustworthy of his servants.

"Very well, my lord," said the coachman, " will not even stir from this spot, my lord, until yo further orders."

"But who drove out the carriage last night asked the footman, when his master was out hearing. "It wasn't you."

"Me ! I think not, indeed. I don't know who drive the carriage last night. It wasn't this o but t'other that stands in the little coach house. went out about midnight with the pair of grey and a nice mess it's in ; all the wheels are clogg with dirt, and, as to the horses, why the greys lo as if they had been driven to death ; but that stan for nothing, you know we musn't whisper a syllable or off we go. The last coachman could tell a pret tale if he chose."

"What Thomas, who left when you came ?"

"Yes. Just after I came to Seawardine."

"What did he know so strange, then ?"

"A good many things ; more than I could ev get out of him, although I've given him many a p of beer, and tried to make him talk in his cups."

"Why did he leave ? What did the earl send hi away for ?"

"He didn't send him away ; Thomas wouldn

stay on no account. He said that Seawardine was haunted."

"He must have been a fool then. I've been there a long time now, and I can swear there isn't any such things as ghosts; I'll take my oath there ain't."

"Don't take any oaths about it. I dare say Thomas was in service as many years as you've been weeks at Seawardine, for the earl don't keep his servants long, particularly when they keep their eyes and ears open a little too far for him."

"Well, but what had Thomas got to say about master?"

"Oh! lots of things. He used to go on awful sometimes when he had a drop of drink. He is in the madhouse now."

"Madhouse!"

"Aye, sure; mad as a March hare, so they tell me."

"Who put him in there, then?"

"Why the lord, to be sure. Who else would trouble themselves about it?"

"And what made him mad?"

"Don't I tell you? He used to say strange things about master, and swear the house was haunted."

"And was that the reason?"

"Truly it was; and, if half be true what he told me, it would have turned *my* head, let alone turning his?"

"And what was it?"

"What was it! You won't whisper a word?"

"Me? Of course not."

"Not to any one? Not even to cook or the housemaid?"

"No! on my honour as a footman."

"Well, then, old Thomas used to say that Earl Penalvon was no lord at all by right, but that he was nobody else than an imposter!"

"Lor!"

"A vagabond!"

"No!"

"And a murderer!"

"The devil!" said the footman in alarm. "A murderer! No, you don't mean to say that?"

"But I do though. He was mad."

"Of course! He must have been to say such things against Earl Penalvon."

"At least, my lord used to say so; but I always took notice that the earl used to shun him when he had a little too much malt in him."

"And he didn't discharge him?"

"Discharge him? No, lad. Why, old Thomas used to go up to his library, and demand two or three guineas at a time; and my lord never refused him, but gave him whatever he wanted, provided he would not remain in the neighbourhood of Seawardine during his sprees."

"And where used he to go to, then?"

"Why, to the very place where master has gone, I suppose; some out-of-the-way spot, where no one knows or heeds him."

"But, what can be my lord's business in such a place?"

"Ah, there you ask too much! That's what I would like to know; but he never took me there, nor anywhere particular. But Thomas used to go about with him as close as a dog at his heels, for master couldn't shake him off do what he would."

"And what did he use to say?"

"Well, he used to rave, and I often used to hear him talking in his sleep about Wild Meg, Thorkil, Lady Julia, and Earl Penalvon, my lord's elder brother, who so suddenly died while out fishing one day."

"But, what was all this?"

"Nothing much as it was, but when he told his rambling tale, it used to make me start up in my bed and look at him; but there he lay fast asleep, and not more aware of what he was saying than the man in the moon."

"But, what was it he did say?" asked the footman, looking very anxious to hear more.

"Won't tell?"

"On my honour."

"Sure?"

"Certain."

"Well, Thomas one night brought master home very late, and Thomas was so drunk he could scarce sit on the box. I was acting as footman then.

"'What makes you drink so much, Thomas?' says my lord, very drily.

"'Oh, nothing particular!' says Thomas, grumpy like. 'Because I like it, I suppose; that's why.'

"'That's no way to speak to me,' says my lord. 'For a button I would knock you off the box!'

"'Do it!' says Thomas, bouncing. 'I shall not be the first man that you knocked over,' says old Thomas, winking at my lord, and rubbing his nose."

"But what did my lord do?" asked the footman.

"Do?" answered the coachman. "Why, nothing. He only laughed like; but I saw that he didn't like it. So that night my lord calls me up into his study.

"'John,' says he, 'has Thomas been saying anything to you?'

"'No, my lord,' says I.

"'Are you sure, quite sure?' he says, looking straight into my face, as if he'd search the very bottom of my heart.

"'Quite sure,' I said.

"'I'm glad of that, John,' he said, smiling, 'because Thomas has been in my service a very long time, and I shouldn't like to part with him, although he does talk so ramblingly occasionally. Haven't you heard any of his strange stories, John?'

"'No, my lord, I haven't, I can assure you.'

"'Strange,' he says, walking about his room, thoughtfully, 'do you occupy the same room as you formerly did at my desire?'

"'I do, my lord,' I says.

"'Your beds are close together, you say, in the same room in fact, and yet you hear nothing of what he says in his sleep?'

"'Quite sure, my lord.'

"'If he does chatter nonsense, John, stop him, wake him up; don't let his old addled brains go wandering, for if he goes on much more, I fear we must place him in a lunatic asylum.'

"That same night when Thomas went to bed, I thought I'd lay awake and hear what he did say."

"Did he talk in his sleep?"

"Oh, he was a famous hand for that when half-drunk; so, to make sure, I gives him a good glass of hot rum and water, and he wasn't in bed more than half-an-hour, when off he goes into a long rigmarole about Wild Meg, Thorkil, Lady Julia, and other things.

"'Dismiss me, will you, eh, my lord?' said he, grinding his teeth. 'I'd like to see you doing it, that's all, my lord. I've got just as much right at Seawardine as you have, and you know it; give me ten guineas to go on a spree, and I won't say another word.'

"After a time he begins to laugh and sing. Then he begins talking again. 'Who'd a thought it?

He an earl too ! What a jolly spree ! If the world only knew all about it, though ; if they only knew where the Lady Julia went to, wouldn't there be a fine hanging scrape ? Well, old Meg knows something about that job ; if she would open her lips, now, it would seal somebody else's besides her own. The poor lady !' he would go on, 'it was a great pity, though, so young and so pretty ; and he would dismiss me, would he, after all that ? I'd like to see him do it. I have driven one corpse to Seawardine, I might drive another from it. You wouldn't be able to hide it in the vaults, and keep the keys, clever as you are. Dismiss me, eh ? So you are going to remove it to your library or museum, are you ? Well, you had better do something with it, it can't tell tales now, there's nothing but white bones left, poor young lady.'"

"Well, what did you imagine he meant by all this talking ?" the footman asked, looking pale and fearful. "You did not suppose for a moment that he accused my lord of anything wrong ?"

"No, I didn't suppose anything. It wasn't my game to suppose anything, you know," said John, the coachman, winking at the footman. "It ain't the place of a good servant, with a good situation, and a good pension in old age, to imagine, let alone suspect, any wrong of my lord his master."

"True," said the footman, "particularly when the grub and pay is good, and little to do, and a good pension in store for faithful servants."

"Just so ; and so next evening, 'My lord,' says I, 'could I speak with you ?'

"'With me, John?' says my lord, surprised. 'Oh, certainly ! Come this way,' he said, 'to the library ; shut the door close, John. And now,' says he, sitting in his easy chair, and playing with his fingers, 'what is it you wish to speak to me about ?'

"It took me much time to explain what I meant ; so after I tells him about Thomas getting drunk and raving in his sleep, my lord's face turns very red and then very pale, and he smiles. You know how he smiles, pressing his lips and biting them till they gets blue again ?

"'Well, John,' says he, 'you say you can't make anything out of Thomas's disordered mental drunken wanderings ; nor more can I. But, do you know—can you imagine anything about this Wild Meg, or this Lady—this Lady—Julia, as he calls her ? Do you form any notions regarding them ? Of course not,' he says, walking about looking awfully annoyed and fretful, 'of course not, nor of this unknown person he calls Thorkil, or the deceased Earl Penalvon ?'

"'No, my lord,' I says, nor more did I.

"'Well,' he says, 'I have had Thomas in my employ many years, and have put up with his nonsense too long. He is demented. He must be looked after. We cannot allow a crazy man to be loose in our household ; he might occasion much mischief and annoyance to all. So, therefore, we must take care of him.'"

"And what did my Lord Penalvon do with him ?"

"Do with him ! Why, next morning Thomas was locked up in one of the strong vaults under the house, and no one was allowed to go near him but master and me."

"Did he go on raving much ?"

"I believe you, he did. If he wasn't crazy before he soon became so, for in less than a month, he was clean gone, and as mad as ever a Bedlamite could be. Oh, what a jolly row he made, to be sure. You never heard such a noise as he made in that cell, and of all the awful stories he told of master, and his goings on at Wild Meg's and at Seawardine,

it would make your hair stand on end to listen to him."

"What did master do with him ?"

"Oh, he was very kind, and used to smile, and went to see him every day. When Thomas clapped eyes on him though, didn't he swear ? 'You are a liar, a thief, and a robber,' he used to say.

"'Mad, you see, John,' master would say, 'mad, you see, John ; quite gone in intellect.'

"'Liar !' roared Thomas, till the vaults re-echoed again. 'Liar ! You know I'm not mad ; you know what I say is true. You are a murderer ; you know it. The bones of your innocent victims are buried not far off.'

"My lord would smile, and sometimes laughed right out, as he said, 'Poor Thomas, I always thought that too much kindness and too much drink, would turn his head. Give him something to eat, John,' he would say, mildly ; 'take care he don't bite or scra'ch you. He's mad, you see ; gone, you see, John ; gone you know, beyond all redemption,' and whenever he turned to leave the grating of the vault Thomas used to rush at it, as if he could tear down the bars with his teeth and hands, so mad was he."

"And what became of him ?" asked the footman.

"Oh, after a few months, he was removed to a private asylum, where he lingered for a few weeks, and died."

"And what did people say ?"

"Say ? What could they say, but that Earl Penalvon had acted very wisely and charitably with his old servant, and deserved all manner of honour for his liberality and magnanimity of heart. Oh, the master is thought a good deal of around Seawardine, I can tell you."

"But what brings him so far away from home to-day ?"

"Didn't he tell you he wishes to meditate and enjoy a quiet walk along these quiet green lanes, that's all. I don't care what he does, or where he goes, as long as he keeps me comfortable. Always speak well of the bridge that carries you over, that's my motto, and always has been."

While Earl Penalvon's servants were busily conversing, the earl himself walked thoughtfully and lowly towards Wild Meg's lonely cottage.

He was deep in thought, and a smile of triumph lit his face as he stood and gazed at the distant cottage, from which wreaths of smoke were curling.

"And Otho," he mused, "I wonder how he performed his office. Did the wench resist much, I wonder ? Ha, ha ! all her resistance is vain when once under Wild Meg's roof. I know her of old ; she was fitted for a tiger-tamer more than aught else. Well, I must reward her well ; she has been faithful to my whims and wishes ; she has been, moreover, _silent_, which is the chief thing, hence I must not forget her."

While Earl Penalvon was slowly approaching Wild Meg's cottage, and meditating calmly on the lovely prospects scattered by bounteous nature hither and thither, on either hand of the copse-fringed road, Wild Meg in her cottage was in an unusually fierce temper, and raised her hand over Nelly Britton in a threatening manner.

"Nay, you must not strike her," said Agger.

"Must not !" said Meg, with a blood-shot eye, flashing with anger. "Must not ! Who stays me if I would ?"

"I will."

"You ! you are a pretty fellow to do Penalvon's

bidding. Where on earth did he pick up such a puling fellow as Otho?"

"Never mind you about Otho," Agger replied; "keep your hand off the girl. Remember, she is *my* charge, not yours."

"Yours! ha, ha! Think you I know not why she was sent hither?—her bright, curly locks, and tear-moistened eyes of blue—ha, ha! Think you I have never seen the likes here before?"

"It matters not why nor wherefore that she came here, but this it is, that you must not use violence with her, at least, not while I am here."

"Then why does she not follow my bidding?"

"Go to your room, girl," said Agger, in a semi-authoritative tone, which Nelly fully understood. "Go to your room, and stay until I call you."

"Why does she not do *my* bidding?" roared the old hag, whose small black eyes flashed with half-drunken rage and vexation. "Why not obey me, I ask? Are you superior to me? Is this my house or yours, pray? Ho, ho! I begin to think that Earl Penalvon has made an error here; he knows not who you are, perhaps. Beware, young man, what you do! Beware, I tell you! Pull the mask from your face, if you wear one, as I suspect, for if you play false to me and Penalvon it's more than your life is worth."

"What do you speak of, old woman?" Agger replied, with firmness, and with a smile of indifference. "You know my orders, perhaps? I am a friend of Earl Penalvon's, that's all; I execute his orders merely, and my name is Otho. Come, no more quarrelling; pass that bottle of rum, you have had more than your share out of it."

His free and indifferent manner completely disarmed Wild Meg's suspicions, who sat opposite to him and began to shriek out all manner of strange speeches.

"She obeys you, it seems, and will not me. Well, we shall see. I have more ways than one to curb her little temper. She is no lady that she need put on such fine stuck-up manners. I'll break her back for her, the little vixen, if she doesn't obey me; she is only a commoner. Think you I don't know why she was sent hither? She ought to feel grateful that a nobleman like Earl Penalvon has cast longing eyes upon her. I was young myself once, and *I* didn't give way to such tantrums. Why don't she dress herself in the silks he sent for her? Does she expect he will befriend her as she is? Why don't she spruce up and make herself agreeable then? Why, he will be here to-day."

"Who?" asked Agger.

"Who! Why, who did you suppose?"

"Oh, no one in particular."

"Why, Penalvon, of course. He'll pay you well for your trouble, young man, never fear; he's not stingy with his money. Did you sleep well last night?"

"No. Why do you ask?"

"Nor I. I have been here alone in this cottage many a year, but I never felt so troubled in dreams before, not in my whole life."

"Why, what should trouble your dreams? You haven't killed any one in your time, have you, that your sleep should be disturbed by phantoms and hobgoblins?"

"Never you mind what I've done in my time, it concerns not you, that I am aware; but suffice it that my sleep *was* disturbed, and strangely too. Did you hear any noises around the cottage?"

"Noises?" asked Agger, with an ill-suppressed smile and well-studied imperturbability of manner. "Noises! No. I only heard the winds shaking the ivy about the house."

"No tapping at the windows or shutters?"

"No."

"Well, I did: and I never hear it but I know that mischief is brewing somewhere."

"Oh, you are superstitious; you are like Thyra and Hylda, two rune-kenners that live in our neighbourhood; they frighten all the wreckers and smugglers round our coast by their strange predictions."

"And you do not believe them?"

"No. Why should I?"

"But I do. One foretold my end."

"Your end! What was it then?" asked Agger, suddenly stopping smoking.

"I went to the White Cliffs one morning, and saw, sitting on a rock, a girl with dark hair and pale face."

"'Twas Thyra!" said Agger, in surprise.

"I know not who it was," said the hag, in a subdued tone of voice, "but she knew me and called me by name."

"And what was that?"

"It matters not to you. 'Go home,' said the girl, 'and pray. Make your peace with heaven; your time is short, your days are numbered.'"

"What meant she?" Agger asked, with open eyes and much curiosity of manner.

"Listen. 'Get you home, the farther you go from Seawardine the happier you. Have no more to do with the man who lives there; he is a whitened sepulchre, his crimes fasten on to and fester in your flesh.' 'Who are you, girl, that speaks thus,' I asked?"

"'No one that you know or care for,' was the answer. 'Get you home; a maid and youth shall shelter 'neath your roof, men shall sleep beneath the floor, your windows shall shake, and your home shall burn while your heart's blood shall flow in the miry ditch.'"

"This was all she said?" asked Agger.

"It was."

"And how long since was this?"

"A year or more."

"But you don't believe it?"

"I cannot, will not," said Wild Meg, laughing hysterically.

"Yours has been a wild and merry life, Meg," said Agger, thoughtfully.

"Why should it not? Earl Penalvon is all in all to me; I never wanted aught since I knew him."

"Nor did he a friend. But what did you, to so merit his bounty and protection?"

"Would you wish to pry into my heart and see?" asked Meg, with a grim smile.

While she spoke, some one tapped at the door.

"'Tis he," said Meg, hurriedly hiding her bottle of rum, and opening the door.

"Welcome, a hundred welcomes," said Meg, bowing obsequiously to Earl Penalvon, as he slowly entered the cottage, and cast his eyes furtively in all parts of the room, as if suspecting that some one unseen lurked in the corners, hidden by the shadows.

"Otho?"

"The same, sir," answered Agger, laying particular stress upon the "sir," which seemed to please the nobleman, who intelligently nodded in approval.

"Otho, you have fulfilled your task?"

"Yes, sir."

"The little one is safe?"

"Perfectly, sir," he answered.

"But not fit to present to you, yet," said Wild Meg.

"Hush, woman!" peevishly spoke Penalvon. "She made no resistance?"

"Not in the least, sir, but seemed rather pleased

to find herself in such pleasant company, particularly when I explained to her fully your liberal intentions towards her."

"Indeed," said Penalvon, pleased and surprised. "Meg, this was more than I dared to expect."

"'Tis truth, sir, believe me ; she came without violence or resistance ; save a maiden's tears there was naught to mar her prospective happiness."

"Do you know her ?" asked Penalvon, looking fixedly at Agger.

"I, sir, I know her ?" said Agger, in well feigned surprise. "I know nothing of her ; we are perfect strangers."

"'Tis well you say so, young man ; I believe you, yet now I look upon you by daylight methinks you are not the person described to me so well by Thorkil."

"The same, sir, believe me."

"Then must Thorkil have been tipsy, for he spoke to me of one he hated much, and his description resembles you ?"

"He must have lied, then, sir, or been beastly drunk, for I am no other than Otho."

"Then, Otho, you may leave us ; go to the lane's end, bid my carriage approach within a stone's throw of the house.

"Have you marked her well, Meg ?" asked Penalvon, when Agger had departed.

"I have. A pretty wench enough ; but what a difference to the Lady Ju——"

"Hush, woman ! Will you for ever prate of her that's now long dead ?"

"Dead ?" asked Meg, with an incredulous smile.

"Dead ! aye, dead ! Will you not believe it ?"

"I must, I suppose, for I never heard of her since that night."

"And why should you ? What concerns it you to know or pry into my affairs ? I have potent reasons for all I do ; further than this it would be dangerous to inquire."

"As you please ; but what, then, is your present pleasure ?"

"Leave that to me. Where is our fair prize ?"

"In yonder room," said Meg, pointing.

"Sleeping ?"

"Sleeping ! No, not she ; she has not closed her eyes since she came, her eyes are red as live coals from weeping."

"We can soon alter that."

"I could if I had my way."

"But you must not ; you must leave this matter to me. It is not appetite alone that prompts me, there is something more potent still that actuates my desire ; revenge, Meg, and you know that I was never yet thwarted in that, cost what it might."

"Revenge against whom ?"

"My bitterest enemy."

"A noble ?"

"No, an outcast, a candidate for any gibbet five minutes after I have secured him."

"And who may he be, this worthless fellow that hunts and haunts the mighty Earl Penalvon?" asked Meg, with a smile, as she gazed on the icy expressionless countenance of her visitor.

"Paul Adair."

"Adair !" Meg almost gasped, as she rose from her seat, turning pale. "Paul Adair ?"

"Adair, aye ; what of him? is he one of thy friends, then ? Speak, I say, you haggard hell-hound ; have I had thee in my keeping for twenty years that you should harbour aught of any one that I knew not ?"

Meg sank upon her seat, and for a moment remained silent.

Removing her hands from her face she gazed upon Earl Penalvon, and both sat mutely scanning each other's countenance.

"No, I do not know him," she said, with an evident struggle to explain herself, "and if I did he would be henceforth an enemy of mine since he is one of yours."

"I am satisfied. Here is a drug, you know how to use it ; make her swallow a mouthful of wine."

Doing as bidden, Wild Meg entered Nelly's room. Nelly was awake, but lay upon her couch, pale and faint with watching.

The old hag smiled and retired.

"'Tis useless to persuade her," she said, "a handkerchief will do."

Taking a handkerchief from her pocket she poured something upon it, and re-entered the room.

"You have been weeping, my poor child," said Meg, in tones of well-affected commiseration. "Dry your eyes, my child," and suiting the action to the word, she wiped Nelly's eyes, and the unconscious girl was almost instantaneously overcome with ether, and fell back upon the couch, with a moan of bitterness and helplessness.

"'Tis done," said Meg, returning to Penalvon, with a wild look of triumph in her flashing eyes. "'Tis done ! potent as ever. Go and take revenge."

Penalvon rose, and went towards Nelly's door.

His steps resembled those of a sneaking thief more than that of a nobleman.

He looked from side to side, as if expecting to meet some phantom, ready to thwart his pleasure and hellish designs.

The rustling of the ivy round Meg's cottage sent a thrill through his frame, and made the blood course through his veins like icicles.

His whole frame shook, and his nerves quivered like a wind-shaken reed.

He saw his prey lying helplessly and unconsciously before him, in all the unhidden charms of maidenhood and virtue.

His lustful eyes gloated with fiendish and tremulous desire, yet though impelled by unseen influences to behold the object of his unmanly revenge, although standing on the threshold of her room, of her for whom he had so long lustfully and unlawfully desired, he seemed unable to proceed a single step further, but stood transfixed with mingled fear and admiration.

Wild Meg watched his stealthy, cat-like movements with looks of womanly derision ; her eyes seemed all aglow with fiendish pleasure and delight.

One moment more of hesitation, and Earl Penalvon entered Nelly's room.

He approached the sleeper, and would have laid unholy hands upon her, but he staggered back from a blow that was given from an unseen hand.

He had not come unarmed, and drew his pistols. The sudden commotion aroused the hag, who rushed to Nelly's room.

"Treachery ! betrayed ! Vile woman, I am betrayed !" Penalvon shouted, and to defend himself against the half dozen or more smugglers, who rushed from beneath the bed, sword in hand, he fired his pistols.

A loud scream responded to his shot, and Meg rushed from the cottage, streaming with blood.

Drawing his sword with a desperate valour, Earl Penalvon laid low more than one of those who opposed his exit, until a youth, powerful and brave, rushed upon him.

"Paul Adair !" gasped Penalvon, rushing upon him.

"I am," was the response, and the next moment the nobleman lay weltering in his gore, while Paul

Adair, picking up the unharmed and unconscious body of Nelly Britton, rushed from the house, which had been set fire to by his exasperated and desperate followers.

Agger, whose mission it was to call Earl Penalvon's carriage, had so arranged his plan that the vehicle might not be very far off when Nelly's rescue should ensue, which, by preconcerted arrangement, he knew would take place, for the taps at the window during the night warned him of the presence of friends, and while Wild Meg slept, unconscious of harm, he had opened Nelly's bedroom window, through which had passed some half dozen or more of Paul Adair's followers, including Paul himself, who patiently waited until a fitting moment to take revenge upon Penalvon.

When, therefore, Paul rushed from the burning house, with Nelly in his arms, the coach was seized by Agger and others, who opened the door for Paul, who, placing Nelly therein, knocked Penalvon's coachman from his place, and drove off, amid the cheers of his followers, who were yelling with delight at the timely and signal rescue of the sweetheart of their chief.

CHAPTER LVI.

THE END OF WILD MEG, THE HAG—DESTRUCTION OF HER HOME BY FLAMES—THE NARROW ESCAPE OF EARL PENALVON—PAUL ADAIR AND NELLY BRITTON—HELP FROM SEAWARDINE.

THE sudden appearance of Paul Adair and some few of his followers would seem unaccountable were it not known that they were in the habit of frequenting the neighbourhood of Wild Meg's cottage for the purpose of secreting goods and treasure.

On the night, therefore, that the coach drew up to Meg's door, several of Adair's followers were loitering about, and being attracted by the appearance of such an elegant vehicle stopping in such an out-of-the-way place, they watched, and satisfied themselves of the fact that it was not only Earl Penalvon's carriage, but that it also contained a female, whose voice and manner betrayed her repugnance and unwillingness to alight.

When all was still, they approached the cottage unobserved.

Peeping through the blinds, they recognised the features of Agger, disguised as he was in livery, and knowing him to be a professed friend of Paul Adair, they signalled with taps upon the shutters, and a series of low whistles, which to untutored ears would sound nothing unlike the night wind, but which, to a weather-beaten wrecker and smuggler as Agger was, convinced him that he had been watched.

When, therefore, Nelly retired for the night, Agger opened her chamber window ajar, and conferred with Adair's men, to whom he explained everything.

Their surprise was great. They had not visited the locality on that night with the remotest idea of what was transpiring ; but as soon as informed of Penalvon's intention, and of the dangerous though magnanimous part Agger was playing, some hurried away to the coast, and informed Adair.

That hot-headed, chivalric smuggler rushed to the spot with the swiftness of the wind, and Agger let them in, unknown to Meg, who, half-stupefied by rum and tobacco, sat in her chair soundly sleeping and snoring.

Secreting themselves beneath Nelly's bed, Paul

Adair and some half-dozen of his chosen followers, waited for the moment of Earl Penalvon's arrival.

It was their intention to capture that nobleman alive, and bear him off to the sea coast, where they might not only punish him for his temerity and guilt, but also impose a heavy sum as the price of his liberation.

His desperate resistance, and the sad havoc the nobleman made among his followers, for a moment disconcerted Adair's coolly laid plans.

The unaccountable calamity to Wild Meg struck him with surprise, for he imagined, and truly, that she was in league with, and the willing instrument of Earl Penalvon in all his past and present schemes of heartless villany.

That he should turn his pistol against her instead of them, struck him with surprise.

Penalvon, however, had a motive in this.

He believed that Wild Meg had concerted with the smugglers to entrap him and rescue Nelly Britton, and he knew besides that she was mistress of so many secrets concerning him and the mysteries of Seawardine, that, should he fall in the encounter, Wild Meg perhaps might reveal all she knew concerning him.

Despite his own personal peril, Paul Adair would fain have suffered wounds himself rather than have Penalvon hopelessly wounded ; but when he perceived the deadly hatred that was in the nobleman's eye when they met face to face, and when he saw the eagerness with which he rushed upon him in the first moments of the fray, he was obliged, for self-protection, to strike him to the earth.

Seizing the unconscious girl, he rushed from the burning cottage, and having secured the earl's carriage, made his way from the scene of conflict in perfect safety, fully believing that both the hag, Wild Meg, and the earl were numbered with the dead, and might be consumed in the conflagration of the dwelling.

His followers, excluding Agger, departed from the scene, in obedience to his orders, while Earl Penalvon's coachman and footman, more terrified than hurt, rushed from the scene of strife in dire alarm, fully satisfied with the kicks and cuffs which Agger and others freely bestowed upon them.

But, contrary to the expectation and wishes of all, Earl Penalvon was not dead.

The blow which felled him to the floor, and the repeated kicks which he received, while prostrate, from the infuriated smugglers, had rendered him insensible indeed to all that was passing around him. He bled profusely from wounds about the head, and his sword lay in fragments beside him, but, when the flames had reached Nelly's chamber, in which he lay, the heat aroused him to a sense of consciousness of his imminent peril, and he aroused himself sufficiently to stagger to the back door and rush, half-frantically, from the flames and crackling roof which every moment threatened to bury and consume him.

Crawling beneath some adjacent shrubbery he lay in pain and agony, a sad witness to the vengeance which had befallen his many crimes and iniquities.

Yet he repented not. His heart was more stony than ever, and, as he writhed in pain from severe wounds, he gnashed his teeth in ungovernable rage, and resolved that, if life was spared him, he would dedicate it to purposes of revenge on Paul Adair, and all who had been concerned in his humiliation and shame.

As he lay moaning he thought of the fate of Wild Meg, the hag. He wished and hoped in his secret soul that she had met her death at his hands, but knew not whether she lived or not.

In a ditch not far from him poor Meg lay writhing in the agonies of death.

Penalvon's shot had proved effective ; it had entered the left breast near the region of the heart, and blood poured from her in purple streams.

She had rushed from the house, screaming with terror and pain.

She staggered as best she could from the scene of conflict, and thought, from the suddenness of the tumult and uproar, that Heaven itself, perhaps, had sent ministering spirits to suddenly avenge and stay for ever her career of crime.

With mind well nigh deranged she gasped in the agonies and throes of death, and fainting, as she moved faintly step by step, she fell into a dry ditch or trench that ran beside her cottage.

Her screams subsided. She had not strength to cry aloud, but, in despair at the thought of her untimely fate, she moaned aloud, and cursed, with bitterest imprecations, the cause of all her wrongdoings and long life of iniquity.

"Who is that ?" asked Penalvon, faintly, as he heard her voice blaspheming the name of her Maker. "Who can that be that is dying ?"

The voice of Meg was audible to him as he lay crouched beneath the shrubbery.

"It is Meg," he thought. "Oh, that it had been Paul or Nelly, and then I should have felt satisfied—delighted."

It was not to be, however.

He still listened to the hag's fearful words ; but at last all was silent, her voice was hushed.

With all the strength that remained to him he dragged himself to the ditch and gazed.

There lay Wild Meg, the hag, in a pool of blood.

Her hair was matted with gore, her face was of ashy paleness.

Her form was curled up as if she had expired in the greatest imaginable torture.

Her eyes were fixed in a horrid stare, and glared at him with stony fixedness.

Her hands were upraised and clenched as if in the act of invoking maledictions on him.

He gazed for a moment, and, bleeding and faint as he was, he felt his heart-strings quiver with horror as he looked upon the one who had been the partner in all his past wickedness and crime.

He shrank from the contemplation of the scene with feelings of intensified horror.

He lay concealed beneath the bushes and shrubbery of the garden.

The flames ravenously devoured the entire dwelling, and Earl Penalvon, from his place of covert, saw the beams give way, heard the roof crash and fall, and soon naught remained of the scene of his many debaucheries and crimes but four bare walls that were red and aglow with intense heat.

So that he lived he cared not.

That his servants would, sooner or later, return to learn his fate, he felt more than certain.

"Once more at Seawardine, he thought, and all will be well. I live no more for pleasures, but for sweet revenge, and if there be power in wealth, influence, or station, I will hunt the coast both far and near to ferret out each and every one of the vile rascals who have brought me to this my present pitiable plight and pain."

Binding up and staunching his wounds as best he could, he remained where he was until evening came.

The sun was low, and birds flew hither and thither as if afraid to approach the smouldering ruins of Wild Meg's cot.

As the moon slowly rose over the distant hills the rumble of carriage wheels fell upon Earl Penalvon's ear.

"Thank Heaven, it is help !" he sighed.

He could say no more ; strength, at last, had failed him, and he sank back upon the garden sward helpless in a swoon.

He had not long so remained, when the sounds of carriage wheels and the tramp of mounted men became more audible each instant.

"This is the place," said one of those who arrived with the carriage, "this is the cottage that was attacked."

Dismounting, they instituted a strict search all about the premises, and, at last, John the coachman discovered Penalvon lying all bloody and helpless.

His shouts and cries soon brought around him all the servants, who raised their hands and eyes in pious horror and astonishment at the sight which the unconscious nobleman presented.

Lifting him carefully from his recumbent position the servants placed him in the carriage, and it drove off as rapidly as possible in the direction of Seawardine.

"But, who is this ?" asked one of the servants who yet remained behind. "Why, here's a woman lying dead in the ditch."

Some fellow-servants soon gathered around him and, between them, they lifted the dead body of Wild Meg from the dry ditch in which it lay, and placed her full length upon the grass.

"Who can she be ?" asked one.

"Can't tell," said another.

"The whole affair seems wrapped in mystery. Perhaps master could explain everything ; but there's not much likelihood of that at present, for he seemed more dead than alive when we lifted him into the carriage, and was perfectly unconscious."

"Well, it is a bad business," said the first speaker "but I wouldn't give many pins for the life of any of them that was concerned in this affair if Earl Penalvon only recovers."

"True, lads ; they will have to pay dearly for all this, you may depend, and if any of the wreckers hereabouts are concerned in it, you may be certain the whole of the King's navy will be soon about the whole coast, and blow every cliff down to the ground, but they will unearth the vile scoundrels who did this."

"Let us take the body to the next village, and send for the coroner."

"Well said, that's all we can do. But, Lord ! what a frightful mess she's in, to be sure. I never saw such a hideous-looking sight in all my life."

"Well, 'tis no use of talking, lads ; we must remove her from this, for if she remains here all night the rats will devour her."

"That's all she seems fitted for, judging from what she looks like."

"Why, now I come to look at her closely, she looks like old Meg—Wild Meg, as she was called."

"Aye, truly, so she does, and an awful old witch she was, so I hear from all accounts—the very terror of all the lasses hereabouts."

"But how did she live ?"

"No one knows. She had a comfortable home, it seems, judging by what remains of it ; but what a careworn, hang-dog look she has, to be sure."

"Well, lads, it's no use of wasting words ; we can't discover anybody else about here. So I suppose the best thing to be done is to sling her across a horse, and take her to Seawardine, and then call in the coroner."

THE DUEL.

"True, lads; but what's this she's got in her pocket? Why, a bundle of letters."

"Give them to me," said the first speaker, who was Earl Penalvon's butler. "Give them to me; when master recovers he may make out what they all mean. That's the best thing we can do."

All the servants concurred in the butler's view of things, who took charge of the bundle of letters, and would allow no one to examine them, for, from the superscriptions, he judged they were in the handwriting of Earl Penalvon himself.

The wary butler did not mention this fact to his fellow servants, nor did he reveal any of his suspicions to them regarding his notions that intercourse of some character had existed between Wild Meg, the hag, and his master.

He saw the body of the woman placed sackwise across a horse, and followed it on its way to Seavardine, saying but little, but revolving in his mind all manner of strange conjectures which recurred to him from time to time owing to the mysterious ways and habits of his wealthy master.

CHAPTER LVII.

THE MIDSHIPMEN AT THE KIDDLEAWINK—THYRA TELLS THEIR FORTUNES—FRANK RAYNER IS TO BE A CAPTAIN, AND REJOICE IN A WOODEN LEG AT GREENWICH HOSPITAL—HARRY HALLIARD IT IS FORETOLD WILL GO TO COURT IN A NOBLEMAN'S COACH—POLRUTH, AFTER HIS JOLLIFICATION, INDULGES IN PIOUS MEDITATIONS—HARRY EMBRACES HIS MOTHER.

WHEN Harry Halliard and Frank Rayner awoke from their pleasant slumbers in the kiddleawink, after the night's rioting and jollification with Polruth's noisy and numerous company, they had unmistakable signs of terrible thirst, accompanied with brain-splitting headache.

They yawned and yawned, and soon emptied the ewer of water which Thyra had thoughtfully placed on the wash-stand.

Descending to the tap early, they found Polruth still fast asleep against the door, pipe in mouth, and bottle in hand.

Here and there were scattered a prostrate form, snoring on benches or on the floor, among the *debris* of the previous evening's entertainment.

The sun was shining through the interstices of the shutters, and cocks were lustily crowing in the garden, in the yards, and on the heath.

Peeping into the back parlour, they saw Thyra sitting fast asleep before a pleasant fire, on which a large tea-kettle was spluttering and boiling.

The little table was neatly laid for breakfast, and bread and butter, eggs and bacon, were all arranged in tempting display for breakfast.

"Poor girl!" said Frank, "she has scarcely slept all night, I am sure, and here she is ready for us with breakfast. What a good lass she is."

"Yes," said Harry, "and always was, Frank."

Without ceremony or hesitation Harry Halliard approached Thyra, and kissed her affectionately upon the cheek.

She awoke full of blushes and confusion, but smiled, as she extended her hand to the two friends who stood good-humouredly laughing at her.

"Good morning, Thyra," said Frank, "very kind of you to think of us so early."

"It is just like Thyra," said Harry, "she always was one of the strangest, kindest creatures that ever lived, and I know she has got a fine breakfast for us, haven't you, Thyra?"

"But why strange, Harry?" asked Thyra, pouring out the coffee, and frying rashers of bacon, "why am I strange?"

"Ah, that's what I cannot fathom, lass; but you are undoubtedly strange and unaccountable in your manners, as all must admit who know you."

"Well, but I simply follow the promptings of my mind, suggestions and promptings over which I can assure you I have seldom little or no controul."

"They say you can foretell fortunes, Thyra," said Frank, laughing, "and if that be so, you must know I am waiting very patiently for another piece of bacon and an egg."

"But, jokes aside, Frank; she can see farther into things than most people, I assure you, and I would rather meet Thyra with a smiling face than any-one's except——"

"Except whose," asked Thyra, thoughtfully, "your mother's, is it not so?"

"Yes; and tell me, dear Thyra, where she is; you say she is well, but why not tell me where she is?"

"You shall know in good time, Harry; I myself will conduct you to her, she is not far from here."

"But why did she remove? She could not have received my letters then."

"Yes she has, every one; I have managed that, and she is supremely happy, I know at this moment, in anticipation of your speedy visit."

Thyra looked very thoughtful, but seemed averse to speaking of family matters before a third person.

This was perceived by Frank who, to dispel the clouds that were gathering on Harry's brow, jocosely observed.

"Well, Thyra, as you can tell fortunes, tell me mine."

"Yours," said Thyra, smiling faintly, "yours, Frank, why that is plainly written on your face, and requires but little scrutiny to explain."

"Then, if it is so easy, let's have it, by all means. I'll give you a guinea, or more."

"Nay, I neither ask for, nor need money," answered Thyra, with a slight frown, "were it anyone else who spoke so, I should be offended. My friends, however—for you and Harry I know are true ones—may speak to Thyra as they please."

"Then forgive me, Thyra, and unlock your secrets.

Tell me, am I destined to find a sweetheart, to become a captain, or what? I feel awfully ambitious since Sir Everard Brandon made me a middy."

"You have already found the first," said Thyra, looking thoughtfully at the fire.

Frank blushed scarlet, and laughed.

"Hullo, Frank! You asked for more than you wished. Go on, Thyra, let's know who it is."

"No names, Thyra," said Frank, still blushing.

"Names! Nay, that is beyond my power; but, as you asked me, I tell you again, you have found the first thing you desired to know, and the first will bring you the second."

"What, make me a captain?"

"Not exactly put a captain's commission in your pocket, but put such ambition and desire into your head and heart as will surely lead you to that in time."

"Anything beyond that?" asked Frank, laughing still, and although not crediting, still enjoying the novelty of feeling which Thyra's prediction aroused within him.

"More than that?" said Harry. "Why, you have grown covetous of late. What more do you want? You surely don't wish to become the First Lord of the Admiralty, do you?"

"You will have more than that," continued Thyra. "You will have a wooden leg."

"A what?" shouted Frank, in amazement, rising from his seat full of youthful enthusiasm. "A what, say you?"

"A wooden-leg," emphatically responded the girl.

"Oh, for the shade of Greenwich Hospital, then," quoth Frank. "Just fancy me hobbling about the park with two medals and a wooden-leg."

"If you serve under Admiral Nelson, you will surely gain both distinction and medals to your heart's content."

"Yes, and a wooden-leg also, mind you," said Harry. "But now that you have foretold things yet to come, in Frank's career, Thyra, why not give me an inkling of what may befall me?"

"I would rather not, Harry. You always were a child of mystery. Your mother coming among us wreckers of the coast, and her subsequent career, has confirmed me in the opinion I have long entertained, that you have a very stormy part in life to play."

"Certainly he has, if he follows the sea," said Frank.

"I don't mean that exactly, Frank. I mean more than that. Before he becomes that to which he is justly entitled; before he escapes the many trials, troubles, and vexations, that shall befall him, he may be prematurely grey."

"Grey! Nay, don't say that, Thyra," added Harry, jocosely. "Because, if I'm grey, I shan't be able to win a wife, no matter how grand I may be."

"The idea of a wife will little trouble you; the great object of your life will be ambition. When you see your path in life clearly defined, you will pursue it with ardour, irrespective of time, place, or circumstance, for none of these will thwart you. Your will and capacity are too great to succumb to the disappointments which would dispirit if not crush ordinary men."

"But what, then, shall I be?—to what shall I attain?"

"That remains, as yet, in the womb of time; but as surely as we know that sunlight approaches when stars begin to pale, so surely do I foresee what you may and will accomplish, through your own indomitable will and purpose. When you ride to Court in a coach with emblazoned panels——"

"What nonsense, Thyra," broke in Harry, blushing and laughing. "Come, come, Thyra, no joking, please."

"When you ride to Court in a coach with emblazoned panels, and bow to the throngs that cheer and wave their hats, remember what poor Thyra, in Polruth's parlour, once told you—remember her, I say, and have compassion and pity on many like me who pass through the unthinking world under the category of half-witted fools, or Bedlamites ; but we must stop this, here comes Polruth. Hear what a noise he's making waking up the sleepers in the tap."

At that moment Polruth appeared at the parlour-door, rubbing his eyes and yawning.

"Hillo, my lads, up so early ? Thyra made you some breakfast ? That's right, my lads. Give me a cup of the same, hot and strong, mind you ; it will act as a sweetner after last night's bout. Don't forget to put a good sup of rum into it, though, lass ; there's nothing like a little of it, lads, after a long night's spree."

"How's your head, Polruth," timidly inquired Frank, with a significant wink at Harry.

"Head ! you jolly young rascals ! Why, thanks to you and your treating everybody, I don't think I've got a head at all ; at least, there's nothing on my shoulders that feels much like one. It aches and sounds more like a water-wheel than anything else. Ah ! lads, I'm not so young as I used to be once ; I could dance and sing, and drink and fight with any one once upon a time ; but I begin to feel like the holy book says, 'it's all vanity and vexation of spirit.'"

"I should think it was, particularly of the head and spirit, considering how much you stowed away in your coppers last night," said Rayner, grinning.

"Aye, aye, Master Midshipman Rayner, it's all very well for youngsters to joke ; but if you'd seen the amount of spirit consumed and wasted that I have in my time, you'd never encourage it much."

"Encourage it ! Why, then, what would become of the 'Jolly Mariners ?'" said Harry.

"What become of it ? Why, turn it over to the Methodists, and make a meeting-house of it, to be sure, what else ?"

"Why it is a meeting-house already, and there's plenty of good and blessed spirits in it yet, I'll be bound, if the revenues did pay you an unwelcome visit last night."

"Aye, true lads, and so they did. If it hadn't been for your advice, though, these same fellows wouldn't have gone from here without broken heads."

"They didn't break into any of your heads, did they ?"

"Aye, true, Harry, they did ; they broke the head of a wine cask, but they didn't find anything but salt junk in it."

"Junk ! rather hard tack that."

"Yes, and they were on the wrong tack, or they wouldn't have mistaken a junk-cask for a cask of wine; but they found a cask of wine, which was just as good, Polruth ; you should have presented all of them a pint each, as a pleasant drink."

"Well they didn't get much out of me, thanks to young Halliard's suggestion, did they ?"

"No, they got cold water for their pains."

"They looked very much afraid of getting other pains though, judging from their looks."

"'Twas better as it was, though," said Harry, "it is better to have respect for law in your own house, than be summoned up to their house before a long bench of big wigs, with the prospect of Van Dieman's Land before you."

"Oh, it isn't the first time they've visited the kiddleawink, by many, owing to master Thorkil's tale-bearing ; but they never bowled me out yet, and never will, I hope. My cellars are not always under the house, lads. I have a jolly good cask or two stowed away, far from where the Revenues would expect it. No one knows half so much about the kiddleawink as I do, and if I like I could stow away a whole ship's cargo, crew and all, for all Thorkil or his sneaks could tell to the contrary."

"Thorkil is no friend of yours ?"

"No ; nor of yours, Harry, as you'll say one of these days, when you know as much as I do about him."

"If ever he comes across my path, I'll slay him," said Harry, with a flashing eye.

"Have nothing to do with him ; he has powerful friends to back him, more powerful than you suppose. There is Earl Penalvon——"

"Who cares for Penalvon !" said Harry, rising indignantly.

"Never mind, lad ; if you don't, I do. 'Tis better for a reed to bow to the storm ; when the winds have passed it rights itself again, and is fresher and greener from being buried for a time beneath the swollen and angry stream."

"Well, 'tis long since I was here before, Polruth, and will not soon forget your kindness. Stay here, Frank, till I return. Thyra and I will take a little walk together. Come, Thyra."

When Harry and Thyra were alone on the heath, he questioned her closely regarding various matters respecting his mother, which Thyra had only hinted at in former conversation.

"Ask me no questions, not to explain anything, Harry," she said ; "suffice it to say that dear Rose is well, and safely protected. If you wish to know more, ask your own dear, devoted mother."

They walked along in silence for some time towards the beach.

The morning was sunny and beautifully clear.

The birds sang their gladdest songs, and sea-gulls sailed through the air with unwonted beauty and grace.

It seemed as if Nature had designed such a lovely morning for the meeting of mother and son.

Dressed in his pretty and becoming midshipman's suit of blue, with a handsome silver-hilted dirk at his waist, Frank walked beside Thyra, with the gait of one who rejoiced in the strength, health, and exuberance of dawning manhood.

His curly hair shook and waved in the freshening sea-breeze that blew from the wide expanse of ocean opening to the view in the receding altitude of the landscape, and his cheeks flushed with pleasure and pride as he looked along the sea-girt coast towards the spot where once was his mother's simple cottage home.

Landsmen and seamen, as they passed, looked with surprise at the handsome young officer escorting the humbly-attired girl by his side, but respectfully raised or touched their caps in salutation, until Harry's figure seemed to imperceptibly gain in height and manliness, as he strode with elastic step beside Thyra, his old and faithful friend.

They had not proceeded far when Thyra stopped and pointed to a small cottage that stood alone close beside and overlooking the sea.

"That's where your mother is, Harry. It is not her own home ; she is staying there on purpose to see you. She dare not make herself known round here, for she has many powerful and bitter enemies."

"Why is all this mystery, Thyra ? What could

I or my father and mother have done to call down the spite or vengeance of great people?"

"I know not, Harry; the Almighty alone can solve that riddle; but so it is. By no means stay after dark."

"But you will come with me, will you not?"

"If you desire it; but I am not suitably attired."

"That should be, and must be, the last and least consideration when you are with me. Thyra, come, I love and honour you as much as I could a princess sparkling in diamonds and satins. Come!"

Hastening their steps to the white cottage on the cliff, Harry knocked at the door, and was answered by a very aged, lady-like person, who opened her eyes in much surprise at the young officer, who, impatient and without ceremony, passed her, and made his way to the parlour.

The door was open.

He entered softly and unnoticed.

At the window sat a fair, and beautifully-formed woman, dressed in black, who, with book in hand, was looking out upon the sea, apparently deeply absorbed in thought, with a tearful, melancholy expression of countenance.

For a moment he stood upon the threshold, and, as if by instinct, Rose turned her head and rose.

A cry of delight escaped her, and, before she could speak or fall into her chair from intense joy and surprise, Harry rushed across the room, caught her in his arms, and the widow's head leaned upon the breast of her handsome son, and she sobbed convulsively.

"Mother!"

"My son!"

Such were the only words uttered; both hearts were full to overflowing with maternal and filial delight, which found vent and expression in long and copious floods of tears.

"Oh, my darling, my darling, God bless you!" Rose sobbed, at length, and fainted helplessly in the arms of her beloved and only child.

Manly as he was in all his actions, he did not attempt to restrain the flow of tears that coursed down his cheek as he laid his mother upon the couch, and bathed her pallid brow, or moistened the parched lips, which, unconscious as she was, were murmuring inaudible blessings upon her darling and long-absent boy.

Thyra and the old lady of the house stood respectfully apart, and gazed thoughtfully upon the holy scene thus presented of the happy meeting, after a long parting, of mother and son.

CHAPTER LVIII.

EARL PENALVON RAVES—THORKIL'S INTERVIEW—ESCAPE OF BLACK WILL—MARRIAGE OF NELLY BRITTON AND PAUL ADAIR—THE MYSTERY OF HARLECK.

EARL PENALVON returned safely to Seawardine.

He was bruised, crushed, and bleeding.

His domestics stood aghast as they beheld their master led, or rather carried from his carriage.

Doctors were sent for, far and near; his injuries were great from various causes, and none could divine the cause or origin of them.

Servants gave different versions of what they knew; but knowing their master's habitual reticence and his love of intrigue the coachman and footman, who had accompanied their master to the lane where dwelt Wild Meg, refrained from passing any remarks that might lead to unpleasant suggestions.

All was mystery.

Earl Penalvon, in his sick chamber, was surrounded by all that luxury could desire or demand.

His brain seemed touched at times from the excitement that followed at Wild Meg's, and he raved incoherently of passing events for hours.

He spoke of Nelly Britton in tones of passion and recrimination.

The name of Paul Adair was continually upon his lips; but never without the accompaniment of fierce and bitter oaths.

He sighed for, and vowed revenge.

Thorkil, when he heard the strange news, was among the first to hurry off to Seawardine with his condolements, and he swore roundly that he would not die until he had dealt out ample revenge upon the heads of all who had participated in the late fray.

"You are a good promiser, Thorkil," said Penalvon, in disgust; "if you were the man you represent yourself to be, or possessed a tithe of the spirit for which I have often given you credit, Paul Adair and his ruffians would not run riot along the coast, and lay violent hands upon noblemen of the land."

"I promise, my lord, that within a week he shall not live."

"I doubt it, Thorkil; your band is worse than useless, mere children compared to those Adair has at his command. However, do your best, and I will reward you."

Bowing to Earl Penalvon, with a flushed face, he retired, and journeyed homewards in a gloomy, revengeful, blood-thirsty mood.

"If Black Will were only here," he said, "or Harleck, I might attempt and achieve something. Money I have, and in plenty, thanks to the earl; but it strikes me he must have something stronger than mere revenge at heart, or he would not be so lavish of guineas. It may be there is more between him and Paul Adair than meets the eye. Well, I can but die once; I would willingly expire if I could but tread upon the neck, and crush this fiery, upstart Paul Adair."

While he mused as he journeyed homewards, a dark figure flitted across his path.

He stopped and listened. He peered into the darkness about him, but he saw nothing.

He felt for his pistols and cocked them; his cutlass, beneath a heavy coat, was unsheathed.

Reassured, he walked forward again, but slowly and cautiously. He thought he saw again the dark shadow that had crossed his path before.

He whistled a signal known only among those who were, or once had been, among his band.

The signal was unanswered. He repeated it a second time, but still no response. Drawing a pistol, he prepared to fire into a small thicket that stood beside the road. He whistled the third time.

It was slowly and distinctly repeated by some one unseen.

"Friend?" shouted Thorkil, interrogatively.

"Friend," was the affirmative reply.

"Trelawny?"

"Thorkil?"

Such were the few words that passed, and ere each could recover from surprise, they stood face to face, hand tightly grasped in hand.

"Let bygones be bygones."

"With all my heart," Black Will answered, gruffly. "I need a friend, now, more than ever."

"And you shall have one; but how comes it that you appear so suddenly and mysteriously?"

"I escaped last night from Paul Adair, and burn to be revenged."

"But how did you effect it?"

"By beating down two of his ruffians who opposed me."

"Know you where it is?"

"I might find it by night; I know not which way I turned when I found myself free. I ran from the coast, and crossed the hills like a wolf, for fear of pursuit and recapture."

"There are more than Trelawny who desire revenge on this same Paul—there is Penalvon, and Joel Britton."

"Joel Britton? Why he should be one of Adair's best friends. He rescued Nelly from the earl at Wild Meg's."

"Oh! that's it, eh?" said Thorkil, whistling in surprise. "Now I begin to see what is what."

"And they are married."

"Married?"

"Aye; and Master Agger gave the bride away."

"Agger say you?" said Thorkil, choking with rage. "My curses follow the traitor's path through life!"

"Rose Halliard dressed her for the occasion, and said that ere long she should visit Seawardine, and act as her daughter there."

"Rose there, too, and to speak so? Why she must be a maniac!"

"I know not that; all I say is, that Paul Adair and Rose seems to know more about Earl Penalvon than most folks."

"Oh, oh! he has not made midnight visits to the manor for nothing; but if you are in the same mind still, Will, we can soon put a stop to all their croaking. The earl has put a price upon Adair's head, dead or alive, and has not been at all miserly in giving the needful to further his ends. We must get a good gang together, and the rest is easy. You know the way by night, and night-time is the best."

"I found out that Paul wants to get hold on Harleck."

"For what?"

"He seems to think that Harleck is the only link in the chain of evidence that is needed."

"Needed for what? What can that ruffian do to injure any of us? A word from Penalvon, and he would decorate a gallows. He is a 'pressed' man in the Navy, and is somewhere away from England; he can never be found, for he passes under another name. No, no, they won't find Harleck in a hurry, nor get him if they do find him; Penalvon has taken good care of him."

Thorkil remained silent for some time, but a cold sweat was upon his brow.

Black Will walked by his side, thoughtful, and uncommunicative.

They reached Thorkil's cavern, and Hylda, though surprised at Trelawny's unexpected appearance, spoke no word but of hearty welcome, for she well knew that her husband had need of such a desperate ruffian, whose strong, remorseless arm, might serve him in coming trials.

Thorkil flung himself upon a rough-looking couch, and remained buried in thought.

His colour came and went from time to time.

His eyes glared like two live coals plucked from the fire.

He was lost in reverie.

His mind was journeying back many, many years.

Scenes passed in review before him that he wished never to recall.

He felt a choking sensation about the throat, but from time to time he gulped down long draughts of rum, and did not heed Trelawny who, stretched full length before the fire, was fast asleep.

Thorkil was unusually moved.

Trelawny's words had awakened strange suspicions and fears and misgivings in his mind.

He felt as if the hand of destiny was laid heavily upon him.

He saw sufficiently into futurity to dimly perceive that the final catastrophe to his life of iniquity was looming in the future.

CHAPTER LIX.

DARK SCENES IN THE LIVES OF EARL PENALVON, THORKIL, AND HARLECK—SOMETHING OF WILD MEG—BLACK WILL'S MOTIVE FOR KILLING CAPTAIN HALLIARD—HARRY A CHILD OF DESTINY.

THE panorama of his life was greatly stained with blood.

Secret deeds that few knew of had their authorship in Thorkil.

Others that none could whisper of against him could be accounted for by the eye of Heaven.

There was one scene in his life, that disturbed him more than all.

It was that one scene, that one deed, which had for ever bound him in the thrall of a merciless noble.

He had been a dupe ever since to Earl Penalvon's wiles and knavery.

The load of crime became heavier and heavier.

It mattered but little what he did, or where he went, there were shadows that tracked him by day and phantoms that hovered around him at night.

The meeting of Trelawny reminded him of the year, the month and the hour.

He remembered the night some thirty years before too well to soon forget it.

He was journeying across the heath, alone and evil-minded.

He was accosted by a stranger.

Soft words and a heavy purse beguiled him.

"You are called Thorkil?" said the muffled stranger.

"I am," was the reply.

"And are a wrecker?"

"True."

"Would money repay you for your assistance?"

"In what?"

"Can I trust you?"

"You may. There are few things that a wrecker might not hazard and attempt. What is it?"

"There is an enemy to his king and country expected to arrive at Seawardine to night."

"What then?"

"He has a son. Neither must ever enter the gates of that ancient mansion, Thorkil, or you will never live to see your next birth-day. He will inform on you; he has done so already."

"And who are you?"

"His enemy, but your firm and lasting friend, Thorkil Penreal."

"And what must I do?"

"The carriage will cross the heath. The rest is easy."

The stranger dropped a heavy purse into Thorkil's not unwilling hand, and departed.

It was midnight, upon the lone dreary heath.

Thorkil and an unknown accomplice were there.

The sounds of carriage wheels were heard.

A vehicle approached.

The horses stumbled, the carriage was overturned.

There alighted from it a gentleman and his little son.

Two men rushed from beside the road with uplifted knives.

In the confusion and darkness the gentleman, driver, and footman were murdered.

The son was caught in the arms of the first ruffian.

The second tossed the murdered men over the cliff.

Thunder rolled, and lightning flashed.

The receding tide carried the bodies far out to sea.

No vestige remained of their identity.

The deed, bloody, sudden, and mysterious murder, was accomplished at dread midnight.

No eye beheld it, save that of Heaven.

The one who had seized the boy disappeared from the scene.

He, like Thorkil, was employed by the unknown stranger, but nought was ever after heard of him.

Months passed, and the estates of Seawardine, with the Earldom of Penalvon, were claimed and secured by another.

His formal possession of the vast estates was attended with every demonstration of joy by old and young, for miles around.

No one had ever before seen him. It was sufficient that he was justly entitled to the title and estates, no one had ever questioned the legality of succession.

This was Thorkil's first acquaintance with Seawardine.

Penalvon ruled there. He was rich, luxurious, carnal, and cruel in his tastes.

'Twas said his wife or sister resided with him; no one had ever seen her. She was reputed mad, and had been sent to a foreign asylum.

Thorkil was summoned to Seawardine.

He knew not the earl, and, hardened wrecker as he was, he trembled before the long, ardent, and stony gaze of Penalvon, who, with a faint smile, welcomed him.

"Thorkil, your hands are stained with blood," were the words of his greeting.

The wrecker's frame shook with astonishment and terror.

"Your life hangs by a single thread—it is in my hands. You slew my brother and his son."

'Twas useless to explain if Thorkil had possessed the will or power.

He stood before Penalvon charmed like a birdling under the serpent's gaze.

"I ask but one thing—seal your fealty by doing my bidding."

"In what, my lord?"

"Follow me."

Down, through long, winding stone passages of the ancient mansion of Seawardine, Penalvon led the way.

Through large, strong, granite vaults, with heavy locks fast bound with gigantic bars of iron, they trod, and their footfalls awoke echoes that rung with solemn sounds.

"Here there is one confined, who must never again behold the light of day," said Penalvon, bestowing upon Thorkil a long, inquisitive glance. "One who may interest you," he continued, unlocking a huge door, that creaked upon its hinges with a dolorous sound.

Seated on the floor was a woman, dressed in rags.

She was the wreck of one once beautiful. Long black hair fell about her shoulders in luxuriant profusion.

She clasped her hands as if in prayer, and looked upon Penalvon with eyes flashing with rage.

The earl pointed to her with a look of pity and contempt.

"There she is."

"Where is my child?" the woman gasped. "Give me back my child! Torture me, kill me, do aught you please with me; but give me back my daughter!"

"Mad, you see," quoth the earl, stoically, "stark mad."

"Murderer as you are——"

Thorkil started at her calmness, and quailed at her glance.

"Murderers you both are! I tell it by the guilty souls peering through your eyes. You killed him, murdered my husband and son, deceived me, and robbed me of my child—my darling daughter."

"Mad, you see, Thorkil. She will not touch her bread and water, although I, myself, supply her personally, day by day. Let us go; she is but a raving, prating woman. You may always gain admittance through this passage, which leads to the park; no one knows it but ourselves," said the Earl, slowly and solemnly.

"And what is this to me, my lord?"

"What to you? Why, this. You have murdered her husband and son; it crazed her brain. Her youngest child, a weakly daughter, was sent to France, to--be educated, the ship was lost upon this coast, several passengers were saved or washed ashore. Watch the coast well; if you do espy a girl of the mother's looks it may be her. It is my wish to restore her to her proper rank in life."

"Is this all, my lord?"

"No. What you have seen and heard tell to no man; I will befriend you through life; always heed my behests. Do now as I bid you."

"And what is that, my lord?"

"Take this knife. If you would escape all vengeance of the law, you might make the maniac's acquaintance. Take this knife to protect yourself."

The moon which slowly rose that night shed faint rays of light through small crevices which seemed to light the maniac's dungeon.

There lay upon the cold stone floor a murdered woman.

Her son and daughter—Alas! where were they then?

The son was *not* murdered, but escaped the vigilance of his guards, and, unknown to the earl, had gone to sea.

The daughter had gone none knew whither.

Whether washed ashore on the rugged coast, in a dreadful storm by night, and saved, or whether the angry waves which lashed the rock-bound shores in fury, had hidden her for ever, none could tell, nor did Penalvon care.

Years followed years, and Penalvon was Lord of Seawardine.

He never married, but his intrigues were numerous and debaucheries disgusting.

He stopped at nothing and stooped to all that was vile to satiate his bestial cravings.

But then arose the figure of a man whose image tortured him,—a dashing, handsome officer in the navy.

He came to Seawardine. He saw Rose, and loved and wooed and married her.

There was not a step that Captain Halliard took but what was quickly reported by spies to Penalvon.

He knew Trelawny's hate. He fostered and

nourished it; he worked his remorseless vengeance through another, but the end was the same.

Halliard fell, was basely, foully murdered by Black Will.

Penalvon rejoiced.

Rose was persecuted and defamed as a woman and widow.

She knew not the cause of all her sufferings, and might have fallen a victim to dishonour and shame.

There was one above, all-seeing and all-wise, who had already pre-ordained Halliard's avenger.

It was his son, the Boy Sailor.

When he had gone to sea on board the Thunderer it was Earl Penalvon's hope that he might be struck down in battle.

It was not thus so to be.

Harleck, the third tool of the Lord of Seawardine, had done dark deeds, he had been a paid spy and ready assassin at Wild Meg's.

He knew too much for Earl Penalvon.

He was rough, vindictive and revengeful; he might, in time, turn virtuous and mischievous.

This must not be.

He was mysteriously taken on board the Thunderer by a press-gang at midnight, and seldom afterwards trod *terra firma*, as we have seen.

It was thought he might do a deed which should rid the Lord of Seawardine of all misgivings.

He was found apt.

He was supplied with money.

Harleck found an easy tool in the "Crawler," and both sought every opportunity to entangle the Boy Sailor in a web, which should eventually strangle him.

Earl Penalvon had resolved on the death of Midshipman Halliard.

He looked upon it as a foregone conclusion.

Noble blood ran through the Midshipman's veins.

A coronet was his by right of succession, and not the arch-impostor and villain who had so long worn it.

CHAPTER LX.

ROSE HALLIARD AND THE BOY SAILOR IN THE WHITE COTTAGE ON THE CLIFF—STRANGE DREAMS AND REVELATIONS—WILD THYRA SPEAKS OF HER CHILDHOOD—THE LOST LOCKET—INTUITIONS OF A BRIGHT AND GLORIOUS FUTURE FOR THE RUNE-KENNER—MIDNIGHT DOINGS OF PAUL ADAIR AT SEAWARDINE.

THE heart of Rose Halliard was full to overflowing, as she clasped Harry to her bosom.

She wept and laughed and wept by turns.

Her tears fell thick and fast upon the upturned face of her darling boy, and she smoothed the curls from his forehead with a tender, affectionate hand, as she softly murmured prayers and wishes for his long life and happiness.

"Oh, that your father, Harry, now so long dead, could clasp, as I now do, his child to his heart. From Heaven he looks down upon us, child; I see his smiles beaming in your eyes. Oh, child, beloved of my heart, embrace me again and again."

"My dear, dear mother," said the brave Sailor Boy, with choking, affectionate emotion. It was all he could say, for tears would flow as he clasped his mother, poor persecuted, long-suffering Rose, to his manly breast.

"Oh, how I have prayed for you, night and day, Harry, my darling! You were never absent from my thoughts for a single moment. I thought I

heard the cannons' roar, and heard the rush of deadly strife, but there was always a good angel that whispered encouragingly in my ear, and I felt certain, nay, I knew, that Heaven had thrown its mantle of protection around you, and that the only son, the hope and joy of his widowed mother, would safely return to her arms once more."

When the feelings of both were calmed—when Rose ceased to caress and fondle him—he sat beside her, and recounted all his adventures and escapes, by land and sea.

The poor woman wept with joy at his candour and open-heartedness. She never tired of gazing upon his every feature, until Thyra crept close to the group, in a timid, bashful manner, and leaned on Rose's shoulder, looking steadfastly at Harry, who, all mirth and good humour, was laughing and joking without interruption.

"I always knew that Harry would safely return," said Thyra, slowly and calmly, without moving a single feature of her thoughtful face. "I prayed for him always, and for you, Rose, also; but I had constant dreams, and such good ones, that honour, fame, and safety would attend him, and here he is, you see, dear, dear Rose, fast rising into manhood, with bright prospects and loving friends surrounding him."

Rose kissed Thyra, as a sister might.

"And what do you think, mother?" said Harry, rising, and playfully putting his arm round Thyra's slender waist. "What do you think? She has been rune-kenning again, and has actually told my and Frank Rayner's fortunes."

Rose laughed.

"She predicts that I am to be a great man, and shall ride to court, bless you, in a grand carriage; that the people will cheer me lustily, and point to my stylish coronet," said Harry, merrily laughing, and looking towards his mother.

"A coronet, Harry?" said Rose, very slowly and thoughtfully. Her colour changed quickly. She alternately blushed and paled, and hung her head bashfully and sorrowfully.

"And so he will," said Thyra, with emphasis. "People may laugh at me, and jeer me, and call me dreamer, but all are not gifted alike. Heaven, which once sent prophets into the world to predict blessings or punishments upon the good or wicked, can do so now."

"Who told you—who taught you to think of carriages and coronets, Thyra?" asked Rose, with a faint smile of pity, compassion and affection.

"I was never taught aught, dear Rose, save what Heaven has given me. Knowledge such as mine comes unbidden."

"Did you never glean anything of your birth or parentage?" asked Rose, affectionately.

"No, dear Rose," said Thyra, kneeling before her, and looking up with almost child-like innocence. "I am what they call an ocean waif."

"But you have relics, at least one, that might some day throw light upon it—the locket I mean?"

"The locket!" said Thyra. "Why I have lost it. It could not have been of much value, or the wreckers would have stolen it long before."

"You have not lost it, Thyra," said Rose, with a smile. "Those who love you most have watched over you in secret. There is a clue to your parentage, Thyra, and the locket, worthless as you may imagine it, will prove a priceless boon in establishing your rights. Who stole it from you?"

"Paul Adair. I was out alone upon the cliffs, gazing on the sea——"

"Rune-kenning again," said Harry, laughing.

"And I had such beautiful visions pass before me; methought I saw my mother. Oh, such a beautiful lady! She passed suddenly from my view. I saw a storm, and I was in it—a helpless child. A mighty wave washed me from the wreck ashore, where I was cared for as a foundling stranger. While visions of light and beauty passed before me, and I was wrapt in their contemplation, Paul stood beside me, and, unperceived, cut the string around my throat that held the locket; it fell to the ground, and when I had gone he picked it up. He never returned it, and that was the cause of our first disagreement."

"Did Thorkil hear of this?"

"Yes; he at first imagined I had found some rare shell, and wore it as a charm; but when I described to him that it contained the half-obliterated miniature of a gentleman, and that I had worn it since the earliest hour I could recollect, he seemed puzzled and annoyed."

"Did you never observe aught else in this locket?"

"It opened by a secret spring at the back, which I by accident discovered. It had contained some mysterious writing I could never understand or decipher; perfectly worthless, I know, or the trinket would never have been left with me so long. I never felt happy or easy without it; there was some charm connected with it that lent a strange pleasure to my heart when wearing it. I have often sighed for it, and begged Paul to return it, but he always smiled, and promised to do so, as he termed it, on a 'fitting occasion.'"

"What was the cause of Paul leaving Thorkil?"

"All concerning me. Penreal called me harsh and wicked names; Hylda abused and ill-treated me. Paul resented this, and a quarrel ensued. Thorkil asked him to be one of the crew that should sail under orders from Earl Penalvon. This he stoutly refused to do, and, getting very much heated and red with anger, swore he would take revenge upon all who should insult or ill-treat me. Penreal threatened his life, and Paul departed."

"Noble fellow!" broke in Harry. "I long to clasp the hand of such a gallant and admirable man. For should any one that breathes, Thyra, dare to insult you in my presence, it would prove the last act of his life."

Rose looked at both Harry and Thyra with an aspect of much concern, but spoke not a word.

"I have always entertained affection towards you, Thyra, from my earliest recollection. You were always my friend in childhood, and I have always felt that a strange if not mysterious tie bound us together, but how, or of what nature, I could never imagine."

"So then let it always be," said Rose, mildly. "Those who invented plots for our ruin and dreamed constantly of unmanly schemes against us, have been foiled by that all-wise Providence, who has ever cared for and guarded the widow and orphan. Had it not been for Penalvon's villany, Rose Halliard would never have known the friendship of Paul Adair, and Thorkil's participation in horrible deeds of blood."

"What deeds of blood?" asked Thyra, reddening suddenly, and clinging still closer to Rose.

Her eyes were all a-glow with fiery animation and excitement.

Her frame upheaved with emotion, and she clutched the arm of Rose with convulsive grasp.

"What deeds of blood? What single particular deed of blood?" she whispered. "Oh, Rose, I have often had horrible dreams concerning hard-hearted cruel Thorkil, that have haunted me incessantly day and night. I once dreamed that my mother was confined in a dungeon, and that at midnight Penreal entered it. I knew him by the faint glimmering of moonlight that stole through crevices; and then, while my poor, harmless, emaciated, half-crazed mother murmured my own and my father's names in troubled sleep, the villain despatched her with a nobleman's hunting knife."

"What names did this visionary woman, your mother, call you by?"

"Oh, dear Rose, 'tis so long ago I forget; but this I know, no music that the waves, or storms, or tides, or birds ever sung was half so sweet to me as the single word which escaped her lips when dreaming."

"Well, Thyra, the world may call you wild or crazy, or what they will, there *is* some truth in your dreams, as time will prove. When I leave here you must come and live with me; there are enemies who would harm you. Under the protection of Paul Adair, and with the affectionate tending of his pretty wife, Nelly Britton, you may rest in peace and comfort, and without fear of ever again being insulted, or within the reach of Thorkil's wickedness and vile machinations."

"But why are you so secret with me, mother?" asked Harry, rather impatiently. "If any one has done you wrong why not let me redress it?" he added, colouring to the temples with ill-suppressed indignation. "We can appeal to law, and should that fail, it can be decided by weapons."

"Patience, child; it would simply be over again the story of the Wolf and the Lamb. When all things are prepared, my son, justice will aid us. I know my sailor boy's single-heartedness and impetuosity too well to trust to your assumed discretion. You must remain with us, and a few days more will make you, not what you are, my beloved son, a single-hearted midshipman, but something grand in the land, and worthy of your forefathers."

CHAPTER LXI.

BLACK WILL AND THORKIL IN SECRET CONFERENCE—STRATAGEM TO ENTRAP PAUL ADAIR—THE MYSTERY OF THE SKELETON AND THE CAULDRON OF BOILING OIL — ROSE, WILD THYRA, AND HARRY LEAVE THE WHITE HOUSE ON THE CLIFF—THORKIL'S VOW AGAINST AGGER—PENALVON'S INTERVIEW WITH THORKIL, AND HIS ASTONISHMENT—PLANS OF BLACK WILL FOILED—THE SPY IS CAPTURED.

"WHAT say you, Trelawny? Do you mean that Rose Halliard and Harry are in the neighbourhood?"

"Yes; have for two days past lived with the old widow in the White House on the cliff."

"How fortunate."

"So I thought; and Thyra is there."

"Then there is mischief hatching. Couldn't we decoy Paul Adair and Nelly there?"

"A capital idea."

"We could bag them all at once."

"Yes, it would be much better than going to unearth him in his cave among his followers."

"True," said Thorkil, biting his lip, as if fully alive to the difficulties, and particularly the danger, that attended open battle with such a foe as Paul Adair, the "Rover of the Phantom Schooner."

"But who could we get to take word to him? No one could find the way but you, Will," said Penreal, biting his nails in deep study.

NOTICE.—The next Number of the Boys' Library will be Published on Friday, September 19th Order early of your Bookseller.

Harry Halliard: or, the Young British Tar.

THE SCENE IN THE DUNGEON.

"*I* go!" said Will, in disgust. "You wouldn't have me thrust *my* head among them again, would you? A cauldron of boiling vitriol would be my portion if once they had me alive."

"Boiling vitriol, say you? Who—why—when—how do you know they would do that?" eagerly asked Thorkil, glaring at Black Will with a flushed face and much excitement. "Who told you this?" he asked, walking to and fro rapidly, inaudibly cursing, and stamping his heavy heels upon the stone floor of his cavern home.

His body shook with a tremor of terror. He clutched his knife, as if at some imaginary foe, and curses loud and deep broke from him, until his mouth was all afoam with rage.

"Boiled in vitriol!" harped Thorkil, laughing sardonically. "Who—when did you hear that strange threat?"

"From Agger, who daily fed me."

"The traitor, Agger?"

"Yes, truly. He is Adair's chief man now. It was through him that Earl Penalvon was wounded, and Nell Britton rescued by Adair, at Wild Meg's."

Thorkil listened with distended eyes.

The news of Agger's systematic and cunning complicity with Paul staggered the ruffian, who ground his teeth in demoniacal rage, and striking the stone floor with his cutlass, broke it into pieces, as he swore solemnly, and with many frightful oaths, that he would never die contented until he had slain the traitor, Agger.

"Now I see it all, Will," he said. "I have been surrounded by spies and tell-tales for years; and all through that tattling, dreaming, rune-kenning hell hag, Wild Thyra. I wish the waves had drowned her rather than cast among us such a whining, pale, seductive witch to betray and destroy us. But how came Agger to use such a strange threat? Had he ever heard of any one being served so?"

No. 15, NEW SERIES   PRICE ONE PENNY.

"He did not say ; nor was I in the humour to speak to him of that or anything. All I know is, that the greatest hatred is entertained against you and Earl Penalvon by the whole gang, and they will leave naught untried to ruin one or both."

"Why should an earl fear such a band of outlaws ? And as to me," said Thorkil, "I will make my mark among them, if once we meet. But who shall be our messenger ?"

"Why not send Otho ? He is the least valuable of your band ; if he does fall it will not matter much. I will lead the way."

While Thorkil busied himself in gathering together his band of desperadoes, which for many months past had scattered far and wide up and down the coast in search of employment more remunerative than wrecking, under Thorkil's guidance, Black Will and Otho departed on their mission to entrap Paul Adair.

The night was dark and stormy.

They could scarcely pick their way along the coast.

The moon rose in a clouded sky, and gave partial light to the ruffians on their journey.

Across wet, marshy heaths, over crags and hills and mountains, they toiled all night, and still were far from the cove where the Phantom Schooner lay safely moored.

Black Will had almost forgotten the path he had pursued but a few days before, and made a long, toilsome *détour* along the coast, ere he arrived within landmarks that confirmed him of his proximity to Paul's rendezvous.

Otho knew not the danger of his mission, and was unsuspicious.

He was jocular ; but Trelawny betrayed more than usual stolidity and gruffness.

He was uncommunicative, and never disclosed, by word, or action, the real purport of their mission.

Otho was informed that Polruth was bent upon mining a mixed cargo in a vicinity well known to Trelawny, and that he required hands to assist him.

Trelawny was represented as unpopular among the sailors of the district, and therefore Polruth had recourse to negotiation by letter.

Towards evening Black Will and Otho rested.

"Let us take a drink of rum, Otho," he said, "and then we will proceed. It is not far from here."

As they sat, they heard the voices of sailors in a neighbouring cove, busily employed in launching a vessel on the rising tide.

"That's they," said Black Will. "Come, follow me."

They advanced along the cliffs for a few hundred yards, and right before them, in their path, a beautiful cove appeared in view, which was almost completely cut off from the broad ocean that heaved and fell with sullen roar upon the cliff-bound gates of the inlet.

From their lofty position, Otho could easily discern the features and attire of those engaged below in launching the schooner on the rising tide.

"See yonder smoke curling from a fissure in the rocks, Otho ? Well, that is where Polruth's friends reside. Take this note ; give it to the man in the red shirt that you see hauling in that line. It is a note for his master. If the master should ask you any questions regarding me, you will of course say nothing. You were directed here from your own knowledge, and by Polruth's orders, for you must know that the captain would deny nothing to the keeper of the kiddleawink, and that is why the letter is signed by him."

This explanation was all sufficient to the unsuspecting Otho, who promised speedily to return, and descended the cliff towards the men engaged in launching the Phantom.

Trelawny watched the progress of Otho with eagerness ; but confident that the ruse would succeed.

"Once within my power," he growled, with an oath, "and I'll clear off all old scores with interest ; he shall never live to see the White House, or his wife again !"

Otho soon descended the cliff, and accosted the seaman in a red shirt, who wiped his hands, and held out his hat to receive the letter.

"For our captain, shipmate ?" said he.

"Yes, I was sent with it from Polruth, the master of the "Jolly Mariners" on the heath ; he's got a job on hand, and wants your captain to lend him a hand in landing the cargo."

"Aye ! aye ! lad ; he's a jolly fellow is that Polruth. How is he ? Well you say ! Right, glad on it, my hearty ; and I'm sure that not only the captain, but every lad he's got will be right willing to help the jolly master of the kiddleawink ; he always treated us well, and I'm sure we'll do the same. Come this way, shipmate ; I dare say we can find a drop of rum to wet your whistle."

"Letter for me, Hardy ?" said Paul, who sat with Nelly beside him, in a snugly-furnished apartment in a cozy rock cottage hid from view by surrounding cliffs and hills. "Who brought it ? Do you know him ?"

"Not I, captain ; never saw him before. He's one of Polruth's friends, so he says."

"You can leave me for a moment, Hardy."

Paul read the letter, and smiled.

Turning to Nelly, who, fresh-coloured and happy-looking, sat beside him, he said,

"Either this is a very affectionate letter from Rose and Thyra, Nelly, or it is a very clever ruse to entrap me."

"To entrap you, Paul ?" said Nelly, in alarm.

"Yes, nothing less. I wonder if the bearer of this knows me ? Nelly, leave me for a short time, I will soon discover the truth. Hardy !" he called, and when that sturdy bandy-legged sailor entered, cap in hand, he said, "Hardy, there is some mystery about this letter, I think."

"Mystery, sir ? Why, the young chap said as how Polruth had a job in hand, and wanted you to help him."

"Yes, so the letter says ; but it says something more, it speaks of Rose Halliard and Wild Thyra. Now I am certain that Polruth doesn't know anything of where Rose is, for I told her to keep it secret. Wild Thyra knows of it, for I sent word to her, with injunctions of secrecy, which, I know, she'd keep inviolably. Say nothing, call the messenger in, and when he is within the door seize him."

Unsuspecting, Otho advanced as bidden into the presence of the "Rover," and was instantly seized and thrown to the ground by the hardy and Vulcanly-built seaman Hardy.

His astonishment was intense ; his eyes stared almost to unsightly protrusion, as he gasped, "Don't kill me ! I'll swear I've done nothing."

"Who gave you this letter, Polruth or Thorkil ?"

"Neither."

"Some one must have given it you. Who told you the way ?"

"Black Will showed me."

"Enough !" shouted Paul Adair, in delight. "The plot is transparent," he said, in a whisper ; and, winking at Hardy, "He has not rested long before seeking revenge. I was a fool not to have hung him to the yard-arm, Hardy, when first we cap-red him." Then aloud to Otho, "Where did you ave him?"

"Is he an enemy of yours?" gasped the prostrate ho, in alarm for his own personal safety, feeling ured now that he had been egregiously deceived Trelawny. "I don't know your name, but I think ave seen you somewhere before."

"There is no fear of any harm to you, young n," said the rover, looking to his pistols, and mining their priming. "Where did you leave ck Will? Tell me quickly!"

"He left me just over the cliffs, and is waiting return."

"The scoundrel! He would slay me, would he, treachery? Well, we will see," he inaudibly ttered. "Hardy, leave this man with me."

He approached, and whispered to Hardy, who ired.

Hardy soon returned, and took charge of the soner.

Paul Adair left the room.

n an adjoining room sat Agger, who rose as air entered.

They conversed in low tones, long and earnestly. "What would you advise?" asked Agger, re- ctfully. "Are you prepared to consummate your ns?"

Not quite; and yet no harm must befall any e at the White House; they are living wit- ses."

If we detain Otho it will convince them that have discovered their plot; this would be very kward."

They ask, in the name of Polruth, for men to ist in landing a French cargo down the coast."

or some time both Paul and Agger remained in p thought, and spoke not a word.

Does Otho know you?" asked Agger.

No."

Well, then, we can undermine them without one discovering that we perceive their inten- n."

How?"

Let Hardy write to Polruth, and tell him that, you are married, and business is dull, you have en up much of your roving, and that nearly all r men have left. Tell him that you will write friend, who will call a dozen or two of hands him."

But I don't know any one."

Send your schooner by night around the coast, land the men. Let Hardy be captain of the g, and you will find that when the right moment es, instead of capturing you and me, Thorkil Black Will, and all his cowardly crew, will find mselves entrapped by Hardy and our party."

A capital plan, by Jove," exclaimed Paul, laugh- , and shaking Agger's outstretched hand, "I n't think you had brains enough to concoct such plot. Hardy shall write the note at once. l him in. No, I will go; you had better ve the room, Agger, Otho knows me. I think has reason to do so, from the ugly scar over his ht eye. Leave the rest to me."

Let him rise, Hardy," said Paul, re-entering stone chamber. "I'm sorry you treated the n so roughly, Hardy, for now that I have read letter a second time, I find I am mistaken; it is n Polruth. Otho, no harm shall befall you; you w how suspicious wreckers and rovers are of es, don't you? Well, that's the reason you were ated so roughly at first. Hardy, get him a stiff ss of grog."

Addressing Otho, whose countenance was now iant with smiles,

"I am sorry to say the captain, Paul Adair, has left here for a few days with his wife, for a trip in the country, but will be back again in a week or two. Nearly all his men have left him, and he thinks of giving up wrecking and roving, but as I can't write, I'll get one of Adair's trusty men to scrawl a note to Polruth. Meantime, you can sit here until he returns.

"Bring the paper and pen, Hardy, and commence to write," he said.

"Write, sir! me write! Why, I have forgot all about it many a long day since. I can handle a cutlass or marling-spike much better than a quill."

With much persuading, Hardy took the pen, rather clumsily, and wrote to Paul's dictation,

"Bill Hardy is the only one as can write, and his respects to Mr. Polruth, and says the captain is away on a cruise ashore with his wife, and nearly all his men has left him. Bill says as how he'll go with Otho himself, and try to get some hands as he knows on, for Master Polruth is a jolly good 'un, particular as he's had a row with the captain, and is tired o' doing nothing.

BILL HARDY.

"Well, that will do capitally," said Paul, laugh- ing. "But you must mind and keep your weather- eye open, for Black Will is waiting for Otho."

"No fear, captain, Trelawny always had a liking for me, somehow, 'cause I gave him tobacco some- times. I'll spin an awful yarn, you'll find, and blind old Thorkil with soft sawder. Don't fail to run the schooner round to-night, and land the lads. I'll meet 'em to-morrow, and I warrant we'll do the trick nicely for all on 'em as means mischief. Only, master, you mustn't doubt me, and do all I tell you for once."

"I know you too well for that, Hardy, my brave old boy. If you knew how important your fidelity was to me in the present instance, you would not, could not, deceive me."

"I know enough on you, captain, and that's sufficient; all I wants you to do is to trust me, bring round the lads, give me some gold chips to treat 'em with, and then if Master Thorkil or big, ugly Black Will and their crew wants a nice little fight, why, then they shall have it with all my heart."

Hardy and Otho were alone.

The bandy-legged sailor plied Otho so liberally with rum and tobacco that he soon forgot the un- pleasantness of their first meeting.

"You see, shipmate, Jack Smith, that young chap as read the letter, is very like our captain, and he thought as you might have been a landshark out on the cruise as a spy on us poor devils of wreckers, do you see, and so, as he couldn't make out the letter right at first, why of course he thinks, very natural, that you landed unknown on the wrong shore; but it's all right now, we understand the tack. Master Polruth is a good fellow, and as I doesn't much care about stopping here any longer, doing nothing, why, I may as well give a turn to a friend as not."

Otho nodded assent.

Hardy added,

"Here, take another drink." And then in a whisper, "You see, shipmate, this young craft as he's sailing with has played the devil with him. All but two or three of his gang have left in disgust. No pay, hard tack, and nothing to do, do you see? So I, like the rest, will turn him up, particular as I thinks he didn't act square with Black Will, as fine a fellow as ever run foul of a reef in shoal- water."

Hardy's eloquence charmed Otho, but the liquor and tobacco much more so.

"Well, lad, since I'm going to leave in a hurry, I might as well help myself, you see."

Hardy winked knowingly at Otho, and began cramming his pockets with bottles of brandy, rum, tobacco, and, to Otho's astonishment, displayed a handful of guineas, which he told Otho in a whisper he had stolen from Paul Adair's private room.

Having laden himself and Otho with eatables and drinkables, both worthies left the cottage very cautiously.

"Because," said Hardy, scratching his nose, "I don't want Jack Smith to know that I've gone with you. I told him I'd give you a note, but that's all —do you see? They're having a snooze, and won't know I've hooked it until it's too late to holler. Oh, won't there be a devil of a row when they finds I've bolted with Paul's tobacco and liquor and money. And see here," said Hardy, laughing boisterously, and striking his thigh in merriment. "Since he'd give me no pay for the last three months, I've paid myself off by stealing the captain's fancy cutlass and pistols."

Otho appeared astonished at Hardy's boldness, and both crept away stealthily from the rock-bound cottage of Adair, and soon made their way to where Black Will lay concealed from observation.

Trelawny started like a hare when he confronted the bow-legged rover; but when the latter offered him his hand in friendship, and proved its sincerity by a liberal bestowal of rum and tobacco, his first suspicions thawed beneath the genial rays of Hardy's merriment and good humour.

After half an hour's talk, and a frequent resort to the bottle of rum, Trelawny began to believe he had found a firm ally and friend in Bill Hardy.

"Hate him! I believe you," he said, with contempt; "and, as to that crawling scoundrel, Agger, I should like to catch him out some dark night, that's all."

"Was Agger there?" asked Otho, in astonishment, and with a sudden change of colour. "I wish I'd known that. Oh! how I would have pounded him if I had but caught sight of him."

"Would you like to have a turn with him, lad?" asked Hardy, laughing at some secret thought. "I should so much like to see him get a good thrashing before I leave. Let's go back; I'll ask him out for a walk, and then, when we gets him a good distance from his pals, why then you can pound him well. Trelawny and I will see fair play."

Otho changed colour; but, although he took several long draughts of liquor proffered by Hardy, he declined the combat, and could not detect the point of sarcasm.

The three worthies journeyed on their way rejoicing; and, ere long, when Hardy had given a long account of the hardships he had suffered at the hands of Paul Adair, and fully endorsed and added to Black Will's narration of the barbarities practised on him during incarceration, they sat themselves down beside the road, and, with pipes and tobacco, and song and tale, they beguiled hours away until the moon was in the full, when they arose and staggered on their journey towards Thorkil's.

CHAPTER LXII.

PAUL'S PLANS — REVELATIONS CONCERNING SEA-WARDINE—WHAT HE SAW AND DISCOVERED IN HIS NOCTURNAL VISITS THERE—PENALVON'S DAYS ARE NUMBERED—THE TRAITOR'S AND MURDERER'S DOOM FORESHADOWED.

"THAT was a capital plan of your's, Agger," said Paul, when they were both alone. "You have a better head than I ever imagined. If I had possessed such 'cuteness as you seem to have, I might have made much better use of time in my ramblings in and around Seawardine."

"I don't think you could have done much better. You have won and secured a beautiful craft to sail with through life, and one, too, that Earl Penalvon took much pains to rob you of."

"He came very nearly doing it, according to my notion. I had, and I still have access to the manor of Seawardine at any time it suits me to go there. I was in the room the very day Penalvon went on his knees to Nelly, and declared his villanous passion for her."

"And could you stand by and look on without moving?"

"It was a trial for Nelly, and I love her ten thousand times more for it than I ever did before. She acted the flirt too much with me when in her father's house, and, although I loved her I scarce knew what to think of her stability or fickleness, but, when tempted, she spoke her mind, and with an eye too, Agger, that flashed with rage."

"You saw the whole scene?"

"Yes; and, were it not that I had Rose Halliard's card in my hands, and that her fame, fortune and rights depended upon my discretion and courage, I should have slain the viper in his own house."

"But did you know of her abduction?"

"I knew that on the excuse of taking Nelly home, the slimy serpent intended to convey her away to Wild Meg's, but a mile or two away; and I also knew that she was to be escorted and guarded by one of Thorkil's hirelings. It was fortunate you acted as you did."

"But it would be dangerous to visit Seawardine again."

"I know it; but it must be done, Agger, and more than that, you must accompany me."

"But the cavern entrance is strongly barred and closed."

"It must be done, nevertheless; if even we have to blow in one of the foundation walls with powder."

"What can you want more than you have already got?"

"What? Much more. I want the letters which he has constantly received from certain French merchants. I already have those he sent, for when I seized that cargo for Polruth I found whole bundles of them on board, for it was the intention of the merchants to have come over shortly afterwards on business. Oh, Agger, my blood curdles and boils both, at times, within my veins when I think of the damnable villany of this Earl Penalvon and his willing slave Thorkil."

"What could there be so very horrible in a correspondence with French merchants about smuggled goods?" asked Agger, innocently.

Paul looked up in surprise.

"French merchants," said he, with a smile of incredulity.

"Well, well, Agger, is it possible that the head which wrought such a pretty plot as that just now revealed and planned cannot apprehend what——"

"Oh, I see now," said Agger, disgusted at his own want of instinct. "Aye, aye, but you don't mean to say that a lord of England would lend a hand to any thing so low as smuggling?"

"Yes I do, though, lad; he has made lots of money by that game, and that's why he can afford to give so large a reward to Thorkil for his services, and offer thousands for my head, whether dead or alive."

"Well, you take all the wind out of my sails

Paul," said Agger, puffing his pipe slowly, and sighing.

"But not only that, Agger, but some of these French merchants he's been so fond of writing to deal in cannon, and ball, and shells, and pistols, all that kind of thing, you know."

"Well, he couldn't sell many of those things here, I think ; it must have been a poor spec for old Thorkil; and they ride in brigs, Agger, fifty gun frigates, and one hundred gun line of battle ships."

"Phew !" whistled Agger, fully realizing the importance of all he now heard. "Why, the d——d traitor !"

"Nothing more nor less, lad. So now, you see, I have had reason to be active in my searches in and out of Seawardine."

"But what good will it do you if you expose him? He's rich, and money will do anything."

"He has no business in that old mansion ; no more right to be lord of Seawardine than you or I have. He killed his elder brother—that is Thorkil and he did—stole his son, and put him under guard at Seawardine, but the little shaver ran away and went to sea ; he saw him when he grew up, and got Black Will to kill him."

"And who was that ? You don't mean——"

"Captain Halliard ! Listen. His brother's wife was travelling in France, and had given birth to a little girl—I have her miniature, stole it from his cabinet. He enticed the wife to England and to Seawardine, the child was to follow soon after with the nurse, and when she arrived he incarcerated her in a dungeon, dark and deep, below the mansion. She went crazy, so 'tis said, but Thorkil was paid a price and killed her."

"Horrible !"

"You have heard me speak of vitriol, eh ? She was boiled, and nothing but her skeleton now remains, and that, white as polished ivory, decorates the monster's museum."

"But the little girl, bless her heart, who or where is she ? Oh, if she were alive I would search all the earth, to be revenged on the inhuman monster. I would slay——"

"Hear me out. Penalvon knew what ship the child was coming over in ; it was described to Thorkil ; his wreckers lured it by night upon the shoals, it was wrecked and all hands were lost."

"But the child?" asked Agger, in an agony of suspense, opening his eyes and gaping with excitement. "It cannot be that——"

"She was, though."

"I thought so," said Agger, with a sigh. "It's always the way, the best sink and the worst swim. Such is life."

"But she didn't sink."

"No !" cried Agger, in rapture.

"She was washed ashore and is safe."

"Safe ! Where, then, is she ? Now, shiver me to splinters if I ain't better pleased than if I had collared and pounded a fifty-gun Frenchman. But can you find her ?"

"I have."

"Where is she? What's her name? Let's go and see her."

"She's with Rose, in the White House on the cliff, and her name is——"

"What ?"

"Wild Thyra !"

This announcement was more than Agger's nerves could bear. He rose from his seat in intense excitement, and capered about the room with all the agility, grace, and ease of a young bear in harvest time.

"But how did you discover all this ?" asked Agger, gazing with stupified amazement at Paul, whom he seemed to look upon with almost awe and reverence, as some supernatural being sent to avenge the wrongs of mankind.

"By a simple act of theft."

"How was that ?"

"By amusing Thyra in conversation, and then robbing her of the locket."

"How then did you proceed ?"

"I knew the features of Rose Halliard's husband, and was struck by its similarity to that of the miniature."

"But what did that avail ?"

"I knew that Earl Penalvon never liked Captain Halliard, and that he had expressed a wish to see 'that curly-headed coxcomb,' as he called him, meet an early death, for Thorkil confessed it in my hearing. The captain's sudden and mysterious death, coupled with the fact of Trelawny being on that occasion very free with an unusually large sum of money, convinced me that there must have been some secret understanding between Seawardine and Thorkil's gang."

"Your industry and perseverance have been remarkable ; but in case all your chain of evidence should occasion Penalvon's downfall, what reward do you anticipate ?"

"Reward, Agger ? I am surprised at such a question from you ! What other reward could any one expect or crave in such a case, more than the consciousness of having done your duty as a man ?"

"Your hand, Paul Adair," said Agger, grasping it with fervour. "I would do your bidding now in aught you please. In the coming conflict some one may fall, and should fortune cast its lot on me, I will willingly lay it down in defence of Rose, Harry, or poor Thyra."

Both were silent. Agger turned his head aside, but Paul never knew that tears sprung to the sturdy seaman's eyes, as he remembered his love for Thyra in times past, and of the rune-kenner's mild and firm rejection of his love-suit.

CHAPTER LXIII.

POLRUTH RELATES JOEL BRITTON'S TRICK UPON THE HIGHWAYMAN — FRANK RAYNER PAYS HELENA A VISIT—FRANK MEETS WITH THE HIGHWAYMAN AND IS ROBBED—THE TABLES TURNED.

WHILE Harry Halliard was at the White House on the cliff, Frank Rayner found the time to hang very wearily on his hands at the kiddleawink, despite the songs, long yarns, and open-hearted hospitality of his burly host, Master Polruth.

Frank yearned for some excitement more genial to his youthful and fiercely-coursing blood than killing time in a country inn, with no sounds but inharmonious skittles, and with no music save the long, drawling, interminable songs of wreckers or sailors to while away the time.

"Take a good jorum of hot rum and water, Mr. Rayner, that's what I always does when I gets into the blues, there's nothing like it."

"Thank you, landlord," Frank, laughingly, answered, "I've been in the the Royal Blues this many a year, and have been laid up in the sick bay more than once ; but Old Sawbones never prescribe old Jamaica for it—the less one has of that medicine the better, I think. But, joking aside, Polruth. Have you ever heard anything of that highwayman that once stopped and robbed Harry and myself when we were last ashore in these parts?"

"Heard of him!" said Polruth, turning up his eyebrows incredulously. "I should think I have. It was only a week or two since he stopped two carriages, and robbed them both. Why do you ask, Frank?"

"Oh, nothing. Only I'm a little larger and stronger than I was then, and I would wager my commission against anything that he wouldn't try it on with me again."

"Lord bless you, my boy, he stops at nothing. He called at old Joel Britton's three months ago, woke the old man up in the dead of the night, made him shoe his horse, then mounted and galloped off without even thanking the good old blacksmith."

"I wish I'd a been there."

"I dare say you do; but if you had, you couldn't have done much better than Joel did, for he had his revenge, and no mistake."

"How was that?"

"'Ain't you going to pay me?' said Joel.

"'Go to the devil!' said the highwayman. 'Ought to think yourself lucky I didn't rob your house while I was about it.'

"Joel didn't say much; but as he patted the robber's noble-looking animal on the back, his ears were very sharp, and he heard some horsemen coming along. The highwayman also heard it.

"'Come, that's enough, blacksmith,' said he. 'Don't you hear some mounted men coming up the road? I must mount, and be off.'

"'Let me strap up your belly-band,' said Joel, and while he did so, he shoved a dozen or two sharp-pointed tacks under the saddle-cloth, unperceived.

"The highwayman started off on the trot; but the tacks began to prick, and the horse commenced to rear, and kick, and plunge about the road, and couldn't be made scarcely to stir, even with whip and spur.

"He had not gone more than a hundred yards, when Joel heard him cursing and swearing; meanwhile three horsemen arrived opposite the smithy.

"'Who are you looking after,' asked Joel, 'nobody? Oh, I thought I would warn you that there's a highwayman a couple of hundred yards in front, and can't get along on account of a lame horse.'

"'The devil there is!' said the gents. 'Let's go and capture him, there's sure to be a good reward, and some fun into the bargain.'

"Off they galloped; but as soon as Mr. Robber hears them coming he whips and spurs, and curses with the fury of a madman.

"The more he whipped and spurred the more the horse kicked and plunged until it reared and lost its balance, and both tumbled over in the road right into the mud.

"The gents saw the accident, and made a rush to capture him; but he was too quick by half, and getting over the hedge as active as a cat, ran across the fields, the gents after him in hot pursuit, bawling and shouting, and firing their pistols after him. He escaped into a thick wood, and there the gents lost sight of him, for though they stopped and beat the bushes for an hour, they thought he had escaped, and when they returned to the road again felt certain of it, for his horse had disappeared.

"The gentlemen went off on their journey disappointed and annoyed; but Joel, between ourselves—for there ain't more than half a dozen of his very particular friends as knows anything about it—sold the horse for £50. So you see you couldn't play a much better trick even if you should chance to fall in with him in your rambles."

"Have you ever heard anything of Helena, Frank's foster sister, Polruth?"

"Lord bless you, yes. When Harry's mother went away from here some time ago, so quietly that nobody ever dreamt, let alone knew it, Miss Helena drives up to this very door, dressed out in all the newest falderals you can imagine, which she bought out of money Harry sent her, and, says she,

"'Mister Polruth, would you be so very polite as to accommodate me with a glass of water?'

"She spoke so very pretty, and her words sounded so much like French, or some other foreign language, compared to the style we folks talk in, that I stands for a minute or two scratching my head, wondering what she really did want. I didn't like to give the lass the worst I had in the kiddleawink, so I says, since she's young Harry's sister, and the adopted child of poor Rose, why I'll give her the very best in the shop. I draws a very stiff glass of old Jamaica, and makes quarter-grog.

"'There, miss,' I says, 'that's what'll do you good this chilly day.'

"'Oh! goodness me, Mr. Polruth!' she says, turning red, and coughing and crying. 'Where am I? I'm poisoned!'

"'Poisoned!' I says, and I had to pity the fine young lady's ignorance, if she is brought up in a fine boarding-school. 'Poisoned,' I says, 'Miss,' and tastes the grog myself; it was made b-e-a-u-ti-ful, Frank, 'and look at me, Miss Helena,' I says, 'look how it poisons me,' and I drinks it up without coughing, and I can tell you, Frank, there's very little of that fine old Jamaica left now, for I took such a fancy to that one-quarter grog for the next three weeks, that I more than once thought I was going to Davy Jones's locker, and no mistake."

"So she's grown a very fine young lady, has she?"

"Fine? I believe you; as tight and fine sailing a little craft as ever ran afore the wind, and no mistake, Mr. Frank."

"Well, I think I shall give her a call before I go to sea again, which will be in a week or two; but if the Scorpion doesn't get her refit in time, it may be a month before we sail."

Frank Rayner *did* give Miss Helena a call, such a one as he never forgot.

Leaving a letter for Harry, telling him, he was obliged to go away for a few days, on urgent business, he hired a conveyance, and made his way to where Helena was at school.

Having paid particular attention to his toilet, for the occasion, he took a long walk, and the flush of health and exercise was on his cheek as he stood at the boarding-school door, in his new uniform, loooking as fine a specimen of a young English naval officer as could be well imagined.

The young ladies were exercising in the pleasure and school grounds at the moment of his call.

Betsy, the housemaid, had caught a glimpse of the fine young officer, and heard his inquiries respecting Miss Helena.

She rushed from the house, and almost breathless exclaimed,

"Oh, Miss! There is *such* a nice young gentleman waiting for you; *such* a beautiful young midshipman, and he *did* blush so, when he asked to see Miss Helena."

"For me, Betsy?" said Helena, blushing, and looking much confused. "Who can it be? Surely it is not Harry? He would have been in the garden long enough ago, and wouldn't stop to ask questions. I must go and see who it is."

"Helena," said Miss Tabitha, the chief of the seminary, advancing with an awful gait of severity, and freezing austerity of manner, "there is a young person who has called to see you. He says he's no relation, and I was about to send him away about his business, but he may be a bearer of some message from your brother Harry, who, I know, is also a sailor."

"Sailor, Miss Tabitha!" said Helena, colouring, and rearing herself up proudly. "An officer in the King's navy, if you please!"

"Well, true; sailors are not officers, but yet officers are sailors. Nevertheless, we will not discuss logic now; but, as I was about to observe until you very unpolitely interrupted me, as it is against the rules of our establishment to permit strangers to interviews, however short, with pupils, I must accompany you, and remain within sight and hearing while conversing with the stranger."

Helena smiled mischievously, and advanced towards the reception-room with an elastic step and graceful carriage.

She entered the apartment, the stern, uncompromising Miss Tabitha close to her heels, in all the dignity of frills and spectacles.

For a moment Frank gazed upon Helena as one might look upon a beautiful phantom in sleep.

The next moment he rushed towards her impetuously, and held her not unwillingly in his arms, and tenderly embraced her.

Miss Tabitha was so astonished that she could but exclaim,

"Helena! Helena, my dear!" and sank upon the sofa in a semi-state of faintness, and hid her wrinkled maiden face in a cambric handkerchief.

"Dear Helena, forgive me," Frank began, "for my rudeness. I have longed to see you for many a day, and you have been the constant object of my thoughts both day and night."

"Oh, dear! oh, dear!" said Miss Tabitha, jerking out her words spasmodically. "This is entirely contrary to the strict rules and regulations of our establishment, and I cannot——"

"Yes, Harry and I had nothing else to speak of except you, Helena, that gave us half so much pleasure, and I made a vow if even I had to travel on wooden legs I would surely come to see you."

"Thank you, Frank. Harry, in his long and pleasant letters, always spoke of you in the most endearing terms. I have always regarded you as a sincere and true friend both of Harry and myself. Your little notes always gave me delight."

"You look upon me as a friend, then, Helena, and you will be a friend to me? I feel happy; I have neither father, mother, relation nor friend in the world that I know, but I shall always prize your friendship and regard as the dearest object of my whole life."

Frank and Helena sat side by side on the sofa, and conversed in low tones, so that the ever-watchful governess might not hear all.

She seemed to understand the stratagem of the young people, for she often coughed and "ahemed" to draw Helena's attention to the clock, but that young lady never heeded the intimation, and, with flushed cheek and sparkling eye, conversed rapidly and confidentially with Frank, and felt her heart beating with pulsations of a strange, new-born pleasure.

Before he went he managed to slip a note into Helena's hand, and, watching his opportunity when Miss Tabitha's back was turned, he imprinted a passionate kiss upon Helena's fair cheek, who blushed scarlet, hung her head, and sorrowfully said "good bye."

Frank's heart felt full to overflowing.

He could have leaped the boundary wall and carried off Helena like some knight of old, but he had misgivings as he said to himself sorrowfully,

"She is too fair and good for a pennyless fellow like me."

Helena, it must also be confessed, felt strangely and peculiarly pleased with the young midshipman, and she hung her head, and felt perplexed to know why it was that tears should involuntarily flow to her eyes.

She went again into the garden grounds and Helena's visitor was the theme of universal remark.

"Oh, I saw him, Helena," said one. "What a nice young man he is, such a rosy face, and bold bearing."

"And don't he look pretty in that nice blue uniform," chimed in another. "I wish I had a brother or cousin, or somebody in the navy. I do love sailors."

Miss Tabitha walked for some time alone, looking cross, and gaunt, and ugly.

"Miss Helena Halliard," she at last said, with much severity and prudishness of tone, "I wish to speak to you for a moment. Your behaviour this morning, miss, was quite contrary to my expectations and desires. Where was your firmness and dignity? Look at me. Where was your grace of deportment, and that engaging winsome manner and pleasant coquetry that I have always endeavoured to instil into the minds of my pupils, and particularly to you, Helena? True, that strange sailor——"

"I beg your pardon. Midshipman, if you please."

"Well, midshipman, was nothing to speak of, but had it been a 'catch,' Helena, your ways would have for ever ruined you."

Helena shrugged her shoulders and smiled.

"When you go out into the world, you must never appear to like individuals, not give the faintest hope of partiality or encouragement to any one, until yourself or friends have discovered, without doubt, that he is in the first place rich, and secondly respectable. These are precepts which were always taught to me: and look at me now," said Miss Tabitha, rearing herself up to a great height, and striding martially like a grenadier. "Look at me! the principal and governess of this seminary, with, I may say, the hopes and fortunes of three dozen young ladies on my hands. The responsibility of my position is very great. You are pretty and somewhat accomplished, Helena; but, you know, are very, very poor. You must take my advice, and not disappoint the expectations of your friends, accept no suitor in the Navy at all, without he is an Admiral at least; but as to toying with and thinking, as I know you long have, of a beggarly midshipman. Ugh! I wouldn't have it said that one of my pupils married so low, for all the world."

Helena was not at all edified by Miss Tabitha's advice; she never sincerely loved the governess, for her many austere, almost masculine ways.

And when at night she told her bosom friend, Fanny Noble, of the conversation, Fanny laughed heartily, and called Miss Tabitha "a cross-grained disappointed old thing."

Frank was destined to meet with adventures on his way home.

His mood was anything but sweet and conciliatory, and as he journeyed to the neighbouring village on foot, he heartily wished that something might occur on his way back to Polruth, which might dissipate the gloominess of his temper.

He wanted a row, or quarrel, or even a fight; his blood acquired a quicker, more impetuous flow. He emptied a small bottle of brandy he carried with him, and looking up to the stars, swore eternal love and fidelity to Helena, and quaffed off the liquor with a relish. A cigar was next in order, and as he puffed the fragrant weed, he eased his lonely walk along the houseless road with snatches of song.

He had not gone far, when he was overtaken by a horseman, muffled in a cloak, who slackened his speed, and walked beside Harry for some time, without speaking a word.

"Fine night, friend," said the horseman.

"It is."

"Do you know anything of an old blacksmith who lives not far from the kiddleawink—Britton, by name, I believe? Is he at the smithy? Is he at home?"

"I really can't say," said Frank, who began to imagine he had fallen foul of his old enemy, the highwayman; "I am a stranger to these parts."

"Rather dangerous travelling for a stranger, without you know the roads well. I should much like to see that old smith once again. He stole a horse from me not long ago. I will be double or quits with him, you may depend."

"I did not think that the worthy old man would have been guilty of such a thing. Besides, it's a hanging matter!"

"It was nearly a hanging matter with me that night, I can assure you. I shan't forget it in a hurry."

"What do you purpose doing?"

"I'm going there now straight; I shall arrive about midnight."

As they walked side by side, Frank was revolving all manner of schemes for capturing the horseman, but before he could arrive at any definite line of action, a roadside public-house loomed in sight.

The windows were all aglow with candle and fire-light, and as they approached he could distinctly hear the voices of a party of singers, who, with stentorian lungs, were bellowing forth the deafening chorus of a popular sea-song of the day.

Frank's heart beat violently. He knew the voices too well to be deceived as to the owners, and quickened his pace.

"Sailors, I should judge," said the horseman.

"Men-of-war's men, just paid off," replied Frank.

"I'll throw my rein across the horse-post then, and take a glass with them. They've got lots of loose change to spare, I know; a little would come very handy to me just now. Are you going in also?" he asked.

"No; I don't mix in such company. My road turns off here."

"But, before you go, my very fine fellow, I'll trouble you for your small change, and any other valuables you may have," he said, pointing a pistol at the midshipman's head. "Hand them over, quickly! I've no time to spare in parley."

Frank smiled, and quietly handed over a few pounds, together with his watch, chain, rings, and aught else he had, for his plans were now matured for the horseman's capture.

"You hand them over very quietly for an officer in the navy," said the robber, with a gruff laugh.

The remark was galling to Rayner's pride, but he turned away down a cross road, and was soon lost to view.

The horseman followed him for some distance, and believing he had gone far on his journey, turned his horse's head again, and trotted off along the hard road towards the inn.

Frank had observed the horseman from a thick hedgerow, behind which he had secreted himself; and when he heard the clattering of the animal's hoofs die away, he turned up his trowsers, laughing, and scampered across the fields towards the inn, directed by the lights in the windows, and the roar of noisy songsters.

He peeped into the window and saw the horseman sitting between two personages who were none other than Joe Juniper and Bill Hawser, who were listening to Konks's song with open mouths and staring eyes.

The robber's plans were self-evident, but Frank determined to frustrate them.

He passed round the back of the house, and barely escaped being bitten by a ferocious dog.

The barking attracted the pot-boy, who left the tap-room to ascertain its cause.

Frank's dress assured the pot-boy of his respectability, and he bowed.

"Could you manage to get one of the seamen here, I wish to speak to him? And should that stranger in the cloak appear anxious to leave, detain him under some pretext."

Within a few moments Hawser came lumbering out of the parlour, half tipsy, and smoking a long pipe.

He mistook his way to the yard, and stumbled into the tap-room where Frank sat.

His astonishment was great. He was upon the point of shouting aloud in joy at finding his young officer so unexpectedly, as he roared,

"Well, blow my——"

"Hush!" said Frank, rushing towards him. "Silence, Bill; that chap in the parlour wants to board you."

"Board us! What, that long-legged sweep think of boarding three of us!" growled Hawser, in disgust.

Rayner briefly explained how they had met now as formerly, and his conduct on both occasions.

"He doesn't know I'm here, you see, so I've made up my mind to serve him out. When you go in, pass the word quietly for Juniper."

Juniper was soon informed, in language the robber could not understand, that the midshipman waited for him in the tap, and after he had gone, Konks, like Juniper, "didn't like his grog and wanted to see the landlord."

Thus, separately and privately, each of the old tars "received their secret sailing orders," as they termed it, and didn't betray by look or word that they were at all aware of the stranger's true character and calling.

Having armed himself with a pair of pistols, Rayner suddenly entered the parlour, and presented a weapon at the astonished robber's head.

"I want satisfaction," Rayner said. "If you stir, a bullet shall whistle through your brain. These three men are my friends; but I don't need their assistance in the matter. I want, and will have, satisfaction for your insults; you took advantage of me just now. We are both on foot, so there's no inequality; these men shall see fair play."

The highwayman turned red and pale by turns.

Konks, Juniper, and Hawser, watched his every motion with almost feline sagacity.

"I have no right to offer you the satisfaction of a gentleman, for any man who could have robbed and insulted two poor sailor-boys, like Halliard and myself once were, cannot be other than a craven-hearted scoundrel," saying which, Rayner lowered the muzzle of his pistol, and slapped the robber's face.

The highwayman fired from beneath his cloak; but the ball simply grazed Frank's cheek.

THE ATTEMPTED MURDER.

In an instant, the active young midshipman closed with his tall and powerful antagonist, and there was a deadly struggle for the fall.

The seamen would have interfered; but Rayner shouted out,

"Hands off, lads, this my quarrel."

And, with a dexterous twist of the leg, he threw the robber violently to the ground, and placing his knee upon the chest, and with a firm grip at the throat, he pointed his pistol at his brain, and the robber, powerful as he might be, was nerveless under him

"Brayvo!—hurrah!—brayvo! my young fighting cock," shouted Juniper, Hawser, and Konks, in wild delight, throwing up their caps in uproarious excitement. "Bravely, fairly down. Let him have it if he don't surrender," shouted Hawser, flourishing a poker, and capering about.

"If he don't ask for quarter, knock his toplights out!" roared Konks.

"I do cry quarter!" said the half-strangled, chopfallen robber. "Don't fire."

"He's run up the white flag. A gallant little brig has walloped a seventy-four. Hurrah for the Thunderer!" shouted Juniper and Hawser, in chorus.

The robber was bound and disarmed, and searched.

His pockets contained all manner of trinkets which had evidently been stolen from females.

"If you hadn't been dastard enough to rob poor defenceless women," Rayner said, with fierceness, "I would have set you free. You are a low-minded cur, and deserve your fate; you shall be handed over to the police."

"Serve him jolly well right, Frank," said Hawser

" And the swab of a landshark ought to think himself lucky he's not got a piece of lead through his red gills, that's all."

The midshipman and his shipmates regaled themselves with grog, and songs, and cigars.

And after an hour or two thus spent in jollity and right goodfellowship, they all departed, Frank, on the robber's horse, leading the way, while the highwayman, with his hands tightly tied behind him, walked between Hawser and Juniper, who with two heavy clubs they had cut from a tree, guarded him with vigilance, enlivening the journey with a song, or a swig of rum, entertaining the robber with a running commentary of oaths, and remarks not at all complimentary to that individual, behind whom Konks walked with a double-shotted pistol.

Thus journeying along, they came in sight of Joel Britton's smithy, just before day dawned, and Frank knocked loudly at the door, which quickly brought the blacksmith down.

" Here he is, Mr. Britton. Allow me to introduce to you the gentleman of the road, who very politely never paid you for shoeing his horse. He was on his way to make your acquaintance last night. He fell into my hands, and meant mischief; but his cowardice has now its reward."

CHAPTER XLIV.

THE GHOSTLY LADY OF SEAWARDINE—PENALVON AND THORKIL IN SECRET CONFERENCE—SHADOWS OF THE ENDING—APPALLING APPARITION.

THORKIL and Hylda were alone.

Age had fast turned the wrecker's locks to grey, and a long career of crime left furrows upon his brow deep and red, and scar-like.

Each day found the heavy, churlish Thorkil, more and more morose and reticent.

He seemed to shun the light of day; he could not bare the glorious glitter and glow of the mid-day sun.

He was brooding over the past, and meditating hellish schemes for the future.

Hylda watched the muscles twitching round his large rapacious mouth, and from the gathering of his heavy beetle brows, full well knew that a storm was gathering of more than ordinary violence.

Like her husband, she had become unusually restless, melancholy, and snappish, during the past few weeks, but neither could divine the cause.

They seldom spoke, and when they did so it was in a growling, snarling tone, like wild, revengeful animals, ready at any moment to pounce and tear each other to pieces.

They felt as if some spell hung over them, as if a powerful hand was laid on them.

It was the hand of Destiny.

Their time had come; their course of crime, a long, long life, spent in wickedness and dark, unmentionable deeds, was near its close, and, though they knew not why, a cold, shivering quiver passed through the frames of both.

" More brandy?" asked Hylda, with a sneer. " What are you now fit for? You have sat idly here, week after week, drinking both day and night. There is but one keg left; what do you want to break into that for?"

" What? Why to drown all care and sorrow, that's why I drink. When this little job is over I shall reform my ways."

" I fear that neither you nor I will ever live to see the day of Penalvon's triumph."

" You are but a silly woman. What wrecker, smuggler or pirate, could withstand the power of all Seawardine?"

" There is a power mightier than Penalvon! Adair is on the seas; I saw his schooner, last night, pass the headland, going before the wind like a flying cloud."

Thorkil laughed hoarsely, as he contemptuously said,

" On the sea? Why, then, so much the better, if it only be so, for the revenue's and king's men are on the look out, and would give anything to catch him. Earl Penalvon's money can do anything."

" Do anything, perhaps, but catch that phantom schooner. Do you think, drunken sot as you are, that any of the heavy, rolling tubs of the king's navy or revenue, could ever overhaul that phantom which Adair commands?"

" Tut, tut, woman; your foolery tempts me to strike you! Adair is not afloat, and never will be again; all his crew have left him. Trelawny and Otho know that, for they have but lately been to his hiding-place, and, before another week passes, I shall have ample revenge. I go to Seawardine tonight."

Thorkil went to Seawardine by night.

He was received with much hauteur by the earl, who, pale and languid, slowly paced his chamber.

" You are here again," he said, eyeing the black-looking wrecker, with a sidelong, sinister glance. " Come with some other plot or plan, a bran new scheme, I suppose, as useless as all others I have foolishly aided you in."

" I come, my lord, to say, that I have perfected a plan to secure your enemy, Paul Adair, and not only him, but Rose Halliard and her son likewise."

" What!" said Penalvon, in sudden flush and surprise, " what, all three? Who told you I wished for the destruction of any but Adair?" asked the earl, with the penetrating glance of a hawk, gazing on Thorkil, with a quivering lip, now of ashy paleness. " Who told you that?"

" I was not so informed, my lord, by any one, but instinct told me as much."

" Instinct! what do you know of instinct?" said the earl, contemptuously snapping his fingers.

" You gave me a knife once, my lord, and——"

" Enough, Thorkil; let that rest with the past," Penalvon said, furtively glancing at the door.

The winds wailed without, sorrowfully and dying.

It seemed as if some unearthly visitor was looked for in that spacious lonely chamber, for both instinctively turned towards the folding-doors that led to the large libraries and museum.

For some moments neither spoke, yet each felt an unearthly chilliness creep over them. At last, Penalvon said,

" If this could be done!"

" Could be? but it shall be."

" And yet there remains another."

" Yet another, my lord?" asked Thorkil, in surprise.

"Yes ; one who as yet roams at large upon the earth—one who visits me nightly in sleep—the daughter ! It is her power and spells, wherever she be, that has thus far foiled me. But come, follow me."

Penalvon led the way to the museum. Thorkil followed.

"I wish to show you something," Penalvon said, and had advanced to the middle of the room, candle in hand.

A sudden gust of wind blew the candle out.

They were in total darkness ; alone, in that chamber of mystery and horror !

The moon shone through the western window, and its light fell upon a single door that opened into a passage leading, by unfrequented passage ways, to the vaults below.

Through some unknown influence the confederates in crime seemed rooted to the spot, and they gazed, with staring eyes, upon the spotless panels of that mysterious door.

Noiselessly it was unlocked by unseen hands, uplifted from its hinges, and fell to the ground with a loud crash, that rent the panels in a thousand pieces ! The skeleton cabinet fell from its pedestal, and was a mass of ruins.

The winds whistled from the dark corridors beyond, and, in the distance, danced a blueish light, like some mystic ignis fatuus.

Astonished, but unable to move or speak, Penalvon and Thorkil gazed with distended eyes and open mouths.

The light slowly approached.

Both could faintly discern the figure of a woman, robed in white.

Slowly it approached ; there were marks of blood about the throat.

Standing in the doorway of the dark corridor, it gazed, long and intently, upon the horror-stricken criminals.

Her features were pale and calm and beautiful ; her hair hung loose about her snowy shoulders, her form and figure seemed transparent like a thing of air, and around her hung a thin haze of luminous light.

She stretched a thin, white hand towards Penalvon, and with the left pointed to a red gash in her throat, at the same time looking at Thorkil with eyes that seemed all a-flame.

" 'Tis Thyra !" said the rough wrecker, horror-stricken.

"Who or what are you ?" gasped Penalvon, in a husky whisper, as he sank to the floor in a state of exhaustion.

"Lady of Seawardine !" was the reply, given in a slow, calm, unearthly tone that sank to the hearts of the trembling culprits.

"And what your mission ?" asked the aged lord, with the voice of one near death.

"To seek revenge. Your time has come !"

In a second the luminous light had faded into darkness.

A loud crash was heard as of a falling mass of bones.

The spectre had vanished !

All was still.

All that remained of that frightful vision was a heap of bones, arms, legs, and ribs that lay heaped together in the doorway.

CHAPTER XLV.

THE BLOOD-STAINED PARCHMENTS — PAUL ADAIR, AGGER, THORKIL AND PENALVON MEET AT SEAWARDINE—THE ROBBERY OF FAMILY PAPERS— THE MYSTERIOUS VOICE—THORKIL SETS OUT ON HIS LAST ENTERPRISE—AGGER'S TERROR.

WHILE the earl and Thorkil stood trembling in the museum, gazing with distended eyes upon the surrounding darkness, irresolute, nerveless and horror-bound to the spot where the spectre had appeared, there were other things transpiring under the same roof, but in a different part of the mansion of Seawardine.

Paul Adair had landed his men along the coast, not far from the White Cliffs near Thorkil's home, and having sent round the Phantom Schooner to anchor in a safe and unfrequented inlet, he and Agger bent their steps towards Earl Penalvon's mansion.

They journeyed rapidly, and were both well armed.

"It is very hazardous," said Agger, as they walked hurriedly along.

"True, but it must be done."

"But if you should fail ?"

"There is no such word as 'fail.' "

"You have been there so often that I fear you will find little chance of entering again ; the long passage that led underground from the park to the mansion is closed. I know, for I told you weeks ago that I had reconnoitred and found it so."

"Well, then, if there is no other way, we must unfasten the windows and get in, that's all."

"Well, you know best ; you are provided with a dark lantern and that will aid us much."

While thus conversing they entered the park of Seawardine.

'Twas past midnight and all was still.

The watch-dogs even were asleep, and no sounds were heard save the sighing of winds.

But a single light was visible in that old and spacious mansion.

"There's but one awake," said Paul, creeping through the trees, "and that's Penalvon himself ; he's in the library. Now for it."

"Which way ?"

"Follow me."

Noiselessly creeping through the thick, low shrubbery that grew around the mansion, Paul Adair cautiously made his way to the east side of the house, which was wrapped in dense shade.

With a chisel he opened the shutters of the drawing-room windows, which were level with the lawn, and entered.

Agger followed, and closed the shutters again.

"You seem to know all about this old place," said Agger, as he observed Paul moving hither and thither through the apartment with a carelessness and ease of manner which bespoke that he was perfectly at home in that apartment.

"What I wish is not here," he said, flinging himself on a sofa, and whispering to Agger. "It must be in his cabinet, or chamber, so, until the old rascal goes to sleep, suppose we have a smoke ?— the old devil always keeps fine cigars. If I don't much mistake, the last time I was here, there were several decanters of choice wine on that sideboard near the window," saying which Paul turned on his dark lantern slightly and soon discovered what he looked for.

Stretching themselves upon costly ottomans or sofas, Adair and Agger smoked and drank at ease, and felt as unconcerned as if they thus disported in mansions of their own.

While thus so pleasantly occupied, the sounds of footsteps were heard approaching the room-door.

"That's not Penalvon's step," said Paul, listening, "'tis too heavy for him. Come, let's secrete ourselves; get under the sofa, Agger, and be as still as a mouse."

Within a few moments the door opened, and Penalvon entered with Thorkil at his heels.

"Yes; this is a much better place to talk in than the other. I never did much like that room upstairs," said Thorkil, seating himself on the sofa.

"We must have been dreaming," said the earl. "And yet how came the door open, and that heap of bones? However, be what it may, it was very harmless; neither of us are dead yet, eh, Thorkil? It will take a little more to frighten two such persons as you and I—dead men tell no tales, they say.

"Nor women either, I think," said Thorkil, half drunk, and laughing.

"Hush! Walls have ears; but what do you intend to do?—are you resolved to finish this business by seizing the whole of them?"

"I am."

"That is if you can."

"Can, eh? Well, if I do not I will perish in the attempt. If he had ten thousand lives, one less would not satisfy my great revenge."

"You speak as if you meant it."

"Yes, and I cannot fail this time. I intend to wipe off old scores with him, or, if I do not, you may take my bones, and stick 'em up in your museum as a curiosity, that's all. But, Lord! how like Thyra that ghost was. I never saw anything so like in all my life."

"Yes, yes," said the earl, who wished to distract Thorkil's attention from all memory of the spectre; "but how do you intend to proceed? You must remember that Adair's gang are a numerous and desperate set of fellows. I have cause to know them from what they did to me at Wild Meg's."

"I don't fear him, he's got no gang now; most of his men have deserted, and I have engaged several of them to help me, who thirst for the villain's blood. If I only had some money now," said Thorkil, thoughtfully, "I could buy up the whole gang, and seize Adair in his own den, surrounded, as he thinks he is, by his friends."

"Money need not stop you. What is money good for, except to gratify our pleasures or revenge?" said Penalvon, walking towards a cabinet, and unlocking it. "Here is money; take these notes, and this bag. There is more if you require it."

Thorkil did as bidden, and took a roll of bank notes, and a small bag of coin, and put them with great care in one of his enormous jacket pockets.

"There's more where that came from," whispered Agger, who, holding his breath, nudged Paul, who pinched his arm in token of silence.

"If you fail in this enterprise, Thorkil, never show your face at Seawardine. I will leave you to plod along alone; therefore, expect my protection no more."

Thorkil blurted out something in reply, and after drinking off half a tumbler of rum at a draught, took his departure.

For some time Earl Penalvon sat moodily alone. He was restless; each rustling of the ivy leaves around the windows caused a tremor to pass through him, and he stalked to and fro, stopping and walking at intervals, until the early cocks began to crow.

During one of these intervals in Earl Penalvon's walks, Paul crept from under the sofa, cat-like and softly, and escaped from the room unperceived.

Agger slipped his boots off and followed the example of his young and daring chief.

"This way, Agger," whispered Paul, when in the large entrance hall, and both rapidly ascended the long and lofty stone staircase, and entered the museum.

The first thing Paul's dark lantern revealed was a heap of human bones which lay upon the floor.

"Poor wretch," said Paul, with a sigh, "so the villains cannot even respect your bones, eh? Great Heavens!"

"Whose are they, Paul," asked Agger, in a whisper.

"A long history; there's no time for that, now. Let's to the library."

"Suppose we are interrupted, what then?"

"We must escape the best we can. No bloodshed yet, that would spoil all. Come."

Once in the library Paul went to a small and elegant writing-desk and burst the lid open.

"The key of his private escritoire is here, if anywhere," he said. "Listen at the door, Agger, and give the alarm."

To his intense surprise and satisfaction he found a bundle of small keys, some of which were labelled. One of them was rusty from disuse.

"This must be it," he said, and instantly tried it on the lock of a very old piece of furniture, half writing-desk, half cabinet, which, from its carving, was evidently some heirloom of the Penalvon family, and of great strength and beauty.

After many endeavours the key forced the huge desk-lid open, and, as it turned on its rusty hinges, it creaked with a piercing sound that much resembled the cry of some animal in intense torture.

Paul involuntarily looked towards Agger, who, pale and excited, was guarding the door.

"D—n the noise," said Adair, in vexation, "it was enough to wake the whole house."

As he turned his lantern inside the desk a mass of mouldy documents met his view, some of paper, some of parchment, which were bound in bundles with red tape.

He looked and looked again, and resolved to carry off them all.

Stuffing his own and Agger's pockets he was about to leave the desk to search elsewhere, when his eye alighted on a last remaining document which was blood-stained and stiff.

"I'll take charge of this," he murmured, with grim satisfaction, and placed it beneath his guernsey for greater security. "It will be stained a little more, I think, before I part with it," he murmured, with a quiet chuckle.

Closing the desk he returned the keys whence taken, and, while fumbling about, touched some secret spring, and several drawers flew open.

His surprise was great.

He found that all were closely packed with letters.

"This is all I ask," said Adair, with a murmur of sincere reverence, as he put them in his pockets.

"If these are from the 'French merchants' I know so much about, then Earl Penalvon may bid a long and last adieu to Seawardine.

Replacing everything as neatly as he could, he closed the second desk as carefully as the first, and left no trace or appearance of its ever having been tampered with.

"What a capital housebreaker you'd make," said Agger, in an approving whisper.

Paul only smiled and darkened his lantern.

They entered the museum again noiselessly.

There sat Penalvon in the moonlight, gazing on the heap of human bones.

He had crept upstairs by a secret passage known to himself alone, and was perfectly oblivious of the presence of any one.

He held a pistol in his hand.

A few more steps would have discovered the robbers.

They retreated into the dense darkness of the library again, and watched Penalvon's actions with almost feline sagacity.

"It was a narrow escape," whispered Agger.

"Hush! he will not remain long there. He is a doomed man!"

Penalvon spoke.

"Why should I destroy myself?" he said. "And yet I care not to live; life is a burden. What is there in those bones that should terrify a living man? Tut! nonsense; it was indigestion. Ghost! Ha! ha!"

And he laughed derisively at the heap of bones scattered on the floor, and spurned the skull with his foot.

At that moment a tremendous sound, as of thunder, rolled through the house.

Strange noises rang along the corridors.

The shrieks of a woman, bound in chains, were heard and repeated with appalling distinctness.

Penalvon rose to his feet.

The sounds approached still nearer and nearer.

The words became more and more distinct.

"Where is my child? Give me my child!" said the voice of one unseen.

The windows shook with violence, loud derisive laughter broke upon the air, as of maniacs scoffing, and then the voice cried out,

"Give me my child! Ah, ha! look at the pale-faced, trembling murderer."

"Damnation!" roared Penalvon, stung to the quick with madness.

He fired in the direction of the voice.

The shot struck the armour-clad figure of some ancient Penalvon, standing with lance in hand on a pedestal, and the whole mass of armour fell to the floor with a loud resounding crash.

"This is awful!" whispered Agger, who now, for the first time in his whole life, felt a true sense of awe and terror. "It is unbearable. The place is inhabited by devils. Let us away."

"Calm yourself. See; here he comes!" Adair whispered. "He must come this way to go to his room. Look at his haggard face as he passes the moonlight."

More like a thing of death than of life, Penalvon walked slowly, and with tottering gait, towards his room.

His hair was all dishevelled, his eyes glared with unnatural ferocity and brilliancy, while his face was ashy pale.

He stalked rather than walked from the museum.

He almost touched Adair, who, crouched in the shade, observed his every motion with supreme indifference and disgust.

He passed the folding-doors, and disappeared through the library, and vanished in the darkness towards his chamber.

Paul and Agger seized the right moment, and disappeared.

They soon reached their first place of concealment, and putting on their boots, decamped from the place expeditiously with their parchments and papers, not forgetting either to help themselves to what spare change remained in the cabinet in the drawing-room, or to drink their own long life and prosperity in right good bumpers of brandy, from decanters on the sideboards.

CHAPTER XLVI.

MIDSHIPMAN RAYNER IS VIOLENTLY IN LOVE—HE DISCLOSES HIS PLANS TO HAWSER AND KONKS—HE "SOUNDS" ROSE HALLIARD ABOUT IT—HER OBJECTIONS—ELOPEMENT AND MARRIAGE.

KONKS, Bill Hawser, and Joe Juniper were snugly installed at Polruth's kiddleawink, but they were restless, and wished to be at sea again.

"Never mind, lads," said Frank Rayner, in his usual good humour and flow of spirits. "The Scorpion won't sail for a month yet, so I heard this morning; but what odds, all our money isn't spent yet, and when it goes, let's trust to luck for more. I'm going to get married."

"Married?" roared the seamen, in stentorian chorus. "Married? A midshipman cast anchor in such stormy times as these? Why, Mr. Rayner, you must be mad!"

"Not quite yet, lads; but the truth of the matter is this: I've always had a liking for a sweet little craft that is docked in a boarding-school not a thousand miles from here, and we've managed of late to pass a great many letters, and exchange friendly signals, so that when I come to compare logs I find that our mutual reckonings and bearings have been truly and accurately taken."

"Aye, aye, Mr. Rayner; you puts the thing right afore us in true talk. Heave ahead, my lad," said Hawser, puffing his pipe. "And now that you've heaved the lead, you find that her anchorage ain't none of the best, eh, very good."

"And, as I was saying, she's given her word that she has no objection to me commissioning her for life, and so I think I'll hoist my flag, and let her stay in dock a little while longer to have her cabin fittings done up with gold and paint, and compasses properly adjusted, in other words, shipmates, marry her privately, and leave her at school for another year or two."

"Perfectly straight, my lad, and well thought on," said Konks, approvingly.

"But when is it to be, then? You'll not have much time to think about it. Are the old folks agreeable, or do they hoist an unfriendly flag?"

"Aye, that's where I drag bottom, lads; the

mother is totally opposed to me yet, although I love the mother almost as much as the daughter, and love the brother still more, perhaps, than either, but, at least, as much. I have resolved that we *shall* get spliced, and trust to luck for the rest, even if I get smashed in the very next action we fight."

"Well, who is the lord of the Admiralty as won't let you commission your favourite little craft ?"

"Harry's mother ?"

"What, Rose ? And is it pretty little Helena that I often hear him speak about ? Why, then, my lad, I'd advise you to study straight sailing in that quarter, because Master Harry isn't very easy to be pleased."

"Why, Harry is my best friend in the matter, and seconds me like a true brother."

"Well done for him, then, lad ; you always were close pals, you know, afloat or ashore, and I should like to see you sail in company still," said Hawser, with many airs of wisdom.

"Yes, and many a good trick they have played me on board the Thunderer," said Konks, smiling rather grimly. "I don't forget my pigtail being nailed to the deck one fine morning, the young rascals."

"They filled my pipe with powder once," said Juniper, "and nearly blew my nose off. However, these are different times, and if the wind's fair we may have a jolly good dance yet before we go on board the Scorpion."

"But what kind of objection could Rose have to your courting or marrying the lass ?" asked Konks, rather indignantly. "You have a commission in your pocket, and that is more than many a young gentleman is worthy of, and if I don't much mistake you'll have plenty opportunities for rising. Admiral Nelson wasn't more than a second luff at your age."

"Well, dear, kind Rose objected on the grounds that, in the first place, we were both too young, and not suitable for each other, for, says she, 'Frank, your position in the world now is that of a gentleman ; there is no knowing what you may not achieve in wealth and greatness ; but as to Helena, my dear adopted daughter, she is entirely dependent upon Harry and myself, and, except her own individual worth, has nothing to recommend her, or advance her in the world.' "

"Plain speaking, shipmates, very plain," said Konks, "and I admire Mrs. Rose Halliard for it more than I ever did ; but I must say, if I were a party in the case, I shouldn't stand at such objections, but take the girl as she was at her own individual worth."

"Which I mean to do, if possible."

Days passed, and still letters came, and went between Helena and Frank. He began to look pale and restless, loss of appetite followed, and Polruth began to imagine that a doctor was necessary to reinstate his good-looking guest to his former state of jollity and robust health.

Harry, who had been hitherto staying at the White House on the cliff, visited but could not comfort him, for Rose Halliard seemed more stubborn than ever to his repeated proposition.

'Twas in vain he begged and beseeched, all was useless. Harry said that, although there were no personal objections in the matter, it was merely a question of time, "for you are sure to have the girl, Frank, and I warrant Helena will remain faithful to her vows if she knew but half of what I do of your true worth and talent."

This balm of praise did not soothe the love-sick middy's mind.

He sat at the window night after night gazing on the rising moon, and at length resolved at all hazards to possess himself of his heart's darling, let the cost or danger be what they might.

His visits to the neighbourhood of Helena's school were frequent, and he sought every opportunity to speak to her.

The postman was bribed, and delivered long and passionately-written letters to the fair prisoner within school walls, while Helena sighed, and tossed many a sweetly-worded, cocked-hat note across the garden wall.

Helena knew not whom to trust in this all-important matter of her lover. The housemaid, however was a willing ally.

Through that faithful domestic's strategy, Frank was duly and regularly informed of the progress of his mistress, and on one occasion she arranged a midnight meeting between the lovers.

Helena crept from her room to the parlour, the window was opened, and in an instant Rayner climbed the garden-gate, and was beside her.

How they embraced, and what sweet words passed between these ardent and youthful lovers, will never be known ; suffice it to say, that they sealed their mutual loves in a long and tender caress, and the following night was arranged for the elopement.

Full of delight, Frank hurried away to a neighbouring village, and hired a coach-and-four for "Falmouth and back," as he gave out, but which was in reality destined to travel in quite a different direction.

The night was beautifully mild and clear.

The moon shone forth with unusual brilliancy, while grand constellations of glittering stars studded the heavens with a calm and holy light.

'Twas midnight !

Helena, with heart wildly beating, sat at her open window, gazing out upon the beauty of the scene.

Tears flowed freely, for she knew that in taking this hazardous step she was disobeying the injunctions both of mother and of brother.

Yet her young and guileless heart was full of love, and she knew not what reason was, in the wild tumult of affection that reigned in her inexperienced heart.

All she knew was that Harry doted on Rayner, and that Frank was the chosen idol of her soul.

Wrapped in a cloak, she sat watching, and listening, and weeping.

The sound of carriage wheels was heard upon the road.

She saw a carriage-and-four appear in sight, and turn up a grassy lane near by.

With pulse madly beating, she heard the steps of her lover approaching.

He was at the gate ; some friendly hand had unlocked it, and in a moment had clambered up to the parlour-window, and clasped Helena to his heart.

"Come, pet, let us away. The carriage awaits."

Helena spoke not ; she could not ; but leaned upon Frank's shoulder, and wept freely.

He tried the room door.

That also was unlocked !

The hall-door stood ajar !

The same friend had done all this out of pure affection for Helena and her gallant lover.

Polly, the housemaid, had proved herself this faithful friend, and while the lovers conversed in low and hurried tones, that trustworthy domestic, in a sort of undress, popped into the moonlit parlour, and beckoned the way.

Frank was not slow to obey.

Helena sat irresolute.

He whispered a word, and before she could reply, he had raised her in his arms, and bore her from the apartment.

A few moments elapsed, and Polly's heart beat with joy when she saw the figures of the midshipman and his loved one flitting across the road to a dense thicket, in the shade of which stood the carriage-and-four.

In a second or two the carriage moved off at a trot, which the postilions, who now for the first time knew their mission, quickly increased into a blood-enlivening gallop, and ere long Polly heard no sound of rolling wheels, for Frank and his intended bride were far upon their journey.

She listened, and then carefully locked the garden gate, the hall and parlour doors, and the whole house being in its usual nocturnal state, she quietly crept up to her bed-chamber again, the highest and smallest part of that large and commodious building.

When morning came, and Helena did not appear in her accustomed place among the pupils, consternation and alarm were on every feature.

The gaunt, irate, masculine principal of the academy, in awe-striking frills and furbelows, was at her wits' end.

She fumed and stamped and stuttered with well-assumed injured dignity and rage.

Governesses looked askance at each other in terror and surprise, while the far greater part of the young ladies themselves whispered confidentially in groups of three or four, and tittered with unaffected merriment and good-humour.

All the servants had warning to leave, and there was much clamour between cooks, kitchen-maids, and others.

"It must have been their fault," the infuriated mistress exclaimed, "or how could Miss Halliard have been spirited away? She might have been abducted and murdered, and no one know anything about it. The academy was totally ruined," she said, in choking tones. "Its long and well-earned reputation had flown to the winds. Rich parents would never confide their daughters to her again; all honour and profit had departed, and she saw no prospect in future but the poor-house."

Polly, of all the servants, appeared the most astonished.

She was astounded. She couldn't draw breath from sheer surprise,

"Miss Helena Halliard run off? Who'd a thought of such a thing, mum? and John, the butcher, says that his master's wife's sister saw a sailor-gentleman hiring a carriage-and-four in the village, just like that young man, mum, as come once to see Miss Helena, and I shouldn't wonder a bit, mum, but as that noise which I heard last night near the house was nothing else but that same carriage as she saw, for it sounded very much like it, and when Jane and me, mum, went across the road this morning, to shake carpets, we saw the marks of wheels quite plain."

Polly did not tell anyone that Frank had made her a present of five guineas, nor did she say what kind of presents Miss Helena had bestowed upon her.

Like most housemaids of buxom rosy appearance and twenty years of age, Miss Polly had cut her wisdom teeth, and never let any mistress command her mind, however much they worked the body.

Polly's good offices, however, were not unrewarded, as the sequel may show.

CHAPTER XLVII.

PAUL ADAIR AND AGGER TAKE REFUGE IN THE KIDDLE-A-WINK—THEY EVADE PENALVON'S EMISSARIES—THORKIL KILLS HYLDA—PAUL ADAIR'S REVELATIONS —THYRA STABS THORKIL.

"WHERE can we best go?" said Agger, when he and Paul Adair had made their escape. "He will be sure to discover the robbery, and will leave no stone unturned to capture and punish us."

"Polruth's is the safest. I know that *he* is a friend, and we can hide there, if need be, until the affair blows over."

"But we must watch Thorkil and Black Will."

"Leave that to me. How cumbersome this load of parchment is."

Journeying across the fields by paths well known to them, they soon came in sight of the kiddle-a-wink, and were heartily welcomed by the burly innkeeper, who bestirred himself to make his visitors comfortable.

"But what is this I hear of you, Paul? Why, Thorkil was up here an hour ago, and, drunk as usual, swore he'd have your life. He laughed like a maniac, said that all your gang had deserted, and had hired themselves to go with him on a secret expedition. There were half-a-dozen fellows with him; he seems to have no end of money.

"There's one particular fellow with him I don't much like, they call him Bow Legs, and, from what he said, one would suppose he thirsted for your very life. What have you been doing to 'em? why, they all rave against you like lunatics. I couldn't put in a word for you edgeways."

Paul laughed.

"So Bill Hardy, or Bow-legs, as they call him, spoke more bitterly than any against me, did he?" said Adair, musing. "Well, Polruth, you need not fear for my safety, for he's the most trusty of all my followers. You must grant us a secret hiding-place for a few days; there will be stormy times at Seawardine shortly.

"I don't pretend to know what your plans or intentions are," said Polruth; "all I know is that you have been a good friend to me, and, as far as is in my power, I will assist you, for I feel confident that the business in hand is perfectly honourable and deserving of countenance by any one who considers himself a man. All that I regret, Paul, is that you should have married Nelly Britton in such a secret way; if you had approached the old man properly I feel certain he would have consented to your union; as it is, the behaviour of his daughter has well nigh broken his heart."

"I feel sorry to have caused any annoyance to old Joel, for not a better man breathes on earth than that worthy, grey-haired blacksmith. Nelly knew me, however; I did not deceive her, or attempt to deceive her. Had her father given me any encouragement I shouldn't have led the wild life I have. However, every dog has his day; meanwhile, Polruth, give us something to eat, and, if any inquiries are made concerning me, you know that I am not——"

"Right, lad; I know nothing of you."

Paul and Agger had scarcely been in the kiddle-a-wink an hour when some of Earl Penalvon's mounted servants rode up to the door.

"A glass of ale, landlord. Have you seen two strange men about these parts, this morning?"

"No. Why do you ask?"

"There has been an audacious robbery at the mansion, and some of the gamekeepers say that they have found the footprints of two men in the grass, and that the direction taken by them led to the heath."

"Robbery!" said Polruth, in well affected astonishment. "What did they steal?"

"Oh, several bundles of very valuable family papers, my lord says; he's in a fine way about it, and would pay any amount in reward for their apprehension."

"Robbed of family papers, eh? Well, then, they must be rather curious robbers, and no mistake, for thieves usually look after money, not family papers."

"Well, since you have not seen nor heard of them, tell me where Thorkil lives. I've a note for him."

Polruth pointed the way to the White Cliffs, whereupon the grooms departed at a gallop.

"They haven't been long in making the discovery," said Agger, laughing; "it will take them much longer to find out our present whereabouts."

"True," said Paul; "nevertheless, when darkness sets in, we must leave this place; 'tis necessary that I should see Harry Halliard and Rose without a moment's delay."

At nightfall Paul and Agger set out for the White House on the cliffs.

The surrounding darkness was impenetrable.

They spoke but little, for fear of being overheard and detected by any of the many loitering sailors who thronged the coast.

As they approached the White House, a man was discovered peeping through the parlour window.

"Hallo, what's this mean?" said Agger. "See that fellow quizzing in there? A good knock on the head would make him less inquisitive for the future, I think. What if it be one of Thorkil's hirelings, taking full bearings of the house?"

"We can soon satisfy ourselves on that point," said Paul, indifferently. "If it be any of Thorkil's own gang, a pistol-shot will soon settle him."

They approached the house still closer, and screened themselves behind the wooden palings of the garden.

Agger cocked his pistol.

Paul placed his hand on Agger's arm to restrain him.

"I know him, or am much mistaken in the darkness. 'Tis 'Bow-legs,' for a million."

He whistled in a peculiar manner.

The man peering through the window instantly turned his head in surprise.

"Bill?"

"I thought it was—in fact I made sure it was—you, captain. I was just taking the bearings to see if you were there or not, because there's mischief brewing, and I wanted to warn you in time."

"I know it, lad, and according to promise, you see I am here, ready for anything."

"What luck, sir?"

"Every success, Bill. You and Agger keep a bright look-out while I go in. Let no one approach within a hundred yards without giving warning."

"There's been the devil to pay with Thorkil and his pals," said Bow-legs, laughing, "nothing less than killing!"

"Killing! say you?" asked Agger, seating himself, and lighting a pipe.

"Aye. It was in this way. It appears that one of the king's men deserted from the receiving-ship, and brought another young chap with him. Well, when Thorkil saw him, he shook him by the hand and they fell to drinking hard.

"'You're the very man I want,' said Thorkil, 'I've got a job in hand that will suit you.'

"Hylda recognised the stranger, and began to curse Thorkil, and call him all the names she could think of.

"He was getting awfully drunk, and struck her. This only aggravated her still more.

"'Do you bring my father's murderer here again?' said Hylda, foaming with passion——"

"The stranger, whose name was——"

"Harleck? I thought so. Well."

"Rose in a frightful passion, and threatened to kill her.

"Thorkil again interfered, and maddened by her tongue, he drew his cutlass, and stabbed her!"

"Killed her?"

"Aye; as dead as a herring."

"Poor wretch! she wasn't half so bad as that fiend, her husband; his day, however, isn't far distant. What then?"

"Oh, he took it quite coolly. He said she had been rune-kenning, and raising spirits from the dead, to thwart all his schemes and plans. He filled out more brandy, drank till perfectly maddened and raving with brandy, and then threw Hylda into the ebbing tide."

"Such is the remorseless villain with whom we have to deal. Nothing would please me more than to plunge my dagger into the monster's heart he's used to killing, however; there's no fear of him ever dying from remorse of conscience. What plans has he in hand?"

"Oh, he, Trelawny, Otho, Harleck, and his companion, Crawley, are as thick as thieves can be. Do you know that two of the king's ships are on the look out for Paul Adair?"

"You cannot mean that!—who informed?"

"Thorkil was sent with a letter from Seawarding to the nearest coast-guard station, and they telegraphed the contents on to Falmouth and Plymouth."

"The pair of double-dyed villains!" shouted Agger, in surprise and indignation. "Vengeance shall overtake them yet; but what of our men?"

"Twenty have joined him. I am their captain," said Bow-legs, laughing. "Oh, Thorkil thinks the world of me."

While this conversation was progressing outside, Harry, Thyra, and Rose, were seated in the comfortable parlour round the fire, spell-bound by the revelations made by Paul.

"This is too horrible to believe, Paul," said one and all, with distended eyes, and open mouth. "Do you mean to say, then, that this Earl Penalvon and Thorkil Penreal are the monsters you represent?—that they could have thus concealed their many crimes and enormities so long."

NOTICE.—The next Number of the Boys' Library will be Published on Friday, September 26th. Order early of your Bookseller.

BOYS' LIBRARY

Harry Halliard: or, the Young British Tar.

THE ACCUSATION

Thyra bowed her head and wept.

"But who was this lady, then, so cruelly murdered thus?"

"Thyra's mother—your father's mother!"
Harry jumped to his feet as if shot.

Thyra screamed and laughed by turns, and fell to the floor in a swoon.

"I knew it, I knew it!" she gasped in a choking voice. "Angels told me so. Men called me mad, wild. I am not. The spirit of my mother visits me in dreams. I could not be—I am not mistaken."

"I did not say this much before," said Paul, calmly, "for I wanted final proof. It is here," he said, producing a crimson-stained parchment from his bosom. "I loathed the sight of Thorkil from the first moment I had reason to suspect him. If I had given mouth to my suspicions, who would

have believed me? I have further proof, documentary evidence of Penalvon's villany. Glance at this bundle of letters, for you can well decipher these French scrawls. He is a traitor, and always has been, to his King and country. These will hang him if nothing else will."

"How can we ever repay you, Paul?" said Harry, pale and nervous.

"Reward, compensation, recompense," said Paul, blushing scarlet, and with a momentary curl on his proud lip, "I did not think——"

"Enough, brave and disinterested friend," said Harry, rising, and grasping the Rover by the hand, "offence was my last thought."

"All I require is, that when the hour of trial comes, you will act as a true man, and let no false notions of mercy and humanity step in between the culprit and his merited reward."

"Mercy!" cried Thyra, rising from her recumbent posture, with a flashing eye and gesture full of heroism, "mercy to one who has acted through his whole life with heartless barbarism towards the poor and helpless! Let me but live to gaze upon him once more," she said, "and if there be steel that can pierce his rocky heart, I will rend it in twain."

She moved towards the door with a look and demeanour full of fiery energy and revenge.

"Stay, Thyra," interposed Paul, who rose and stood before the door, "you must not leave us yet."

"Yes," she said moodily and dreamily, "yes, within another hour it may be too late. Thorkil and his minions are on the move; let all begone, then I will remain."

She had scarcely spoken, when Agger and Hardy, without, whistled long and shrilly.

"'Tis the signal," said Paul. "Come, we must away from this. Nay, no resistance, Harry; now is not the time."

"Fly before such a dastard crew of cut-throats and hirelings?" said Harry, in a contemptuous tone. "What do you take me for?"

"For as brave a lad as ever walked the quarter-deck; a true type of a gallant British Sailor Boy; but discretion is the better part of valour. You fear not for yourself truly, but you would not have your mother and Thyra imperilled. Let us fly; our turn will come speedily; one false step now would undo all that has been done."

Persuasion prevailed.

All departed from the White House, and hid themselves among the rocks and cliffs, securely screened from view.

Shortly there arose strange noises on the air.

They came nearer and nearer.

Presently Thorkil's voice was heard, leading a numerous and villanous band towards the house.

They surrounded the dwelling as if by preconcerted movement, while Thorkil rushed to the door, and dashed into the passage, cutlass in hand.

All was darkness.

He entered the parlour, naught was there save bright moonbeams that fell upon the floor.

"Escaped! foiled!" he roared, in drunken, delirious anger. "Search every room. I myself will stand in the passage; no one dare pass this way."

Thorkil stood alone, some feet in front of the dark stairs, cutlass in hand, and looked straight before him.

He peered into the darkness, and perceived the figure of an unknown, defenceless woman.

Her eyes gleamed with fiery rage.

She did not attempt to escape or stir.

Thorkil glared upon the object with eye-balls distended by surprise and satanic hate.

"You here? Ha! ha!" he screamed, with barbaric pleasure. "One caged at last, eh?"

He rushed upon her with uplifted weapon.

The blade fell upon naught but air.

The dark figure glided past him noiselessly like a shadow.

In an instant Thorkil fell to the ground with a heavy oath, cursing, and foaming with rage and impatience.

"Stabbed!" he shrieked, and tried to rise, "murdered! Help!—here men, in the parlour! Quick! they will escape!"

Those of his followers near by raised him from the ground.

Blood flowed freely.

No one was found in any part of the house.

"Oh! that I may live to repay this!" he roared, with many strange and impious oaths, and was carried out into the open air, and borne away upon an unhinged door.

"Why did you leave us? Where have you been? We thought you were mad or foolish, and returned to fall a prey to Thorkil's madness and fury," said Paul, deprecatingly.

"Where have I been?" said Thyra, with a trembling, nervous utterance, as she rejoined the secreted party. "Where have I been? I have been there!" she said, with a flashing eye, displaying, and admiringly gazing on a blood-dipped dagger glistening in the moonlight. "I have been there—to his heart, I hope!"

CHAPTER XLVIII.

JOEL BRITTON VISITS THE KIDDLEAWINK, WHERE HE DISCOVERS HIS DAUGHTER — THE RECONCILIATION.

"Come in, Joel," said Polruth, as the worthy blacksmith passed the "Three Jolly Mariners" at sunset one evening. "You are the very one I wish to talk to. Have you seen or heard anything of Nelly, lately? Come, don't frown old fellow, and look so angrily; I did not ask the question to pain you. I have seen her, and moreover I have talked to her, and a fine young woman she has grown, too, since last she passed the kiddleawink on her way to Seawardine."

"It was a luckless day that she ever left it," said Joel, seating himself in Polruth's cosy parlour.

"Luckless, Joel! Don't say that till you hear both sides of the question. I think from what Paul Adair told me that it was a very lucky day for her, and for you, and for all of us."

"Did you hear that the king's men are after him, and that he and his wife are fugitives? Is that what you call lucky, Polruth, to be obliged to fly like a villain from the face of the king's officers?"

"Well, there's two sides to that question also,

Joel. If you knew only half as much of him as I do, you'd feel proud of having such a son-in-law."

"Feel proud to know, perhaps, that a noble of the land, no less than Earl Penalvon, has set a price upon his head, either dead or alive! You must be mocking me."

"Well, well, Joel, I never was much hand at arguing; but all I know is that neither Paul nor Nelly are a thousand miles from here; 'tis true she left her own snug little home for a time until the storm blows over, but——"

"Where is she?" asked Joel, shading his face to hide the tears fast falling. "Whether fortunate or otherwise, she is still my daughter. I forgive her follies from the bottom of my heart. All I desire is to see her happy. If I could but place my arms around her neck and kiss her once more, I would gladly lay down and die."

"Father!" said Nelly, weeping copiously, emerging from her place of concealment, and throwing her arms around the old man's neck; "father, here is Nelly, your own Nelly, father; forgive me, forgive me!"

She fell upon her knees before him and wept in his lap.

Polruth tried to whistle or cough down the feelings that involuntarily rose with a choking sensation to his throat, but after turning very red, and looking very moist and sheepish about the eyes, he exclaimed, striking the table,

"The best girl in the world, Joel. I *told* you she wasn't a thousand miles off," and rushed out of the parlour.

For some time neither father nor daughter spoke; tears alone and choking sobs told too well the unutterable thoughts and feelings of both.

He raised her tear-dewed face with a gentle hand, and gazed into her upturned, sinless eyes long and affectionately, and kissed her a hundred times.

Kneeling as she was, with clasped hands and quivering lip, before him, she poured out the whole burden of her heart and soul.

She briefly but eloquently pleaded in her own and Paul's behalf, narrating with great force Penalvon's evil designs upon her, and of her husband's love, faith, and long-tried constancy.

Joel's eyes enlarged with astonishment and rage as he listened, with open mouth and clenched fist, to the simple but touching story of his daughter's wrongs and trials.

"And did he do this?" gasped Joel, striking the table heavily, "Would he have destroyed my daughter's honour? Oh, the canting, slimy, hypocrite! would that his head were under my sledge-hammer, that I might pound it to powder!"

"Yes, this he did, my father dear. You will believe your Nelly's words? I never told you a lie except when denying my constant love for dear, dear, brave, good, Paul!"

The old man sighed.

"This he did, father, and much, much more, that I will speak of at some other time, and had it not been for my husband——"

"Where is Paul Adair?" said Joel, rising suddenly. "Where is he, that I may thank him and bless him for all he's done for you?"

"Here, Mr. Britton," said the Rover, respectfully, approaching and extending his hand to the astonished blacksmith, who knew not, nor perceived that he had stood unobserved in the background, "Here is your son, father, and let's be for ever friends. The devil isn't so black as he's painted, they say; perhaps in time you may live to learn what I truly am, and forgive all my shortcomings."

Perceiving the happy reunion, Polruth ventured to place refreshments before the trio, and slunk away into the tap again, so highly delighted with the happy and agreeable turn things had taken that he commenced to whistle and sing with great noise and gusto.

Paul, Joel, and Nelly remained for hours in confidential chat.

Joel laughed and wept alternately, but when Adair recounted some of his strange midnight adventures at Seawardine, and the true purpose of them, the blacksmith's face elongated to a ludicrous degree, and he listened in speechless, almost motionless, awe and wonder.

"If this be true," he said, at last, "oh, the devil incarnate! I would give ten years of my life to have the pleasure of making the chains that should dangle him from a roadside gibbet as food for carrion crows or vultures."

"You may have that pleasure yet, but the time is scarcely ripe; there is one thing you can do, to enable us to complete the chain of evidence against the arch traitor."

"Name it, lad; anything, I don't care what it is; I am ready and anxious to be up and doing."

"There are some strong vaults at Seawardine that I have not yet examined."

"You don't mean to visit that place again?" interposed Joel, turning pale.

"The doors are bound with huge locks and bars."

"Well."

"You can undo them."

"Easiest thing in the world, lad, for me; but we should be discovered, and then——"

"At all hazards it must be done. I know that they contain secrets that have never yet known the light of day, and——"

"Couldn't this be done after the exposure?" said Joel, apologetically coughing, "because, you know, two men ain't much of a match for such a villain and all his household."

"It must be done," said Paul, "if even I do it myself. As to the precise time, that depends on favourable circumstances. I may not live to see him hung, for I have many enemies, but while I live I shall never rest until he is repaid a hundredfold for a few of his many villanies and crimes."

"True, my brave lad; true. Never fear, if you fall, it will not be alone; I'll make one to put a nail in that rascal's coffin, and the sooner the better. Here's your health, Paul, and long life to you and Nelly!"

CHAPTER XLIX.

THORKIL AND HIS GANG CONCOCT A PLAN TO CAP-
TURE PAUL ADAIR—TRELAWNY AND HARLECK
EXPLORE THE SECRET CAVERNS, AND WHAT THEY
SAW THERE.

"BLACK WILL, bind up my wound. Oh! that I knew the villain that stabbed me in the dark," said Thorkil, as he lay on his couch, cursing with rage.

"It is a mystery to me," said Otho, "who could have done it, but it seems we must have been watched."

"Yes; and some one must have been waiting for the opportunity."

"Oh! don't talk," said Thorkil, angrily; "it was some agent of Paul Adair's, no one else could have done it."

"Perhaps, Agger," said Black Will.

"Perhaps the devil," said Thorkil, in increasing rage, and with contempt. "Perhaps it was a woman."

"A woman!" exclaimed both Will and Otho in surprise.

"Aye, a woman; no man could have approached me so closely, unperceived. Some female in the pay of Paul Adair. Never mind, we will soon settle with that imp."

"When do you propose to storm his strong-hold?"

"Why, to-morrow. Is all prepared? Where is old Bow-legs."

"Hardy, do you mean? He is the strongest and bravest fellow I ever saw," said Otho, in admira-tion.

"Here is Bow-legs, captain," said Hardy, entering the cavern. "Sorry to hear of what happened. You know I was first on the spot, and told you that the lights had been put out rather suddenly, but I hadn't the least idea that any one should have laid in wait for you. Nasty wound certainly, but not dangerous, only painful."

"Only painful," growled Thorkil, petulantly. "Well, if I only lay eyes on Mr. Paul Adair, or any

of his friends, I warrant that some of them will have to pay dearly for this."

"That's the way to talk, captain," said Hardy, approvingly. "No one wishes to settle off old scores with Adair more ardently than I do, and if you'll only give us a chance, I will do more than my share of the work, however bloody it may be."

"That's a true man," said Thorkil, grinning, "and so you shall. How do the lads take to the expedition—the new ones, Adair's old gang?"

"They? Oh, they are better pleased with the idea of having it out with Paul than if you had given them five pounds each. We had such a jolly spree at Polruth's last night."

"So I heard, and am glad that the lads are in good temper. Who are those strange people there?"

"Strange people? I never saw any one."

"There are strangers there, for Polruth wouldn't have his kitchen so well supplied with meat, other-wise, I know."

"Oh, travellers, I suppose."

"But there are some king's men there."

"Oh, yes, so there are. They belong to one of His Majesty's ships. They are on a land cruise after that scamp of a Paul Adair."

"You don't mean to say that?" asked Thorkil, in delight. "They don't give him much time or peace. His days are numbered, Hardy," said Thorkil, drinking rum freely, as usual. "Yes, his days are numbered, thanks to my friend and patron the great Earl Penalvon, of Seawardine. Let's drink to his health, lads; a better man don't breathe than the Lord of Seawardine, and when we have caged Paul Adair, and delivered him over to the earl, there is to be a thousand guineas dis-tributed amongst Thorkil's gang."

This news was received with cheers by those surrounding him.

"How many men have we, all told?"

"Thirty," answered Black Will. "Quite enough to clear out half-a-dozen such fellows as Adair, don't care how many friends he has."

"Well, let all assemble to-night; we must journey quietly, or he may get scent of our inten-tions."

"True. Hardy knows the way; he'll lead us."

"True, lads, and so I will; I will pilot all the gang to the spot, and if we don't get Paul Adair, hang me to a gibbet. We meet then here at nine to-night; I will gather all my old shipmates, and we will sure to be punctual," said Hardy, leaving the cavern.

As he went his way a peculiar smile lit his features.

"It is a hazardous game, but I will play it out," he said, "for the sake of Nelly and Paul Adair. This Thorkil is a monster in human shape; but who could have stabbed him in the dark? A woman, so he says. She must have been a plucky one. An inch lower, and Thorkil wouldn't have lived five minutes."

So thought Hardy as he rambled on the beach.

"Thirty men all told, eh?" said Thorkil, when Bill Bow-legs had left, "and most of them are Adair's old gang. What do you think, Will? What do you think, Harleck?"

"Well, I think this much," said Trelawny, in a gruff, heavy voice, "that I wouldn't trust myself on this venture with so many new-made friends."

"Do you suspect them?" asked Thorkil, with a flashing eye. "Do you scent treachery?"

"No, not that exactly, but it's well to have a few more of your own choosing, that's all, for it might happen that Paul has influence at work that might disarm all of his former gang who go with us. This Hardy is——"

"A true man, think you?"

"Y-e-s; I don't exactly doubt him, but now and then I think I see a peculiar light in his small, grey eyes, a lurking devil or two that might prove unpleasant and mischievous in emergencies."

"Well, then, he must be watched and——"

"Leave that to me; if he move but a foot the wrong way," said Black Will, maliciously, "he shall fall on the instant. Let me go out and gather a few more men in case of need."

"That's a man for you," said Thorkil, admiringly, when Trelawny left his presence. "He's the man to do things with a will."

"Since there are blue-jackets about," said Harleck, "it wouldn't be foolish to disguise ourselves a little, Dan."

"True, my brave runaways; there's plenty of slops in that cavern to the right; make yourselves up in any style you like. Alter your figure-heads, for they'd be sure to recognise you. I mean to do well by you, Harleck, although we've had a tiff or two in our time."

Harleck and the Crawler soon made a transformation in their attire, and so altered were their looks with false hair, whiskers, and the like, that Thorkil broke out into roars of drunken laughter on their re-appearance.

Trelawny had returned, and looked well pleased.

"What success?" asked Thorkil.

"Thanks to your money, I have secured a dozen or more right good fellows that we may depend upon."

"Good news. Now we may fear nothing."

"We had better look after our arms. We must provide weapons for all comers, for few of them are provided."

Thorkil led the way, and followed by Trelawny, Harleck, Crawley, and Otho, they entered a sort of cellar beneath the cavern, where Thorkil, since the lesson taught by the Phantom Schooner's shot, was wont to deposit his powder and arms.

Several chests of pistols were opened; but when they entered the powder-room, they found a large quantity of powder scattered over the floor, while many of the powder kegs had their heads knocked in.

"Hullo! who's been here?" said Trelawny, suspiciously, and cautiously retreating to the door. "Why, here's the powder laid out as if ready to blow us all up."

Thorkil shuddered.

"And just under me!" he exclaimed, with many savage oaths. "What scoundrel could have done this?"

"What scoundrel could have stabbed you, and done so many things that neither you nor the earl can account for?" replied Black Will, somewhat contemptuously. "Come, don't stand there staring, Thorkil. Let's gather enough to supply us, and the rest may remain where it is for the present."

Cutlasses were ground almost to the sharpness of razors.

Pistols were reflinted and loaded.

Belts were arranged.

Knives, daggers, and dirks were sharpened.

"We have quite enough, I think," said Black Will, "to suit all comers; so let's put all shipshape for to-night."

Excited by what they saw in the powder chamber, Trelawny and Harleck resolved to explore the whole region of cellars and caverns, which led one to another right down to the water's edge.

The first cavern that they entered, contained the refuse parts of several small cargoes of goods obtained from vessels which had been decoyed and destroyed upon the Fin's Back, and the treacherous reefs near the White Cliffs.

Flour, wine, tobacco, and general merchandise lay scattered about in waste and confusion.

The next place explored contained something more horrible.

The place was dark and damp.

Water trickled from the granite walls.

The atmosphere was loathsome, noisome in the extreme.

Rats darted hither and thither when the door was opened.

Slimy creeping things crawled from beneath the intruders' feet into cracks and crevices.

Mosses and strange plants hung dank and mildewed from the walls.

When the lantern's light was shed upon the interior rays of various hues were reflected in strange and brilliant colours from the uneven surface of the rocks.

Black Will and Harleck hesitated for a moment.

A strange unearthly cold and dampness thrilled their frames.

They felt that they stood in a chamber which Thorkil dreamed would never see the light.

They entered.

Harleck stumbled.

The light was lowered.

Bones of arms and legs and ribs lay scattered about, while skulls broke into pieces at the slightest touch.

"It is as much as our lives are worth to be discovered here," said Black Will; "let us go."

"Thorkil is dark," said Harleck.

"And bitterly revengeful, these bones could tell a tale."

"If he saw us here we should never leave the place alive."

The lantern was dimmed, the door refastened, and both departed, busied with strange thoughts of the past and future.

CHAPTER L.

HARRY HALLIARD RECEIVES A LETTER FROM FRANK RAYNER ACQUAINTING HIM WITH HIS MARRIAGE WITH HELENA—HARRY'S SURPRISE—THE MEETING ON THE PHANTOM SCHOONER.

"WHAT, Konks, Hawser, and Juniper here?" said Harry, in surprise, as he entered the kiddleawink towards evening, and discovered those rosy-faced worthies enjoying themselves.

The meeting was boisterously hearty, for though the seamen had been there many days, he was unaware of it.

"But where's Frank?"

"Frank? Didn't you hear the news?"

"What news?" asked Harry, in surprise.

"Why, he is married."

"Married! and so young! Why he must be mad!"

"And so he is—in love," said Hawser, laughing.

"And to whom?"

"Well, that I don't pretend to know anything about; but Polruth has got a letter for you which may explain everything."

The letter ran:—

"DEAR HARRY.—I leave you for a week or more, for I am married. I am nothing else but your brother. Helena is my wife, and I am a happy man; I couldn't help it. I am sorry for having offended Rose or you; but my passion grew so strong and irrepressible day by day, that my very life and existence seemed to depend upon securing and making dear Helena mine. Do with me as you will, we have always been brothers, let us be so still, and all through life. I beg a thousand pardons of dear Rose, my mother, for anticipating her wishes by two years; but in a moment of violent love, in a moment of passion, almost amounting to despair, in contemplating the change and

fortunes of fleeting time, and the possible loss of my dearly loved prize through cruel delays, I prevailed upon Helena, I overwhelmed all her sense of filial duty with earnest words and resistless passion. She listened to the tempter, dear Harry, and scarcely knowing what she did, eloped with me. I am happy and miserable, if you can understand it—I am steeped in felicity with my dear girl, but I am unhappy to think that, perhaps, I may have forfeited your love, and the friendship of dear Rose by my headlong rashness. Helena is not to blame; the fault is mine. Forgive me—forgive us both; tell me that you and dear Rose do so, and, like penitent, wayward children, we will return, and on our knees crave pardon, and promise that a whole life of duty, fidelity, and love, shall scarcely repay for our reinstation in your inestimable affection and regard.

"Believe me, Harry, in life or death,

"Your true brother,

"FRANK RAYNER."

"Well, this is news!" said Harry, astonished. "And who delivered this letter, Polruth?"

"Paul Adair, Harry, my lad, and right heartily he laughed over it. Here comes Paul."

As he spoke, Adair entered.

"You look astonished, Harry."

"And well I may," was the reply, as he fumbled the letter.

"Well, come, come; don't look down on account of it. I'm sure if I had a sister I shouldn't fret to see her elope with such a fine young fellow as Frank Rayner."

"I don't fret, as you say, on my own account, but mother will——"

"Say nothing about it. I have explained all; she is perfectly satisfied, and willingly forgives them."

"But both are so young."

"What of that? You wouldn't have them wait till they get old, would you? I made a runaway match of it myself with Nelly, but I've had no occasion to regret it. Your turn will come next; one of the daughters of Admiral Sir Everard Brandon, perhaps. But come, let us all have a bumper to the long life and happiness of Frank Rayner and his pretty young bride; and let us all hope that when Mr. Midshipman Halliard picks a wife, he may be as fortunate as his constant friend and bosom companion, Frank."

The bumper was drunk with rounds of applause.

Harry beckoned Hawser, Konks, and Juniper into the parlour.

"Do you know him?" he said, alluding to Adair, who had ascended the stairs to his room.

"Know him? Well, I've heard something about him, and what little I have heard say, convinces me that he is your true friend, and as such I admire him," said Hawser, bluntly.

"People do say," quoth Konks, winking, "that he is looked after by some of us blue jackets rather sharply."

"Let them say what they will; he is a true friend to me, and if I live to see another week, his character shall be fully vindicated in an open court of justice, and then the world will know who and what Paul Adair really is. Listen!" he said. "Shut the door."

Bill Hawser was on his feet in a moment, and barred the door firmly.

The seamen looked at each other with anxious inquisitive features, as if expecting to hear some interesting disclosures regarding Paul Adair.

Harry spoke for some time in very low tones, and the narration worked up his auditors to the highest pitch of excitement, enthusiasm and indignation, as he briefly recounted the doings of Adair, Thorkil, and Earl Penalvon.

"You don't mean *that!*" roared Hawser, striking the table violently, and throwing up his cap in exultation.

"Hurrah, my lad ! Long life to your honour !" said Konks, grasping Harry's hand, and almost crushing it in his vice-like grip.

Juniper contented himself with drinking up Hawser's grog and capering round the room. Snapping his fingers he shouted out lustily,

"I always knew it, my lad. I knew there was good blood in you, and as to giving a helping hand to drag up these rascals to be hung, why of *course* I will, and so will all of us ; there isn't a man in the whole British fleet, from Admiral Nelson to Joe Juniper, as wouldn't."

When evening set in, Paul, Polruth, Harry, and the three seamen, set out on some secret expedition. Each and all were in the best possible spirits, and laughed and joked right heartily at the prospective work in hand.

"Why, does the lubber think he's going to storm your castle, Paul, without a fight ?" shouted Hawser, hitching up his trousers, and squirting tobacco juice in great wrath.

"No, no, Hawser, my messmate, that black-looking scoundrel knows there will be a fight, and a pretty tough one, and has, therefore, raked together all the scoundrels along the coast to assist him."

"A d do you mean to say that Harleck and the Crawler have escaped from the receiving-ship, and joined him ?" asked Konks, in indignant surprise. "Why, shiver me, then, that Mr. Thorkil has got a fine crew together, and no mistake."

"Nothing could please me more than to knock that sneaking Crawler on the head," said Juniper, in disgust, "and I'll do it, too, if I get a chance."

After several hours' walk, Paul and his companions reached a small, secluded cove, in which lay, snugly anchored, the Phantom Schooner.

"A pretty little craft, Paul," said Harry, admiringly.

"A regular racer, I should judge," said Konks, looking at the craft with a professional eye.

"None of the king's craft could overhaul her, I think."

"Sits the water like a duck," said Hawser, hands in pockets, gazing with pleasure on the clean make and rig of the schooner.

Paul shouted to those on deck, and soon the lamp at her stern was dipped thrice, in token of recognition and readiness.

As they approached, the sounds of moving chains caught the seamens' ears, and they knew that some on board were almost noiselessly raising anchor.

Paul and his party were soon on board.

Harry perceived two figures standing aft, in deep conversation.

Paul laughed.

"Allow me to introduce to you Harry——?"

The strangers turned sharply round.

It was Frank and Helena.

Helena gave a little scream of surprise and pleasure. Next moment, she was fast locked in her foster-brother's arms.

Frank stood by, and clasped Harry's hand.

Neither spoke, but as thus they stood mute and wrapt in thought, Rose Halliard and Nelly emerged from the cabin, and completed the family group.

Sails were set, and winds were fair.

The Phantom Schooner glided from the cove with the grace and ease of an aërial thing of life and beauty.

Stars shone forth with unwonted brilliancy, while foam-crested waves sparkled with diamond-like beauty.

The moon in fulness and silvery brilliancy rose o'er the waves.

The schooner's white sails filled in the freshening breeze, and the swift little craft bounded gracefully, and ploughed through the dark blue flashing waves as if instinct with sense and life.

Hawser, Konks, and Juniper, were in their glory, they took a hand at the ropes, and tacked the craft with much judgment and precision.

Hawser was uneasy, he would stand at the wheel, and eye the man at the helm with looks of envy, while Konks and Juniper stood on the forecastle keeping watch as carefully and importantly as if on board his Majesty's ship the Thunderer.

"Will you take the helm, Hawser ?" said Paul, who had watched that seaman's uneasiness ; "I'm sure the lad will be much obliged to you. And do you stand by and watch him," continued Paul, to his man. "See there ! see how close Hawser runs to the wind !" and so it did.

Hawser was in his glory, and made the Phantom shoot through the water with redoubled ease and speed.

"Hullo, there," roared Konks, who instantly perceived that the craft was now steered by some old and experienced hand. "Hullo, there, Bill, I knew it were you ; that ain't fair. My turn next, hearty."

"Lor, how be-a-utifully she steers," sighed Juniper, who squatted upon the deck, and lit his pipe.

While things were thus transpiring at sea, Thorkil was busily engaged in fitting out and arranging his expedition to capture Paul Adair.

At the appointed hour Thorkil's hirelings assembled.

Thorkil himself, though much weakened by his recent wound, was able to accompany the party.

The nearer his arrangements were completed the more fierce and bombastic he became.

He liberally plied all hands with liquor, and among those who were boisterous and noisy in their humour, none was more so than Bill Hardy or Bow-legs.

The whole gang departed in squads of half-a-dozen, but before they went he briefly addressed the gang and told them that he was bent on the capture of a noted pirate, who had long been a bitter enemy to all honest wreckers on the coast, and had a commission from the great Earl Penalvon to secure him whether dead or alive, and that on the completion of the task every man engaged would be liberally rewarded.

———

CHAPTER LI.

THORKIL AND HIS GANG START ON THEIR EX-
PEDITION AGAINST PAUL ADAIR—THEIR PLANS
ARE FRUSTRATED BY BILL HARDY.

THORKIL'S band approached the object of their journey.

It was yet day, and wanted some hours of sunset.

His men halted in a wood, and awaited for the darkness of night.

Thorkil, Trelawny, and Black Will set out alone to reconnoitre.

They approached the rocky inlet with the greatest caution.

The schooner was there safely anchored.

Smoke slowly curled from Paul's cottage, and no sounds were heard save the beating of tide waves as they rolled and dashed upon the sandy beach.

"Just as I wanted it," said Thorkil, "it couldn't be better, we will divide our party, approach his house and caverns in several gangs, and make a rush upon the upstart from different sides, and at once."

Trelawny proposed that they should wait till the dead of night.

This plan was cursed down by Thorkil, who, now all oaths and blasphemy, drank brandy continually, and increased his rage and passion to an ungovernable pitch.

"Bow-legs" was to pilot Thorkil's own immediate gang.

Black Will volunteered to head another squad.

The various parties divided, and stealthily pursued different paths towards the house.

"This is rather a difficult game to play," thought Bow-legs, " there are only eight of Paul's men here beside myself ; Thorkil's crew are two dozen or more. It's too late to alter matters now though, but if I had known he was going to bring so many, I should have advised Paul, and beat a retreat home. I fear Trelawny is a little suspicious of me ; no matter, here we are, and all I hope is that Paul's men will keep together, and obey the signal when given."

Thorkil's party were within a hundred yards of the house.

A long shrill whistle was heard.

"This way, Thorkil," said Bow-legs, "follow me."

"What did that whistle mean?" asked Thorkil, who, intent upon looking forward, did not notice that several of Hardy's men had slunk behind, and left the party.

The long, shrill whistle was again repeated.

Hardy stood in the shade of a rock, near a log-house used by Paul's crew when on shore.

He fired a pistol, as if by accident, and fell to the ground with a loud groan.

The report had scarcely died away, when a scattering volley was delivered into Thorkil's gang by an opposing force.

Shrieks, and shouts, and yells succeeded, with deafening sounds.

Vollies from pistols succeeded in another direction, which were again returned by others approaching by diverging paths.

By a ruse, Hardy had fired into Black Will's gang, who, in the darkness, could not distinguish friend from foe.

Stray shots had fallen among Otho's gang, and these again replied by firing on Harleck, who, with the Crawler, were stealthily approaching Paul's house in a different direction.

All was darkness and confusion.

Shouts and oaths, and screams and yells were heard on every side.

Thorkil and Trelawny's voices were heard loud above the din and roar of battle.

"There is treachery," said Thorkil, who literally foamed at the mouth with fury and disappointed revenge. "Advance, men, to the house!" he shouted, in stentorian tones.

Trelawny, in deep anger at the disastrous turn things had suddenly taken, gathered his men together, and made a sudden rush at Adair's house.

Thorkil, blinded by fury, cared not which way he approached the cottage, so that he might sate his revenge.

Rushing headlong forward both gangs assailed the stone-built place with great ardour.

Paul Adair and his companions, now joined by Bill Hardy, were quietly awaiting the wild, ill-planned attack of the ruffians, and cocked their weapons with all the coolness imaginable.

When the several diverging parties had joined they stopped for a moment to regain breath.

Thorkil, Black Will, Harleck, and Otho rushed to the front, and thinking that but feeble opposition awaited them, felt confident of making an easy and safe capture of the house, and all who were in it.

They approached still nearer.

It was absolutely necessary that they should run across an open piece of ground before reaching the cottage.

They gave a wild yell, and rushed to the attack.

The schooner's colours were suddenly run up, and its guns belched forth vollies of grape shot upon the assailants.

Cries, groans, and shrieks rent the air.

Again and again were the schooner's guns discharged, with frightful accuracy, by the men-of-war's men, who had charge of the cannon, while Paul Adair, and a small party within the house, kept on firing guns and pistols into the terrified mob without.

At a preconcerted signal Konks, Hawser and

Juniper, together with a few others, landed from the schooner, cutlass in hand, and attacked the assailants in the rear.

Paul Adair, Harry, Frank, Bill Hardy, and others assailed them vigorously in front.

The shrieks and oaths and yells of the wounded and dying rent the air with appalling sounds.

One man, more bold than all the rest, rushed to the front, cutlass in hand.

It was Black Will.

There was one of the defenders who eagerly went forth to meet him.

It was Harry Halliard.

Their swords clashed with frightful violence in the onset of the contest.

"Die like your dastard father!" roared Black Will, with a frightful oath, recognising the brave and fearless youth before him, and making a desperate lunge.

The stroke was dexterously parried.

"My father's blood is on your head, villain!" said Harry, in reply.

As if entranced at the sight of this desperate duel taking place midway between them, both parties, for a time, ceased from hostilities.

Harry's strength was unequal to the ferocious onslaughts of his opponent.

All he could do was to ward off Trelawney's blows.

Sparks flew from their weapons as if from a forge.

Nearer and nearer Trelawney's sword played around the young midshipman's head.

One moment more and he would have been slain.

He slipped on his knee from faintness.

Black Will rushed at him with the ferocity of a tiger.

Harry watched for a favourable opportunity.

Trelawney made, as he imagined, a last and fatal blow at the brave Sailor Boy, but his weapon missed its mark.

The next moment Harry's sword passed through his body in the region of the heart.

Black Will gave a frightful yell and jumped into the air.

The next instant he fell to the ground with heavy violence.

A tremor passed through his stalwart frame.

With foaming mouth and curses on his lips he groaned and expired.

The sudden and unexpected fall of Trelawney, at the hands of a mere boy, sent a thrill of fear and horror through his partizans.

Before Thorkil's men could recover from astonishment, they were attacked with redoubled fury in front and rear.

"There he is! there he is!" roared Juniper, who, cutlass in hand, was wielding it without mercy among Thorkil's now dispirited followers. "There he is! I know him," continued Juniper, cutting his way through towards two particular individuals. "I told you so, Hawser; there's Harleck and the Crawler. I can't mistake their ugly mugs in ten thousand."

So saying Hawser and Juniper redoubled their exertions to kill or capture their two old enemies.

Konks had singled out Otho, who, cornered by the gallant sailor, fought desperately for life.

Harleck and the Crawler perceived the burly forms of the two brave blue jackets approaching, and Dan endeavoured to escape.

His attempts were useless.

Juniper pounced upon him with the ferocity of a wolf.

"Spare me! spare me!" whined the Crawler. "Spare me, Mr. Juniper!"

The gallant tar did not reply, but dealt him one desperate blow across the brow that split his skull in twain.

Hawser's attack on Harleck was not so successful, for that ferocious fellow was as strong as a giant, and more than a match for Hawser with the cutlass.

Perceiving his shipmate in great danger, Juniper rushed to the rescue and felled Harleck to the earth with a blow across the shoulder.

"Secure him! Don't kill him!" shouted Harry, who was witness to the scene.

Harleck was safely bound and placed in Paul's cottage under guard.

Konks and Otho had a long bout.

The seaman was too impetuous for his young and active antagonist.

Konks puffed and blowed like a grampus with his unusual exertions, and cursed and swore till fairly blue in the face.

By a happy chance Otho slipped and fell to the ground. He held up his hand in token of surrender.

"I won't kill you, you ugly swab," growled Konks, with a deep and heavy oath. "You know how to handle a cutlass, I see, and it's a pity the king shouldn't have the benefit of your services on board ship. I'll take care of you, my man. If you only fight the French half as well as you fought me, you'll pass muster anywhere."

So saying, Konks conducted his prisoner of war to Paul's cottage, and placed him in care of the guard placed there.

The battle, however, was not yet over.

Scattering shots were heard in all directions, but it was evident that Thorkil was disheartened, and that his once numerous party, now much thinned, were stubbornly retreating before Paul Adair's victorious followers.

Frank Rayner was foremost and in the thickest of the fray.

Hawser, Juniper, Bill Hardy, and Harry Halliard remained as close beside each other as possible.

It was the ambition of all to capture Thorkil alive.

Paul Adair moved hurriedly hither and thither in the hope of espying that black-hearted chieftain.

Thorkil was too cunning to present himself as a conspicuous mark, for when he perceived the discomfiture of his friends, he craftily withdrew from the fray, and was the first to retreat.

His followers, however, made one more gallant stand.

Having reached the hill top which overlooked the cove, they planted themselves against the rocks, and seemed for a time to bid defiance to all Paul's party.

Foremost among them was Thorkil, who, thinking his position unassailable, waved a black handkerchief in token of defiance.

Adair's intrepid band, however, were resolute, and rushed up the hill at their enemies, despite the storm of shot that assailed them.

Frank Rayner was far to the front, cutlass and pistol in hand.

He was warned back by Adair and Harry, but would not retreat a foot.

He was desirous of capturing Thorkil.

A shot was fired; he fell.

Harry and Paul ran to his assistance.

"Oh, it's nothing, Harry," said he, laughing, "only a flesh wound in the leg, I scarcely feel it; bind it up with a handkerchief, and I shall be all right again."

Wounded and weak as he was, he speedily rose again, undaunted and full of hilarity.

He kept his eye on Thorkil, who, with his handkerchief tied to a sword, was waving it in defiance.

Creeping on his hands and knees, Rayner approached him unperceived, and sprang at him with the bound of a panther.

He knocked down the black flag, and secured it.

A dozen or more immediately assailed him with unabated fury.

Konks, Hawser, Juniper, and Harry were quickly on the spot, and saved him from certain death.

Thorkil had again escaped.

The last attack was short and fierce.

Beaten at all points by much inferior numbers, Thorkil and his party made a hasty retreat.

They ran in wild confusion from the scene of the deadly fray.

Caps, swords, and pistols lay about here and there in confusion.

Some dead and others dying, were scattered over the spot, giving eloquent tokens of the fierceness of the fight.

Moans and groans were heard in all directions.

Black Will lay in a pool of blood.

His hand grasped the cutlass with the firmness of a vice.

His eyes were wildly staring, and his mouth was firmly set in a hideous grin.

Dan Crawley, the Crawler, was not far from him, with his skull cleft in halves.

His features, as he lay all gory, were repulsively idiotic.

As best he could, Paul gave immediate orders to his men to provide for the wounded.

He jumped into a boat, and pulled off to the schooner, and informed Helena, Nelly, and Rose, of the whole affair, and calmed their fears by saying that not one of his party were seriously hurt.

The dead were buried, and ere midnight all was calm and quiet, as if naught had transpired in that tranquil cove.

"We have not done yet," said Paul Adair, after a refreshing bath and supper; "we haven't quite done with them yet. There's something more to do, before this miserable business is finished."

Giving all necessary orders, and seeing that Rose, Helena, and his wife were safely provided for, he bid them all adieu for a few days, saying that pressing business called him along the coast.

Weighing anchor in the dead of night the schooner glided with the tide, having Hawser, Juniper, Konks, Harry, Frank, and Bill Hardy on board.

"We've quite enough with us," said Harry, who understood the nature of the expedition. "So that mother and the others are perfectly safe, I don't care what befalls me."

"No harm shall befall ye, lad, while I've a leg to stand on," said Hawser, who was at his favourite occupation of steering.

"Don't let's begin to feel moody, after giving the lubberly crew such a dressing as we have," said Konks. "And, by your leave, Mr. Paul, I think we might as well splice the main-brace, on the strength of it."

"Anything you like, my lads," said Adair, smiling. "I never had such a bit of fun in all my life."

"Nor I, master," chimed in Bill Hawser. "We've seen some toughish kind of work in our time, haven't we, Harry?" said he, hitching up his trousers. "I think Sir Everard could give a good account of the Thunderer's crew; but in ne'er a cruise I ever had did I enjoy it more than that little scrape with old Thorkil's gang."

"If there's anything more on hand of the same sort," said Juniper, "I should like to be one of 'em on your side."

While they thus pleasantly chatted, and recounted each his deeds in the late affray, Bill Hardy descended to the cabin, and soon reappeared on deck with two or three bottles of prime old Jamaica rum.

The wind was fair, and, with Hawser at the helm, the Phantom Schooner shot through the water with more than accustomed speed, as if the trim little craft was conscious of the all-important mission of her captain and crew.

Konks and Juniper stretched themselves on deck, pipe in mouth, and kept on criticising the build and bearings of the vessel.

Frank and Harry were seated on the bow, looking forth upon the boundless sea, taking note of the various signal lights along the coast, that twinkled in the distance like luminous stars.

"There's a light yonder that I never saw in the Channel chart," said Harry, pointing in the direction of the Fin's Back.

"I dare say not," answered Paul, grimly. "And never will be in the chart. That's a wrecker's light."

"You don't mean that!" said Juniper, with an oath. "Why, it looks for all the world like a regular beacon."

"Yes, true, shipmates; but it's not, for all that. That's no more nor less than one of old Thorkil's signal fires."

"Well, d—n him, then! But why do you carry that large black cross in your mainsail?" asked Hawser. "I never saw anything like that before."

"A mystery is attached to that. There's a long, sad story connected with it."

"A yarn," said Frank, all attention; "let's have it, then, by all means."

"Aye, aye, lads; let's have the yarn. Pay it all out," said Konks, introducing his red nose into a pannikin of rum.

"It can be told in a few words. You have learned from Harry, perhaps, something about the villany of this so-called Earl Penalvon?"

"No more a lord than our ship's cook," grunted Juniper, in disgust.

"Well, then, this large black cross, simple as it is, might be taken, and it is taken, for naught else but as a common signal of some merchantman along the coast, whose owners wished to have the safety of their schooner reported during her regular trip."

"I see," said Konks; "I always thought it. These Frenchers and Dutch always have jim-crack notions; they paints ther craft with all the colours of the rainbow. Heave ahead, Master Paul."

"But there is one man in the land who knows it is not a merchantman's signal, and that man is Penalvon. He always hated me from the first day I saw him talking privately to Black Will and Thorkil, for what I did not know, nor could I guess. Since I have known him, however, in his true colours, I am positive he detests me; yes, and fears me, too, more than he does the very devil himself. I knew that he understood this signal, and that's the only reason I adopted it. From the moment that he heard of me upon the waters with this simple large black cross upon my mainsail from that same instant he secretly vowed and determined on my destruction, if he could, in any way, effect it by fair means or foul."

"And why, Master Paul?" asked Hawser, impatiently.

"Let's 'bout the schooner first, lads; she's getting too close in upon the land; and then I will explain."

All hands soon put the gallant craft upon another tack, and Paul continued,

"I discovered among other things regarding Earl Penalvon that when he had resolved upon the destruction of his brother's daughter—your aunt Thyra, Harry—he gave the foreign merchant so much to land the child near the Fin's Back. 'In order that you may be recognised,' Penalvon wrote, 'and be seen a good distance off shore by the pilot that I shall send to guide you in, paint a large black cross on your main-sail.'"

"This was done, but instead of sending out a pilot he instructed Thorkil, and paid him heavily, to decoy the unlucky craft upon the Fin's Back, which resulted in her total destruction."

"I wish I had his head here!" swore Juniper, striking the deck heavily with his clenched fist. "I'd give him the Fin's Back, and no mistake, the cowardly swab!"

"When Penalvon heard of the destruction of the ship, and total loss of all hands, he was satisfied. But he little thought, and does not dream even now, that Thyra is the child that was washed ashore with nought in the world but a small locket that hung from her neck; but such is the fact."

"Villainy will come to light at some time," said Frank, "and all I ask, Harry, is that I may be permitted to put a pretty large nail in your uncle's coffin, for, from all I can gather, he is the most cold-blooded scoundrel, Thorkil excepted, who ever trod the earth."

"Patience, my lad," said Paul; "I have laid a train for him that shall hoist him higher than any yard-arm in all the British fleet."

"Glad to hear you talk that way," said Konks. "Please the Lord and fair weather—and I don't say that except on special occasions—I'll give that same Mr. Penalvon such a dressing as he never had in his whole life!"

"Wouldn't you like to have him on board, and lashed to the gratings for half an hour?" said Frank, with a grin.

"Aye, true, lad, I do," he answered, "d——d if I don't! and if I didn't lay the cat on him in true style, then may Konks never wet his whistle with a messmate again."

"Ship a-ho!" shouted Juniper, who alone on the forecastle kept a sharp look-out. "Ship a-ho!"

"What course, Joe?" asked Harry, in haste.

"Bearing nor'-nor'-west," said Paul Adair, with a smile, "and bearing right down on us. A King's ship, ain't it?"

"How did you know that?" asked Hawser and Konks in surprise. "How could you tell, Master Paul?"

"Easy enough. I gave them sailing directions, that's all," he said, with a good-humoured laugh. "People think that the Phantom Schooner fears to meet one of the King's ships, and here we are sailing out to meet one."

"You don't mean to say that you are going to run right into the jaws of the blue jackets, Paul?" said Harry, in surprise. "You know what the world says of you?"

"I know it, my lord," replied Paul, with a laugh; "but you'll see that instead of them putting me in irons they'll shake me by the hand, and give us lots of grog."

This announcement filled all on board with surprise.

The seamen Konks, Hawser, and Juniper couldn't understand it; they were as much befogged as Harry and Frank, who looked uneasy.

"It's all up with us, Harry," said Frank, "if they find us in company with Adair, for you know

his reputation is rather black, that is judging from common report."

"Never mind common report," said Paul, who had overheard the remark; "the devil isn't so black as he's painted."

"I beg pardon, Paul; but you know we hold commissions in the navy," said Frank, apologetically.

"Being found in my company won't hurt your parchments, lads, don't fear. When Lieutenant Frazer steps on board the schooner, I know he'll be glad to see you both."

"Frazer!" said Harry, in surprise. "Why, he is in command of the Scorpion."

"Not a bit of it."

"What mean you, then?"

"I mean that the Admiralty, through me—me mind, the rover, Paul Adair—has hastily equipped the six-gun sloop of war Racehorse, and sent her out, under Lieutenant Frazer, to meet me, and, more than that, to act under my instructions."

"The devil!" said each and all, in surprise, "you must be dreaming, or mad."

"Perhaps so," answered Paul, laughing; "but a few moments will tell. Hardy, fire those three rockets, as quick as possible."

In a few moments three red, white and blue rockets ascended in rapid succession, and burst in the air into a shower of star-like sparks.

"Now watch for the answer," said Paul, pointing to the sloop which looked no more than a black speck upon the distant waters.

In a few seconds the king's craft also threw up rockets, but very slowly.

"D——d if it ain't so!" roared Hawser, at the helm, in surprise. "See how careful she is to be understood though; just like Frazer, ain't it, lads?" he continued. "Slow, but v-e-r-y sure, as he always was."

"We'll give them three more to let them know that we perceive them," said Paul.

This time three red rockets were sent up, one after another, but slowly.

"What's that? What does that mean?" roared Konks, in wonder, as the booming of a gun came rolling over the water. "D——d if they ain't firing at us."

"No fear, my hearty. It's only a blank cartridge to warn us that they fully understand what I mean. Close to the wind, Hawser shipmate; they are watching our seamanship. There's many a dozen eyes looking at us from their decks at this moment, I know, for they've often heard of the 'Phantom Schooner' and her sailing qualities."

"You just let him alone, Master Paul," said Joe Juniper, in a loud whisper. "You'll see he'll surprise 'em; there ain't a man on board the British fleet can steer better nor closer to the wind than Bill Hawser, eh, Konks?"

"No, there ain't," said Konks, in reply. "If he can't get nine knots out of her, there isn't a man breathing that can."

Being thrown upon his honour, Hawser pulled off his coat, and kept the beautiful craft so close to the wind that her sails were as tight as a drum, and she rushed through the water with so much speed that Paul Adair and Bill Hardy looked at each other in wonder.

"No mistake about him, captain," said Bow-legs, approvingly, alluding to Hawser's steering; "they'll think we're some flying cloud."

"Give me my night-glasses, Hardy," said Paul. "I want to see how the Racehorse carries the wind."

He took a long look, and then burst out laughing.

"They are doing all they know to keep close up in the wind, but have fallen off two points already."

"Don't mean that?" asked Hawser, laughing, who, red and perspiring, was holding on to the wheel with redoubled energy. "Well, they can't say that much of us, I think," he added, as he gave the helm another turn, and brought the beautifully-modelled schooner so close to the wind that her ropes whistled again.

"We must show 'em a little bit of steering," said Harry. "Go it, Hawser! You'll get an extra rating when you rejoin, for with these glasses I perceive all the officers of the sloop watching you"

The man-of-war seemed to perceive the beautiful manner in which the fast-sailing schooner was handled, and in rivalry Lieutenant Frazer worked and tacked his ship in the most scientific style.

"Hullo, hullo, Hawser!" said Konks, laughing, "the first luff has cast a weather eye over his quarter, he ain't going to let us beat him. See how he's reefing; it will take some time before we can hail him or come alongside, the wind's too high."

While the Phantom Schooner and her gallant crew were engaged in exhibiting their seamanship to the admiring gaze of the Racehorse, events were transpiring at Seawardine that merit our attention.

CHAPTER LI

THORKIL ACQUAINTS EARL PENALVON OF THE
FAILURE OF HIS SCHEMES.

It was midnight.

Earl Penalvon was alone in his library, walking to and fro in great perturbation of spirit.

"Have you seen any signal fires along the headlands to-night?" he petulantly inquired of a servant. "But one, say you?"

"Yes, my lord, we have been on the roof for many hours, but did not discern more than one."

There was cause for Earl Penalvon's anxiety, and his very soul was shaken with strange fears.

No one knew better than he did the importance of Paul Adair's death.

He paced his apartment anxiously hour by hour, yet no tidings of Thorkil's success arrived.

He had arranged with that black-hearted wrecker chief to have signals posted along the coast, as tokens of the success of his expedition.

As yet but one fire glowed, and that was indicative of nought decisive.

The earl sat in his chair, weary and worn with watching.

He was tired of life. Wherever he went, strange noises rang in his ears, and phantoms seemed to dance across his path.

A voice seemed to whisper, "Your hour has come!"

He shook off all sense of fear by frequent visitations to a richly-cut decanter of brandy, and even tried to hum an old tune, as if indifferent to impending fate.

"What if he does know aught of the past," thought my lord; "who would believe him?—a poor worm of the earth; a wrecker, smuggler, pirate, and what not. What would his name weigh in the balance with mine? Ha! ha! what sound is that?" he said, rising, and going to the window. "I hear a horse's hoofs approaching. It comes at a gallop."

The sound came nearer and nearer.

The hall bell was rung violently.

A rider dismounted hastily.

It was Thorkil!

He rushed past the servants and ascended the stairs. He entered Earl Penalvon's apartment, breathless and muddy.

His head was tied up; the bandages were bloody.

"The result, Thorkil?" asked Pelalvon, anxiously.

"All is lost; we have been beaten back with loss—most of my men are killed, wounded, or dispersed."

"And Adair?"

"Is alive."

"Young Halliard and Rose?" he hurriedly inquired.

"Also live."

"Damnation!" said Penalvon, stamping his foot in rage.

"They will soon be here, I fear!" said Thorkil.

"Here! say you?" gasped the earl, pale, and in alarm, "they would not dare———"

"Dare!" said Thorkil, with a gruff laugh. "If you saw how they fought, you would think they would dare anything. He has several men-of-war's men with him."

"What had we better do?" inquired Penalvon.

"Anything—everything. I fear that all is lost."

"We must appeal to law—seek protection from these out-laws."

"Law!" grunted Thorkil; "that is the last argument for such as we. Gather your servants, bolt and bar the gates and doors, arm every man, woman and child; we must fight," he added fiercely; "they shall never live to take me alive."

"I will fly," said Penalvon, in alarm.

"Stay, old man!" said Thorkil. "We have played our parts together through life—you have been the lord, and I the cut-throat. I see it all clearly enough now; you must not stir, you cannot, you dare not, every avenue to Seawardine is watched and guarded."

"But there is the secret gallery into the park—no one dreams of that."

"Not so fast. Listen! When my party were beaten I stole several horses from a grazing drove; my men rode hither with me. They are already in the gallery, and must be admitted. I, myself, rode boldly to the hall door, and had to fight my way through a chain of desperate men who have encircled, and are now watching the house."

"Encircle and watch my mansion, say you?"

"Aye, don't be surprised—they are not wreckers nor pirates."

"What say you? Who, or what are they?"

"Several boats' crews of men-of-war's men. The Racehorse is anchored in the roads."

For a moment, Earl Penalvon looked like a man who had been suddenly paralysed by lightning. "It cannot be," he said, stamping with rage and fury. "What! can they know aught of what has been almost forgotten?"

"All I know is," said Thorkil, "that there's been some powerful agent at work, who has been quiet, secret, and determined on your destruction for years. That he knows more than he pretends, is clear. We are undone; he has enlisted the imps of justice on his side; men-of-war's crews wouldn't lend their aid for trivial causes."

Penalvon was petrified. It seemed as if all the remorse of a lifetime had returned upon him in an overwhelming flood.

His colour changed alternately from a deep flush to deathly pallor, as he walked the room, and eyed Thorkil askance, with looks of bitter disappointment and hate.

"I want some brandy," said the wrecker chief, unceremoniously, going to a small cabinet and helping himself.

"You make yourself very free, Thorkil Penreal," said the earl, with a curling lip. "Do you know in whose presence you are ?"

"Yes ; in face of th· very devil himself," answered the wrecker, doggedly, tossing his muddy boots carelessly across a silk-covered ottoman. "You are the devil, or I shouldn't have been what I am at this moment."

"Have I not paid you well for all that you have done ?" asked the earl, in a bitter tone.

"Nothing can pay me for all in which I've committed myself for you, my l-o-r-d," said Thorkil, with peculiar emphasis, and a satanic glow about his eyes. "We are here, and caged at last, it seems. I will go, and admit my faithful companions. Escape is impossible without bloodshed. We must fight ! The more there are to help us the better."

"What, cornered like a dog !" exclaimed Penalvon, blue with rage and anger. "Am I to die iike a felon, tracked by limbs of the law ? Never ! I will die first. If my time *has* come, I will end my existence as bravely and fearlessly as I began it. Hark !" said he, turning deadly pale.

The sound of some mysterious, unseen voices was heard upon the air.

"Penalvon, Lord of Seawardine, your time has come !" echoed through his lonely room.

"What's that ?" exclaimed the carl, as the unnatural sounds fell upon his unwilling ear.

"Penalvon, Penalvon, Lord of Seawardine, your time has come !" was again re-echoed.

He rushed frantically to a closet, and seized a bright Damascus blade, and flourished it with a practised hand.

"Who calls upon Penalvon ?" he asked, in deep, guttural tones. "Earl Penalvon fears nought of earth or air !"

"Penalvon, Penalvon, so, Lord of Seawardine, your hour has come !" repea'ed the voices, in long-drawn, sorrowful accents, and the sounds died away.

Penalvon sank upon the sofa.

The sword fell powerless from his grasp.

He felt as if choked by ten thousand demons.

"Bolt and bar the gates and doors !" he frantically shouted to his astonished servants. "Arm yourselves every one to the teeth ; we are set upon by outlaws and scoundrels ! A thousand pounds for the head of Paul Adair, the Rover !"

CHAPTER LIII.

ATTACK ON SEAWARDINE—PENALVON IS ASKED TO SURRENDER ON THE CHARGE OF MURDER AND TREASON—MURDER OF THE NAVAL MESSENGERS—ATTACK OF THE SEAMEN AND MARINES — AWFUL DEATH OF EARL PENALVON AND THORKIL.

WE left the Phantom Schooner stiff in a fresh breeze, and steered by the gallant blue-jacket, Bill Hawser.

"I think they are signalling," said Frank, who observed a lamp dipping at the side of the sloop.

"True, lad, so they are," said Paul. "We must lower our boat, and go on board."

Harry Halliard repeated the signals of the sloop of war, and Lieutenant Frazer squared his yards in order to enable a boat from the Phantom Schooner to approach him.

Paul and Harry, together with Konks and Juniper, soon lowered a boat, and pulled lustily towards the sloop.

"Boat a-ho !" shouted Konks, in stentorian tones.

The signal was repeated and heeded.

A rope was thrown to the schooner's boat, and it was soon alongside.

Paul and Harry, quickly followed by Konks and Juniper, soon clambered up the ship's side, and trod the deck with a firm, elastic step.

"What, Harry ! Hullo, Konks ! and Juniper, too !" said Lieutenant Frazer, in surprise. "Why, how's this, eh ? You are Paul Adair, eh ?" said he, addressing the Rover, and bowing. "I imagined so. Your pretty, swift little craft answers her helm splendidly."

"No wonder, sir," said Konks, bowing respectfully and profoundly ; "Bill Hawser's at the wheel."

"What !" said Frazer, in still greater surprise, "you don't mean to say that ?"

"But I do though, lieutenant, and he, like all of us, seems determined to stick to young Harry here."

"Step this way, sir," said Frazer to Adair, "I wish to speak to you."

They retired to the cabin, and after a long, confidential conversation returned.

"This is the most astonishing piece of news I ever heard," said Frazer, with a flushed countenance. "Mr. Halliard, allow me to congratulate you on your accession to the estate and title of Earl Penalvon, Lord of Seawardine."

"Not yet, lieutenant," replied Harry, blushing, "there is to be bloodshed, I fear. I think some of us will fall in the encounter."

"As to that," said Frazer, indifferently, "I have no fear. The letters forwarded to the Admiralty prove beyond doubt that this so-called Earl Penalvon has been in constant secret correspondence with the French naval authorities, and has been heavily paid for all the information which Thorkil and his gang have given them. My orders are imperative. I have to secure him, whether dead or alive."

The schooner was signalled to make way in shore, which, under Bill Hardy's pilotage, was soon and safely accomplished.

The sloop and schooner lay side by side.

Several boats' crews were told off, and they disembarked from their boats in quiet order, making their way towards Seawardine under the direction of Paul Adair.

They had just arrived within a mile of the mansion, when, as has been narrated, Thorkil burst through them, and rode headlong to the hall.

Having placed his men at a respectable distance from each other, with imperative orders to allow no one to pass, Lieutenant Frazer held a council of war.

"I will send two men with a note," said Frazer, "calling upon Earl Penalvon to make an unconditional surrender of himself."

Two seamen were chosen for this purpose, and presented themselves at the hall door.

"Two seamen want *me* ?" asked Penalvon. "What can they desire, Thorkil ? "

"Admit them and see," answered the wrecker chief, with indifference. "I should like to hear what they have to say," he added, playing with his cutlass.

"Admit them," said Penalvon, to his servant, "and be sure to bar the doors. Are your men all prepared ?" he asked of Thorkil.

"Yes, ready for anything. They know the king's men are outside ; they know, also, that we have all been entrapped. It will make them fight all the harder, that's all."

Two seamen were admitted to Earl Penalvon's presence.

They presented a large doument, which the earl read, changing colour every instant.

"Accused of murder, and treason, eh?" he muttered, with a quivering lip. "And asked to surrender myself. Ha, ha! What do the Admiralty take me for, a coward, or a poltroon?" he said. "Penalvon can die, but will never surrender to a gang of ruffians under the leadership of such a vagabond as the pirate, Paul Adair!"

"We are seamen, my lord," the messengers said, respectfully, "and not vagabonds."

"Liars!" roared Penalvon and Thorkil, rushing upon the two unsuspecting men, and cutting them down, without a word of warning.

"So be it with all who would disturb or dishonor me!" said Penalvon. "Pitch their worthless bodies out of the window to the dogs, Thorkil. Let us die, they can but kill us; but I warrant we will make more than one vile rascal bite the dust first. Gather your men; have you primed them with rum? We will fight from the hall door to the roof; not a man of us shall ever surrender. If all comes to all, I'll ignite the vault of powder, which is well stored, and blow all the piratical scoundrels to eternity."

While he spoke, the sound of voices reached him.

It fell upon his ear like a death-knell.

"They are coming, Thorkil!" said the earl, nervously. "They must have seen their comrades' bodies fall into the court-yard; let us meet them in the hall. We had better fall sword in hand, than be tried before a gaping rabble, and consigned to a gibbet."

So saying Thorkil and Penalvon drank a large glassful of brandy each, to stay their failing spirits, and descended to the hall.

Lieutenant Frazer waited long and patiently for his messengers to return, but they did not.

"It cannot be," he said, "that harm could have befallen them."

"More likely than not," answered Paul. "A man of his antecedents is not over scrupulous in hours of danger. Besides, the letter you sent is quite enough to convince him of the great net-work of evidence which we have weaved around him. He is perfectly conscious that escape is impossible from the meshes of the law."

"I never dreamt; in fact, was astounded to learn that the traitor had such extensive dealings with the enemies of our country; to think that he has been corresponding for years with Frenchmen of note! the idea is awful."

"Almost as awful as the fate that awaits him, should we be fortunate enough to capture him alive."

"I fear we shall be forced to resort to violence," said Frazer, "'Tis farthest from my wishes; but if resistance is made, I would not give a farthing for the lives of any who are with him, my men are already infuriated beyond all controul."

"You heard, of course," said Harry, "that a party of horsemen were seen to approach and enter the Manor gates?"

"I did, and judge it must be some of Thorkil's desperate gang, including perhaps the cunning old chief himself."

"What say you?" said Paul, impatiently; "it is fast becoming dark, we had better advance and attack the place in full force; the sooner done the better."

Frazer gave the order for his men to move forward.

They were but a quarter of a mile from the mansion.

The boats' crew received the order to advance with great shouts and hurrahs.

One party, headed by Lieutenant Frazer, attacked the front gates, and tore them down in a few moments.

Paul Adair, with a second squad, went round to the rear of the premises, and was equally successful in gaining admission to the court-yard.

When both assailing parties were united they sent up loud shouts that rent the sky.

Their cheers were answered from a numerous party within the mansion, with a long volley of guns and pistols from windows and from the roof.

Several of the assailants fell dead.

Thorkil's voice was heard loudest of all, amid the noise and confusion.

Lieutenant Frazer attempted to force the hall door.

It was strongly barred and firmly bolted, resisting every attack.

With natural instinct and without orders, several of the sailors seized hold of carriage poles and battered down the heavy oaken door, which fell into the spacious hall with a loud crash.

Pistols and guns were discharged at the assailants by those stationed in the hall.

Again did several brave blue jackets fall to rise no more.

Lieutenant Frazer, exasperated beyond control by the loss of his men, rushed to the front, sword in hand.

He clambered over the ruins of the massive door, closely followed by Frank and Harry, and cut his way into the midst of a crowd of desperadoes, who thronged the spacious hall.

Paul Adair and his party, at the same moment, dashed in from the rear, and the fight became general.

The defenders, finding themselves surrounded, slowly retreated up the wide stone stairs, firing and fighting as they went.

Foremost and among the most desperate were Thorkil and Earl Penalvon.

"Surrender!" shouted Frazer. "'Tis useless to resist!"

"Never!" shouted Penalvon, at the top of his voice. "Oh! that I could pick off that rascal Adair," he hoarsly swore, as he repeatedly fired from the top of the landing; "three have already dropped, and yet I hear his voice."

"Surrender, villains, surrender!" roared Paul, foaming with rage.

Bill Hardy lay bleeding and moaning at his feet.

"You shall pay dearly for this, dastard as you are," he said, rushing upstairs, in ungovernable fury.

"Follow!" said Frazer, "or he is lost!"

The rush of the assailants was irresistible.

The defenders were stricken down at every step.

The stairs were literally blocked with wounded men.

The defenders, losing heart, retreated into various rooms, determined to sell their lives as dearly as possible.

The doors were burst open.

Of those inside some had clambered out of window, and endeavoured thus to escape, while others had piled the furniture into miniature barricades and defended themselves desperately to the last.

While Lieutenant Frazer and his men were thus engaged in clearing various rooms of their infuriate defenders, Paul Adair, Harry, and Frank rushed hither and thither in the hope of capturing Penalvon and Thorkil, who now could nowhere be found.

Room after room was burst open.

Cabinets, beds, closets, chairs, and sofas were a mass of fragments, whither soever they went.

The shouts of assailants and curses of defenders mingled with the clash of cutlasses and report of fire-arms.

Penalvon and Thorkil had escaped.

The thought was bitter and repugnant to the feelings of those in seach.

"Follow me," shouted Paul Adair, rapidly descending the stairs, "delay is dangerous; another moment may see us all blown into eternity."

Leaping downstairs Paul, closely followed by Harry and Frank, were soon on the ground-floor.

They descended still lower by a long flight of narrow stone steps, which Adair knew of old. This secret staircase led to a number of stone vaults and cellars.

"Off with your shoes; no noise!" said Paul, "Penalvon is in the powder-room."

Doing as they were bidden Harry and Frank noiselessly followed their brave, intrepid leader, and quickly passing through a long, stone passage, which was but dimly lighted, they dashed into a large stone vault which contained many kegs of powder.

A slow match was burning, another moment and it would have ignited the whole mass.

Rayner snatched up the match and extinguished it.

"Not here, then," panted Paul, like a bloodhound on the trail.

"They cannot be far off," said Harry.

"No, here they are," said Thorkil, aiming a frightful blow at Paul, as he and his companions dashed into an adjoining vault."

Rayner was quick, and warded off the blow, which, had it fallen on Adair, would have slain him; next moment Penalvon fired a pistol, and Frank fell senseless to the ground.

"Now we are equal!" growled Thorkil, desperately fencing with Adair, while Harry, cutlass in hand, made frequent but unsuccessful attacks on Earl Penalvon.

It was a fierce, desperate fight for life or death.

Paul fell; Thorkil, with a wild, demoniacal shout of triumph, rushed upon him.

With the agility of a panther Adair eluded the thrust; he jumped to his feet, his own sword cut the air with a whistling sound; Thorkil gave a loud scream, his skull was cleft in twain.

Though successful himself, Paul was wounded, and so weak that he fell helplessly to the ground, nor could he do more than sigh as he witnessed the unequal contest of Harry with so skilled a swordsman as Penalvon.

Harry was wounded in several places, yet he fought on with the courage and tenacity of a lion.

He was faint from loss of blood, and tottered on his feet.

Penalvon's eyes glistened with demoniacal rage and pleasure as he looked upon his fast fainting victim.

"Die, bastard, die!" shrieked Penalvon, as Harry fell weak against the wall. "Die like your braggart father!"

He gathered himself up as for a final effort.

He glared upon the pale and wounded youth like a tigress about to despatch her timid and mangled prey.

He poised his sword with a glistening eye, and measured his distance.

He aimed directly at the heart.

Harry raised his weapon feebly in defence.

Penalvon rushed at him with his whole force.

His foot slipped.

He fell upon the point of Harry's sword, and was pierced to the heart.

He gave a loud groan.

Blood spouted from him in crimson streams.

His eyes were wildly staring.

A quiver passed through his frame, and he was no more.

Exhausted and unconscious of all that passed, Harry Halliard fell upon his prostrate foe, insensible of all around him in that bloody, gloomy vault.

As he fell, the sound of strange voices caught his ear.

He knew not what they were, but it seemed to him as if they were echoes from the inhabitants of the grave, who rejoiced at the horrible scenes they had there seen enacted.

CHAPTER LIV.

WITH THE DEATH OF EARL PENALVON AND THE FALL OF SEAWARDINE ENDS THE CURRENT OF OUR STORY.

As if the charm of some gigantic spell had been rent asunder, the conflict in the mansion ceased on the fall of its terrible master, Earl Penalvon.

Frazer and his men secured their prisoners, and went in search of Paul, Harry, and Frank.

They were horrified to find them where they were, in that dimly-lighted vault, all gory and helpless. They were instantly conveyed away, and the affrighted female servants, who had hitherto concealed themselves in cellars and out-houses, now issued forth, weeping and wailing.

They attended, however, to the wants of the wounded, but could not understand the cause, the nature, nor the meaning of the bloody fray which had so suddenly and unexpectedly taken place in the mansion, and with such terrible consequences.

Frazer and his men at once began a systematic search of the vast old hall from roof to cellar, and from cellar to cells, and still deeper vaults beneath the earth.

Wherever they went they were filled with wonder.

Doors which had not been opened for years were burst open, and chests and bales, and bundles of letters and dispatches brought to light—that which fully proved Penalvon's long complicity in plots to betray the British fleet, and to warn French and Dutch authorities of all movements of English admirals.

Penalvon's body, all gory and disfigured as it might be, was sent to London.

Frazer's evidence, coupled with that of the intrepid Paul Adair and Joel Britton's exploration of the vaults was conclusive as to the guilt of the recreant nobleman.

His corpse was publicly exposed, and was ordered to be hung from a gibbet on the White Cliffs near the Fin's Back.

Nor did it take legal authorities long to fully investigate and establish Harry Halliard's claim to the estate and title of Seawardine, to which, as the grandson of the rightful heir, he was legally entitled.

Great was the surprise, and vast the wonder, which this astounding news created for many long miles along the coast, and throughout the country.

Village bells rang out merry peals of joy, rustics and sailors waved their hats and shouted, as a carriage, containing Rose, Wild Thyra, Nelly, and Paul, drove up to the Hall.

NOTICE.—The next Number of the Boys' Library will be Published on Friday, October 3rd. Order early of your Bookseller.

BOYS' LIBRARY

Harry Halliard: or, the Young British Tar.

A second carriage quickly followed, having for occupants, Lieutenants Frazer, Armitage, Frank Rayner, Joel Britton, and Polruth. Behind this came still other vehicles of divers kinds, filled with noisy, boisterous sailors and bands of music, which were decked with ribbons and banners, inscribed with the devices, "Long life to Harry Halliard, the brave Sailor Boy!" "Success to the young Lord of Seawardine!" "Hurrah for the Navy, and her gallant lads!" "Nine times nine, and a bumper to the Rover, Paul Adair!" "Success to the Phantom Schooner!" "Down with Thorkil, and all such murderous gangs!" &c., &c.

Great rejoicings were at the Hall for many days. Noblemen and gentlemen, for many miles round, drove up and left notes of congratulation.

Yachting excursions and fishing parties occupied the day, the Phantom Schooner being ever in request and gaily decked with flags.

Balls and parties were the order of the evening and among those who honoured Rose Halliard with his presence was no less a personage than the gallant and distinguished naval officer, Sir Everard Brandon.

Tears filled the old man's eyes as he grasped Harry heartily by the hand, and whispered, "God bless you, lad, may long life, distinction in the navy, and superabundant happiness attend you."

Foremost among all who jigged and danced in the great hall of Seawardine were Bill Hawser, Joe Juniper, old Konks, and bow-legged Bill Hardy. Their mirth and jollity, and awkward attempts, as fair ladies condescended to dance with them, was the cause of unceasing merriment and laughter, but no one seemed to enjoy the joke more heartily than those brave, weather-beaten old tars themselves.

They often made their escape, however, from the glittering lights and dazzling beauty which graced the drawing-room, and descended below stairs, or as they called it, "atween decks," where Bill Hardy produced such excruciating music from an old violin that servant-maids, footmen and grooms danced and capered about with unrestrained hilarity and merriment.

In the midst of all the great rejoicings and festivities that attended Harry Halliard's installation as the rightful Earl Penalvon and Lord of Seawardine, Wild Thyra moved with a modest, bashful, bewitching grace and motion which won the admiration of all who saw her.

Her pale, thoughtful face, and large, lustrous eyes and luxuriant raven tresses were admired by all who beheld her.

Decked as she was in rich attire, and attended at every turn by Rose and her faithful, obedient servants, she walked the drawing-room, or gathered flowers in the shrubberies, with a queenly manner that even struck Harry with mute surprise.

She smiled on her nephew with the looks of one who had now realised her life-dream, and had found a long-sought brother.

Rose, with Helena and Frank, were supremely happy, and if there was one thin cloud that shadowed the happiness of her overflowing heart it was a sigh of regret that her dear, departed husband was not by her side to share the universal joy, and counsel her son and Frank to bid adieu to roving in the navy.

Not being of age, Harry was restless and ambitious.

Providence had raised him, without any effort of his own, to one of the highest positions in the land, but when he read daily of the gallant deeds of Nelson, of Collingwood, and a host of other naval heroes, he sighed to achieve distinction on the sea.

Such wishes and aspirations were whispered in confidence to his inseparable bosom friends, Frank and Paul Adair. He sought an interview with Sir Everard Brandon.

"I care not for position nor money," said Harry, as he held the old man's hand. "I sigh for the honours and rewards which a grateful country can bestow upon her brave and successful defenders."

The old man smiled approvingly, as he said, emphatically,

"And if you live, you shall have it. I will leave you for a moment in the drawing-room here. I have several distinguished Admiralty lords waiting on business below. I will mention your wishes to them."

This was not the only, or perhaps, the *real* cause of Harry's visit to Plymouth, or the anxiety he felt to call on Sir Everard at Clarence Terrace. There was a blushing, witty beauty living there, whose charms had long before enslaved his heart. He could not, nor would he forget for worlds, he thought, the entrancing being whose hand was placed so confidingly and lovingly in his on a previous visit. It was *her* words which had prompted the vast ambition for distinction which now possessed him.

As he stood alone in the drawing-room, gazing with love and admiration at the portrait of Sir Everard's youngest daughter, light footsteps were heard approaching. He turned; there stood Annie before him. Instinct, ungovernable and impulsive, impelled him to rush towards her.

He clasped her hands in his and sank on his knee.

The surprised and bashful maiden quivered in every limb.

For some time all was silence. Neither dare look at or speak to each other. Tears gushed to Harry's eyes, but he knew not why. He kissed her hand ardently, devotedly; he looked up to her pale face and felt her tremble as he did so. Another moment passed, she was locked in his arms, and he kissed her a hundred times, passionately, fondly.

"How cruel not to have come before," she sighed.

"You never answered my many letters, Annie," whispered Harry, as she leaned and sobbed upon his shoulder.

"How could I? Father never dreamed of our attachment; yet you always knew that——"

"You returned my love?" asked Harry, passionately, still clasping the trembling girl to his heart.

A slight pressure of the hand was the mute but eloquent reply.

Harry Halliard was happy.

Sir Everard's surprise was extreme. Neither himself nor Lady Brandon ever dreamed that young Halliard had loved their young and favourite daughter Annie. Clara did, however, and when she heard the news of Harry's proposal and acceptance, she embraced her sister affectionately, and turning to Lieutenant Frazer, to whom she had been married but a fortnight before, she said, playfully,

"Didn't I say so, husband?"

She kissed Harry.

The lieutenant grasped his hand, saying, as he did so,

"I'm right glad of this, my brave boy, and nothing gives me greater pleasure than to call you brother-in-law of mine; but would you might sail with me in the Scorpion, as lieutenant; she hoists anchor for a cruise in a week."

Neither Rose, Thyra, nor Sir Everard had any objections to the wedding; but both parents proposed that it should be postponed for a few months, which, after many long and affectionate consultations, was finally agreed to by Harry and Annie.

Those few months, however, were fraught with many changes. War, fierce and bloody, was then waged between France and England.

Lieutenant Frazer was burning with ambition to distinguish himself.

The Admiralty were urged by Sir Everard's friends, and soon got the "Scorpion" undocked, and ready for sea.

She was one of the best equipped, and fastest sailing frigates in the British Navy, and right proud did Frazer feel, when pacing her snowy quarter-deck.

When it became known through Plymouth that Sir Everard Brandon's son-in-law was placed in command of such a staunch-made and clipping frigate, seamen volunteered in dozens, all anxious to sail with such a well-known and reliable officer.

Hawser, Juniper and Konks, were on board as petty officers, while through powerful influence Harry and Frank were rated as second and third lieutenants.

Brave old Hawser was in his glory, and was eternally singing.

Juniper and Konks, like himself, paid much attention to the composition of the crew, and made it a point to have, as far as practicable, only such men upon the ship's books as had proved themselves of good character.

These worthy old tars knew full well that the best soldiers, as well as the best sailors, are to be found among steady men, and not loud-mouthed braggarts.

Hence it was that when the Scorpion sailed from Plymouth harbour she was vociferously cheered by thousands who lined the shore and gazed with admiration on the beautiful vessel, as with white snails flowing, and colours gaily flying, she gracefully rocked in the gentle breeze, and put forth to sea.

Rose, Helena, Annie, Clara, and Thyra were the last to leave the dock-head.

They watched the gallant ship intently, and with pride, but each and every one of them had tear-dewed eyes.

Helena sobbed aloud, and leaned on Thyra's shoulder.

Clara cheered Annie's drooping spirits with words of hope with a flushed face foretelling the brilliant career of that noble ship, now fast fading from view.

Thyra spoke not a word.

She stood upon the sandy beach waving her hand-kerchief, and her face was flushed with a delicate crimson hue.

She smiled, and her lips moved as if in prayer, while Helena clung to her, and looked upon her as she stood majestically waving her hand like some prophetess of old.

The Scorpion disappointed the hopes of none. She was lustily cheered by every craft she met, whether large or small for there was something about her build and trim that bespoke the ability and dash of her officers and crew.

She had no positive orders, so that with such latitude Captain Frazer cruised about the channel in search of adventure.

Frenchmen were loth to leave their harbours to form the Scorpion's acquaintance.

Frazer, taking advantage of a foggy night, ran his ship close in upon Brest harbour, and cut out a sloop of war, which he captured under the very nose of the citadel guns.

This act of daring and defiance caused the greatest excitement among French naval officers, who instantly sailed out of harbour to chastise the impudent British ship which had displayed such impudence and pugnacity.

The Scorpion and her gallant crew were not loth to try conclusions with any *two* French ships, as Frazer wisely remarked; but it was not discreet to hazard his vessel with half a dozen opponents. The Frenchmen, consequently, were not accommodated with a fight. They were half a dozen in number, but would not divide their force.

A heavy gale sprang up during the night, and dispersed the French fleet.

The Scorpion's crew were not loth to seize this advantage, and pursued it to the utmost.

Three vessels were successively overhauled, and compelled to strike their colours before others could succour them.

The Scorpion did not escape scathless. In three successive fights, on the same day, she was much battered, and her rigging and spars were all a wreck.

In this state, and with three prizes, Captain Frazer sailed within full view of Brest harbour, flaunting his colours, and firing guns of defiance in the very teeth of the greatest dockyard and arsenal of France.

The reception of the Scorpion at Plymouth was of the most extraordinary character. The town was literally drunk with uproarious enthusiasm. Here was a vessel which had not been at sea more than two weeks, and yet she brings in four prizes, won from the enemy in fair battle !

Bells rang, and flags floated from every steeple. Business was suspended for the day, and all went forth to view the gallant Scorpion, which, battle-blackened and riddled with shot, lay proudly at anchor in the harbour.

Lieutenant Frazer, together with his officers and men, were publicly honoured with a grand banquet, at which admirals, generals, and all the wealth and nobility of the country attended.

Though her successive quick, sharp battles had resulted in some loss to the gallant crew, it is pleasing to learn from records of the ship that none of our old acquaintances were in any way dangerously injured.

'Tis true that a stray splint of wood struck Konks heavily across his very prominent nose, which slightly indented the bridge of that valuable organ, for which, when he retired from the service many years subsequently, he received an increase of pension.

Hawser and Juniper had slight wounds, the first received a pistol shot, which came within an inch of striking a vital part ; but from which, under careful treatment, he recovered within a week or two.

Juniper had a sword cut in the thigh, but not of a dangerous character.

Frazer, Harry, and Frank luckily escaped without a scratch.

Government was not slow to recognize the merits of Captain Frazer and his subordinates.

While the Scorpion was under repair he was given another ship, and, with his former men and officers, set sail again in search of honour and renown.

Again and again was the Spitfire signalled off the harbour's mouth with prizes in tow, until it became quite a byeword among the people of Plymouth to say, " Oh ! it's only Frazer with two more ships in tow !"

Harry and Frank were not forgotten by the Lords of the Admiralty, who were not slow to recognise the true merits of those young and daring lieutenants.

It was difficult to separate two such friends. Harry was appointed captain of the frigate Neptune, and Frank was also offered the command of a fine ship, but he could not brook the idea of parting with his brother, and volunteered to go as first lieutenant in the Neptune.

He took one voyage with Harry, in that subordinate capacity; but the admiralty forced him to accept a ship, so that finding himself under stringent orders. she sailed alone.

Hawser and Juniper remained with Harry, while Konks and Bill Hardy were prevailed upon to sail with Frank.

These life-long companions were parted, but frequently met, and their exploits were the theme of conversation, and praise among all the fleet.

They were rivals and strove to outshine each other, until at last their brilliant career won the thanks of Parliament for their many deeds of heroism.

Harry, now Earl Penalvon, rapidly rose in the list of daring leaders, and after the ever-memorable battle of Trafalgar, fought under the immortal Nelson, as captain of the frigate Neptune, was gazetted Rear-Admiral of the Blue, and went to Court with his lovely wife, as Thyra, in days long past, had truthfully predicted—with a coronetted coach, and richly emblazoned panels, with stars, and orders, and decorations on his breast, amid the deafening plaudits of an admiring multitude, who thus rendered deserving national honour to the gallantry and prowess of one of Old England's brave and lion-hearted Sailor Boys.

With him, and in the same coach, rode Post-

Captain Frank Rayner, who, having been maimed in battle, now rejoiced in a cork leg, and was roundly joked by his pretty, loving wife, Helena.

The gallant Paul Adair, through Harry's influence, rose to be chief of all the coast-guard on the Cornwall coast, a position which much pleased him, assisted as he was by those veteran tars, Hawser, Juniper, and Konks, who, having lucrative positions and ample pensions, enjoyed their honours and old age with all the vivacity of renewed youth, and many a time on the sly would they drag in old Joel Britton along with them, rouse Polruth from a nap in the snug parlour of the kiddleawink, and make the house re-echo with their joyous songs and shouts.

Harleck confessed his guilt, and, together with Otho, were transported for life, a fate well deserved by all of Thorkil's gang, which was dispersed to the four winds of heaven.

Thus did Providence guard the welfare and fortunes of those brave lads who, helpless and friendless, had once trod the decks of the Thunderer.

Seawardine was always honoured with the presence of the noblest and greatest in the land.

Rose lived to a good old age, loved and revered by rich and poor.

Thyra, true to the supernatural instincts with which she was endowed, gave ebullition to her natural feelings of piety in attending the poor, sick, and fatherless, and although she remembered Agger's love, she never married, but died like some fair spirit that had for a time deserted her etherial home, and sighed to return to it again.

Yet Agger was not forgotten.

Earl Penalvon procured him a firm position in the Customs, and never forgot the love and fidelity which his conduct in a great measure had been providentially instrumental in raising him from the humble position of a simple Sailor Boy to the grand and lofty station of Earl Penalvon, the world-wide renowned, charitable, hospitable, and historically famed Lord of Seawardine.

[THE END]

www.ingramcontent.com/pod-product-compliance
Lightning Source LLC
Chambersburg PA
CBHW081323020726
47506CB00005B/1166